दबंग दादी

दबंग दादी

लेखक
डेविड वॉलियम्स

अनुवाद
मनीशा तनेजा

चित्र
टोनी रॉस

हार्पर
हिन्दी

हार्पर हिन्दी
(हार्परकॉलिंस पब्लिशर्स इंडिया) द्वारा 2018 में प्रकाशित

कॉपीराइट लेखक © डेविड वॉलियम्स 2011
कॉपीराइट अनुवादक © मनीषा तनेजा 2018

लेखक इस पुस्तक के मूल रचनाकार होने का नैतिक दावा करता है।
इस पुस्तक में व्यक्त किये गये सभी विचार, तथ्य और दृष्टिकोण लेखक के
अपने हैं और प्रकाशक किसी भी तौर पर इनके लिए जिम्मेदार नहीं है।

हार्पर हिन्दी हार्परकॉलिंस पब्लिशर्स इंडिया का हिन्दी सम्भाग है
पता: ए-75, सेक्टर-57, नौएडा—201301, उत्तर प्रदेश, भारत

P-ISBN: 978-93-5302-303-4

टाइपसेटिंग: निओ साफ़्टवेयर कन्सलटैंट्स, इलाहाबाद
मुद्रक: थॉम्सन प्रेस (इंडिया) लि.

MIX
Paper
FSC FSC® C010615

This book is produced from independently certified FSC® paper to ensure
responsible forest management.

फ़िलिप ओनयांगो के लिए ...

... मुझे मिला अभी तक का सबसे बहादुर बच्चा।

आभार

मैं कुछ लोगों के प्रति अपना आभार व्यक्त करना चाहता हूँ।

सबसे पहले, प्रतिभाशाली टोनी रॉस, अपने जादुई रेखाचित्रों के लिए। निक लेक, मेरे मेहनती सम्पादक और दोस्त। बेहतरीन डिज़ाइनर जेम्स स्टीवेंस और ऐलोरीन ग्रांट, जिन्होंने पुस्तक के कवर और टैक्स्ट पर काम किया। सतर्क कॉपी एडिटर लिज़्ज़ी राइली। समांथा व्हाइट, मेरी किताबों के बढ़िया प्रचार के लिए। तान्या ब्रेननान्ड-रोपर जो ऑडियो संस्करण तैयार करती हैं। और मेरे अति-सहायक लिटरेरी एजेंट, पॉल स्टीवेंस।

मगर सबसे अधिक मैं आप सब बच्चों को धन्यवाद कहना चाहता हूँ, मेरी किताबों को पढ़ने के

लिए। यह मेरे लिए बहुत गर्व की बात है कि आप साइनिंग पर आते हैं और मुझसे मिलते हैं, मुझे पत्र लिखते हैं और मुझे चित्र भेजते हैं। मुझे आपको कहानियाँ सुनाना बहुत पसन्द है, और मैं उम्मीद करता हूँ कि मैं और नयी कहानियों की कल्पना करके आपके लिए लिखूँगा। पढ़ते रहिये—यह आपके लिए बहुत फ़ायदेमन्द है।

1

बन्दगोभी-सी

"पर दादी कितनी बोरिंग हैं," बेन बोला। नवम्बर की ठंडभरी शुक्रवार की शाम थी, और हमेशा की तरह वह कंधे झुका कर अपने माता-पिता की गाड़ी में पीछे बैठा था। एक बार फिर वह अपनी भयानक दादी के घर रहने जा रहा था। "सारे बुज़ुर्ग होते ही डरावने हैं।"

"अपनी दादी के बारे में ऐसा मत बोलो," बाबा ने धीरे से कहा; उनकी तोंद परिवार की छोटी भूरी गाड़ी की स्टीरिंग व्हील से पिचकी हुई थी।

"मुझे उनके साथ वक्त बिताना अच्छा नहीं लगता है," बेन ने विरोध किया। "उनका टीवी नहीं चलता, उनको सिर्फ़ स्क्रैबल ही खेलना पसन्द है और उनसे

बन्दगोभी की बदबू आती है!"

"वैसे सच कहा जाये तो उनसे वाकई में बन्दगोभी की बदबू आती है। यह ठीक ही बोल रहा है," माँ ने ऐन वक्त पर अपनी लिपस्टिक लगाते हुए हामी भरी।

"तुम कुछ मदद नहीं कर रही हो, जान," बाबा बड़बड़ाये। "ज़्यादा से ज़्यादा मेरी माँ से उबली हुई सब्ज़ियों की हल्की-सी गन्ध आती है।"

"क्या मैं आपके साथ नहीं आ सकता?" बेन ने विनती की, "मुझे वो—जो भी है डांस बहुत पसन्द है," उसने झूठ बोला।

"उसको बॉलरूम डांस बोलते हैं," बाबा ने सही किया। "और तुम्हें वो पसन्द नहीं है। तुमने कहा था और मैं दोहराता हूँ, 'यह बकवास देखने से तो अच्छा है कि मैं अपने गूँगे खा लूँ'।"

बेन के माँ और बाबा को बॉलरूम डांस बहुत ज़्यादा पसन्द था। कई बार बेन सोचता था कि उनको यह डांस अपने बेटे से भी ज़्यादा पसन्द था। माँ और बाबा हर शनिवार शाम को आने वाला टीवी शो,

स्ट्रिक्टली स्टार्स डांसिंग, कभी भी देखना नहीं छोड़ते थे। इस में बड़े-बड़े कलाकार बॉलरूम डांस करने वाले नर्तक के साथ भाग लेते थे।

बेन को पक्का यकीन था कि अगर कभी घर में आग लग जाये और उन्हें हिट शो में आने वाले सांवले-सलौने, दिलकश इटालियन डांसर फ़्लावीओ फ़्लावीओली के सुनहरे, टैप डांसर जूते और इकलौते बेटे में से किसी एक को बचाना हो तो वो यकीनन जूतों को बचायेंगी। आज रात, उसके माँ और बाबा मंच पर *स्ट्रिक्टली स्टार्स डांसिंग* को लाइव देखने जा रहे थे।

"पता नहीं बेन, तुम प्लम्बर बनने का अपना मुश्किल इरादा क्यों नहीं छोड़ देते और नाच को ही अपना पेशा बनाने की क्यों नहीं सोचते?" माँ बोलीं। गाड़ी की ऊबड़-खाबड़ हिचकोलों से उनकी लिपस्टिक उनके गालों पर घिसट कर फैल गयी थी। माँ को गाड़ी में मेकअप करने की आदत थी, जिसका मतलब था कि वह अक्सर जोकर बनकर पहुँचती थीं। "हो सकता है, तुम टीवी पर आ जाओ!" माँ ने जोश में आकर कहा।

"क्योंकि ऐसे उछल-कूद करना बेवकूफ़ी है," बेन बोला।

माँ थोड़ा रिरियाई और टिशू पेपर की तरफ़ हाथ बढ़ाया।

"तुम अपनी माँ को नाराज़ कर रहे हो। अब बस अच्छे बच्चों की तरह चुप बैठो, बेन," बाबा ने सख़्ती से कहा और साथ ही रेडियो की आवाज़ तेज़ कर दी। ज़ाहिर है एक ही सीडी बज सकती थी। प्रसिद्ध टीवी कार्यक्रम स्ट्रिक्टली स्टार्स डांसिंग के 50 सुनहरे

गाने। बेन को इस सीडी से चिढ़ थी, क्योंकि उसने यह लाखों बार सुनी हुई थी। असल में, उसने इतनी ज़्यादा बार सुनी थी कि अब उसे सुनना किसी यातना से कम नहीं था।

बेन की माँ शहर के ही नाख़ूनों के पार्लर, 'गेल्स नेल्स' में काम करती थीं। अब चूंकि वहाँ ज़्यादा ग्राहक तो आते नहीं थे, इसलिये माँ और वहाँ काम करने वाली दूसरी महिला—गेल—पूरा दिन एक दूसरे के नाख़ून ही सजाती रहती थीं। चमकाना, साफ़ करना, छोटा करना, क्रीम लगाना, कोट लगाना, आकार देना, रोगन लगाना, नकली नाख़ून लगाकर लम्बा करना और नेलपॉलिश लगाना। वो दोनों एक दूसरे पर पूरा दिन यही करती थीं (अगर फ़्लावीओ फ़्लावीओली दिन में टीवी पर ना आये तो)। इसका मतलब यह था कि माँ हमेशा अपनी अँगुलियों के छोर पर कुछ ज़्यादा ही लम्बे रंगीन प्लास्टिक एक्सटेंशन लगाये घर आती थीं।

बेन के बाबा लोकल सुपरमार्केट में गार्ड थे। उनके बीस साल की नौकरी में आज तक की सिर्फ़ एक ही

उपलब्धि थी—एक बुज़ुर्ग को रोकना, जो मक्खन के दो डिब्बे अपनी पतलून में छिपाकर ले जा रहा था। हालाँकि बाबा किसी चोर के पीछे दौड़ने के लिए बहुत ज़्यादा ही मोटे थे, लेकिन वह उनको गेट पर तो रोक ही सकते थे। बाबा माँ से जब पहली बार मिले थे, तब उन्होंने माँ पर चिप्स का पैकेट उठाने का ग़लत आरोप लगाया था, और फिर एक साल में ही उनकी शादी भी हो गयी।

गाड़ी ग्रे क्लोस मोहल्ले के मोड़ पर घूमी, जहाँ दादी का बंगला उकड़ूँ बैठा था। उस पूरी गली में छोटे-छोटे उदास से घरों की पंक्ति में ज़्यादातर बुज़ुर्ग रहते थे।

गाड़ी रुकी, और बेन ने धीरे से अपना सिर बंगले की तरफ़ मोड़ा। ड्राइंग-रूम की खिड़की से दादी बेसब्री से झांक रही थीं। इन्तज़ार। इन्तज़ार। वह हमेशा खिड़की पर उसके आने का इन्तज़ार ही करती रहतीं थीं। *कितने समय से वह वहाँ हैं?* बेन ने सोचा। *पिछले हफ़्ते से?*

बेन उनका इकलौता पोता था और जहाँ तक उसे पता था, और कोई कभी भी उनसे मिलने नहीं आता था।

दादी ने हाथ हिलाया और बेन मुस्कुराया, फूले मुँह के बावजूद।

"ठीक है, हम में से एक तुमको कल सुबह ग्यारह बजे लेने आ जायेगा।" बाबा ने अपनी गाड़ी बन्द नहीं की थी।

"दस बजे नहीं हो सकता क्या?"

"बेन!" बाबा गरजे। उन्होंने चाईल्ड लॉक खोला और बेन बेमन से दरवाज़ा खोल कर बाहर निकला। बेन को चाईल्ड लॉक की ज़रूरत तो नहीं थी: वह ग्यारह साल का था और शायद ही चलती गाड़ी में दरवाज़ा खोलता। उसे लगता था कि बाबा ने सिर्फ़ उसको दादी के घर जाते हुए गाड़ी से ना कूदने के लिए लगाया था। 'क्लिक', जैसे ही दरवाज़े से आवाज़ आयी, गाड़ी फिर से दौड़ पड़ी।

दबंग दादी

इससे पहले कि वह घंटी बजाता, दादी ने फ़ट से दरवाज़ा खोल दिया। बन्दगोभी का एक बड़ा-सा झोंका बेन के मुँह पर आया। वह बदबू के ज़ोरदार थप्पड़ सरीखे था।

दादी एकदम किताबी दादियों की तरह थीं:

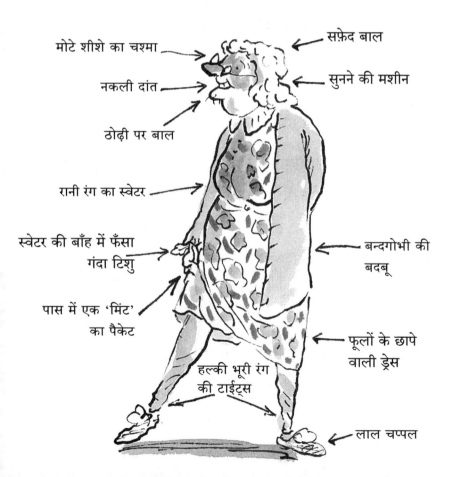

मोटे शीशे का चश्मा

नकली दांत

ठोढ़ी पर बाल

रानी रंग का स्वेटर

स्वेटर की बाँह में फँसा गंदा टिशु

पास में एक 'मिंट' का पैकेट

हल्की भूरी रंग की टाईट्स

सफ़ेद बाल

सुनने की मशीन

बन्दगोभी की बदबू

फूलों के छापे वाली ड्रेस

लाल चप्पल

"माँ-बाबा अन्दर नहीं आ रहे?" उन्होंने निराशा से पूछा। दादी की अनगिनत चीज़ें बेन से बर्दाश्त नहीं होती थीं और उन में से एक थी बेन से बच्चों की तरह बात करना।

ब्रूम-ब्रूम-ब्रूरोओओओओओओम

बेन और दादी ने एक साथ उस छोटी भूरी गाड़ी को स्पीड ब्रेकर पर उछलकर तेज़ी से जाते हुए देखा। बेन की तरह ही, माँ और बाबा को भी दादी के साथ समय बिताना पसन्द नहीं था। उनका घर बस बेन को हर शुक्रवार शाम को छोड़ने के लिए ठीक था।

"नहीं, वह ... मुझे अफ़सोस है दादी..." बेन बड़बड़ाया।

"अच्छा, फिर भीतर चलो," वह धीरे से फुसफुसाईं। "मैंने स्क्रैबल का बोर्ड लगा दिया है और खाने के लिए मेरे पास तुम्हारा मनपसन्द बन्दगोभी का सूप है।"

बेन की शक्ल और उतर गयी। *नहहहहहहहहहीं! अब तो गया,* उसने सोचा।

2

एक बतख़

कुछ ही देर में दादी और पोता एक दूसरे के सामने खाने की मेज़ पर बैठे थे और दोनों के बीच पसरा था गहरा सन्नाटा। हर शुक्रवार शाम की तरह।

जब उसके माँ और बाबा *स्ट्रिक्टली स्टार्स डांसिंग* टीवी पर नहीं देख रहे होते, तब या तो वो बाहर खाना खाने जाते या फ़िल्म देखने जा रहे होते थे। शुक्रवार की शाम उनकी 'डेट की शाम' होती थी, और जहाँ तक बेन को याद था, वे हमेशा उसको दादी के पास छोड़कर बाहर जाते थे। अगर वह *स्ट्रिक्टली स्टार्स डांसिंग मंच पर लाईव!* नहीं देखने जा रहे होते थे, तो

वह ताज महल जाते (बड़ी सड़क पर भारतीय रेस्तरां, सफ़ेद संगमरमर का प्राचीन भारतीय स्मारक नहीं) और अपने वज़न जितना पापड़ खा लेते।

और, यहाँ दादी के मकान में, घड़ी की टिक-टिक के अलावा प्यालों पर चम्मचों की टक-टक और हर थोड़ी देर में दादी के कान की मशीन की सीटी सुनाई दे रही थी। वह ऐसा यंत्र था जिसका काम दादी को सुनने में मदद देने से ज़्यादा, दूसरों को बहरा बनाना था।

यह दादी की उन चीज़ों में से एक थी जिनसे बेन को नफ़रत थी। बाक़ी थीं:

1) दादी हमेशा स्वेटर की बाँह में खोंसे गये टिशु में थूकती थीं, और उसी से अपने पोते का मुँह भी साफ़ कर देती थीं।

2) 1992 से उनका टीवी बन्द था। और उस पर जमी धूल की मोटी परत अब रोयेंदार फ़र जैसी लगती थी।

दबंग दादी

3)   उनका घर किताबों से भरा हुआ था और
     पढ़ने से चिढ़ने वाले बेन को हरदम वह
     पढ़ाने की कोशिश में जुटी रहती थीं।

4)   वह पूरे साल सर्दी का मोटा कोट पहनने
     पर ज़ोर डालतीं, चाहे कितनी गर्मी क्यों
     ना हो। वरना तुम्हें "फ़ायदा" नहीं होगा।

5)   उनसे बन्दगोभी की बू आती थी। (अगर
     किसी को बन्दगोभी से एलर्जी हो, तो
     वह उनसे दस मील दूर भी नहीं खड़ा हो
     सकता था।)

6)   दादी के लिए रोमांचक दिन का मतलब
     था तालाब की बतख़ों को बासी, फ़फ़ूंद
     लगी ब्रेड के टुकड़े खिलाना।

7)   वो बार-बार पाद मारती थीं। और फिर
     स्वीकार भी नहीं करती थीं।

8)   उनकी पाद से सिर्फ़ बन्दगोभी की ही

नहीं बल्कि सड़ी हुई बन्दगोभी की बास
आती थी।

9)   वह इतनी जल्दी सोने भेज देतीं कि सुबह
उठना भी बेकार लगता था।

10)   वह अपने इकलौते पोते को क्रिसमस पर
कुत्ते और बिल्लियों के पिल्लों वाला
स्वेटर बुनकर देतीं, और उसके माता-
पिता जबरदस्ती पूरी छुट्टियाँ उसको वह
स्वेटर पहनने पर ज़ोर देते थे।

"तुम्हारा सूप कैसा है?" दादी ने पूछा।

पिछले दस मिनट से बेन टूटे प्याले में पड़े, हल्के
रंग के पानीदार सूप में चम्मच घुमा रहा था, इस उम्मीद
में कि शायद वह ग़ायब हो जाये।

हुआ नहीं।

अब तो वह ठंडा भी हो रहा था।

बन्दगोभी के टुकड़े, बन्दगोभी के ठंडे पानी में तैर रहे थे।

"अर्र यह, यह स्वादिष्ट है। धन्यवाद," बेन ने जवाब दिया।

"अच्छा है।"

टिक टॉक टिक टॉक।

"अच्छा है।" बूढ़ी औरत ने फिर से दोहराया।

क्लिंक। क्लिंक।

"अच्छा है।" दादी को बेन से बात करने में उतनी ही मुश्किल होती थी जितनी बेन को उनसे बात करने में होती थी।

क्लिंक क्लैंक। सूँ...

"स्कूल कैसा है?" उन्होंने पूछा।

"बोरिंग," बेन बड़बड़ाया। लोग हमेशा बच्चों से उनके स्कूल के बारे में ही पूछते हैं। वही एक चीज़ है जिसके बारे में बच्चों को बात करना बिल्कुल भी पसन्द नहीं है। स्कूल के बारे में तो स्कूल में भी बात करने का मन नहीं करता है।

"अच्छा," दादी बोली।

टिक टॉक क्लिंक क्लैंक सूँ टिक टॉक।

"मुझे अवन में देखना चाहिए।" कुछ पल बाद दादी बोलीं, जो खींच कर कुछ ज़्यादा ही लम्बा लम्हा बन चुका था। "मैंने तुम्हारी मनपसन्द बन्दगोभी की कचौड़ी बनायी है।"

वह धीरे से अपनी कुर्सी से उठीं और रसोई की ओर गयीं। हर क़दम के साथ उनके लटके हुए पिछवाड़े से हवा का बुलबुला फूलता हुआ बाहर आया। बतख़ की आवाज़ जैसा। या तो उनको अहसास नहीं होता था, या फिर वह अहसास ना होने का ढोंग अच्छे से कर लेती थीं।

बेन ने उनको जाते हुए देखा और चुपके से कमरे की दूसरी ओर खिसक गया। यह बहुत मुश्किल था क्योंकि किताबों का ढेर हर जगह था। बेन की दादी को किताबें बहुत ही ज़्यादा पसन्द थीं, और हमेशा उनकी नाक एक में घुसी रहती थी। उनके शेल्फ़ में किताबों की थप्पी लगी थी, खिड़कियों पर कतारें थीं, और कोनों में भी ढेर लगा था।

अपराध कथायें उन्हें बेहद पसन्द थीं। डाकू, बैंक लुटेरे और माफ़िया की कहानियाँ। बेन दबंग डाकू और माफ़िया डॉन में फर्क तो नहीं जानता था, लेकिन दबंग ज़्यादा दुष्ट लगता था।

हालाँकि बेन को पढ़ना पसन्द नहीं था, लेकिन

उसे दादी की किताबों के कवर देखने में मज़ा आता था। उन पर तेज़ गाड़ियाँ, बन्दूकें और लुभावने अन्दाज़ में सुन्दर औरतें बनी हुई थीं, और बेन को यक़ीन नहीं होता था कि उसकी बूढ़ी बोरिंग दादी को ऐसी रोमांचक किताबें पढ़ना पसन्द था।

इनको दबंगों में क्या दिलचस्पी है? बेन ने सोचा। *दबंग डाकू बंगलों में तो नहीं रहते, ना ही स्क्रैबल खेलते हैं। उन में से तो बन्दगोभी की बू भी नहीं आती होगी।*

बेन बहुत धीरे पढ़ता था, और उसके टीचर उसे बुद्धु होने का अहसास कराते क्योंकि वह सबके साथ बराबरी नहीं कर पाता था। प्रिंसिपल मैडम ने तो उसको एक साल छोटी कक्षा में भी डाल दिया था, इस उम्मीद से कि वह छूटी हुई पढ़ाई पूरी कर लेगा। इस वजह से उसके सारे दोस्त दूसरी कक्षा में थे। इसलिए वह स्कूल में भी उतना ही अकेला महसूस करता था जितना कि घर पर, क्योंकि उसके माँ-बाबा को तो केवल बॉलरूम डांस की परवाह थी।

एक ख़तरनाक पल के बाद जिस में वह असली अपराध के उपन्यास के ढेर से टकराते हुए बचा, वह कोने में पड़े पौधे के पास पहुँचा। जल्दी से उसने बचे हुए सूप को पौधे में उड़ेल दिया। वह पौधा पहले से ही अपनी आख़िरी साँसें गिन रहा था, और अगर नहीं भी मरने वाला होता तो दादी के बन्दगोभी के ठंडे सूप से तो ज़रूर मर जाता।

बेन को जैसे ही दादी के पिछवाड़े की चूं-चूं पास आती सुनाई पड़ी, वह तेज़ी से मेज़ की ओर दौड़ा। वहाँ बैठ, हाथ में चम्मच और मेज़ पर ख़ाली प्याले के साथ शराफ़त का ढोंग करने लगा। "मैंने सूप ख़त्म कर दिया, धन्यवाद दादी। स्वादिष्ट था!"

"अच्छी बात है," हाथ में कढ़ाई लिये दादी धीरे से मेज़ की ओर आते हुए बोलीं। "तुम्हारे लिए मेरे पास और सूप है!" मुस्कुराते हुए उसके लिए एक और कटोरी सूप डाल दी।

बेन डर के मारे सूप सुड़कने लगा।

3

प्लम्बिंग वीकली

"**मुझे** *प्लम्बिंग वीकली* नहीं मिल रही, राज।"
बेन बोला।

अगले शुक्रवार को यह लड़का मोहल्ले
में अखबार वाले की दुकान में पत्रिकाओं के शेल्फ़
की तलाशी ले रहा था। यह पत्रिका पेशेवर नलसाज़ों
के लिए थी और बेन को पन्ने-पन्ने पर पाइप, नली,
नलके, टंकियाँ, बॉयलर और नालियाँ मंत्रमुग्ध कर
देती थीं। एक यही पत्रिका थी जो उसे पढ़नी अच्छी
लगती थी—वो भी क्योंकि तस्वीरें और नक़्शे ठूँस-
ठूँसकर भरे थे।

जब से बेन ने चीज़ों को पकड़ना शुरू किया था

तभी से उसे ठीक करना पसन्द था। जब दूसरे बच्चे बतख़ के साथ टब में खेलते थे, तब बेन ने अपने माता-पिता से नली के छोटे टुकड़े माँगे थे और पानी पहुँचाने की जटिल व्यवस्था बना डाली थी। अगर कोई नल बह रहा होता है तो, बेन ही उसे ठीक करता है। अगर कोई शौचालय रुक जाता है तो, बेन को उबकाई नहीं आती, बल्कि वह बहुत खुश हो जाता है।

वैसे, बेन के माता-पिता को उसके प्लम्बर बनने पर ऐतराज़ था। वे चाहते थे कि बेन अमीर और मशहूर बने और जहाँ तक उन्हें मालूम था, आज तक कोई भी प्लम्बर अमीर और मशहूर नहीं हुआ था। बेन पढ़ने में जितना कच्चा था उतना ही हाथों की कला में माहिर था और किसी भी प्लम्बर को नल ठीक करते देखने में उसे खूब मज़ा आता था। वह उसको मोह लेता था, ठीक उसी तरह जैसे कोई जूनियर डाक्टर किसी बड़े सर्जन को ऑपरेशन करते देखे।

उसके माता-पिता को तो वह हमेशा मनहूस ही लगता था। उनको तो बस चाहिए था कि उनका बेटा बॉलरूम डांसर बनने का उनका सपना पूरा कर दे जो

वह खुद नहीं पूरा कर पाये थे। बेन के माता-पिता का बॉलरूम डांस के लिए प्यार देर से जागा था, जिसकी वजह से वे दोनों कभी विजेता नहीं बन पाये। दरअसल, सच तो यह था कि उन दोनों को भाग लेने से ज़्यादा, पसर कर टीवी देखने में अधिक दिलचस्पी थी।

वैसे, बेन अपने शौक को अपने तक ही रखना चाहता था। अपने माता-पिता को निराश ना करने के लिए *प्लम्बिंग वीकली* को वो अपने बिस्तर के नीचे छिपा देता। उसने अखबारवाले राज के साथ भी साँठ-गाँठ कर ली थी कि वह हर हफ़्ते उसकी पत्रिका अलग रख दे। लेकिन, अभी उसको कहीं नहीं मिल रही थी।

बेन ने *केरॉंग* और *हीट पत्रिका* के पीछे, यहाँ तक कि महिलाओं की पत्रिका *द लेडी* के पीछे भी अपनी पत्रिका तलाशी, लेकिन सारी मेहनत बेकार गयी। राज की दुकान में किताबों का उल्टा-पुल्टा ढेर लगा रहता था, हर तरफ़ किताबें बिखरी रहती थीं, फिर भी लोग मीलों दूर से उसकी दुकान में खरीददारी करने आते थे क्योंकि वह सबके चेहरों पर मुस्कुराहट ला देता था।

राज सीढ़ियों पर चढ़ कर क्रिसमस की सजावट लगा रहा था। वैसे तो मैं इसे 'क्रिसमस की सजावट' बता रहा हूँ, लेकिन असल में वो 'हेपी बर्थ-डे' का बैनर लगा रहा था। हालाँकि उसने बर्थ-डे को मिटा कर, टेढ़े-मेढ़े तरीक़े से क्रिसमस लिख दिया था।

बेन की मदद करने के लिए राज सीढ़ी से उतरा।

"तुम्हारी *प्लम्बिंग वीकली* ... वो हम्ममम ... सोचने दो, तुमने बोनबोन की टॉफ़ियों के पास देखा?" राज ने पूछा।

"हाँ।" बेन ने जवाब दिया।

"चित्रकारी की किताबों के नीचे भी नहीं है?"

"नहीं।"

"और क्या तुमने चुइंग गम के मर्तबान के पीछे भी देखा?"

"हाँ।"

"यह तो रहस्यमय है। मुझे याद है कि मैंने तुम्हारे लिए एक मँगवाई थी, छोटे बेन। हम्म ... बड़ी अजीब

बात है," राज बहुत धीरे से बोला जिस तरीके से लोग सोचते हुए बोलते हैं। "मुझे माफ़ कर दो बेन, मैं जानता हूँ कि तुम्हें वह बेहद पसन्द है, लेकिन मुझे मालूम नहीं कि वह है कहाँ। वैसे, मेरे पास आइसक्रीम पर विशेष ऑफ़र है।"

"राज, नवम्बर चल रहा है और बाहर कड़ाके की ठंड है!" बेन बोला "आइसक्रीम कौन खायेगा?"

"हर कोई, जब वह मेरा ऑफ़र सुनेगा! रुको, पहले तो तुम सुनो, तेईस आइसक्रीमों के साथ एक मुफ़्त!"

"मैं पागल हूँ क्या जो मैं चौबीस आइसक्रीम लूँगा?" बेन हँसते हुए बोला।

"वैसे तो, मुझे नहीं पता, तुम शायद बारह खा सकते हो और बाकी अपनी जेब में डाल कर, बाद में खा सकते हो।"

"यह बहुत ज़्यादा आइसक्रीम है, राज। तुम इनसे छुटकारा क्यों पाना चाहते हो?"

"यह कुछ दिनों में ख़राब हो जायेंगी," राज बोला और फिर लड़खड़ाते हुए फ्रीज़र का दरवाज़ा खोला और आइसक्रीम का डिब्बा निकाला। एक ठंडा-सा फुहारा एकदम से दुकान को धुँधला कर गया। "देखो! 15 नवम्बर से पहले इस्तेमाल करें।"

बेन ने डिब्बे को ध्यान से देखा, "इस पर तो 15 नवम्बर 1996 लिखा है।"

"अच्छा," राज बोला, "अब तो विशेष ऑफ़र देना ही पड़ेगा। सुनो बेन, मेरा आखिरी ऑफ़र। एक डिब्बा आइसक्रीम के साथ दस बिल्कुल मुफ़्त!"

"राज, बहुत शुक्रिया, लेकिन नहीं," बेन बोला। उसने फ़्रीज़र के अन्दर घात में बैठी चीज़ों के बीच झाँका। उसमें हमेशा बर्फ़ जमी रहती ... कभी पिघलाई नहीं गयी थी और बेन को आश्चर्य नहीं होता अगर वहाँ पर कोई हिम युग का मैमथ सुरक्षित रखा मिलता।

"रुको," उसने आइसक्रीमों पर जमी बर्फ़ को हटाते हुए कहा। "यहाँ है! *प्लम्बिंग वीकली!*"

"शुक्र है! मुझे अब याद आ गया," राज बोला। "मैंने वहाँ तुम्हारे लिए ताज़ा रखने के लिए रखी थी।"

"ताज़ा?" बेन बोला।

"नौजवान, यह पत्रिका मंगलवार को आती है, और आज शुक्रवार है। तो मैंने फ़्रीज़र में उसे तुम्हारे

लिए ताज़ा रखने के लिए रखी थी। मैं नहीं चाहता था कि वह आइसक्रीमों की तरह बासी हो जाये।

बेन यह तो नहीं जानता था कि कैसे कोई पत्रिका आइसक्रीम की तरह ख़राब हो सकती है, लेकिन उसने अखबारवाले का शुक्रिया अदा किया और कहा, "आप बड़े दयालु हैं, राज। और मुझे रोलोस की गोलियों का एक पैकेट चाहिए।"

"मैं तुमको तिहत्तर रोलोस की गोलियों के पैकेटों को बहत्तर के दाम पर दे सकता हूँ!" अखबारवाले ने उत्साह से कहा और मुस्कुरा कर उसको ललकारने की कोशिश की।

"नहीं, धन्यवाद, राज।"

"एक हज़ार रोलोस की गोलियों के पैकेटों को नौ सौ निन्यानवे के दाम पर दूँ?"

"नहीं, धन्यवाद," बेन ने बोला।

"बेन क्या तुम पागल हो? इतना बेहतरीन ऑफ़र है। अच्छा अच्छा, ठीक है, तुमको और अच्छा सौदा

चाहिए। दस लाख सात रोलोस की गोलियों के पैकेटों को तुम दस लाख चार के भाव से ले जाओ। इससे तीन पैकेट मुफ़्त।"

"मुझे सिर्फ़ एक पैकेट और पत्रिका ही चाहिए, धन्यवाद।"

"ज़रूर, नौजवान!"

"मुझे आज *प्लम्बिंग वीकली* पढ़ने का बेसब्री से इन्तज़ार है। मुझे आज फिर से अपनी बोरिंग दादी के घर पूरी रात बितानी पड़ेगी।"

पिछली भेंट हुए एक हफ़्ता भी हो गया था और आज फिर से शुक्रवार दनदनाते हुए आ गया था। उसके माता-पिता आज एक रोमांटिक फ़िल्म देखने जा रहे थे। रोमांस और चुम्मा और वो सारी गू। छी छी छी।

"च, च, च," राज अपना सिर हिलाते हुए बोला और बाकी के पैसे दिये।

बेन को अचानक ही शर्मिंदगी महसूस हुई। उसने अखबारवाले को पहले कभी ऐसा करते नहीं देखा था।

सारे बच्चों की तरह बेन भी यह ही सोचता था की राज उन में से नहीं बल्कि हम में से एक है। वह ज़िन्दादिल था और माता-पिता, अध्यापकों, अन्य सभी बड़ों से कोसों दूर था जिन्हें लगता था कि वे आपको कुछ भी बोल सकते हैं, महज इसलिये क्योंकि वे आपसे बड़े हैं।

"सिर्फ़ इसलिए की तुम्हारी दादी बूढ़ी हैं, नन्हें बेन," राज बोला, "इसका मतलब यह नहीं है कि वह बोरिंग हैं। मैं भी बूढ़ा हो रहा हूँ। और मैं जब भी तुम्हारी दादी से मिला हूँ, मुझे तो वह बहुत दिलचस्प लगीं।

"लेकिन—"

"उन पर इतनी भी सख़्ती मत करो बेन," राज ने निवेदन किया। "हम सब एक दिन बूढ़े हो जायेंगे। तुम भी। और मुझे यक़ीन है कि तुम्हारी दादी का भी अपना कोई ना कोई राज़ ज़रूर होगा। बुज़ुर्गों के हमेशा होते हैं।"

4

रहस्य और आश्चर्य

बेन को बिल्कुल नहीं लगता था कि दादी के बारे में राज की बात सही हो सकती थी। इस रात भी फिर वही कहानी। दादी ने बन्दगोभी का सूप, फिर बन्दगोभी की कचौड़ी और बन्दगोभी की मिठाई परोसी। उनको तो भोजन के बाद खाने वाली बन्दगोभी के स्वाद वाली चॉकलेट* भी कहीं से मिल गयी थी। भोजन के बाद, दादी और बेन, हर बार की तरह फ़फ़ूँदीदार पुराने सोफ़े पर बैठ गए।

"स्क्रैबल खेलने का वक्त हो गया है," दादी खुशी से चहकी।

---

* बन्दगोभी के स्वाद वाली चॉकलेट उतनी अच्छी नहीं है जितनी सुनने में लगती है, और वैसे तो वो सुनने में भी अच्छी नहीं है।

बहुत बढ़िया, बेन ने सोचा। *आज की रात पिछले शुक्रवार से लाख गुणा और बोरिंग होगी।*

बेन को स्क्रैबल से घृणा थी। उसका बस चलता, तो वह रॉकेट बना कर, दुनिया के सारे स्क्रैबल बोर्ड को उड़ा देता और अन्तरिक्ष में भेज देता। दादी ने धूल से ढके स्क्रैबल के पुराने डिब्बे को अलमारी से निकाला और खेलने के लिए बिछा दिया।

बेन ने एक ठंडी आह भरी।

सदियों सरीखे लगने वाले कुछ पल तक, जो हकीकत में कुछ घंटे ही थे, बेन अपने हाथ आये अक्षरों को ताकता रहा। फिर उसने बोर्ड पर बने शब्दों पर नज़र दौड़ाई। अब तक उसने बनाया था:

BORING

ANCIENT

QUACK (दुगने स्कोर वाला)

POINTLESS

PONGY (इसे शब्दकोश में देखना पड़ा)

WRINKLES

CABBAGESICK (तिगुना स्कोर)

ESCAPE

HELP

IHATETHISSTUPIDGAME (दादी ने इसे माना नही क्योंकि यह एक शब्द नहीं था)

"ठीक है, अब तो आठ बजने वाले हैं, बेटा," दादी ने अपनी छोटी सी-सुनहरी घड़ी को देखते हुए कहा। "मुझे लगता है छोटे बाबू के सोने का वक्त हो गया है।"

बेन अपने आप से बड़बड़ाया। *छोटे बाबू! मैं बच्चा नहीं हूँ।*

"लेकिन मुझे तो घर पर भी नौ बजे नहीं सोना पड़ता!" उसने विरोध किया। "और जब अगले दिन

स्कूल ना हो तब तो दस बजे।"

"नहीं बेन, अभी चलो तुम बिस्तर में।" दादी को जब सख़्ती दिखानी होती तो वह बख़ूबी दिखाती थीं। "और ब्रश करना मत भूलना। मैं बस आ ही रही हूँ, अगर तुम चाहो तो तुम्हें कहानी-किस्से सुनाने। सोने से पहले तुम्हें कहानी सुनना हमेशा से अच्छा लगता है।"

कुछ देर बाद बेन, बाथरूम के सिंक के सामने खड़ा था। यह कमरा ठंडा और गलन भरा था, न ही इसमें कोई खिड़की थी। काफ़ी टाइलें तो दीवार से गिर भी रही थीं। बस एक घिसा हुआ पुराना तौलिया था और एक पुराना साबुन था, जो साबुन कम फ़फ़ूँद ज़्यादा लग रहा था।

बेन को ब्रश करने से नफ़रत थी। तो उसने ब्रश करने का ढोंग किया। यह ढोंग करना बहुत ही आसान था। अपने माता-पिता को मत बताना कि मैंने तुम्हें यह बताया, लेकिन अगर तुम्हें कोशिश करनी है तो तुम बस क्रमबद्ध तरीके से इस विधि का पालन कर सकते हो:

रहस्य और आश्चर्य

1) ठंडे पानी का नल खोलो

2) ब्रश को गीला करो

3) अपनी अंगुली पर थोड़ी-सी टूथपेस्ट लगाओ और अंगुली को मुँह में डालो

4) अपनी जीभ से टूथपेस्ट को दाँतों पर लगाओ

5) थूको

6) नल को बंद कर दो

देखा? कितना आसान था। एकदम दाँतों को ब्रश करने जितना आसान।

बेन ने शीशे में अपने-आप को देखा। वह ग्यारह साल का था, लेकिन अभी भी उसके हिसाब से उसका क़द कम था, इसलिए वह अभी अपने पंजों पर खड़ा था। बेन बेसब्री से बड़ा होना चाहता था।

बस कुछ साल और, बेन ने सोचा, फिर वह लम्बा होगा, घने बाल होंगे और उसका रंगबिरंगा अन्दाज़ होगा। और उसकी शुक्रवार की शाम बहुत ही अलग होगी।

उसे अपनी बोरिंग बूढ़ी दादी के साथ समय नहीं बिताना पड़ेगा। बदले में बेन शहर के बड़े बच्चों वाली रोमांचक चीज़ें कर पायेगा:

जब तक डांट ना पड़े तब तक वह अपने दोस्तों की टोली के साथ वो सारे काम कर पायेगा जो वैसे मना हैं।

या फिर वह बस अड्डे पर ट्रैक सूट पहनने वाली लड़कियों के साथ बस चूइंग गम चबाते हुए समय

बितायेगा जहाँ दरअसल कोई भी बस नहीं पकड़ता है।

यकीनन, रहस्यों और चमत्कारों से भरी दुनिया उसका इन्तज़ार कर रही थी।

लेकिन, अभी, बाहर अँधेरा भी नहीं हुआ था और कुछ लड़के पास के पार्क में फ़ुटबाल खेल रहे थे, और बेन के सोने का वक्त हो गया था। एक सख़्त बिस्तर में, एक सीले हुए छोटे कमरे में, अपनी दादी के छोटे-से पुराने बंगले में। जिस में से बन्दगोभी की बदबू आती थी।

थोड़ी-सी नहीं।

बहुत ज़्यादा।

आह भरते हुए बेन कम्बल में घुस गया।

उसी समय, दादी ने हल्के से दरवाज़ा खोला। उसने जल्दी-से अपनी आँखें बन्द कर सोने का ढोंग किया। वह धीरे-धीरे चलते हुए बिस्तर की तरफ़ आयीं। जिस तरीक़े से वह वहाँ खड़ी थीं, बेन उनकी उपस्थिति महसूस कर सकता था।

"मैं तुम्हें कहानी किस्से सुनाने वाली थी।" वह फुसफुसाई। उसकी बूढ़ी दादी ने पहले भी उसे बहुत सारे समुद्री लूटेरों, तस्करों और शातिर चोर-उचक्कों की कहानियाँ सुनाई थीं, लेकिन अब वह इन सब बकवास के लिए बड़ा हो गया था।

"ओह, तुम सो गये!" उन्होंने कहा। "मैं सिर्फ़ तुम्हें बताना चाहती थी कि मैं तुमसे कितना प्यार करती हूँ। शुभ रात्रि मेरे नन्हें बेनी।"

उसे 'बेनी' नाम से भी नफ़रत थी। और 'नन्हा'।

बुरा सपना खत्म नहीं हुआ था, बेन को महसूस हुआ की दादी झुकीं और उसको चूमा। उनकी कांटेदार बालों वाली ठोड़ी बेन के गालों पर ख़ुदरती हुई गयी। फिर उसने उनके चूं-चूं करते हर क़दम की वजह से पिछवाड़े से बतख़ की वही आवाज़ सुनी।

चूं-चूं करती हुई वह दरवाज़े की ओर गयीं और उसे बन्द करते ही सारी बदबू अन्दर ही समा गयी।

बस, बेन ने सोचा, *मुझे यहाँ से भागना पड़ेगा!*

5

थोड़ी निराशा

खर्*ऱऱऱऱऱऱऱऱऱऱऱऱऱऱऱऱऱऱऱऱऱऱऱऱऱऱऱऱऱऱऱ*
ऱऱऱऱऱऱऱऱऱऱऱऱऱऱऱ ...

नहीं, मेरे पाठक, तुमने ग़लती से स्वाहीली भाषा
की किताब नहीं खरीदी है। बेन को तो बस इस आवाज़
का इन्तज़ार था।

दादी के खर्राटों का।

वह सो गयी थीं।

खर्ऱऱऱऱऱऱऱऱऱऱऱऱऱऱऱऱऱऱऱऱऱऱऱऱऱऱऱऱऱऱऱ
ऱऱऱऱऱऱऱऱऱऱऱऱऱऱऱ ...

बेन दबे पाँव कमरे से निकला और हॉल में फ़ोन

की तरफ़ गया। पुराने ज़माने का फ़ोन था, जिसे डायल करने पर बिल्लियों की आवाज़ निकलती थी।

"माँ?" वह फ़ुसफ़ुसाया।

"मुझे कुछ सुनाई नहीं दे रहा है!" उन्होंने चिल्लाते हुए कहा। पीछे ज़ोरों से जैज़ संगीत चल रहा था। माँ और बाबा फिर से मंच पर *स्ट्रिक्टली स्टार्स डांसिंग लाईव* देखने गये थे। शायद उनको फ़्लावीओ फ़्लावीओलि को ठुमकते और उनकी उम्र की हज़ारों औरतों का दिल तोड़ते देख, मुँह में पानी आ रहा था। "क्या बात है? सब कुछ ठीक है ना? वह बूढ़ी चमगादड़ मर तो नहीं गयी?"

"नहीं, वह ठीक हैं, लेकिन मुझे यहाँ रहने से नफ़रत है। आप मुझे घर नहीं ले जा सकते? प्लीज़?" बेन फ़ुसफ़ुसाया।

"फ़्लावीओ अभी तक दूसरी बार नाचा भी नहीं है।"

"प्लीज़," उसने विनती की। "मुझे घर जाना है। दादी एक दम पका देती हैं। यहाँ समय बिताना बेहद

तकलीफ़दायक है।"

"अपने बाबा से बात करो।" जैसे ही माँ ने फ़ोन बाबा को दिया, बेन को एक दबी हुई आवाज़ सुनाई दी।

"हेलो?" बाबा चिल्लाए।

"प्लीज़ धीरे बोलो!"

"क्यों?" वह फिर से चीखे।

"शश। धीरे बोलो। आप दादी को जगा दोगे। बाबा, आप मुझे यहाँ से ले जा सकते हो? प्लीज़? मुझे यहाँ रहने से नफ़रत है।

"नहीं, हम नहीं आ सकते। यह हमारी ज़िन्दगी का सबसे अनूठा अनुभव है जो दोबारा नहीं आयेगा।"

"पिछले शुक्रवार को तो देखा था आपने!" बेन ने विरोध किया।

"अच्छा तो दो बार ज़िन्दगी में।"

"और आप ने बताया था कि आप अगले हफ़्ते फिर से जायेंगे।"

"सुनो, अगर तुम यह बदतमीज़ी जारी रखने वाले हो, तो तुम क्रिसमस तक वहीं रहोगे। बाय-बाय।"

यह बोलते ही, उन्होंने फ़ोन रख दिया। बेन ने ध्यान से फ़ोन रखा और फ़ोन से हल्की-सी *टिंग* की आवाज़ आयी।

लेकिन उसे अहसास हुआ कि दादी के ख़र्राटों की आवाज़ बन्द हो गयी थी।

क्या उन्होंने मेरी बात सुन ली? उसने पीछे देखा और उसे लगा कि उनकी परछाईं थी जो अब जा चुकी थी।

यह सच था कि बेन को वह अत्यन्त बोरिंग लगती थीं, लेकिन वह नहीं चाहता था कि उनको यह बात पता चले। आख़िरकार वह एक बूढ़ी विधवा थीं, और उनके पति बेन के पैदा होने से पहले ही गुज़र चुके थे। शर्मिंदगी से बेन दबे पाँव कमरे में चला गया और सुबह का इन्तज़ार करता रहा।

नाश्ते पर दादी कुछ बदली हुई लग रही थीं।

अजीब-सी चुप्पी थी। शायद थोड़ी और बूढ़ी। और थोड़ी निराश भी।

उनकी आँखें लाल थीं, ऐसा लग रहा था कि वह

रात भर रो रही थीं।

क्या उन्होंने सुन लिया था? बेन ने सोचा। *काश उन्होंने ना सुना हो।*

वह अवन के पास खड़ी थीं और बेन रसोई के छोटे से मेज़ पर बैठा था। दादी अवन पर लगे कैलेंडर में दिलचस्पी दिखाने का ढोंग कर रही थीं। बेन को उनका ढोंग समझ आ रहा था क्योंकि कैलेंडर में कुछ भी मज़ेदार नहीं था।

दादी की अत्यन्त व्यस्त ज़िन्दगी का एक हफ़्ता कुछ ऐसा था:

सोमवार: बन्दगोभी का सूप बनाओ। अपने विरुद्ध ही स्क्रैबल खेलो। किताब पढ़ो।

मंगलवार: बन्दगोभी कचौड़ी बनाओ। एक और किताब पढ़ो। हवा छोड़ते रहो।

बुधवार: 'ताज्जुब से भरी चॉकलेट' पकवान बनाओ। ताज्जुब की बात यह थी कि उस में कोई चॉकलेट नहीं थी। सिर्फ़ 100% बन्दगोभी ही थी।

गुरुवार: मिंट की गोलियाँ पूरा दिन खाओ।

(वह एक गोली को पूरी ज़िन्दगी खा सकती थीं।)

शुक्रवार: अभी भी मिंट की गोलियाँ चूसते रहो। मेरा लाजवाब पोता आता होगा।

शनिवार: मेरा लाजवाब पोता चला गया है। फिर से आराम से बैठो। एकदम थकी हुई।

रविवार: तन्दूरी बन्दगोभी के साथ उबली हुई बन्दगोभी। पूरा दिन हवा छोड़ो।

कुछ ही देर में दादी ने कैलेंडर छोड़ा। "तुम्हारे माँ-बाबा तुम्हें लेने के लिए आते ही होंगे," आखिर में उन्होंने अपनी चुप्पी तोड़ी।

"जी," बेन ने अपनी घड़ी देखते हुए कहा। "बस कुछ और मिनट।"

वह कुछ मिनट घंटे जैसे लग रहे थे। दिन भी। महीने!

एक मिनट बहुत लम्बा लग सकता है। यकीन नहीं होता? तो अपने कमरे में अकेले बैठो और साठ सेकंड गिनने के अलावा कुछ भी मत करो।

किया तुमने? मुझ पर यकीन नहीं है? मैं मज़ाक नहीं कर रहा। मैं सच में चाहता हूँ कि तुम यह करो।

मैं यह कहानी आगे नहीं बढ़ाऊँगा जब तक तुम यह नहीं करोगे।

तुम मेरा समय ख़राब नहीं कर रहे हो।

मेरे पास तो पूरा दिन है।

अच्छा, तो तुमने कर लिया? ख़ूब। अब कहानी को आगे बढ़ाते हैं।

ग्यारह बजने के कुछ ही देर में, एक छोटी भूरी गाड़ी दादी के घर के सामने आ कर रुक गयी। माँ ने इंजिन बन्द ही नहीं किया। ऐसा लग रहा था कि जल्दबाज़ी में बैंक में डकैती डालने आयी हैं। आगे झुककर उन्होंने दरवाज़ा खोला ताकि बेन तेज़ी से गाड़ी में घुस जाये और वह वहाँ से भागें।

बेन पाँव घसीटते हुए गाड़ी की तरफ़ जा रहा था जब दादी दरवाज़े पर खड़ी थीं। ''तुम चाय के लिए अन्दर आओगी, लिंडा?'' उन्होंने ज़ोर से आवाज़ दी।

"नहीं, धन्यवाद" बेन की माँ बोलीं। "भगवान के लिए जल्दी करो बेन!" इंजिन गुर्रा रहा था। "मुझे इस बुढ़िया से बात नहीं करनी।"

"शुश!" बेन बोला। "उन्हें सुनाई दे जायेगा!"

"मुझे लगता था कि तुमको दादी पसन्द नहीं हैं?" माँ बोलीं।

"मैंने ऐसा नहीं बोला माँ। मुझे वह बोरिंग लगती हैं, लेकिन मैं नहीं चाहता कि यह बात उन्हें पता चले, है ना?"

54

माँ ने हँसते हुए ग्रे क्लोज़ मोहल्ले से गाड़ी दूर भगाई। "चिन्ता करने की ज़रूरत नहीं है बेन, दादी को नहीं समझ आयेगा। जो तुम बोलते हो वो उनके सिर के ऊपर से उड़ जाता होगा।"

बेन ने त्यौरी चढ़ायी। उसे इस बात पर सन्देह था। उसे बिल्कुल भी ठीक नहीं लग रहा था। उसे नाश्ते के समय उनकी उतरी हुई शक्ल याद आ रही थी। अचानक उसे महसूस हुआ कि दादी को वह सब समझ आ गया था जो उसने ख़ुद भी नहीं सोचा था।

6

ठंडा गिलगिला अंडा

अगर बेन अपनी पत्रिका लाना भूल जाता, तो यह शुक्रवार की रात भी पिछली बार की तरह एकदम पकाऊ होने वाली थी। एक बार फिर माँ-बाबा ने अपने इकलौते बेटे को दादी के यहाँ पटक दिया था।

जैसे ही बेन पहुँचा, वह उनके समीप से भागते हुए अपने ठंडे सीलन भरे कमरे में गया, दरवाज़ा बन्द किया और अपनी *प्लम्बिंग वीकली* पढ़ने लगा। उसमें बहुत सारे रंग-बिरंगे चित्रों के साथ एक आधुनिकतम बॉइलर लगाने का अद्भुत तरीका दिया हुआ था। बेन ने उस पन्ने को हल्का-सा मोड़ लिया। अब उसे पता था कि उसे क्रिसमस के लिए क्या चाहिए था।

पूरी पत्रिका पढ़ने के बाद, बेन ने आहें भरीं और ड्राइंग-रूम में गया। वह जानता था कि वह पूरी शाम इस कमरे में नहीं बिता सकता था।

दादी ने उसकी ओर देखा और मुस्कुराईं। "स्क्रैबल खेलें!" बोर्ड पकड़ कर वे प्रसन्नता से बोलीं।

अगले दिन सुबह एक घोर चुप्पी छायी हुई थी।

"एक और उबला अंडा दूँ?" दादी ने अपनी छोटी-सी, पुरानी, घिसी-पिटी रसोई में पूछा।

बेन को उबले अंडे पसन्द नहीं थे और ना ही उसने अपना पहला ख़त्म किया था। दादी तो साधारण खाने को भी बर्बाद कर सकती थीं। अंडे हमेशा ही पिलपिले होते थे और उबले अंडों के साथ खाने वाले सोल्जर ब्रेड हमेशा की तरह काली जली होती थी। जब बूढ़ी दादी देख नहीं रही होती थीं, तब बेन चम्मच से अंडे को झटके से खिड़की के बाहर फेंक देता और ब्रेड के टुकड़ों को रेडियेटर के पीछे रख देता। अब तक तो वहाँ ब्रेड की दुकान तैयार हो गयी होगी।

"नहीं, शुक्रिया दादी। मेरा पेट भर गया है," बेन ने जवाब दिया। "स्वादिष्ट उबले अंडे थे। धन्यवाद।"

"म्म," बूढ़ी औरत को यक़ीन नहीं हो रहा था। "आज कुछ ठंड-सी है। मैं एक कार्डिगन पहन लेती हूँ," उन्होंने बोला, जब कि उन्होंने दो पहले से ही पहने हुए थे। दादी भारी क़दमों के साथ बतख़ों की आवाज़ निकालते हुए कमरे से निकलीं।

बेन ने बचे हुए अंडों को भी खिड़की से बाहर फेंक दिया और कुछ और खाने के लिए ढूँढना शुरू किया। वह जानता था कि दादी ने चॉकलेट बिस्कुट का एक डिब्बा रसोई की अलमारी के ऊपर छिपा रखा था। दादी उसके हर जन्मदिन पर एक चाकलेट बिस्कुट देती थीं। जब दादी की बन्दगोभी के पकवान उसे एक भेड़िए की तरह भूखा छोड़ देते थे, तब बेन कभी-कबार एक-दो बिस्कुट चट कर ही लेता था।

उसने जल्दी से अलमारी के साथ कुर्सी लगायी और बिस्कुट के लिए उस पर चढ़ गया। उसने बिस्कुट के डिब्बे को उठाया। वह ख़ास बिस्कुटों का डिब्बा

था जिसके ढक्कन पर एलिज़ाबेथ द्वितीय की तस्वीर थी, जिसका रंग उड़ गया था। डिब्बा बहुत भारी था। हमेशा से ज़्यादा भारी।

अजीब है।

बेन ने डिब्बा थोड़ा हिलाया। ऐसा लग नहीं रहा था कि उस में बिस्कुट पड़े थे। बल्कि उसमें पत्थर और कंचे पड़े लग रहे थे।

और भी अजीब।

बेन ने ढक्कन घुमाया।

वह घूरने लगा।

और फटी आँखों से वो घूरता ही रह गया।

उसे अपनी आँखों पर यक़ीन नहीं हो रहा था।

हीरे! अँगूठियाँ, चूड़ियाँ, मालाएँ, बालियाँ, सब कुछ बड़े-बड़े चमकते हीरों के साथ। हीरे, हीरे और हीरे!

बेन को कुछ ख़ास पता नहीं था लेकिन उसे समझ आ गया कि इस बिस्कुट के डिब्बे में पड़े आभूषणों की

क़ीमत तो हज़ारों पाउंड की होगी, शायद लाखों।

अचानक बतख़ की आवाज़ निकालती हुईं दादी कमरे में आयीं। हड़बड़ी में टटोलते हुए उसने डिब्बा बन्द किया और वापस अलमारी के ऊपर रख दिया। उसने छलांग मारी, झटक कर कुर्सी को खींचा और मेज़ पर बैठ गया।

खिड़की पर सरसरी नज़र डाली तो देखा कि बगीचे में फेंका अंडा पूरे शीशे पर फैला हुआ था। अगर वह सूख गया तो दादी को ब्लोटॉर्च का इस्तेमाल करना पड़ेगा। फ़टाफ़ट वह खिड़की की ओर भागा, और ठंडे गिलगिले अंडे को चूस लिया, फिर अपनी कुर्सी पर बैठ गया।

उसको निगलना इतना अजीब था कि घबराहट में बेन ने उसको अपने मुँह में ही भरकर रखा।

दादी पैरों को धीरे-धीरे घसीटते हुए वापस रसोई में अपना तीसरा स्वेटर पहन कर आयीं।

अभी भी बतख़ की आवाज़ें निकालते हुए।

"बेहतर होगा अगर तुम अपना कोट पहन लो, नौजवान। तुम्हारे माँ-बाबा पलक झपकते ही आते होंगे।" वह मुस्कुराईं।

बेन ने ना चाहते हुए ठंडे गिलगिले अंडे को निगल लिया। वह उसके गले से फिसलता हुआ उसके अन्दर जा रहा था।

छी, छी, छी! "जी," वह बोला और उलटी के डर के मारे अंडा वापस खिड़की पर चिपका दिया।

अंडे की भुर्जी।

7

खाद के बोरे

"क्या मैं आज रात दादी के घर फिर से रह सकता हूँ?" बेन ने अपने माँ-बाबा की छोटी भूरी गाड़ी की पिछली सीट में बैठे हुए पूछा। बिस्कुट के डिब्बे में पड़े हीरे इतने उलझाऊ थे कि वो उनकी जासूसी करने को उतावला हो रहा था। शायद दादी के बंगले का चप्पा-चप्पा छानना पड़ेगा। यह सब बेहद रहस्यमय था। राज ने कहा था कि दादी के एक-दो राज़ होंगे। और अब लग रहा था कि वह सही था! और जो भी दादी का राज़ था, उसको समझने के लिए हीरों का दिलचस्प रहस्य भी सुनना होगा। क्या पता उनके पास अनगिनत पाउंड रहे हों? या तो उन्होंने हीरों के खान में काम

किया हो? या किसी राजकुमारी ने उन्हें दिये? बेन को पता लगाने का बेसब्री से इन्तज़ार था।

"क्या?" बाबा ने अचम्भित हो कर पूछा।

"लेकिन तुमने तो कहा था कि वह बोरिंग हैं," माँ भी अचम्भित थीं और साथ ही साथ चिढ़ भी रही थीं। "तुमने कहा था कि सारे बुज़ुर्ग बोरिंग होते हैं।"

"मैं तो मज़ाक कर रहा था," बेन बोला।

बाबा ने रियरव्यू मिरर से अपने बेटे को ध्यान से देखा। उनके लिए अपने प्लम्बिंग के शौक़ीन बेटे को अच्छे समय में भी समझना मुश्किल था। अब तो बेन बिल्कुल ही समझ के बाहर हो गया था। "अच्छा ... अगर तुम यही चाहते हो तो, बेन..."

"मुझे जाना ही है बाबा।"

"मैं घर पहुँचकर उन्हें फ़ोन करता हूँ। क्या पता वह कहीं बाहर जाने वाली हों।"

"बाहर जाना!" माँ हँसी। "वह बीस सालों से बाहर नहीं गयी हैं!" माँ कुड़कुड़ाईं।

63

बेन को समझ नहीं आया कि इसमें मज़ाक की क्या बात थी।

"मैं एक बार उनको सेंट्रल पार्क लेकर गया था।" बाबा ने कहा।

"वह सिर्फ़ इसलिए क्योंकि तुम्हें खाद के इतने सारे बोरों को उठाने के लिए मदद चाहिए थी," माँ ने कहा।

"लेकिन वह एक शानदार दिन तो था ना," बाबा ने नाराज़गी दिखाते हुए बोला।

बाद में बेन अपने बिस्तर में अकेला बैठा था। उसका दिमाग़ दौड़ रहा था।

दुनिया के किस कोने से दादी को वह हीरे मिले?

कितने के होंगे?

अगर वह इतनी अमीर थीं, तो वह ऐसे छोटे से बंगले में क्यों रहती हैं?

बेन जवाब ढूँढता ही रहा लेकिन कुछ समझ नहीं आया।

फिर बाबा कमरे में आये।

"दादी को कोई काम है। उनका बहुत मन था तुमसे मिलने का, लेकिन आज वह बाहर जा रही हैं।" उन्होंने बताया।

"क्या?" बेन गुस्से में बड़बड़ाया। बेन ने दादी के कैलेंडर में देखा था कि वह तो बहुत ही कम बाहर जाती हैं। यह रहस्य और गाढ़ा होता जा रहा था।

8

एक मर्तबान में नकली बाल

बेन दादी के घर के पास वाली झाड़ियों में जा छुपा। जब उसके माँ और बाबा नीचे ड्रॉईंग रूम में टीवी पर *स्ट्रिक्टली स्टार्स डांसिंग* देख रहे थे, तब बेन अपने कमरे की खिड़की के साथ लगे पाइप से नीचे उतरा और पाँच मील दूर, दादी के घर साइकिल से जा पहुँचा।

यह अपने आप में ही उसकी दादी के प्रति उत्सुकता का प्रतीक था। उसको साइकिल चलाना पसन्द नहीं था। उसके माता-पिता उसे हमेशा कसरत करने के लिए उत्साहित करते रहते थे। कहते थे कि पेशेवर डांसर बनने के लिए ज़रूरी था कि वह तन्दुरुस्त रहे। लेकिन क्योंकि बेन को सिंक के नीचे लेट कर नयी

पीतल की पाइप लगानी पड़ती थी, इसलिए उसे और कोई कसरत करने की वजह नहीं दिखती थी।

अब तक।

अगर दादी बीस साल में आज बाहर जा रही थीं, तब बेन को जानना था कि कहाँ। क्या पता इस से उसको कोई सुराग मिल जाये कि दादी के पास बिस्कुट के डिब्बे में इतने हीरे कैसे थे।

बेन ने अपनी सारी जी-जान से हाँफते-हाँफते नहर के साथ-साथ अपनी चूँ-चूँ करती पुरानी साइकिल को तेज़ी से भगाया, जब तक कि वह ग्रे क्लोज़ मोहल्ले नहीं पहुँच गया। यह तो अच्छा था की नवम्बर का महीना था, जिसकी वजह से पसीने में भीगने की जगह, बेन हल्का-सा नम था।

उसने पैडल फुर्ती से चलाये क्योंकि वह जानता था कि उसके पास ज़्यादा वक्त नहीं था। वैसे तो ऐसा लगता था कि *स्ट्रिक्टली स्टार्स डांसिंग* घंटों तक चलता था, दिनों तक भी, लेकिन आज बेन को साइकिल पर आधा घंटा हो गया था और जैसे ही कार्यक्रम ख़तम

होगा, माँ उसको चाय के लिए नीचे बुलायेंगी। बेन के माता-पिता को नाच के सारे कार्यक्रम पसन्द थे, जैसे *डांसिंग ऑन आईस स्केटस, सो यू थिंक यू केन डांस ए बिट?* लेकिन उनको *स्ट्रिक्टली स्टार्स डांसिंग* का फ़ितूर सवार था। उन्होंने एक-एक एपिसोड रिकार्ड किया हुआ था, और उनके घर में इस शो से जुड़ी वस्तुओं का जबरदस्त संग्रह था, जिसमें थे:

- हल्के हरे रंग की पतली थौंग चड्डी, जो फ़्लावीओ फ़्लावीओलि ने एक बार पहनी थी। उसके साथ ही एक तस्वीर है जिसमें उसने यह पहनी हुई है।

- *स्ट्रिक्टली स्टार्स डांसिंग* का असली लेदर बुकमार्क।

- किसी खिलाड़ी के पैरों के पाउडर का डिब्बा जिस पर फ़्लावीओ की डांस में साथी रही ऑस्ट्रियाई सुन्दरी एवा बन्ज़ ने हस्ताक्षर किये थे।

- *स्ट्रिक्टली स्टार्स डांसिंग* के आदमियों और

औरतों के गरम पायजामे।

• गानों की एक सीडी जो कार्यक्रम में इस्तेमाल होने वाली थी।

• एक मर्तबान में कार्यक्रम के उद्घोषक सर डर्क डोडरी का विग।

• फ़्लावीओ फ़्लावीओलि की आदमकद तस्वीर, जिस के होठों पर माँ की लिपस्टिक लगी थी।

• एक मर्तबान में मशहूर प्रतिभागी और सांसद, डेम रेचल प्रेजुडिस के कानों की मैल।

• एवा बन्ज़ की महक वाले हल्के भूरे रंग के टाइट्स।

- एक नैपकिन पर दुष्ट जज, क्रेग मोलटेसर-वूडवर्ड द्वारा बनाया हुआ चित्र।

- *स्ट्रिक्टली स्टार्स डांसिंग* के लिए खास बने प्याले।

- फ़्लावीओ फ़्लावीओलि द्वारा इस्तेमाल की हुई आधी राक्सजेक्स की ट्यूब।

- क्रेग मोलटेसर-वूडवर्ड का छोटा-सा हाथ-पैर हिलाने वाला खिलौना।

- एक हवाईयन हॉट पिज़्ज़ा का टुकड़ा जो फ़्लावीओ ने झूठा छोड़ा था। (यह साबित करने के लिए एवा बन्ज़ का हस्ताक्षर किया हुआ एक पत्र भी।)

शनिवार का दिन था, इसलिए कार्यक्रम के बाद परिवार को चीज़ और सॉसेज खाना था। ना माँ और ना ही बाबा खाना पकाना जानते थे, इसलिये बेन की माँ बने-बनाए भोजन को फ़्रीज़र से निकालतीं, काँटे से मारतीं और गरम करने के लिए तीन मिनट के लिए माइक्रोवेव में रख देतीं। यह उसका मनपसन्द खाना था। बेन को

भूख लगी थी और वह अपना मनपसन्द खाना छोड़ना नहीं चाहता था। इसका मतलब था कि उसको जल्द ही दादी के घर से वापस जाना था। अगर आज सोमवार की रात होती, तब वह चिकन टिक्का का लज़ान्या खाता, बुधवार को डोनर कबाब पिज़्ज़ा, और अगर रविवार होता, तो मीनू में दूध, आटे और अंडे से बने यार्कशायर पुडिंग के साथ चाऊमीन* होता। शायद उस दिन बेन को खाने की चिन्ता नहीं होती।

रात ढल रही थी। वैसे भी नवम्बर की रात होने के कारण ठंड और अँधेरा जल्द हो जाता था, और बेन झाड़ियों में बैठा अपनी दादी पर जासूसी करते हुए ठिठुर रहा था। *वह कहाँ जा सकती हैं?* बेन ने सोचा। वे मुश्किल से ही कभी कहीं बाहर जाती होंगी।

बंगले में उसने एक परछाई को हिलते हुए देखा। फिर दादी का चेहरा खिड़की पर दिखा और बेन एकदम

---

* जिस सुपरमार्केट में बेन के बाबा काम करते थे, वहाँ के लोगों को दो देशों के पकवानों को मिलाकर, माइक्रोवेव में गर्म करके रेडी-टू-ईट खाना बनाना पसन्द था। दो देशों के भोजन को मिला कर शायद इस बँटी हुई दुनिया में अमन-चैन आ जाये। या शायद नहीं।

छुप गया। झाड़ियों में से सरसराहट हुई। *शशऽऽऽऽ!* बेन ने सोचा, *अगर दादी ने देख लिया होता तो?*

कुछ देर बाद धीरे से सामने का दरवाज़ा खुला और ऊपर से लेकर नीचे तक काले कपड़ों में कोई बाहर निकला। काला स्वेटर, काली पतलून, काले दस्ताने, काली जुराबें, शायद काली ब्रा और पेंटी भी। पूरी शक्ल ढकने वाली टोपी ने उनका भेष और बदल दिया था, लेकिन उनकी झुकी कमर से बेन को पता चल गया कि वह दादी ही थीं। वह अपनी मनपसन्द किताबों से निकली हुई कोई किरदार लग रही थीं। वह बूढ़े लोगों के लिए खासतौर से बने एक सीट वाले स्कूटर पर चढ़ीं और उसे चालू किया।

हे भगवान! वे आखिर कहाँ जा रही हैं?

बड़ा प्रश्न तो यह था कि यह जापानी खूनी निन्जा के भेष में क्यों थीं?

बेन ने अपनी साइकिल को झाड़ी के साथ लगाया और अपनी दादी का पीछा करने के लिए तैयार हो गया।

यह तो उसने सैकड़ों साल में भी अपने सपने में नहीं सोचा था।

जैसे एक मकड़ी छुपने के लिए बाथरूम में फुर्ती से भागती है, ठीक वैसे ही दादी ने अपना स्कूटर दीवारों के साथ-साथ चलाया। बेन पैदल ही उनका पीछा चुपचाप कर रहा था। उनके साथ-साथ चलना ज़्यादा मुश्किल नहीं था क्योंकि उनके स्कूटर की सबसे अधिक गति थी चार मील प्रति घंटा। अचानक दादी को लगा कि उन्होंने कुछ सुना। जैसे ही उन्होंने पीछे देखा, बेन तुरन्त पेड़ के पीछे छिप गया।

अपनी साँस रोक कर वह इन्तज़ार करने लगा।

कुछ नहीं।

कुछ देर बाद, उसने धीरे से पेड़ के तने की ओट से बाहर झाँका तो पाया कि दादी सड़क के अन्त तक पहुँच चुकी थीं। उसने पीछा करना जारी रखा।

जल्द ही वह मुख्य सड़क के पास थे। वह एकदम सुनसान थी। क्योंकि शाम का धुँधलका था, सारी दुकानें बन्द हो गयी थीं और पब और भोजनालय को

रात के लिए खुलने में अभी समय था। दादी सड़क की बत्तियों से दूर, इधर-उधर भटकती रहीं और थोड़ी देर में फिर अपनी मंज़िल पर पहुँच गयीं।

जहाँ उन्होंने अपना स्कूटर रोका, उस जगह को देख कर बेन की साँसें रुक गयीं।

यह एक जौहरी की दुकान थी।

खिड़की पर मालाएँ और अँगूठियाँ और घड़ियाँ जगमगा रही थीं। बेन को अपनी आँखों पर विश्वास नहीं हो रहा था कि दादी ने स्कूटर की टोकरी से अपने बन्दगोभी के सूप का टीन का डिब्बा निकाला। इधर-उधर नाटकीय ढंग से निगाह डाली और दुकान का शीशा तोड़ने के लिए अपना हाथ उठाया।

"नहहहही!" बेन चिलाया।

दादी ने डिब्बा गिरा दिया। वह ज़मीन पर गिरा और सारा बन्दगोभी का सूप बहने लगा।

"बेन?" दादी ने फुफ़कार कर कहा, "तुम यहाँ क्या कर रहे हो?"

9

काली बिल्ली

बेन अपनी दादी को काले कपड़ों में जौहरी की दुकान पर खड़े एकटक देखता रहा।

"बेन?" दादी ने फिर पूछा। "तुम मेरा पीछा क्यों कर रहे हो?"

"मैं तो बस … बस…" बेन इतना चौंक गया था कि उससे एक वाक्य भी बोलते नहीं बन रहा था।

"अच्छा," दादी बोलीं। "तुम यहाँ जो भी करने आये हो उसके बावजूद पुलिस यहाँ बस आती ही होगी। बेहतर होगा कि हम यहाँ से जल्दी चलें। जल्दी, स्कूटर पर चढ़ो।"

"लेकिन मैं नहीं..."

"बेन! हमारे पास सिर्फ़ तीस सेकंड हैं कैमरा शुरू होने से पहले।" उन्होंने फ़्लैटों की दीवार पर लगे कैमरे की तरफ़ इशारा किया।

बेन उनके स्कूटर पर चढ़ गया, "आपको पता है कि कैमरे चल जायेंगे?" उसने पूछा।

"ओह," दादी बोलीं, "तुम ये जानकर चौंक जाओगे कि मैं क्या-क्या जानती हूँ।"

वह स्कूटर चला रही थीं और बेन उनकी पीठ को देखता रहा। बस अभी ही तो उसने उनको एक जौहरी की दुकान में चोरी करने की कोशिश करते हुए देखा था, अब और *कितना* चौंका सकती थीं? लेकिन अब ये तो स्पष्ट था कि जितना बेन सोच सकता था, उससे कहीं ज़्यादा रहस्य थे दादी के!

"पकड़ कर बैठो," दादी ने बोला। "अब मैं स्कूटर को उड़ा ले जाऊँगी।"

उन्होंने इतनी तेज़ी से स्कूटर का हेंडल घुमाया कि बेन को कुछ समझ ही नहीं आ रहा था। रात के अँधेरे

में वह दोनों स्कूटर पर, 3 मील प्रति घंटे की गति से भिभिनाते हुए गये।

"काली बिल्ली?" बेन ने दोहराया। आखिरकार दोनों दादी के ड्राईंग रूम में बैठे थे। दादी ने चाय बनाई और चॉकलेट बिस्कुट के साथ परोसा।

"हाँ, सब मुझे इसी नाम से जानते हैं," दादी ने जवाब दिया। "मैं दुनिया की सबसे कुख्यात आभूषण चोर हूँ।"

बेन का सिर सैंकड़ों सवालों से फट रहा था। *क्यों? कहाँ? कौन? क्या? कब?* इतने सारे सवाल थे कि उसे समझ नहीं आ रहा था कि पहले कौन-सा पूछे।

"बेन, तुम्हारे अलावा कोई भी नहीं जानता," दादी ने बताया। "तुम्हारे दादा भी यह जाने बिना कब्र में गये। तुम क्या एक राज़ रख सकते हो? तुमको कसम लेनी होगी कि तुम किसी को भी नहीं बताओगे।

"लेकिन..."

उस वक़्त दादी का चेहरा उग्र लग रहा था। उनकी

आँखें डँसने वाले नाग जैसे काली और पैनी हो गयीं।

"तुमको कसम खानी पड़ेगी।" बूढ़ी दादी की ऐसी उग्रता बेन ने कभी भी नहीं देखी थी।

"हम चोर अपनी शपथ को गम्भीरता से लेते हैं। काफी गम्भीरता के साथ।"

डर के मारे बेन ने थूक गटकते हुए कहा, "मैं कसम खाता हूँ कि किसी को नहीं बताऊँगा।"

"अपने माता-पिता को भी नहीं!" दादी ऐसे गरजीं मानो उनके नकली दाँत बाहर ही गिर जायेंगे।

"मैंने कहा ना कि किसी को भी नहीं बताऊँगा," बेन वापस गरजा।

बेन ने स्कूल में हाल ही में, वेन रेखाचित्र सीखा था। जब उसने किसी को ना बताने की कसम खाई थी, तो उसने सोचा, 'किसी को' अगर हम 'क' खंड समझ लेते हैं, फिर तो माँ और बाबा भी इसी खंड के भाग होंगे, और ज़ाहिर है कि उपखंड होंगे।

इसलिए दादी को बेन से दूसरी कसम खिलवाने की कोई ज़रूरत नहीं थी।

चलो, एक बार आसान रेखाचित्र को देख ही लेते हैं:

लेकिन बेन को लग रहा था कि दादी अभी तो किसी भी रेखाचित्र में बिल्कुल दिलचस्पी नहीं दिखायेंगी। क्योंकि वह अभी भी बेन को डरावनी आँखों से घूर रहीं थीं। बेन ने एक आह भरी और बोला, "अच्छा, ठीक है, मैं माँ और बाबा को भी नहीं बताऊँगा।"

"तुम अच्छे बच्चे हो," दादी बोलीं। उनकी कान की मशीन फिर से सीटियाँ मारने लग गयी थी।

"लेकिन, सिर्फ़ एक शर्त पर," बेन ने साहस किया।

"कैसी शर्त?" दादी उसके साहस से चौंक कर बोलीं।

"आपको मुझे सब कुछ बताना होगा..."

10

सब कुछ

"मैं तुम्हारी उम्र की ही थी, जब मैंने अपनी पहली हीरे की अँगूठी चुराई थी," दादी बोलीं।

बेन हक्का-बक्का रह गया। एक तो इसलिए कि यह यक़ीन करना नामुमकिन था कि दादी कभी उसकी उम्र की भी थीं, और दूसरा इसलिए क्योंकि ज़ाहिर था कि ग्यारह साल की लड़कियाँ हीरे नहीं चुरातीं। चमकने वाली स्याही के पैन, बालों के क्लिप, शायद कुछ लड़कियों के खिलौने भी, लेकिन हीरे तो बिल्कुल नहीं।

"मुझे मालूम है कि तुमको मुझ में सिर्फ़ स्क्रैबल, बुनाई करना और बन्दगोभी का शौक ही दिखता होगा,

जिसकी वजह से मैं तुम्हें कोई बूढ़ी बोरिंग अम्मा लगती हूँ।

"नहीं..." बेन ने थोड़ा हिचकिचाते हुए कहा।

"बच्चे लेकिन तुम भूल रहे हो कि मैं भी कभी जवान थी।"

"आप ने सबसे पहले कौन-सी अँगूठी चुराई थी?" बेन ने बेसब्री से पूछा। "क्या उस पर एक बड़ा-सा हीरा था?"

बूढ़ी दादी हँसीं। "इतना भी बड़ा नहीं था! वह मेरा पहला था। अभी भी मेरे पास ही कहीं होगा। बेन, तुम ज़रा रसोई में जाओ और अलमारी से सिल्वर जुबली वाले बिस्कुट का डिब्बा लाओ।

बेन ने कंधे उचकाये और ऐसे नाटक किया जैसे मानो उसको सिल्वर जुबली वाले बिस्कुट के डिब्बे और उसके अन्दर पड़ी अद्भुत सामग्री के बारे में कुछ मालूम ही ना हो।

"है कहाँ वह, दादी?" बेन ने ड्रॉईंग रूम से जाते हुए पूछा।

"बेटे, वह कोठार के ऊपर ही पड़ा है," दादी ने

आवाज़ दी। "जल्दी-जल्दी करो। तुम्हारे माँ और बाबा जल्द ही तुम्हें ढूँढने लगेंगे। बेन को याद आया कि उसे घर पर चीज़ी बीन्स और सॉसेज खाने के लिए जाना था। लेकिन एकदम से सब कुछ बिल्कुल ही महत्त्वहीन लगने लगा। उसे तो अब भूख भी नहीं लग रही थी।

बेन डिब्बा लेकर दुबारा कमरे में लौटा। डिब्बा तो पहले से कहीं ज्यादा भारी लग रहा था। उसने डिब्बा अपनी दादी को पकड़ाया।

"मेरा अच्छा बच्चा," उन्होंने अपनी खोज शुरू करते कहा और एक ख़ास चमकती हुई खूबसूरत चीज़ को निकाला।

"हाँ! यही है!"

बेन को अधिकतर हीरे की अँगूठियाँ एक ही जैसी दिखती थीं। मगर ऐसा लग रहा था कि दादी तो एक-एक को अपने करीबी दोस्तों की तरह पहचानती थीं। "कितनी सुन्दर है," उन्होंने अँगूठी को परखने के लिए अपनी आँखों के पास ला कर बोला। "यही है वह जो मैंने पहली बार चुराई थी, जब मैं बस एक नटखट बच्ची थी।"

बेन अनुमान भी नहीं लगा पा रहा था कि दादी

बचपन में कैसी होंगी। वह तो उन्हें सिर्फ़ एक बूढ़ी औरत की तरह जानता था। उसे तो यहाँ तक लगता था कि वह बूढ़ी ही पैदा हुई थीं। मानो सालों पहले, अस्पताल में जब उनकी माँ ने उनको जन्म दिया होगा

और नर्स से पूछा होगा कि लड़का है या लड़की, तब नर्स ने बताया होगा, "एक बूढ़ी औरत!"

"मैं एक छोटे-से गाँव के ग़रीब परिवार में पली बढ़ी हूँ।" दादी ने आगे कहा। "और पहाड़ी के ऊपर एक आलीशान घर था जहाँ लॉर्ड और लेडी डेविनपोर्ट रहते थे। जंग के बाद के ही दिन थे और उन दिनों

हमारे पास खाने को कुछ ज़्यादा नहीं था। मुझे भूख लगी थी, तब एक दिन, आधी रात को जब सब सो रहे थे, मैं अपने माता-पिता की छोटी-सी कुटिया से दबे पाँव निकली। अँधेरे का लाभ उठाते हुए, मैं जंगलों से डेविनपोर्ट निवास वाली पहाड़ी पर पहुँची।"

"आपको डर नहीं लगा?" बेन ने पूछा।

"बिल्कुल लगा। रात के अँधेरे में जंगल में अकेले होना बहुत ही खौफ़नाक था। पहाड़ी वाले मकान पर तो पहरा देने के लिए कुत्ते भी थे। विशाल काले डोबरमैन। मैं चुपचाप बिना आवाज़ किये पाइप से ऊपर चढ़ी और एक खुली खिड़की पर पहुँची। मैं अपनी उम्र के लिए भी बहुत छोटी-सी थी। इसलिए मैं उस छोटी-सी खिड़की से आराम से अन्दर घुस गयी और एक मख़मली परदे के पीछे आ पहुँची। जैसे ही मैंने परदे को पीछे किया तो देखा की वह तो लॉर्ड और लेडी डेविनपोर्ट का कमरा था।"

"नहीं!" बेन बोला।

"हाँ," दादी ने आगे बताया। "मुझे लगा था कि

मैं बस कुछ खाना ले जाऊँगी, लेकिन फिर मेरी नज़र पलंग के सिरहाने इस खूबसूरत चीज़ पर पड़ी।" उन्होंने उस अँगूठी की ओर इशारा किया।

"तब आप ने उठा ली?"

"विश्व प्रसिद्ध आभूषण चोर होना कोई आम बात नहीं है बच्चू," दादी बोलीं। "बड़े साहब और उनकी पत्नी बहुत ज़ोर-ज़ोर से खर्राटे मार रहे थे, लेकिन अगर वह जाग जाते तो मेरी तो शामत आ जाती। बड़े साहब हमेशा अपने पास एक बन्दूक रखकर सोते थे।"

"बन्दूक?" बेन ने पूछा।

"हाँ, वह रईस थे, और उनको तीतर मारना पसन्द था, इसलिए उनके पास बन्दूक थी।"

बेन के डर के मारे पसीने छूट रहे थे। "लेकिन वह उठे तो नहीं ना आपको मारने के लिए?"

"सब्र करो, बेटा। हर चीज़ का अपना वक्त होता है। मैं दबे पैर लेडी डेविनपोर्ट के बिस्तर की तरफ़ गयी और चुपके से अँगूठी उठा ली। मुझे यकीन नहीं हो

रहा था कि वह कितनी खूबसूरत चीज़ थी। मैंने अपनी ज़िन्दगी में कभी भी इतनी खूबसूरत अँगूठी नहीं देखी थी। मेरी माँ तो ऐसा कुछ लेने की कल्पना भी नहीं करती थीं। 'मुझे गहनों की ज़रूरत नहीं है,' वह हम बच्चों को कहा करती थीं। 'तुम सब मेरे नन्हे से हीरे हो।' मैं उस हीरे को अपने हाथों में लेकर, विस्मय में डूब गयी। वह मेरी ज़िन्दगी की सबसे भव्य चीज़ थी। फिर, अचानक, एक बहुत ज़ोरदार आवाज़ हुई।"

बेन की भौंहें तन गयीं। "वह क्या था?"

"लॉर्ड डेविनपोर्ट बहुत लालची आदमी था। उन्होंने ज़रूर ठूँस-ठूँस कर खाना खाया होगा, इसलिए उन्होंने बड़ी ज़ोर से डकार मारी!"

बेन हँसने लगा और दादी भी हँसने लगीं। वह जानता था कि डकार मज़ाकिया बात नहीं थी, लेकिन उसकी हँसी रुक ही नहीं रही थी।

"कुछ ज़्यादा ही बड़ी थी!" दादी अभी भी हँसते हुए बोलीं।

“डकाऽऽऽऽऽऽऽऽऽऽऽऽऽ ऽऽऽऽऽऽऽऽऽऽऽऽऽऽऽऽऽार्र!!!”

उन्होंने नकल उतारी।

हँसते-हँसते बेन के पेट में दर्द होने लगा था।

“वह इतनी ज़ोरदार थी कि,” दादी आगे बोलीं, “मैं चौंक गयी और अँगूठी लकड़ी के चिकने फ़र्श पर गिरा दी। सागौन से बने फ़र्श पर गिरने से इतनी ज़ोर से आवाज़ आयी, कि लॉर्ड और लेडी डेविनपोर्ट जाग गये।”

“उफ़्फ नहीं!”

“अरे हाँ! तब मैंने अँगूठी झपटी और खुली खिड़की की ओर भागी। मैंने पीछे देखने की हिम्मत नहीं की, क्योंकि लॉर्ड डेविनपोर्ट अपनी बन्दूक़ का घोड़ा चढ़ा रहे थे। मैंने घास पर छलाँग लगाई और एकदम से घर की सारी बत्तियाँ जल गयीं और कुत्ते भौंकने लगे और मैं अपनी जान बचाने के लिए भागी। फिर एक और कान फोड़नेवाली आवाज़ आयी...”

"एक और डकार?" बेन ने पूछा।

"नहीं, इस बार उनकी बन्दूक थी। लॉर्ड डेविनपोर्ट मुझ पर निशाना साध रहे थे लेकिन मैं पहाड़ी से नीचे दौड़ते हुए जंगल के अन्दर घुस गयी।

"फिर क्या हुआ?"

दादी ने अपनी छोटी-सी सुनहरी घड़ी को देखा, "मेरे लाडले, अब तुम्हें घर जाना चाहिए। तुम्हारे माँ और बाबा चिन्तित होंगे।"

"मुझे तो नहीं लगता," बेन बोला। "उन्हें तो सिर्फ़ उस बेकार बॉलरूम डांस की पड़ी है।"

"ऐसा कुछ नहीं है," दादी अचानक बोलीं। "तुम जानते हो कि वह तुमसे प्यार करते हैं।"

"मुझे कहानी का अन्त सुनना है।" मायूसी से बेन ने कहा। उसको जानने की उत्सुकता थी कि आगे क्या हुआ।

"एक दिन ज़रूर बताऊँगी।"

"लेकिन दादी..."

"बेन तुम्हें घर जाना पड़ेगा।"

"यह नाइंसाफी है।"

"बेन, अब तुम्हें जाना चाहिए। मैं तुम्हें एक दिन ज़रूर बताऊँगी कि क्या हुआ।"

"लेकिन!"

"आगे देखेंगे," उन्होंने कहा।

11

चीज़ी बीन्स और सॉसेज

तेज़ी से साइकिल दौड़ाते हुए बेन घर की ओर भागा, उसे ना ही अपनी टाँगों की जलन के बारे में होश था और ना ही अपनी छाती के दर्द के बारे में। वह तो बस तेज़ी से अपनी साइकिल चला रहा था। वह इतना तेज़ चला रहा था कि उसे इस बात का डर था कि कहीं पुलिस तेज़ चलाने की वजह से उसका चालान ना काट दे। जिस तरीके से उसके पहिये घूम रहे थे, ठीक उसी तरीके से उसका दिमाग़ भी घूम रहा था।

क्या उसकी बोरिंग बूढ़ी दादी सच में दबंग थीं?

एक दबंग दादी?

शायद उनको दबंग डाकुओं की कथायें भी इसलिए बेहद पसन्द थीं क्योंकि वह खुद दबंग थीं!

इससे पहले कि किसी को पता चले, वह पीछे के दरवाज़े से अन्दर घुस गया। ड्रॉईंग रूम से *स्ट्रिक्टली स्टार्स डांसिंग* का संगीत सुनाई दे रहा था। वह समय रहते ही घर पहुँच गया था।

लेकिन जब बेन ऊपर जाने ही वाला था, ये ढोंग करने के लिए कि वह अब तक अपने कमरे में होमवर्क कर रहा था, उससे पहले ही माँ रसोई में तूफ़ान की तरह घुसीं।

"तुम क्या कर रहे हो?" उन्होंने उससे पूछा। "पसीने में पूरे लथपथ हो।"

"नहीं, कुछ नहीं," बेन अपने पसीने को महसूस करते हुए बोला।

"देखो अपने आप को," माँ ने उसके पास आते हुए बोला। "तुम्हें तो सूअर की तरह पसीना आ रहा है।"

बेन ने कुछ सूअर तो देखे थे लेकिन उन में से किसी का भी पसीना नहीं निकल रहा था। बल्कि सुअर के जानकार बताते हैं कि सूअरों के शरीर में

पसीना निकालने वाली ग्रंथि होती ही नहीं है, इसलिए उनका पसीना नहीं छूटता।

वाह! यह किताब तो बहुत ज्ञानवर्धक है!

"मेरा पसीना नहीं छूट रहा," बेन ने विरोध किया। इस पसीने के आरोप ने उसका और पसीना छुड़वा दिया।

"तुम्हारा पसीना *निकल* रहा है। तुम क्या बाहर भाग रहे थे?"

"नहीं," अब और भी पसीने में डूबे हुए बेन बोला।

"बेन, मुझसे झूठ मत बोलो, मैं तुम्हारी माँ हूँ," उन्होंने अपनी ओर इशारा करते हुए बोला ही था कि उनका नकली नाखून उड़ता हुआ गिरा।

उनके नकली नाखून बहुत गिरते थे। एक बार बेन को माइक्रोवेव में बनाने वाले स्पैनिश व्यंजन, पायेल्या बोलोनिज़ में भी नकली नाखून मिला था।

"बेन, अगर तुम बाहर भाग नहीं रहे थे, तब तुम्हें इतना पसीना क्यों आ रहा है?"

बेन को जल्दी से कोई बहाना बनाना था। *स्ट्रिक्टली स्टार्स डांसिंग* भी ख़त्म होने वाला था।

"मैं नाच रहा था!" उसने कह डाला।

"नाच रहे थे?" माँ ने ना मानते हुए कहा। बेन कोई फ़्लावीओ फ़्लावीओलि नहीं था। और ज़ाहिर था कि उसको बॉलरूम डांस में भी कोई दिलचस्पी नहीं थी।

"हाँ, मैंने बॉलरूम डांस के बारे में अपनी राय बदल ली है। मुझे बेहद पसन्द है।"

"लेकिन तुमने कहा था कि तुमको उससे नफ़रत थी," माँ ने शक की नज़र से तुरन्त जवाब दिया। "एक बार नहीं, बहुत बार। कुछ ही दिन पहले तुमने कहा था 'यह बकवास देखने से अच्छा तो मैं अपनी ही नाक के गूँगे खा लूँ।' यह कहते ही तुमने मेरे दिल को चूर-चूर कर दिया था।"

माँ यह सोचते हुए और भी उदास हो रही थीं।

"मुझे माफ़ कर दो माँ, सच में।"

बेन ने उनको दिलासा देने के लिए हाथ आगे

बढ़ाया और एक और नकली नाखून गिर पड़ा। "लेकिन मुझे अब सचमुच बहुत पसन्द है, मैं तो बस दरवाज़े की दरार से *स्ट्रिक्टली स्टार्स डांसिंग* देख कर सारे डांस स्टेप्स की नक़ल कर रहा था।"

माँ की छाती गर्व से फूल गयी। ऐसा लग रहा था मानो उनकी ज़िन्दगी का अब कोई मकसद था। उनके चेहरे पर खुशी और उदासी, दोनों थीं, मानो यह ही तक़दीर हो।

"क्या तुम," उन्होंने साँसें भरीं, "एक डांसर बनना चाहते हो?"

"मेरा चीज़ी बीन्स और सॉसेज कहाँ हैं, जान?" बाबा ने ड्रॉईंग रूम से आवाज़ दी।

"तुम चुप करो, पीट!" माँ की आँखों में खुशी के आँसू आ गये थे।

वह आखिरी बार इतना तब रोई थीं, जब दो साल पहले फ़्लावीओ को कार्यक्रम से धक्के मारकर निकाल दिया गया था। फ़्लावीओ को ज़बरदस्ती थुलथुली डेम रेचल प्रेज़ुडिस के साथ भाग लेना पड़ा, जिसकी वजह

से वह रेचल को मंच पर बस घसीटता ही रहा।

"अच्छा। वैसे तो।" बेन इस परिस्थिति से निकलने की पूरी कोशिश कर रहा था। "हाँ।"

लेकिन बात यहाँ ख़त्म नहीं हुई।

"मैं जानती थी!" माँ रोईं। "पीट, अन्दर आओ एक मिनट। बेन तुमको कुछ बताना चाहता है।"

बाबा पैर घसीटते हुए अन्दर आये। "क्या हुआ, बेन? सर्कस में भाग लेने का इरादा तो नहीं है ना? हे

भगवान! तुम्हें कितना पसीना आया है।"

"नहीं, पीट," माँ ने धीरे-धीरे, हर शब्द पर ज़ोर देते हुए कहा मानो वह पुरस्कार देने के लिए विजेता के नाम की घोषणा करने वाली थीं।

"बेन को अब कोई फ़ालतू प्लम्बर नहीं बनना।"

"शुक्र है भगवान का," बाबा बोले।

"यह चाहता है..." माँ ने अपने बेटे को देखा, "बेन, तुम बताओ।"

बेन ने अपना मुँह खोला ही था कि माँ ने सुर में सुर मिलाते हुए बोला, "बेन बॉलरूम डांसर बनना चाहता है!"

"इस दुनिया में भगवान हैं!" बाबा चिल्लाए। उन्होंने तम्बाकू के दाग़ से भरी छत की ओर कृतज्ञता से नज़र उठाई इस उम्मीद में कि शायद दिव्यता के दर्शन हो जायें।

"अभी यह रसोई में अभ्यास कर रहा था," माँ उत्साह से बोलीं। "कार्यक्रम के नाच के हर कदम की नक़ल उतारकर।"

बाबा ने अपने बेटे की आँखों में देखा और मर्दों की तरह उससे हाथ मिलाया। "यह बहुत अच्छी ख़बर है, मेरे लाल! वैसे भी तुम्हारी माँ और मुझे ज्यादा कुछ नहीं मिला है। वह भी जब तुम्हारी माँ नाख़ूनों को पॉलिश करती हैं।"

"मैं नाख़ूनों की तकनीशियन हूँ," माँ ने उनको टोका। "ज़मीन आसमान का फ़र्क है, पीट, तुम्हें पता है।"

"नाख़ूनों की तकनीशियन। मुझे माफ़ कर दो। और मैं ख़ुद भी सिर्फ़ एक बूढ़ा गार्ड हूँ क्योंकि पुलिस में होने के लिए मैं काफी मोटा हूँ। रोमांच के नाम पर मैंने सिर्फ़ व्हीलचेयर पर बैठे, कम्बल में कस्टर्ड का डिब्बा छुपाकर ले जा रहे एक आदमी को रोका है। लेकिन तुम जब बॉलरूम डांसर बनोगे, यह, यह हमारी ज़िन्दगी की सबसे विशेष बात होगी।"

"सबसे ज़्यादा विशेष!" माँ बोलीं।

"सबसे सबसे ज़्यादा विशेष!" बाबा ने हामी भरी।

"सच में, यह है ही सबसे सबसे सबसे विशेष," माँ बोलीं।

"अब बस 'अत्यन्त विशेष' पर राज़ी हो जाते हैं," बाबा ने थोड़ा तंग आकर बोला। "लेकिन मैं तुम्हें सचेत करना चाहता हूँ कि यह आसान नहीं है। अगर तुम अगले बीस सालों तक, दिन में आठ घंटे निरन्तर अभ्यास करोगे, तब जाकर तुम टीवी पर आ सकोगे।"

"शायद यह अमेरीका वाला जीत सके!" माँ ज़ोर से बोलीं। "पीट, ज़रा सोचो, हमारा बेटा अमेरीका का सितारा!"

"अच्छा, जल्दबाज़ी मत करो, जान। अभी तक तो यह ब्रिटिश भी नहीं जीता है। अभी हमको इसे जूनियर प्रतियोगिता में भाग दिलवाना होगा।"

"तुम ठीक कह रहे हो, पीट। गेल ने मुझे बताया था कि क्रिसमस से पहले टाउनहॉल में एक प्रोग्राम होगा।"

"वाइन की बॉटल खोलो, मेरी जान। हमारा बेटा चा-चा-चा डांस का विजेता बनेगा!'

बेन को सिर्फ़ अपशब्द सूझ रहे थे।

इस मुसीबत से वह अब कैसे बाहर निकलेगा?

12

प्यार का बम

रविवार का पूरा दिन माँ बस बेन का नाप ही लेती रहीं। वह उसके नाचने के लिए एक पोशाक बनाना चाहती थीं। पूरी रात जागकर, उन्होंने सारे डिज़ाइन के चित्र बना डाले।

माँ के दबाव में, बेन को एक पसन्द करनी पड़ी, तभी उसने हिचकिचाते हुए सबसे कम भयानक दिखने वाली पोशाक की ओर इशारा किया।

माँ के बनाये सारे चित्र लज्जाजनक से लेकर अपमानजनक तक थे।

उन में थे:

जंगल

फलों की टोकरी

गरज और बिजली

दुर्घटना और आपातकाल

बर्फ़ और फ़ाँक

झाड़ी और बिज्जू

क्वालिटी स्ट्रीट की टॉफ़ी

अंडा और हैम

कंफ़ेटी

जलपरी

प्यार का बम

प्रेम जलन

चीज़ और अचार

सौर-मंडल

पियानो मैन

लेकिन जो बेन के मुताबिक सबसे कम खराब पोशाक थी, वह थी, प्यार का बम:

"इस प्रतियोगिता के लिए हमें एक अच्छी-सी नौजवान साथी ढूँढ निकालनी होगी!" माँ खुशी से बोलीं और उनका एक नकली नाखून ग़लती से गिरा और सिलाई मशीन के अन्दर आ कर फट गया।

बेन ने साथी के बारे में सोचा नहीं था। उसको अब सिर्फ़ नाचना ही नहीं, बल्कि एक लड़की के साथ नाचना पड़ेगा! वो भी कोई आम लड़की नहीं, बल्कि

एक नकली चमक-दमक से भरी, अपनी उम्र से बड़ी की गयी, ढेर सारे मेकअप से चुपड़ी, छोटे कपड़ों में घिनौनी-सी लड़की...

बेन की उम्र अभी भी उतनी ही थी जिस में उसे लड़कियाँ मेंढक के अंडे जितनी आकर्षक लगती थीं।

"नहीं, मैं अकेला ही नाचूँगा।" बेन गुस्से में बड़बड़या।

"अकेले!" माँ बोलीं, "एकदम अनोखा!"

"असल में, मैं यहाँ पूरा दिन बातों में नहीं गुज़ार सकता। मुझे जाकर अभ्यास करना चाहिए," बेन बोला और ऊपर अपने कमरे में चला गया। उसने दरवाज़ा बन्द किया, रेडियो चलाया और खिड़की से कूदकर, दादी के बंगले की ओर अपनी साइकिल पर दौड़ पड़ा।

"तो आप जंगलों में भाग रही थीं जब लॉर्ड डेविनपोर्ट ने आप पर गोलियाँ चलायीं," बेन ने उत्सुकतापूर्वक दादी से पूछा।

लेकिन अभी दादी को कुछ भी याद नहीं आ रहा था।

"मैं क्या?" दादी ने हैरानी से पूछा।

"आप ने कहानी कल यहीं खत्म की थी। आपने कहा था कि आपने अँगूठी डेविनपोर्ट के कमरे से चुराई और आप जंगल में भाग रही थीं जब आपने गोलियाँ चलने की आवाज़ सुनी।"

"अरे, हाँ, हाँ," दादी का चेहरा एक नयी रोशनी से जगमगाया और वह बड़बड़ाईं।

बेन खुल कर मुस्कुराया। उसको याद आ गया जब वह छोटा था तब कैसे उसे दादी से कहानियाँ सुनना और एक अलग जादुई दुनिया में जाना पसन्द था। एक ऐसी दुनिया जहाँ आप अपने मन में सारी फ़िल्मों या टीवी के कार्यक्रमों या वीडियो गेम से भी ज़्यादा रोमांचक चित्र बना सकते थे। कुछ हफ़्ते पहले ही वह सोने का ढोंग कर रहा था ताकि दादी उसको कहानी किस्से ना सुनाये। ज़ाहिर है कि वह भूल गया था कि दादी कितनी रोमांचक थीं।

"मैं भागी ही जा रही थी," दादी ने कहानी हाँफते हुए शुरू की, जैसे वह अभी भी भाग ही रही हों, "फिर मुझे गोली चलने की आवाज़ सुनायी दी। फिर एक

और। मुझे लग रहा था कि यह आवाज़ ज़रूर राइफ़ल की नहीं शॉटगन बन्दूक की ही है।"

"इन दोनों में फ़र्क क्या है?" बेन ने पूछा।

"राइफ़ल एक ही गोली मारती है लेकिन निशाने से चूकती नहीं। लेकिन एक शॉटगन बन्दूक एक साथ सौ छोटे जानलेवा शीशे की गोलियाँ छोड़ती है। कोई भी नासमझ आदमी तुमको मार सकता है, अगर उसने शॉटगन बन्दूक से निशाना साधा।"

"और क्या उन्होंने शॉटगन से गोली चलाई थी?" बेन ने पूछा। उसकी मुस्कुराहट मिटने लगी थी। उसको सच में घबराहट हो रही थी।

"हाँ, सौभाग्य से तब तक मैं बहुत दूर पहुँच चुकी थी इसलिए मुझे कुछ नहीं लगीं। मुझे कुत्तों के भौंकने की आवाज़ भी सुनाई दे रही थी। वह मेरे पीछे थे और मैं तो सिर्फ़ एक छोटी-सी बच्ची थी। अगर उन्होंने मुझे पकड़ लिया होता, वह शिकारी कुत्ते मेरे चिथड़े उड़ा देते।

बेन धक्क-सा रह गया। "तो आप बचीं कैसे?" उसने पूछा।

"मैंने जोख़िम उठाया। मैं जंगलों में उनको पीछे नहीं छोड़ सकती थी। दुनिया के सबसे तेज़ धावक भी उन कुत्तों को पछाड़ नहीं सकते थे। लेकिन मुझे जंगल के रास्ते अच्छे से मालूम थे। मैं अपने भाई-बहनों के साथ वहाँ घंटों खेला करती थी। मैं जानती थी कि अगर मैंने नदी पार कर ली, तब कुत्तों के लिए मेरी गन्ध नष्ट हो जायेगी।"

"ऐसा कैसे?"

"कुत्ते पानी में गन्ध को नहीं पहचान सकते। और नदी के ठीक उस पार एक विशाल शाहबलूत वृक्ष था। अगर मैं उस पर चढ़ जाती, तब मैं बिल्कुल सुरक्षित होती।"

बेन अपनी दादी को सीढ़ियाँ चढ़ने की कल्पना भी नहीं कर सकता था, पेड़ तो भूल ही जाओ। जहाँ तक उसे याद था, दादी इस बंगले में ही रह रही थीं।

"जब मैं अँधेरे में नदी की तरफ भाग रही थी तो गोलियों की और बरसात हुई," बूढ़ी दादी आगे बोलीं। "और तभी मैं रात के अँधेरे में गिर पड़ी। एक पेड़

113

की जड़ से ठोकर खाकर मैं मुँह के बल गिर पड़ी। मैं उठी, पीछे मुड़कर देखा तो लॉर्ड डेविनपोर्ट के नेतृत्व में घोड़ों पर एक फ़ौज खड़ी थी। उनके हाथों में मशालें और बन्दूकें थीं। मशालों की आग से पूरा जंगल जगमगा रहा था। मैंने नदी में छलाँग मारी। उस समय ठिठुरती सर्दियाँ थीं और पानी भी बर्फ़ीला था। उस ठंड ने मुझे हिला दिया और मैं साँस भी मुश्किल से ले पा रही थी। मैंने अपने हाथ से मुँह बन्द किया ताकि मेरी चीख़ दब जाये। मुझे कुत्तों के भौंकने की आवाज़ आयी। नज़दीक, और नज़दीक से सुनाई दे रही थी। ज़रूर दर्ज़न-भर कुत्ते रहे होंगे। मैंने अपने पीछे देखा और मुझे उनके नुकीले लम्बे दाँत रात की चाँदनी में चमकते हुए दिखे।

"मैंने नदी पार की और पेड़ पर चढ़ना शुरू कर दिया। मेरे हाथ मिट्टी से सने थे, मेरे पैर गीले थे और मैं बार-बार फिसलती जा रही थी। मैंने हड़बड़ी में अपने कपड़ों से हाथ साफ़ किये और फिर से चढ़ना शुरू किया। गिरते-पड़ते, जैसे-तैसे मेहनत करके पेड़ की सबसे ऊपरी डाली पर चढ़ गयी और एकदम चुप बुत की तरह बैठी रही। मुझे कुत्तों और डेविनपोर्ट की फ़ौज की दूसरी ओर जाने की आवाज़ सुनाई दी। कुत्तों के भौंकने का खौफ़नाक शोर दूसरी दिशा में जाता सुनाई दिया और थोड़ी देर बाद, मशालें भी दूर जाती टिमटिमाती दिखीं। मैं सुरक्षित थी। मैं उस पेड़ पर घंटों ठिठुरती रही। मैंने सुबह होने का इन्तज़ार किया, पेड़ से नीचे उतरी और अपनी कुटिया में वापस चली गयी। मैं फिर बिस्तर में दबे पाँव घुस गयी और वहाँ लेटी रही।"

बेन हर एक चीज़ का चित्र अपने दिमाग में बना रहा था। दादी ने उसे मन्त्रमुग्ध कर दिया था।

"क्या वह आपको ढूँढने आये?" उसने पूछा।

"किसी ने भी मुझे अच्छे से देखा नहीं था, इसलिए

डेविनपोर्ट ने अपने आदमियों को पूरे गाँव की तलाशी लेने भेजा। उन्होंने हर एक कुटिया को अस्त-व्यस्त कर दिया।"

"आपने कुछ नहीं बोला?"

"मैं बताना चाहती थी। मुझे बहुत अफ़सोस हो रहा था। लेकिन मैं जानती थी कि अगर मैंने गुनाह कुबूल कर लिया तो मैं भारी मुश्किल में फँस जाऊँगी। लॉर्ड डेविनपोर्ट मुझे पूरे गाँव के सामने कोड़े मारते।"

"फिर आपने क्या किया?"

"मैं ... उसे निगल गयी।"

बेन को विश्वास नहीं हो रहा था। "अँगूठी, दादी? आपने अँगूठी निगल ली?"

"मुझे लगा उससे बेहतर छिपाने का कोई तरीक़ा ही नहीं था। मेरा पेट ही था। कुछ दिनों बाद, मैं टॉयलेट गयी और वह बाहर आ गयी।"

"बहुत दर्द हुआ होगा!" बेन बोला। उसका पिछवाड़ा तो यह सोचकर ही दर्द कर रहा था। "एक

बड़ी-सी हीरे की अँगूठी..."

"बहुत दर्द हुआ। असल में, अति दु:खदाई था।" दर्द के बारे में सोचकर दादी का मुँह ऐंठ गया। "अच्छी बात तो यह थी कि उन लोगों ने ऊपरी भाग से निचले भाग तक छान मारा, मेरा मतलब कुटिया का निचला भाग, मेरा नहीं।" बेन हँसने लगा। "लॉर्ड के आदमी ढूँढने दूसरे गाँव चले गये। इसलिए मैं एक रात जंगल में गयी और अँगूठी छिपा दी। मैंने ऐसी जगह रखी थी जहाँ कोई भी उसे ढूँढ ना पाये। नदी में एक पत्थर के नीचे।"

"चालाकी की आपने!" बेन बोला।

"लेकिन वह अँगूठी बहुत अँगूठियों में पहली थी, बेन। उसकी चोरी मेरी ज़िन्दगी का सबसे बड़ा रोमांच था। और हर रात मैं और बहुत सारे हीरों को चुराने का सोचती रहती थी। वह अँगूठी तो बस एक शुरुआत थी।" दादी ने दबी हुई आवाज़ में बेन की मासूम आँखों में देखते हुए बोला, "जुर्म से भरे एक जीवन की..."

13

जुर्म से भरा जीवन

कई घंटे ऐसे फुर से बीते जैसे कुछ ही मिनट बीते हों,
जब दादी ने अपनी हर एक चमचमाती चीज़ को कमरे
में फैलाकर, उनकी चोरी के किस्से-कहानियाँ पोते को
सुनाना शुरू किया।

ये बड़ा-सा मुकुट अमरीका के राष्ट्रपति की बीवी
का था। दादी ने बेन को बताया कैसे पचास साल पहले
एक बड़े जहाज़ में वो अमरीका गयीं जहाँ वाशिंगटन
डीसी में राष्ट्रपति के निवास, व्हाइट हाउस, से चोरी
करके लायी थीं। और जब वह घर लौट रही थीं, उन्होंने
जहाज़ में सफ़र कर रही हर अमीर औरत के गहने चुराए
थे। यह भी बताया कैसे जहाज़ के कप्तान ने उन्हें रंगे

हाथों पकड़ा था और वह सारे गहनों को अपनी निकर में छिपा कर पानी में कूद गयी थीं। फिर कैसे उन्होंने इंग्लैंड पहुँचने के लिए अटलांटिक महासागर के कुछ आख़िरी मील तैर कर पूरे किये थे।

दादी ने बेन को बताया कि इतने सारे जो उनके छोटे-से बंगले में पन्ने की चमकती हुई बालियाँ थीं, उनकी क़ीमत दस लाख पाउंड से भी अधिक थी। वह एक अत्यन्त रईस भारतीय महाराजा की महारानी की बालियाँ थीं। उन्होंने बताया कैसे उन्होंने हाथियों के एक झुंड की मदद से उनको चुराया था। उनको बहला-फुसलाकर एक लम्बी सीढ़ी बनाने के लिए हाथियों को एक-दूसरे के ऊपर खड़ा कराया। फिर वह भारत के किले की दीवार पर चढ़ीं ताकि वह शाही कमरों से बालियाँ चुरा सकें।

सबसे गज़ब की कहानी नीले रंग के बड़े से हीरे और नीलम के बने ब्रोच की थी, जो अब दादी के घिसे हुए कालीन पर चमचमाता पड़ा था। उन्होंने बेन को बताया कि वह रूस की आख़िरी महारानी के थे, जिन्होंने ज़ार, रूस के बादशाह के साथ, 1917 के रूसी

क्रांति से पहले राज किया था। बहुत सालों तक दोनों आभूषण सेंट पीटर्सबर्ग के हर्मिटेज संग्रहालय में अभेद्य काँच की अलमारियों में थे। जांबाज़ रूसी जवानों की एक पलटन, दिन के चौबीस घंटे, हफ़्ते के सातों दिन, साल के तीन-सौ पैंसठ दिन उनकी रखवाली करती थी।

इसकी चोरी के लिए विस्तार से योजना बनानी पड़ी थी। दादी को लगभग एक-सौ साल पुराने, महारानी कैथरीन के ज़माने के कवच में छिपना पड़ा। जब तक वह ब्रोच के पास नहीं पहुँचीं, वह जवान का कहीं और देखने का इन्तज़ार करतीं और फिर अपने

धातु के कवच में कुछ मिलीमीटर आगे बढ़तीं। इस तरह उनको एक हफ़्ता लग गया।

"क्या, मतलब कछुए से भी धीमी, दादी की चाल?" बेन ने पूछा।

"हाँ, बेटे!" दादी ने जवाब दिया। "मैंने फिर चाँदी की कुल्हाड़ी से शीशा तोड़ा और ब्रोच उठा लिया।"

"आप भागीं कैसे, दादी?"

"अच्छा प्रश्न है, तो अब मैं कैसे भागी?" दादी अपनी ही कहानी में खो गयीं। "मुझे माफ़ कर दो, बेटा। मेरी उम्र की वजह से मैं चीज़ें भूल जाती हूँ।"

उनका साथ देते हुए बेन मुस्कुराया। "कोई बात नहीं दादी।"

जल्द ही दादी की याददाश्त वापस आ गयी। "अरे हाँ, मुझे याद आया," वह बोलीं। "मैं आंगन में पहुँची, एक बड़ी-सी तोप में घुस गयी और अपने आपको उड़ा लिया।"

बेन ने एक मिनट लिया और सोचा, *मेरी दादी*

खूँखार रूस के मध्य में, एक प्राचीन कवच में हवा में उड़ रही थीं। यक़ीन करना मुश्किल था, लेकिन आखिर और क्या हो सकता था कि आज इस छोटी-सी बूढ़ी औरत के पास इतने सारे अनमोल रत्न थे?

बेन को दादी के जोशिले किस्से बहुत पसन्द थे। घर पर, बेन कोई भी कहानी नहीं पढ़ता था और ना ही किस्से सुनता था। उसके माता-पिता काम से घर आकर, टीवी चला कर सोफ़े पर पसर कर बैठ जाते थे। दादी के किस्सों में इतना मज़ा था कि वह अपना घर छोड़, दादी के घर पर ही रहना चाहता था। दादी की कहानियाँ वह पूरा दिन सुन सकता था।

"दुनिया में ऐसा कोई भी आभूषण नहीं होगा जो आपने ना चुराया हो!" बेन बोला।

"नहीं बेटा, एक है। रुको। वो क्या था?"

"क्या क्या था?" बेन ने पूछा।

दादी ने दहशत भरी शक्ल बना कर बेन के सिर के पीछे इशारा किया। "वह है। वो।"

"क्या?" बेन पीछे घूमने की हिम्मत ना कर सका। उसके रौंगटे खड़े हो गये।

"तुम ने जो करना है करो," दादी बोलीं, "बस पीछे नहीं मुड़ना।"

14

ताँक-झाँकिया पड़ोसी

बेन अपनेआप को रोक नहीं सका और उसकी आँखें खिड़की की ओर एकाएक पड़ीं। कुछ देर तक उसको एक अटपटी-सी टोपी पहने काली परछाई घर के अन्दर ताकती हुई दिखी। लेकिन जल्द ही वह ग़ायब भी हो गयी।

"एक आदमी खिड़की से अन्दर ताँक-झाँक कर रहा था," घुटी हुई सांस से बेन ने कहा।

"मैं जानती हूँ," दादी बोलीं। "मैंने तुम्हें वहाँ देखने से मना किया था।"

"क्या मैं बाहर जा कर देखूँ कौन है?" बेन अपना डर छिपाते हुए बोला। लेकिन असल में तो वह चाहता

था कि दादी बाहर जायें और देखें कौन है।

"मैं शर्त लगा सकती हूँ कि यह ताँक-झाँकिया, श्रीमान पार्कर हैं। सात नम्बर के घर में रहते हैं, पोर्क पाई आकार की गोल-सी टोपी पहनते हैं और हमेशा मेरी जासूसी करते रहते हैं।"

"क्यों?" बेन ने पूछा।

दादी ने कन्धे उचकाये। "मुझे नहीं पता। शायद उनको सिर पर ज़्यादा ही ठंड लगती होगी।"

"क्या?" बेन बोला। "नहीं, नहीं। टोपी नहीं। मेरा मतलब था कि वह आप की जासूसी क्यों करते रहते हैं?"

"वह फ़ौज़ में मेजर थे। अब वह ग्रे क्लोज़ में मोहल्ला चौकीदारी योजना चलाते हैं।"

"मोहल्ला चौकीदारी क्या होता है?" बेन ने पूछा।

"यह यहाँ के लोगों का एक समूह है जो आस-पड़ोस पर नज़र रखते हैं ताकि चोरी ना हो। लेकिन ताँक-झाँकिया महाशय श्रीमान पार्कर ने तो सब पर जासूसी करने के लिए इसको एक बहाना बना लिया

है। मैंने कई बार देखा है कि जब मैं सुपरमार्केट से अपने बन्दगोभी के पैकेट लेकर आती हूँ, तब यह जाली के परदों के पीछे दूरबीन लेकर मेरी जासूसी करते रहते हैं।"

"क्या उनको आप पर शक है?" बेन थोड़ा घबराया हुआ बोला। चोर को सहायता और उकसाने के जुर्म में वह जेल नहीं जाना चाहता था। उसको इसका मतलब नहीं पता था, लेकिन यह ज़रूर जानता था कि वह एक गुनाह था और जेल जाने के लिए वह खुद अभी बहुत छोटा था।

"उसको सब पर शक होता रहता है। हमें उस पर नज़र रखनी पड़ेगी, बेटा। यह आदमी मुसीबत है।"

बेन खिड़की की ओर गया और बाहर झाँका। उसको कोई भी नहीं दिख रहा था।

ब्रिन्न्न्न्न्न्न्न्न्न्न्न्न्न्न्न्न्न्न्ग् ग् ग् ग् ग् ग् ग् ग् गगगगग!!!!

बेन को झटका लगा। सिर्फ़ घर की घंटी ही थी, लेकिन अगर श्रीमान ताँक-झाँक घर में आ गये तब

उन्हें दादी और बेन के ख़िलाफ़ सारे सबूत मिल जायेंगे और वह पुलिस के सामने सारे जुर्म साबित करके उन्हें जेल भेज देंगे।

"मत खोलो!," बेन कमरे में सारे आभूषणों को जल्दी से डिब्बे में डालते हुए बोला।

"तुम क्या कहना चाहते हो? ना खोलूँ? उन्हें पता है कि मैं घर में हूँ। अभी तो उन्होंने खिड़की से देखा था। तुम जाकर दरवाज़ा खोलो और मैं आभूषण छिपाती हूँ।"

"मैं?"

"हाँ तुम! जल्दी करो!"

ब्रि न् ऱ् ऱ् ऱ् ऱ् ऱ् ऱ् ऱ् ऱ् ऱ् ऱ् ऱ् ऱ् ऱ् ऱ् गगगगगग!!!!

इस बार घंटी और भी ज़ोर से बजी। उन्होंने इस बार घंटी पर हाथ ज़्यादा देर रखा। बेन ने एक लम्बी साँस ली और दरवाज़े की ओर जाने लगा। धीरे-धीरे उसने दरवाज़ा खोला।

बाहर एक आदमी अटपटी-सी टोपी पहने खड़ा

था। यक़ीन नहीं होता? देखो कितनी अटपटी थी:

"हाँ जी?" बेन ने किकियाते हुए कहा। "क्या मैं आपकी कोई मदद कर सकता हूँ?"

श्रीमान ताँक-झाँक ने अपना पैर चौखट में अटका लिया ताकि वह दरवाज़ा ना बन्द कर सके।

"तुम कौन हो?" वह नाक से गरजे।

उनकी नाक बहुत बड़ी थी, जो उन्हें हर किसी के मामले में नाक अड़ाने में खासी मददगार सिद्ध हो रही थी। क्योंकि उनकी इतनी बड़ी नाक थी, उनकी आवाज़ भी नाक से ही निकलती थी। इसकी वजह से वह जो भी बोलते थे, जितना मर्ज़ी गम्भीरता के साथ क्यों ना हो, थोड़ा बेहूदा लगता था। लेकिन उनकी आँख यमराज की तरह सुर्ख लाल थी।

"मैं दादी का दोस्त हूँ," बेन ने जल्दी से कहा। *मैंने ऐसा क्यों बोला?* उसने सोचा। असल में, वह बुरी तरह से घबराया हुआ था और उसकी ज़ुबान बस भागी चली जा रही थी।

"दोस्त?" श्रीमान ताँक-झाँक दरवाज़े को धक्का देते हुए गरजे। वह बेन से ज़्यादा मज़बूत थे और ज़बरदस्ती अन्दर घुस आये।

"मेरा मतलब पोता, श्रीमान पार्कर," बेन ड्रॉईंग रूम की ओर जाते हुए बोला।

"तुम मुझसे झूठ क्यों बोल रहे हो?" उन्होंने कहा, और उतने ही कदम आगे लिये जितने बेन ने पीछे

लिये। ऐसा लग रहा था कि दोनों टैंगो नाच कर रहे थे।

"मैं झूठ नहीं बोल रहा!" बेन कलपा।

दोनों ड्रॉईंग रूम के दरवाज़े तक पहुँच गये।

"आप अन्दर नहीं जा सकते!" बेन आभूषणों के बारे में सोचकर चिल्लाया।

"क्यों नहीं?"

"वह ... वह ... क्योंकि दादी अन्तवस्त्र पहने योगा कर रही हैं!"

बेन को कोई प्रभावशाली बहाना चाहिए था, श्रीमान ताँक-झाँक को कमरे में ज़बरदस्ती घुसने और गहनों को देखने से रोकने के लिए। उनको यक़ीन था कि उनकी लॉटरी निकल आयी थी लेकिन अब वह रुके और उनके चेहरे पर शिकन दिख रही थी।

लेकिन ताँक-झाँकिया को अभी भी सन्देह था।

"अन्तवस्त्र में योगा?! सच में! मुझे तुरन्त तुम्हारी दादी से बात करनी है। मेरे रास्ते से हटो पिल्ले कहीं के!" उन्होंने बेन को यह कहते हुए, उसको धक्का दिया और ड्रॉईंग रूम में घुस गये।

दादी ने बेन को दरवाज़े की दूसरी तरफ़ से सुन

लिया होगा, इसलिए जब श्रीमान ताँक-झाँक कमरे में झटके से घुसे, दादी अपने अन्तवस्त्र में पेड़ की तरह वृक्षासन में खड़ी थीं।

"श्रीमान पार्कर क्या आप यहाँ से जायेंगे?" दादी ने तिरस्कार और भय से बोला क्योंकि उन्होंने दादी को ऐसी दशा में देख लिया।

श्रीमान ताँक-झाँक भी इधर-उधर बगले झाँकने लगे। उन्हें समझ नहीं आ रहा था कि वह कहाँ देखें इसलिए वह अब खाली पड़े कालीन को ताकने लगे।

"मुझे माफ़ करियेगा, लेकिन क्या आप मुझे बता सकती हैं कि वह सारे आभूषण जो अभी यहाँ पड़े थे, कहाँ गये?"

बेन ने रजत जयन्ती के बिस्कुट के डिब्बे की झलक सोफ़े से देखी। नज़र बचाते हुए उसने अपने पैर से उसे छिपा दिया।

"कौन से गहने, श्रीमान पार्कर? क्या आप मेरी जासूसी कर रहे थे?" दादी ने बड़े आत्मविश्वास से उनसे पूछा हालाँकि वह आधी नंगी खड़ी थीं।

"मैं तो वह..." वह बड़बड़ाए। "मेरे पास कारण था। मुझे शक था कि मैंने एक नौजवान को आपके घर में घुसते देखा। मुझे लगा कोई चोर होगा।"

"मैंने ही उसको घर में आने दिया।"

"बहुत ही मनमोहक चोर होगा। उसने अपने भ्रामक शब्दों से ही आपका विश्वास जीत लिया होगा।"

"वह मेरा पोता है। हर शुक्रवार की रात वह यहाँ रहता है।"

"अच्छा!" श्रीमान ताँक-झाँक विजयी भाव से बोले। "लेकिन आज तो शुक्रवार नहीं है! इसलिए आपको समझ आ गया होगा कि मेरी शक की सुई क्यों घूमी। ग्रे क्लोज़ के मोहल्ला चौकीदार योजना का प्रमुख होने के नाते, मुझे पुलिस को हर सन्देहास्पद चीज़ की रपट देनी पड़ती है।"

"मुझे तो अब यह लग रहा कि मुझे पुलिस में रपट लिखवानी पड़ेगी, श्रीमान पार्कर!" बेन बोला।

दादी ने उसको जिज्ञासापूर्वक देखा।

"किस चीज़ के लिए?" वह आदमी बोला। उसकी आँखें अब इतनी लाल सुर्ख हो गयी थीं कि मानो उसका दिमाग़ जल रहा हो।

"एक बूढ़ी औरत की जासूसी करना जब उसने पूरे कपड़े भी नहीं पहने थे!" बेन ने विजयी भाव से कहा। दादी ने बेन को आँख मारी।

"उन्होंने सारे कपड़े पहने हुए थे जब मैंने खिड़की से देखा था," श्रीमान ताँक-झाँक ने विरोध किया।

"सब यही बोलते हैं!" दादी बोलीं। "अब मेरे घर से निकल जाओ इससे पहले कि मैं तुम को ताँक-झाँक करने के लिए गिरफ़्तार करवा दूँ!"

"मैं ऐसे हार नहीं मानूँगा। अलविदा!" श्रीमान ताँक-झाँक बोलते ही मुड़ गये और कमरे से बाहर चले गये। दादी और बेन को घर का दरवाज़ा धड़ाम से बन्द होने की आवाज़ आयी। दोनों खिड़की की ओर भागे और उन्हें अपने घर की ओर भागते देखा।

"मुझे लगता है कि हमने उनको डरा दिया," बेन बोला।

"लेकिन वह फिर से आयेगा," दादी बोलीं। "हमें सावधानी बरतनी होगी।"

"हाँ," बेन थोड़ा और सतर्क हो कर बोला। "हमें इस डिब्बे को कहीं और छिपा देना चाहिए।"

दादी ने एक मिनट के लिए सोचा। "हाँ मैं फ़र्श के नीचे छिपा देती हूँ।"

"ठीक है," बेन बोला। "लेकिन पहले..."

"बोलो बेन?"

"आपको कपड़े पहन लेने चाहिए।"

15

दुस्साहसी और जोशिला

जब दादी ने अपने कपड़े पहन लिये, वह और बेन सोफ़े पर बैठ गये।

"दादी, श्रीमान ताँक-झाँक के आने से पहले आप मुझे बता रही थीं कि एक आभूषण है जो आपने कभी नहीं चुराया," बेन फुसफुसाया।

"कुछ ऐसा ख़ास है जो इस दुनिया के सारे बड़े चोर पाना चाहते हैं। लेकिन यह नामुमकिन है। यह हो ही नहीं सकता।"

"ऐसा हो ही नहीं सकता कि आप ना कर पाओ, दादी। आप तो दुनिया में आज तक की सबसे बड़ी शातिर चोर हो।"

"धन्यवाद बेन, लेकिन मैं हूँ नहीं, शायद थी। और इन आभूषणों की चोरी करना हर एक बड़े चोर का सपना है। लेकिन यह बिल्कुल ही नामुमकिन है।"

"आभूषणों? एक से ज़्यादा हैं?

"हाँ बच्चे। आख़िरी बार तीन-सौ साल पहले किसी ने इनको चोरी करने की कोशिश की थी। कप्तान ब्लड शायद। मुझे नहीं लगता महारानी ख़ुश होंगी।" वह हँसी।

"आप यह तो नहीं कहना चाहती कि...?"

"यूनाइटेड किंगडम के शाही आभूषण, हाँ मेरे लाल।"

स्कूल में शाही आभूषणों के बारे में बेन ने इतिहास में पढ़ा था। इतिहास एक ऐसा विषय था जो उसे पसन्द था, इसलिए क्योंकि उसमें पुराने ज़माने के ख़तरनाक, ख़ौफ़नाक दंड होते थे। "हैंग्ड, ड्रॉन और क्वॉर्टर्ड" उसका सबसे मनपसन्द था। इसमें घोड़े पहले गुनहगार को फाँसी की जगह घसीटकर ले जाते हैं, फिर फाँसी पर चढ़ाकर आख़िर में उसके चार हिस्से कर देते हैं। लेकिन उसे मौत की चक्की, जलाने से मौत और

धातु की गरमागर्म छड़ी को पिछवाड़े में घुसाना भी पसन्द था।

किसको नहीं पसन्द यह सब?

स्कूल में बेन ने सीखा था कि शाही आभूषण में मुकुट, तलवारें, राज-दंड, अँगूठियाँ, चूड़ियाँ और गोले थे और इन में से कुछ हज़ार साल पुराने भी थे। जब भी नये राजा और रानी का अभिषेक होता था, तब इनका इस्तेमाल होता था और 1303 (साल, समय नहीं) से उन पर ताला लगा हुआ था और चाबी लंदन टावर में थी।

बेन ने अपने माता-पिता से बहुत विनती की थी कि वह उसको यह देखने के लिए ले जायें, लेकिन उन्होंने कहा था कि लंदन बहुत दूर है (जब कि इतना दूर नहीं था)।

सच तो यह है कि वह कहीं भी एक परिवार की तरह नहीं गये थे। जब वह छोटा था, बेन सोचता था कि क्लास में शो-एंड-टेल के दौरान कैसे उसके सहपाठी अनगिनत यात्राओं का वर्णन, किसी निशानी के साथ करते थे। समुद्र-तट, म्यूज़ियम और देश के बाहर भी छुट्टियाँ। लेकिन जब उसकी बारी आती तो

उसके पेट में गाँठें पड़ जाती थीं। वह बहुत शर्मिंदा होता यह बताने में कि पूरी छुट्टियों में उसने बस माइक्रोवेव में बना खाना खाया और टीवी देखा। इसलिए वह पतंग उड़ाने, पेड़ चढ़ने और महलों में जाने के किस्से गढ़ता था।

लेकिन अब उसके पास सबको सुनाने के लिए सबसे बढ़िया कहानी थी। उसकी दादी एक अन्तरराष्ट्रीय आभूषण चोर थीं। एक दबंग डाकू! लेकिन अगर उसने कुछ भी दिखाया या बताया, तो उसकी प्यारी दादी को कोई जेल में डाल देगा और उसकी चाबी भी फेंक देगा।

बेन को लगा कि यह सबसे बड़ा मौका था दुस्साहस और जोश दिखाने का।

"मैं आपकी मदद कर सकता हूँ," बेन ने बिना हिचक और शान्ति से कहा, हालाँकि उसका दिल धौंकनी की तरह तेज़ी से धड़क रहा था।

"किस चीज़ में मदद?" बूढ़ी दादी ने आशंकापूर्वक पूछा।

"शाही आभूषणों को चुराने में!" बेन बोला।

16

नहीं मतलब नहीं

"नहीं!" दादी चिल्लाईं और उनके कान की मशीन ज़ोर से कुकर की तरह सीटी मारने लगी।

"हाँ!" बेन चिल्लाया।

"नहीं!"

"हाँ!"

"नहीं ना!"

"हाँ ना!"

"नाऽऽऽऽऽऽऽऽऽऽऽऽऽऽऽऽऽऽऽऽऽऽऽऽऽऽऽ ऽऽऽऽऽऽऽहीं!"

"हाऽऽऽऽऽऽऽऽऽऽऽऽऽऽऽऽऽऽऽऽऽऽऽ ऽऽऽऽऽऽऽऽऽऽऽऽऽ!"

यह कुछ मिनटों तक चलता रहा, लेकिन पन्ने बचाने के लिए और उसे बनाने के लिए पेड़ और फिर जंगल और फिर पर्यावरण, मतलब दुनिया बचाने के लिए मैंने छोटे में ही निपटाने की कोशिश की है।

"मैं किसी भी हालत में तुम्हारी उम्र के लड़के को डकैती पर अपने साथ नहीं आने दूँगी! और शाही आभूषण तो हरगिज़ नहीं! वो भी जब यह नामुमकिन है! यह नहीं हो सकता!" दादी चिल्लाईं।

"कोई तो तरीका होगा," बेन निवेदन करने लगा।

"बेन, मैंने बोला ना, नहीं। तो अब बस!"

"लेकिन..."

"मुझे कोई लेकिन नहीं सुनना, बेन। नहीं। नहीं मतलब नहीं!"

बेन बहुत ज़्यादा निराश था लेकिन दादी अड़ गयी थीं। "मुझे जाना चाहिए फिर," उसने मायूसी से कहा।

दादी भी थोड़ी दु:खी हो गयीं। "हाँ बेटे, तुम्हें जाना चाहिए। तुम्हारे माँ और बाबा तुम्हारे लिए चिन्तित होंगे।"

"वह नहीं होंगे।"

"बेन! घर! अभी!"

दादी को बड़े लोगों की तरह वापस बोरिंग बनते देख, बेन बहुत निराश था। ख़ासतौर से जब वह दिलचस्प बनना शुरू ही हुई थीं। लेकिन उसने तब भी उनकी बात मान ली। वह यह भी नहीं चाहता था कि उसके माता-पिता को शक हो, इसलिए वह तेज़ी से घर गया, पाइप से अपने कमरे की खिड़की पर पहुँचा और फिर वहाँ से ड्रॉईंग रूम।

उसे कतई आश्चर्य नहीं हुआ जब उसने देखा कि उसके माँ और बाबा को उसकी बिल्कुल भी चिन्ता नहीं थी। दोनों अपने बेटे के प्रसिद्ध डांसर होने के इतने सपने संजो रहे थे कि उन्होंने देखा ही नहीं कि वह घर पर नहीं था।

बाबा अंडर-12 नाच की प्रतियोगिता के नम्बर पर तब तक फ़ोन पर फ़ोन लगाये जा रहे थे, जब तक फ़ोन लगा नहीं और उन्होंने अपने बेटे के लिए एक

स्थान सुरक्षित नहीं कर लिया। माँ ने सही कहा था कि कुछ ही हफ़्तों में टाउनहॉल में प्रतियोगिता थी। समय व्यर्थ ना हो, इसलिए माँ ने अपना सारा वक़्त उसकी पोशाक, प्यार का बम, बनाने में निकाल दिया।

"अभ्यास कैसा चल रहा है, बेटा?" बाबा ने पूछा। "ऐसे लग रहा है कि तुमने बहुत पसीना बहाया है।"

"ठीक है, बाबा। पूछने के लिए धन्यवाद।" बेन ने झूठ बोला। "मैं सचमुच इस प्रतियोगिता के लिए एक लाजवाब नाच का अभ्यास कर रहा हूँ।"

बेन ने अपनी ही बेलगाम ज़बान को कोसा।

कुछ लाजवाब?

शुक्र हो अगर वह गिर कर बेहोश ना हो जाये।

"हम बेसब्री से देखना चाहते हैं! ज़्यादा समय नहीं है!" माँ ने अपनी सिलाई मशीन से आँख उठाये बिना कहा। वह लाइक्रा के कपड़े से बनी पतलून पर एक लाइन से सैकड़ों चमकते हुए लाल दिल की सिलाई कर रही थीं।

"माँ, मैं अभी अकेले में ही अभ्यास करना चाहता हूँ," बेन घबराते हुए बोला। "कम से कम पूरी तरह से तैयार होने तक।"

"हाँ, हाँ, मैं समझती हूँ," माँ बोलीं।

बेन ने चैन की साँस ली। उसको और समय मिल गया था।

लेकिन बस थोड़ा-सा ही समय था।

कुछ ही हफ़्तों में बेन को मंच पर पूरे शहर के सामने नाचना होगा।

बेन अपने बिस्तर पर बैठा और अन्दर से छिपी हुई *प्लम्बिंग वीकली* निकाली। पिछले साल के एक लेख "प्लम्बिंग का संक्षिप्त इतिहास" के पन्ने ऐसे ही पलट रहा था। इस में लंदन की सारी पाइपों पर प्रकाश डाला गया था। बेन हड़बड़ी में कुछ ढूँढ रहा था।

मिल गया! यही था जो वह ढूँढ रहा था।

सैंकड़ों साल पहले थेम्स नदी के तट पर, जहाँ लंदन टावर था, वहाँ एक खुली सीवेज की पाइप थी।

(तकनीकी रूप से सीवेज पाइप का मतलब यह था कि उस में बहुत सारा मल-मूत्र होगा।)

नदी के तट पर बाकी इमारतों के टॉयलेट एक बड़ी पाइप से सीधा नदी से जुड़े थे। पत्रिका में लंदन के कई सारे प्रसिद्ध इमारतों के विस्तार से ऐतिहासिक नक़्शे बने हुए थे। वहाँ दिखा रखा था कैसे सब नदी से जुड़े हुए हैं।

और!

बेन की नज़रें नीचे कुछ ढूँढ रही थीं।

हाँ। लंदन टावर की पाइपों का एक नक़्शा था।

यह थी शाही आभूषणों को चोरी करने की चाबी। एक पाइप एक मीटर चौड़ा था, और एक बच्चा उस में आराम से तैर सकता था। और शायद एक बूढ़ी औरत भी।

लेख में यह भी लिखा था कि प्लम्बिंग सिस्टम आधुनिक था और व्यवस्थित सीवरेज सिस्टम बना था लेकिन बहुत सारे पुरानी पाइपों को ऐसे ही छोड़

दिया गया था क्योंकि उनको खोद कर बाहर निकालना
आसान न था।

यह सब सोच कर बेन का सिर घूम रहा था। यह
मुमकिन था कि वहाँ एक बड़ी-सी पाइप थी जो थेम्स
नदी से लंदन टावर तक जाती थी और ज़्यादातर लोग,

प्लम्बिंग के शौकीनों को छोड़कर, यह भूल गये थे। बेन को भी नहीं पता चलता अगर वह लम्बे समय से *प्लम्बिंग वीकली* का ग्राहक नहीं होता।

वह और दादी पाइप में तैर कर ऊपर लंदन टावर तक जा सकते थे।

माँ और बाबा ग़लत थे। उसने सोचा। प्लम्बिंग भी रोमांचक हो सकती है।

हाँ, यह एक सीवेज पाइप थी, जो बहुत अच्छी तो नहीं थी, लेकिन जो भी मल-मूत्र अभी भी होगा, वह सौ साल पुराना होगा।

बेन नहीं जानता था कि यह ठीक था या ग़लत।

फ़िलहाल, उसे किरकिराने की आवाज़ सुनाई दी और उसके कमरे का दरवाज़ा खुल गया। माँ के हाथ में लाइक्रा का बड़ा-सा कपड़ा था जो बदक़िस्मती से पोशाक प्यार का बम लग रही थी।

घबराकर बेन ने पत्रिका को आनन-फानन में बिस्तर के नीचे छुपा दिया।

"मैं सिर्फ़ देखना चाहती थी कि तुम पर कैसी लगती है," माँ बोलीं।

"अच्छा, हाँ," बेन अपने बिस्तर पर अजीब तरीक़े से बैठ कर बोला। साथ ही साथ वह सारी *प्लम्बिंग वीकली* को माँ की तेज़ नज़रों से छिपा रहा था।

"यह क्या है?" वह बोलीं। "तुमने मेरे आने पर क्या छिपाया? क्या वह *नट्स* पत्रिका थी?"

"नहीं," बेन ने ग्लानि में थूक गटकते हुए कहा। स्थिति तो ज़्यादा ही खराब थी। ऐसा लग रहा था मानो वह कोई अश्लील पत्रिका अपने बिस्तर के नीचे छिपा रहा था।

"यह कोई शर्मिंदगी की बात नहीं है, बेन। मुझे लगता है कि स्वास्थ्य के लिए अच्छा है कि तुम लड़कियों में दिलचस्पी दिखा रहे हो।"

अब तो गया! बेन ने सोचा। *मेरी माँ मुझसे लड़कियों के बारे में बात करेंगी।*

"लड़कियों में दिलचस्पी रखना शर्मिंदगी की बात नहीं है, बेन।"

"हाँ, है! मुझे लड़कियों से घिन्न आती है।"

"नहीं बेन, यह ज़िन्दगी की वास्तविकता है।"

यह रुक ही नहीं रहीं!

"जान, खाना बन गया है!" नीचे से आवाज़ आयी। "तुम ऊपर क्या कर रही हो?"

"मैं बेन से लड़कियों के बारे में बात कर रही हूँ," माँ ने कहा।

बेन का चेहरा टमाटर सरीखा लाल था।

"क्या?" बाबा ज़ोर से चीखे।

"लड़कियाँ!" माँ ने आवाज़ दी। "मैं हमारे बेटे से लड़कियों के बारे में बात कर रही हूँ।"

"अच्छा, ठीक है!" बाबा नीचे से बोले। "मैं अवन बन्द कर देता हूँ।"

"तो बेन, अगर कभी तुमको ज़रूरत हो..."

ट्रिंग ट्रिंग। ट्रिंग ट्रिंग।

माँ का मोबाइल फ़ोन उनकी जेब में बज रहा था।

"मुझे माफ़ करना बेटा," उन्होंने फ़ोन उठा कर बोला। "गेल मैं क्या तुम्हें वापस फ़ोन करूँ? मैं बेन से लड़कियों के बारे में बात कर रही थी। ठीक है, धन्यवाद। बाय!"

उन्होंने फ़ोन रखा और बेन के तरफ़ पलटीं।

"मुझे माफ़ करना, मैं कहाँ थी? हाँ, अगर तुमको कभी लड़कियों के बारे में बात करनी हो, तो ज़रूर करना। भरोसा रखो कि मैं किसी से कुछ नहीं कहूँगी।"

17

लूट की योजना

अगले दिन ज़िन्दगी में पहली बार बेन सुबह स्कूल नहीं गया।

अपने प्लम्बिंग के प्यार की वजह से उसने पिछली रात लंदन टावर की कमज़ोरी जान ली थी। दुनिया की ऐसी इमारत जहाँ घुसना नामुमकिन था, जहाँ देश के सबसे ख़तरनाक गुनहगारों को बन्दी बनाया गया था और फाँसी पर चढ़ाया गया था, उस में एक ज़बरदस्त कमी थी। एक बड़ी सीवेज पाइप जो सीधा थेम्स नदी से जा मिलती थी।

वह प्राचीन पाइप, उसका और दादी का टावर में अन्दर और बाहर जाने का मार्ग बनेगी! यह एक बहुत

ही शानदार योजना थी और बेन अपना उत्साह चाह
कर भी छुपा नहीं पा रहा था।

इस वजह से वह आज स्कूल नहीं गया था।

अब वह शुक्रवार रात का इन्तज़ार नहीं कर पा
रहा था जब उसके माँ और बाबा उसको फिर से दादी
के घर छोड़ देंगे।

तब वह बूढ़ी दादी को मना पायेगा कि वह
दोनों एक साथ शाही आभूषणों की चोरी कर सकते
हैं। बेन अपने साथ लंदन टावर के सीवेज सिस्टम
का *प्लम्बिंग वीकली* में बना नक़्शा उनको दिखाने के
लिए ले जायेगा। दोनों पूरी रात जागकर हर जानकारी
की मदद से दुनिया की सबसे दुस्साहसी लूट पर काम
कर सकेंगे।

दिक्कत तो थी—पूरा एक हफ़्ता पाठों, अध्यापकों
और गृहकार्यों से भरा, अभी और शुक्रवार रात के बीच
में खड़ा था। लेकिन बेन ने फ़ैसला कर लिया था कि
वह इस पूरे स्कूल के हफ़्ते का बुद्धिमानी से काम लेगा।

कम्प्यूटर की क्लास में उसने शाही आभूषणों को इंटरनेट पर ढूँढा और हर एक जानकारी को याद कर लिया।

इतिहास में, उसने अपने अध्यापक से लंदन टावर पर प्रश्न और उसमें आभूषणों का स्थान पूछा। (वह आभूषण घर होगा।)

भूगोल में, एक ब्रिटिश द्वीप का नक़्शा ढूँढा और जाना कि थेम्स नदी पर टावर कहाँ था।

शारीरिक शिक्षा में, हर बार की तरह जान-बूझकर, ग़लती से अपना किट नहीं भूला, बल्कि उसने कुछ ज़्यादा ही व्यायाम किया ताकि उसकी बाँहें अपने आप को टावर की ओर सीवेज पाइप में खींचने के लिए मज़बूत हो जायें।

गणित में उसने अध्यापक से पूछा कि पाँच अरब पाउंड (जो शाही आभूषणों की क़ीमत बतायी जाती है) में वह रोलोस की कितनी गोलियाँ खरीद पायेगा। रोलोस की गोलियाँ बेन की सबसे मनपसन्द गोलियाँ थीं।

उत्तर था, दस अरब पैकेट या चौबीस अरब गोलियाँ। एक साल के लिए बहुत थीं।

और राज ने भी कुछ और पैकेट मुफ़्त में देने का आश्वासन दे दिया था।

फ्रेंच भाषा की कक्षा में बेन ने "मैं चोरी के बारे में कुछ नहीं जानता, 'शाही आभूषण' को क्या बोलते हैं, मैं तो बस एक ग़रीब किसान का लड़का हूँ" बोलना सीखा ताकि अगर उसको घटनास्थल से भागना पड़े तब वह ग़रीब किसान का बेटा होने का ढोंग कर सके।

स्पेनिश भाषा में उसने "मैं चोरी के बारे में कुछ नहीं जानता, 'शाही आभूषण' को क्या बोलते हैं, मैं तो बस एक ग़रीब किसान का लड़का हूँ" बोलना सीखा ताकि अगर उसको घटनास्थल से भागना पड़े तब वह ग़रीब किसान का बेटा होने का ढोंग कर सके।

जर्मन भाषा में उसने सीखा ... अब आप समझ ही गये होंगे।

विज्ञान में, बेन ने अध्यापक से अभेद्य काँच को

भेदने के बारे में पूछताछ की कि कैसे आप गोली-सहने वाले शीशे में छेद कर सकोगे। अगर आप आभूषण घर में पहुँच भी गये, आभूषणों को वहाँ से लेना आसान नहीं होगा क्योंकि वह एक इंच के शीशे के पीछे थे।

कला की कक्षा में, उसने माचिसों से लंदन टावर का पूरा नमूना तैयार किया ताकि वह इस दुस्साहसी चोरी का ड्रेस रिहर्सल कर सके।

लूट की योजना

स्कूल में कभी इतना मज़ा नहीं आया था और पूरा हफ़्ता कहीं उड़-सा गया। सबसे महत्त्वपूर्ण था कि अपनी पूरी ज़िन्दगी में बेन पहली बार दादी के साथ समय बिताने का बेसब्री से इन्तज़ार कर रहा था।

शुक्रवार दोपहर को स्कूल खत्म होने पर, बेन को लगा कि उसके पास इस हैरतअंगेज़ चोरी को अंजाम देने की सारी जानकारी थी।

शाही आभूषणों की चोरी की कहानी हफ़्तों तक टीवी और वेबसाइटों पर दिखायी जायेगी और हर देश के हर अख़बार के पहले पन्ने पर जगमगायेगी। लेकिन, किसी को भी, दुनिया में किसी को भी शक नहीं होगा कि चोर एक बूढ़ी औरत और ग्यारह साल का एक लड़का थे। वह दोनों सदी की सबसे बड़ी चोरी करके लोगों की आँखों में धूल झोंकने में सफल हो जायेंगे।

18

मिलने का समय

"तुम आज रात दादी के साथ नहीं रह सकते," बाबा बोले। शुक्रवार दोपहर के चार बज रहे थे और बेन स्कूल से बस अभी आया ही था। कुछ अटपटा था क्योंकि बाबा इतनी जल्दी घर आ गये थे। आमतौर पर बाबा काम से आठ बजे से पहले नहीं आते थे।

"क्यों नहीं?" बेन ने बाबा के चेहरे पर शिकन देखते हुए पूछा।

"बात तो यह है कि मेरे पास एक बुरी ख़बर है।"

"क्या?" बेन ने प्रश्न उठाया और उसके भी चेहरे पर शिकन आने लगी थी।

"दादी अस्पताल में हैं।"

*

कुछ देर बाद जब उनको गाड़ी खड़ी करने की जगह मिल गयी थी, बेन और उसके माता-पिता अपने आप खुलने वाले दरवाज़े से अन्दर घुसे। बेन को लग नहीं रहा था कि यहाँ माँ और बाबा कभी भी दादी को ढूँढ पायेंगे। यह अस्पताल हद से ज़्यादा बड़ा, बीमरियों के लिए एक विशाल स्मारक था।

यहाँ लिफ़्ट थीं जो दूसरी लिफ़्टों की ओर ले जाती थीं।

मीलों लम्बे कॉरिडोर थे।

ऐसे-ऐसे साइन बोर्ड लगे थे जो बेन को समझ नहीं आ रहे थे:

कोरोनरी केयर यूनिट

रेडियोलॉजी

प्रसूति-विज्ञान

क्लीनिकल निर्णय विभाग

एमआरआई स्कैन क्षेत्र

बौखलाए हुए मरीज़ों को ट्रॉली या व्हीलचेयर पर पल्लेदार ले जा रहे थे। डॉक्टर और नर्स भी भागे जा रहे थे। लग रहा था कि बेचारे नींद से वंचित थे।

जब उनको आख़िर में उन्निसवीं मंज़िल पर एक क्षेत्र में दादी मिलीं, तब बेन उनको पहचान भी नहीं पा रहा था।

उनके बाल चपटे थे, उन्होंने अपना चश्मा नहीं पहना था, और ना ही अपने नकली दाँत। दादी ने अपने ख़ुद के कपड़े भी नहीं पहने हुए थे, बल्कि अस्पताल की दी गयी सरकारी नाइटी पहनी हुई थी। ऐसा लग रहा था मानो जो चीज़ें दादी को उसकी दादी बनाती थीं, वह सब उनसे ले लीं गयी थीं और अब वह बस एक ढाँचा भर थीं।

बेन को उन्हें इस हालत में देखकर बहुत बुरा लगा लेकिन उसने यह छिपाने की कोशिश की। वह दादी को उदास नहीं करना चाहता था।

"हेलो, मेरे बच्चों," उन्होंने कहा। उनकी आवाज़ मेंढक सरीखी थी और उनकी बोली अस्पष्ट। बेन को

अपने आँसू रोकने के लिए एक लम्बी साँस लेनी पड़ी।

"आप कैसे हो, माँ?" बेन के बाबा ने पूछा।

"कुछ ख़ास नहीं," उन्होंने जवाब दिया। "मैं गिर गयी थी।"

"गिर गये थे?" बेन बोला।

"हाँ, मुझे कुछ ज़्यादा याद नहीं है। मैं सीढ़ियों पर अपना बन्दगोभी का सूप लेने के लिए चढ़ने लगी थी, अचानक से पता नहीं कैसे मैं लिनोलियम के फ़र्श पर गिरी और छत को देख रही थी। मेरी चचेरी बहन एड्ना ने बहुत बार डिस्पेन्सरी फ़ोन किया। उसको कोई जवाब नहीं मिला, इसलिए उसने ऐम्बुलेंस बुलायी।"

"दादी आप गिरे कब थे?" बेन ने पूछा।

"मुझे सोचने दो, मैं रसोई के फ़र्श पर दो दिनों तक थी, उस हिसाब से बुधवार सुबह। मैं फ़ोन तक भी नहीं पहुँच पा रही थी।"

"मुझे माफ़ कर दो माँ," बाबा ने धीरे से कहा। बेन ने कभी भी अपने बाबा को इतना मायूस नहीं देखा था।

"पता है, मैं आप को बुधवार को फ़ोन करने वाली थी, यूँ ही बातें करने के लिए और आपका हाल-चाल जानने के लिए," माँ ने झूठ बोला। उन्होंने आज तक अपनी ज़िन्दगी में दादी को कभी भी फ़ोन नहीं किया था, और अगर कभी दादी फ़ोन करती थीं तो माँ शिकायत करतीं कि दादी बहुत बोलती थीं।

"तुमको कहाँ ही पता चलता, मेरे बच्चों," दादी बोलीं। "उन्होंने आज सुबह हर प्रकार की जाँच की। जानने के लिए कि मुझे हुआ क्या है; एक्स-रे और स्कैन और वो सब। कल सुबह रपट मिलेगी। मैं उम्मीद कर रही हूँ कि मुझे यहाँ ज़्यादा देर तक ना रहना पड़े।"

"मैं भी यह आशा करता हूँ," बेन ने कहा।

वहाँ एक अजीब-सी चुप्पी छा गयी।

किसी को भी समझ नहीं आ रहा था कि क्या बोलें और क्या ना बोलें।

माँ ने बाबा को कोहनी मारी और घड़ी की तरफ़ इशारा किया।

बेन जानता था कि अस्पतालों से उनको बेचैनी होती थी। जब दो साल पहले बेन का अपेंडिक्स

निकाला था, वह उसे सिर्फ़ एक-दो बार मिलने आयी
थीं, तब भी उनके पसीने छूट रहे थे और वह कुलबुला
रही थीं।

"अच्छा, तो अब हमें जाना चाहिए," बाबा
ने कहा।

"हाँ, हाँ, तुम जाओ," दादी बोलीं, उनकी आवाज़
में एक हलकापन था लेकिन आँखों में उदासी भी थी।
"मेरी चिन्ता मत करना। मैं ठीक हो जाऊँगी।"

"क्या हम कुछ देर और नहीं रुक सकते?" बेन
ने कहा।

माँ ने उसको दुख भरी आँखों से देखा, जो बाबा
ने भी देखा।

"नहीं, चलो बेन, दादी को आराम करने दो,"
बाबा ने खड़े होकर कहा। "मुझे अभी बहुत काम है, मैं
सप्ताहान्त को आने की कोशिश करूँगा।"

उन्होंने अपनी माँ के सिर पर हाथ फेरा जैसे एक
कुत्ते पर फेरते हैं। यह काफ़ी अटपटा था, क्योंकि बाबा
गले नहीं मिलते थे।

वह जाने के लिए मुड़े और माँ धीमे से मुस्कुराईं और फिर वहाँ से जाना ना चाह रहे बेन का हाथ पकड़कर वार्ड से ले गयीं।

उस दिन शाम को बिस्तर में बेन उस हफ़्ते की स्कूल से इकट्ठा की गयी सारी जानकारी को छाँट रहा था।

हम उनको दिखायेंगे दादी, उसने साहस के साथ सोचा। *मैं आपके लिए यह करूँगा।* अब जब दादी बीमार थीं तब बेन का इरादा पहले से भी ज़्यादा दृढ़ था।

उसके पास इतिहास की सबसे बड़ी चोरी की योजना बनाने के लिए चाय के समय तक का वक़्त था।

19

एक छोटा विस्फ़ोटक यंत्र

अगली सुबह जब माँ और बाबा बेन की जल्द ही होने वाली प्रतियोगिता के लिए संगीत खोज रहे थे और एक के बाद दूसरा गाना चला रहे थे तब बेन चुपचाप घर से भागा और साइकिल पर अस्पताल जा पहुँचा।

जब उसको आखिरकार दादी का वार्ड मिला, उसने एक ऐनकवाले डॉक्टर को उनके बिस्तर के किनारे बैठे पाया। फिर भी वह खुशी से दादी की ओर भागता हुआ गया ताकि वह उनके साथ योजना बना पाये।

डॉक्टर ने दादी का हाथ पकड़ा हुआ था और धीरे-धीरे बात कर रहा था।

"बेन हमको कुछ वक़्त अकेला छोड़ दो प्लीज़," दादी बोलीं। "मैं और डॉक्टर अभी, क्या कहते हैं, औरतों की चीज़ों के बारे में बात कर रहे हैं।"

"अच्छा, ठीक है," बेन बोला। वह वहाँ से बाहर गया और टेक अ ब्रेक पत्रिका के पन्ने पलटने लगा।

डॉक्टर उसके सामने से वार्ड से निकलने से पहले बोले, "मुझे माफ़ कर दो।"

माफ़? बेन ने सोचा। इनको माफ़ी क्यों चाहिए?

हिचकिचाता वह दादी के बिस्तर की तरफ गया।

दादी टिशू से अपनी आँखें साफ़ कर रही थीं। लेकिन जैसे ही बेन आया, वह रुक गयीं और उसको अपनी नाइटी की बाँह में छिपा दिया।

"दादी क्या आप ठीक हो?" उसने प्रेम से पूछा।

"हाँ, मैं ठीक हूँ। मेरी आँखों में कुछ है।"

"फिर डॉक्टर ने 'मुझे माफ़ कर दो' क्यों बोला?" दादी घबराई हुई लग रही थीं।

"वह ना, मुझे लगता है उन्होंने तुम्हारा समय व्यर्थ किया इसलिये कहा होगा। वैसे भी मैं तो बिल्कुल ठीक हूँ।"

"सच में?"

"हाँ, डॉक्टर ने जाँच के परिणाम बताये। और मैं तो पहाड़ी बकरी की तरह तन्दरुस्त हूँ।"

बेन ने यह बात पहले नहीं सुनी थी, लेकिन उसको लगा की इनका मतलब बहुत, बहुत दुरुस्त होगा।

"यह तो बढ़िया ख़बर है, दादी," बेन खुशी से झूम उठा। "अब, मैं जानता हूँ कि आपने पहले मुझे 'नहीं' कहा था..."

"बेन, क्या तुम उसकी बात कर रहे हो जो मैं सोच रही हूँ?" दादी ने टोका।

बेन ने सिर हिलाया।

"मैंने सौ बार 'नहीं' बोला था।"

"हाँ, लेकिन..."

"लेकिन क्या?"

"मुझे लंदन टावर में एक कमज़ोरी मिली है। और मैं पूरा हफ़्ता आभूषणों की चोरी की योजना पर ही काम कर रहा था। मुझे लगता है कि यह सम्भव है।"

यह सुनकर दादी की जिज्ञासा जाग उठी। "परदे खींच दो और धीरे बोलो," दादी फुसफुसाई और अपनी कान की मशीन को एक दम तेज़ कर दिया।

बेन ने तेज़ी से दादी के कमरे के सारे परदे खींच दिये और उनके साथ बैठ गया।

"तो फिर, हम दोनों ठीक आधी रात को साँस लेने के लिए स्कूबा डाइविंग की ड्रेस पहनकर, थेम्स में तैरते हुए प्राचीन सीवेज पाइप को ढूँढने निकलेंगे, यहाँ," बेन उनको *प्लम्बिंग वीकली* के पुराने प्रकाशन में बना नक्शा दिखाते हुए फुसफुसाया।

"हमको एक सीवेज पाइप में तैरना पड़ेगा?! मेरी उम्र में!" दादी बोलीं। "पागल मत बनो!"

"धीरे। धीरे बोलो," बेन बोला।

"मुझे माफ़ करो," दादी फुसफुसाई।

"और यह पागलपन नहीं है। यह बेहतरीन है। पाइप इतनी चौड़ी है कि, देखो यहाँ।"

दादी अपने तकियों से ज़रा ऊपर उठीं और *प्लम्बिंग वीकली* के और पास आयीं। उन्होंने नक़्शे को ध्यान से देखा। वह सच में उतना चौड़ा लग रहा था।

"अब, अगर हम दोनों पाइप से ऊपर तैरते हुए टावर तक पहुँचें तो हमें कोई नहीं देख पायेगा," बेन ने आगे कहा। "इस इमारत के इर्द-गिर्द, हर जगह सशस्त्र पहरेदार, कैमरे और लेज़र सेन्सर हैं। अगर हम कोई भी दूसरा रास्ता अपनाते हैं तब हम बिल्कुल भी कुछ नहीं कर सकते।"

"हाँ, हाँ, हाँ, लेकिन ऐसा कौन-सा तरीक़ा है जिस से हम आभूषण घर तक पहुँचेंगे जहाँ आभूषण रखे हुए हैं?" दादी ने धीमी आवाज़ में पूछा।

"सीवेज पाइप इस पाखाने पर खत्म होती है।"

"माफ़ करना, लेकिन क्या?"

"पाखाना एक पुराना शब्द है शौचालय के लिए।

"अरे हाँ।"

"पा़खाने से बस भागते हुए हम..."

दादी ने गला साफ़ किया।

"मेरा मतलब चलते हुए आँगन से आभूषण घर तक जायेंगे। ज़ाहिर-सी बात है कि रात को दरवाज़े पर

ताले और फिर उस पर दूसरे ताले लगे होते हैं।"

"शायद तीसरे भी!" दादी को यक़ीन नहीं हो रहा था।

"दरवाज़े मज़बूत स्टील के हैं, इसीलिए हम छेद करने वाली ड्रिल मशीन से तालों को खोलेंगे।"

"लेकिन बेन, सारे मुकुट और राजदंड और बाकी सब भी एक अभेद्य शीशे के पीछे होंगे," दादी बोलीं।

"हाँ लेकिन बम तो शीशे को तोड़ सकता है ना। हम एक छोटा विस्फ़ोटक यंत्र लगाकर शीशे को चूर चूर कर देंगे।"

"विस्फ़ोटक यंत्र?" दादी तुरन्त बोलीं। "हम दोनों को कहाँ से मिलेगा?"

"मैंने विज्ञान की कक्षा से चुपके से रसायन उठा लिये थे।" बेन खुद पर गर्व करते हुए बोला। "मुझे लगता है कि मैं उस शीशे को तोड़ने के लिए एक धमाका कर सकता हूँ।"

"बेन, लेकिन अगर पहरेदारों को धमाका सुनाई दे

गया तो? नहीं। नहीं। मुझे माफ़ करो, लेकिन यह नहीं हो सकता!" दादी ने धीमे से कहा।

"मैंने उसके बारे में सोचा था," बेन अपनी चतुरता पर कुछ क्षण खुश होते हुए बोला। "आपको लंदन के लिए एक ट्रेन में जाना पड़ेगा और एक प्यारी-सी बूढ़ी औरत का ढोंग..."

"मैं हूँ ही एक प्यारी-सी बूढ़ी औरत!" दादी ने कहा।

"मेरा मतलब," बेन ने आगे मुस्कुराते हुए बोला, "स्टेशन से आपको अठहत्तर नम्बर की बस लेनी होगी, लंदन टावर तक। फिर आप उन हट्टेकट्टे पहरेदारों को चॉकलेट केक खिला देना जिस में नींद की दवा मिला हो।"

"हाँ, मैं अपनी विशेष जड़ी बूटियों वाली नशे की दवा मिला दूँगी!" दादी बोलीं।

"हाँ। बढ़िया," बेन बोला। "तो वह पहरेदार चॉकलेट केक खाकर रात भर गहरी नींद में होंगे।"

172

"चॉकलेट केक?" दादी ने विरोध किया। "मुझे लगता है कि उनको चॉकलेट केक से ज़्यादा मेरे हाथों से बना बन्दगोभी का केक पसन्द आयेगा।"

दादी के बन्दगोभी केक बनाने की विधि:

छ: बड़ी बन्दगोभी लें

बन्दगोभी को अपने आलू पीसने के यन्त्र से पीसें

पिसी हुई बन्दगोभी को बेकिंग ट्रे में रखें

तब तक इसे पकायें जब तक कि आपका पूरा घर बन्दगोभी की महक से भर न जाये

इसके बासी होने का एक महीना इन्तज़ार करें

काटें और परोसें (उल्टी के लिए बाल्टी वैकल्पिक)

"वो..." बेन छटपटाया।

वह दादी को नाराज़ नहीं करना चाहता था, लेकिन यह तो निश्चित था कि दादी के करीबी भी दादी के बन्दगोभी के केक का एक टुकड़ा मुश्किल से खा पाते थे और वो भी शायद दादी की नज़रें हटते ही फेंक देते थे।

"मेरे हिसाब से सुपरमार्केट से लिया हुआ चॉकलेट केक बेहतर होगा।"

"ऐसा लगता है कि तुम सब कुछ सोच समझ कर आये हो। मुझे तुम पर नाज़ है। पुरानी पाइपों को इस्तेमाल करने का विचार अद्भुत है।"

बेन गर्व से फूला नहीं समा रहा था। "धन्यवाद।"

"लेकिन तुम को इसके बारे में कैसे पता था? तुम्हें यह सब स्कूल में तो नहीं सिखाते हैं ना? सीवेज पाइप और यह सब?"

"नहीं," बेन बोला। "मुझे प्लम्बिंग शुरू से बेहद पसन्द है। मुझे याद था कि इन पाइपों का ज़िक्र मेरी मनपसन्द पत्रिका में होगा।" उसने *प्लम्बिंग वीकली* उठाई। "मेरा सपना है कि मैं एक दिन प्लम्बर बनूँ।"

उसने अपनी नज़रें नीची कर लीं यह सोचकर की दादी भी उसको मना करेंगी या उसका मज़ाक उड़ायेंगी।

"तुम ज़मीन क्यों ताक रहे हो?" दादी ने पूछा।

"मैं जानता हूँ कि एक प्लम्बर बनना बेवकूफ़ी भरा और बोरिंग है। मुझे पता है कि मुझे कुछ और दिलचस्प बनना चाहिए।" बेन को एहसास था कि उसका चेहरा लाल हो रहा था।

दादी ने उसकी ठोड़ी पर हाथ रखा और प्यार से उसका मुँह ऊपर किया। "बेन तुम जो भी करोगे वह कभी भी बेवकूफ़ी भरा या बोरिंग नहीं होगा," उन्होंने कहा। "अगर तुम प्लम्बर बनना चाहते हो तो तुमसे यह कोई भी छीन नहीं सकता। तुम समझ रहे हो ना? तुम अपनी इस ज़िन्दगी में बस अपने सपने पूरे कर सकते हो। नहीं तो तुम बस अपना समय बरबाद कर रहे हो।"

"शायद।"

"बिल्कुल। सच में! तुम कह रहे हो कि प्लम्बिंग बोरिंग है, लेकिन भगवान के लिए एक बार देखो, तुम शाही आभूषणों को चुराने की योजना बना रहे हो, और

175

यह सब कुछ प्लम्बिंग से जुड़ा है!''

बेन मुस्कुराया। शायद दादी सही थीं।

''लेकिन मेरे पास तुम्हारे लिए एक प्रश्न है, बेन।''

''जी?''

''हम भागेंगे कैसे? ऐसी योजना का क्या फ़ायदा होगा, मेरे लाल, अगर तुम रंगे हाथों पकड़े गये।''

''मैं जानता हूँ दादी, इसलिए मुझे लगता है कि जिस रास्ते से हम अन्दर आयेंगे, उसी रास्ते से, यानी सीवेज पाइप से ही वापस थेम्स नदी में जायेंगे। वह सिर्फ़ पचास मीटर लम्बा है और मेरे पास सौ मीटर तैरने का प्रमाणपत्र भी है। चुटकियों में हो जायेगा।''

दादी ने अपने नाखून चबाने शुरू कर दिये। ज़ाहिर था कि उनको यह काम चुटकियों में हो जाने वाला नहीं लग रहा था, और खास तौर पर एक ज़ोर से बहती नदी में तैरना।

बेन ने दादी की ओर आशा भरी नज़रें घुमाई।

''दादी आप यह करोगे? क्या आप अभी भी दबंग हो?''

ऐसा लग रहा था मानो वह किसी ख्याल में डूब गयी थीं।

"प्लीज़?" बेन ने विनती की। "मुझे आपके रोमांचक किस्से सुनना बहुत अच्छा लगा है और मैं सच में आपके साथ इस लूट पर जाना चाहता हूँ। और यह अत्यन्त ख़ास होगी क्योंकि यह शाही आभूषण हैं। आपने ही कहा था कि यह हर बड़े चोर का सपना है। तो, दादी क्या आप यह करोगे?"

दादी ने अपने पोते के उल्लास से चमकते हुए चेहरे को देखा। कुछ देर बाद वह बोलीं, "हाँ।"

बेन ने अपनी कुर्सी से छलाँग मारी और उनको गले लगा लिया। बहुत सालों बाद, आज दादी ने उसे वाक़ई गले से लगाया था।

"लेकिन मेरी एक शर्त है," बूढ़ी दादी ने संजीदा निगाहों से देखते हुए बोला।

"क्या?" बेन फुसफुसाया।

"हम उनको अगले दिन वापस रखने जायेंगे।"

20

धक धक धक धक

दादी की बातों पर बेन को यकीन नहीं हो रहा था। ऐसा कैसे हो सकता था कि वह खतरा मोल लें, शाही आभूषणों की चोरी करें, और फिर अगली रात वापस रख दें?

"दादी उनकी क़ीमत लाखों, अरबों में है..." वह कुड़कुड़ाया।

"मैं जानती हूँ। हम जैसे ही उनको बेचने की कोशिश करेंगे हम पक्का पकड़े जायेंगे।

"लेकिन..."

"कोई 'लेकिन' नहीं, बेटा। हम उनको अगली रात वापस रखेंगे। क्या तुम जानते हो मैं इतने साल

जेल से कैसे बची? मैंने कभी भी कुछ नहीं बेचा। मैं सिर्फ़ रोमांच के लिए चोरी करती थी।''

''लेकिन आपने अपने पास रखे हैं,'' बेन बोला। ''आपने बेचे नहीं, लेकिन आपके बिस्कुट के डिब्बे में सारे आभूषण पड़े हैं।''

दादी ने आँखें झपकाईं। ''हाँ, मैं तब छोटी और नादान थी,'' उन्होंने बोला। ''अब मैंने सीख लिया है कि चोरी करना ग़लत बात है। और तुमको भी यह समझना पड़ेगा।'' उन्होंने बेन को गम्भीरता से देखा।

बेन छटपटाया। ''मैं समझता हूँ, यकीनन समझता...''

''तुमने एक चतुर योजना बनायी है, बेन, सच में। लेकिन वह आभूषण हमारे नहीं हैं ना?''

''नहीं,'' बेन बोला। ''नहीं हैं हमारे।'' अब उसको भी थोड़ी-सी शर्म आ रही थी क्योंकि वह एक बार आभूषणों को लौटाने की बात से डर गया था।

''और यह मत भूलना की देश की सारी पुलिस, और शायद दुनिया की भी, शाही आभूषणों को ढूँढ़ेगी। लंदन पुलिस का मुख्य कार्यालय, स्कॉट्लैंड यार्ड,

हमारे पीछे होगा। अगर उन्होंने हमें पकड़ लिया, तो हमें जेल में पूरी ज़िन्दगी के लिए डाल देंगे। मेरे लिए चाहे वह बहुत लम्बी नहीं होगी, लेकिन तुम्हारे लिए सत्तर-अस्सी साल होंगे।"

"आप ठीक बोल रहे हो," बेन बोला।

"और महारानी कितनी प्यारी-सी लगती हैं। हम दोनों की उम्र दरअसल एक ही है। मुझे बहुत बुरा लगेगा अगर मैंने उनको ठेस पहुँचाई।"

"मुझे भी," बेन बड़बड़ाया। उसने महारानी को हज़ारों बार समाचार में देखा था। जब अपनी विशाल बग्गी में पीछे बैठकर, मुस्कुराते और हाथ हिलाते हुए सबका अभिवादन करतीं तो वह एक प्यारी-सी बूढ़ी औरत लगती थीं।

"इसको हम सिर्फ़ रोमांच के लिए करते हैं। ठीक है?"

"ठीक है!" बेन बोला। "हम कब कर सकते हैं? एक शुक्रवार रात को ही हो सकता है, जब माँ और बाबा मुझे आपके पास रहने ले आयेंगे। क्या डॉक्टर

ने बताया कि आप कब अस्पताल से जा सकती हैं?''

"वह, अरे हाँ, बताया था, उन्होंने कहा कि मैं कभी भी जा सकती हूँ।''

"बढ़िया!''

"लेकिन हमको जल्द ही करना होगा। अगले शुक्रवार करें?''

"यह बहुत जल्दी नहीं है?''

"बिल्कुल भी नहीं, तुम्हारी योजना का हर पहलू ग़ौर से सोचा गया है, बेन।''

"धन्यवाद,'' बेन गर्व से बोला। उसको पहली बार लग रहा था कि किसी बड़े को उस पर गर्व था।

"जैसे ही मैं यहाँ से निकलूँगी, मैं सारे सामान को इकट्ठा करने में जुट जाऊँगी। बेन, अब तुम जाओ और मैं तुमको अगले शुक्रवार हमेशा के समय मिलूँगी।''

बेन ने परदे खोल दिये। श्रीमान पार्कर, दादी के ताँक-झाँकिया पड़ोसी, वहाँ ही खड़े हुए थे!

भौचक्का बेन कुछ कदम झिटककर बिस्तर की ओर पीछे हो गया और जल्दी से उसने अपनी *प्लम्बिंग*

वीकली अपने स्वेटर में छिपा दी।

"आप यहाँ क्या कर रहे हैं?" बेन ने पूछा।

"मुझे बिस्तर में नहाते हुए देखने आये होंगे!" दादी बोलीं।

बेन हँसा।

श्रीमान पार्कर निःशब्द हो गये। "नहीं, नहीं, मैं..."

"नर्स! नर्स!!" दादी ज़ोर से चिल्लाईं।

"रुको!" श्रीमान पार्कर घबरा गये। "मुझे सच में लगता है कि मैंने आप दोनों में से एक को शाही आभूषणों के बारे में बात करते हुए सुना है..."

बहुत देर हो गयी थी। नर्स, जो हमेशा एक लम्बी बड़े पैरों वाली औरत होती है, गिरते फिसलते वार्ड की तरफ़ तेज़ी से आयी।

"जी?" नर्स ने पूछा। "कुछ हुआ क्या?"

"यह आदमी परदों के पीछे से मेरी जासूसी कर रहा था!" दादी बोलीं।

"सच में?" नर्स ने श्रीमान पार्कर से ग़ुस्से से पूछा।

"वो, मैंने इन लोगों को सुना..." श्रीमान

पार्कर ठिनकनाए।

"पिछले हफ़्ते मेरी दादी जब अपने अन्तर्वस्त्र में योगा कर रही थीं, तब भी यह जासूसी कर रहे थे," बेन ने दादी का साथ देते हुए पिछली घटना बताई।

नर्स लाल-पीली हो गयी। "सूअर के बच्चे, अभी के अभी मेरे वार्ड से निकल जाओ!" वह चिल्लाई।

शर्मिंदा श्रीमान पार्कर नर्स से पीछे हटे और वार्ड से शीघ्रातिशीघ्र चले गये। वह बाहर निकलने से पहले दरवाज़े पर रुके और दादी और बेन पर चिल्लाये, "देखते जाओ, आगे-आगे मैं तुम दोनों के साथ क्या करता हूँ!"

"मुझे ज़रूर बताना अगर यह आदमी वापस आये तो," नर्स ने कहा, और अब उसके चेहरे का रंग वापस आ रहा था।

"ज़रूर," दादी ने नर्स के जाने से पहले जवाब दिया।

"उन्होंने शायद सब सुन लिया होगा!" बेन फुसफुसाया।

"शायद," दादी ने कहा। "लेकिन मुझे लगता है नर्स ने उनको अच्छे से डरा कर भगाया है!"

"भगवान करे ऐसा ही हो।" बेन इस दुर्भाग्यपूर्ण घटना से चिन्तित था।

"क्या तुम अभी भी यह करना चाहते हो?" बूढ़ी दादी ने पूछा।

बेन को लग रहा था कि वह एक टेढ़े-मेढ़े झूले, रोलर-कोस्टर, पर बैठा था जो धीरे से ऊपर जा रहा था। वह उतरना भी चाहता था और बैठे भी रहना चाहता था। ख़ौफ़ और आनन्द दोनों ही उसको झूला झुला रहे थे।

"हाँ!" उसने कहा।

"शाबाश!" दादी बेन को देखकर मुस्कुराते हुए बोलीं।

बेन जाने के लिए मुड़ा और फिर वापस पलटा। "मैं ... मैं आपसे प्यार करता हूँ," उसने बोला।

"और मैं भी तुमसे प्यार करती हूँ, बेनी," दादी ने आँख मारते हुए बोला।

बेन ने मुँह बनाया। उसके पास अब दबंग दादी थी, और यह बहुत बड़ी बात थी, लेकिन अभी भी उनको बेन बोलना सिखाना पड़ेगा!

*

बेन कॉरिडर में भागता गया। उसका दिल ज़ोर-ज़ोर से धकधक कर रहा था।

धक धक धक धक।

वह जोश में था। ग्यारह साल का एक लड़का, जिसने आज तक अपनी ज़िन्दगी में कुछ भी महत्त्वपूर्ण नहीं किया था, बस एक बार झूले में अपने दोस्त के सिर पर उलटी करने के अलावा, अब दुनिया में अब तक की सबसे रोमांचक चोरी में भाग लेने वाला था।

वह अस्पताल से बाहर निकला और साइकिल की चाबी को टटोलने लगा। फिर, जब उसने ऊपर देखा तो उसके होश उड़ गये।

वहाँ उसकी दादी थीं।

यह कुछ अनोखा नहीं था।

दबंग दादी

लेकिन अनोखा तो यह था कि—

दादी रस्सी के सहारे अस्पताल की दीवार से उतर रही थीं।

उन्होंने बड़ी सारी चादरों को बाँधा हुआ था और वह बिल्डिंग से उतर रही थीं।

बेन को अपनी आँखों पर यक़ीन नहीं हो रहा था। वह जानता था कि उसकी दादी अच्छी ख़ासी दबंग थीं, लेकिन यह तो कुछ ज़्यादा ही हो रहा था।

"दादी, आप यह क्या करने की कोशिश कर रहे हो?!" बेन कार पार्क से चिल्लाया।

"लिफ़्ट नहीं चल रही थी, बेटा! अगले शुक्रवार मिलते हैं। देरी मत करना!" वह ज़मीन पर पहुँचते हुए चिल्लाई। फिर वह अपने स्कूटर

186

पर बैठीं और उसको उड़ाते हुए घर ले गईं।

*

कभी भी हफ़्ता काटना इतना भारी नहीं पड़ा था।

बेन ने पूरे हफ़्ते, शुक्रवार का इन्तज़ार किया। हर एक मिनट, हर एक घंटा, हर एक दिन ख़त्म होने को ही नहीं आ रहा था।

बस अजीब था आम लड़के होने का ढोंग करना, जबकि असल में तो वह दुनिया की अब तक की सबसे बड़ी योजना बनाने में सफल हुआ था।

आखिरकार, शुक्रवार शाम आ गयी। बेन के कमरे के दरवाज़े पर खटखट हुई।

टक-टक-टक

"बेटा, तुम तैयार हो?" बाबा ने पूछा।

"जी," बेन ने शरीफ़ होने का नाटक करते हुए कहा, जो असल में बहुत मुश्किल था क्योंकि उसके भीतर बवंडर चल रहा था। "आपको कल सुबह मुझे

जल्दी लेने आने की ज़रूरत नहीं है। मैं और दादी स्क्रैबल बहुत देर तक खेलते हैं।"

"बेटा आज तुम स्क्रैबल नहीं खेलोगे," बाबा बोले।

"नहीं?"

"नहीं बेटा। आज तुम दादी के घर बिल्कुल नहीं जाओगे।"

"नहीं!" बेन बोला। "क्या वह अस्पताल में हैं?"

"नहीं, वहाँ नहीं है।"

बेन ने चैन की साँस ली लेकिन उसको एक चिन्ता सता रही थी। "फिर मैं उनके घर क्यों नहीं जा रहा?"

योजना भी बनी हुई थी और बरबाद करने के लिए समय बिल्कुल नहीं था!

"क्योंकि," बाबा बोले, "आज तुम्हारे अंडर-12 नाच की प्रतियोगिता है। आखिरकार, छा जाने का समय आ गया है।"

21

टैप डांस का जूता

बेन अपनी 'प्यार का बम' वाली पोशाक पहनकर, छोटी-सी भूरी गाड़ी में पीछे चुप-चाप बैठा था।

"आशा करती हूँ कि तुम इस प्रतियोगिता के बारे में भूले नहीं थे, बेन," माँ ने अपना मेकअप करते हुए कहा। तभी गाड़ी मुड़ी और उनकी लिपस्टिक उनके गाल पर घिसटती हुई गयी।

"नहीं माँ। ऐसा कैसे हो सकता है?"

"तुम चिन्ता मत करो बेटा," बाबा बोले। वह गर्व से गाड़ी चलाकर अपने बेटे को प्रतियोगिया के लिए ले जा रहे थे। "तुमने अपने कमरे में इतना अभ्यास किया है कि मैं जानता हूँ सारे जज तुमको सबसे ज़्यादा अंक

देंगे। दस में से दस!"

"दादी का क्या होगा? वह मेरा इन्तज़ार नहीं कर रही होंगी?" बेन ने चिन्तित होकर कहा।

आज शाही आभूषणों को चुराने की रात थी, लेकिन उसके बजाय वह नाच प्रतियोगिता में भाग लेने जा रहा था, वह भी जब वह अपनी पूरी ज़िन्दगी में एक बार भी नहीं नाचा था।

पिछले दो हफ़्तों से उसने इस प्रतियोगिता के बारे में सोचा भी नहीं था, लेकिन अब समय आ गया था।

यह सच में होने वाली थी।

उसको मंच पर अकेले नाचना होगा।

जिसकी तैयारी उसने नहीं की थी।

लोगों से भरे एक थियेटर में...

"तुम दादी की चिन्ता मत करो," माँ बोलीं। "वह नहीं जानतीं की आज कौन-सा दिन है!" वह हँसी, गाड़ी लाल बत्ती पर आ कर अचानक से रुक गयी और माँ की आँखों का मेकअप, मस्कारा उनके पूरे सिर पर फैल गया।

वह टाउनहॉल पहुँचे। बेन ने इमारत में रंग-बिरंगे लाइक्रा के कपड़ों की एक नदी बहती हुई देखी।

अगर स्कूल में किसी को पता चल गया कि वह यहाँ गया था, तो वह शर्म से मर जायेगा। यह तो स्कूल के सारे गुंडों के लिए गोलाबारूद होगा जिससे वह उसकी ज़िन्दगी हमेशा के लिए नरक बना देंगे। उसने एक बार भी अभ्यास नहीं किया था। एक बार भी नहीं। उसको बिल्कुल भी अनुमान ही नहीं था कि वह क्या करने वाला था।

यह नगर के सबसे अच्छे डांसर को ढूँढने की प्रतियोगिता थी। एक पुरस्कार सबसे बेहतरीन जोड़ी के लिए था, एक अकेली महिला के लिए, और एक अकेले आदमी के लिए था।

अगर यहाँ आप जीत जाओ, आपको देश की प्रतियोगिता में भाग लेने का अवसर मिलेगा, और अगर वहाँ जीते तो अन्तरराष्ट्रीय प्रतियोगिता में।

यह पहला कदम था अन्तरराष्ट्रीय और प्रसिद्ध डांसर बनने के लिए। और मेज़बान और कोई नहीं बल्कि *स्ट्रिक्टली स्टार्स डांसिंग* का चितचोर और माँ

का मनपसन्द फ़्लावीओ फ़्लावीओलि था।

"आज, इतनी सारी खूबसूरत स्त्रियों को देखकर हम खुश हो रहें हैं," इतालवी लहज़े से उसने कहा।

फ़्लावीओ असल में और भी ज़्यादा चमचमाता था। उसके बाल काले और चिकने थे, उसके सफ़ेद दाँत जगमगा रहे थे और उसकी पोशाक उसके बदन पर चिपकी हुई थी। "तो अब क्या हम रूम्बा नाच करने के लिए तैयार हैं?"

पूरी जनता चीख़ी, "हाँ!"

"फ़्लावीओ को सुनाई नहीं दे रहा, मैंने कहा, 'क्या हम रूम्बा नाच करने के लिए तैयार हैं?' "

"हाँ!!" सब पहले से ज़्यादा ज़ोर से बोले।

बेन मंच के पीछे घबराया हुआ बैठा था। उसको एक औरत की आवाज़ चिंघाड़ती हुई सुनाई दी, "मुझे तुमसे प्यार है फ़्लावीओ!" उसको शक था कि यह उसकी माँ ही थीं।

बेन ने ड्रेसिंग रूम में इधर-उधर देखा। लग रहा था मानो दुनिया में सबसे ज़्यादा चिढ़ पैदा करने वाले बच्चों का सम्मेलन था। सारे बरदाश्त से बाहर थे।

ऐसा लग रहा था कि बड़ा लगने की कोशिश में भद्दे तरीक़े से चूक रहे थे क्योंकि उन्होंने लाइक्रा के भड़कीले कपड़े पहन रखे थे, भारी मेकअप पोता हुआ था और उनके दाँत इतने मोतिया सफ़ेद थे कि अन्तरिक्ष से भी दिख जाते।

बेन ने व्याकुलता से अपनी घड़ी देखी, जानते हुए कि दादी से मिलने में बहुत देर हो जायेगी। वह इन्तज़ार और इन्तज़ार करता रहा। मेकअप वाले डांसर थिरके, वॉल्ट्ज़ नृत्य किया, विएना का भी वॉल्ट्ज़ किया, टैंगो नृत्य किया, फ़ॉक्सट्रॉट नृत्य भी, और फिर चा-चा-चा भी किया।

आख़िर में बेन की बारी आयी। वह मंच से कुछ ही दूर खड़ा था जब फ़्लावीओ ने उसका नाम पुकारा।

"अब वक़्त है इसी नगर के लड़के का, जो हम सब को अकेले नाच कर मनमोहित कर देगा। बेन का स्वागत कीजिए!"

फ़्लावीओ मंच से खिसक गया और बेन पैर घसीटते हुए, मुश्किल से पिछवाड़े पर टिकी लाइक्रा की प्यार के बम वाली पोशाक में मंच पर आया।

दबंग दादी

बेन डांस मंच के बीचों-बीच अकेला खड़ा था। स्पॉट लाइट उस पर थी। गाना शुरू हुआ। वह यहाँ से भाग जाने के तरीक़े के लिए प्रार्थना कर रहा था। वह चाह रहा था कि उस पल कुछ भी हो जाये, मतलब:

अग्नि चेतावनी की घंटी बज जाये

भूकम्प आ जाये

तीसरा विश्वयुद्ध छिड़ जाये

एक और बर्फ़ीला युग अभी छा जाये

एक जानलेवा मधुमक्खियों का झुंड आ जाये

एक बाह्य अन्तरिक्ष का उल्का जो धरती को मार कर उसको उसके अक्ष से हिला दे

ज्वार की लहर आ जाये

फ़्लावीओ फ़्लावीओलि पर सैकड़ों मांसाहारी प्रेतों का आक्रमण हो जाये

समुद्री तूफ़ान या बवंडर (बेन को दोनों में अन्तर नहीं पता था, लेकिन इस वक़्त कुछ भी चलता)

धरती से बाहर से आये लोग बेन का अपहरण करके ले जायें और हज़ारों सालों तक उसे वापस ना लायें

डाइनोसॉर किसी टाइम-स्पेस पोर्टल से धरती पर छत तोड़ते हुए वापस आ जायें और अन्दर सब को खा जायें

ज्वालामुखी पहाड़ फट जाये, जबकि यहाँ आस पास बदकिस्मती से थे नहीं

एक बड़े से घोंघे का आक्रमण हो जाये

एक मध्यम लम्बाई का घोंघा भी चलेगा।

बेन ज़्यादा नहीं माँग रहा था। इनमें से कोई एक चीज़ भी स्वीकार थी। लिखी हुई कोई भी चीज़ होना काफ़ी था।

गाना काफ़ी देर से चल रहा था और बेन को एहसास हुआ कि उसका शरीर एक बार भी नहीं हिला था। उसने अपने माता-पिता को देखा। वह अपने इकलौते बेटे को आखिरकार मंच पर देखकर गर्व से दमक रहे थे।

उसने मंच से कुछ ही दूर फ़्लावीओ को देखा। वह उसको प्रोत्साहन भरी मुस्कुराहट से देख रहा था।

प्लीज़, अब धरती फट जा...

नहीं फटी।

अब और कोई चारा नहीं था कुछ तो करना पड़ेगा।

बेन ने अपनी टाँगें हिलाना शुरू किया, फिर बांहें और फिर सिर। उसके शरीर का कोई भी अंग समय के साथ या क्रम में नहीं था, और अगले पाँच मिनट तक उसने अपना जिस्म मंच पर खुला छोड़ दिया और ऐसे हिलाया कि कोई भूल ना पायेगा। वह ऐसा ना भूलने वाला समय था जिसको आप चाहे कितना ही भूलाना चाहो, लेकिन आप कभी नहीं भूल सकते।

अन्त में जब गाना खत्म ही होने वाला था, बेन ने कूदने की कोशिश की और धम

से ज़मीन पर गिर गया।

चुप्पी। कानफोड़ू चुप्पी।

फिर बेन को एक जोड़ी हाथ की तालियों की आवाज़ सुनाई दी। उसने ऊपर देखा।

उसकी माँ थीं।

फिर साथ में एक और जोड़ी आयी।

उसके बाबा थे।

पल भर के लिए उसको लगा की यह पल उन फ़िल्मों जैसा था जिस में कम क्षमता का व्यक्ति सम्भावनाओं के परे विजय पाता है। जल्द ही भवन के सारे लोग अपने पैरों पर खड़े होकर इस आम लड़के के लिए तालियाँ मारेंगे, जिसने ना केवल अपने घर वालों का सिर गर्व से ऊँचा किया था बल्कि नाच को भी नयापन दिया था।

समाप्त।

नहीं। ऐसा नहीं हुआ।

कुछ देर बाद, उसके माता-पिता को शर्मिंदगी हुई क्योंकि सिर्फ़ वह दोनों ही तालियाँ मार रहे थे और वह रुक गये।

फ़्लावीओ मंच पर वापस आया।

"अच्छा, यह थी, यह थी..." पहली बार इतालवी हीरो के पास बोलने के लिए शब्द नहीं थे।

"जज, क्या हम आपके दिये गये अंक देख सकते हैं प्लीज़?"

"शून्य," पहला बोला।

"शून्य।"

"शून्य।"

अब बस एक और जज बाकी थी। क्या बेन चार ज़ीरो लायेगा?

लेकिन आख़िरी जज को शायद बुरा लगा होगा इस छोटे-से पसीने से लथपथ लड़के को देखकर, जिसने अपने गुणहीन प्रदर्शन से ख़ानदान की सारी पुश्तों को लज्जित कर दिया था। उसने अंक देने वाले तख़्तों को मेज़ के नीचे, उलटा और पलटा। "एक," उसने एलान किया।

जनता ज़ोर-ज़ोर से छी-छी, नहीं-नहीं चिल्लाने लगी, तब उसने अपने अंक को ठीक किया। "मुझे माफ़ करना, मेरा मतलब शून्य था," उसने अपनी इच्छा

अनुसार पहले वाली तख़्ती उठायी।

"जज लोगों ने ज़रा निराशाजनक अंक दिये हैं," फ़्लावीओ ने अपनी मुस्कान रोकते हुए कहा। "लेकिन बेन, अभी भी सब खत्म नहीं हुआ है। क्योंकि तुम इकलौते लड़के थे जिसने आज अकेले नाचने के लिए भाग लिया था, तुम ही विजेता हो। मैं तुमको इस प्लास्टिक की मूर्तिका से सम्मानित करता हूँ।"

फ़्लावीओ ने सस्ती दिखने वाली एक नाचते हुए लड़के के आकर में बनी ट्रोफ़ी बेन को दी।

"देवियों और सज्जनों, लड़के और लड़कियों, बेन के लिए ज़ोरदार तालियाँ!"

फिर से एक चुप्पी। माँ और बाबा ने भी तालियाँ बजाने की हिम्मत नहीं की।

फिर से लोग छी-छी करने लगे, फिर हँसी उड़ाने और फिर और तिरस्कार। चिल्लाने की आवाज़ें आ रहीं थी: "शर्म आनी चाहिए तुमको!" "नहीं!" और "फिक्सिंग थी!"

फ़्लावीओ मुस्कुराया। वह बेन की ओर नीचे झुका और उसके कान में बोला, "तुमको यहाँ से जाना

चाहिए, इससे पहले की यह लोग तुम्हें मार डालें।"

उसी समय दर्शकों में से किसी ने टैप डांस का एक जूता फेंका। वह तेज़ी से उड़ता हुआ आया। शायद उनका निशाना बेन ही था, लेकिन वह फ़्लावीओ की आँखों के बीच में लग गया और वह बेहोश होकर गिर गया।

वक़्त आ गया है बहाना बना कर यहाँ से खिसकने का, बेन ने सोचा।

22

मृत्युदंड देने वाली लाइक्रा टोली

गुस्से से तमतमाती बॉलरूम नाच के शौक़ीन लोगों की एक टोली, छोटी भूरी गाड़ी के पीछे लग गयी। उन्होंने काफ़ी दूर तक पीछा किया। पिछली खिड़की से बाहर देखते ही बेन ने सोचा कि यह इतिहास में पहली बार ही हुआ होगा कि बकायदा मृत्युदंड देने वाली एक टोली ने लाइक्रा के कपड़े पहने हों।

बाबा ने कार दौड़ाई।

व्‌ व्‌ व्‌ व्‌ व्‌ रररररररररररउउ उउउउमममममममममममम!

... और वह अगले चौक से मुड़े और सबको पीछे

छोड़ दिया।

"शुक्र है कि मैंने फ़्लावीओ को जीवनदान किस दे दी!" माँ ने आगे वाली सीट से कहा।

"वह सिर्फ़ बेहोश हुआ था। उसकी साँसें नहीं रुकी थीं, माँ," बेन ने पीछे से बोला।

"तुम्हें कैसे पता," माँ अपनी लिपस्टिक फिर से लगाते हुए बोलीं। उन्होंने अपनी अधिकतर लिपस्टिक फ़्लावीओ के होठों और चेहरे पर जो पोत दी थी।

"एक शब्द में कहूँ तो तुम्हारा प्रदर्शन भयानक और लज्जाजनक था," बाबा बोले।

"यह दो शब्द हैं," बेन ने उनको टोका। "तीन अगर आप 'और' को भी गिन लें।"

"मज़ाक़ करने की कोशिश भी मत करो तुम," बाबा फट पड़े। "यह कोई हँसने की बात नहीं है। मुझे शर्मिंदा कर दिया है। शर्मिंदा।"

"हाँ, शर्मिंदा," माँ ने सहमति जतायी।

बेन तो सिर्फ़ किसी तरह वहाँ से गायब होना चाहता था। माँ और बाबा के साथ गाड़ी के पीछे ना बैठना पड़े, इसके लिए वह अपना अतीत और भविष्य

त्यागने को तैयार नहीं था।

"मुझे माफ़ कर दो, माँ," बेन बोला। "मैं चाहता हूँ कि आपको मुझ पर गर्व हो, सच में।" चाहे कितनी बार वह उनको बेवकूफ़ समझता था, बेन अपने माता-पिता को कतई शर्मिंदा नहीं करना चाहता था।

"वैसे, तुम्हारा बड़ा ही मज़ाकिया तरीक़ा है यह दिखाने का," माँ बोलीं।

"मुझे नाचना पसन्द नहीं है, बस।"

"यह मुद्दा नहीं है। तुम्हारी माता ने तुम्हारे लिए पोशाक बनाने में घंटों लगाये," बाबा बोले।

अजीब बात है कि हर बार जब हम मुसीबत में होते हैं, और उस दौरान माता-पिता को एक-दूसरे को सम्बोधित करना होता है, तब वह एक दूसरे को 'माता' या 'पिता' बोलते हैं, ना कि, 'माँ' या 'बाबा'।

"तुमने मंच पर किसी भी प्रकार की कोशिश तक नहीं की," बाबा ने आगे कहा। "मुझे नहीं लगता कि तुमने एक बार भी अभ्यास किया होगा। एक बार भी नहीं। मैं और तुम्हारी माता दिन-रात काम करते हैं,

तुमको वह मौका देने के लिए जो हमको भी नहीं मिला था और तुम हमारे साथ ऐसा बर्ताव करोगे।"

"तिरस्कार के साथ," माँ बोलीं।

"तिरस्कार!" बाबा की आवाज़ गूँजी।

बेन का एक आँसू टिप-टिप करता गालों पर गिरा। उसने अपनी जीभ से उसको पकड़ लिया। ख़ारा था। गाड़ी घर की तरफ़ खड़खड़ाती हुई जा रही थी और सब चुप बैठे थे।

बिना एक शब्द बोले वह गाड़ी से निकले, और घर में घुसे। जैसे ही बाबा ने दरवाज़ा खोला, बेन अपने कमरे की ओर गया और दरवाज़ा बन्द कर लिया। प्यार का बम की पोशाक में वह अपने बिस्तर पर बैठ गया।

बेन को भी इतना अकेलापन पहले महसूस नहीं हुआ था। दादी को मिलने के लिए उसने घंटों देरी कर दी थी। उसने सिर्फ़ अपने माँ और बाबा को ही निराश नहीं किया था, बल्कि उसने उस इंसान को भी निराश किया था जिसको वह सबसे ज़्यादा प्यार करने लगा था, उसकी दादी।

अब वह कभी भी शाही आभूषणों की चोरी नहीं

कर पायेंगे।

उसी वक़्त, खिड़की पर खटखट हुई।

दादी थीं।

स्कूबा-डाइविंग की पोशाक पहन कर यह बूढ़ी औरत सीढ़ियों से अपने पोते के कमरे की खिड़की तक पहुँच गयी थी।

"मुझे अन्दर आने दो!" उन्होंने नाटकीय ढंग से कहा।

बेन अपनी मुस्कुराहट रोक नहीं पा रहा था। उसने खिड़की खोली और बड़ी मछली खींचते मछुआरे की तरह उनको बलपूर्वक अन्दर खींचा।

"तुमने बहुत देर कर दी," दादी ने बेन का सहारा लेते हुए बिस्तर पर जाते हुए डाँटा।

"मैं जानता हूँ। मुझे माफ़ कर दो," बेन बोला।

"हमने सात बजे बोला था ना। अभी साढ़े दस हो रहे हैं। जो नींद की दवाई मैंने टावर के पहरेदारों को दी उसका असर खत्म होने वाला होगा।"

"मुझे सच में माफ़ कर दो, लम्बी कहानी है," बेन बोला।

दादी बेन के बिस्तर पर बैठीं और उसको ऊपर से नीचे तक देखा। "और तुम ऐसा बावलों वाला वैलेन्टाइन कार्ड क्यों बने हुए हो?" उन्होंने पूछा।

"जैसे मैंने कहा, लम्बी कहानी है..."

दादी को अपनी स्कूबा डाइविंग की पोशाक, वेटसूट और गोता लगाने वाले चश्मों में देख बेन ने सोचा, उल्टा चोर कोतवाल को डाँटे। लेकिन अभी इस में घुसने का वक़्त नहीं था।

"जल्दी करो बेटा, अपना सूट पहनो और मेरे पीछे सीढ़ियों से नीचे आ जाओ। मैं स्कूटर पर बैठ कर तुम्हारा इन्तज़ार करूँगी।

"क्या हम सच में शाही आभूषण चुरायेंगे?"

"हमें कोशिश तो करनी पड़ेगी!" दादी ने मुस्कुराते हुए कहा।

23

मामा ने पकड़ा

दोनों शहर से फरफराते हुए निकले। दादी स्कूटर चला रही थीं और बेन ने कसकर उन्हें पकड़ा हुआ था। दोनों ने अपने वेटसूट और गोता लगाने वाले चश्मे पहने थे, और साथ में मीलों लम्बे प्लास्टिक से लपेटा हुआ दादी का झोला आगे की टोकरी में बैठा था।

दादी ने राज को अपनी अख़बार की दुकान बंद करते हुए देखा।

"हेलो राज, मेरे लिए मिंट की गोलियाँ रखना मत भूलना!" वह चिल्लाई।

राज ने दोनों को देखा और उसका मुँह खुला का खुला रह गया।

"पता नहीं इसको क्या हुआ है, आम तौर पर तो बड़ा बातूनी है!"

लंदन का रास्ता लम्बा था, ख़ासकर ऐसे स्कूटर पर जिसकी अधिकतम गति तीन मील प्रति घंटे (दो लोगों के भार के साथ) थी।

थोड़ी देर बाद बेन ने देखा की सड़क चौड़ी, और
चौड़ी होती जा रही थी: दो लेन, फिर तीन लेन।

"उल्लू का पट्ठा! हम मोटर गाड़ियों के रास्ते पर
आ गये हैं!" पीछे से बेन चिल्लाया जैसे ही एक दस-
टन की लॉरी, स्कूटर को लगभग गिराते हुए, उड़ती
चली गयी।

"तुम जानते हो, तुमको गालियाँ नहीं देनी चाहिए बेटा," दादी बोलीं। "अब मैं और तेज़ी से चलाने वाली हूँ, इसलिए अच्छे से पकड़ लो!"

कुछ देर बाद, एक पेट्रोल टैंकर, उनके बगल से कुछ ही इंच दूर, अपना हॉर्न बजाते हुए गरजी।

"कमीना," दादी बोलीं।

"दादी!" चकित बेन बोला।

"अरे, ग़लती से ज़बान फिसल गयी!" दादी बोलीं। बड़े लोग कभी भी उदाहरण बनकर नहीं जीते।

"मुझे माफ़ कर दो दादी, लेकिन मुझे नहीं लगता कि यह स्कूटर इस एक्सप्रेस-वे के लिए बना है," बेन बोला। उसी वक़्त एक और, पहले से भी बड़ी, लॉरी धमाका करते हुए गुज़री। बेन को महसूस हो रहा था कि स्कूटर के पहिए सड़क से एक सेकंड के लिए उठ गये।

"मैं अगले एग्ज़िट से उतर जाती हूँ," दादी बोलीं। लेकिन इससे पहले की वह यह कर पातीं, नीली बत्तियाँ चमचमाते हुए उनके पीछे आने लगीं। "नहीं, यह तो मामू है! देखते हैं हम उससे आगे दौड़ सकते हैं या

210

नहीं।" उन्होंने अपना पैर एक्सिलरेटर पर और ज़ोर से मारा और स्कूटर ने तीन मील प्रति घंटे से साढ़े तीन मील प्रति घंटे पर छलाँग मारी।

पुलिस की गाड़ी उनके साथ ही चल रही थी और अन्दर बैठे ऑफ़िसर ने ग़ुस्से में रुकने का इशारा किया।

"दादी, बेहतर होगा कि आप रोक दें," बेन बोला। "हमारा खेल खत्म।"

"मुझे सँभालने दो, बेटा।"

दादी ने जैसे ही आपातकाल लेन में रोका, पुलिस की गाड़ी उनका रास्ता रोकने के लिए आगे आकर खड़ी हो गयी। वह बहुत बड़ी गाड़ी थी और उसने स्कूटर को बौना कर दिया जैसे एक लम्बे इंसान के सामने कोई छोटा आदमी।

"मैडम, क्या यह आपका वाहन है?" पुलिस ऑफ़िसर ने पूछा। वह मोटा था और उसकी छोटी-सी मूँछ उसके उस मोटे मुँह को और भी मोटा बना रही थीं। उसके चेहरे पर दम्भी तेवर और लोगों को डाँटने का उसका शौक साफ़ झलक रहा था। साथ ही डोनट

के लिए उसका प्यार भी। उसकी वर्दी पर नाम लिखा था, एम.के. लड्डू।

"कोई दिक्कत, ऑफ़िसर?" दादी ने मासूमियत से पूछा और इतनी हलचल से उनके गोता लगाने वाले चश्मे अब तक भाप से भर गये थे।

"जी, एक दिक्कत है। इस रास्ते पर स्कूटर चलाना सख़्त मना है," पुलिस ऑफ़िसर ने कहा।

(निम्नलिखित वाहन एक्सप्रेस-वे पर मना हैं:

स्केटबोर्ड

डोंगी

पहियेदार स्केट

गधे

ठेला

इकपहिया साइकिल

बर्फ़ वाहन, स्लेज

रिक्शॉ

ऊँट

मामा ने पकड़ा

जादुई कालीन
बच्चों की घोड़ा-गाड़ी

"अच्छा, मुझे बताने के लिए शुक्रिया ऑफ़िसर। हम अगली बार याद रखेंगे। अब अगर आप हमें जाने की आज्ञा दें, हम ज़रा जल्दी में हैं। नमस्ते!" दादी ने खुशी से कहा और अपना स्कूटर चालू कर लिया।

"क्या आपने पी हुई है, मैडम?"

"मैंने निकलने से पहले बन्दगोभी का सूप पिया था।"

"मेरा मतलब शराब से था," पुलिस वाले ने गहरी साँस ली।

"मैंने मंगलवार को एक ब्रांडी की चॉकलेट खायी थी। उसको गिनोगे?"

बेन अपनी हँसी नहीं रोक पाया।

एम.के. लड्डू ने अपनी आँखें छोटी की। "तब आप मुझे समझा सकती हैं कि आपने स्कूबा डाइविंग की पोशाक क्यों पहनी है और आपके झोले पर इतना

क्लिंगफ़िल्म क्यों है?

अब कुछ तो समझाना ही पड़ेगा।

"क्योंकि, क्योंकि," दादी बोलने में लड़खड़ा रहीं थीं।

हो गया काम।

"क्योंकि हम क्लिंगफ़िल्म समालोचना सभा से हैं," बेन ने कहा।

"मैंने तो कभी भी नहीं सुना इसके बारे में!" एम.के. लड्डू ने कहा।

"हम अभी नये हैं," बेन बोला।

"बस दो ही सदस्य अभी तक," दादी ने झूठ को आगे बढ़ाते हुए कहा। "और हम अपनी सभा को अभी छोटे स्तर पर रखना पसन्द करते हैं, इसलिए हम अपना सम्मेलन पानी में रखतें हैं, इसलिए वेटसूट।"

पुलिसवाले का सिर घूम गया। दादी ने अपनी बातें नहीं रोकीं, इस मकसद से कि वह उसका दिमाग़ और घुमा देंगी।

"अब, अगर आप हमें आज्ञा देंगे, हम ज़रा जल्दी में हैं। हमे लंदन में एक ज़रूरी सम्मेलन में बुलबुला

214

लपेटन समालोचना सभा से मिलना है। हम दोनों संस्थाओं को मिलाने का सोच रहे हैं।

एम.के. लड्डू अब बिल्कुल ही नि:शब्द हो गया था। "उसके कितने सदस्य हैं?"

"बस एक," दादी बोलीं। "लेकिन अगर हम एकजुट हो गये तब हम चाय और फ़ोटोकापी और पेपर क्लिप जैसी चीज़ों पर पैसे बचा पायेंगे। अलविदा!"

दादी ने एक्सिलरेटर पर पैर रखा और उनका स्कूटर झटका खाते हुए चल पड़ा।

"वहीं रुक जाओ!" एम.के. लड्डू ने अपना थुलथुला हाथ अपने सामने रखते हुए कहा।

बेन डर के मारे सुन्न हो गया। अभी वह बारह साल का भी नहीं हुआ था, और वह अपने आगे की पूरी ज़िन्दगी जेल में बिताने वाला था।

एम.के. लड्डू आगे झुका और अपना चेहरा दादी के चेहरे के सामने किया।

"मैं आपको छोड़ देता हूँ।"

24

काला पानी

"बस यहाँ," दादी ने पुलिस की गाड़ी में पीछे बैठे इशारा किया। "बस, टावर के सामने। आपका बहुत धन्यवाद।"

एम.के. लड्डू ने गाड़ी की डिक्की से स्कूटर निकालते हुए पूरा ज़ोर लगा दिया। "अगली बार प्लीज़ याद रखना कि आपका यह स्कूटर सिर्फ़ पैदल पथ के लिए बना है, ना कि सड़कों के लिए, और बड़े वाहनों की हाईवे के लिए तो बिल्कुल भी नहीं।"

"जी, ऑफ़िसर," दादी ने मुस्कुराते हुए जवाब दिया।

"अच्छा, आप दोनों को शुभकामनाएँ, आपके

जो वो ... क्या ... क्लिंगफ़िल्म और बुलबुला लपेटन के गठबन्धन के लिए।'' और यह बोलते ही, एम.के. लड्डू रात में तेज़ी से ग़ायब हो गया। उसने दादी और बेन को हज़ारों साल पुराने लंदन टावर के सामने, नदी के तट पर छोड़ दिया था जहाँ से वह उसको निहारते रहे। आज कुछ ज़्यादा ही शानदार रात थी, चारों गुम्बदाकार टावर चमक रहे थे, और उनकी परछाई ठंडी काली थेम्स में जगमगा रही थी।

किसी ज़माने में यह टावर जेल हुआ करता था, पूर्व कैदियों की शानदार सूची में कुछ थे, महारानी एलिज़ाबेथ प्रथम, साहसी सर वॉल्टर रैली, आतंकवादी गाए फ़ॉक्स, बड़े नाज़ी रूडोल्फ़ हैस, जेडवर्ड[*]। अब, टावर एक म्यूज़ियम था और इस में एक विशेष इमारत बनी थी, आभूषण घर, जहाँ सारे शाही आभूषण थे।

अभूतपूर्व दबंग डाकुओं का एक जोड़ा नदी के तट पर खड़ा था। "क्या तुम तैयार हो?" दादी ने पूछा।

---

[*]   मैंने आख़िरी वाले का झूठ बोला, लेकिन जेडवर्ड को गानों की ख़राबी के अपराध में, हमेशा के लिए इस टावर की सलाख़ों के पीछे देखना चाहता हूँ।

पुलिस की गाड़ी में पीछे बैठने से उनके गोता लगाने वाले चश्मों में भाप भर गयी थी।

"जी हाँ," बेन उत्तेजना से काँप रहा था। "मैं तैयार हूँ।"

दादी ने बेन का हाथ पकड़ा और गिनती शुरू की, "तीन, दो, एक," और एक पर दोनों ने पानी में गोता लगा लिया।

पानी में वेट सूट पहनने के बावजूद कड़ाके की ठंड लग रही थी, और कुछ देर तक बेन को सिर्फ़ अँधेरा ही नज़र आ रहा था। यह अनुभव सामान्य पैमाने पर ख़ौफ़नाक और रोमांचकारी, दोनों ही था।

काला पानी

जब उन दोनों का सिर झटके से ऊपर आया, बेन ने अपनी साँस लेने वाली पाइप को मुँह से निकाला।

"क्या आप ठीक हो दादी?"

"मैंने आज से पहले कभी भी खुद को इतना जीवन्त नहीं पाया।"

दोनों ने तैरने के नाम पर कुत्तों की तरह पैर हिलाते हुए नदी पार की। बेन एक अच्छा तैराक नहीं था और हमेशा थोड़ा पीछे रह जाता था। अन्दर ही अन्दर वह सोच रहा था कि काश वह अपने तैरने में मदद करने वाले बाजूबन्द या कम से कम फुलाने वाली नाव तो लाया होता।

दबंग दादी

बगल से एक जहाज़ छप-छप करके गुज़रा। उस पर पार्टी चल रही थी। ज़ोर से गाने बज रहे थे और नौजवान चिल्ला रहे थे। दादी उससे आगे निकल गयीं और बेन को वह कहीं भी दिख नहीं रही थीं।

नहीं!

कहीं जहाज़ ने उनको कुचल तो नहीं दिया था?

क्या दादी थेम्स नदी के नीचे, जल समाधि में समा गयी थीं?

"अरे, ज़ोर लगाओ, कछुए!" दादी चिल्लाई जैसे ही जहाज़ सामने से निकला और दोनों ने एक दूसरे को देखा। बेन ने चैन की साँस ली और कुत्तों की तरह तैरते हुए गहरा काला गन्दा पानी पार किया।

उसके *प्लम्बिंग वीकली* के नक़्शे के अनुसार, सीवेज पाइप विश्वासघातियों के द्वार के बाएं पर था। (यह टावर का एक ही ऐसा द्वार था जो नदी से जुड़ा था। यहाँ से बहुत से कैदियों को आजीवन कारावास के लिए या मौत की सजा देने के लिए ले जाया जाता था। आजकल विश्वासघातियों के लिए दरवाज़े पर एक

ईंटों की दीवार थी, इसलिए सीवेज पाइप ही अब टावर को नदी से जोड़ती थी।)

फिर, पाइप मिलते ही बेन ने चैन की साँस ली। वह कम पानी में थी। उसमें भी घोर अँधेरा था, और उसको लहरों के टकराने की आवाज़ गूँजती हुई सुनाई दे रही थी।

अचानक बेन का मन डांवाडोल होने लगा। प्लम्बिंग चाहे जितनी पसन्द थी, लेकिन उसको इस प्राचीन सीवेज पाइप में रेंगने की कतई इच्छा नहीं थी।

"चलो भी अब बेन," दादी ने कहा। वह अपना मुँह पानी में अन्दर बाहर कर रही थीं। "हम इतनी दूर हार मान लेने के लिए नहीं आये हैं।"

अच्छा, बेन ने सोचा। *अगर एक छोटी-सी बूढ़ी औरत यह कर सकती है, तब मैं तो ज़रूर कर ही सकता हूँ।*

बेन ने एक लम्बी साँस ली और खुद को पाइप में ठेलना शुरू किया। दादी कुछ ही दूरी पर पीछे-पीछे आ रही थीं।

पाइप के अन्दर माहौल काले से भी ज़्यादा गहरा काला था और कुछ मीटर के बाद उसको किसी चीज़ के रेंगने का अहसास हुआ। उसको एक ईक-ईक की आवाज़ सुनाई दी और उसे लग रहा था जैसे कोई उसका सिर खुजला रहा था।

किसी के पंजे लग रहे थे।

उसने सिर पर हाथ रखा।

उसका हाथ किसी बड़ी रोयेंदार चीज़ पर पड़ा।

तभी उसे कड़वे सच का अहसास हुआ।

वह एक चूहा था!

एक विशाल चूहा जो उसके सिर पर था।

"आऽऽऽऽऽऽ!!!"

बेन चीख़ा।

25

भूतों से भरा

पूरी की पूरी पाइप बेन की चीख से गूँज उठी। उसने चूहे को हाथ मारा और वह पीछे आ रही दादी के सिर पर उछल कर जा पहुँचा।

"बेचारा छोटा-सा चूहा," उन्होंने कहा। "प्यार से पेश आओ, बेटा।"

"लेकिन..."

"वह यहाँ पहले था, अब चलो, हमें जल्दी करना पड़ेगा। नींद की दवाई का असर पहरेदारों पर जल्द ही खत्म होने वाला होगा।"

वह जोड़ा रेंगते हुए पाइप में आगे बढ़ा। गीली और चिकनी पाइप, और बहुत ही ज्यादा बदबूदार।

(बेन और दादी की बदकिस्मती थी कि इतना पुराना मल अभी भी बू मारता था।)

कुछ देर बाद, बेन को अंधेरे में एक धुँधला-सा शाफ़्ट दिखा। वह सुरंग का अन्त था, आखिरकार! उसने अपने आपको प्राचीन पत्थर के पाख़ाने से खींचा और फिर दादी को मदद करने के लिए हाथ दिया। दोनों सिर से पैर तक गन्दे बदबूदार काले कीचड़ में लथपथ थे।

एक ठंडे, काले टॉयलेट में खड़े बेन ने बिना शीशे वाली खिड़की से ताँक-झाँक की। दोनों कठिनाई से ऊपर चढ़े और टावर के आँगन की ठंडी गीली घाँस पर उतरे।

दोनों कुछ देर वहाँ लेटकर चाँद और तारों को एकटक देखते रहे। बेन ने अपना हाथ दादी के हाथ में डाला। उन्होंने उसे ज़ोर से पकड़ लिया।

"यह बहुत ही अद्भुत है," बेन बोला।

"चलो बेटा," दादी फुसफुसाईं। "हमने अभी तो शुरू ही किया है!"

बेन खड़ा हो गया और दादी की भी मदद की।

दादी ने जल्दी से क्लिंगफ़िल्म खोली जिस से उन्होंने अपने झोले को पानी से बचाया हुआ था।

इस में बहुत समय लग गया।

"मुझे लगता है कि मैंने कुछ ज़्यादा ही क्लिंगफ़िल्म लगा दी। लेकिन, बाद में पछताने से क्या होता, जब चिड़िया चुग जाये खेत।"

कुछ देर बाद, एक मील लम्बी क्लिंगफ़िल्म उतर गयी और दादी ने नक्शा निकाला। बेन ने यह नक्शा अपनी पुस्तकालय की किताब से फाड़ा था। इसके सहारे यह दो शातिर चोर आभूषण घर ढूँढ पायेंगे।

लंदन टावर में रात बहुत ही डरावनी थी।

कहा जाता है कि टावर में यहाँ मारे गये लोगों के भूत मँडराते हैं। बहुत बार ऐसा भी हुआ है कि डर के मारे पहरेदार काम छोड़कर चले गये क्योंकि उनके अनुसार रात में उन्होंने काफ़ी सारे मरे हुए ऐतिहासिक हस्तियों के भूत देखे थे।

अब तो यहाँ आँगन में और भी कुछ अजीब चीज़

घूम रही थी।

वेटसूट में दादी!

"इधर चलो," दादी फुसफुसाईं, और बेन एक कॉरिडर में उनके पीछे हो लिया। बेन का दिल इतनी ज़ोर से धक-धक कर रहा था मानो फट ही जायेगा।

कुछ देर बाद दोनों आभूषण घर के सामने खड़े थे। हरे टावर और उस स्मारक के सामने जहाँ लोगों के सिर काट दिये जाते थे या उनको फाँसी दे दी जाती थी। बेन सोच रहा था कि क्या उसको और दादी को भी मारा जायेगा अगर उन दोनों को शाही आभूषणों की चोरी करते हुए पकड़ लिया गया। इस विचार से ही उसकी रूह काँप उठी।

रानी के दो अंगरक्षक ज़मीन पर गिरे हुए थे और ज़ोर से खर्राटे मार रहे थे। उनकी काली और लाल वर्दी जिस पर अंग्रेज़ी में 'ई आर' लिखा था, गीली ज़मीन पर कीचड़ से लथपथ थी। दादी की विशेष जड़ी बूटियों से बना केक अपना काम कर रहा था।

लेकिन कितनी देर तक?

जैसे ही दादी उनके सामने से निकलीं, उनके पिछवाड़े से फिर बतख़ों वाली आवाज़ निकली। एक पहरेदार ने बदबू के मारे नाक सिकोड़ी।

बेन ने अपनी साँस रोक ली। सिर्फ़ बदबू से बचने के लिए नहीं, लेकिन इसलिए भी क्योंकि उसको डर लग रहा था।

क्या दादी का पाद उन पहरेदारों को उठा देगा और सब खत्म हो जायेगा?

ऐसा लगा कि सदियाँ गुज़र गयी हैं।

पहरेदार ने एक आँख खोली।

नहीं!!

दादी ने बेन को पीछे कर दिया और अपना झोला उठाया और उससे उनको पीटने को हुईं।

बस अब हो गया, बेन ने सोचा। *हमको फाँसी दे देंगे!*

लेकिन पहरेदार ने अपनी आँख फिर बन्द कर लीं और खर्राटे मारने लगा।

"दादी प्लीज़ अपने पिछवाड़े को रोकने की कोशिश करो," बेन फुसफुसया।

"मैंने कुछ भी नहीं किया," दादी ने भोलेपन से कहा।

दोनों पंजों पर चलकर आभूषण घर में बड़े से

स्टील के दरवाज़े के पास पहुँचे।

"अब, बस मुझे तुम्हारे बाबा का ड्रिल चाहिए..." दादी ने अपने झोले को टटोलते हुए कहा। घरघराने की आवाज़ के साथ उन्होंने दरवाज़े पर लगे तालों पर छेद करना शुरू कर दिया। एक के बाद एक ताले टुकड़े-टुकड़े होने लगे।

पहरेदारों ने अचानक बहुत ज़ोर से खर्राटे मारना शुरू कर दिया।

ज़्र् ज़्र्!

बेन सुन्न हो गया और दादी ने ड्रिल लगभग गिरा ही दी। लेकिन पहरेदार सोते रहे और कुछ दिल दहलाने वाले पलों के बाद, आखिरकार दरवाज़ा खुल गया।

दादी थकीं लग रही थीं। उनके सिर से पसीना चू रहा था। वह थोड़ी देर के लिए एक छोटी-सी दीवार पर बैठ गयीं और थर्मस निकला।

"बन्दगोभी का सूप?" उन्होंने बेन से पूछा।

"नहीं, धन्यवाद दादी," बेन ने जवाब दिया। वह अपनी जगह पर बेचैनी से हिला। "पहरेदारों के उठने से पहले हमें चलना चाहिए।"

"जल्दी, जल्दी, जल्दी, आज कल के बच्चे सिर्फ़ यह ही करते हैं। सब्र का फल मीठा होता है।" उन्होंने बन्दगोभी का बचा हुआ सूप पिया और चलने के लिए खड़ी हो गयीं।

"स्वादिष्ट! चलो, अब आगे का काम करते हैं!" उन्होंने कहा।

बड़ा स्टील का दरवाज़ा खोलने पर किरकिराने लगा और बेन और दादी आभूषण घर में घुस गये।

अँधेरे में काले पंखों का झोंका दादी और बेन के मुँह पर लगा। बेन इतना चौंक गया कि उसकी चीख निकल गयी।

"चुप!" दादी बोलीं।

"वह क्या थे?" बेन ने पूछा और देखा की पंखों वाले प्राणी काले आसमान में ग़ायब हो गये थे।

"चमगादड़?"

"नहीं बेटा, काले कौए। यहाँ बहुत सारे हैं। काले कौए इस टावर में सैंकड़ों सालों से रह रहे हैं।"

"यह जगह ख़ौफ़नाक है," बेन ने कहा। उसके पेट में डर की वजह से गाँठें पड़ रही थीं।

"रात को ख़ासकर," दादी ने हामी भरी। "अब तुम मेरे पास रहो, बेटा, क्योंकि अब और भी ख़ौफ़नाक होने वाला है…"

26

अँधेरे में आकृति

उनके सामने एक लम्बा-सा घुमावदार गलियारा था। यहीं पर पूरी दुनिया से आये लोग शाही आभूषणों को देखने के लिए कतार में खड़े होते थे। बूढ़ी औरत और उसका पोता पंजों के बल चुप-चाप वहाँ से जा रहे थे और दोनों ही थेम्स के बदबूदार बर्फीले पानी से बास रहे थे।

आखिरकार उस कमरे में पहुँचे, जहाँ सारे आभूषण थे। जैसे घने बादलों में से सूरज खिल जाता है, ठीक उसी तरह आभूषणों ने बेन और दादी के चेहरे को प्रकाशित कर दिया।

चोरों का यह जोड़ा ठिठक गया। खजाने को देख

वह भौंचक्के रह गये। कोई इंसान कल्पना भी नहीं कर सकता था कि वह कितने आलीशान थे। सही अर्थों में मूल्यवान वस्तुओं का यह संकलन सबसे शानदार था।

प्रिय पाठक, वह सिर्फ़ खूबसूरत ही नहीं, बल्कि अमूल्य भी थे क्योंकि वह सैंकड़ों सालों के इतिहास के प्रतीक थे। उस में बहुत सारे शाही मुकुट थे:

- सेंट एड्वर्ड का मुकुट जिसे पहनाकर नये राजा या रानी का राज्याभिषेक कैंटरबरी के प्रधान पादरी करते हैं। वह सोने से बना और नीलम और पुखराज से सजा है। क्या चमक है!

- तीन हज़ार अद्भुत रत्न वाला शाही राजकीय मुकुट, जिसमें अफ्रीका का सितारा (दुनिया के सबसे बड़े हीरे से कटा कीमती पत्थर) भी था।

- छह हज़ार हीरे और शानदार नीलम और माणिक से सजा हिन्दुस्तान का अद्भुत

ताज। दुर्भाग्य से वह मेरे नाप का नहीं था।

- बारहवीं सदी में बना सोने का शाही चम्मच जिससे राजा या रानी पर धार्मिक तेल डाल कर अभिषेक किया जाता था। नाश्ते में दूध के साथ कोको पॉप्स सिरियल के लिए नहीं था।

- एम्प्युला को नहीं भूलते जो एक सोने की गरुड़ के आकर की बोतल थी, जिस में धार्मिक तेल रखा जाता था। रईसों का थर्मस फ़्लास्क जैसा।

- और अन्त में प्रसिद्ध गोला और राजदंड। यह कुछ ज़्यादा सामग्री नहीं है?

अगर कभी अरगोस की पुस्तक-सूची में शाही आभूषण प्रकाशित हुए तब वह शायद कुछ ऐसे लगेंगे :

शाही आभूषण डालने के लिए दादी ने अपने झोले से सुपरमार्केट का थैला निकला।

"बस, अब हमें इस शीशे को तोड़ना है," वह फुसफुसाई।

बेन ने उनको अविश्वास से देखा। "मुझे नहीं लगता हम सारे आभूषणों को इस में डाल सकते हैं।"

"मुझे माफ़ कर दो बेटा," उन्होंने धीमी आवाज़ में जवाब दिया। "आजकल, दुकान से पाँच पेन्स का एक प्लास्टिक का पैकेट मिलता है, इसलिए मैं एक ही लायी।"

शीशा एक इंच मोटा था।

अभेद्य।

बेन अपनी विज्ञान की कक्षा से कुछ रासायनिक यौगिक छिपा कर ले आया था और जैसे उनको मिलाया आवाज़ आयी:

काऽऽऽऽऽऽऽऽऽऽऽऽ बूबूबूबूबूबूम्म्म्म्म्म्म्म्म्म्!! !!!!!!!!!!!!!!!!!!!!!!!!

उन्होंने रसायन को काँच पर ब्लूटैक से चिपकाया।

236

फिर दादी ने एक गुलाबी ऊन के धागे को एक सिरे से ब्लूटैक से जोड़ा। (ऊन सबसे अच्छा फ़्यूज़ होगा।) उन्होंने फिर माचिस जलाई। उनको सिर्फ़ धमाके से दूर रहना था। वरना वह दोनों भी उड़ जाते।

"ठीक है, बेन।" दादी फुसफुसाई। "अब हमें शीशे से दूर हो जाना चाहिए।"

दोनों ऊन को खोलते हुए पीछे गये, दीवार तक।

"क्या तुम फ़्यूज़ को जलाओगे?" दादी ने पूछा।

बेन ने सिर हिलाया। उसको करने का बहुत मन था, लेकिन उसके हाथ उत्सुकता से इतने काँप रहे थे कि उसको पता नहीं था कि वह यह कर पायेगा या नहीं।

बेन ने माचिस की डिब्बी खोली। अन्दर सिर्फ़ दो तीलियाँ थीं।

उसने पहली जलाने की कोशिश की, लेकिन उसके हाथ इतने काँप रहे थे की, वह दो हिस्सों में हो गयी।

"अरे बाबा," दादी फुसफुसाई। "एक और है।"

बेन ने दूसरी तीली उठाई।

उसने जलाने की कोशिश की लेकिन कुछ नहीं हुआ। नदी का कुछ पानी उसके वेटसूट की बाँह में से निकला। अब दोनों, माचिस और माचिस की डिब्बी पूरी तरह से गीले थे।

"नहीं!!" बेन तड़पता हुआ रोया। "माँ और बाबा ठीक ही बोलते हैं। मैं निकम्मा हूँ। मैं एक माचिस भी नहीं जला सकता!"

दादी ने अपने पोते को गले लगा लिया। लगाते ही, उनके वेटसूट से चूं-चूं की आवाज़ आयी।

"ऐसा मत बोलो बेन। तुम गज़ब के इंसान हो। सच में। जब से हमने साथ में इतना वक़्त गुज़ारना शुरू किया है, तब से मैं सौ गुना ज़्यादा खुश हूँ।"

"सच में?" बेन बोला।

"सच में!" दादी ने जवाब दिया। "और तुम बहुत चतुर हो। तुम ने यह सारी अनोखी चोरी की योजना

ख़ुद बनाई और अभी तुम सिर्फ़ ग्यारह साल के हो।"

"मैं बारह का होने ही वाला हूँ," बेन बोला।

दादी हँसीं। "लेकिन तुम्हें मेरी बात समझ आयी। तुम्हारी उम्र के कितने बच्चे ऐसा हिम्मती काम करने की योजना बना सकते हैं?"

"लेकिन अब हम शाही आभूषण चुरा नहीं पायेंगे और सब कुछ एक बड़े पैमाने पर समय की बर्बादी होगी।"

"अभी कुछ खत्म कहाँ हुआ है," दादी ने कहा और अपने झोले से बन्दगोभी का डिब्बा निकला। "हम थोड़ा पुराने ज़माने का बाहुबल लगा सकते हैं!"

दादी ने डिब्बा अपने पोते को पकड़ाया। बेन ने मुस्कुराते हुए लिया और अलमारी की ओर गया।

"यह मारा!" बेन बोला और ज़ोर से उसने शीशे पर डिब्बा मारा।

"कृपया ऐसे मत कीजिए," अँधेरे से एक आवाज़ आयी।

दबंग दादी

बेन और दादी डर के मारे सुन्न पड़ गये।

क्या वह एक भूत था?

"कौन है?" बेन ने आवाज़ दी।

एक आकृति सामने आयी।

वह महारानी थीं।

27

महारानी के साथ भेंट

"आप, आप यहाँ क्या कर रही हैं?" बेन ने पूछा। "वो ... मेरा मतलब था कि आप यहाँ क्या कर रही हैं, महारानी साहिबा?"

"जब हमें नींद नहीं है आती तो हम यहाँ आ जाते हैं," महारानी ने जवाब दिया। वह अपने प्रचलित शाही ठाठ से बोल रही थीं। नाईटी और रोएंदार पिल्ले सरीखी कोर्गी चप्पल को देखकर, बेन और दादी चौंक गये थे। उन्होंने अपना मुकुट भी पहना हुआ था। वह सारे शाही आभूषणों में सबसे ज़्यादा आलीशान था। 1953 में जब वह महारानी बनी थीं, तब कैंटरबरी के प्रधान पादरी ने उनका राज्याभिषेक इस मुकुट से किया

था। यह मुकुट 1661 का था, जो सोने से बना था और हीरे, लाल मणियों, मोतियों, पन्ने और नीलमों से अलंकृत था।

यह दृश्य प्रभावशाली था, यहाँ तक कि महारानी के लिए भी!

"हम यहाँ सोचने आते हैं," महारानी ने आगे कहा। "हमने ड्राइवर से कहा कि बेंटली कार में बकिंगहम पैलेस से यहाँ पहुँचा दे। कुछ ही हफ़्तों में हम क्रिसमस के मौके पर लोगों को सम्बोधित करेंगे, और हमें सोचना होगा कि हमें क्या बोलना होगा। जब भी मुकुट पहना हो, सोचना आसान हो जाता है। लेकिन मसला यह है कि आप दोनों यहाँ क्या कर रहे हैं?"

बेन और दादी ने एक दूसरे को शर्मिंदगी से देखा।

किसी से डाँट खाना किसी भी समय बुरा लगता है, लेकिन महारानी से डाँट खाना तो एक दूसरे पैमाने की बात थी। एक आसान-सा रेखा-चित्र यह दर्शाता है:

"और आप दोनों में से पू-पू की बदबू क्यों आ रही है? हम्म?" महारानी साहिबा ने पूछा। "हम इन्तज़ार कर रहे हैं।"

"यह सारा दोष मेरा ही है, महारानी साहिबा," दादी ने सिर झुकाते हुए कहा।

"नहीं, ऐसा नहीं है," बेन ने कहा। "वह मैं था जिसने शाही आभूषण चुराने के लिए कहा था। मैंने इनको मजबूर किया था।"

"यह सच है," दादी बोलीं, "लेकिन मेरा मतलब यह नहीं था। सब कुछ तब शुरू हुआ, जब मैंने अन्तरराष्ट्रीय आभूषण चोर होने का ढोंग किया।"

"क्या?" बेन चिल्लाया।

"माफ़ कीजिए?" महारानी बोलीं। "हमें कुछ भी नहीं समझ आ रहा।"

"मेरे पोते को मेरे साथ हर शुक्रवार रात रहने से नफ़रत थी," दादी बोलीं। "मैंने इसे एक बार रात में अपने माता-पिता को शिकायत करते हुए सुना था कि मैं कितनी बोरिंग हूँ—"

"लेकिन दादी, अब मैं ऐसा नहीं सोचता!" बेन ने आपत्ति जतायी।

"ठीक है, बेन, मैं जानती हूँ कि चीज़ें तब से बदल गयी हैं। लेकिन बात तो यह है कि मैं बोरिंग थी। मुझे सिर्फ़ बन्दगोभी खाना और स्क्रैबल खेलना पसन्द था और मैं अन्दर ही अन्दर यह भी जानती थी कि तुमको इन चीज़ों से नफ़रत थी। इसलिए मैंने जो किताबें पढ़ी थीं, उनसे तुम्हारे मनोरंजन के लिए एक कहानी बना ली। मैंने तुम्हें बताया कि मैं बदनाम आभूषणचोर, 'काली बिल्ली'..."

"लेकिन उन सब हीरों का क्या जो आपने मुझे दिखाये थे?" बेन भौचक्का था क्योंकि उसके साथ धोखा हुआ था।

"उनकी कोई क़ीमत नहीं है," दादी ने बताया। "काँच के बने हैं। एक लोकल दान देने की दुकान के आइसक्रीम के डिब्बे से निकले थे।"

बेन ने उनको घूरा। उसको यक़ीन नहीं हो रहा था। सब कुछ, सब कुछ बस एक अद्भुत मनगढंत

कहानी थी।

"मुझे यक़ीन नहीं हो रहा कि आपने मुझसे झूठ बोला!" उसने कहा।

"मेरा, मेरा मतलब..." दादी ने हिचकिचाते हुए कहा।

बेन ने उनको गुस्से से घूरते हुए कहा, "तो आखिरकार आप मेरी दबंग दादी नहीं हो।"

फिर आभूषण घर में सन्नाटा छा गया।

उसके बाद एक ऊँची और थोड़ी ठेठ खाँसी की आवाज़ आयी। "और हम्मम," एक शाही आवाज़।

28

कुटाई, फाँसी और चार टुकड़े

"टोकने के लिए अफ़सोस है," महारानी ने कहा, "लेकिन क्या हम ज़्यादा ज़रूरी मुद्दे पर बात कर सकते हैं? हमें अभी भी समझ नहीं आ रहा कि आप दोनों लंदन टावर में, आधी रात को पू-पू की बदबू में हमारे आभूषणों की चोरी करने क्यों आये।"

"एक बार जब मैंने शुरू किया, तो झूठ बढ़ता ही चला गया, महारानी साहिबा," दादी ने बेन से आँख चुराते हुए कहा। "मैं नहीं चाहती थी कि यह हो। मैं शायद भावनाओं में बह गयी। अपने पोते के साथ थोड़ा ज़्यादा समय बिताना अच्छा लग रहा था। मुझे उस वक़्त की याद दिलाता था, जब मैं इसको कहानियाँ

पढ़ कर सुनाती थी। तब मैं बोरिंग नहीं लगती थी।"

बेन भी कुछ परेशान होने लगा। उसको भी शर्मिंदगी महसूस होने लगी थी। दादी ने उसकी वजह से झूठ बोला था, और हालाँकि यह गलत था, लेकिन उन्होंने ऐसा सिर्फ़ इसलिए किया था क्योंकि वह निराश थीं कि बेन उन्हें बोरिंग समझता था।

"मुझे भी मज़ा आया," वह फुसफुसाया।

दादी उसको देखकर मुस्कुराईं। "यह सुनकर अच्छा लगा, मेरे बेनी। मुझे माफ़ कर दो, मुझे सच में—"

"हम्म," महारानी ने टोका।

"हाँ," दादी बोलीं। "इससे पहले कि मैं कुछ सोच पाती, बात बड़ी तेज़ी से बढ़ गयी और हम दोनों एक हिम्मती चोरी की योजना बना रहे थे। वैसे, हम दोनों सीवेज पाइप से ऊपर चढ़े। हम से ऐसी बदबू आमतौर पर नहीं आती, महारानी साहिबा।"

"उम्मीद तो यही है।"

"ㄣㄣㄣㄣㄣㄣㄣㄣㄣㄣㄣㄣㄣㄣ ㄹㄹㄹㄹㄹㄹㄹㄹㄹㄹㄹㄹ!!!!"

बेन को अब सच में अफ़सोस हो रहा था। चाहे दादी कोई अन्तरराष्ट्रीय आभूषण चोर रही हों या नहीं, वह बोरिंग तो बिल्कुल नहीं थीं। उन्होंने उसकी चोरी की इस योजना में मदद की थी, और अब दोनों लंदन टावर में आधी रात को महारानी से बात कर रहे थे।

मुझे इनकी मदद करने के लिए कुछ करना पड़ेगा, बेन ने सोचा।

"यह चोरी मेरा सुझाव था, महारानी साहिबा," उसने कहा। "मुझे माफ़ कर दो।"

"प्लीज़ मेरे पोते को जाने दीजिए," दादी बीच में बोलीं। "मैं इसकी ज़िन्दगी खराब नहीं करना चाहती हूँ। प्लीज़, मैं आपसे विनती करती हूँ। हम ने तय भी किया था कल रात को शाही आभूषण वापस कर देंगे। भरोसा कीजिए।"

"बिल्कुल, बिल्कुल," महारानी बड़बड़ाईं।

"यह सच है!" बेन बोल उठा।

"आप जो चाहे, मेरे साथ कीजिए, महारानी साहिबा," दादी ने आगे कहा। "मुझे यहाँ ही, इस टावर में हमेशा हमेशा के लिए बन्द कर दीजिए, लेकिन मैं आप से दया की भीख माँगती हूँ, इस लड़के को जाने दीजिए।"

महारानी ख़यालों में खो गयीं।

"हम नहीं जानते हमें क्या करना चाहिए," महारानी ने आख़िरकार कहा। "आप की कहानी हमें छू गयी। जैसा आप जानते होंगे, हम भी एक दादी हैं, और हमारे भी पोते और पोतियाँ अक्सर हमें बोरिंग समझते हैं।"

"सच में?" बेन ने पूछा। "लेकिन आप तो महारानी हो!"

"हम जानते हैं," महारानी हँसीं।

बेन हैरान हो गया। उसने कभी भी महारानी को हँसते हुए नहीं देखा था। आमतौर पर वह अत्यन्त गम्भीर रहती थीं, और बेन ने उनको कभी भी क्रिसमस के दिन टीवी पर, या संसद के पहले दिन, यहाँ तक कि रॉयल वैराइयटी शो, जिस शाही कार्यक्रम द्वारा पैसे दान किये जाते हैं, उस में हास्य-कलाकार को देखकर

भी हल्का-सा मुस्कुराते तक नहीं देखा था।

"लेकिन उनके लिए हम सिर्फ़ एक बोरिंग बूढ़ी दादी हैं," महारानी ने आगे बताया। "वह भूल जाते हैं कि हम भी कभी जवान थे।"

"और यह भी कि वह भी एक दिन बूढ़े होंगे।" दादी ने बेन को देखते हुए जोड़ा।

"वही तो, डियर!" महारानी ने हामी भरी। "हमें लगता है कि आजकल की पीढ़ी को बुज़ुर्गों के साथ थोड़ा ज़्यादा वक़्त गुज़ारना चाहिए।"

"मुझे माफ़ करना, महारानी साहिबा," बेन ने कहा। "अगर मैं इतना स्वार्थी नहीं होता और अगर मैं बूढ़े लोगों को बोरिंग बोल कर कलपता नहीं, तो यह सब कभी भी नहीं होता।"

चुप्पी कुछ चुभ रही थी।

दादी ने अपना झोला टटोला और मीठी गोलियों का एक पैकेट निकाला। "मिंट, महारानी साहिबा?"

"जी, ज़रूर," महारानी बोलीं। उन्होंने उसे खोला और अपने मुँह में डाला। "वाह वाह, ना जाने कितने सालों से हमने यह नहीं खाया है।"

"मेरे मनपसन्द हैं," दादी बोलीं।

"और यह खत्म ही नहीं होतीं," महारानी ने उसको चूसते हुए कहा, और फिर महारानी सरीखा बर्ताव करने के लिए शान्त हो गयीं।

"क्या आप जानते हो कि उस आदमी का क्या हुआ था जिसने आखिरी बार शाही आभूषण चुराने की कोशिश की थी?" महारानी ने पूछा।

"क्या हुआ उसको? घसीटकर फाँसी दी गयी और

चार टुकड़े कर दिये गये?'' बेन ने उत्तेजित होकर पूछा।

''मानो या ना मानो, उसको क्षमा कर दिया गया था,'' महारानी ने मुँह बनाते हुए कहा।

''क्षमा, महारानी साहिबा?'' दादी बोलीं।

''1671 में एक आयरलैंडवासी, कर्नल ब्लड ने चोरी करने की कोशिश की थी, लेकिन उनके भागने से पहले पहरेदारों ने उनको पकड़ लिया। उन्होंने यह मुकुट ही अपने चोग़े में छिपाया था और बाहर निकलते ही पहरेदारों ने उनको पकड़ लिया। महाराजा चार्ल्स II कर्नल ब्लड की हिम्मती कोशिश से इतना प्रसन्न हुए कि उन्होंने उनको छोड़ दिया।''

''यह तो मुझे गूगल करना चाहिए,'' बेन बोला।

''मैं नहीं जानती गूगल करना क्या होता है,'' दादी बोलीं।

''हम भी नहीं,'' महारानी हँसीं। ''इसलिए शाही परम्परा का मान रखते हुए, हम भी यही करेंगे। आप दोनों को क्षमा करेंगे।''

''धन्यवाद महारानी साहिबा,'' दादी ने उनका हाथ चूमते हुए कहा।

बेन घुटनों पर गिर गया। "धन्यवाद, धन्यवाद, बहुत-बहुत धन्यवाद, महारानी साहिबा..."

"ठीक है, ठीक है, गिड़गिड़ाओ मत," महारानी ने गुरूर से कहा। "हम गिड़गिड़ाना नहीं सह सकते। हमें हद से ज़्यादा ही गिड़गिड़ाने वाले मिलते हैं।"

"मुझे माफ़ कर दीजिए, महारानी साहिबा," दादी ने कहा।

"हमारा मतलब यही था! अब आप गिड़गिड़ा रही हैं!" महारानी ने कहा।

बेन और दादी ने एक दूसरे को डर से देखा। महारानी साहिबा के सामने बिना थोड़ा गिड़गिड़ाए बात हो ही नहीं सकती थी।

"चलो चलो, दौड़ो दौड़ो, प्लीज़," महारानी बोली, "इससे पहले कि हर जगह से पहरेदार उमड़ आयें। और हमें क्रिसमस के दिन टीवी पर देखना मत भूलियेगा।"

29

सशस्त्र पुलिस

सुबह होने वाली थी जब दोनों भारी कदमों से ग्रे क्लोज़ पहुँचे। इस बार उन्हें छोड़ने वाली पुलिस की कोई गाड़ी भी नहीं थी। दादी के स्कूटर पर लंदन से घर तक की दूरी और भी लम्बी थी। सड़कों के स्पीड ब्रेकर पर वह ऊपर-नीचे, ऊपर-नीचे, हिचकोले खाते हुए दादी के घर पहुँचे।

"क्या रात थी!" बेन ने आह भरी।

"बिल्कुल! हे भगवान, इतनी देर बैठ कर बदन अकड़ गया है," दादी ने कहा और अपने बुढ़ापे तथा स्कूटर से थके शरीर को आराम दिया। "मुझे माफ़ कर दो बेन," उन्होंने कुछ देर ठहर कर कहा। "मैं

तुम्हें आहत नहीं करना चाहती थी। तुम्हारे साथ वक़्त बिताना इतना अच्छा लग रहा था कि मैं रुकना नहीं चाहती थी।"

बेन मुस्कुराया। "ठीक है," उसने कहा। "मैं समझ सकता हूँ कि आपने क्यों किया। और चिन्ता मत करो। आप अभी भी मेरी दबंग दादी हो!"

"धन्यवाद," दादी ने धीरे से कहा। "अच्छा, इस एक जन्म के लिए काफ़ी रोमांच हो गया। मैं चाहती हूँ कि अब तुम घर जाओ, प्यारे बच्चे, और अपनी प्लम्बिंग पर ध्यान दो..."

"मैं दूँगा, मैं वचन देता हूँ। और कोई चोरी नहीं," बेन हँसा।

एक दम से दादी सुन्न हो गयीं।

उन्होंने ऊपर देखा।

बेन को एक हेलिकॉप्टर की आवाज़ आ रही थी।

"दादी?"

"चुप..." दादी ने अपने कान की मशीन ठीक की

और ध्यान से सुना। "यह तो एक से ज़्यादा हेलिकॉप्टर हैं। यह तो कई सारे हेलिकॉप्टरों की आवाज़ है।"

वू-वू-वू-वू-वू!

पुलिस की गाड़ियों के भोंपुओं की भी आवाज़ हर जगह से आ रही थी, और कुछ ही देर में ढेर सारे सशस्त्र पुलिसवाले घर को हर कोने से घेर चुके थे। दादी और बेन को अब आस-पास का कोई भी बंगला दिख नहीं रहा था क्योंकि अब उन दोनों के सामने बुलेट प्रूफ़ जैकेट पहने सैकड़ों पुलिसवाले दीवार बन कर खड़े थे। पुलिस के हेलिकॉप्टरों के घरघराने की आवाज़ इतनी तेज़ थी कि दादी को अपनी मशीन धीमी करनी पड़ी।

एक हेलिकॉप्टर से बड़े भोंपू की आवाज़ आयी। "आपको घेर लिया गया है। अपने अस्त्र-शस्त्र छोड़ दो। मैं दोहराता हूँ, अपने अस्त्र-शस्त्र छोड़ दो नहीं तो हम गोली चला देंगे।"

"हमारे पास कोई अस्त्र-शस्त्र नहीं है!" बेन चिल्लाया। उसकी आवाज़ अभी तक भारी नहीं हुई थी और कुछ लड़कियों सरीखी तीखी निकली।

"उनके साथ बहस मत करो बेन। बस अपने हाथ ऊपर कर लो!" दादी उस शोर में चीख़ीं।

दबंग जोड़े ने अपने हाथ ऊपर कर लिए। कुछ बहादुर पुलिसवाले बेन और दादी की तरफ़ बन्दूक ताने आगे बढ़े। उन्होंने दोनों को धक्का देकर ज़मीन पर

बैठा दिया और अपना निशाना साधे रखा।

"हिलो मत!" हेलिकॉप्टर से आवाज़ आयी। बेन
ने सोचा, जब एक हट्टे-कट्टे पुलिसवाले ने पीठ पर टेक

लगाया हुआ है, तो मैं कैसे हिल सकता हूँ?

चमड़े के दस्ताने पहने हुए हाथों का एक गुच्छा आया और उनके शरीरों को टटोला। उसने दादी के झोले को भी पलटा।

अगर वह इस्तेमाल किये हुए टिशू ढूँढ रहे होते तो आज तो लॉटरी लग जाती, लेकिन उनको कोई अस्त्र-शस्त्र नहीं मिले।

उन्होंने बेन और दादी को हथकड़ी पहनाई और खड़ा कर दिया। पुलिस की दीवार के पीछे से एक बूढ़ा आदमी एक बड़ी नाक और पोर्क पाई के आकार की गोल टोपी पहने निकला।

वह और कोई नहीं, श्रीमान पार्कर थे।

दादी के ताँक-झाँकिया पड़ोसी।

30

चीनी का एक पैकेट

"क्या सोचा था तुमने, शाही आभूषण चोरी करके बच जाओगे?" श्रीमान पार्कर ठिनकनाए। "मैं तुम्हारी दुष्ट योजना के बारे में सब जानता हूँ। लेकिन, अब सब ख़त्म। ऑफ़िसर, इन को ले जाओ। और इनको अन्दर बन्द कर दो और चाबी फेंक देना!"

पुलिसवाले ने दोनों बन्दियों को पुलिस की दो गाड़ियों की ओर ढकेला।

"एक सेकंड रुको," बेन चिल्लाया। "अगर हम ने शाही आभूषण चोरी किये हैं, तो वह हैं कहाँ?"

"ज़रूर, ज़रूर! सबूत! बस वही तो चाहिए तुम दोनों दबंगों को सलाख़ों के पीछे डालने के लिए। इनके

स्कूटर की टोकरी में देखो। अभी के अभी!” श्रीमान पार्कर ने कहा।

एक पुलिसवाले ने टोकरी में छानबीन की। उसको क्लिंगफ़िल्म में लिपटा एक बड़ा गीला-सा पैकेट मिला।

“यह रहे, यही होंगे आभूषण,” श्रीमान पार्कर को पूरा विश्वास था। “यहाँ दो।”

श्रीमान पार्कर ने दादी और बेन को घूरा। उसकी आँखों में जीत का ग़ुरूर था। उसने पैकेट को खोलना शुरू किया।

जब तक वह बड़ा पैकेट एक छोटा पैकेट नहीं बन गया, वह खोलते रहे। आखिरकार श्रीमान पार्कर क्लिंगफ़िल्म के अन्त तक पहुँचे।

“बस, अब खुल ही गया!” उन्होंने ऐलान किया और तब ही एक बन्दगोभी के सूप का डिब्बा ज़मीन पर गिरा।

“क्या आप मुझे वह दे सकते हैं, श्रीमान पार्कर?” दादी बोलीं। “यह मेरा दोपहर का भोजन है।”

"इसके बंगले की छान बीन करो!" श्रीमान पार्कर गरजे।

कुछ पुलिसवालों ने दरवाज़ा तोड़ने के लिए कंधे से धक्का दिया। दादी उनको देख रही थीं। अचानक, मुस्कुराते हुए, उन्होंने कहा, "मेरे पास चाबी है, अगर आपको चाहिए हो!"

एक पुलिसवाला उनके पास आया और लज्जित होते हुए चाबी ली।

"धन्यवाद, मैडम," उसने नम्रतापूर्वक बोला।

दादी और बेन एक दूसरे को देखकर मुस्कुराए।

जैसे ही उन्होंने दरवाज़ा खोला, सैकड़ों पुलिसवालों ने घर पर हमला-सा कर दिया। एक हड़बड़ी के साथ, उन्होंने तलाशी ली, लेकिन कुछ ही देर में खाली हाथ बाहर निकल आये।

"मुझे अफ़सोस है, साहिब, यहाँ कोई भी शाही आभूषण नहीं हैं," एक पुलिसवाले ने कहा। "बस एक स्क्रैबल का खेल और बन्दगोभी के सूप के कुछ डिब्बे।"

श्रीमान ताँक-झाँक का चेहरा गुस्से से लाल हो

गया। उन्होंने देश की आधी पुलिस को बुलाया था, वह भी व्यर्थ में।

"अब, श्रीमान पार्कर," एक पुलिसवाले ने कहा, "आप अपनी खुशकिस्मती समझिए कि हम आपको पुलिस का वक़्त ख़राब करने के लिए गिरफ़्तार नहीं कर रहें हैं।"

"रुकिए!" श्रीमान पार्कर बोले। "चाहे इनके पास घर में आभूषण नहीं हैं, इसका मतलब यह बिल्कुल नहीं है कि इनके पास हैं ही नहीं। मुझे पता है मैंने क्या कहा था। ढूँढो ... बगीचे में! हाँ! खोदो!"

पुलिसवाले ने शान्त कराने के लिए अपना हाथ उठाया। "श्रीमान पार्कर, हम यह बिल्कुल नहीं—"

अचानक ही श्रीमान पार्कर की आँखें जीत की आशा से जगमगाने लगीं। "एक मिनट। आपने इन से यह नहीं पूछा कि यह शाम से कहाँ थे। मैं जानता हूँ कि यह शाही आभूषण चुराने गये थे। और मुझे पक्का पता है कि इनके पास कोई उत्तर नहीं होगा!"

पुलिसवाले ने क्रोध में बेन और दादी की ओर देखा। "वैसे यह ठीक ही बोल रहे हैं, क्या आप मुझे

बता सकते हैं कि आप आज शाम कहाँ थे?" श्रीमान पार्कर अब बहुत ही दमक रहे थे।

तब ही, एक पुलिसवाला ठुमकते हुए उनकी ओर आया। वह कुछ जाना-पहचाना लग रहा था, और जब बेन ने उनकी मूँछ देखी, तो याद आ गया।

"साहिब, आपके के लिए एक फ़ोन आया है—" एम.के. लड्डू ने वाकी-टाकी पकड़े हुए कहा। वह एकाएक रुक गया, और बेन और दादी को घूरने लगा।

"अच्छा!" उसने कहा। "तो यह हैं क्लिंगफ़िल्म के लोग!"

"एम.के. पेड़ा!" बेन ने कहा।

"लड्डू!" लड्डू ने उसे टोका।

"माफ़ कीजिए, लड्डू। आपको मिलकर खुशी हुई।"

बड़े ऑफ़िसर को कुछ भी समझ नहीं आ रहा था। "माफ़ कीजिए?"

"यह लड़का और उसकी दादी। दोनों क्लिंगफ़िल्म समालोचना सभा से हैं। आज यह अपने वार्षिक सम्मेलन के लिए लंदन गये थे। असल में, मैंने ही

इनको छोड़ा था।"

"तो यह शाही आभूषण चोरी नहीं कर रहे थे?" साहिब ने पूछा।

"नहीं!" एम.के. लड्डू हँसा। "वह बुलबुला लपेटन समालोचना सभा के साथ मिलने वाले हैं। और शाही आभूषण, ज़रूर, ज़रूर!" बेन और दादी को देखकर मुस्कुराया। "वॉट ऐन आयडीआ, सरजी।"

श्रीमान पार्कर जलभुनकर राख हो चुके थे। "लेकिन ... लेकिन ... इन्होंने किया है! यह दोनों

बदमाश हैं, मैं बता रहा हूँ ना!"

वह गुस्से में बड़बड़ा रहे थे, तब ऑफ़िसर ने वाकी-टाकी एम.के. लड्डू से लिया। "जी। हम। ठीक है। धन्यवाद," उन्होंने कहा। उन्होंने फिर बेन और दादी को कहा, "स्पेशल ब्रांच से फ़ोन था। मैंने उनसे बोला था कि वह देखें अगर शाही आभूषण वहाँ हैं, या नहीं। पता चला कि वह वहीं हैं। मुझे माफ़ कर दीजिए, मैडम। और बेटा। हम तुरन्त हथकड़ी खोल देते हैं।"

श्रीमान पार्कर कंधे झुकाए मुरझा गये थे। "नहीं, ऐसा नहीं हो सकता..."

"मुझे अब अगर एक चूँ की भी आवाज़ आयी ना, श्रीमान पार्कर," पुलिस अफ़सर ने कहा, "मैं आपको जेल में फेंक दूँगा!" वह ज़ोरदार ढंग से अपनी एड़ियों पर मुड़ा और अपनी गशती गाड़ी की तरफ़ गया। एम.के. लड्डू उनके पीछे चल दिये।

बेन और दादी हथकड़ियों के साथ श्रीमान पार्कर के पास गये।

"जो आपने सुना था, वह सब सिर्फ़ कहानियाँ

थीं," बेन ने कहा। "मेरी दादी मुझे सिर्फ़ कहानियाँ सुना रहीं थीं। श्रीमान पार्कर मुझे लगता है कि आपकी कल्पनाएँ आप पर हावी हो जाती हैं।"

"लेकिन, लेकिन, लेकिन...!" श्रीमान पार्कर हड़बड़ा गये।

"मैं? एक अन्तरराष्ट्रीय आभूषण चोर?!" दादी हँसीं।

पुलिसवाले भी हँस रहे थे।

"ऐसी बात पर विश्वास करने के लिए आपके कुछ स्क्रू ढ़ीले होंगे!" उन्होंने कहा। "माफ़ करो बेन," दादी ने बेन के कान में फ़ुसफ़ुसाकर कहा।

"कुछ नहीं होता!" बेन वापस फ़ुसफ़ुसाया।

पुलिसवालों ने हथकड़ियाँ खोल दीं और अपनी गाड़ियों में बैठ कर ग्रे क्लोज़ से तेज़ी से चले गये।

"आपको तंग करने के लिए खेद है, मैडम," एक पुलिस अफ़सर ने कहा। "आपका दिन शुभ हो!"

हेलिकॉप्टर भी आसमान में ग़ायब हो गये।

जैसे ही उनकी गति बढ़ती गयी, श्रीमान पार्कर की कीमती पोर्क पाई की आकार की गोल टोपी कीचड़ में गिर गयी।

दादी श्रीमान पार्कर के पास गयीं, जो अब बिना टोपी के खड़े थे।

"अगर कभी भी आपको एक पैकेट चीनी की ज़रूरत पड़े..." बड़े प्यार से बोलीं।

"जी..." श्रीमान पार्कर ने कहा।

"मेरे दरवाज़े पर मत खटखटाना, नहीं तो मैं पूरा पैकेट आपके पिछवाड़े में डाल दूँगी," दादी ने एक मीठी-सी मुस्कान के साथ कहा।

31

सुनहरी रोशनी

सूरज उग गया था, ग्रे क्लोज़ सुनहरी रोशनी में नहा चुका था। ज़मीन पर शबनम थी और कोहरे से ढके बंगले जादुई लग रहे थे।

"वाह," दादी ने आह भरी। "अब तुमको घर भागना चाहिए, नन्हे बेन, इससे पहले कि तुम्हारे माता-पिता जागें।"

"उनको मेरी परवाह नहीं है," बेन ने कहा।

"ज़रूर है," दादी ने कहा और अपने पोते को गले लगा लिया। "बस उनको जताना नहीं आता।"

"हो सकता है।"

बेन ने अपनी ज़िन्दगी की सबसे बड़ी उबासी

ली। "ओह, मैं बहुत थक गया हूँ। आज की रात लाजवाब थी!"

"मेरी ज़िन्दगी की सबसे रोमांचक और अभूतपूर्व रात थी, बेन। मैं दुनिया में किसी भी चीज़ के लिए इसको नहीं छोड़ती," दादी ने कहा और एक झिलमिलाती हुई मुस्कान दी। उन्होंने एक लम्बी साँस ली।

"इसको ही जीना कहते हैं।"

फिर उनकी आँखों में आँसू आ गये।

"दादी, आप ठीक हो ना?" बेन ने प्यार से पूछा।

दादी ने पोते से अपना चेहरा छिपाया। "मैं ठीक हूँ बच्चे, सच में।" उनकी आवाज़ भारी थी।

बेन समझ गया था कि कुछ गड़बड़ है।

"दादी, प्लीज़, आप मुझे बता सकते हो।"

उसने दादी का हाथ पकड़ा। उनकी त्वचा नरम और कोमल लेकिन बूढ़ी हो रही थी। नाज़ुक।

"अब…" दादी हिचकिचाते हुए बोलीं। "एक और चीज़ है, जिसके बारे में मैंने झूठ बोला था बेटा।"

बेन का दिल बैठने लगा।

"वह क्या है?" उसने पूछा और उनका हाथ और

ज़ोर से कसकर थामा।

"डॉक्टर ने मुझे पिछले हफ़्ते जब जाँच की रपट दी थी और मैंने तुमसे कहा था कि मैं ठीक हूँ। वह झूठ था। मैं ठीक नहीं हूँ।" दादी रुक गयीं। "सच तो यह है कि मुझे कैंसर है।"

"नहीं, नहीं..." बेन बोला और उसकी आँखों में आँसू आने लगे। उसने कैंसर के बारे में इतना सुना था जिस से उसको यह समझ आ गया था कि यह एक जानलेवा बीमारी है।

"जब तुम उनसे अस्पताल में मिले थे, तब ही उन्होंने मुझे इस बीमारी के बारे में बताया था और यह काफ़ी बढ़ चुकी है।"

"आप के पास कितना समय है?" बेन बड़बड़ाया। "क्या उन्होंने बताया?"

"उन्होंने कहा था की मैं क्रिसमस से पहले ही ..."

बेन ने दादी को ज़ोर से गले लगाया, यह सोचकर कि शायद उसके शरीर की ताकत दादी में चली जाये।

उसके आँसू रुक ही नहीं रहे थे।

यह कितना अनुचित था। अभी कुछ ही हफ़्ते

पहले उसने दादी को सही मायने में जानना शुरू ही किया था और अब वह उनको खोने वाला था।

"मैं नहीं चाहता कि आप मरें।"

दादी ने बेन को कुछ देर देखा।

"हम में से कोई भी हमेशा के लिए नहीं जी सकता ना, मेरे बच्चे। भगवान करे तुम मुझे कभी भी ना भूलो। तुम्हारी बूढ़ी बोरिंग दादी!"

"आप बिल्कुल भी बोरिंग नहीं हो। आप तो दबंग हो! हमने बस शाही आभूषण चुरा ही लिये थे, याद है ना आपको!"

दादी हँसीं।

"हाँ, लेकिन इसके बारे में किसी को पता नहीं चलना चाहिए, प्लीज़। अभी भी तुम मुसीबत में पड़ सकते हो। यह हम दोनों के बीच का रहस्य ही रहना चाहिए।"

"और महारानी का भी!" बेन ने कहा।

"अरे हाँ! वो कितनी प्यारी बूढ़ी औरत थीं।"

"मैं आपको कभी नहीं भूलूँगा दादी," बेन ने कहा। "आप मेरे दिल में हमेशा रहोगे।"

"इससे प्यारी बात किसी ने कभी नहीं कही मुझे," बूढ़ी दादी ने कहा।

"मैं आपसे बहुत प्यार करता हूँ, दादी।"

"मैं भी तुमसे प्यार करती हूँ, बेन। लेकिन अब तुम को जाना चाहिए।"

"मैं आपको छोड़ कर नहीं जाना चाहता।"

"तुम बहुत ही प्यारे हो बेन, लेकिन अगर उठने पर तुम्हारे माँ-बाबा को तुम नहीं मिले तो उन्हें तुम्हारी बहुत चिन्ता होगी।"

"नहीं होगी।"

"ज़रूर होगी। अब बेन, अच्छे बच्चे बनो।"

बेन अनिच्छापूर्वक उठा। उसने दादी को भी सीढ़ी से उठने में मदद की।

उसने फिर उनको गले लगाया और उनके गाल पर एक चुम्मी दी। उसको उनकी बालदार ठोड़ी से कोई आपत्ति नहीं थी। वास्तव में, उसको बेहद अच्छी लगी।

उसको दादी की कान की मशीन की सीटी बहुत पसन्द थी। उसको उनसे आती बन्दगोभी की भी महक

अत्यन्त पसन्द थी।

और उसको सबसे ज्यादा पसन्द था कि बिना
जाने वह हवा छोड़ती रहती थीं।

उसको उनकी हर एक चीज़ से लगाव था।

"अलविदा," उसने धीरे से कहा।

"अलविदा, बेन।"

32

परिवार का सैंडविच

जब वह घर पहुँचा, बेन ने देखा कि उनकी छोटी-सी भूरी गाड़ी घर पर नहीं है। अभी दिन की शुरुआत ही हुई थी।

उसके माता-पिता कहाँ गये हो सकते हैं?

फिर भी, पाइप से वह ऊपर चढ़ा, और खिड़की से अपने कमरे में घुस गया।

यह चढ़ाई एक कठिन परिश्रम थी। वह पूरी रात जागने से थक गया था और वेटसूट का वज़न भी भारी पड़ रहा था। बेन ने *प्लम्बिंग वीकली* को एक तरफ़ किया ताकि वह वेटसूट को बिस्तर के नीचे छिपा सके।

फिर, उसने कम से कम आवाज़ करते हुए पायजामा पहना और बिस्तर में घुस गया।

जैसे ही उसने अपनी आँखें बन्द की, उसको गाड़ी आने की तेज़ आवाज़ आयी। फिर घर का दरवाज़ा खुला और माँ और बाबा के रोने का शोर आया।

"हमने उसको हर जगह ढूँढा," बाबा ने नाक से साँस लेते हुए कहा। "मैं नहीं जानता अब मैं क्या करूँ।"

"यह मेरी ही बेवक़ूफ़ी थी," माँ ने अपने आँसू पोंछते हुए कहा। "हमको उसे डांस प्रतियोगिता में भाग नहीं दिलवाना चाहिए था। वह घर से भाग गया होगा..."

"मैं पुलिस को फ़ोन करता हूँ।"

"हाँ, हाँ, ज़रूर, हमें यह कुछ घंटों पहले ही कर देना चाहिए था।"

"हमें पूरे देश को उसे ढूँढने में लगाना होगा। हेलो, हेलो, मुझे पुलिस से बात करनी है, प्लीज़, मेरा

बेटा। मुझे मेरा बेटा नहीं मिल रहा..."

बेन को दुख भरी शर्मिंदगी महसूस हो रही थी। आखिरकार उसके माता-पिता को उसकी परवाह थी।

बहुत ज़्यादा।

वह बिस्तर से उछला, अपने कमरे का दरवाज़ा खोला और सीढ़ियों से नीचे, सीधा उनकी बाहों में चला गया। बाबा के हाथ से फ़ोन गिर गया।

"ओ, मेरा बेटा! मेरा बेटा!" बाबा ने कहा।

उन्होंने बेन को ज़ोर से गले लगाया। माँ ने भी अपने बेटे को बाहों में लिया, और वह सब एक बड़ा-सा सैंडविच बन गये, जिस में बेन बीच का हिस्सा था।

"ओ बेन! शुक्र है कि तुम वापस आ गये!" माँ रो रहीं थी। "तुम कहाँ थे?"

"दादी के साथ," बेन ने बताया, आधा सच छिपाते हुए। "वह ... वह बहुत बीमार हैं," उसने दुख से कहा। लेकिन उसको अपने माता-पिता की सूरत देख कर लग नहीं रहा था कि उनके लिए यह कोई ताज्जुब की बात थी।

"हाँ..." बाबा बैचेनी से बोले। "मुझे डर है

कि वह—"

"मैं जानता हूँ," बेन ने कहा। "मुझे विश्वास नहीं हो रहा कि आपने मुझे नहीं बताया। वह मेरी दादी हैं!"

"मैं जानता हूँ," बाबा ने कहा। "वह मेरी माँ हैं। मुझे माफ़ कर दो कि हमने तुम्हें नहीं बताया बेटा। हम तुम्हें दुःखी नहीं करना चाहते थे..."

बेन को अपने बाबा की आँखों में दर्द दिखा। "कोई बात नहीं बाबा," उसने कहा।

"मैं और तुम्हारी माँ पूरी रात जागे हुए थे और

तुमको ढूँढ रहे थे," बाबा ने आगे कहा और ज़ोर से जकड़ लिया। "हमने सोचा ही नहीं कि हम को दादी के घर पर भी देखना चाहिए। तुम हमेशा कहते थे कि वह बोरिंग हैं।"

"वह, वह बोरिंग नहीं हैं। वह दुनिया की सबसे अच्छी दादी हैं।"

बाबा मुस्कुराए। "यह कितनी प्यारी बात है, बेटा। लेकिन तुम हमको बता सकते थे कि तुम कहाँ हो।"

"मुझे माफ़ कर दो। आपको डांस प्रतियोगिता में निराश कर, मुझे लगा था कि आपको मेरी फ़िक्र नहीं है।"

"तुम्हारी फ़िक्र?" बाबा चकित हो गये। "हम तुमसे प्यार करते हैं!"

"हम तुमसे बेहद प्यार करते हैं, बेन!" माँ ने कहा।

"तुमको कभी भी कुछ और नहीं सोचना चाहिए। किसको फ़र्क पड़ता है एक बेवकूफ़ों वाली प्रतियोगिता का जिसका मेज़बान फ़्लावीओ फ़्लावीओलि हो? मुझे

तुम पर गर्व है, चाहे तुम कुछ भी करो।''

"हम दोनों को,'' बाबा बोले।

अब सब रो रहे थे और मुस्कुरा रहे थे और यह जानना मुश्किल हो गया था कि यह खुशी के आँसू हैं या दुख के। क्या फ़र्क पड़ता है।

"हम दादी के घर चाय के लिए चलें?'' माँ बोलीं।

"हाँ,'' बेन बोला। "अच्छा होगा!''

"और मैं और बाबा बात कर रहे थे,'' माँ ने बेन का हाथ पकड़ते हुए कहा। "हमें तुम्हारी *प्लम्बिंग वीकली* मिलीं।''

"लेकिन...'' बेन बोला।

"कुछ नहीं होता,'' माँ ने आगे कहा। "तुमको शर्मिंदा होने की ज़रूरत नहीं है। अगर यह तुम्हारा सपना है, तो इसको साकार करो!''

"सच में?'' बेन बोला।

"हाँ,'' बाबा ने गुनगुनाते हुए कहा। "हम बस यह चाहते हैं कि तुम खुश रहो।''

"बस..." माँ बोलीं, "मुझे और बाबा को यह लगता है कि, अगर प्लम्बिंग का काम नहीं चला, तब तुम्हारे पास कोई दूसरा उपाय होना चाहिए..."

"उपाय?" बेन ने पूछा। अच्छे से अच्छे वक़्त में उसको अपने माता-पिता समझ नहीं आते थे, अब तो छोड़ ही दो।

"हाँ," बाबा बोले। "और मैं जानता हूँ बॉलरूम नाच तुम्हारे लिए नहीं है।"

"नहीं," बेन ने हामी भरी और राहत की साँस ली।

"तो, बर्फ़ पर नाचना कैसा रहेगा?" माँ ने पूछा।

बेन उनको घूर रहा था।

कुछ देर तक माँ भी उसको एकटक देखती रहीं और आखिरकार उनकी हँसी छूट गयी और वह ज़ोर-ज़ोर से हँसने लगीं। और फिर बाबा भी हँस रहे थे और अभी तक बेन के चेहरे पर आँसू थे, लेकिन वह भी हँस पड़ा।

33

चुप्पी

उसके बाद, बेन और उसके माता-पिता का रिश्ता बेहतर हो गया। उसके बाबा तो उसके लिए प्लम्बिंग के यंत्र लाये और दोनों को दोपहर में एक ख़राब पाइप को ठीक करने में बहुत मज़ा आया।

फिर, क्रिसमस से एक हफ़्ता पहले, उन तीनों को एक फ़ोन आया।

कुछ घंटों बाद, बेन, माँ और बाबा, दादी के बिस्तर के पास खड़े हुए। वह मरणासन्न रोगियों के अस्पताल में थीं, जहाँ वह लोग जाते थे जिनका इलाज अब अस्पताल और नहीं कर सकता था। उनके पास अब और वक़्त नहीं था। शायद कुछ ही घंटे। नर्स ने

कहा कि वह कभी भी जा सकती थीं।

बेन दादी के बिस्तर के पास व्याकुल बैठा था। उनकी आँखें बन्द थीं और ऐसा लग रहा था कि वह बोल नहीं पायेंगी। उस कमरे में बैठना गमगीन था।

बाबा बिस्तर के सिरे पर आगे पीछे चल रहे थे। उनको समझ नहीं आ रहा था कि उनको क्या करना चाहिए।

माँ भी बैठी देख रही थीं, बेबस महसूस कर रही थीं।

बेन ने दादी का हाथ पकड़ा।

वह नहीं चाहता था कि दादी अँधेरे में अकेले ही चली जायें।

वह उनकी रुकती हुई उखड़ती साँसें सुन रहे थे। बहुत ही भयंकर आवाज़ थी। लेकिन उस से भी ज़्यादा बदतर एक आवाज़ थी।

चुप्पी।

जिसका मतलब था कि वह चली गयीं।

फिर दादी ने आँखें झपकायीं और फिर खोलते ही सबको चौंका दिया। जब उन्होंने तीनों को देखा, वह मुस्कुराई। "मैं ... भूख से मर रही हूँ," उन्होंने कमज़ोर आवाज़ में कहा। उन्होंने अपनी चादरों में से क्लिंगफ़िल्म में लिपटा हुआ कुछ निकाला और उसको खोलने लगीं।

"यह क्या है?" बेन ने पूछा।

"बस बन्दगोभी के केक का एक टुकड़ा," दादी ने कष्ट से साँस ली। "असल में यहाँ का खाना गले से नीचे नहीं उतरता।"

थोड़ी देर बाद, माँ और बाबा कॉफ़ी लेने बाहर गये। बेन दादी को एक सेकंड के लिए भी नहीं छोड़ना चाहता था। वह आगे बढ़ा और उसने उनका हाथ पकड़ा। वह रूखा और हल्का था।

धीरे से दादी ने उसकी ओर देखा। बेन को अहसास था कि उनका वक़्त खत्म हो रहा था। उन्होंने आँख मारी। "तुम हमेशा मेरे छोटे बेनी रहोगे," वह फ़ुसफ़ुसाई।

बेन को लगता था कि उसको इस नाम से नफ़रत थी। लेकिन अब उसको यह नाम बेहद पसन्द था। "मैं जानता हूँ," उसने मुस्कुराकर कहा। "और आप हमेशा मेरी दबंग दादी रहोगी।"

*

कुछ देर बाद, जब दादी जा चुकीं थीं, माँ और बाबा अस्पताल से वापस घर जा रहे थे, बेन गाड़ी में चुप-चाप पीछे बैठा था। सब रो-रो कर थक गये थे। इसी दौरान लोग क्रिसमस की खरीददारी कर रहे थे, सड़कें गाड़ियों से भरी थीं और सिनेमाघर के बाहर लम्बी कतारे थीं। बेन को यक़ीन नहीं हो रहा था कि ज़िन्दगी साधारण तरीक़े से चल रही थी, जबकि उनके साथ इतनी बड़ी घटना हो गयी थी।

गाड़ी मुड़ी और छोटी दुकानों के मेले की तरफ़ गयी।

"मैं क्या अखबारवाले के यहाँ जा सकता हूँ, प्लीज़?" बेन बोला। "मुझे ज़्यादा वक़्त नहीं लगेगा।"

बाबा ने गाड़ी लगायी, और क्योंकि हल्की-सी बर्फ़ गिर रही थी, बेन राज की दुकान में अकेले ही गया।

डिंग! जैसे ही बेन ने दरवाज़ा खोला, घंटी बजी।

"आह! हमारा बेन!" राज ने पुकारा। अखबारवाले को उसके चेहरे का दुख दिख गया। "क्या हुआ?"

"हाँ, राज अंकल..." बेन बड़बड़ाया। "मेरी दादी अभी गुज़र गयीं।" जैसे-तैसे, बोलते ही उसका रोना फिर से शुरू हो गया।

राज दुकान की मेज़ के पीछे से निकला और बेन को ज़ोर से गले लगाया।

"अरे बेन, मुझे बहुत अफ़सोस है। वह कुछ समय से आयी नहीं थीं, तो मुझे लगा कि वह ठीक नहीं होंगी।"

"नहीं। और मैं कहना चाहता था, राज," बेन ने लम्बी गहरी साँस खींचते हुए कहा, "मुझे उस दिन डाँटने के लिए शुक्रिया। आप ठीक ही कह रहे थे, वह

बिल्कुल बोरिंग नहीं थीं। वह बेहतरीन थीं।"

"मैं तुम्हें डाँटने की कोशिश नहीं कर रहा था, बेटा। मुझे तो बस यह लग रहा था कि शायद तुमने अपनी दादी को जानने के लिए वक़्त नहीं निकाला था।"

"तुम सही थे। उन में इतनी सारी ऐसी चीज़ें थीं, जिनकी मैं कल्पना भी नहीं कर सकता था।" उसने अपनी बाँह से अपना नाक साफ़ किया।

राज अपनी दुकान में कुछ ढूँढने लगा। "अब ... मेरे पास एक टिशू का पैकेट था। कहाँ है? अरे, हाँ, फुटबाल के स्टिकर के नीचे। यह लो।"

अखबार वाले ने पैकेट खोला और बेन को दिया। उस लड़के ने अपनी आँखें पोंछीं।

"धन्यवाद, राज अंकल। क्या दस टिशू के पैकेट नौ के दाम के हैं?" उसने मुस्कुराते हुए पूछा।

"नहीं नहीं नहीं!" राज हँसा।

"पन्द्रह पैकेट, चौदह के दाम पर?"

चुप्पी

राज ने बेन के कन्धे पर हाथ रखा। "तुम समझ नहीं रहे," उसने कहा। "यह मुफ़्त हैं।"

बेन उसको देखता रहा। इतिहास में लिखा था कि राज ने कभी भी कुछ भी मुफ़्त नहीं दिया था। यह कुछ अनोखी बात थी। यह पागलपन था। "बहुत धन्यवाद राज," उसने जल्दी से कहा, और उसकी आवाज़ नम हो गयी। "मुझे अपने माता-पिता के पास वापस जाना चाहिए। वह मेरा इन्तज़ार कर रहे होंगे।"

"हाँ, हाँ, बस एक मिनट," राज बोला।

"मेरे पास तुम्हारे लिए क्रिसमस की एक भेंट यहीं कहीं थी, बेन।" अपनी उथल-पुथल दुकान में उसने और उथल-पुथल मचा दी। "अब, कहाँ है?"

बेन की आँखों में एक नई चमक थी। उसको तोहफ़े बहुत पसन्द थे।

"हाँ, हाँ, ईस्टर ऐग के ही पीछे है। मिल गया!" राज चिल्लाया और मिंट की गोलियाँ निकालीं।

बेन थोड़ा निराश हो गया लेकिन उसने छिपाने की पूरी कोशिश की।

"अरे वाह! धन्यवाद राज," बेन ने कहा "एक मिंट का पूरा पैकेट।"

चुप्पी

"नहीं, सिर्फ़ एक मिंट," राज ने बोला पैकेट खोलते हुए और एक मिंट की गोली बेन को पकड़ाई। "यह तुम्हारी दादी को बेहद पसन्द थे।"

"मैं जानता हूँ," बेन ने मुस्कुराते हुए कहा।

ज़िम्मर फ़्रेम

क्रियाकर्म क्रिसमस से एक दिन पहले था। बेन ने पहले कभी क्रियाकर्म नहीं देखा था। उसको सब कुछ विचित्र लग रहा था। जैसे ही शवपेटी को चर्च के सामने रखा, वहाँ उपस्थित लोग अंजाने से भजन गाने लगे और पादरी, जो दादी से मिला भी नहीं था, उसने उनके बारे में एक थकानेवाला लम्बा भाषण दिया।

पादरी की कोई ग़लती नहीं थी, उसका तो काम ही यह था। वह उदास और उबाऊ तरीक़े से बोलते जा रहा था। वो भी प्राचीन चर्च जाने में दादी की रुचि और जानवरों के साथ उनके दयालू बर्ताव के बारे में।

बेन का चिल्लाने को मन कर रहा था। वह माँ-

बाबा, चाचा-चाची, मामा-मामी, सब को बताना चाहता था कि दादी कितनी अद्भुत थीं। कैसे वह सबसे ज़्यादा हैरतअंगेज़ कहानियाँ सुनाती थीं।

सबसे ज़्यादा तो, वह सबको शाही आभूषणों की चोरी और महारानी के साथ भेंट का अभूतपूर्व अविस्मरणीय अनुभव बताना चाहता था।

लेकिन कोई भी यक़ीन नहीं करता। वह केवल ग्यारह साल का था। उनको लगता कि वह कहानी गढ़ रहा है।

जब वह घर पहुँचे, चर्च से काफ़ी सारे लोग उनके घर आ गये। एक चाय के बाद एक और चाय पिये जा रहे थे, एक प्लेट सैंडविच के बाद एक प्लेट सॉसेज के रोल खाये जा रहे थे। क्रिसमस की सजावट भी अजीब लग रही थी। शुरू में सब दादी के बारे में बात कर रहे थे, लेकिन कुछ ही देर में उन्होंने दूसरी चीज़ों के बारे में गप्पें मारनी शुरू कर दीं।

बेन सोफ़े पर अकेला बैठा था और बड़े लोगों की बातें सुन रहा था। दादी ने अपनी सारी किताबें उसके

नाम कर दी थीं, और अब ऊँचे-ऊँचे ढेर उसके कमरे में थे। उसका मन इन किताबों में छिप जाने का कर रहा था।

कुछ देर बाद एक बूढ़ी औरत हाथ में चार पैरों वाले वॉकर के सहारे धीरे से चलती हुयी आयी और बेन के पास आकर आराम से बैठ गयीं।

"तुम बेन होगे। तुम्हें याद तो नहीं होगा कि मैं कौन हूँ?" बूढ़ी औरत ने पूछा।

बेन ने कुछ देर उनको देखा।

बात तो उनकी ठीक थी।

"आख़िरी बार मैंने तुमको तुम्हारे पहले जन्मदिन पर देखा था," उन्होंने कहा।

तब ही तो मुझे याद नहीं हैं! बेन ने सोचा।

"मैं तुम्हारी दादी की चचेरी बहन एड्ना हूँ," उन्होंने कहा। "मैं और तुम्हारी दादी बचपन में, क़रीब-क़रीब तुम्हारी उम्र में ही, एक साथ खेलते थे। कुछ साल पहले मैं गिरी थी, और मैं अपनी देखरेख नहीं कर

पा रही थी। तब मुझे एक वृद्धाश्रम जाना पड़ा। तुम्हारी दादी ही थीं जो मुझे वहाँ मिलने आती थीं।"

"सच में? हमें लगता था कि वह कभी भी बाहर नहीं जातीं," बेन ने कहा।

"नहीं, वह महीने में एक बार आती थीं। उसके लिए आसान नहीं था। उसको चार बार बस बदलनी पड़ती थी। मैं उसकी बहुत आभारी रहूँगी।"

"वह बहुत ही ख़ास थीं।"

"वह तो है। हद से ज़्यादा दयालु और संवेदनशील भी थीं। मेरे ख़ुद के कोई बच्चे या पोते-पोतियाँ नहीं हैं, इसलिए मैं और तुम्हारी दादी वृद्धाश्रम की बैठक में घंटों स्क्रैबल खेलते थे।"

"स्क्रैबल?" बेन ने कहा।

"उसने मुझे बताया था कि तुमको भी बहुत पसन्द है," एड्ना ने कहा।

बेन अपनी मुस्कान छिपा नहीं पा रहा था।

"जी, मुझे बेहद पसन्द है," बेन ने कहा।

आश्चर्य की बात तो यह थी कि वह झूठ नहीं बोल रहा था। अब याद करने पर उसे लगा कि उसको सच में स्क्रैबल बेहद पसन्द था।

अब उसकी दादी जा चुकी थीं, और अब उनके साथ बिताया हर एक पल अनमोल था। शाही आभूषणों से भी ज़्यादा अनमोल।

"वह तुम्हारे बारे में बात करना बन्द ही नहीं कर सकती थीं," एड्ना ने कहा। "तुम्हारी प्यारी-सी दादी कहा करती थीं कि तुम हर शुक्रवार को उसके साथ रहने का बेसब्री से इन्तज़ार करते थे। उसके लिए यह हफ़्ते का सबसे अच्छा दिन होता था।"

"मेरे लिए भी हफ़्ते का मनपसन्द दिन होता था," बेन ने कहा।

"अगर तुमको स्क्रैबल पसन्द है, तो तुम्हें वृद्धाश्रम ज़रूर आना चाहिए," एड्ना ने कहा। "क्योंकि दादी नहीं रहीं, मुझे एक नये साथी की ज़रूरत है।"

"ज़रूर, मज़ा आयेगा," बेन ने कहा।

उस शाम जब उसके माता-पिता *स्ट्रिक्टली स्टार्स डांसिंग* की विशेष क्रिसमस प्रस्तुति देख रहे थे, तब बेन अपने कमरे की खिड़की से पाइप के सहारे नीचे उतरा। बिना आवाज़ किये, उसने गराज से अपनी साइकिल निकाली और दादी के घर आख़िरी बार गया।

बर्फ़ गिर रही थी। साइकिल के पहिए के नीचे पिस रही थी। बेन ज़मीन पर धीरे से गिरती बर्फ़ को देख रहा था, और रास्ते पर उसका ध्यान कम ही था। उसे यह रास्ता अच्छे से याद हो गया था। पिछले कुछ महीनों से वह दादी के घर इतनी बार जा चुका था कि उसको सड़क के हर गड्ढे और दरार का पता था।

दादी के छोटे बंगले के आगे उसने अपनी साइकिल रोकी। छत पर भी बर्फ़ फैली हुई थी। चिट्ठियों का ढेर भी लगा हुआ था, सारी बत्तियाँ भी बन्द थीं और "बिकाऊ" का बोर्ड लगा हुआ था।

बेन को लग रहा था कि दादी खिड़की पर बैठीं उसका इन्तज़ार कर रही होंगी।

अपनी छोटी-सी आशाजनक मुस्कान के साथ

उसकी राह देख रही होंगी।

लेकिन, वह वहाँ नहीं थीं। वह हमेशा के लिए जा चुकी थीं।

लेकिन वह उसके दिल से नहीं गयी थीं।

बेन ने एक आँसू पोंछा, लम्बी साँस ली और घर चला गया।

उसके पास अब एक लाजवाब कहानी थी अपने पोते-पोतियों को सुनाने के लिए।

अनुलेख

"क्रिसमस साल का खास समय होता है," महारानी ने कहा। वह हमेशा की तरह प्राचीन कुर्सी पर बकिंगहम पैलेस में शालीनता और गम्भीरता से बैठी थीं। आज एक बार फिर वह देश को वार्षिक सन्देश दे रही थीं।

माँ, बाबा और बेन ने अभी क्रिसमस का खाना खत्म ही किया था और सोफ़े पर चाय के प्याले के साथ पसर कर बैठे, महारानी को टीवी पर देख रहे थे।

"परिवार के साथ मिलजुल कर उत्सव मनाने का समय है," महारानी साहिबा ने आगे कहा।

"लेकिन, हमें बुज़ुर्गों को भूलना नहीं चाहिए।

कुछ हफ़्तों पहले लंदन टावर में हमारी मुलाकात हमारी हमउम्र एक महिला और उनके पोते से हुई।"

बेन अपनी जगह पर छटपटा रहा था।

उसने अपने माता-पिता को देखा लेकिन वह तो टीवी देखने में मग्न थे।

"उन्होंने हमें सोचने पर मजबूर कर दिया कि नौजवानों को बुज़ुर्गों के प्रति करुणा दिखानी चाहिए। अगर कोई नौजवान यह देख रहा है, तो हम उन्हें कहना चाहेंगे कि अपनी बस की सीट किसी बुज़ुर्ग को ज़रूर दो। या उनका थैला पकड़ने में मदद करो। एक स्क्रैबल का गेम भी खेल लेना चाहिए। कभी-कभार, हमारे लिए एक मिंट की गोलियों का पैकेट क्यों नहीं ले आते? हम बूढ़ों को एक मिंट चबाने में बड़ा मज़ा आता है। और सबसे ज़्यादा ज़रूरी, देश के नौजवानों, हम बुज़ुर्ग लोग बोरिंग नहीं हैं। क्या पता एक दिन हम भी आप लोगों को चौंका दें।"

फिर, एक नटखट मुस्कान के साथ, महारानी ने पूरे देश के सामने अपनी स्कर्ट उठाई और यूनियन जैक

(ब्रिटेन का झंडा) का अंडरवियर दिखाया।

आश्चर्य से माँ और बाबा के मुँह से चाय कालीन पर उलट गयी।

बेन सिर्फ़ मुस्कुरा रहा था।

महारानी भी एक असली दबंग हैं, उसने सोचा। एकदम उसकी दादी जैसी।

SILENCE

John Arden was [...] 1930 and now liv[...] Ireland. While [...] bridge University [...] Edinburgh College of Art, he began writing plays, three of which were produced at the Royal Court Theatre, London, in its heyday under George Devine. These were *The Waters of Babylon* (1957), *Live Like Pigs* (1958) and his best-known play, *Serjeant Musgrave's Dance* (1959), which was successfully revived at the National Theatre in 1981. A fourth early play, *The Workhouse Donkey* (1963), was staged at the Chichester Festival Theatre by the then National Theatre Company under Laurence Olivier. *Armstrong's Last Goodnight* was first seen at the Glasgow Citizens' Theatre in 1964 and subsequently at the National Theatre. *Left-Handed Liberty* was performed at the Mermaid Theatre in 1965 to commemorate the 750th anniversary of Magna Carta.

Arden has frequently worked in collaboration with Margaretta D'Arcy. Among the fruits of this collaboration are *The Happy Haven* (1960), *The Business of Good Government* (1960), *The Royal Pardon* (1966), *The Hero Rises Up* (1968), *The Island of the Mighty* (1972), *The Ballygombeen Bequest* (1972), *The Non-Stop Connolly Show* (1975), *Vandaleur's Folly* and *The Little Gray Home in the West* (both 1978).

A volume of essays by Arden published in 1977, *To Present the Pretence*, shows the development of his views on the theatre and its public. For radio Arden's work includes *The Bagman* or *The Impromptu of Muswell Hill* (1970), *Pearl* (1978), *Garland for a Hoar Head* (1982) and a two part adaptation of *Don Quixote* (1980). *Silence Among the Weapons* is his first novel. It was short-listed for the 1982 Booker Prize.

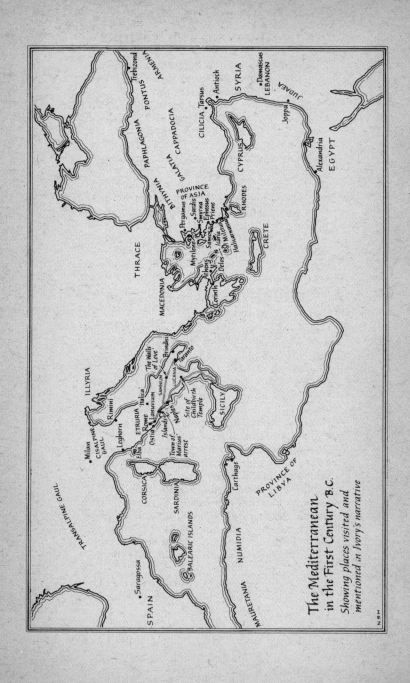

The Mediterranean
in the First Century B.C.

Showing places visited and
mentioned in Ivory's narrative

SILENCE
AMONG THE WEAPONS

*Some events at the time of the failure of a
republic*

JOHN ARDEN

'When the twelve eagles circled round the Palatine Hill, they
ushered in the kings: the new eagle which Gaius Marius be-
stowed on the legions proclaimed the advent of the emperors.'
Theodor Mommsen, *The History of Rome*

METHUEN · LONDON

DEDICATION

To the Subject Peoples –
  subjected, that is to say,
  to their own rulers,
  to someone else's,
  to ours;
  to *us* . . .

First published in Great Britain in 1982 by Methuen London
Ltd, 11 New Fetter Lane, London EC4P 4EE
This revised and corrected Methuen Paperback edition first
published in 1983
Copyright © 1982, 1983 by John Arden
ISBN 0 413 52310 1
Printed in Great Britain by
Richard Clay (The Chaucer Press) Ltd,
Bungay, Suffolk

The quotations from Theodor Mommsen's *The History of Rome*
are taken from the abridged version by C. Bryans and F. J. R.
Handy published by Peter Owen Ltd, London.

Contents

Historical Note

Ivory's thirty-fifth birthday (Book One: Chapter 2) was in 91 BC.
Irene wrote her letter to King Mithradates (Epilogue) in 81 BC.
The events of the main narrative fall between these years.

Some of the people in Ivory's story are known to the historians.
Many of them are referred to in the text by nicknames. Their real
names are given here in parentheses:

The *ACOLYTE* (Lucius Cornelius *Merula*):
　Roman politician, of the Aristocratic party.
ASHES (Lucius Cornelius *Cinna*):
　Roman politician, of the Popular party.
BOCCHUS:
　King of Mauretania (North Africa).
HARMONY (Marcus Livius *Drusus*):
　Roman politician, associated with the Popular party.
MULE-DRIVER (Gaius *Marius*):
　Roman general, and politician, of the Popular party.
GNAEUS *OCTAVIUS*:
　Roman politician, of the Aristocratic party.
REDHEAD (Publius *Rutilius* Rufus):
　Roman colonial administrator, and politician, opposed by the
　Popular party.
QUINTUS *ROSCIUS* GALLUS:
　Italian actor.
PUBLIUS *SEXTILIUS*:
　Roman governor of the Province of Libya.
The *STAIN* (Lucius Cornelius *Sulla*):
　Roman general, and politician, of the Aristocratic party.
STRYCHNINE (*Mithradates* VI):
　King of Pontus (Asia Minor).

Although Ivory's story is supposed to have been written in Greek,
I have not troubled to give the precise Greek versions of place-
names and personal names (e.g.: 'Aischulos' for 'Aeschylus') as

this can lead to an unpalatable academicism. Nor have I given all the ancient names of places if the modern ones seemed likely to be easier to the reader. This course is open to objections; but any alternative appeared to involve, at some stage, awkward inconsistencies. 'Rome', for example, and 'Athens', are usages that can scarcely be dispensed with: though the inhabitants of those cities, both in ancient times and today, have always had their own notions about what the names ought to be . . .

J. A.

BOOK ONE

The Stain

'The problem of governing this new empire was not wholly mis-understood, though it was by no means solved. The idea of Cato's time that the state should not extend beyond Italy, and that outside that limit a mere protectorate should be exercised, had proved untenable; the necessity of substituting a direct sovereignty, that should preserve the liberties of the various communities, was generally recognized. But this policy was not adopted firmly and uniformly.'

'The family to which Sulla belonged had remained for many generations in comparative obscurity, and his character at first gave no promise of an extraordinary career.

His tastes made him incline to a life of cultivated luxury, some-times descending to debauchery. He was a pleasant companion in city or in camp, and even in the days of the regency would unbend after the business of the day. One of the most curious traits in his character was a vein of cynicism, which showed itself in the play-ful but dangerous irony of many of his acts.

Whenever Sulla and Marius had come into competition the result had always been loss of renown to the elder general, and increase of reputation to the younger.

Sulla's worst fault was the unscrupulous and cynical violence with which his work is defiled.'

Mommsen

1 His Exact Words

What he actually said – his exact words, I have been told;
in his own thunderous language – the blood-fouled old general, seven times consul, Gaius Marius the Mule-driver,
staggering in the last malodorous days of his last term of
office, from his bed to the latrine on swollen septic feet to
heave out his bowels – his life indeed, the undigested in-
digestible gobbets of his failed ambition – from both ends
at the same time (and most of it spattered on his sheets or
his nightshirt before he could get there, according to his doctor
– who ever heard these days of a discreet doctor? they tell
everything to everyone these days in case someone accuses
them of poisoning people) – his exact words were as follows:

'*Inter Arma Silent Leges*': 'Once the weapons are out, the
laws fall silent.' And by god so they do.

Under whatever form of government we are at present
surviving (or will in the future survive, god knows whether
any of us will – at this point I slide my hand under my
shirt-front and finger my private parts beneath the edge of
my desk – there's a furtive superstition it's supposed to
withhold bad luck – in my business we're all superstitious,
it makes more sense than religion) – a democracy? an auto-
cracy? a republican oligarchy? an imperial tyranny? – whatever it may be called, and the theoretical professionals argue
it in-and-out day-by-day in their damned impotence – I
know only the one thing about it that is of any serious
concern to me here as I attempt to compile this record –
fragments of a record – I dare not tempt the future so far as
to call it a *book*! – the non-barbarous nations of the world are
presently experiencing government by informers for informers for the torturers gaolers and hangmen: and nobody
is safe.

I know so much about it because I have been part of it:

and I must be insane to be even thinking of putting pen to paper on the subject.

I have not told my wife what I am doing. She is supposed to believe that my hours in my study are devoted to the regulation of the theatre's profit-and-loss, and the calculation of next season's repertoire, so many productions from the resident company, so many visiting troupes, so many special presentations for municipal festivals and so on – of course she does *not* believe it. But she does not dare enquire and I do not dare tell her. And the rims around her worried eyes are even blacker than the cosmetic she uses to blacken them and to make them seem sensual, untroubled, the calm ox-eyes of a gentle ministrant to the pleasures of decisive men.

If I *could* decide to tell her, perhaps we would both be the happier for it. But then, under torture, who knows what she might reveal? She understands that as well as I do: and therefore will ask no questions.

So why do I write? Write, and then hide the writings?

Perhaps, first, because I have a daughter. It is just possible she will live in a world where people will be able to read about the state of the world she was born into. Of this I have no confidence.

But then again, there is a woman called Irene. Now I do know that Irene is alive after all (I'll explain the 'after all' in due course: if ever I am able to carry the story so far): and maybe she is clever enough to stay alive. Alive, however, where? In the kingdom of Pont. No theoretical problems about the government of Pont. Pont is not pleasant. A voluptuous military despotism; you love it, or leave it – if they let you. Would it endanger Irene to receive these papers? I doubt it. Either she is well enough established in that nerve-racking country to brazen out any diggings-up of her ambivalent past (she is the sort of person to take pride in them, anyway, and even use them to strengthen her position): or she is already in danger, in which case revived memories from the hand of an old friend will make little difference. In any event I don't suppose I will be able to get them to her in the immediate future. I have tried to send her a non-committal message – a hint, as it were, conveyed by word-of-mouth – just to say where I am, whom I am married to, and why . . .

Because of 'the instability' (murder and so forth), it is not yet practicable to post a regular letter, but I daresay my message will eventually reach her. If she replies to it in any hopeful form, I will know whether or not I should make any consequent arrangements about my papers: or even – and god I pray it may not come to that – about my family; about, even, myself.

If she were to give me assurances that we would be safer in Pont than Italy (it is just possible: a hunter's snare would seem safer for a calf than soft quarters in an abattoir – unless the hunter was also a cattle-rustler), then I must persuade myself to trust her (she was never at all trustworthy). Because what other hope would be left? But even so, I am afraid events will by then be moving so quickly that I may have to make more urgent dispositions.

And yet, here I am, a day's journey from the City; and there she is, on the borders of Persia: half the world lies between us. And I dream day and night of bridging it with – with little pieces of my own history, as though I were great Hannibal, after his defeat, before his suicide, putting together (for the intellectual advantage of the next strong conqueror) the complexities of his achievement, good and bad – an exemplar – a monument – oh, at worst, the synopsis of a consoling graveside eulogy.

I have, you see, this perverse idea that Irene ought to be told so many things about me, and how things fell out in my life, because I fear that unless she knows of all these events she will be despising me even more than I deserve: I could not bear to think of her doing that. You see, I must make clear to her to what an extent I was unable to help myself. In due course you'll hear why.

I observe already I'm saying 'you'. But who is 'you? It is not Irene: nor is it my daughter. Nor my wife. And surely it is not the world at large – I envisage no *publication* of my writings, not even private readings to groups of literary connoisseurs, though I do try to keep my Greek prose decorous, if only out of a sense of personal responsibility to the muses. No: I think *you* can only be a part of *me*, the part that used once to live in Ephesus, held the law in (some) respect, was (up to a point) content. I think 'you' need to be informed about what's happened since.

So: I justify myself, to my daughter, to Irene, to my own self. And I put myself in peril by attempting it. I do know that all my life I have taken sudden and unwise decisions, now and then, all in a rush and a flounder, quite against my regular habit of life. In a way it belongs to my superstition, I daresay: the powers that control, if they do control, our good and bad luck, require, now and then, the odd irregular *act* from their creatures to remind them that we *are* creatures with certain inconsistent characteristics, and would they please not continue to treat us as though we were no more than a grazier's livestock in copulating defecating bulk! We did not make ourselves; but being made, we have our dignities, even the silliest amongst us have some little warmth in our clenched hands that derives, at a long remove, from the firebrand of Prometheus (about whom there was a play written, though it would not be suitable, not be safe, for production in my theatre this present season, oh dear no).

In another way my decisions, all arbitrary and self-defeating as they are, must be related to my profession. Comedy. It needs a constant series of reversals of expectation: it needs a constant sense of ill-timed careful timing. If I was at all successful at it, I must have been granted such a sense. No doubt the commencement of this memoir came to my mind as a piece of ludicrous plot-construction to diversify the predictable last act of my life. Who will be there to applaud?

The informers? Well, in order to throw them off whatever scents they can snuff up, I have disguised some names of people and places; though I know very well that informers are never called upon for *proof*. If the papers to hand are not good enough for them, they'll manufacture their own papers – didn't I do it myself? The only important question for them is: against *whom* will they need papers? No-one can foresee that, except god, or gods, or the goddess, or whoever . . . Are there indeed such beings? I have met many who have thought so.

But tap on the wooden top of my desk first with the left hand then with the right, how many times? Say, seven. The stage-manager in Ephesus used to do it three times over, twenty-one in all: but he was, we all said, quite needlessly apprehensive. He once saw three little boys (flying Cupids) fall crash onto the stone-paved stage from the forty-foot crane, and of course it had unnerved him: though not even the licensing authority held him responsible.

The point is, yes it is, and with all these digressions I have been avoiding it like a scorpion in the corner of the bathroom, the point is: I do not know, I do not even dare to know, how many of these corpses every day up and down the streets are to be thought of as in some fashion (if only by default – and 'default', dammit, means de*fault*) my own responsibility.

That unhappy man in Ephesus had to sit in the prompt corner and watch the hawsers of the crane slowly parting high up in the air, there was nothing he could do to avert the appalling accident: he had indented four times for new cords and each time the accountant had vetoed the expenditure: and the backers had gone over his head and insisted on a flying ballet when he swore to the world it was not safe – three screaming naked children, with absurd golden wings on their delicate shoulders, plunging to destruction before the gape of a huge audience (one of them killed outright, one of them a permanent cripple, and the third in a coma for weeks and then only fit for sweeping the dressing-room): and yet he was exonerated.

In my case, they say thousands, thousands upon thousands, in village after village after town after city, to reckon nothing of the One City: and I am not to be exonerated.

Can we make this quite clear? I intended nothing of the sort. Except when, as I have explained, I was in the grip of one of my now-and-then urges – *lusts* would be a better word – to take some immediate and unadvised and would-be-decisive action, I have spent my life doing the next thing to the thing I had been doing: and at the time there seemed no alternative.

So I cannot account for my political history by simply stating how Marius fell out of power and then came back in and sat down to make away with the partisans of Sulla, who in turn came back in to dispose of Marius's people; and that as I was necessarily mixed up with all this (being a taxpayer and thus, it might be thought, an automatic partisan) I pursued my civic duty and assisted the state authorities, insofar as I recognized some of them to be legitimate: and that this assistance, at a time of public crime, inevitably involved me willy-nilly in crime as well.

The point is, I recognized none of them, I was a partisan of neither faction, I did *not* want them to rule over me: or over anyone else. Yet I seemed to have helped them both to perpetrate what they have perpetrated. If you find me speaking now and again, with the discomfortable jocosity so common among subject peoples, of Gaius Marius as 'the Mule-driver', of Lucius Cornelius Sulla as 'the Stain', don't let it deceive you. No bonhomie is intended. They are *not* 'dear old fellows', uncles of the commonwealth. They are – were – only one of them so far is dead – brimstone out of Tartarus and ought never to have been permitted by humankind to erupt themselves amongst us.

As I say, I did permit. And in order to show how, I must go back a few years – say, ten years or so, god I don't remember, but about ten. Recapture what happened at Ephesus. Bits of it. In the days when the laws were not silent: at least, I thought not. And it seems to me that what people think about the laws is more effective than what the laws actually are. If you believe yourself secure, you will in fact be secure. Up to a point.

Let me remember about that point.

2   *A Birthday and Some Games*

It was the point that confronted me a few days before my thirty-fifth birthday. Word came to Ephesus that the army was marching in: and the word alone, long before any soldiers were visible, long before any dust from their boot-nails was kicked up along the distant road, the word alone abolished law. Nor was it even the army of an enemy. Our magnanimous protectors put some regiments into column-of-route: and that was the end of our grasshopper Greek lives. Ants, you see (remembering your Aesop), are not only diligent: they are also damned frightening and they march in column-of-route, they do not need to be *seen* in order to overcome, only to be *heard of*. Here is how I heard of them.

I must tell you first who I was. What I did. Where.

I was content in the town of Ephesus. Beautiful spring weather, strong sunshine. I rented a pair of rooms in the portico of the theatre – well, not exactly in the portico, under a penthouse attached to the building next door, you could walk from one to the other without going more than two yards into the open street. A position to have potential clients come to me instead of my being forced to go in search of them. I operated as an agent for actors, dancers, musicians and the like, occasionally circus-artists: the theatre porch was their market-place, where they put themselves on hire and were brought into contact with managers and impresarios from both Ephesus itself and the country-towns within a distance of up to fifty or sixty miles inland. There was also a good deal of business done with Samos and Icaria and several of the other islands.

The theatre itself was a municipal enterprise and really rather too grand for the sort of performers I normally dealt in: but now and then I was able to help them to someone unexpectedly recondite and valuable, and my relations with the administration there were on the whole good. For special festival presentations at the theatre, or at the temple of the Mother of Ephesus, with large choruses and troops of extras, I could rely on being called upon to furnish whole wagon-loads of part-time personnel.

I also did a slightly shady but remunerative business in girls and boys for grandees' private parties: but I was in no way a vulgar pimp. They had to be more than sexual receptacles, I insisted on properly-trained artists – flute-players, singers, tightrope-dancers – and I had to be assured of their talents in such lines before I would allow them on my books. Prostitutes plain and simple could be obtained from any one of a hundred hags and ruffians up and down the town.

I had given up the stage myself about five years earlier,

after the accident that dislocated my hip, and made me unfit for any characters except aged beggars and wounded soldiers. It was no spectacular dramatic catastrophe, like the breaking of the crane-ropes I have already mentioned: indeed it had caused the biggest laugh of the show, and at the time I had even laughed at it myself. What happened was this: we were playing a silly farce in a little backwoods fit-up theatre in central Anatolia. As usual I had a woman's role – the dimwit tart who is always finding herself in the wrong gentleman's bedroom, and being hidden in closets, rolled up in laundry, and sat upon in sofas.

In one scene I had to make a quick getaway from a balcony by a rope-ladder that wasn't there, and land with a lot of squawking and splashing in a coincidentally-placed tub of water. The idiot who should have unhooked the ladder had been so full of himself after a round of applause he had extracted for a totally unauthorized ad-lib with his leather phallus, that he forgot all about it, and made his exit from the top level of the stage-booth without any of the concomitant business needed to set the scene for my episode.

So out I came as rehearsed, puffing and blowing, my artificial tits billowing every which-way, I vaulted the balcony rail with exactly the technique I knew would get me safe into the tub without being hurt: I caught my left foot in the bloody rungs of that damned ladder.

I fell all askew, cut my jaw on the edge of the tub, broke a wrist under my elbow: and discovered when I tried to stand up that something had gone really wrong with my leg where it joins onto the pelvis. I thought for a few days that it was only a strain. I gradually came to realize it was permanent: and very sadly, very very sadly (for I rejoiced in physical comedy, the setting-up of a whole sequence of somersaults, farts, kicks in the stomach, verbal gags and double-takes and drunken totterings, to build the laughter stage-by-stage until the final explosion: the delight of getting it *right*. I loved it), I allowed myself to be persuaded to change my whole manner of life.

I had tended to despise agents. But they *are* part of the theatre: and a necessary part: and indeed there is much real pleasure to be obtained from the work they do. I have tried to accommodate myself.

I rented these rooms in Ephesus and looked up all my old contacts. It was difficult enough at first, but after a year or so I began imperceptibly to make ends meet and to achieve a small reputation. Small enough, and I won't deny it: but I could flatter myself that I was *known*. My one problem was that I never seemed to make enough money at any one time to be able to invest it to permanent advantage. I did back a few shows not always with bad results: but in the end I made the cardinal mistake of putting all my profits in one lump into a troupe of very high-class ballet-dancers who were setting off to tour the western provinces of Persia, just as all of Armenia, Cappadocia and Galatia erupted into full-scale war. The dancers were trapped beyond the fighting and never came back. I heard that they had all been taken onto the regular entertainment-strength of the Great King's local satrap, which was a relief to me from the personal point of view – many of them were my close friends – but of course every penny had disappeared with them for ever.

My only piece of realizable property remaining in Ephesus (which I had absolutely no intention of turning into cash) was a young woman bequeathed to me from the effects of a dead tragedian (a man called the Raven) whom I had handled for about twelve months. He had bought her as a child and trained her to play the pipe-and-tabor for an accompaniment to his solo recitatives, which had been in great demand at the more cultural kind of banquet. She was very skilful at this, and had taken the trouble to learn all the Raven's speeches, and a good many others besides. She could deliver them with great ferocity and he sometimes used her as a speaking partner in dialogue passages (in the Greek language only. He was a considerable polyglot: but he wanted no rival – least of all his own pupil – in *that* particular field).

She was a soft-footed, round-headed, straight-necked black girl, born, so she believed, far to the south of Upper Egypt. She could barely remember – had probably never

really learnt – her native tongue; and in all respects, save
for her colour, she seemed as Greek as you or I. (You will
discover later on just how Greek *I* can claim to be). Her
real name was unpronounceable anywhere down-river from
the first cataracts of the Nile. We called her Cuttlefish in
the profession – for her clinging affections, her sudden
rapidity of movement and mood alternating with long per-
iods of deceptive placid drifting; and, of course, for her dark
skin, impregnate, as it were, with her own self-concealing ink.

She and I lived together as man and wife. Our home was
the inner of my two rooms: the outer room was my office. I
usually saw clients in the street or the portico, but I needed
somewhere to keep the books. Cuttlefish acted as my secretary: very competent in general, though if she disapproved of
any particular transaction she had a bad habit of sabotaging
the book-keeping on it and ultimately making me so tired of
trying to sort it out that I would cease to pursue the matter.

She had had her face under the cheekbones cut into tribal
marks when she was a baby. This sometimes had an alarming effect upon strangers, but when you knew her you no
longer noticed it. She had no idea what the scars signified.
She thought she remembered her mother with the same
disfiguration, or was it her mother? She could not be certain. The first years of her life were so very confused for
her: she hated to talk about them. Whatever had happened,
and a great deal must have happened between the hidden
rivers of deep Africa and the crowded childrens' pen – as
squalid as a cow-byre – in the market of Antioch where the
Raven had so happily taken note of her, it had terrified her
out of her memory and there was nothing more to be said.

She had only commenced to become a human being, she
supposed, at about the age of five. Prior to that – a black
Ethiop, blameless, stark naked, beloved of god: but outside
the rim of the world.

I ought to be getting on to my birthday and the news of
the marching ants. But recollection of my Cuttlefish is working through all my nerves, disorders my literary instinct,
with a dredging at sexual memories, grapnels in the valves
of my heart – I have to say some more about her first.

It was over eighteen months since Raven had died and left her to me: the proviso in his will had been not a little disconcerting.

My esteemed assistant *Cuttlefish*, inasmuch as she has no immediate prospect of marriage by reason of the intense selfishness with which I have held her so many years to myself and the pursuit of my art, should not be afforded her immediate liberty (as otherwise I would have wished) lest she fall into the power of unscrupulous persons and become even less capable of exercising free choice as to her manner of life than her present condition prescribes.

I therefore most earnestly request my friend colleague and business-agent – known in the profession as *Ivory* (from the colour of the girls' masks he commonly assumed when he too trod the boards) – to accept full responsibility for the aforesaid *Cuttlefish* with the ultimate intention of freeing her as soon as he can conscientiously take oath before a competent magistrate that he is capable of vouching that she will be properly provided for.

I am aware, and have long been aware, though no-one knows I have been aware, that certain surreptitious carnal passages have already taken place between the aforesaid *Ivory* and *Cuttlefish* the aforesaid. I pride myself, however, that I have been, as an interpretative artist, at all times responsive to the emotional requirements of the poets I have honoured in my repertoire – the majestic Aeschylus, the profound Sophocles, Euripides the ever-ambiguous, and, in the Latin tongue to which these debased days have regrettably and politically compelled us, the not-inconsiderable Ennius and Pacuvius – and I have thus conditioned myself to transmute my own temporary passions – in particular the rage of jealousy – into the material of my work, and have allowed them no access among the companions of my private life.

Let *Ivory* take care that he cherish this girl as ardently and firmly as he has already pledged to her: in such fashion he will amply render me his posthumous reparation for the usurpation of my bed. He may not know it, but I loved her: and still shall: and if ghosts walk, as many distinguished philosophers have maintained, mine will be unerringly watchful for the felicity of my *Cuttlefish*.

Let her play the pipe-and-tabor (air: 'Agamemnon's Triumph') at my funeral obsequies: and let her also declaim a portion of the chorus from *The Suppliants* of Aeschylus: beginning –

> O mountain land of Argos, whose great king
> Protects our suppliant plight, where shall we fly?
> What pitchy cave will hide our heads of terror?

down to –

> I had rather on the gallows hug with Death
> And tumble with him in the straining noose
> Than launch a hated husband at my flesh:
> Sooner than man-sperm, sterile bone of Death!

If she can utter that without faltering in the presence of *Ivory*, and if *Ivory* can hear her and embrace her afterwards in all sincerity, I shall know in the Further World that my trust is not misplaced. If not: then they deserve each other, let their pains be no greater than mine.

Item: I also give and bequeath to my friend colleague and business-agent – known in the profession as *Ivory* etcetera – my mask of *Heracles Raving,* as a keepsake; my working scripts, as written out in her own hand by the *Cuttlefish*; two small frying-pans and the oil-bottle with the green glass stopper: and all feminine effects, trinkets, and fal-de-lals bought at any time by me for *Cuttlefish*'s pleasure and still fit for her use.

He had had the assistance of no lawyer to construct this document, I could see that well enough: and the expression on the face of the attorney who read it out to the assembled friends, relatives, dependants and servants, would have made a comic mask in itself.

As for me, Raven's mischievous perversity had exactly the effect it was presumably designed to: I did not know where to look, most certainly I could not meet the wide eyes of the Cuttlefish, and afterwards I had great difficulty in speaking to her. She likewise. We had both been so sure that our heated little assignations had been kept thoroughly secret, and I think neither of us had considered them anything more than instantaneous satisfactions of a transient desire. Now, however, we were forced to enter into a relationship of a far more inclusive nature. How well we succeeded in this will appear in due course.

On the whole, though, we retained more harmony than distemper in our inevitably confined cohabitation. We decided from the beginning that she was not to be made pregnant: I could not cope with children. Two rooms, reduced business, an extremely uncertain future ... let alone all the legal problems about status and citizenship. She said, 'My mother was commercial property and they sold me away from her: they had the right to, you see. I'm opening no doors to the same thing happening again. If it does I will tell the Raven. He'll know what to do about it.' Well, yes, a sort of joke, she said it snuggled up to me, running her finger-nail across the back of my neck. But I could not deny that it was a joke with a hard edge to it: we agreed to leave it alone, and we did not speak of it again. I knew she had told me her mind. I had no wish to challenge it.

I don't need to say anything more now about the Cuttle-fish.

Right then, my birthday. I thought it would be pleasant to look out as many of my old friends as I could find at that time in Ephesus and invite them to a small party. We would have an after-dinner cabaret, highly extravagant – there was a trio of young Syrians, sisters, who performed in a very spare costume – jewels in their navels, veils across their faces, ankle-bells, now and then transparent trousers, that's all. I had seen their act and marked it down as ideal for 'a small audience that knew how to behave itself'. Poetic dances and postures, to be contemplated at length by sensual but cultivated men who felt at peace with the world. They were between engagements and, as they were on my own books, I might manage to persuade them to accept a reduced fee ... Well, maybe not. Anyway, find some guests.

I took my stick and limped out.

The first I ran into was an old fellow called Shoulderbone – a more or less retired actor-manager who had given me my start in the profession, and to whom I had always felt a particular debt of gratitude. He had just emerged from the stage-door of the theatre, and looked very grim. I told him about the birthday.

'Oh yes: oh yes? Thirty-five? Half-way through life, unless you live longer than any actor has a right to these days. You have climbed, my dear child; and now you can go nowhere but down. Syrians, with little ankle-bells? Why not? Oh why not indeed? When we've all of us enjoyed them we can take them around the block and chop them into bleeding cutlets.'

'What on earth are you talking about? I always thought these eastern women appealed to you – *thought* they did? – I *know* they did – remember that time in Smyrna with the Sidonian contortionist, you missed three whole performances because you couldn't unwind yourself from her – '

'Dear child, this is no occasion for your complacent greenroom humour. Don't you know what's been happening in there?' He jerked his thumb towards the theatre, and spat viciously into the dust. After a few ponderous but vague denunciations of the age and the men who made it, he condescended to tell me his news.

It appeared that he had entered into a verbal agreement to play a small role ('a cameo, dear child, but a rich one, very rich: they won't have it that I have the stamina for a leading-man any more: but I do know my own value, and so, I fondly believed, did they') in a new comedy that was about to go into rehearsal. He had just now called in to the manager's office to complete the contract, only to be told that the production was cancelled. ('Cancelled! I said, my dear sir, I had your word that the engagement was positive: your word, sir, as between gentlemen. You cannot mean *cancelled*. *Postponed*, I would accept . . .'). The theatre people were in fact as angry and distressed as he was, though you wouldn't know it, the way he vilified them.

The root of the trouble was finance: they owed an enormous amount of back-taxes to the provincial governor's treasury. They had been ludicrously over-assessed, and were confident that their formal appeal, put through the correct channels nearly a year ago, would in the end be upheld. So of course they hadn't paid. Now, all of a sudden, and with absolutely no chance of staving it off, the officials in charge had sent in their 'security-enforcement' to seize all the moveables on the premises, and – quite without rhyme or reason (for how could the theatre pay its debts unless it could achieve audiences?) – had ordered the freezing of all contracts until the money was forthcoming.

This was the point beyond which the law in Ephesus ceased to have meaning, though I did not of course realize it just then. What I did realize, as I put my head through the stage-door, was that a peculiar violation of our profession and its established domicile was unaccountably taking place. The stage was littered with costumes, musical instruments and heaps of gaudy furniture, some of the actors and backstage staff were standing around in knots, their faces pale, their hands gesturing in frustrated frenzy, while a number of wooden-visaged jacks-in-office from the revenue department were taking inventories, pricing items, and throwing valuable material onto the heaps with no regard for possible damage. I saw two of them hauling out the beautiful tapestried screen, all hung with little glass mirrors, that had been used as the background to the *Marriage of the Amazons* ballet, I knew it had cost a fortune. They pitched it down into the orchestra, it caught on the rim of the stage, the cloth ripped into a wicked three-cornered tear, and an entire cluster of mirrors cracked and smashed against the marble. One of the enforcement-men kicked it back into place with his hobnailed boot and broke off a gilded ornament from the edge of the frame. Superintending this barbarity was a stout man with documents clipped onto a board. He saw me and waddled over to me, irritably flapping his bunch of papers towards my face.

'No, no, out you go, no-one allowed in here except registered employees and the responsible officials – responsible officials – why isn't there a guard on that door? – you, stand at the door and keep all of these people out.'

I reluctantly retreated, and the door was slammed behind me. A heavy-set thug took post upon the threshold, his arms folded across his chest cradling his government-issue bludgeon.

Shoulderbone shrugged: 'You need not have bothered: I could have forewarned you what would happen if you tried to go in. They threw *me* out of the office before I'd even said the half of what I was proposing to tell them.'

'But, surely, they can't do this? This sort of thing hasn't been legal since, since, oh since I was a boy. Oh I know it always used to be the usual practice, but surely, surely, it's all been changed. I remember Redhead himself told me personally that it was all changed. He told me personally when I went to see him about the choirmen for his public festival – I'd had a bit of trouble with my own arrears of stamp-duty on a whole load of artists' contracts, I thought a word in the right ear at the right time – he told me personally: and he told me the truth. Those arrears were all nonsense and I never had to pay them.'

'Redhead,' said my old friend solemnly, 'Redhead was a gentleman. His word was his bond.'

'What do you mean, *was*? Is he dead? Why haven't I heard?'

'Because no-one has heard, dear child, except those bastards in there and the bloodsuckers who give them their orders. Oh yes, they told *me*. They had to tell me something to get me out of the building. Burn the bastards' balls off. Redhead has been recalled!'

I should explain at this point that Redhead was a Roman. A senior administrator of the Province of Asia in which we all dwelt and did our best to pretend we had no knowledge of its existence. He was one of the very few Romans that any of us had ever been given cause to respect. He was, as Shoulderbone said, a gentleman, entirely honest, devoid of rapacity. Single-handed, more or less, he had reformed our entire revenue service. If we did not, theoretically, recognize the right of his City to govern us, at least we had been able for some considerable time to recognize him, in practical terms, as a person to whom it was no disgrace to afford obedience. He had almost made some of us believe that government was essentially benign: and now, decent man, he was recalled.

'For god's sake, why?'

'Dear child, they have laid charges against him, in the City: malversation of public funds, embezzlement, bribery, god knows what.'

'Nonsense!'

'Of course it's nonsense: all of their politics is nonsense. I thought you knew that already.'

'But he cannot be guilty – Redhead? Not on your life.'

'Not a question of *my* life. *His*. Impartial though he may have appeared to us while he was here, he was a member of a party: appointed here by his party: and his party is out of power.'

'Do you know what was his party?'

'Does it matter? That republic of theirs is founded on some sort of principle of eternal irrigation as befits their drear ambition to be military engineers and nothing else: one bucket down the well, one bucket up. When the one at the bottom comes up, the one at the top has to drop. One of them's called "we've-got-it" and the other one "we-mean-to-have-it". Redhead was able to be honest because his people were we've-got-it. Now the other ones want their chance. They are reforming the corrupt echelons of privilege and power; of bloodsucking and trample-the-public-face: so they have to trample *our* face to prove to their under-privileged voters that they mean business. They begin by getting rid of anyone who thinks different. And this' – (jerking his thumb again and spitting as before) – 'this is only the start of it. Oh it's no use you tickling your wee prick, my dear child – ' (I hastily withdrew my hand from inside my clothes: not pleasant to have one's superstitions observed, even by a friend) ' – if the bad times are coming onto us, there's nothing your fingers can do to rub them away.'

I was still bewildered. His analysis of the City's party-system may have been accurate but it was scarcely en-lightening: what Roman voter can actually have *desired* the dissolution of our theatre? For what reason? Was it believed to be *subversive*, that they needed to close it?

'Oh no, not *close* it, no no no – don't you see, they put the pressure on to have it open again *for their own purposes*?'

'Purposes?'

'Cutlets, bloody cutlets, what did I tell you? Bring out your little Syrians, chop them up into the smoking sand. Sword-fighters, net-and-trident butchers, hooligans from the steppes of Scythia hacking at bears and crocodiles with slash-hooks and sledge-hammers. If there's anyone in the gaols whom they don't want to go to the trouble of feeding any longer, fetch 'em out, strip their clothes, watch how

long it takes a squad of lions to finish 'em off. Have you
ever seen a lion pulling his meat out of a live man's rib-
cage? It it's a woman, how much the better: hang her up by
one foot from a pole and have half-a-score of famished
wolves leaping on step-ladders to see can they grab at her
paps. Oh yes, the Roman Games: men and beasts and beasts
and men, and after three hours of it, who's going to be able
to tell the difference between them?'

I was so shocked I became tongue-tied, just as I used to
when I was a boy. 'But, but, but this is a – a – theatre –
we – '

'It is a theatre not a fighting-ring: it is a theatre where
there are to be no plays!' He crouched violently towards me
and entered into a ferocious stage-whisper (First Murderer
from *The Death of Ibycus* revealing the plot to his confederate): 'Except in so far as some dreadful pantomime from
Corinth – from the garrison theatre, would you believe? –
have you heard of them, "The Five Hot Pockets"? – except
in so far as they are being brought in to perform *Eros in
Spring* as a series of interludes while the blood is being
sluiced out of the orchestra.'

'*Eros in Spring?* What's that?'

'Bucks and does, boars and sows, stallions and mares, all
the four-footed folk of moor and marshland doing what
they do in the green of the year. Can't you just imagine
it?'

Yes, I had heard of 'The Five Hot Pockets'. Two couples,
of indeterminate sex, and one left over; they wore an assort-
ment of animal masks and performed stuffed with aphrodisiac to ensure that nothing was simulated. The only element of drama in their shows was who was going to get the
one left over and by means of which orifice. They were the
personal property of a wealthy ship-chandler who had been
run out of the Province by Redhead's office for supplying
putrid salt pork to the fleet. He had tried once to have me
find engagements for them and Cuttlefish had persuaded
me to be unsuccessful in my search. But, a garrison theatre?
Had he sold them to the army? And if he had, why should
the army – ? But, surely –

'Will you stop saying *surely*! You stand there with your

mouth open like the very first time I ever put you on a stage and you forgot every word of your part. Surely what, boy, surely *what*?' He was beginning to shout and quite a crowd had collected. A small man of the name of Jampot who ran a very disreputable agency from a booth in a nearby back-alley was standing at my elbow. I moved away from him and he sneered at me. I recollected that he had for a time handled the 'Pockets' on behalf of the corrupt chandler. I tried to get some final sense from the apoplectic Shoulderbone.

'But who's going to buy tickets? It costs so much a seat to keep this theatre out of the red, we both know that, if they lower the prices for the class of crowd that want that class of show – '

'Oh there'll always be such a crowd, always some foul audience for cruelty and shit if you take the trouble to scoop deep enough!'

'No, you don't take my point: the cost of admission – '

Then Jampot put in his oar: 'I don't think you'll find there's going to be any costs of admission. They distribute the tickets buckshee to the soldiers on payday: two to each man so they all bring their little friends. I've got a bulk invoice for twelve-year-old Armenians in my office this minute. Don't you know there's a war on?'

So that was it. That was the news. There was the explanation that poor old muddled Shoulderbone had not managed to elucidate. The Roman Army was coming in through the Province into Ephesus for the first time for forty years: and we would have to accommodate it. Some general had won a victory, out east, where I had lost my ballet-dancers: from what Jampot was saying it was apparent that the Armenians had suffered. If he was importing children, there must also be a large number of captive adults. I thought of the wolves and lions: I thought of Cuttlefish and the Antioch market-place.

I wondered what sort of man the general would be. Whatever was going on among the administration at this juncture, it would have to be put a stop to, before our entire profession along the coast was utterly ruined. Tax-racketeers *and* the military: we could never cope with both at once. In my lifetime we had never had to. It was, I thought, just possible that the general might not be personally responsible. Could not someone make some careful approaches to him? I had a vague idea he was known as 'the Stain', which sounded sinister: it certainly did not suggest another Redhead. I said as much to Shoulderbone, dropping my voice. He looked warily at Jampot.

'Not here, dear child, too much dog-dung on the steps of this portico. We'll talk about it at your party. I've no doubt you'll be inviting the right sort of people: I can give you a few names of one or two whom I know will be in town. We won't do this through the Guild. It affects far more artists than the high-falutin classical bastards in this theatre here. Legit *and* non-legit: I'll give you a few names . . . Back-taxes indeed; I've never heard of such a pretext. In my small opinion, there is vindictive jealousy here at work.' He still seemed to half-believe the whole affair had been set up in order to deprive him of his cameo-role: I watched him stumble furiously away down the street, spluttering and muttering, his hunched right shoulder casting its lumpy shadow on the white walls as he went.

My old friend had perhaps forgotten: but he ought to have known that I knew rather more about back-taxes than most people would have suspected. Back-taxes, cruelty, shit. Devote a few pages to remind myself how.

3   Memories of Tax-avoidance

I was only thirteen when I ran away from home in order to become an actor.

My father was a tax-collector. He called it the 'civil service'. He was in fact a commercial speculator who bought the right to collect taxes from a given area of the Province at whatever rate he saw fit to impose upon the public. All that government required of him was that the money he sent in to head-office should equal the amounts voted in the annual budget of the One City – he called it the Great City, so greedily and self-importantly, though I never heard he had ever been there. He said the civil service always used such a term.

Our home was in a small town not very far from Pergamus. Pergamus had once been the capital of the kings who had sold us to Rome. Now it was a regional administrative centre for the northern half of Asia.

My father said he was a sort of Arab; my mother was half-Persian, half-Greek-Paphlagonian, a very stilted person, not at all agreeable. My schoolfellows said my father had bought her out of a brothel in settlement of the proprietor's revenue-debts. I became extremely tired of being the son of the most unpopular man in the district.

One day, I spent an afternoon's truancy watching a comedy performed by a professional touring company in a village-square down the next valley but one. I never dared attend any public entertainment in our town, the best I could hope for if I did was to be stoned on the way home, and at worst I would be humiliatingly ordered out by the organizers in the middle of the show because I was creating a riot simply by being there.

On this particular day, when the play was over, I was none too anxious to set out for home until the sun began to set. I might meet the schoolmaster, who would flog me the next morning, and, moreover, be strongly supported for it by my father. ('Discipline must be maintained, government servants have an example to set. You and I, boy, *and* your elder brother – and why in god's name don't you cultivate his company, he could teach you so much? – we are the only three men in this town who can honestly claim to be more than mere provincials. I was *posted* here, dammit. Why, even the mayor is a native. So's the police-chief, and he's supposed to be *my* man, dammit.')

The elder brother was already at work as assistant in the tax-office, doing very well out of it, thank you very much. He kept a smelly yellow-skinned slant-eyed dwarf whom he had acquired as a part of a transaction with a camel-train operator, something to do with the latter's road-user's duty. The dwarf spoke no word of any known language but was adept at applying tourniquets of knotted string to the temples of suspected tax-evaders when the security-enforcement brought them in to my father's 'back room'. My father had the highest opinion of my brother's initiative and went out of his way to reward him by finding him a wife, the daughter of a colleague from Mytilene over the water ('good for your career, boy, and warm enough, greasy enough, dammit, to keep you out of disease-ridden dives where they'll know you for a civil servant and try to take advantage'). She was a very superior young lady who never condescended to notice me. She and my mother did not get on. She shared some secret with the dwarf. They used to go into the 'back room' to confer about it when the house was supposedly empty (I could be very self-effacing when I chose). She would whisper: and he would bark what sounded like abrupt orders in his outlandish tongue. It was a change from the squeals of pain that usually came out from behind that ill-omened small door. Sometimes she would seem to be singing to him. Such noises never came from the room she shared with my brother. It was all very odd. I used to think about telling my brother. I used to hug the thought and roll it about in my mind. But I was too fearful of the dwarf to pursue the notion any further.

If I got home from the play successfully my father would give me a sick-note for the schoolmaster in order to show the schoolmaster that the civil service can look after its own. He would of course flog me himself. But he did not hurt. The dwarf would have hurt. He would not use the dwarf on me, though, because that would degrade the civil service, or at any rate degrade the posteriors of a son of the civil service: and the provincials might get to hear of it.

But I did not get home successfully. I had to hang around the village so long waiting for dusk that I felt it necessary to drop in to the wine-shop in case people started asking questions. This was, I well knew, part of my father's catchment-area. I had just enough money saved (stolen: abstracted from the kitchen dresser when the cook was, as usual, drunk) for one cup of wine. There was a middling crowd of country people there who had come to see the play and to celebrate the religious festival of which it made part. Outside in the dusty square the actors were dismantling their stage and awnings, and packing up costumes and masks into exciting hampers. Seven of them – three men, and two boys; and two young women who had not acted in the play itself (the female roles had been played by the boys) but had done a song-and-dance act with tambourines during the intervals, for which they had not worn masks. I thought them friendly jolly girls it would be good to talk to: though when they all came into the wine-shop and sat down in a laughing chattering huddle I was far too nervous to approach them.

I was at a table by myself at one corner of the terrace, half-hidden by a screen of poles with vines straggling across and over it. Not the most comfortable place – the waiter kept pushing past me on his way in and out of the bar, and a lot of men came backing against my table with their cups in their hands, as they crowded round the rustic repartee that was going on between the more important villagers (official hosts to the entertainers) and the theatre company. There was roaring and shoving, the more boisterous as it grew darker. The waiter stood on my table without apology to hang a bunch of lanterns from the trellis. Inside the bar an argument was going on, getting louder and louder. Rude agricultural voices denounced the state fiscal system: I felt it was high time for me to leave.

But every now and then I could catch a glimpse of one or other of the dancing-girls through the vine-leaves and thronging elbows: they were laughing and sweating and drinking, so much at ease with all these raucous men that I felt tortured and delighted all at the same time.

And pefectly incapable of getting up to go.

'You seem to have a nice little corner to yourself, do you mind if I join you?' I turned round in a panic. It was one of the actors, a youngish man with long dark hair who had played the extortionate Parasite – a character that might have been modelled feature by feature upon my own brother, with certain traits of my father thrown in. He looked tired and held a large jug of wine, from which he was drinking very thirstily. 'You saw the show, yes? Of course you did – front row, stage-right, and when Chloe came round with the tambourine for contributions, you pretended you'd lost a button or something and went down on all fours. Yet you were clapping and laughing more than anyone else. What's the matter with you people here – don't you believe in paying good money for good work? Oh I'm sorry, I've embarrassed you – why would you have any money? You slipped away from school or the boss's shop-counter, don't tell me, I know the story. No, tell me though – you saw the show – did you really enjoy it?'

'Oh yes,' I said, 'yes . . . yes . . .' I began to stammer. 'It was *wonderful*,' I said. He looked at me carefully, as though suspecting me of laughing at him.

'You really thought so? Yes, you did, you did really think so. Tell me, it's nice and quiet here, we don't have to join the boys and girls in all the brawling and I'm far too fagged anyway – tell me: do you see a lot of shows? Have you standards of comparison? You're obviously an educated man.' I was most obviously by no means a man, educated or otherwise: and I could not decide whether he was now laughing at *me*, or merely being kind and trying to put me at ease. It turned out to be the latter. For half an hour we talked theatre together – I gave him the benefit of my immature opinions and criticisms, indeed (how it shames me now to admit it) I ventured to offer him a number of my imitations of actors I had seen at different times over the years. In return he told me extraordinary stories about life in the profession: he was getting a little high on the wine he kept gulping down, and his anecdotes became more and more scandalous. His voice dropped to an intimate malicious murmur and he kept filling my cup from his jug. I wonder now, was he trying to seduce me? I was really very innocent. My involuntary role as pariah of the community had prevented my being initiated into the sexual confidences and tentative activities of boys of my own age, and nobody had ever visited the house who had not talked exclusively about money, administration and status.

This actor was the first person who actually spoke to me like a friend. If there was anything more to it, it completely passed me by.

The moon came up, very large, very low, a bright golden shield in the sky over the thatched gable of the little shrine across the square. Two dogs down the empty street started to fight. The crowd in the wine-shop surged and bellowed and a line of men stood up to dance with white handkerchiefs in their hands. The two theatre-girls clattered their tambourines for them. Then the girls began to sing – a high-pitched erotic song – something about –

> Herostratus: how long and how far
> Will you carry your crackling fire
> Herostratus away from my bed?
> Herostratus I am shaking and trembling
> Unscorched yet such hope for your kindling,
> Untouched in the dark by your torch
> Its long flame, its red head
> Herostratus don't you hear what I said – ?
> I want you now Herostratus, here, here
> To my neck to my breast to my mouth, to my eyelid my ear –
> O my dear do not fear
> I want you now to my hand my wet cunt I can't wait:
> Herostratus come soon Herostratus
> It will soon be too late . . . !

– and so on – on and on – the two voices wailing and yearning: one of them (Chloe, a tall dark woman who swayed about rolling her head up and down to swing her black glistening hair in front of her face and over her bosom) howled out the 'Herostratus' repetitions with a vast distortion of the long vowels – 'Hai-ai-airo-straa-aa-aaa-tus . . .!': and the other one (Irene, my new friend had told me she was called: a small twisting orange-haired creature with prominent pale eyes) listed the parts of the body (hundreds of them as the song progressed, all equally craving for Herostratus, and always concluding with the same one, and a great gasp) in short exclamatory pants and grunts: and then together they sang the intermediate lines, Irene putting in the high notes, Chloe growling the low ones, until one might have thought there was an entire chorus at work. I had never heard anything like it, except now and then when a Phrygian funeral passed the house.

If this was what love was all about to adults it seemed

incredibly desolate and awful: I was not at all sure I wanted
to have anything to do with it: I could not reconcile it with
the bouncings-about and buttock-slappings and tumblings-
upon-bolsters that had made up so great a part of the play I
had just seen.

All round the terrace the men were clapping their hands
to the rhythm of the song: there was a breathlessness, a sort
of dangerous tension growing appreciably throughout the
crowd as though they knew something was going to happen
that ought not to be happening in a well-conducted community but they couldn't stop it and didn't want to stop it.
I was all of a sudden very frightened and aware, all of a
sudden, that I had got helplessly drunk. I was horrified
that these two obviously warm-hearted girls should be singing so demonstratively of such profound and private
emotions in the midst of so many crude strangers. I hated
them for their insensitivity, I hated their audience for goad-
ing them on to it, I hated myself that I had been too shy to
make friends with them earlier, so that I could have withdrawn them from this atmosphere: I stood up to plunge
away on my own and unobserved into the darkness, tripped
heavily over a stool, clung to one of the trellis-poles to save
myself, and started to be sick.

I was revolvingly aware that the young actor was still
beside me and was holding my head. I muttered something
to him – 'go away, bugger off, leave me alone' – something
very far from gracious: and then I slumped down and passed
out.

When I next looked about me it was bright daylight and
for a while I could not assemble myself, where I was or
how I came there.

I was in fact on a pile of sacks, on the ground, under the
actors' wagon. It was parked in a scrubby field a little way
outside the village, the mule that hauled it was grazing in
the middle distance with a hobble on its legs, two or three
of the company were lying stridently asleep beside me; and
Chloe, looking very pulled-about and cross-tempered, was
attending to a camp-fire with a kettle hung over it. I sat up
cautiously: she saw me.

'Oh,' she said, 'there you are. One of you's awake at any rate. Here, come and blow at these twigs, boy. Come on, boy, look sharp, can't you, where the hell is that Irene, we're supposed to be on the road already, will you look where the bloody sun's got to.'

'Will you look,' she said again, and started tugging at the legs of the man next to me, 'will you look at the bloody sun, we'll never get to where we're going to, you'd think it was for our entertainment, not theirs, we spend all night doing this and that.' I felt mazy in the head and not at all clear what she thought about me, whether she knew who I was, or whether she was so used to seeing new faces under the wheels of a morning that she had ceased to enquire. I knelt at the fire and blew. The ash came up into my face and I coughed and spluttered.

An elderly man with a sharp nose and a crooked shoulder – I recognized him as the Miser in the comedy, the one whose daughter was always running away with debauched young noblemen – put his head out from the tilt of the wagon.

'Where the hell is Irene?' he said. 'And will you look at that bloody sun.' He saw me. 'Oh,' he said, 'there you are. So you stayed after all.' I goggled at him. He laughed. 'I am informed by my young friend Proteus that you showed some concern for an entry into the profession.' His voice had suddenly become ponderous and rhetorical: he adopted a deliberate pose. Although he was unshaven and in his underwear, he was definitely impressive. 'Of course,' he continued, 'my acceptance of your talents is conditional upon confirmation by the execrable Ganymede of his resignation from my troupe. Ganymede, I speak to you! Wake him up.'

Chloe gave a sharp poke with a stick of firewood into the ribs of a boy who was curled snoring under a blanket. He sat up and scowled.

'Ganymede,' said the elderly man, 'you told me yesterday you had had a better offer in Sardis. Is that still true today, or were you merely endeavouring more than usually to aggravate my mistrust of you?' The boy looked at Chloe, looked at me, looked at his master.

'Bellerophon the fire-eater needs a patter-boy for his act.
He's paying twenty-five which is three more than I get from
you even at the top of the season. I was out of my appren-
ticeship two and a half months ago. You can't hold me so
don't try it.'

'My dear child, I have no intention of trying it, still less
of succeeding. I don't like you, you see: and yesterday, *twice*,
you cut in on me before the laugh came. Sardis lies *that*
way: our road, *this*. Here's your money, count it, it's all
there.' (He whisked out a handful of coins from nowhere in
particular with the panache of a conjurer). 'Eat fire to your
heart's content, and when friend Bellerophon gets too drunk
to do more than set light to his waistcoat, heap coals of it
upon your head and remember where you would have got
to had you had more than one half-ounce of basic human
gratitude! Stupid infant – go!' Ganymede picked up his
blanket, rolled a few personal possessions into it, and set off
down the road without another word. As he went, he looked
at me again, sharply, and laughed, like a dog barking.

Chloe said: 'Proteus told me that his father's a tax-man.
Fine,' she said, 'right: so he's got a pretty face, just the
thing to put into a mask, he's got not an inch of experience,
and his father's a tax-man. D'you suppose it's worth the
effort?' The manager pulled his nose sideways, blew some
snot between his fingers, scrambled out of the wagon, went
over to the fire, poured hot water from the kettle into a
bowl of oatmeal, and started to eat.

After two or three mouthfuls: 'No and it is not worth it.
Dear child, it is not. Interfering with the family of a bloodsucking thieving bureaucrat: you're quite right, they'd call
it kidnapping, and they'd crucify the lot of us. So . . .' And
he looked at me carefully, weighing me up. 'So: most unsafe,
you will appreciate, if we tried to take you with us out of
your own home-district. Yet I need a boy: and you need a
life, and an art, and a chance for self-expression to do justice
to the pretty face. Proteus says you're comical: we're a
comedy company. I'll tell you what, I have a plan. You can
join us at Priene. You can get there by yourself, it shouldn't
take you more than – oh – a few days' fast walking: you join

us there at the end of next week. Can you do it? Of course
he can: he's a trouper: more than anxious to prove himself.
Dear child, you'll need expenses.' Once again, the swift
conjurer's movements, and a clutch of loose change was in
my hand. I found out later it was just about sufficient to
buy a loaf of bread.

'Now then,' went on the manager, 'you can breakfast here
with us, and set out on your road. Good god look where the
sun is already! Here's the agreement.' There and then he
explained to me that at half of a trained boy's normal share
in the profits (when there were any), at three-quarters of an
adult's share of the communal provisions, and in return for
my guaranteed silence as to my provenance and parentage,
I would receive his personal instruction in the rudiments of
my art – I could start off wearing the Ingenue's mask when
she didn't have more than a line or two of dialogue, and if I
showed any promise he would promote me to the Yellow-
haired Courtesan (Ganymede's speciality, and with important roles in several plays). He even got out the masks to
show me: but he did not let me put them on. I would also
be responsible for washing and folding the costumes,
caring for the properties and scenery, grooming the mule,
buying the food, posting up the playbills, sweeping the
acting area, washing the ordinary clothes of the company,
running delicate and personal errands for Chloe and Irene
(apparently a notable task), ensuring the camp-fire stayed
burning all night when they slept out of doors ('Wolves,
dear child; mountain-cats: bandits'), massaging the
manager's right shoulder when it ached badly, and making
myself generally available at all times to be called upon.

'All this,' he said solemnly, 'all this on condition you pick
us up at Priene. If you do, I shall be confirmed in my in-
fallible intuition: you and no-one else are the right man for
us.' Incredible as it may seem, at that moment I believed
him absolutely. After all, why would I not become an actor?
Why wouldn't I earn my living by doing all those things for
the public I had done for the last few years for nobody but
myself in the privacy of my own room?

Since I discovered that I could represent, with only my
voice and my face and a tarnished old mirror I bought from

a pedlar at the back door, a whole world of amazing persons I had never met but knew all about because I invented them to come to talk to me, I had almost ceased to talk intelligibly to anyone else. I felt immensely courageous: and also disturbingly scared.

I set out without waiting for Proteus to wake up or Irene to come back from wherever she had spent the night. I could get to know them all in Priene. If I ever got to Priene ... A few furlongs beyond the fork in the road I paused: and thought seriously about going straight home.

I could not bear to face my home: my father glowering and muttering at all hours over the rat's-nest of papers on his desk; his rapacious snarl, the ostentatious gold tooth that eerily illuminated the gloom of his closed-in features; his drooping eyelids; the bunches of skin on his gobbling throat: my mother in her icy silence staring out through bead-curtains at the passers-by in the street as though she were trying to become an assistant gorgon by sheer will-power and had in mind to petrify the entire town: my brother and his horrid dwarf squatting obsessed either side of a chest of money, erecting all the coins one by one into neat little piles like light-houses: my sister-in-law yawning and posturing from one room to another, dabbing perfume behind her ears, into her armpits, trying on rings, scarves, head-dresses, bows of ribbon, flouncing about in them, taking them off again, tossing them onto all the occasional tables all over the house: the cook crapulous among the dirty dishes, his boy tormenting a stray dog with a rusty spit: the porter at the front door contemptuously denying everybody entrance unless they were government officers when he would practically wash their feet with his wreathed fingers: a barefoot maid blubbering secretly under the stairs because my brother had done something cruel to her in the angle of the bedroom corridor.

I could not bear to face them: and yet, apart from them, the world, as far as I knew it, was so wide open, so arbitrary, so dismissive of the sort of person I thought that perhaps I might really be, that I could not bear to face it either.

I sat down on a stone and looked miserably along the valley to where it broadened out with a view of the sea. There was a ship, headed away from the coast, its white sail catching the sun, the gilt carving on the poop winking brightly against the blue. I wondered if the sailors understood exactly where *they* were going – the captain would obviously know, and no doubt his more seasoned subordinates – but might there not be a boy or two on board who had begged to be taken along and now were wishing helplessly they had never left dry land? They were indeed about to vanish over the rim of the world . . . Absurd, of course, I had no reason to believe that the vessel was bound for anywhere further than one of the offshore islands . . .

A footstep and heavy breathing behind me: I turned round: it was Chloe. 'If you think you've got to Priene, may I tell you you haven't? Do you want to go or don't you?' She was still very untidy, and I now noticed a black bruise under her eye that had not been there the previous evening: but her savage expression had left her. She was smiling at me – the sort of smile she had given the other actors when they all sat down in the wine-shop, not at all like the smile she had had on offer to the villagers who came pressing around. Without her face-paint she was older than I had at first thought, perhaps at least twenty-five.

'I saw how much money he gave you, old Shoulderbone, mean old bastard, look here, if you make haste you'll be at the Horse-bridge before sunset, you can't miss it, the police-barracks has a carving of the Love-goddess over the gate, don't ask me why: but it always makes me laugh. Don't go to the inn there, they'll cheat you, I know them. There's a saddler's shop at the corner of the square just opposite the fountain: ask for Longlegs, he's a friend of mine, and tell him I'm telling him to let you sleep in the store-room. If he don't believe you, show him this – ' She gave me a small knob of some shiny stone with a love-knot engraved on it, she took it from a hook on her necklace. Then she went on to explain about similar arrangements I was to make with other old friends in nearly every town along the Priene road. (She chose her men well, Chloe – as it turned out not one of them refused me what she asked). She made sure I repeated her elaborate directions: and then she gave me a hug and a kiss, which astonished me.

'Make sure you get to Priene, boy: he ought never to have set it up with you this way. But we none of us like tax-men, and *you* don't, and we're solid. Burn the bastards' balls off, and you can take that however you like. And make sure you give them back – ' (the tokens to her old friends, she meant) ' – you give them me in Priene: sweetheart, make sure that you get there.' Then she pushed her hair out of her eyes – she had to stoop to look at me at my own level – and scampered away from me sideways, jerking her big bum like a goat, down over the fields to the other road where it bent westwards, where I could just see the top of the wagon lurching off on its separate journey through a clump of low thorn-bushes.

I was now in no doubt that I would never go back home. That the rim of the world, dangerous, improbable, would be after all worth the search. I set out for it. Before long I was even to be thinking I had found it.

Have I explained all you need to know about myself and the revenue-service? I hope I have made it clear that when Shoulderbone suggested that the 'right sort of people' be invited to my birthday-party I no longer intended we should do nothing but eat and drink and play jig-a-jig with belly-dancers. Shoulderbone himself might not in his old age be good for much but fulmination: but I was an experienced agent, I knew how to fix things, I knew what I wanted fixed.

I did not relish the notion that after all these untroubled years I had been helplessly returned to the yellow dwarf, the 'back room', the one gold tooth.

4 *My Birthday-party (1)*

The birthday began with a quarrel with Cuttlefish. Well, not so much a quarrel, I should say rather an exchange of views from opposed standpoints. It was still very early in the morning, the pork she had bought smelt fresh, and I said so.

'Of course it is fresh. When did I ever bring you rotten

food? Do you think I don't know good pork from bad? You're changing the subject. I said why haven't you asked any women? The profession is full of them: I know you're very fond of them: don't they rate any status for so grand an affair as this? Of course I do know they're not members of your marvellous Guild. Or perhaps you don't think they would enjoy the Syrian Sisters?'

'I was going to invite women, half and half, indeed more than half.' I refused to lose my temper. (The theatre has always permitted a certain equality in social intercourse between the sexes, at least since it ceased to be a primarily religious activity. I approve of such a practice, though to most people outside the theatre it is only evidence of moral instability. We were not however here dealing with solely theatrical affairs). 'Don't you see, I didn't know it was going to get so political. We shall have to talk seriously, talk seriously tonight about *what is to be done.*'

'Oh I do see. And of course women would not be capable. Will the Syrian Sisters be lending a hand with the patriotic intrigue then? I do know the eldest one has a head as well as a backside.'

'How long do you reckon that pork will take to cook? I've cleaned the fireplace in the back yard: it had better be done there or we'll stink out the whole premises. I want to clear my office and lay down cushions and my carpet, leave a space in the corner for the dancing once we've finished the food. We won't have guests in our own inner room, use it for serving and preparation, stacking the dirty dishes and all that . . .'

She rose ominously to her feet, smoothed her tight beaded braids of hair with both hands even closer to her skull than they normally lay – a gesture that always preceded some statement of intent.

'If you are seriously telling me you have laid the choice of guests entirely in the hands of that begrudging old tyrant Shoulderbone (who never allowed a woman to advise him in anything but what sort of hair-oil he should put on his bald head), then all I can say is – it is your own birthday and the pork can roast itself for all I'm having to do with it.'

This was serious. Some proprietors would have taken a

strap to her there and then. But I recollected Raven, crosssd
myself to prevent him listening. She saw it and grinned
maliciously.

I said: 'That's all very well, but it's too late to do anything
about it now. But some of them will be bringing their girl-
friends with them anyway. You'll not be the only woman
present, I promise. Will that satisfy you?'

'No it won't. But never mind,' she looked away from me,
shifty, 'never mind, it's all attended to.'

'What d'you mean, attended to? Would you look me in
the face! You've been up to something. What?'

She played with her pebble necklace. 'Before I went to
the market I called at a few houses. Not everyone was at
home, but at least I got hold of Chloe. You ought not to
have forgotten Chloe, she's a very old friend: and she
promised to bring someone else. I was serious, by the way,
about the eldest Syrian: she used to live with a judge in
Damascus and she prepared all his verdicts for him. No, I
don't want you to kiss me. Put a big pot of hot water to be
boiling on the stove, please. We've a great deal of work to
get through . . .'

I might have guessed that Chloe would arrive at least an
hour too early. Our ancient acquaintance gave her the right,
she believed, to take these casual liberties. She had abandoned the stage to get married, oh maybe a decade ago:
since then she had been widowed twice. Both of her husbands had been mild hard-working master-craftsmen and
she had had a great many children. She inherited from her
second man a stage-costumier's business, which she ran
with immense verve and success, achieving almost a
monopoly of the trade in the district. She had grown extremely stout, and for some quirkish reason (she was by no
means a mournful widow) she always wore black, with a
mass of black kerchiefs on her head and shawls round her
shoulders. Her hair, when she let it be seen, was as abundant
as ever, unmarked with any grey. She had the delusive
appearance of an old peasant wife at a country fair.

She came barging in through the door just as Cuttlefish
had retired into the back room to take a bath and change

her dress. The food was all cooking nicely and I was putting the final touches to the décor of the front room. It still looked like an office. But an office with flowers and gay fabrics, and a range of inviting wine-pitchers, saucers of nuts, fruit, raisins, all that.

'Ivory, my sweetheart: how are you? Thirty-five, is it, *already!* thirty-five! How come that you're older than I am? It didn't use to be so – or did it?' She panted and fanned herself. She trotted wherever she went. 'Right: fine: where's the Cuttlefish, where's my lovely blackbird – Cuttlefish indeed, hideous name for a beautiful girl – where is she, I must talk to her!' She plunged through the bead-curtain across the door between the rooms. Cuttlefish, a polished statue of ebony standing in a basin pouring the water over her head, squealed with delight at the sight of her, and they embraced with unembarrassed ardour. Chloe, dripping wet all down her frontage, suddenly rounded on me and sent me to the street door – 'I've a friend coming after me; poor creature, she couldn't keep up: go and greet her, boy, sharp, you'll never guess who it is!'

On the doorstep a most elegant apparition, teetering in on high pattens, which she kicked off inside the house. At first sight, without them, a miniature Persian princess, in a positive rainbow of swirling silks, with a painted-faced pageboy in a brocade turban holding a sunshade over her head. I stared in consternation. She smiled at me, well, simpered, a delicate movement of the mouth-muscles too slight to disturb her make-up, and a butterfly tremor of her jet-black false eyelashes.

Good god it was Irene. I hadn't even seen her since I was sixteen. If I was thirty-five, she must be thirty-eight or thereabouts: but she looked no more than twenty. Her hair no longer orange, was it any longer her own hair? Her page-boy with difficulty removed all the swathings of oriental cloth from it and left nothing but a species of wire diadem (silver and emeralds!) amongst a sea-green tangle of in-credible serpentine curls. Ear-rings like silver soup-plates, her breasts half-exposed among the loose folds of her dress, their nipples precisely picked out in red ochre and gold.

She smelt like a temple where the incense had been burning
all night.

And this was the acrid high-pitched slut who used to
squall out her forlorn lust for fire-bearing Herostratus, who
had pulled me up into old Shoulderbone's wagon when the
rest of the company were out on the town after a show, who
had stripped my unhandled body and clutched me and
bitten me till I feverishly began, for the first time ever, to
do the same thing to her, who had compelled me when it
was all over to say 'I love you' in ten different ways, and
then had slapped me on the face and told me all of them
were bloody lies. I was so genuinely intimidated by her new
guise that I do not think I could even have kissed her, had
she not jumped up and kissed me instead. Her hard little
arms went round my back, her finger-nails dug into my
buttocks. 'Blood of the bull, you've got fat,' she said. 'Oh
god but your leg, why didn't Chloe tell me! Why didn't you
tell me?' The massive Chloe was watching me and leering
from the back room: 'And what's the matter with fat?' she
said. 'As for the leg, we've all got used to it, no regrets any
longer, the man works damn well for all of us. D'you know
where she's been, this bitch of an Irene? D'you know where
she's been, sweetheart? All the way to the far corner of the
Black Sea, no less, Trebizond, would you believe, making
love to the King of Pont!'

The King of Pont was something of a joke to us in those
days (we were later to know better) – an eastern barbarian
who wanted to be Greek and civilized, and poisoned or
strangled every relative he had. He himself (it was said)
took poison every day with his breakfast in order to render
himself immune. We called him King Strychnine and spe-
culated lewdly on his sexual habits – his harem was the size
of a regiment. Could it really be that Irene had lived there?
Yes it could: and the story she told of her adventures once
she got out of it, buying her way westward through the
assorted armies of the Cappadocian battlefront with no more
resources than her own golden flesh (and a dress-hem sewn
full of jewels), would have astonished an Arabian bard.

At this point Cuttlefish joined us, fully dressed, or rather revealed, in an assemblage of feathers and scarlet strapwork. She saw my raised eyebrows. 'It is after all your birthday. I don't want your *oldest* friends to claim *all* your attention. And besides, Chloe made it. Her birthday present for *you*.' She and Irene were sizing one another up. Fortunately they both seemed, more or less, to defer disapproval of what they saw.

In due course the other guests arrived. There were in all about twelve of them and they crammed my small room to bursting point. They included another agent (circus-acts rather than theatre business, and therefore not exactly a *rival*), an aged philosopher who wrote commercially-successful farces under an assumed name, a few actors from the municipal theatre, and a licensing-officer from the town hall who took bribes from all the theatre people and therefore was classed as a friend. And of course Shoulderbone. The latter brought along an Italian actor none of us had seen before. He was called Roscius. His modest demeanour and taciturn manner were misleading. Once he got going no-one could stop him: but among strangers he was made shy by a most unprepossessing squint. Shoulderbone introduced him to us as 'the best Pantaloon in the business', adding, in an undertone, 'alas, only in the Latin plays'. Indeed his Greek was hesitant – until he got going. The philosopher had a silly tart under his arm: he incited her to ask condescending questions of Roscius, implying the negligible nature of the Italian theatre. The reply was modest enough:

'Let me say first of course that we are altogether imitation – our Plautus and Terence are very euphoric to Italian publics: but from the text of your Menander they have made notorious piracy for every good concept.'

He was embarrassed when pressed to explain the differences in production-styles: 'We do not – pray excuse, gentle ladies, to mention such a circumstance – we do not wear the phallus to ornament our roles: such costume in the eye of government would be thought of much indecency.'

The philosopher then made a sneering mention of 'The Five Hot Pockets' – government and indecency seemed nestling tight enough in the one eye, he thought, there?

Roscius was even more embarrassed, explaining that soldiers' theatre was something quite different, not at all representative, and not indeed particularly Italian – he had
heard, had he not, that the 'Pockets' came originally from
Smyrna? The philosopher – who perhaps knew more about
Italy than he let appear – then asked after the theatre in
the One City, its size, age, financial arrangements and so on.

Roscius looked him full in the face with one eye and
allowed the other to roam remorsefully round everyone else
– an effect of irresistible burlesque, a guilty pickpocket
caught in the act, pretending his hand was nowhere near
the victim's purse. 'Ah,' he said, 'the City's theatre . . . how
can I confess there is no such a thing? A few years, not long
ago, there was one almost nearly complete. But government
made order that every stone to be pulled down, pull it down,
pull it away, no theatre, nothing.'

We were all horrified and naturally wanted to know
more.

Roscius told us that the City had said a permanent theatre
would 'feminize the strong people: create buggery with little
boys – all such nonsense of course, Cato-nonsense: not representative.'

The philosopher alone seemed to have heard of Cato. He
described him as 'the archetypical moral of Rome, though
happily deceased.' He nuzzled the bared breasts of his tart
and inveighed against Cato's zeal for the destruction of
Carthage, which had happened, so he said, 'the very same
year they also destroyed Corinth. Today, what is Corinth?
A military cantonment and a garrison-entertainment-troupe
of a highly obnoxious nature. Oh indeed, not representative:
my dear sir, we must accept your statement. But when we
shall observe their debased and soulless posturings on the
desecrated stage of our own theatre: how will that bring
consolation?'

Now it was most disagreeable to have this old artichoke
baiting my foreign guest in such a way, especially as Shoulderbone had hinted that the Italian might be of very
material help to us if he were handled right. But on the
other hand it was perhaps no bad thing that Roscius should
be apprised so rapidly of the strength of feeling prevalent in

Ephesus. I was still debating with myself how to deal with the unpleasantness, when, to my surprise, Irene swooped to the attack. Her eyes were pink and furious: she rounded on the philosopher, swearing what she told me later were Persian oaths of a highly pious nature, though in Greek they sounded plain rude.

'Blood of the bull,' she barked, 'how dare you! This sweet little man has made it perfectly clear he is totally opposed to everything we are opposed to: they've hurt him just as they're trying to hurt us! Why, he does all these plays out of Menander – he said so – and they won't even allow him a building to do them in, so nobody comes and he's bankrupt – blood of the bull, I call it heroic!'

She had gone too far the other way and Roscius had to assure her that it was only in the City that 'the publics are inimical: in the south towns, dear lady, many thousands complete our audience . . .' But she took no great notice; and, by the time she had finished, the philosopher's girl was weeping drunkenly and being sick across Chloe's lap in the corner, while the old man had upset an entire platter of roast fish in his discomfiture and was grovelling on the floor trying to find his brooch (somehow mixed up in the spilt sauce). Cuttlefish was most of the time in the inner room dishing up. The rather gentle young tart who had come with the licensing officer obligingly offered to help her with this, which meant that she fell about amongst us where we lay spread out upon the cushions, passing hot plates of food over our heads, and far more jugs of wine than was altogether wise at this stage of the evening.

Despite the philosopher's malice and its well-merited reversal, we had become loudly convivial very quickly. Too quickly. Our nerves were all on edge, and there was a danger that the essential politics would soon be obliterated by feckless self-indulgence. I saw two of the actors threatening to come to blows over the pretty boy that belonged to one of them, and the circus-agent and *his* pretty boy had obviously forgotten that there were other people in the room. Once fingers had begun to creep miscellaneously into the underclothing, there would be no more serious talk. I must catch Shoulderbone's attention, and directly. He was mumbling god knows what senile reminiscences of earlier, more virile, days into the warm folds of Chloe's neck: and I put a sharp foot against his kidneys. He knew what I meant, and levered himself round to wink at me – reassuring, confident, the old trouper about to resume control of his dissolving rehearsal. He swung his disengaged hand (containing a greasy rib of pork) towards Roscius, who, thank heaven, seemed to be ready for it, cue, prompt, or whatever he took it to be. The Italian politely removed the licensing-officer's tart's arm from his waist and rose gracefully to his feet. Shoulderbone clapped for silence; a sort of silence was achieved.

Roscius had a revelation for us: and Shoulderbone was stage-managing it for us.

'Please, gentle ladies, gentle men: I am asked here with so much honour among your notable Greek culture because it is known I am more passionate than I can express for what shall happen to your theatre in Ephesus. Now, I beg you, believe me: there is danger, yes, and great confusions – but not altogether whence you think! We have drunken, we have talked, I have heard so many of you saying this past hour, 'oh the curses on this Roman general for the troubles he will bring with him!' I have heard. Please: let Roscius tell you, it is *not with the general* that the troubles are about to come, for believe me one-and-all the general is in all ignorance, he must be, I am certain of it, for I, Roscius, am his chosen friend, and it is only because of him I am in the Province of Asia at all!'

Well, this was not what any of us had expected. Except Shoulderbone: he had known about it, and now he sat like a crooked cross-legged idol, basking in the anticipated applause. But before Roscius could explain himself more fully, Cuttlefish suddenly upstaged him, rattling in through the bead-curtain, unfastening her apron, sprinkling scent on her shining cleavage, clapping her hands for silence all unaware that Shoulderbone's dramatic silence was still in force. Uneasily conscious from her scalding kitchen recesses of the imprudent speed with which the licensing-officer's doxy had been dispensing the liquor, she had determined to batten down a few hatches with some cultural coolings-off. 'Birthday first,' she announced, 'politics later, and you can wait till after that before you all roll yourselves to rack and ruin. I haven't blistered my own self with fat pork for three-quarters of the day to be deprived of all decency afterwards as well as bored to death with pointless going over-and-over what we all know already about the villainy of generals.

'Some singing,' she announced, 'recitation; dancing, with propriety – if anyone can find room. It's Ivory's birthday, and we are here to honour him, as colleagues, as fellow-artists. We should offer him our accomplishments, those of us who have any.'

This rebuke, from a censorious female of low status to some of the most conceited men in the Province, needed to be softened by good humour if no-one was to take offence. I therefore, despite my recumbent posture, offered my own offering to my own birthday – a skittish, and (truth to tell) second-rate, patter-song from a play that I knew had been written by the aged philosopher. After that, Shoulderbone performed some of his ponderous feats of prestidigitation, Chloe and Irene sang about Herostratus, and one of the actors gave us about three hundred lines of Pindar in praise of nude athletic youth. Cuttlefish demanded something Latin from Roscius. The latter's revelation about his chosen military friend had been effectively, if unintentionally put aside: but he accepted the situation, realising no doubt that Shoulderbone had mistimed his introduction. He refused us a comic speech because he said we wouldn't know where to give him his laughs, instead he would demonstrate the potential of his language with an oration of Cato's upon decadence and corruption. He made it more than clear by his expression where he needed the laughs with this one: we supplied them in good measure. 'Carthago est delenda' was the final line, reiterated several times with huffings, puffings, and misconceived cadences: we nearly burst our bladders at it, he was so ludicrous. He then told us what it meant.

'Carthage must be destroyed': what Greek these days does *not* know what it means? But, remember, this was ten years ago . . . We stopped laughing. We nodded our heads as the aged philosopher crowed like a cock with an I-told-you-so flourish of his fish-smeared whiskers. We assured ourselves we were now beginning to feel seriously political, and the licensing-officer told his girl to 'put down that bottle and sit quiet'. Cuttlefish and Roscius, even though at cross-purposes, had at last brought the gathering into an appropriate sense of its true function.

'First,' I said, 'we need to know about this general. Our friend informs us he is – he is in some way his employer? Could we hear exactly how?'

So we heard. The general (yes, he was the Stain, Cornelius Sulla, a strenuous commander) was, unlike most Romans, a lover of the arts – the Greek arts, our arts: and also of artists. Roscius was one of the artists whom he loved, both ideally and physically. Indeed Roscius thought his invitation to travel from Italy to meet the general here was primarily personal: the general's bed was often filled as the result of abrupt messages sent over immense distances, that was the general's style. But there was more to it than this. If the Stain called for a Latin artist to prepare the cultured inhabitants of a Greek town for his arrival, it could only be that he had some intention to reconcile the Province to Roman control by patronizing its artisitic institutions. Perhaps he even had in mind to dignify the Ephesian theatre – or rather ('profuse apologies, gentle ladies, gentle men, please condemn my poor use of your language') to dignify the Latin drama by having Roscius perform on our stage.

But, in that case, as the licensing-officer pointed out, why had the revenue-office been behaving like such a parcel of offal? And why had the secret police laid hold on all the files in his department of the town hall? 'The whole building's bloody pullulating with them – three of my clerks already taken down to the barracks for extended interrogation. They're only waiting for one of the poor sods to implicate me, I know it too damned well, they'd have me there myself already except that my wife's father was one of their own cherished informants and the old devil still has an influence – I don't even understand what it is they want to implicate me with . . .'

An actor chimed in with an account of how the secret police had searched the theatre green-room and had questioned him for two hours about the alleged subversive significances of a Braggart Soldier costume they found hanging in a closet.

The licensing-officer rambled on about how his father-in-law had once exposed a revenue-office extortion plot to Redhead's people, and how his wife was now terrified that this would be discovered by those in the secret police who had acted this last month against Redhead, who had, as surely we all knew, been given the chop for belonging to the very same party as this Stain man who was in love with Roscius: and so what conclusions were to be drawn? 'First,' he said, 'nobody in government in the City is at all pleased by your general's success in the east. The revenue people and the secret police are acting here against his interests: and the City has told them to do it. And what about this victory anyway? My information is that it's no more than a patched-up settlement to get the Stain home with his reputation in his own party just sufficiently augmented for him to be given the political leadership of the 'old crowd' in the forthcoming elections there. The 'new crowd' is on the way out, public feeling's turned against them, that king-prick of theirs, the other general – you know who I mean, the old sweat they call the Mule-driver – he was consul time and again and he never managed to hold his position. Now they think he might be slipping down for good and all.'

The philosopher said, 'He even had to go into voluntary exile not so long since, I met a man who met him in these parts – Halicarnassus, I think. He didn't like us, couldn't even speak Greek: well, they say he got back home rehabilitated. But if this Stain is leading the hue-and-cry against him, he's bound to feel threatened . . .'

'Threatened enough to order the civil service to demolish all good feeling between us natives and the Stain? Just to keep things nice and nasty?' I was beginning to detect a shape of probable intrigue among all the gossip and prejudiced speculation. But even so, for whose benefit –

'For whose benefit,' shouted the circus-agent above all

the voices talking together, 'for whose benefit do they now organize these barbarian vomit-displays in our theatre? They've given me orders for fifteen assorted items, jugglers, rope-dancers, a woman who dances with an elephant, to take place amongst the sword-fighting acts: and by god if I don't think they'll be putting my artists in physical danger! Comic relief, they said, they want the elephant woman with no clothes on for god's sake, and poor creature, she's past forty: and they were asking how long would the rope-dancers be able to perform while the fighters were firing arrows at them! I've always run a clean business, far cleaner – if I may say so – than a number of friend Ivory's little sidelines, though I've nothing against him or I wouldn't be here at his birthday, would I?'

He was wandering from the point in a way I chose not to indulge. I cut him short and placed the issues firmly. Why should the civil administration make such a disruptive effort to pander to the debased tastes of the Stain's soldiery if they wanted to discredit the Stain?

Shoulderbone said it was a civil-service cockup, they were fouling each other's boghouse without even knowing they were doing it.

The pretty boy who belonged to one (or two?) of the actors disputed this with a sudden vehemence. It seemed he too had been questioned in the green-room and as far as he was concerned there was no cockup: the men had come there to hurt him, body and soul, and they had succeeded. He showed us some sufficiently horrible bruises all down his side and between his thighs. 'Oh they knew what they were doing,' he said, 'They didn't choose to explain why, but I can tell when bastards like that are acting to a prearranged plan. When they're only out for their fun-and-games the atmosphere's quite different.' He kissed both his friends and relapsed into a self-pitying silence. Chloe stroked his shoulder with absent-minded kindness: she too had fallen silent, and she looked carefully round the room as though wondering whether she really ought to speak absolutely freely. The licensing-officer's admission about his father-in-law's activities had disconcerted her, I guessed. Were we all in truth at one in this discussion? The boy's bruises were upsetting: his white skin had been broken here and there and there were scabs of dried blood sticking to his flank.

'No,' said Chloe, after a pause, 'this is not fun-and-games. But it's a sight more than the tail-end of a City faction-quarrel – "new crowd", "old crowd", elections, and all that. These people – all of them – believe they have god's authority to rule the world: and whether they reconcile this Province by patronizing our theatre, or whether they torment us into submission by *this* sort of thing – ' (she lifted the boy's hem again to show us once more his ugly marks) ' – there is one and the same policy behind it all the time. Of course they contradict each other: and they get in each other's way. But by and large they are our stage-managers: they have given us one mask to wear – the mask of the Obedient Subject People. Whatever the plot of the play, we enact the role that the mask dictates. The only difference is, that the Stain, if we believe Roscius, speaks agreeably to his cast: and the civil service don't.'

Roscius appeared most disconcerted, even ashamed, at this uncompromisingly underdog viewpoint from the Greeks he so much admired: but he had the sense not to contest Chloe's interpretation of his general's vaunted culture. He rolled his squint-eye downwards and applied himself to a dish of fruit. But of course none of this had got us any further forward towards our main goal of the evening: what on earth could we devise that would preserve our profession against its Roman enemies? The more unpredictable and inconsistent these enemies were shown to be, the less chance we had of countering them – or so it seemed to me.

Cuttlefish, a little diffident, because she was afraid she had been too bossy earlier on, put forward her own analysis. An acute analysis, too. She asked us to consider what we would do if we were the Stain. He has not really won a war, he has patched up a dubious peace and called it a victory. But his troops know exactly what it has been; they have to, they have looted no towns, and in any real victory there must always be abundance of loot. Armenian children were of no importance – anyone could capture children and herd them into stockades. (Her face as she said this went very hard and bony.)

The Stain (she continued) required the complete loyalty of his men for whatever military exigencies emerged from his political intentions in Italy. They had therefore to be compensated for the shortage of plunder, for the shortage of all those pleasures deriving from the search for plunder. Ephesus was not at war: but Ephesus outside the war was the nearest substitute for the real thing that could be found for the regiments at short notice. 'Don't tell me,' she added savagely, 'that these Games of theirs will be confined to the theatre.'

'That's what the *Stain* proposes,' Chloe agreed with her, and then advanced the argument: 'and the revenue-men *know* he proposes it. They know too – and they hope – that troops let loose are not so easily brought to heel, they know too – and they hope – that if the Stain proves unable to control them here, he'll never dare to bring them to Italy to threaten the "new crowd" – they won't have the discipline to hold a battle-line against the regiments of a regular old war-elephant the like of Mule-driver. So they've set the whole thing up so it'll all go too far: first to discredit the Stain as a soldier, second as a faction-boss; and the blood that his feet are intended to slip in is *our* blood, no-one else's.'

The philosopher's bed-girl said something intelligent from the haze of her wine-lees: 'One way we are caught, the other way they catch us. So what to do?' Then she needed to make water in a hurry, failed to get to the backyard in time, and Cuttlefish had to run for a saucepan and intercept her just at the bead-curtain. After we had all settled ourselves again, and the licensing-officer's tart had very courteously obliged with a mopping-up cloth improvised from the philosopher's scarf, we endeavoured to consider a plan.

I am sorry to say it was not a very decisive plan. In fact it was what Irene (who had had surprisingly little to offer, I thought, considering her international experience) called a 'thoroughly *subject-people* plan, disgusting, demeaning', though she raised no final objection to its being carried out. We all relied on Roscius. He assured us that if the Stain were to be told exactly what we had deduced about the state of affairs in Ephesus, and told it before he reached the town, he would infallibly change his arrangements, and

without doubt to our advantage. He (Roscius) would therefore take horse first thing in the morning and ride as fast as
he could to meet the army on its march. He would be
buggered by his amorous general the next night in camp, if
that seemed to be called for: and at all costs he would persuade him of the dangers of his situation. Would we trust
him?

We had no choice . . .

We considered all this, shrugged our shoulders,
wondered what had happened to the famous subtlety of the
Greek intellect, and then wondered – or at least Shoulderbone did – what had happened to the Syrian Sisters? He
understood they were to be the crowning glory of my party,
so where the devil were they then? Cuttlefish told him they
were in the back yard, with their musicians, only waiting
for our call. We called.

Cuttlefish took Chloe into the back room for some private
chat of her own. She wanted Irene to come too: but Irene
refused, saying that she took as much pleasure as any of the
men did from the sight of gleaming young arses and de-
pilated crotches undulating through a layer of gauze, it
reminded her of the Trebizond harem. We sprawled about
then, and stared at the undulations for maybe an hour. The
Syrians permitted the caresses of my guests to the extent
specified in their contract. Having been refreshed by food
and drink (also in the contract), they showed signs of relax-
ing their business-discipline a little, consonant with the
nature of the night – I was, after all, as much a friend as an
agent, and birthdays in Syria are occasions of unbridled
generosity: the dances grew more heated and the music
more inflamed until the municipal watchman knocked on
the door to say that there were complaints all up and down
the street about the shrillness of the woodwind, and if there
was any more of it he would have to call the real police.
Didn't the gentlemen know what time it was?

The gentlemen did: and one by one they all went home,
bringing their bedfellows with them. One of the Syrians
stayed: I didn't know why, but if it was to sleep with me
she was reckoning without the Cuttlefish . . .

5 *My Birthday-party (2)*

I was alone for a few minutes amid the squalid wreckage of
my front room – alone, that is to say, except for Irene's
little page, fast asleep on cushions in the corner, and Irene
herself, who suddenly put her hand between my legs and
her teeth too near my ear-lobe. Her make-up had run, she
was tired, and, I thought, worried as well. So was I. This
was no time . . .

'No no, don't be scared, I'm not offering you *that*. Just a
gesture of good luck: we're both superstitious. But I am
making an offer, it's perfectly genuine. I'm going back into
the business. I want a manager. I thought the job might
suit you. Travelling: get out of Ephesus: bring your little
black squid with you, you haven't much else to bring, I
know that. But Ephesus is no place: all they can do here is
rely on a general's bum-boy to save their souls: it's all nonsense.'

She looked her age. I asked where would she travel.

'Italy. I have capital. King Strychnine has been bountiful
and I brought most of it out. Have a word with your squid,
she's no fool. You can tell me in a few days. You know
where I'm staying: Chloe's place. Don't make up your mind
now.'

I was tempted. To be Irene's manager: or to be with
Irene?

Cuttlefish, Chloe, and the eldest Syrian (Miriam), came
in from the back room. Miriam, now in her street clothes,
heavily-veiled from head to foot, resembled a pile of washing: but two very bright black eyes peered at us through a
small gap, and the speed of her mobile fingers, covered with
rings, more than made up for the concealment of her
features. It was evident that her continued presence had as
much to do with the Cuttlefish as with me. I felt boozily
aggrieved. Her fingers and eyes said she was part of the
plot, whatever plot had been hatching in there.

Irene seemed to know all about it, anyway, even though

she had been fomenting her own small plot with me. There was a certain disturbing female telepathy going on, which I was not quite sober enough to catch hold of. (No, to be frank, I was really considerably fuddled). Irene was beginning to talk about generals, enlarging upon her scepticism of the effectiveness of Roscius and his alleged influence over the Stain. She said, 'Oh, it's one thing for him to expect the Stain to unburden all his cares to him, between his legs, between the sheets – that's easy enough, I've done it myself, I know all about it. Quite another to think that these monumental manslaughterers will amend their considered policy by the dimension of one whip-flick, no not for the sake of the smoothest buttock between here and the hill of Troy they won't: *unless it suits their purpose*. The Stain's purpose is to find a means of outwitting the Mule-driver . . .' She was smiling demurely to herself: and then, swiftly, she showed her teeth, a pair of tight white fences with a sharp red tip of tongue, a glowing coal, between them.

'Mule-driver. Why the name? Because he was the first City general to look for his soldiers among the rubbish of the gaols and labour-gangs: he offered them a life where before they had nothing but pigswill and bludgeons. And then he drove them, like mules, till he made 'em into an army that saved his precious City from the wild men of the north. And after that, they were *his* soldiers, not the City's at all – but the City never knew that: they have thought him all this time the only one true patriot; while the Stain, for all his cleverness, his tactical successes (he's had more of them than Mule-driver) has never seemed alive to anything beyond his own instant advantage. If this Stain could once find proof that Mule-driver's republican virtue was as hollow as his own, and could be publicly *exposed* as being as hollow as his own, then we might see some results: and even that squint-eyed Roscius might be surprised at what might happen. You see, I've met the Mule-driver, and he told me his corruption himself.'

She had achieved the big effect that Roscius had been baulked of by Shoulderbone's cack-handedness earlier on. Chloe slapped her big palms together, the Cuttlefish whistled softly, Miriam jerked herself indefinably inside her veils: I refrained from taking another last drink. Irene went on:

'I didn't mention it before – very few of your friends, Ivory, are to be trusted with this sort of gossip. But, 'voluntary exile', were we told, Halicarnassus? Oh further away than that – Trebizond, the court of Pont: and that's where Irene was, too. Mule-driver came to Strychnine to work him up to war – war against the Stain in this Armenian complication, which otherwise King Strychnine was determined to keep out of. Mule-driver wanted the Stain's army well-mauled by Strychnine – that's to say, a *Roman* army, and he wanted it *mauled*. Then the City would have to recall the Stain and put Mule-driver in to replace him. Mule-driver would then defeat Strychnine, saving the City yet again, you see – and after that, no end to his acclaimed rule over all the world! Of course the last part of the arrangement was not confided to King Strychnine. But, of course, being the man he is, he more than suspected it. So when he had all these specious promises made him by his deferential Roman visitor, all conditional (do you follow me?) upon Pont moving troops into Armenia and Cappadocia for a most ill-defined purpose, he naturally asked Irene to find out what it was all about. I was only sometimes behind the harem-curtain in that palace, Strychnine had several other uses for me. Well, I uncovered the profound calculations of the distinguished exile, informed the king, and then waited to see from which poison-bottle he would dose the Mule-driver's kouss-kouss. He was too sharp to do any such thing: he thought such a crude intriguer would work more damage to Rome alive than dead, so he kissed him, promised him everything, bade him a polite good-bye: and immediately set about finding a means to stop the war as soon as possible – a patch-up peace (as we have heard) which the Stain can call a victory, if he wants to: and Pont's involvement revealed to nobody – except maybe to the King of Persia, but that's not really germane . . .'

Indeed it was not. We impatiently demanded what we all wanted to know – how had she persuaded Mule-driver to betray himself? She had already told us her poor opinion of attempts to affect great generals through their genitals –

surely such a veteran commander would never talk freely to
a foreigner's concubine?

'No of course not, he didn't talk to me, he talked to himself. He never found out I could understand a bit of Latin;
not much, but it made sense of his ramblings – blood of the
bull, though, did he ramble! He used to get so very tired –
thick build, varicose veins – bladder trouble, poor old sod,
and it hurt him. He would suck himself full at bedtime with
the filthiest Crimean wine that'd sicken a carthorse, and
then get me to sponge his temples while he lay back on his
mattress and belched. Then I'd have to toss him off – he
wouldn't actually offer to come inside me in case Strychnine
took it amiss (he had the oddest notion of what was due to
his host's ladies) – and while I was doing it, he would talk.
Rehearsing the justification of his acts that he would one
day be delivering to some assembly. "Revered and most
honourable Roman Fathers," he used to say – wait a
moment, let me show you just how . . .'

She fell back across a pair of cushions and went into an
acutely disgraceful comedy routine:

' "I took occasion to conduct this unofficial embassy on
your behalf to the kingdom of Pont, knowing full well that
its ruler was implacable in his enmity to this City – no no,
woman, no – higher up, two fingers only – there we are
there we are *there* – touch it with your tit, woman, slowly,
woman, slowly – implacable in his enmity and therefore
ripe to be destroyed – and – oh, now the mouth, mouth,
girl, damn you, *quick* – oh, I did destroy him, I did I did I
did – aaah . . .!" '

As soon as she had completed her performance, Irene
sprang lightly to her feet and looked round with hauteur.

'There you are, that was Mule-driver. Now you know
who he is. Now we all know what we ought to do next.'

Her red tongue out again, flicking backwards and for-
wards. We all thought about it as we looked at it . . . But
the immediate political application of her anecdote seemed
less easy to imagine. I stumbled out through the bead-
curtain to put my head in a water-jar. I had a feeling that I
was about to be called upon to commit myself to something serious: and at this late hour I would have preferred

to postpone it. When I returned it was apparent that Cuttle-fish and Chloe had made all manner of deductions from the Mule-driver's singular pillow-talk.

Chloe was saying: 'Treason, conspiring to have a City army defeated in the field, oh certainly treason – but the Mule-driver's back in Italy among his own people, how would the Stain hearing of what he was up to in Trebizond do any good for us, here, now? – it's all far too fanciful, and suspect moreover. Irene, as always, you think your oily old bed-ropes make a noise the whole wide world is clamouring to listen to. It's not true.'

Cuttlefish said, 'If Mule-driver committed treason, and is no doubt still committing it, there must be someone in Ephesus who can be linked to it – the revenue department?'

'Oh surely,' Chloe sounded cross, 'but who, how? For god's sake let's think clearly, I'm as drunk as a bloody Gaul. Who is there in this town who can *precisely* be shown to be working to damage the over-riding interests of the Senile and Posturing Querulousness of Rome? These soldiers won't do a thing without we can give them proof, but once give them proof, goddammit they will be *merciless*. Who? If we knew who, the how would be simple enough.'

I couldn't see this, but I forebore to speak. Cuttlefish clutched hold of my wrist, and waved it up and down to reinforce her own gesticulations – she was hot on the scent. 'When Mule-driver went home again he must have left arrangements here for his people to get news to him independent of the official mails. If one of the letters addressed to him came adrift in its passage and fell into the hands of the Stain – say, a letter from a confederate in the revenue-office – '

'Ah!' I came in here, at last I saw where we were. 'The civil service would never send that sort of letter through any sort of civil service connection, they'd use a commercial operator whom they had some crooked dealings with in the line of their daily business.' I had it, I had it. 'Jampot! Oh yes, he's very well in with the hostage-and-captives depart-ment, and there's deals he's pulled off that could only have been made through collusive tax-arrangements, which means close friends in *that* office as well. But how to use him to set them up? Oh really, Chloe, what do you mean, "the how would be simple enough"? Do you expect me to search his premises?'

The Syrian finger-nails were shooting away in all directions. 'Listen,' Miriam hissed, 'Before we came onto your books, we were for a while, for a short while, being so ignorant of which men were making which filth in this town, we were handled by Jampot. He tried to divide us – imagine, please, we are sisters, he made effort to divide us one from the other – a merchant from India had seen Rachel and discovered lust for her: Jampot asked him for purchase-money. And Abigail he was contriving to insert her for a good price into the pleasure-gardens at Antioch. But we are free people – I am mother to these two young girls – ' (she was about eighteen, her sisters one year and three years younger) ' – I am mother and they shall not be taken from me except for very advantage of marriage! When I found out what was his trick I had to buy out all our contract complete, before we could get loose from him. But I do know he has always wanted us back. Every time I meet him, he says to me, to come back – he will make us all three as rich as Queen of Sheba. You and I, Ivory, could we not have this quarrel? I go back therefore to the Jampot, and then I find out all his doings and put upon him the letter-of-fraud?'

'Wait a minute, you're going too fast. What letter?'

'Whatever letter you think best, of course,' snapped Chloe.

'Maybe one to the Mule-driver, or to one of the Mule-driver's friends, from a chief revenue-officer here, telling him – oh, telling him – ' The Cuttlefish was running out of ideas but she kept on repeating herself until someone else caught up with her. It was Irene, snarling with impatience: 'Telling him the Stain's troops are indeed on the verge of mutiny, *all according to plan*, the King of Pont is in touch and about to march into the Province – oh for god's sake telling him anything so long as it shows that Asia is falling apart and the sodding tax-man abets and aids, does all that he can to make catastrophe: for the City, catastrophe, chaos! Ivory writes the letter – don't pretend you're not clever enough, Ivory – Miriam plants it: then word is passed to the Stain when he gets here that it's where he can find it if he looks: and there we are!'

She smacked her page to wake him up (Cuttlefish gave him a sweetmeat, which was more effective), and that was the end of the first stage of our conspiracy to bring liberty to all the Greeks. Oh, we Greeks had invented democracy: in these dreadful days of its erosion and eradication we had no right to stand aloof . . .

When Cuttlefish had had too much to drink she would wrap her arms around me and talk about housework. Tonight, once all the others had gone, she talked about how the housework should be deferred until the morning, foul though the whole place was. Leave the cushions were they were, we had a use for them. Because of the injury to my hip, the way we made love was this: I would sit back against a pile of cushions with one knee crooked sideways, the right knee. The left leg would have to stretch out straight, or as straight as it would go.

Then Cuttlefish would squat facing away from me as it were in the triangle made by the crook of my right knee. She would work herself asymmetrically backwards into my groin, her hand behind her buttocks, gently raising my courage up, then her buttocks after the hand, sliding their cleft up and down, until she felt a shape of strength that would go into her. We had found any other arrangement almost always gave me excruciating cramps. Sometimes she got cramps as well, as she lifted herself up, with the palms of her hands on the floor, high enough to fit herself onto me without hurting my hip-joint. My own hands would be round her belly and breasts and then go down into her crotch to help tighten things up down there. When all went well it worked well, tonight though nothing significant could be found to augment itself. She became an angry panting jockey for a few minutes and then gave up, shaking her head, more sadly than spitefully, not so much contempt as regret. Of course I was apprehensive to almost the point of diarrhoea, and she knew that, perhaps she was too. I hadn't felt so scared since the day I set out for Priene.

Maybe we shouldn't be trying any more of this love-blunder till the crisis was resolved. What crisis? She had a different notion perhaps from mine. She said, before she fell asleep, 'I find you all these lovely women and your imagination quails. Or your blood quails, or something. Maybe it's the Raven? He sees, when I don't, where that Irene will be putting her hand.' And she took hers away, firmly, for the rest of the night.

6   *Notched Pennies*

I had to visit Jampot, give some colour to the story that Miriam would be telling him. Cuttlefish brooked no delay – 'She'll have been there to see him very early, a most determined girl, you ought to take pattern from her: the way she looks after her sisters is heroic, get down there directly and follow it up for her, quick sharp.'

'There' was his alleged office, a hole in the wall of a sordid tenement building, like a low-class cobbler's shop. A badly-lettered signboard said 'Import-export and negotiations undertaken'. Inside the booth were lockers and shelves stacked with dirty papers, a charcoal brazier that made the eyes run in such a confined space, and two stools occupied by Jampot himself and a crony (whose face was in shadow) drinking some hot infusion and talking in low voices. They fell silent when I rapped on the counter for attention. Jampot glanced up at me sideways with yellow eyes: the other man looked into his cup.

'Why, who do you think, my dear old Ivory, the Queen of the vanished boards!'

I pretended to be boiling with rage. 'Look here, Jampot, this is not good enough, grossly unethical, you have absolutely no business to – '

'Ah: I knew you'd be coming, and in such a mood too. But really, my dear old Ivory, it's not going to get you anywhere. Young Miriam and her sisters are of an age to know their own interest. You treated them downright shabby, and so of course they come back to uncle. You've been a bleeding pimp to them there girls, whatever your highfly sentiments, so don't come the artistic superior over me! Expecting them to perform gratis for all your kinky friends – "ho culture, we do a very naice laine in elegant and refained terpsichore, if you want to feel their quaint little *quims*, me deah fellah, you pay *me* not the properties – ho yes . . ." ' He enjoyed himself for a minute with these imitations, while his friend in the corner sniggered. I felt almost as foolish as though the whole thing were genuine. Miriam's sincerity had clearly been persuasive and Jampot was triumphing in its aftermath. It was therefore not hard for me to simulate the intense rage I was here to make him feel I was feeling. I banged my stick on the counter and abused him. As he had called me a pimp first – with his usual adroitness – it was a problem to know what to call *him*, except a collaborator with the common enemy, so I called him that: and then wished I hadn't. It cut him short in mid-return-flow of abuse: he stared at me in an envenomed silence. Two fang-like teeth appeared in the corner of his mouth, his pointed features slowly slid into a demoralizing omniscient grin. The man in the shadows seemed frozen in mid-snigger. Their deathly stillness cut me short as well.

For an appreciable while the three of us might have been posing for a genre-study by a realistic artist – 'A picturesque corner of the old bazaar', perhaps. Then, as softly as a lizard, he unhooked the flap of his counter and beckoned me into the booth. He pulled a third stool out from under somewhere and mutely invited me to sit on it. I did, and began to cook myself uncomfortably against his brazier. Rather as though he were talking to some dog-eared old invoices pinned to the wall instead of to a contiguous human being, he said, 'Oh yeah, so that's what it is . . . a bit late to think about it now, seeing as the procession's already rolling half-way up the street. However there might just be room for a little one to jump up into the arse of the chariot. Always supposing such a limp-leg can jump . . . and always supposing you cared, at moderate expense, to propose some discreet small arrangement. Just a minute, I'll close the shop. More or less through with clients for the morning, wouldn't you say?' He got up, hauled in his awning, and pulled folding wooden shutters across the top of the counter, enclosing us in an almost-dark fumey box lit only by the glow of the charcoal and some ventilation holes near the ceiling.

The other man leaned forward to toss the dregs of his drink into the brazier and I recognized him – a well-known local faction-boss, called the Hook (from the favourite weapon of his young militants in street-fights): he controlled the warehouse-men and stevedores down at the port and had a name for unscrupulous labour-agitation, always very much to his personal advantage. Nothing could move in or out of Ephesus without his say-so, we were told, and the provincial government was supposedly terrified of him. I had never thought of him as in any way connected with the sort of business Jampot undertook, but I supposed anyone involved in any kind of shipping transaction would have to meet his terms sooner or later.

Jampot said, 'Right. You said "collaborator". Why not? Only two alternatives to it. A bleeding bankrupt, or a cruci-fied rebel. I happen to know that you're neither: oh yeah, you're a piece of shite, but even so you're no moron. You want in, with what's going: you came to the right slot for it – Jampot nicked your Syrians from you, but Jampot's got the fingers that'll put your fingers back into far more sugary quims, provided you see him right, and remember all the time that he's the uncle and you're nothing, however much you pay for it, you'll never match Jampot's stake, I know *that* much about your commercial capacity. Right.'

This was so enigmatic it took me a while to interpret. I read it as an invitation to buy my way in to some syndicate that Jampot wanted me to think he ran, which was exploit-ing the requirements of the City, specifically in relation to the imminent arrival of the Stain's soldiers. It seemed to be pretty much what I was after. But I needed to hear rather more.

The Hook in the meantime was mumbling something. He had started mumbling when Jampot repeated the word 'collaborator', as though the repetition hurt his feelings. 'When the masses are confronted by two contradictory op-pressive forces, let them strike at the immediate one even if this means forging a temporary and tactical alliance with the more remote. The remoter force can then be isolated and crushed at leisure . . .' seemed to be the gist of it. This was more than enigmatic: it was entirely incomprehensible. I ignored it. I waited for Jampot's precise proposition.

But it didn't come. Instead Jampot's face was suddenly thrust so strongly into mine that I was bent over backwards till the burning charcoal singed my coat. 'Nice party did you have last night? A very unexpected high class of a lady-guest among the other ones, young Miriam didn't catch her name, too busy shaking her tits into your eyeballs I daresay: but I saw her in the street when she arrived, yardage of silks and a kid with a parasol. Persian at a rough estimate. Am I right?'

The Hook had levered himself forward from his stool, and, as Jampot finished his question, he shot out an arm like a crowbar and seized hold of my wrist, bending me back even more. Another ounce of pressure and my hand would have been in the coals. I opened my mouth to yell, but Jampot clapped a greasy lump of cloth into it: and there I was, held. 'Now,' breathed the Hook, 'before we talk any more business, you answer the man's questions: answer them right, and no more problems. Try to shout, and who'll hear you? We've got very good friends in this building.'

The cloth was removed. I steadied myself against the wall by the hand the Hook was not holding. The stool was kicked from under me, throwing all my weight upon my bad leg. If I fell now a good deal more of me than my hand would be in the brazier. I croaked fatuously, 'Yes, Persian . . .' Jampot nodded his head to the Hook and the Hook pressed my hand against the red-hot metal. Cloth in my mouth again, I couldn't scream, I smelt myself frying. Then an easing of the pressure, cloth momentarily out of my mouth, I gasped for breath and groaned. 'No,' said Jampot wearily, 'them silks was Persian all right, but not her. The kid gave her away, you see. She never picked him up east of the Euphrates. Libyan, or my name and goods have never been known in Alex. Peculiarity of the trade, you know, they don't sell Libyan kids in Persia, I don't know why. Blackies, yeah, Circassians certainly: but that kid was bought nearer west.' This was acute of him. Irene had mentioned that the

pageboy came from a market in Egypt: but then – not so
acute, Jampot – he wasn't hers. Chloe had found a friend
who had lent him to her for the evening. 'Egypt,' said
Jampot with a leer, 'the bint was Egyptian, right?'

'Right,' I moaned, 'Egyptian.' He seemed well satisfied,
confident that I was now thoroughly intimidated. (Indeed I
was, but I was also bewildered, and desperately trying to
work out a way to outmanoeuvre his apparently meaningless
manoeuvres.) He hovered over me, sweltering me with more
questions: 'She didn't come here by ship, she'd have been
noted at the docks – ' 'She'd have been noted,' said the
Hook, 'I've some very smart men there.' 'And if she came
by ship to some other port along the coast and then to
Ephesus by the post-road, it was no Gyppo ship brought
her: there's an epidemic in the Delta all this past month
and no vessels allowed to leave. So where *did* she come
from, and *why is she bloody well here?*'

The one thing I was not going to tell him was anything
about Pont. I knew where we were now: we were in military
(or political) intelligence, and Irene's affairs in Trebizond
were not for publication. I said, 'I don't know – ' and the
Hook kicked me hard under the stomach, dropping me in
agony across the fire and all over the floor. When they
picked me up again I held out my burnt hand plaintively,
'Please, let me finish, I really don't know – but I know she
talked to Miriam. I never met her before, you see, she's a
friend of big Chloe's – ' 'Right, that's what Miriam said.' 'I
– I understood her to say she's been working the southern
coast – Cilicia, around Tarsus, Cyprus perhaps . . .' 'Hit
him again, Hook, he's a liar.' 'She's a song-and-dance girl,
she does work the circuits, but oh god I'm not a liar, *she's*
the liar if anyone is, she told different stories to everyone,
she – ' Jampot was smiling: 'Right, she *is* a liar, she did tell
Miriam different. Told Miriam she'd been in Trebizond.
Was it a lie or was it true?'

Miriam's idiocy? Miriam's treachery? Good god I was so
shocked I could say nothing. I gibbered. Fortunately he
thought it was the pain that caused me to do it. He answered
his own question: 'A lie, of course, it has to be. Because we
know she comes from Africa, and we know why she bloody

comes.' (I had had so little experience of the sort of world I was unexpectedly getting myself into that of course I did not realize that characters like Jampot actually *prefer* to believe lies, and pursue a principled process of never believing the truth. It makes their whole business so much the more worth while. If the truth, you see, were true, government would not need to pay for thousands of Jampots to check it and re-check it and analyse it and contradict it, they would find it out fairly quickly and then act upon it without fuss: three-fourths of all bureaucracy would be out of a job. No, Miriam had been very wise).

'Didn't hurt you too much, did we?' He was suddenly changing his approach. 'We only wanted to see was you involved or just stupid. Stupid, right, we know it now: but then again, you're no moron. So listen at this. She comes from Mauretania, from a wog king called Bocchus. We've been expecting her, or someone like her, all these last few weeks. Now she's living with big Chloe and apart from your party last night, she's never put her nose out o' doors. A gaudy tart of that class of cunt-consciousness, if she was all above-board, she'd be in her sedan-chair parading the avenues from her first night in town, letting all the noble gentlemen have a glimpse of the goods. But she hides away from all of us and only goes out to a fat little half-solvent limp-leg who happens, yeah, just happens to invite to his birthday not only nearly all the top showbiz of Ephesus, but the Stain's pet actor from Italy into the bargain. You didn't know I knew that? You know nothing, darling, fuck-all.' I nodded, I fully agreed with him.

He was still talking. 'I'm now going to tell you why you had that party and what was to be fixed at it. *Then* you will appreciate why it's far better for you to work with us rather than arsehole around trying to fuck us up, right? King Bocchus is an old friend of the Stain, did him a big favour in an African war years back and thereby wiped the eye of Mule-driver – you've heard of Mule-driver? He's ready now to do him another one. The Stain is supposed to bring his army back to Italy. But the governor of Asia here is one of the "new crowd" and the Stain belongs to the "old". Embarrassment in the Province. No general ever wants to leave hold

of an army in being: *but* our lord the governor's had orders
to make sure that this army is left in Asia – transferred to
his own command – while the Stain goes home alone; alone,
d'you see, and impotent. He won't be able to fight such an
order without a big excuse.

'Now what could be a big excuse? Like, a message from
Bocchus that there's rebellions in Africa and no troops there
to prevent 'em. Who in the City, among the Servile and
Popular Quibblers and Rioters, right, could blame any
strong general that moved the first immediately-available
regiments lickety-spit to the centre of trouble? But to fix it
takes time, and Bocchus won't be writing to him in anything
like detail – no, he'll send an agent, and knowing Bocchus
it'll be a woman, it always is. So for the last few weeks
we've kept a regular lookout for her. I was daft enough to
think he'd send one of his nig-nog princesses to sleep direct
with the general, just like he's done before; not any
common-or-garden provincial song-and-dance-bint-made-
good who'd go straight in amongst her old circles only just
around the corner from your old uncle Jampot.

'That Eyetalian comic had his general's orders to contact
her as soon as he got here: and dear old Ivory, my old darling – *you* was the sucker set up to provide the safe-house
and the cover for the meeting. Oh you didn't know it and
now I know you didn't know it, but that's how it was.'

Not only did he refuse to believe the truth when it was
told him, he also made a point of making up his own lies
and believing *them* from start to finish. If the whole administration was conceived on these lines, no wonder the
public was permanently bemused. Unless, of course the
Bocchus story *was* the truth, and Irene had told us nothing
but lies. But in that case . . . I was in such agony, I decided
not to try and think any more: just wait for what came next.

What came next was a mixture of threat, promise, and –
at last – proposition. 'Seeing how your whole arrangement
is blown, darling, what d'you reckon you ought to do about
it? The general is not yet in town: the provincial government
very much is. We could have you down the security-enforcement in less than five minutes, hung up by the thumbs,
waiting all night for the red-hot irons to come clipping your

pubic wrinkles, but *you* don't want that, *you're* a man of sense, *you're* going to listen to a sensible programme of work and I swear to you you'll gain goodies out of it. You come on the strength, on the pay-roll – we pay well, we pay regular – you tell us what we want, when we want, where we want it: and until you hear further, you carry on just like you have been with whatever you'll be asked to do by the Eyetalian or any other of 'em. What d'you say?'

'You keep talking about this "we". Who are you and whose is the pay-roll?'

'Oh crafty, I knew he was; of course, he's in the business. The Sordid and Pretentious Quorum of Realists, that's who: government, boy, all branches of it – *except* for this king-prick general who very shortly is not going to know what's hit him . . . So what d'you say?'

There and then, with the minimum of ceremony, I became an official agent of the One City's secret service. A double-agent, I suppose, though who my other employer was did not seem very clearly established. Perhaps it was myself: in which case it was high time I made up my mind what cause I represented. In the meantime it was my duty to myself to gather all information possible. To start with, there was the Hook. How many more grassroots guarantors of our native rights and liberties were similarly employed to ensure the subject people remained always subjected? How many hundreds of innocently City-hating labouring men and their families had been, for how long, so cruelly deceived? Hundreds? Probably thousands. . . .

But that could keep. I had this letter-of-fraud to fabricate: now I knew who Jampot was I might make a better job of it. I was given a peculiar notched penny – the token, they said, of my enrolment. It thrilled me, in a childish way.

7   *Letter-of-fraud*

Cuttlefish was all bandages, boiling water, ointment and compassionate tears. I can tell you I was in need of them. It was amazing I had no bones broken. Oh, the Hook knew how to damage a man in the most economical fashion. She kissed my wounds and blamed herself. I blamed her, if it came to that, but restrained myself from actually saying so. I showed her the penny and told her the whole story. This coin had a tiny hieroglyph scratched on to its face and an equally tiny notch cut into the rim. You wouldn't have noticed it at all unless you looked for it. They had told me to wear it round my neck on a string (with the various other charms and amulets I always wore), and to show it to any-body I thought might need to know about it. Both Jampot and the Hook carried very similar pieces.

After the compassion Cuttlefish turned to criticism: of course. 'I cannot imagine how you let him seduce you actually into his shop. A baby three weeks old would not have fallen for that one . . .' and so on. Then she fetched a wax tablet and I began to draft the letter. I made several attempts. When I thought I had it right I read it over to her: she put her head on one side and listened with great attention, her tongue sticking out in the adorable way she had when things were important. If I had been in better condition, I might even have postponed business and reversed last night's amorous failure: but things *were* im-portant, the letter must come first.

'I don't think it should seem to be going direct to the Mule-driver – he's too big. Better if it's addressed to someone of no great status, an information staging-post, as it were, in the City . . . What do you think of a shyster lawyer, someone of that sort whom the Mule-driver relies on for his more doubtful bits of business?'

'But you don't know his name?'

'I don't need to. All such things'd be bound to be anony-mous. How about this?

Sir, to let you know, and through you, his lordship – '

'Do they call each other lordships? I thought they were a republic?'

'So they are, and they don't. It's a nickname and it indi-cates a man of power.

Sir, to let you know, and through you, his lordship, that so far all goes well in Ephesus. *He* and his soldiers not yet arrived but expected daily. Reports about their discipline etcetera unfavourable to his credit. Your friends in the regiments expect manifestations –

Manifestations is a better word than *mutiny*? More mysterious, a little wary: he don't want to incriminate himself more than need be.

– to appear as soon as troops are subjected to inevitable relaxations here, followed by equally inevitable use of military police to control them. I anticipate appropriate delay in furnishing troopships.

I picked that up from the Hook. They've a problem here. The Stain's supporters want his army moved swiftly to Italy: *but* his opponents intend it to hang about in Ephesus long enough to make trouble. The stevedore-shipwright element will secure the right timing. But then, too long a delay, and it would make it easier for the Stain if he really wants to ship the troops to Bocchus in Africa. Goodness, the complexities of the seditious conspirator . . .!

Reports from Pont –

Pont crossed out, replaced by initial 'P', but crossing-out still leaves it legible.

– suggest that royalty is not yet ready to comply with our hopes: your patron's visit there, however, has clearly had effect: return messages not unhelpful.

That ought to fix it strong enough onto Mule-driver.

In the meantime this department has implemented all instructions for renewed coercive policy. Public feeling towards City deteriorating in consequence: *he*, as chief representative of City (when he gets here with troops) will certainly bear brunt. PG –

Provincial governor: they'll understand the abbreviation.

– in meantime will not leave his regional HQ in P.'

'In Pont?'

'No, Pergamus. Oh dammit, same initial for both places. How about "regional HQ in Statue-town"?' (Pergamus was famous for its sculptures).

'So all manifestations here will be seen clearly to derive from where your friends want them derived. Bocchus business – '

'Bocchus? Use his name?'
'Yes. Everyone in the City has been dealing with Bocchus. The suggestive bit comes immediately after:

> Bocchus business carefully monitored: an agent or agents presently under surveillance: expect results soon.

No signature: but initials –

> – P.Sp: provincial revenue.

Then I cross out 'provincial revenue' as though having second thoughts again . . .'
There was a real Publius Splintho in that department: he had once been a particularly slimy subordinate of my father's. I had no scruples about getting *him* into some very murky waters – knotted string, even, red-hot irons at his pubic wrinkles, I owned someone some pain, dammit.

Cuttlefish suggested minor modifications and set to work to concoct the finished copy, as her handwriting was more flexible than mine. We used the Aramaic language, suggestive of all sorts of Levantine complications, and wrote it in blurry violet ink on a strip of glazed Egyptian linen, very hard to decipher. We then rolled it up into a tight little cylinder the size of a thick toothpick and covered it with hot wax (which would be melted off by whoever was to open it).
I was trysted to pass it to Miriam, later on, after sunset.
My injuries were throbbing and stinging, all my bones and joints were one spread of disabling ache. I asked Cuttlefish to massage my hip-connection, where of course the hurt was worst. She was sweet and tender about it, understood what I wanted and took off her light housework-shift (all she was wearing on this hot afternoon) to afford herself greater ease. She made little jokes about being retained by the secret service for the secret service's secret service and could she have a notched penny too? She told me where she might wear it, and asked me to explore the appropriate recess. Desire was not lacking: but only my eyes and the

fingers of my unburnt hand received much satisfaction. We fell, briefly, asleep.

She woke me with a soft touch on my shoulder: 'It's nearly dark already, Ivory: oughtn't you to be on your way?' I kissed her and put on my clothes. As I looked at her lying there I suddenly saw that her eyes were full of fear. I was aware for the first time that I was proud of her, proud that I loved her, afraid for her too, I could never live without her. I kissed her again: a tear ran down her scarred cheek.

'Ivory, if anyone's following you, don't go, for god's sake don't go. Miriam can always be reached in some other way – please! Oh I beg you to look after yourself!' And this, from my own property. Ridiculous, degrading arrangement: oh one of these days it would have to be rectified. Then she sat up and said: 'I never gave you your birthday present. It's such a small present, as you know, I don't own, I am owned. It's the gift of your own ownership, my assets towards your profession.' I did not understand her. Then she showed me.

She swung her feet to the floor, caught up a bright multi-coloured scarf, and draped it loosely about her neck and breasts, winding the end round her haunches, elegant, lascivious. Then she adopted a theatrical pose – graceful, without self-consciousness – as though in front of an audience of thousands – flattened her palms together and bowed, the way I have seen Indian artists acknowledge their public – and launched into Helen's famous speech from the last book of *The Iliad*. Quiet, compelling, a hard intensity of delivery laid over the obvious pathos:

'Hector, Troy's hero,
    held highest in my love
Among battalion of brothers,
    bold bairns of King Priam:
Though not you but Paris pursued and pressed me to him
    (would god I had first perished).
In all the years since I yielded him my honour,
    only from you
Not one cruel glance of contempt
    nor coarse word in this country of strangers.

Intense insult from so many,
  I was impotent to face it
Had not you, gentle Hector,
  held back the hard chill of it
With kindness and courtesy always.
  Now you are killed:
And I weep both for you and the lone waste
  of my wantonness unfriended
Here in empty Troy: endless from today
  I must ever eat my heart
Amid jerking of heads and jibing away
  from my jaunts, as they call them,
Here, in this town.' And her tears fell,
  and those of all Trojans, turbulence of grief . . .

She knelt in front of me, palms together again, bowed her head to the floor, as though receiving a standing ovation. I could neither applaud nor say anything. She put out her hand for her pipe-and-tabor and began an ancient country-dance tune from the islands, with which she had been in the habit of playing the public out at the end of the Raven's performances. A slow stately little air, with a kind of jump in the rhythm by itself sufficient to bring tears to my eyes when I heard it. This tune sometimes had words to it:

My love my love, if you must go
Then go you must, go now and don't look round.
Till you return, how shall I know
Your golden feet will still be treading on the ground?
My love my love, every step they take
They tread my heart to let it quake:
However far, my love, however near,
You tread my lonely heart and hurt it like a spear.

I knew that she knew I knew these words. I slipped out, and left her there, on my diminutive square of Persian carpet, crouched on her knees, dark, delicate, immeasurably vulnerable, placing the notes of her music after me, one by one, a charm – so it seemed – for my safety.

I was no sooner out in the dark street than I knew I was being followed. With my limp and my stick anyone could spot me a quarter of a mile away, even at night. There was nothing to be done except to do what came next.

8   The Seven Sleepers

The shrine of the Seven Sleepers has existed on a hillside behind Ephesus since time immemorial – it is a cave up a winding track with very little in it except dark walls and a large number of votive offerings hanging on them – strips of ribbon, wax dolls with wounds marked in red paint, miniature crutches and tiny silver figurines – each one indicating some sick or injured person to whom the virtue of the cave has afforded relief.

There is a story about it, of course: seven beautiful young boys, lovers of our great goddess, the Mother of Ephesus, were once in mortal danger from a local tyrant who had attempted to ravish the goddess, and who had been repelled by their valour. They fled to the cave, hoping to stay there for a day or two and then make their escape once the hunt for them had died down. But the hunt did not die down and they dared not emerge. At last, by grace of the Mother, they fell asleep. They did not wake up for years and years: and were amazed, on their return home, to discover all their contemporaries dead (including the tyrant), and the city under the beneficent rule of the Mother herself and her devoted servants. They themselves, needless to say, were still as young as ever, and even more beautiful. They thereupon built the first of the succession of resplendent temples to the Mother that they have made Ephesus famous through all the world. As I hobbled nervously through the town, with my sinister follower a block or two behind me, I dearly wished something of the same sort could happen to me.

I was in a bad enough condition altogether to make it thoroughly plausible that I was visiting the shrine for my health. I made a point of mentioning it to the constable on duty at the postern in the town wall as I went out: and indeed he saw me pulling myself along by painful clutches at pillars and posts. The steep walk up the hill was torture, but I completed it.

The cave, when I reached it, was marked by an old lady

squatting outside under an arch of lanterns, holding a begging-bowl. My contribution was a large one: I wanted the man behind me to understand that I was in search of a really comprehensive cure. I supposed he would know what the Hook had done to me, so he would not think there was anything strange about my nocturnal excursion.

Inside the cave there were more lanterns and a heavy smell of incense to cover up the smell of the devotees. The procedure was that you waited here all night, spread out face-down on the stone floor, and by morning, if you were lucky, the grace of the Mother would have entered your blood and bones. Chronic invalids spend night after night there. At the far end of the cave was a vine-root twisted by nature into an approximately female shape, almost hidden under garlands. It was said to be an image of the Mother placed there by the Sleepers before they went to sleep. If it could indeed work miracles, perhaps it had already fetched Miriam up here safely (as arranged) before everything got so awkward. I had not ventured to send word to her since my beating-up.

Well, I say nothing against vine-roots from this day forward. As I shuffled through the people, trying to find a vacant place, and genuflecting towards the image, a shapely hand stole out from a heap of shawls and mantles and took me softly by the ankle. I knelt down, and bowed my head to the ground, muttering what I hoped sounded like the proper prayers. In the middle of all this I inserted a few short words, apprising Miriam quickly of the main course of events, and imploring her to be careful. 'I know,' she whispered back, 'Jampot made me these questions all of one hour. But I knew he would not go to beat *me*, oh no not *me* – so greedy he is for the money he thinks I will bring him.' She uttered in her own language an intensely foul word about Jampot that seemed unsuitable to the sacred place, until I remembered the legendary tyrant, and decided the Mother would approve. The letter-of-fraud was passed into Miriam's hand, and whipped at once into an interior recess of her voluminous garments. We resumed our prayers.

★

I had become aware that a new worshipper had entered
the cave behind us. If he knew Miriam he could scarcely
recognize her in all her coverings, but it would not be safe
for me to leave her side too suddenly, nor vice versa. We
had to wait this out for some length of time. The opportunity came when a young priestess emerged from a
curtained alcove to perform a sacred dance. I watched her
with a professional eye: she was clumsy and repetitive, but
ultimately hypnotic, and her dance lasted literally for hours.
It communicated its steady frenzy to the crowd, who began
heaving and tossing all around me in an ecstasy. Their eff-
luvium was appalling. At the climax, amid arms shooting
up out of rotten rags, toothless mouths foaming and spluttering, screams, cries, hysterical invocations, the priestess
fell backwards in a fit, arching her body and rolling all over
the floor. When all was quiet again, Miriam and I were well
separated: but I still dared not leave until morning. I was
cramped, bored to death, chilled to the bone, and still in
pain. Perhaps I had negated my cure by using the cave for
political intrigue. Don't tell me it had never been done there
before: is it not the one activity we Greeks are all supposed
to be expert in?

When the first rays of the sun appeared through the entrance, I rose creaking to my feet, and made my way out,
still facing inwards to the image, bowing and ducking in the
ardent fag-end of my night's supplications. I could not dis-
cern whether or no I was followed any more. At least I did not
see him. Perhaps he had had enough of the discomfort of the
shrine and had gone home hours ago to his bed, lucky bugger.

The next stage of the plot would depend upon Miriam.
With the general so near at hand there was no time to be
lost.

When I was about half-way down towards the town-wall,
something caught my eye along the valley to the east. It was
a cloud of dust among the olive-groves, such as might be
set up by a marching column of men.

With the general upon us already, there was no time *at
all* to be lost. I heard the faint braying of a cavalry trumpet,
peremptory beyond the distant trees.

9   *Professional Responsibilities*

I did not personally go to witness the arrival of the regiments into Ephesus. I was far too knocked about. As soon as I reached home I gave instructions to Cuttlefish to turn any clients away and pin up a notice that the office was closed. I was going to bed for a few hours' much-needed sleep. In the meantime, I would be obliged if she could go out into the town and observe events. She also should explore an arrangement to receive an up-to-date bulletin from Miriam, if this was possible. She did not comment on these orders.

I woke up in hot oppressive thunderstorm weather, early afternoon; had some wine and bread-and-garlic: and decided to visit the public baths. Cuttlefish had not returned. As I crossed the threshold I heard thunder, crackling and rumbling through a livid sky behind the mountains. In a few minutes the storm would be on top of us. I wrapped myself up accordingly. There was another noise too, a hubbub of shouting some way off, down-town in the direction of the main square. By the time I reached the baths – a small establishment frequented by actors and the less pretentious sort of literary man – the rain was coming down as though god had kicked over a washtub. Was I still under surveillance? Oh dammit, what the hell . . .?

The porter at the baths took my money in silence, helped me off with my dripping oilskin, and gave me the key to a cubicle. His silence was unlike him: I asked if he had any news. 'No sir, afraid not, sir. Nobody's given me any, so I've none to pass on. Hardly any customers today, sir, they'll all have gone out to the temple, you see.'

'The temple? What temple?'

'The temple of the Mother, sir.' (This lay outside the walls in its own extensive precinct). 'The general went direct there to celebrate his victories.'

'I see. I wasn't well this morning. So he hasn't come into town at all, then?'

'Not yet, sir, and by all accounts he isn't going to, nor yet any of his men. They've been pitching camp up the valley there, well clear of the town.'

'Then what was all that shouting? It sounded as though it came from the square?'

'Oh yes, sir, that was the public meeting. One or two of the faction-bosses, that chap they call the Hook from down the docks, Bully Brisket from the red-light district, old Mother whatsit who runs the operation in the vegetable-market, you know who I mean – they've been up making speeches to the street-gangs – what an insult to the trade of the town it is that the troops have been kept away, and how the general wants to bankrupt the tradespeople and so on. No-one'll care though.'

'Won't they? Why not?' For a man with no news he was singularly well-informed.

'Because all them sharks in the temple-precinct are making a packet out of today, souvenir-selling, catering, girls for the soldiers – oh the lads have been given a measure of leave: to attend the temple for approved pious purposes, offering thanks just the same as their general: but no-one's to come a yard nearer the town than that, dead strict. You see how it all sets up.'

I did indeed. The council was only under serious threat from the people's discontent if the factions among the temple-dependants were united with those inside the walls. Ephesus was primarily a pilgrimage town, and the temple carried far more political weight than the rest of the place. If the Hook and his friends had thought that the general at odds with the town-council would be an opening they could exploit, they were already out-manoeuvred. Someone, I thought, had been giving the general some excellent advice. Had I under-rated Roscius? I tipped the porter and went on into the baths.

There was no-one I knew in the hot rooms: I lay about in the steam for a while, submitted to a massage, which did me some good, and then passed through to the cold plunge. The first person I saw was Roscius himself, having his wiry dark body towelled down by an attendant. I was amazed, I had supposed he would be with the army, and said so.

'Oh no no, no no,' he replied, shaking globules of water out of his close-cropped hair. 'I was with them, yes: but today is the general on duty, and I am on duty. As soon as I am restored from the bath I commence rehearsal. You will watch?' He laughed at my astonishment. 'Complete achievement: your great theatre in three days, four days perhaps, but I hope sooner, grand gala performance of Plautus, for the general; Menander, for all you good Greek-people, double-bill, triple-bill, I thought some chorus-dance from Aristophanes. But who shall direct? Plautus, of course, me – the actors Latin amateurs from the general's private troupe: our friend Shoulderbone the Menander-piece, he shall use the regular theatre-company: for the chorus, can you suggest? All to be ready in enormous great haste. Did I not say my general would turn trump? Complete achievement for the intrigue of Roscius. All Roman Games and Cato-nonsense to be in the camp and nowhere else. Let the hooligans do what they want inside there: sword-fighters, temple-girls, wild animals, Armenian captives, wagons of wine from up-country: no damage to your town at all! Congratulate me, Ivory!'

I did. He pranced about flapping his towel, an innocence and self-conceit that was hard to resist. I would guess his age at about thirty: he was as lively as a child of seven. He made me promise to call in at the theatre later on – 'I assure you, a great honour. Besides, I shall need your help. Oh these will be such jealousies, temperaments; and you know all the people here: you will tell me which ones to despise. And, please, do contrive me a good chorus-master for the Aristophanes.' He skipped off into the gymnasium for half-an-hour of vigorous handball, while I gave myself up with a shudder into the icy cold water. It occurred to me that everything I had gone through during the past twenty-four hours had been utterly pointless – this intense little squinting Italian with one word in the right ear had done the whole business for us. For *us*, yes indeed – the purposes of my birthday party were apparently abundantly fulfilled. But how far were they in truth *my* purposes?

It had been Shoulderbone's idea that my party should be turned into a political cabal, and the 'intrigue of Roscius' had been its successful result. The *improvement* upon this, the framing of Jampot, was an elaboration which I could have checked had I had all my wits about me: but no, I did not check it, and it now had become *my purpose*.

Did I need any more to pursue it? I had my own very particular feud with the men of the tax-office: I had a yellow torturing dwarf in the back of my memory, a brother who made servant-girls cry, a father with a gold tooth. No reason to think that any of them still lived in the province: but their life-work was once more extant, and it had to be brought down in ruin. Whatever I had begun was to be continued. To be finished. For *me*. (Maybe better, after all, had we left it all to our politically-moribund Guild . . . ?)

As I hurried home through the diminishing rain, I ran smack into Cuttlefish at a street-corner. Her eyes snapped at me, her mouth was a rigid slit.

'Where the hell have you been?'

'I went to the baths, why wouldn't I? Look, Roscius was there and he said – '

'I got home and you'd gone. The least you could do was to leave a note on the table.'

'I'm sorry, I didn't think. There's a change in the situation. Roscius has already managed to – '

'Why didn't you tell me Irene had asked you to go with her to Italy?'

'What? Who told you that?'

'I got home and you'd gone, the whole place was completely empty, god I thought that they'd taken you, how could you be so goddam thoughtless! Chloe told me, who else? I don't mind, why should I mind: you've a right to improve your career, you'll either take me with you to cook for you and enter your books up, or you'll dispose of me before you go, you've a right to do either. Miriam has already put the letter onto Jampot. She left word with Chloe an hour ago. She went to Jampot's office with her sisters to talk business, and took her chance to lift up his felt cap from the counter while Abigail got Rachel to let him feel her breasts and so on . . . the letter has been slipped into the rolled seam of the cap. He never goes out without it on his head, he won't notice the letter because the seams are stiffened anyway with bits of bone to make it sit sharp like a cockscomb. So there you are. What are you doing?'

We had come back into my office and I was searching through my ledgers for names. A chorus-master for the Aristophanes. I told the Cuttlefish and she offered some pertinent advice. And then:

'I suppose this means you'll drop the whole Jampot thing?'

'I'm dropping nothing. I have my reasons.'

'Oh god. And I know you have. Oh god, can't you forget them?'

'No. Now these are the names I have jotted down as a set of possibles, but some of them may not be in town. I can't chase them all up myself, I told Roscius I'd attend his rehearsal. Find out who's available and come and tell me at the theatre.'

'You had every chance to mention to me that Irene had invited you: you bloody well said nothing. Have you told her yet you accept her offer?' I was silent. 'I said have you told her? If you don't give me an answer I'll find not one chorus-master and when you look for me I'll be gone. Then you will have to advertise me as "run" and put the reward out. But would you dare? You would not: you'd be ashamed. I want an answer!'

'I have told Irene nothing. I have not made up my mind.'

'Then bloody well make it up. In Ephesus you're a notched penny and they watch you wherever you go. Get out of here, go to Italy, use your wits, you hobbling bastard: that woman is well aware of what's good for you, she guessed what might happen. Take me or don't, I don't care: you're fat enough in the gut to be comfortable anywhere, and a meagre thing like her could slide inside that crooked hip for as long as you want.'

I went over to the theatre with my mind in a turmoil. For the next few hours, until well after sunset, I had more than enough to think about; I tried my best to concentrate upon professional responsibilities. They needed more than a chorus-master, they needed chorus-boys and musicians, and

Chloe (who was doing the décor) required sheaves of notes
and verbal instructions. Cuttlefish turned up, in the event,
with an excellently put-together schedule of available people
and then went out again to do the same for the chorus-boys
and music – she knew the job better than I did in some
ways and Roscius congratulated me upon her extreme
efficiency. She made no reference to her earlier outburst:
and was cool and polite in everything she had to say to me.

10   Gala Performance

For three days I was privileged to watch Roscius create his
programme. That is to say I sat in the middle of a sort of
equinoctial storm (metaphorically and literally – it sluiced
with rain at unpredictable intervals, the stone seats of the
theatre were intermittently turned into a cascade from an
ornamental garden and the stage-floor steamed between
showers): Roscius ran up and down, shouted, sang, jumped
onto the stage and pushed and pulled his actors about; he
skidded off into corners with individual performers and
whispered ferocious things into their ears; he put on everyone else's mask and demonstrated in a rage how each
character should be rendered; he cursed, kissed, and cooed
and dashed his head against pillars, screaming like a sea-
gull.

His actors were literate and largely Greek-speaking young
NCOs from the headquarters company of the Stain's force.
They were not at all bad – I gathered Roscius had had
something to do with their original training. They were
a complete contrast to the Menander company, which
Shoulderbone directed in a solid old-fashioned manner as
befitted a group who were all playing parts they had played
hundreds of times before and knew exactly what was
expected of them. The main tensions of the work arose when
Shoulderbone and Roscius quarrelled over who should rehearse in the theatre at any given time. The stage-manager
had worked out an alternating arrangement with a small
roofed concert-hall at the far end of town, and neither party
wanted to have to use it. *The Frogs* chorus (we decided

on *The Frogs* because the theatre had a set of admirable costumes only partially damaged by the revenue-office men) was taken away to a gymnasium outside the walls, to the annoyance of the aristocratic athletes who normally occupied it. That too caused trouble, and our neurotic stage-manager fell into repeated despairs, accusing all of us of sabotaging his theatre's reputation.

At night cressets of fire illuminated the orchestra and there was somebody at work by their light upon stage nearly all night every night until dawn. I found myself general production assistant for everyone. I did manage to slip home for erratic intervals of sleep, and Cuttlefish brought my meals into the theatre. She spent most of the time racing round town on essential errands, that were really none of her responsibility. The regular theatre-staff, though, had proved itself totally inadequate. It consisted largely of silly boys whom the stage-manager liked to caress: whereas Roscius was, I suppose, a genius; and Shoulderbone had derived his years of experience from the improvisatory patchworks of down-at-heel touring companies. They both made demands that these young urban exquisites were unable to fulfil, and Cuttlefish bore the brunt.

On the third day – the day of the dress-rehearsal – the hysteria had reached crisis. The Plautus company were on stage doing a final run-through without costumes: the Menander company were disputing their costumes in high voices with two of Chloe's assistants: the *Frogs* boys were brek-ek-ekking at some last-minute vocal variations up at the top of the seat-tiers: and more of Chloe's girls were on step-ladders all over the place hanging up decorations and squabbling with the scene-shifters and stage-carpenters, whose hammerings, sawings, and bad language (extra loud, to show their independence) reverberated through the whole auditorium. Chloe herself was striding about with her skirts kilted to the thigh, yelling at her employees and now and then abusing Shoulderbone.

Irene and the Cuttlefish were on the upper stage having an argument. I gathered that in some bewildering way Roscius had hired them both to present a prologue of de-

clamation and song, and was expecting them to work
out their own material. I was exhausted and had a headache:
but for the moment I had nothing to do. I contemplated
the chaos from half-way up the tiers.

I saw a person walking in at one of the entrances. The
rain had begun again, though none of us noticed it any
longer: but this man had pulled his hood over his head and
wrapped his cloak around him. A strong-bodied, upright,
graceful figure. I assumed he was from the front-of-house
staff (newly appointed for this special occasion). He walked
up the tiers and sat down a few yards away from me. He
looked sharply this way and that. I don't think anyone else
had observed him. After a while the rain stopped and the
theatre steamed yet again. Chloe, stopping on the steps,
wrung water out of her heavy skirts with both hands.

'There's some of us going to enjoy rheumatism after this,'
she announced: 'I just hope it rains tomorrow and lays up
that damned general.' Then she saw the stranger. 'Who's
that?' she said to me. I shrugged. 'Then he oughtn't to be
in here. No public in at dress-rehearsal unless invited and
no-one's been invited. This is a private rehearsal. Will you
kindly get out.'

The man had folded his hood back when the rain left off.
He had a huge maroon birthmark running all down one
side of his face from eye to jowl as though someone had
splashed paint at him. His hair was thick, tufted, going grey
at the temples. He seemed mild-mannered, sensitive, perhaps
a little diffident. Then I saw his eyes. Ice-blue and utterly
terrifying. They never changed, whatever expression moved
elsewhere on his face.

'I am so sorry if I am intruding, madam, but I understood
from the artistic director it would be possible for me to be
here if I did not get in the way.' Roscius, lifting his mask,
took a squint at what was happening: 'That's quite in good
order; the gentleman is permitted.' And then he continued
in his role as the Uxorious Usurer. Chloe snorted, turned
away to her work. I sat up in alarm and adjusted my attire.
That birthmark, Roscius's permission? Of course – and they
called him the *Stain* . . .! Was there a specific penalty for
insulting an incognito senior officer? I thought it more than

probable. My father would have known, my father would have been oiling the man's buttocks by now – oh god, the bloody Stain was coming across to talk to *me*. What on earth was I to say?

'Excuse me, you are Ivory, I think? I understand that the general will be inviting a few people – artists, musicians, people like that – to an informal gathering at his quarters tomorrow night, after dinner. He has commissioned me to enquire if you would care to make one of them?' I replied that I was most honoured and would certainly attend the general. I spoke rather less deferentially than I would have done had he really been the general's social secretary. I've no objection to incognito, but I resent its being *flaunted* at me. Like the stage-carpenters, I too had some independence to maintain. He smiled, quite a warm smile (but not including the eyes), moved quietly across the stage through the Plautus (the soldier-actors showed no awareness, no doubt they knew his methods), gave a polite nod to Roscius, and disappeared into the greenroom.

A little later I saw him chatting, very smoothly, to the Cuttlefish and Irene. I crossed my fingers.

The dress-rehearsal, immediately afterwards, passed off with no more than the usual number of stomach-churning disasters. One incident was interesting. As a gesture of courtesy to the practices of our Greek theatre, Roscius had ordered Chloe to provide the phallus for the Plautus costumes. Just before his company got their work under way, an assertive young warrant-officer of the engineer-corps (who played the Bald Old Man, and rather well) came forward and said that the men regarded these lolloping appendages as degrading to the One City and they were refusing to have anything to do with them. They were men and they were soldiers and such filthy tricks were only fit for . . . Roscius hastened to cut him short, but too late. Shoulder-bone came roaring-in that the phallic costume had the most ancient and sacred associations, and that the sapper was offering a deliberate insult to his hosts in the theatre and to the entire culture of Homer, Plato and Pythagoras. Everybody else joined in, phrases like 'Greeko ratbags' and 'imperialist dogsbodies' were flung about regardless.

The Stain came out of the greenroom, stalked softly across the stage, and spoke – in Greek – in a low voice to the warrant officer, with his quick pleasant smile, just as before. But what he said was in strong contrast to his demeanour. 'You: come here, please, here. My friend Roscius has decided, for reasons that do not concern you, that you are all to dress yourselves upon this stage like a crowd of sex-starved sausage-pricked balloon-ballocked fucking donkeys. Please do what he asks. You are to hang, with enthusiasm, these red-and-yellow school-girls' dream-sweeteners to swing about between your legs for all the Greeks to giggle at. I want it done. So do it. Thank you.' He then left the theatre. The sapper was as pale as his shirt and trembling from head to foot.

After that there were no more inter-cultural difficulties, and Shoulderbone apologized handsomely to Roscius for having accused him of 'colonizing the Ephesus theatre'.

I need not describe the Gala Performance itself, except just to state that it was an enormous success. In my opinion the prologue, by Irene and Cuttlefish, was the best part of it. Probably because (a) it was the only part played by women, and (b) it was new. Menander and Aristophanes I knew backwards: and Plautus struck me as quite devoid of originality – but then I could not follow the Latin dialogue in any detail, though I dare say it was witty. The prologue was a compilation of light classical verses, sprightly traditional tunes, and some delicately salacious dancing. Its theme was 'the war is over: welcome the blessings of peace (most of them are erotic)'.

They played it with an excellent technique, as I would have expected: but what gave it its particular piquancy was the very vivid sense conveyed to the audience that the two women were – well, not exactly quarrelling, but in some concealed way *disputing* their script and their stage-business between them even as they presented it to the public. They performed without masks: Chloe had got up exquisite costumes. Irene was a young man in the hunting-dress of a mountain-clan, sombrero hat and skin-tight blue riding breeches. I had never seen her in anything like a 'role' before: she was stunning. The Stain applauded her with especial energy. (Roscius told me that it was at the Stain's personal insistence that the prologue was allotted to women. It seemed he liked them as much as men). Cuttlefish wore a semi-transparent shepherdess costume and showed far greater sense of comedy than I am sure her old Raven had ever suspected.

There was another point about this prologue, which, oddly, never struck me until it was all over – I had been altogether too rushed off my feet during the hectic days-and-nights of preparation to be able to look at all judiciously at what was being prepared . . . Women, *in the public theatre*, without masks, exchanging dialogue (as opposed to merely exhibiting themselves in ballet or declaiming a certain type of choric interlude), were an unprecedented innovation. Chloe and Irene, as members of Shoulderbone's old company, for instance, never appeared in a regular town-auditorium. Village-festivals and private performances in somebody's house were quite a different matter. I suppose conservative colleagues, such as Shoulderbone himself, were so relieved to see the army actors wearing our Greek phallus in a Greek-derived comedy, that they forgot to be outraged: but in a sense this elegant prologue was as disruptive to our Ephesus habit-of-life as the 'Hot Pockets' would have been . . . 'Colonizing our theatre' . . .? I don't think so. It was just as much an innovation to Roscius as it was to us. If it had not been for subsequent and *really* disruptive events, we could have constructed an entire avant-garde theatrical climate out of it. Now I never thought of myself as at all avant-garde. But all the theatre work I have been involved in since this extraordinary gala has been in one sense or another a development of the women's prologue: so maybe I ought to be better known to the cultural historians? No: of course not . . . the direct credit belongs to Roscius. And, I must admit it, to that blood-thirsty murderer, the Stain. 'Forgive him, Muse, his thousands upon thousands of butchered innocents: he re-animated the sluggish stage.' *There's* an epitaph.

After the performance, in the emerging crowds, somebody jogged my elbow, it was Jampot, in his absurd cockscomb cap. 'Nice show, very nice, ho yes. That Eyetalian knows his business. Hey, who was the bint in the blue breeches? Very sharp, very brisk little curve to her backend.' If he had not recognized Irene (she had been wearing high pattens the last time he saw her and her hair today was worn short, blonde and uncovered), I was not going to tell him. He showed his fangs. 'Right then, keep her a secret. But if she's at the general's rave-up tonight, watch out for old Jampot: I'll be having them sky-blue strides off of her before you can addle an egg.' He merged into the crowd and was off. I had not thought the Stain would have invited Jampot. Possibilities?

11   *The Stain's Hospitality*

The general was staying at the provincial governor's residence (the governor himself, as I had guessed, was sulking in Pergamus) – more a villa than a palace, in the outer suburbs beyond the Mother's temple. As I limped along there after dinner in gathering dusk, I noticed the temple precinct was full of soldiers in walking-out dress, most of them drunk, all of them noisy. Raucous music and the screaming of girls. I thought one or two of them had begun to scream in earnest. It relieved me to see a large number of military police assembling in the shadows outside the sacred gardens, bludgeons at the ready; they looked as though they meant business. I was glad Cuttlefish was not with me. I didn't know what privileges of disorder were permitted the custodians of soldiers' order in a foreign town. But no-one accosted me.

The residence was exuberantly illuminated, house, gardens, and all. Butler at the hall-door receiving me like a prince: though he vexed me by trying to park my walking-stick in the cloakroom – I *need* it on staircases, dammit. A footman led me through half-furnished (governor in Pergamus, of course) rooms into a wide saloon with too much statuary. Upon divans amid the marble disc-hurlers and nymphs-burst-in-on-in-the-bathroom were gathered the more raffish representatives of our artistic and cultural élite, as well as associated chancers such as the Jampot and some moderately refined courtesans. None of them looked much more at their ease than I was.

Irene was there, in a very demure dress: and beside her – good god – the Cuttlefish. Damn the black bitch, not one word to me beforehand. I had been away from home since the show – I had dined with some clients – and, as far as I knew, Cuttlefish was not going out this evening. But here she was and in the very outfit she put on for my birthday. I congratulated her in a bitter whisper upon the democratic geniality of our host.

'Don't believe a word of it:' between her teeth, poker-faced. 'He is proving to all of us that all of *our* class-distinctions are altogether beneath his notice.' I was served with fancy rubbish on a dish, and a drink, thank god, by a flunkey. Roscius was behind him: 'Ah, Ivory, so good that you came. Oh dear me, he was delighted, *such* delight, beyond all hope – and to *you* the greatest share of the credit, I have told him.'

'Where is he then?'

'Still at dinner, with horrible staff-officers. Apologies to us all: but affairs of state have created delay. Aha, here he comes.'

The Stain, flushed and resplendent, swung in through the double doors. He was talking strenuously to a staff-officer, to whom he had apparently just handed a sheaf of papers. This man saluted and went away. The doors were closed behind him, and the Stain came into our midst. He held out his arms in a gesture of humble welcome. He made a most graceful speech, sat down and asked us to sit. He called for music. We then enjoyed for the next three hours what proved to be, all in all, a conventional 'artistic' party of the sort we had all been to many times before.

The Stain chatted in an intimate and unfailingly court-eous manner with nearly everyone (including myself). His talk was interesting and appropriate, he did not condescend. Enough wine was served for a number of people (who ought to have known better) to grow slightly tipsy. Jampot, alas, was not one of them. On the other hand, the Stain was – at least, he gave that impression. The unmarked side of his vivid face (normally very pale) broke out into red blotches, and his loose evening robes became progressively looser as he played little amorous games with his fingers on exposed areas of male and female skin (Cuttlefish was not exempt, but what could I say?).

At one point Jampot got hold of me and led me aside.

'It's *her* of course, of course it is, why didn't you tell me?' He was looking at Irene.

'You didn't ask me.'

'Don't come clever. Remember what happened the last time. Is she going to get him into her letter-box tonight then, or isn't she?'

'Who?'

'Who d'you think? Our parti-coloured jocular Greek-lover, that's who.'

'I don't know.'

'Then fucking find out, me old darling. Jerk your ear in the right place when he's having his next little whispers with her. What else d'you think you're paid for?'

'Why don't you do it? You're paid for it as much as me.'

'I'm paid a sight more, which entitles me to delegate dodgy jobs. I don't want to be anywhere near him: he gives me the creeps. Go on, you do what I tell you, I'll see you tomorrow. I want to hear the full chapter-and-verse – if not, you know what'll happen.'

Now and then during the evening an officer or secretary would slip in with a confidential communication for the general. He dealt with these briefly, very quiet, very business-like, very far from tipsy. Now and then I could hear footsteps and busy voices in other parts of the house: and at times a harsh outbreak of military orders from beyond the garden terrace. Eventually – while we were all taking part in rowdy and promiscuous dancing (even me with my bad leg – ridiculous hop-skip-jump: some of the ladies said they loved it) – an aide-de-camp entered with an important-looking document. The Stain at once stopped dancing: 'Dear ladies, gentlemen, I am forced to make my excuses to all of you: my official duties once more compel me. I have been honoured and stimulated indeed by your presence here tonight. May I thank you for your acceptance of my presumptuous invitation?'

We thanked him – some of us unduly effusively – and moved en masse towards the cloakroom. I had done nothing about Jampot. Something must be done. And where was the Cuttlefish? Ah, there she was. She was coming home with me and with nobody else – we had to discuss . . .

A man stepped in front of me, an agreeable fat man, I had noticed him telling anecdotes to Irene about Italian actresses. I assumed he was one of the Stain's entourage, but he was not introduced to anyone. Now he cut me out, as it were, from the crowd, and manoeuvred me into a side-passage before I realized what was happening. His hand on my upper arm was soft but firm.

'I don't want you to go home just yet,' he said. 'The butler will tell your girl that there is a carriage for her and the other lady: come with me, please, this way.' He spoke as though there was no question of my disputing his instruction. I did not dispute it. We went up some back stairs into a small box-room, full of piles of discarded furniture. He sat down on a camp-stool at a folding table, motioned me to sit opposite.

His podgy hand was out palm-uppermost on the table. A notched penny was lying in it. 'This fell down from your neck in the course of the dancing,' he said. 'If you are wearing one of these, it is very foolish not to look after it. You had too much to drink and that is not at all what we expect of you.' I made myself look stupid.

'Don't pretend you don't understand me,' he said. He brought his other hand up to the table, an identical penny was there.

'Now,' he said, 'who recruited you, when was it done, and for whom do you imagine you are working?' I had thought him agreeable: I was now changing my opinion. But this time there was no Hook in the room to knock me about. I said something about being over-tired after the heavy work in the theatre. I said I had been recruited by a

man in Ephesus and that he had given me to understand I
was to work for the security of the One City, which I very
much wanted to do, on account of the One City being the
only defence against our external and internal enemies.

'Bullshit,' said the man. 'You are in it for the goodies like
everyone else of our provincial recruitment. The question
is, whose goodies? What did he ask you to find out, this
"man in Ephesus"?' I was, oh dear, not quite sober. I tried
hard to thrust myself into condition of intensive thought.
This fat man had participated in the Stain's private relaxations: he had unchallenged access to a room in the Stain's
house: the butler ordered carriages at his say-so. Could I
risk the assumption that he was an operator in the Stain's
political interest? If not, I was finished. But if so: then by
god I could deal with Jampot, and I would.

12   Six Legs in a Bed

I said: 'The man who recruited me said to me what I just
said to you, all right, let's call it bullshit. But at the time –'
   'When?'
   'Last week.'
   'Ah-ha. Carry on. At the time?'
   'At the time I believed him. If we don't have your army
here King Strychnine or the Persians will make a grab for
us and *we* can't keep them out. We're a very rich town, we
face west, so we work for the west. I was happy to join
because, as you said – goodies. But general goodies, for the
town as well as me. Don't misunderstand me. I'm not an
idealist. But I'm not one of your cheap crooks, like the
Jampot.'
   'Who's the Jampot?'
   'The man who recruited me.'
   'How do you know he's a cheap crook?'
   This was it. Do I tell him now, or don't I? His face had
no expression on it. It was just fat. I could not read him,
any more than I could read his master: if the Stain *was* his
master. I prevaricated. I was a coward. The Cuttlefish
would have despised me. 'Because,' I said, 'I know him:

we're in the same business and he cheats me out of my clients.'

'That would not necessarily have anything to do with his work on behalf of the City. It might be a cover he's been carefully building up. He might even be an idealist.'

No, I must get it over with. 'He might, but he isn't. I happen to know that he works for at least *two* Cities. One of them within the other. I can't tell you exactly how. I work for him and I do what he tells me. If he tells me to copy and translate the draft of a private and very ambiguous letter and roll it up tight enough for him to hide it in the stitches of his cap, I don't ask any questions. But if the City in fact wants to support the overt policy of your general and to use him here to protect its assets, then it is going about it an odd way: I say no more.'

He sat in silence for what seemed ages. It must have been at least ten minutes. Then he went out, leaving me alone (except for a silent soldier whom he called into the room to watch me). I waited for what seemed ages. It must have been at least two hours. Then he came back and fetched me by several corridors into a small lobby with sentries in it. Through a half-open door I saw a tangle of bare legs among bed-sheets. The fat man, gone in through this door, was speaking softly. The legs disentangled themselves, and four of them came to the floor, followed by their respective bodies – two young women, trying to grasp a few clothes around them. The fat man brought them out into the lobby and propelled them down the corridor. They ran out of my vision, their knock-knees moving very fast.

The owner of the remaining legs was out of bed too, striding naked across the room and also out of my vision: it was the Stain. The door was closed and I waited among the sentries, until the fat man called me into the room. The Stain had put a dressing-gown half-on half-off, he looked like one of the more suggestive statues downstairs. His body was white, almost hairless, his eyes appalling.

'Sit down,' he said. I did so. 'I would have preferred not to have been interrupted just at this moment,' he said. 'They have been out and collected your Jampot. It would have saved trouble, saved *me* trouble, had we known before he left the premises. Let us see if you told us the truth.'

A knock on the door: a military policeman with Jampot's cap.

'Of course what you say was put into it may not be still there. If it isn't we can always ask him – *and* you – if it ever really was. You will tell us.' As the Stain spoke, he ran his finger over the seams. He picked up a razor from his dressing-table, slit one of the seams, and there was the letter. But before he found it, something happened to me: I knew what to be touching just now, and my hand was under my shirt. I felt warm water between my fingers. Everything I had intended to have had done was being done, and I was leaking with terror in the general's bedroom. My shameful pool spread on the polished floorboards. Neither of them took any notice: I daresay they were used to it.

The wax of the letter was warmed over a candle, and the fat man cautiously unrolled the linen strip. 'Aramaic, sir.' 'Can you read it?' He could and did.

'When does he say he was told to write this?'

'Last week.'

'It's already out-of-date and it hasn't been sent. "He (underlined) and his soldiers not yet arrived but expected daily" . . . Perhaps he had a courier to go with it on a particular ship and we got here before the ship was due to leave, in which case he'd be writing a new one. He could, I suppose, have forgotten he still had it in his cap. Probable?'

'Incompetent,' said the fat man. 'Some of our provincial recruitment is extremely incompetent.' They both looked at me.

'I suppose there is no doubt who is meant by "his lordship"?' said the Stain.

'No, sir: though we haven't actually heard him referred to as that before.'

' "PG" . . .? How deeply can we assume *he* is implicated? Of course he's sympathetic . . .'

'May I suggest it would be judicious to ignore PG for the time being? Have a look at this "P.Sp.", though, and everyone else in associated departments. Have a very thorough look at our provincial recruitment too.' He swung round to

me. 'I wonder how much more *you* know?' Four eyes
burned into me, relentless, contemptuous.

'Keep your leg still,' said the Stain. And then, to the fat
man: 'He has his motives for telling us this: straight, bent,
does it matter? He's ours now, until someone gives him an
excuse for more motives. Tell him to go home.' He went
over to a full-length mirror, tossed his dressing-gown into
the bed, and began to rearrange his dishevelled hair. 'Oh,'
he said, 'start your business directly, if you'd be so good. I
want all these people *depreciated* by first thing tomorrow
morning. And send those two back in again.'

At the far end of the corridor were the two girls, shivering. (At least, they were not Cuttlefish and Irene . . .) The
fat man clapped the bare bottom of one of them and sent
them scuttling towards the bedroom. His hand was on my
arm all the way downstairs to a back door, and a sentry
looked after me in the same fashion as far as the garden
gate.

I was overtaken on the road into town by a column of
horse, riding fast . . . Outside the temple was a scene of
dereliction, overturned tables, torn clothes, scattered
flowers and broken bottles, a girl weeping by the edge of
the road, some pools of vomit (and one of blood), and three
sodden soldiers being beaten by military policemen. Everyone else had disappeared . . . At a small villa between temple
and town some of the cavalry horses were stamping about
on the flowerbeds. Troopers pulled a corpulent figure in
a nightshirt down the front steps. I recognized the tax-
officer whom I had seen a few days before taking inventory
at the theatre. His wife stood in the doorway shrieking and
trying to pull him back. One of the troopers knocked her
down.

Inside the town I could hear the hoofs of the cavalry
echoing through the streets on all sides. Round the corner
of a side-street that led to the harbour came a number of
them clattering out of the shadows. The last horse had a
man tied by the feet to its tail, his body jerking and bouncing
over the cobbles. The face was unrecognizable with blood
and filth, but I thought I knew the shaven head and the big

fists at the ends of the sinewy arms. Could they have discovered the Hook so soon after my disclosure, or had he
been marked down at the time of his public meeting? I had
very much the feeling that the Stain had had a well-prepared
contingency plan, and that my contribution to it was no
more than incidental.

When I knocked on my own front door and fell shuddering into the room, I was rounded on at once by Cuttlefish,
and by Irene, who had been sitting with her for hours, convinced that I was dead, convinced that the Cuttlefish would
be sold off at once by public auction as the sequestrated
property of a treasonable conspirator. Irene had said she
would help Cuttlefish escape. This would have subjected
Irene to an equal jeopardy. Neither of them were in a
rational state at all. Cuttlefish hit me six or seven times in
the face.

I burst into tears: 'You treacherous grinning liquorice-
stick, whether you like it or you don't like it, I am accepting
here and now Irene's offer to go to Italy and – '

Irene ground her teeth. 'Does the offer still stand? I'm
not taking you anywhere if the only reason you want to
come is that you've got into a paralysed panic and watered
your pants. I need a man in Italy who can do my business
for me as it needs to be done, a cool head, you hysterical
bugger, clear thinking, that's what I need. If you can give
me that I don't mind about your double chin. I don't mind
your slob-belly like a sackful of gutter-sludge, I can even
put up with your daddy-longlegs bloody limp. But *can* you
give it me? Or will you wait for the moment of crisis and
then get yourself weeping drunk?'

A man in the street came running, shouting 'help help'
and pounding on doors. We all three froze and clutched
each other. No door was opened to him, whoever he was.
The horsehoofs came after him, there was a furious tumbling struggle and a noise like wet washing being thumped
and slapped on the riverbank. The horses went away again,
more quietly, almost a pretty jingling.

I lurched into the yard, to drop off my clothes and to
pour cold water over myself. Cuttlefish came after me,
helped me to dress again, and told me it was all right: Irene

would take me, she had already asked her to, there was a
boat for the Heel of Italy in four days' time and Chloe knew
the captain. Irene wanted Cuttlefish to come to Italy too.
We then talked in a calmer fashion, had something to eat,
had a great deal to drink, and at last went to bed. I thought
Irene should stay with us: at least *I* didn't dare escort her to
Chloe's.

In the end we all got into bed together because we seemed
to need each other's company. The mattress was scarcely
wide enough. But the two women went off to sleep at once,
curled up under and over me with all their clothes on. They
snored, out of time with one another. I lay on my back, felt
the entire night spin drunkenly round and round. If I had
to get up and go out again into the yard, I did not know
how to do it without waking the pair of them up. It was as
though we were devising a careful parody of the Stain's
sleeping habits. Perhaps we were. Gradually the wine had
its effect. I fell into unconsciousness like an ill-shaped
boulder rolling down a terraced hillside . . .

The following morning a number of individuals, some of
them well-known, others obscure, were discovered by the
police to have suffered mysterious street-accidents during
the night. A notice appeared outside the town hall, signed
on behalf of the provincial governor, promising full compensation for any wrongful decisions (particularly upon
matters of taxation) affecting the rights of the public.
Several dozen government officers were 'replaced' or 'superannuated', and immediately vacated their commodious
houses. One of them was seen moving his family and effects
into the tenement where Jampot had had his 'office'. Jampot
himself was never seen again on this earth. A consortium
from Delos took over his business.

No security-enforcement personnel were included in
these cautiously-welcomed reforms: and indeed the town-
hall notice made it clear that compensation was not on offer
for any of their transgressions. The same old predatory
figures were seen, as always, patrolling the streets.

Chloe, down at the docks to organize our sea-passage,

noticed a long line of brutal-looking men, in fetters, descending the gangplank of a freighter just in from the mouth of the Danube. She was told they were sword-fighters, for the soldiers' Games in the Stain's camp. Later we heard that a whole regiment, collectively disgraced by court-martial, had had to match every tenth man, unarmed, against these newcomers. It was rumoured that this was in punishment for the dreadfully disorderly behaviour of the troops that had been entertained at the Mother's temple. Two flute-girls had died, it seemed, and a priestess had been grossly abused in attempting to prevent the desecration of an altar. But we never heard a reliable account. The soldiers, from then on, remained strictly behind their stockade.

Roscius kept out of our way: but on the eve of our departure I ran into him again at the baths. He said that the Stain had had charges of extortion laid against him in the City, that he was happily making ready to journey there and confront them, confident in the outcome. The regiments were to remain in Asia, split up into small units among widely-dispersed garrisons. Arrears of pay had been supplied, and the men were to be allowed to find wives and bring them with them. There was a new political situation in Italy. Roscius thought that the 'new crowd' administration had developed a split in it, something to do with franchise-rights for the allied towns: anyway, the Stain was taking no precipitate action.

We, on the other hand, were. For we discovered that unaccountable obstacles were being put in our way – a writ was suddenly served on Irene for a debt she swore she had never incurred – ages ago, according to the document, some ancient bill drawn in Tarsus for the supply of cosmetics, enough to keep a whole brothel in mascara and lipstick for years. She would have to go to court and we would miss our sailing. We were sure this was a notched-penny trick: and we determined to circumvent it. In the end we boarded the ship disguized as an Indian priest with his two wives – myself and Irene in blackface, Cuttlefish well whitened-down, and my limp concealed by putting me on a stretcher and claiming that I was in 'the sacred trance of Kali', whoever Kali might be. Irene got the name from a man she had

known in Trebizond who happened, by pure chance, to be
in Ephesus running a series of spirit-raising seances from a
wine-vault next door to Chloe's workshop. The ship-captain
was furious. Chloe and Irene had to pay him an enormous
sum to cover the risk. Nearly as much as the cosmetic bill
itself. Some of it came out of Irene's precious capital: the
rest, I think, was Chloe's. I say 'I think', advisedly. The
preliminary financial arrangements for our tour were extremely *occult*. To be enigmatic, for Irene, was a principle
of life: and Chloe was — Chloe was a first-rate Ephesus
business-woman, with all that that implies. I was already
beginning to wish I had not agreed to come. I was supposed
to be leaving home in order to secure my safety. With Irene,
in Italy or anywhere else, I could not think I would ever be
safe . . .

BOOK TWO

The Walls of Love

'It might have been thought that the senate and the conservative party objected, not to the demands of the Italians, but to the revolutionary schemes of those by whom these demands were supported: but in 95 BC the deliberate policy of the oligarchy was made clear by a consular law (Lex Licinia-Mucia) which prohibited under penalties any non-burgess from laying claim to the franchise. With Drusus hope arose once more for the Italians; Drusus accomplished nothing but his own destruction, and now no resource was left but an appeal to arms.'

Mommsen

1   On Board the 'Lady Ruth'

A good deal of what happened in Italy cannot be written, not exactly as it fell out, at least; if these papers *are* to be used in evidence-against (and how can I prevent it, if that is what god, or the gods, or the goddess etcetera has – have – determined for me? Tap the table, tickle the prick, criss-cross dregs-and-dross charm-and-alarm keep-us-from-harm . . . all of that once again, yes), then it had better be evidence against *me* and not against good friends. So what I am to describe as having happened for example in the place I call the Walls of Love, let you understand *did* happen, but not all in the one town, and not all in the same order of events. More or less. That's the important bit, anyway. I want to get on to it. The earlier chapters can wait. I have a few notes for them. Something about the voyage: there was of course much more to the voyage than this, but at present this is all I can remember . . . care to remember. . . .

★

The Raven had not been pleased by my treatment of my Cuttlefish – his Cuttlefish – *our* Cuttlefish, when the Stain came to Ephesus. That's why he travelled with us to Italy and why I saw him every day sitting in the stern of the ship – the *Lady Ruth* of Joppa (Captain Habbakuk). He wore his tragedian's huge black cloak, the one he always wore when he played the demented Ajax, it was smeared with the blood of the innocent beasts the hero butchers in the belief that they were men. He sat behind the helmsman, secretly con-ning the ship for him, his hooked nose pointing forward, shifting slightly to right or left every time the wind shifted, and each time it did so, the helmsman leant on his tiller and the ship's head would come round to the same line. Oh yes, I could see him. Nobody else could.

Except perhaps Cuttlefish. If she did, she never men-tioned it. But her eyes reverted constantly to the poop as she sat or strolled with Irene in the waist. The helmsman became embarrassed and complained to the mate, who passed it on to the captain. The captain had a word with me about it. Female passengers must not distract the pilot: it brought the voyage bad luck. He was a weatherbeaten man with oily black hair tied back into a tangled pig-tail and one gold ear-ring. He thought Cuttlefish was playing sexy games. I could not tell him the truth.

'Sailormen is a funny crowd, and the Heel of Italy run is always awkward with squalls coming down on us, and pirate cutters prowling out from behind the islands. The young woman's your property, right? It's up to you to be responsible. If not I'll give an order to have her confined to the hold till we make port.'

'If he wants me to go below, I'll go below', she said; and that was that. She had anyway decided not speak to me throughout the voyage, she didn't condescend to tell me why. Irene bothered me too. She kept talking to Cuttlefish about a notion she had that the Italian tour should not be just Irene singing songs, doing her dances and erotic monologues, which was the original idea; but that Cuttlefish should also appear with her, something of the same sort of thing the two of them had done for Roscius at the Stain's Gala. *That* had not brought us much good luck, I kept saying: in vain. I kept my hand under my shirt during these conversations.

Irene spoke to me one day, on the foredeck (Raven seemed to have left the poop for a while, so I could relax, or I thought I could). 'Ivory,' she said, 'you used to be such a pretty boy, so straight and *precise*, despite your awkward manners. A bad leg flying out at all angles doesn't *have* to be copied inside of your mind, you know. You've allowed that notched-penny nonsense to twist you about north south and centre. Now you are working for me, you work according to *my* business, and that's as straight as I can make it. I want *this*, and I tell you about it, and you fix it for me: if I change my intention and decide I want *that*, then you take account of the new circumstances and adjust yourself without fuss. I want Cuttlefish to perform with me in one or two numbers. We offer ourselves to the managements as a flexible arrangement and see what they think. She was trained by a tragedian – don't keep looking back at the steersman, look at me when I'm talking to you, please – and it might be an idea to see what she can do in that line as well as the comic-erotic. She's your property, and I pay you what she earns, in the usual manner. How much of it you give her is your business: but I see no reason why it should make *me* any difficulties. Understood?'

2   *The South Towns*

Roscius was right. The 'south towns' of Italy were euphoric for our profession. Maybe less so than formerly, but there was good money to be made by foreigners, especially Greeks, many of the towns being of Greek foundation, and, even today, almost entirely Greek language. Samnite and Lucanian settlements were a different matter – here the language was similar to Latin, and the tastes of the people were very strongly towards the barbarous Games which had caused us so much trouble in Asia. Oddly, though, these were the people most hostile to the City. Like rivalling like, I suppose.

★

Irene bought a wagon and had brilliantly coloured paintings made on its canvas cover. Two mules, with bright red harness. Her costumes and scenery had been sold her in Ephesus by Chloe: there had been a row with Chloe over their cost, but it had ended in kisses, and mutual embracements, and some very fudged figures in the books – I suspect there was another dubious deal on the side here, to which I was not privy. Irene said, 'if *you* don't know, there's no chance of the tax-man finding out: burn the bastards' balls etc.' Chloe was involved in the fig-trade, and I'm sure she also smuggled silk.

★

Irene bought the pair of them at Brindisi – a muscular young Celt to look after the wagon and mules – his name was Horsefury: and a Spanish girl called Snowflake, dark, pale, shy, hardly ever spoke. She was Irene's personal maid. Both of them helped with any stage-management work that was needed.

*

Private performances: gentry or peasants, said Irene, but she was not going to diminish herself by giving a good name to the dinner tables of ignorant usurers. If they wanted her they could come to the theatre like other decent people. But she used to patrol the streets and squares in any of the towns we visited, with Cuttlefish and Snowflake, all three of them dressed-up like herbaceous borders, and Horsefury to strut beside them in a blue footman's coat flourishing a spear. Young noblemen set her letters of assignation: she said she returned these immediately. Far too soon, she said, to hobble herself with a patron. She would organize herself exactly as she wanted herself organized, under no obligation to anyone.

*

Why did she keep disappearing for a day or two at a time? She never missed a performance, but . . .

*

Cuttlefish began to take part in more and more of the bill. Irene seemed to need company on the stage. She spent far more time with Irene than with me. Their double acts were unquestionably successful. The young noblemen sent their letters to Cuttlefish too. This was difficult for me. Irene said, leave it to her, she'd look after Cuttlefish. But then she would be off again, mysteriously, for a day and a night, and was I expected to keep the Cuttlefish under guard?

*

Taranto was our first bad experience. 'Political troubles'; the management of the theatre was controlled by a faction that had made itself extremely obnoxious the week before our arrival, and our audience consisted largely of opponents bent on wrecking the building. We were lucky to escape with our lives. I got the blame for this fiasco. It was, partly, my fault. My sources of advance information about the state of the town had, I think, deliberately misled me, for 'political reasons'. I ought to have detected it. I was supposed to have a flair for such matters. I was getting over-confident, things had been going so well.

In the autumn we moved further north. Here the 'political troubles' seemed more intense, though to begin with we did not suffer any direct inconvenience. We decided to stay in one place during the winter, and rented a house in a town called the Walls of Love. The first shows we did at the theatre there had been very well-liked, as had the short tours we made into the villages of the surrounding countryside. The population was very mixed, Latin, Greek, some disgruntled Samnites (all related to mountain bandit-clans), Etruscans – not many – and a curious group of hirsute 'Aboriginals' who had been there since the primeval flood. Main language spoken, Latin: but Greek known to all educated classes: and Greek theatre generally popular. But by this time we were working up some comedy numbers in dog-Latin which caused amusement. We normally shared the bill with all sorts of other touring troupes and individuals – the worst being an African with a dozen performing apes, which got loose and pulled our act to pieces, literally – Irene's costume was dragged right off her in the middle of the orchestra. Horsefury killed the ape responsible. Great arguments about who was to pay. The magistrate took our side, thank god.

*

When we were inspecting the house in the Walls of Love, Irene bounced like a child on the big bed in her room.

'Do you know,' she proclaimed, 'Ivory: I am at last my own mistress! I haven't slept with anybody all this trip, except gentlemen whom I told to get lost the next morning and by god they got lost. Congratulate me, Ivory – I am thirty years old – ' (at least eight years short, but why be malicious? Because the two stones between my legs are pebbles of old hard jealousy, when I think of those days, that's why), ' – and at last I have found myself where I once hoped to be at the age of eighteen. Blood of the bull, can *you* say that?'

*

There was subterranean tension between Irene and Cuttlefish which often proved positive, in that it enlivened their stage-relationship and set the public agreeably on edge – nothing was ever entirely predictable, and predictability in the theatre always makes for boredom.

But off-stage the negative aspects were more in evidence. The Cuttlefish, for instance, had found that some audiences in these cultural backwaters had a strong taste for high-minded philosophical poetry – the sort that old-fashioned schoolmasters exalt. She was therefore anxious to prolong her declamations from Athenian tragedy, and indeed to augment them with some solemn dance numbers in long robes with Snowflake and Horsefury beating drums. Irene did not like this, she said it killed the lighter parts of the show. And besides, bloody Horsefury was getting above himself, in that idiotic mountain village his drum-solo had got two whole rounds of applause for itself alone, who did he think he was?

Cuttlefish said it wasn't *her* fault that those particular mountainy-men happened to be specialists at making and playing their own unique kind of goatskin drum, they had appreciated Horsefury as a kindred spirit. Irene said I had been careless, I should have warned her about this. I said I *had* warned her but she had taken no notice. Snowflake, who was in love with Horsefury, went off in a flood of tears; while the flamboyant Celt took his drum out onto the hills and played there all night to the memory of his heroic ancestors in the north, chanting long-drawn-out laments and terrifying the shepherds.

3   Antigone Striding Out

Irene said, 'Who is in charge of this company, damn you: me or your young woman?'

The theatre of the Walls of Love was a very pretty auditorium, its stage-building unchanged for three hundred years, the old simple style of flat-roofed, white-washed adobe with no more than the minimum of 'architecture'. The tiers of seats climbed the hill of the 'high-town', on the top of which was a disused citadel and a temple to the Love-goddess. The overgrown slopes of the hill, above the theatre, were a favourite place for lovers. (From the top one could see between the hills almost to the eastern sea. The post-road from Taranto cut a brilliant white line through the valley below the town. It by-passed the Walls of Love by about a mile – the army engineers who built it were not interested in detours for the benefit of local commerce. Troops on the march were consigned from garrison to garrison. No garrison had been needed in the Walls of Love since the Great War, when the citadel had successfully defied the formidable Hannibal.) Oh yes, the theatre was an enviable place to work in.

On this particular morning, Irene lost her temper. She and Cuttlefish were blocking-out an Apollo-and-Daphne routine – Irene as Apollo (with lifts in her boots) pursues Cuttlefish until Cuttlefish in despair turns into a tree. Irene wanted Snowflake to walk on as the Virginity-goddess with some practicable foliage and envelop Cuttlefish in it. The Cuttlefish said this was far too cumbersome and the tree (and the goddess) could more easily – and artistically – be *imagined*. Did Irene suppose her incapable of miming a tree? Or did she think we were playing to a community of bloody fools?

She should not have shouted. Irene went white with anger and said that if the audience came especially to see Cuttle-fish, most of it would consist of bequeathed bloody bond-women and usurers' indentured concubines, such self-conceited half-wits needed every visual aid they could get. Snowflake, who had been looking forward intensely to her unexpected appearance on stage in a character-costume, crumpled up against the wall. I suggested that we were all getting tired, perhaps we should break for lunch. Horsefury slammed our wine-jug and food-hamper down in the middle of the stage and went off to comfort his sweetheart. I ignored Irene, selected what I wanted to eat, and carried it to the upper tiers.

Oh, Cuttlefish, of course, had walked out. Into the green-room, anyway: maybe out at the back and home, but that remained to be seen.

I became aware of Irene creeping almost guiltily up the tiers towards me, holding the wine-jug. She sat down beside me, folding her vigorous neat legs under her bottom, and grinding her teeth.

'You forgot to bring yourself anything to drink. Here's the bottle, damn you: take it.' I drank and passed it back. She drank. 'What the devil are we going to do with that girl of yours, Ivory? Beyond a joke the way she spoke to me. We need three people in the Daphne piece – the number before had both of us in it, and so does the one immediately after. Bad structure to run items on and on without variation of the groupings: didn't the Raven ever teach her any of these elementary principles?' I was certain he had: I was equally certain that in this instance the Cuttlefish was quite right. She *could* mime the scene to excellent effect, and the laurel-boughs had looked ridiculous, tatty. But I did not want my own row with Irene. The solution, of course, was to alter the programme-order. But tomorrow would be a better time to bring that up.

We sat in silence for a few tense minutes. A multitude of birds was wheeling over the haunch of the high-town, northerners already assembling for the next stage of their journey to the land of no winter, the land of my Cuttlefish perhaps – if she were to go with them, would she recognize it when she got there? The way she had walked off the stage just now, one might have thought she would not stop till she went over the rim of the world . . . Clytemnestra de-

parting from the murderous bathroom, Antigone striding
out to find her subversive pick-and-shovel. Had she learned
that proud march from the Raven as a technical exercise, or
had she always had the strut of it in her own jet-black ham-
strings?

'I want you to drink some more of this, boy,' said Irene
suddenly. 'I've something to say to you: you might as well
be sozzled, then you won't knock my head off . . . Don't
you think it's about time you gave your wee squid her freedom?'

To such a totally improper interference in my private
affairs I could make no immediate response: I stuttered, of
course. 'No I don't.' I knew my face was filling with blood.
'I don't see how I can, how I possibly can. Of course I
would always want to, but – '

'But that ranting hook-nosed cuckold left her to you on
condition you were to provide for her until you can swear
that she is otherwise provided for. Well, wouldn't you say
now that she was?'

'How can she be?' I muttered furiously, 'How can she be
when here she is on the very edge of getting thrown out
from your programme, and what have I to endow her with?
If you can't work with her any more, then how can I work
with *you*? If I tried it, and still lived with her, we'd be
cutting each other's throats in no time. And if I leave you,
I've not yet any more saved than would keep me and her
for a fortnight! Her *freedom* – good god, I was thinking that
I might even have to put her for sale . . .'

The corners of Irene's eyes were blurring with vivid red.
'If you were to do that, boy, I will tell you what I will do. I
myself will cut throats; one throat: yours.' She shook herself, like a wet terrier-bitch. 'Oh no, let's keep it rational. If
you let her go, she could certainly work with me. We would
draw up a regular contract. If she didn't like the conditions
we could shout and shout and go through the bazaar-
bargaining number until she was satisfied. Oh look at me
and Chloe. I had in mind a sort of partnership.'

'She's got no capital.'

'I'll loan her some. At the rate we've been earning she'll

soon earn enough to pay it back and draw profits in addition, I'm damn sure she'll *save* a sight better than you do. I won't charge her interest, well – not all that much: I can't abide usury. As you know. We could include these two incapables – ' (Snowflake and Horsefury) ' – as part of the assets, she could have her share in them. And then they would have to do as she told 'em – when and *only* when they were working specifically in connection with her act. Anyway, all the details – for *you* to ravel out: you know more than is good for you about contracts and all of that. What do you think of it?'

We were interrupted by a throng of young girls giggling and chattering on their way down the high-town path just above us – bouncing bosoms, white thighs among the bushes – they had been up to the temple to make offerings no doubt in the hope of handsome husbands. When they had gone past –

I said, 'What about me?'

'What *do* you mean, Ivory, what the hell do you mean?'

'You know what I mean.'

'Oh yes, if she *is* free, then what guarantee she will be living with *you* as well as working with *me*? There's a quick answer: none at all. That's what freedom's all about. How can *I* tell you what she'll feel? Suppose you tell *me*. When did she last put her socket on top of your rod?'

'That's none of your business.'

'Yes it is, you've just made it my business. Well, will you tell me? I can't hear you. Open your mouth.'

'I said "Taranto" and be damned. You've no right to force me to – '

'I've every bloody right. She told me about Taranto. You were so bloody relieved, the pair of you, to be safe and sound out of that riot, you put it up for her five times without pulling your boots off, and then forgot all about it for the rest of the summer.'

I exploded into a recrimination about all the travelling, the rehearsing, the difficult managements, the Samnite indifference, the political atmospheres, all the tensions they imposed on me everywhere we went – she didn't let me finish:

'You were working too hard. So was she. And Ivory, my dear: Ivory: don't you realize the poor child *did not know who she was working for*? You? Me? Her own self? How could she be expected to spread her legs for *anyone* in that sort of state?' She looked down towards the stage: 'Oh god will you just observe that greedy black whoor – every morsel of the cold fowl, and I hadn't had a single bite at it!' Cuttlefish had re-appeared from the greenroom or wherever, and was crouched beside the lunch-basket, her fists and cheeks full of food. Irene began to laugh.

'Go on, boy: you go and tell her. We won't rehearse any more today anyway. I'll walk up to the temple with Snow-flake. Snowflake – ! Come up, child, I want you!'

I went straight down through the tiers, across the orches-tra, planked down the ferrule of my stick in front of Cuttlefish. She gaped at me, defiant, her open mouth bulg-ing with roast chicken. I said at once, without preliminary, that she was now a free woman: I would get out the docu-ments the minute I reached home and tomorrow first thing we would go to the magistrate for the bureaucratic formalities. Perhaps I should not have omitted some preliminary: at any rate she misunderstood, her eyes widened in horror.

'You're throwing me away,' she said, choking. It took me some time to explain that I was not. When she had thor-oughly grasped the situation, she still stood motionless, tears streaming down her face.

'I must go to the temple,' she cried, and started away up the hill, in such haste to catch Irene and Snowflake that she was scrambling on all fours among the shrubberies. When they saw her climbing after them, they stopped and waited for her at a bend of the zig-zag path. I told Horsefury to tidy the stage and lock away our gear before he came home: I was returning to the house directly.

In the street outside the theatre I saw a man I had noticed there the day before and the day before that. A lean sec-retarial sort of person with silver-grey hair and a stoop. He made a half-hearted bow to me, as though perhaps he knew me. As I did not know him, and had a great deal on my mind, I ignored him. I was half-way home when it suddenly struck me that maybe he was following me. But his presence in the street was so vaguely-defined that I might have been mistaken. The possibility was nevertheless alarming in the extreme: I'd had more than enough of that in Ephesus.

4   Notched Pennies Again

It now being the heat of the day, I went to my room and lay down to sleep. I had a dream – not about the Raven, I hadn't seen him since the ship – but about Cuttlefish: she was in reality a cuttlefish, and harpooned upon my sexual organ, which was so fiercely erect and sharp it might have been forged out of steel. Her tentacles enveloped it, sucking hard, and her pierced body flapped grotesquely. I tossed and turned and woke up. I could not bear to have her mine and yet not mine – nor could I endure to have her free and yet not be assured that she could also be mine. My memory kept returning to the sweet precision of her legs with the slit in between them so elegantly and exactly placed, as though drawn there by the light finger-nail of the Love-goddess from her house in the high-town: and I thought of all this in juxtaposition to the hideous crank-angle made by my own legs and injured pelvis, the dangling sac, the sweaty tufts, the self-pitying worm lopsided and so rarely stirring itself; and yet, like a malicious sleeping-partner in a dis-reputable commercial enterprise, now and then issuing orders and expecting me to bloody jump to them . . .

To get rid of these thoughts I sat down to my ledgers and began to work out an acceptable Irene-Cuttlefish contract, and also to draft the document-of-liberty for the magistrate. But noises from the back yard interrupted me – I recognized the voice of Horsefury, no doubt with some tiresome drinking-companion – this must be put a stop to during my working-hours: I went out to tell him off.

He was sitting on the shaft of our wagon with a man – the same silver-haired man I had seen in the street. 'Appalling bloody noise,' I snapped. 'Be so good as to go elsewhere if you want to argue and shout.' The silver-haired man made deprecating gestures: Horsefury stood up and met my glare. He answered with a curious kind of insolent innocence, you would call it 'courtesy' if you had been offered it by a social superior.

'Indeed, sir, and surely I beg your pardon, so I do – ' (his baroque variations of Greek were always pleasant to hear) ' – but here is a poor man has been seeking a short word with the mistress not for a week, no, but for more than a month, and himself has no more than the leather of his shoes between his feet and the street, so what could I do but bid him welcome and take account of his trouble?'

This sounded like a fancy way of saying that Horsefury was accepting a bribe from someone who wanted something from Irene: and I said so. Horsefury bowed his head and went into his quarters behind the kitchen. The stranger twitched at me: 'I do apologize, most ungraceful to be caught tampering with the staff: but also important I discovered how the land lay before I approached you direct. I happen to know of course that 'the mistress' has gone up to the temple and she will not be home until tomorrow.'

This was a surprise. 'Indeed? Where will she be then?'

He shifted his eyes: 'No doubt she will tell you when she returns. Do you think we might go indoors? A private room, out of earshot from the household, perhaps? I won't keep you very long.'

I led him in through the kitchen into my study. Before taking a seat he crept swiftly round the room, checking window, door, and cupboards for possible eavesdroppers. 'I do apologize, in my job we do have to be particular.' He put his clothes aside at the neck and showed me his notched penny. 'You still have possession of yours, I take it? Or did you lose it in the flurry of getting aboard the *Lady Ruth*?'

'I had no call to think I was going to require it any more. You've been sent after me by the Stain's people? I have a bone to pick with them – do you know (of course you damn well know) how they tried to stop us leaving Ephesus – '

'Let me make it quite clear I am not employed by the Stain, nor by any other military commander. We regard them as our *colleagues* in our joint service of the One City,

and only take orders from them when ordered to do so.' I
felt as thought a warehouse-full of featherbeds had been
quietly lowered onto my face – suffocation of silent despair.

He went on talking in his maddening consequential flow.
He told me that the Stain had spent the summer in the
City, preparing his defence against the charges that had
been brought. That this had involved an examination of
secret service records relating to the operations in Asia,
nothing concrete had emerged to incriminate the general,
and that in all likelihood the charges would be dropped –
they were, after all, only a 'political gambit' and now more
inclined to advantage the Stain himself than his opponents
– 'but, of course, with all this, we in the service have nothing
to do.'

However, in the process, my name had turned up, and
the circumstances had seemed anomalous. 'We thought it
advisable to follow through some research.' Ah yes, he was
thinking I might have come to Italy to do dirty work for the
Stain. How on earth would I convince him otherwise? I did
my best. He frowned and then smirked again. 'Yes: well, I
daresay if you are not telling the truth you will appreciate
we will already be largely aware of it. Did you happen to
hear, by the way, what they did to that fellow in Ephesus –
what was his name, now? – the Hook . . .? Well, shall we
suppose that for the time being we accept your account?
How long have you known Madame?'

'I knew her fifteen years ago. Met her again in Ephesus
in the spring.'

'And she at once invited you to manage her affairs?'

'Why not, it's my profession.'

'Why not indeed. Loyalty to old friends. Pleasant if in all
professions we could say the same thing.' He stopped talking and busied himself with the meticulous spearing of a fly
with my paper-knife. I thought of my recent dream. 'Tell
me,' he said, 'tell me – you have heard of this man they call
"Harmony"?' I had – very much in passing. A City politico,
his real name was Drusus, bidding his way to become another king-prick, supposedly a member of the 'old crowd'
but of late up to one or two things that had made people
suspect he was changing party-allegiance, not quite in the

way that might have been expected. In the 'south towns' people had spoken of him with some excitement – he was supporting their interests, it seemed.

'Quite so, but what *are* their "interests"? Do you know?' I didn't, not absolutely. Indeed, even today I'm not sure, despite everything: but I *think* it ran something like this. These towns were in theory independent of the City, in alliance with it: and by the terms of the alliance they paid certain taxes (you may be sure!), supplied quotas of men to certain City regiments, and refrained from a foreign policy of their own. In return for this they received 'protection', but since Hannibal's time they had been under no immediate outside threat. The virtues of this Jampot-like arrangement had long ceased to be noticeable to them, their inhabitants were demanding more of a genuine quid-pro-quo, and the City was refusing it. Even though many among the populations of the 'south towns' were of Latin origin (i.e. from the City or its close neighbourhood), they had lived so long apart that their old loyalties had inevitably lapsed. Samnites and Etruscans had never felt other than alienated from the Romans; and the Greeks, of course . . . well, the Greeks . . . no doubt they felt much as I did. All of them wanted, primarily, voting rights in the City legislature. This agitation had been going on for years, I knew that much. I had assumed it would go on for many more years without any heavy eruptions. But apparently this Harmony, reassuring nickname or not, was beginning to create earth-tremors.

'Quite so. And he's coming here. At the weekend. Did you know? Perhaps you didn't. Well, he is. He'll be holding public meetings, addressing some closed committees. We want you to get to know him, loosely enough, oh loosely. Attach yourself to his activities until he leaves town. No need to let it interfere with your work: your spare time, quite sufficient. We think we know what he will be saying to people. We need you to tell us what the people have to say to him, and also what they decide to do about it after he has gone. I won't be here then: but a means will be found for you to pass on your report to the proper quarters. You know, that chap, the Hook, he wasn't killed by the horse-dragging, not quite. They spent another forty-eight hours with him, in a small place, before they decided they would let him die . . . Apologies for my intrusion . . .'

He stooped his way out of the house, close to the wall, like a dead leaf in a gentle breeze.

Before nightfall Snowflake came home alone. She told me that the Cuttlefish was going to spend all night in the temple: the priestess there had told her of certain devotions appropriate to her situation, a vigil of some sort. Would I go there at dawn to meet her and escort her down again? I had never known Cuttlefish express interest in divinity, except insofar as it was handled by the tragic poets. A message to collect her from a sacred edifice, indeed, as though she were a prim lady of the middle-class, what Irene would call a 'usurer's madam'! Whom did she intend to impress? Snowflake was impressed: *she* was a regular sponge when it came to absorbing religious sentiment.

'It is so beautiful in the house of Our Lady, sir, so high up above the town.'

'Yes. Where is Madame?'

'Sir, I do not know. She did tell she will not be home tonight too, but she did not stay with Our Lady.'

I had all these documents to complete, to make Cuttlefish a free woman. I must do it before I went to bed. I had promised. It was clear that, as a free woman, she was going to be quite a *new* woman. Not, I hoped a maudlin one. God knows, you can never tell.

I was so frightened by the notched-penny man that I put him right out of my mind. I would *not* bear him in mind, until this 'Harmony' came to town. I supposed I should tell Cuttlefish. I was sure I should tell Irene. But I couldn't tell them, could I? Oh god they were not here. If she had not been Horsefury's girl, I would have made an attempt to spend the night with little Snowflake. I couldn't tell *her* anything, but at least she would have been company. As it was, my only company was nightmare, unrelieved.

5   *The House of Our Lady*

The temple of the Love-goddess was indeed beautiful, and at sunrise it was also poetic and mysterious. There were misty clouds all round the high rock, which the rising sun cut into slivers, and made one think that the goddess herself was wafting about up there, damaging and enhancing human beings according to her arbitrary fancies. The porch of the temple faced east and caught the first rays of the red dawn. It was comforting to be there when it caught them, made me feel that maybe most of my fears were less serious than the night had made them seem.

It was a very old building, steep-roofed, with timber columns, the green and gold paint flaking off them at capital and base. On the peak of the roof was a fire-red terracotta statue of the Lady – a tall slim figure in straight pleated robes, her enigmatic face set in a half-smile peering out towards the sea and eventually Cyprus where she had been born. One hand was outstretched, pointing – the other one held a brazen wand tipped with gold lilies.

Cuttlefish was standing waiting for me on the steps of the porch, with one of the Aboriginal temple-servitors, a broad-shouldered youth, shaggy as a bear. She looked exhausted, and her casual rehearsal costume (loose tunic and eastern trousers) was crumpled and seemed to be slipping off her slumped shoulders. She was smiling, like the statue over her head. I paid the Aboriginal his requisite tip.

'Would you like to come inside,' she said, 'Come inside and see where I've been.' Inside it was still half-dark. The walls were hung with an immense array of smoke-blackened gifts to the goddess – ancient shields, crowns, sceptres, plates and cups, womens' head-dresses, tapestries, ropes of jewels, all gleaming faintly in the light of one or two guttering torches. There was another statue here, almost a duplicate of the one on the roof, but made of ivory with precious metal inlay, draped with long green silk and hung with flower-garlands.

★

An upright grey-haired lady came to meet us from behind the statue: Cuttlefish whispered that this was the priestess. She looked me up and down with a speculative eye, and I thought her cheekbones were just like those of her goddess, too sharp for my ease of mind. 'So here is the man,' she said. I made haste to give her enough money for a high-class sacrifice, a pair of white doves (which can come expensive – grey ones are sufficient for most normal occasions). She took it without remark. She still surveyed me, up and down.

'He is not beautiful,' she said. 'He should eat less and restore the line of his jaw. The crooked leg and receding hair cannot be helped, of course. Our Lady will make allowances for age and a genuine accident. But she will not excuse disharmony of temper brought about by self-conceit. Now, sir:' fixing me like a scholastic examiner, 'the liberty you have afforded this girl is not to be abused. She has been cleansed by Our Lady of the coercive pollution you imposed upon her during her servitude. She is, in effect, a virgin once again. *I* cannot prevent you – once you both leave this precinct – from doing whatever you choose to do with her. The civil law will ensure that certain limits are observed: but the goddess has her own standards – your behaviour will be watched, and, if necessary, chastised. Do I make myself clear? If not, I am sure this young woman will inform you fully of what I mean.'

I gulped, but made some assurances of a singularly cringing nature. Hard to say which was worse, this censorious old whetstone or Irene. And what the hell had Cuttlefish been telling her all last night?

Cuttlefish asked her, timidly, if she might show me the garden. 'I think he would like to see it, it would help him to understand.'

'It is not usual, but as you tell me he did not demand a price for your liberation, I think it may be permitted. Our Lady makes allowance for genuine affection.' She escorted us out of the temple, and unlocked the gate of a high-walled open-air sanctuary cut into a ledge at the edge of the steep rock, and overlooking the houses of the lower town. She then left us there (with the Aboriginal to keep an eye on us) and returned to her business. Cuttlefish explained softly that she had spent half the night in the temple itself, and then had been taken, after moon-rise, into these gardens, for some very strange proceedings.

'They gave me this purgative, my stomach ran out like water, behind the rose-bushes there – don't go over there, it'll still be stinking. I got thorns stuck in my bum. . . . Here I was scourged,' she said.

'*What?* What on earth did they do that for?'

'It didn't hurt. Not much. I think it left marks on my back, though. . . . Here they made me take the bath.' A grotto with dolphin-spouts and a pool.

(There was water on the rock, drawn up from a complex of cisterns by prolonged turning of a heavy wooden wheel set into the wall beside the pool. The principle was that of the ingenious Archimedes: tourists were told that the people of the high-town had discovered his 'hydraulic screw' years before he was born, and that he had fraudulently stolen the notion from here. Perhaps).

'Here there were some other things done: but I mustn't tell you what.' A rough image, here, hacked out of oiled wood, a two-legged creature like an unnaturally skinny man with a sort of stag's head and an erected prick, very long, very shiny. I thought again of my dream; and looked suspiciously at the Aboriginal, who was whistling a traditional sacred melody as he gazed out over the wide countryside . . .

'Here they gave me the second bath.' In the middle of another pool, yet another statue of the goddess, naked this time, round and plump, modelled in an unusual style (I took it to be eastern). Black bronze, with the hair on the head and in the groin picked out with gold, the squat body enamelled all over with a speckle of multi-coloured flowers.

'If you ever tell anyone what it is like here, Our Lady will drain you of your blood and you will die. When she first came to this town, she put her trust in a young man and let him lie with her, just there beside the pool. He betrayed her by boasting of it. The next time he came up to meet her here again, she put two teeth into his neck, at the very moment when he thought he would be spurting inside her.

His blood all ran out into the water, look at it, it is still red. It is a sign, and that is why they built the temple and called the town by her name. The life of this town depends on the trust given to it by the goddess. She trusts *you*. You won't betray her.'

There was indeed a discernible rusty tinge in the water.

On the way down the hill, she folded her arm into mine, and held me very close to her.

6 *Scourgings*

I made an effort to get her to tell me what she felt about going on living with me. I had found the whole goddess-atmosphere aphrodisiac and also intimidating: I naturally wanted to know where we stood, in its aftermath. But she evaded my hints, and spoke only of the great age of the temple, the charm of the garden and so on. I was baffled, but played it carefully. I kept glancing round to see could I detect any token of the Raven and his constant watch: but there was nothing. Perhaps the goddess had taken over from him now. The idea of Cuttlefish being scourged, bathed, and subjected to god-knows-what in front of that stag-headed image, was strongly arousing my flesh, if I let it: I felt I should not let it. There were too many forces observing me. Did the goddess distribute notched pennies, by any chance?

We called in at the house (Irene had not returned), collected the legal papers, and went to the town hall to register the liberation. I knew the procedure, I had helped clients with it in Ephesus. But this morning, there was a hitch. The courtyard of the town hall was surprisingly busy for so early in the day – policemen running about and disappearing into doorways, officials and clerks conferring in worried groups, one or two town notables arriving hastily in sedans. A most objectionable young man in the white gown of the City's formal dress was holding forth in Latin in a high-pitched whine – 'Absolutely intolerable,' he kept repeating, 'I expected inefficiency, good god, but this is *obstruction*! I won't stand for it, do you hear! Do you hear, I won't stand for it, I suppose you do know who my father is – ?' and all that. I took him for a tourist who had been overcharged at the inn . . .

In the office a bothered clerk told me he didn't think anything could be done for us this morning, something had come up, please come back this afternoon, no regular business just yet . . . We left the papers with him, frustrated. As we went out, it occurred to me to take him by the arm and announce, very breathless: 'I insist before I go that I state here and now with you as witness that I regard this young lady as totally free, even though the legal forms have not yet been ratified.' Cuttlefish looked pleased at this, but the clerk was not impressed.

'Total freedom, what does it mean?' he snarled. 'I'll tell you what it means, friend, it means any snot-fed pansy-boy in a milk-white gown can tear away your whole life, house, family, children, the lot, just so that he himself remains the son of the red boots of his father – oh come back this afternoon . . .'

We returned home, in disappointment and depression, ate an irritable meal, and decided to go to bed. Cuttlefish was worn out. She said, 'Please, Ivory: don't ask to come into the same bed, not just yet, I need to think about it.'

'I thought you thought about it in the temple.'

'Oh I did, and all night. I am very confused. Our Lady was helpful, she made me see that I do not have to make up my mind until my mind is prepared to be made up. You do understand what I mean, my dear?' She had never called me her 'dear' before. She used the term as though we had a mother-and-son relationship. But my mother had not been that sort of mother, so I am only guessing that that was what it was. I took a cat-nap on the couch in the study. Cuttlefish slept upstairs in the room that I thought of as 'ours'.

We hurried to the town hall in the afternoon by the shortest route, through narrow back lanes; empty except for scavenging dogs, which was unusual. This time the courtyard was quiet, the verandahs quite devoid of their regular swarms of petitioners. We found a magistrate on duty in an office, he was preoccupied and unshaven as though called

away from home before he'd had his breakfast, and unable
to make up the time all day. He went through the formalities
in a dull monotone; and at the end, when he had to place a
red cap-of-liberty on Cuttlefish's head, he put it there
wrong way round and let it fall to the floor. He shook hands
with us: absent-minded, automatic. He all but kissed Cuttlefish, as though she were a bride and he was conducting
the civil portion of a wedding-ceremony. A pretence at an
apology and he hurried away. We had hoped for Irene there
to be our witness, but she was still missing. The clerk had
to do instead.

It was all dreadfully deflating.

None the less, we decided to enjoy the occasion somehow,
a lively dinner of whitebait and fizzy wine, we thought,
there was a row of eating-houses along the main square, one
of them was famous for its fish dishes, we would go there
and indulge ourselves regardless of all the let-downs. But
when we turned the corner into the square, we stopped short
in consternation. Immediately in front of the very eating-
house we had chosen we saw the most horrifying sight.

There was a scaffold surrounded by a thick press of armed
men in the uniform of the highway police (a notorious gendarmerie responsible only to the One City and with absolutely no jurisdiction inside the town. They specialized in
harassing travellers – we had had our own experiences with
them). These in turn were surrounded by a vast and completely silent crowd. On the scaffold, a post. Tied to the
post, the brown figure of a man, square-bodied, crop-
headed; his bow legs quivering under him; his arms hauled
taut above his head; his back, rump, and upper thighs half
cut to pieces and dropping thick trickles of blood on to the
floorboards.

A beefy executioner had paused to take breath, to wipe
sweat from neck and face. He held a whip of several thongs,
each of them equipped with a series of metal fragments.
Blood dropped from all of these. The man at the post
exhaled in great agonized gurgles, we could hear him right
across the square.

All in the one moment I recognized him, and so did

Cuttlefish. 'Oh god,' she whispered, 'Ivory: look. O my god
. . .' He was a Latin farmer, a free man, who had entertained
us only two weeks before, when we had played in his village.
The chairman of the village-assembly, a famous drinker and
sportsman, with a big family and prosperous olive-groves,
he had sung songs and told stories to us all night, he had
adored the Cuttlefish: the Queen of Africa, he had called
her, black Dido come back alive to rescue Italy from the
sons of her dirty seducer.

'They are to beat him till he dies,' a low but fierce voice
in the crowd close beside me: 'for the hard word that he put
upon their City. One word and that is all.' Horsefury:
rawboned features distorted with emotion, his yellow
moustache gripped in between his teeth. 'All he did, sir,
was to answer the gentleman when he was asked the right
road to a certain place: sure he answered with an understanding of the ignorance of the bloody man, it is true he
was after firing a laugh at him for it too, and a strong laugh
at the ignorance of the City he came from. But to beat him
till he dies: would you describe that as justice, sir?'

'No.'

'I am glad, so, to hear you say it. It is a good thing at all
events to have agreement in the one house. The mistress,
too, will be making her own opinion.'

Cuttlefish asked him who was the 'gentleman'? He
pointed out an individual standing among the police. The
young man, of course, from the town hall that morning: his
expression was vindictive.

'You see, sir,' continued Horsefury, 'it appears they have
no right to do such things in this town. The magistrates
were over-ruled by the highway police. It is not the poor
man only, but the whole town is to be punished, by this
whip, and that blood, and the torture and murder. I have
heard some people wondering, sir, that it was not by any
accident they chose this week for such a business . . .' He
slipped into the crowd and disappeared. The scourging
began again. We watched it: for about four or five terrible
deliberate lashes. Cuttlefish was ready to faint (or if she
wasn't, I certainly was), so I hurried her away.

★

As we went, I glanced up, purely by chance, to a first-floor window above one of the restaurants. Irene was standing in it, no emotions on her face, a sort of wax-image like the goddess in one of her street-corner shrines. There was someone behind her in the shadow: I saw a man's head bent forward to whisper in her ear. Silver-grey hair, the unmistakable stoop ... I said nothing to Cuttlefish about this: but I was going to have to tell her about the notched penny sometime soon. So much to bewilder, so much to terrify. None of it made sense.

The flogged man was now screaming, and screaming.

In front of our house, which was very near the town gate, we found soldiers gathered, standing-easy, with arms piled. A corporal informed me brusquely that they were the advance-party of a detachment sent into the town to reinforce the highway police in case of trouble after the scourging. More of them on the paved track leading up from the post-road. They were well under control and took but small notice of us. We could hear them up and down the streets all night: in the morning they had departed. There had been no disturbances, which was strange. I was expecting a riot. That crowd had been so still: but its compressed collective rage had hung in the air like steam.

7   *Agitations*

After the torture to death of a free man in the Walls of Love, things happened, one after the other. Fragments of these happenings: I got to find out a little too much, better not to put it all down in detail.

*

I think Cuttlefish thought this:

They drained him of his blood and he died. But it was not the goddess who did it. The highway police are not part of her trust. Why does she not kill them, she has the power? He had named me Queen of Africa, called his daughters in from the kitchen to praise the black bells of my breasts: I saw lumps of his flesh fly out through the air when the whip spun.

If she will not do what needs to be done for her town, she is not likely to do it for *me*, even though I have washed in her pools. But if she does not do it, who does she mean should be doing it? She must mean *someone*. And the way they will set about it, will it please her? This morning I was made free . . . free to do – *nothing*?

★

I think I was thinking this:

Cuttlefish told me of a whip and the marks on her body, and I rose up under my clothes, in secret, at the thought of it. She has not shown me those marks and I do not want to see them now. Obliterated in my memory by grooves, furrows, oozing black-red ditches in the body at the post.

'Not the poor man only but the whole town is to be punished . . .' and Silver-hair needs his work done here . . . and Irene was with Silver-hair. Horsefury knows that this week was *chosen*: Horsefury was *chosen* by Irene: the Walls of Love was *chosen* by Irene as well. Now: was she *chosen* by Silver-hair to stand in the window, or had she *chosen* him? Did she guess I would look up and see her? She saw me, I am sure she did, and yet she made no sign of – even – embarrassment at it.

I am therefore expected to ask her about it. She will destroy all my life with one word, if her answer is what I fear it will be. She pulled me into Shoulderbone's wagon when I was thirteen years old and her thin savage hand jerked into my breech-clout like a quack-dentist's pincers . . . what she wants she will take, and I have been *chosen*. Whether or not, I *must* ask her.

★

Song made, and sung, in his own language, by Horsefury while grooming the mules. (Later on he told me what the words meant: I am not sure about some of the names):

> Little black mule, little red mule,
> No-one ever gave you your freedom:
> And the shape you were made in,
> Neither proud horse nor honest ass,
> Was caused for you before you were born.

My shape is the shape of Cor an da Eala beside Loch Orbsen:
Wild bog, swept yellow in April with the gorse, made my hair;
The knotted roots of the blackthorn in the wood of Creag
Came in under my skin to twist with the muscles of my loins;
Creaking tree-limbs around Brigid's well at Tonagarraun
Have penetrated every long bone;
And the two swans from the brimming river beneath the bridge
　　of Baile Chlair
Flew into the caves of my skull to flourish whiteness behind
　　my eyes.
Male and female the two swans live and love all their lives
No such promise for myself and Snowflake:
Who can tell when they will divide us?
Little mules, when they brought me in chains to this free
　　country,
Did they think I would scrub your unfree pelts for ever?

*

*Part of a conversation between me and Irene, when she came home,
late at night, haggard and trembling.*

I put the obvious question to her.

She did not try to evade it. 'Of course I knew him. How
come you didn't? He's been about town all of a fortnight.
Never was such a secret bastard so open in his secrecy.
Incompetent or deliberate? I don't know. My guess: he
wants people to know he's here, but not know exactly why.'

'Do you know why?'

'Yes. To play off both sides. Which means that *he* is a
side and can himself be played-off. So I did.'

This was a clever remark: but she did not look clever.
She looked to me to be in a despair.

I said, 'How is it our business?'

She turned on me at that as though I was somehow to
blame for her having led me over the hatch of this damned
trap. 'It is yours because you were caught into it at Ephesus.
Mine, because I am here and attempting to earn a living.
Our living, damn you. How can we do that when they are
making kebabs in the market-place from the blood and fat
of our audience? Have some sense.'

One would think it had been *me* who had complained to
the highway police of the farmer's rudeness on the road.

But I wasn't going to argue. I tried, instead, to 'have some sense'. 'Why don't we find another town?'

Well, maybe not so sensible . . . 'Shite-house, boy, what makes you think there *is* any other town? Do what you're paid for, sort out my ledgers.'

'Paid for? I'm paid by Silver-hair – ' (was I? I certainly hadn't been, not yet at all events: and now I came to think of it, I never saw the colour of Jampot's cash either. No doubt I was credited, somewhere, with moneys due. I wonder which department? I daresay they are still due . . .) ' – paid by Silver-hair to inform upon Harmony. Am I to do it then, or will it ruin your box-office?'

Now she was clever: clever and sharp as usual. 'Oh do it by all means: but not one word of any information to him until you have first told it to *me*.'

'Why?'

'Because you work for me, that's why, and I've a right to know if you're moonlighting in some other fart-face's trade. I mean it: not one word.'

I sat very still and looked at her. I did not like to say this, but . . . 'How do I know I can trust you?'

She said, 'Put your hand on my breast.' And undid her gown so I could do so. 'Ivory, your hand, put it *here*.' She still looked haggard, but was no longer trembling. I was trembling. After so many years and I still quivered. 'There we are,' she was whispering: 'I was sixteen years old when I took this fat hand – in those days, not fat, light and nervous as a humming-bird – and put it *here*, just like this. Have you thought about it, since? Of course not, he thinks only of his Cuttlefish, and now she will not suffer him. Is she free, by the way? I *told* you: did you do it?'

Cuttlefish's red cap was on top of the wall-cupboard. I rolled my eyes toward it so that Irene saw it. Otherwise I did not answer her. She said, 'Sit still. Feel my heartbeat. Through all these past years, what have I done to make you feel you cannot trust me?'

The honest reply would have been 'everything you possibly could.' I gave her a dishonest one: 'Nothing.'

She said, 'Leave it there. The question, you lecherous limp-leg: not your hand.' As she was fastening up her dress,

I fetched some hot water and made her a drink with honey and lemon: the night was cold. She asked me to add wine. She had not evaded my question. Nor, I now realized, had she answered it.

★

Two notices posted up over the top of the regular playbill at the theatre box-office.

(a) PERFORMANCES POSTPONED UNTIL FURTHER NOTICE.
(b) PUBLIC MEETING! TOWN'S CHARTER IN DANGER!
   There will be a public meeting in this auditorium 6 am Saturday Nov 4th to discuss erosion of Civil Liberties and highway police brutality issues.
   Speakers: leading local political and community personalities (names to be announced).
   plus
   visiting speaker from City legislature: *M. Livius Drusus T.P.** – noted fighter for Italian rights.
Meeting organized by Walls of Love ad-hoc Civil Rights Action Committee (CRAC). Don't fail to attend!
(Security for public meeting guaranteed by CRAC volunteer defence group).

★

Report to Irene by Snowflake early in the morning the day after the scourging:

   Because Horsefury did not come to me all night, and because of the man in the market-place – oh madam I saw his blood and do you know they did exact the same thing to my uncle in Saragossa, beat him to his death, madam, but that time I did not *see it* – I was afraid and what could I do but go up to the temple to talk to Our Lady about it? Oh madam all the soldiers. In the old castle before you walk into Our Lady's house, they have built their huts and tents among the broken walls of the castle and they are drinking from Our Lady's springs – even with the red blood in the water from her miracle, and the temple is all shut up, the priestess has a hairy-man there to turn the people away, he said they will not dare to violate the altar but the priestess and her ladies have locked themselves in the sanctuary and what are we to do?

★

* *T.P. – Tribune of the People (for those whose Latin isn't up to it)*

An announcement from the town hall:

The council and magistrates wish to assure all free residents of the Walls of Love that they are making the most urgent representations to the appropriate military authorities about the installation overnight of a garrison of regular infantry in the citadel and the disturbance this has occasioned to law-abiding worshippers at the temple.

The commanding officer has replied with assurances to the effect that the action has been taken solely in the interests of security until such time as law and order may be effectively replaced in the hands of the municipal police. He will not guarantee that the highway police be removed outside the town, as had been requested.

The council and magistrates cannot regard this statement as entirely satisfactory: but they urge all residents to make every effort to avoid attempts by unrepresentative bodies to create disruption.

The public meeting announced for the theatre on Saturday may be held, on condition the following safeguards are observed:

    (a) No unauthorized policing of the meeting by any groups except those designated by the municipal chief constable.

    (b) No parades or marches to precede or follow the meeting.

    (c) Names of intended speakers to be approved by this office.

Any free resident proposing to arm his/her servants is hereby reminded of public ordinance (Walls of Love internal jurisdiction – no. IV/BX) prohibiting this practice under severest penalties. (Special Circumstances licenses for bona-fide applicants may be obtained upon submission of requisite pro-forma to this office.)

★

Horsefury to Irene:

    Of course if the mistress should say I am not to carry my spear for the safeguarding of our cart and mules and of herself, then I have a right not to carry it, but the spear makes his own opinion and he will be thinking very poorly of such work.

★

Irene to Ivory:

I shan't be at the meeting – or at least not in public view. It's an Italian matter: everyone knows I'm not Italian. *You* will be there though. Write down everything you hear and see. You'll not be the only notched penny there, of course: he wants your report as an outsider's check on everyone else's, which will be locally biassed one way or the other. I'll read it over and tell you what you're to put in the final draft you are to send him. Never mind my sodding reasons, boy, I'm in charge of this tour and you do my paper-work, you can take it from me that this is all part of it. By the way, Cuttlefish needs your help: she has a speech from Euripides they've asked her to do at the meeting.

*

Argument between me and the Cuttlefish:

'What speech,' I shouted, 'who asked you, what the hell is Irene up to? By god this is absolutely *no business of ours*, it could be very dangerous!

She comported herself with nearly as much disdain as her preceptress up in the temple. 'If you are a notched penny, of course it's your business. Take care to inform your masters of the new costume I shall be wearing.'

'I said what speech: and why?'

She stopped her infuriating pacing about the room, sat down, and began to deal with me as I sometimes saw the Raven deal with *her* when she was at her most temperamental. Controlled simmering patience, but a twitching hand to strike hard if the patience was not responded to. I did my best to respond to it. 'The Love-goddess from *Hippolytus*,' she said, flatly. 'The priestess has shut herself up in the temple. Someone has to speak for Our Lady. There are soldiers in this town and people are afraid of them: we need to remind them that soldiers in turn can be – should be – afraid of the goddess. Snowflake and Horsefury will play drums – Irene has agreed to it.'

*

A note of the costume devised by Irene and Cuttlefish for the latter's speech. Costume made up by Snowflake.

Buskins: reaching to just below the knee, of bottle-green felt with gold laces and trimmings, red soles 3″ thick.

Legs: bare.

Gown: pale yellow with gold-braid border. Pulled up on one side high enough to reveal thigh. One white wide-puffed lawn sleeve (left arm). Bosom largely exposed. Embroidered girdle, 4″ wide, grass-green, edged with silver-braid.

Mantle: green/blue shot-silk. Wrapped round shoulders and draped over left shoulder. Long enough to trail on ground behind. Powdered all over with spangles.

Mask: gold with blue lips and eyebrows. Expression of unrelenting power (from theatre-stock – an Apollo-mask modified).

Wig: red-gold, piled 12″ high with eighteen long braids coming down to waist. Silver disc representing full moon worn in centre of brow.

Accessories: gold-tipped spear, two wings (gold, silver, white feathers) made of leather – also from stock, from a Pegasus-costume, modified.

Length of time taken by Cuttlefish to practise walk, gestures, speech, in above accoutrements: three hours.

Cost of persuading theatre's stage-manager to practise swinging Cuttlefish in on crane: two hours' overtime wages and a free meal with drinks. Cost of retaining stage-manager's services (plus assistant) at theatre during public meeting: nil – labour volunteered as a community service.

*

The Euripides speech as rehearsed by Cuttlefish:

> I am Aphrodite, from the shore
> Of Cyprus rising to prevail in power
> Upon all mortal men and to make splendid
> The deathless flesh of god. Through all this earth
> From sunrise orient to the western gloom
> That towers each night from out the ocean stream
> My sovereignty compels all life breeding
> Beneath huge heaven. I smile upon with joy
> And kindly stroke to vibrant warmth such creatures
> As do me reverence. But self-sufficient
> Haughty pride I shall drive down and trample.
>
> Baleful sun or flame of star
> I swear to you, you need not fear

Not half so much as Aphrodite's dart
That makes insane the human heart:
Flung from the murderous hand of Love
Stark daughter of great god above,
Terror, terror, here she shall come
To make the love-bed or the tomb,
Swift as the bee which carries sweetness forth
Yet stings to madness those who cross its course:
Direct and fierce her power shall fly
Straight to the blindest eye . . .

There you are, what do you think of it? Ivory, you are *not
to touch me*: I am preparing to wear her mask: I shall be, as
it were, *her*. Not to touch me, not to speak to me, except to
tell me with what strength I am pronouncing the lines. I
have explained to you the effect she requires.

8   Public Meeting

It finished about noon. Back at the house I found Irene,
impatiently waiting for me so that she could spring at me
and demand a sight of my (supposedly verbatim) notes. I
cannot manage an effective shorthand. She made me read
them to her before I had copied them out. She crammed
herself over my shoulder as I sat at the table, one of her
knees was *on* the table, and her wig got in between my eyes
and the note-tablets. To start with she listened in silence, a
very heavy-breathing silence which caused me frequently to
lose my place and stutter. I won't report those passages. I
had tried to keep the notes methodical.

Attendance: vast. All theatre seats and aisles filled, many standing around edge of auditorium. Women, children, free, unfree.
'Democracy' – would one call it? If anything comes of it, yes.

Security: a few municipal police, diffident. Dominant presence,
despite town hall ordinance, of CRAC volunteer guards, young
men of apprentice and student type, with clubs, green armbands
(the goddess's colour).

Platform party: the mayor, looking as though he wished he
wasn't. Three or four councillors. Several faction-bosses (not
necessarily councillors). Two visiting representatives of neigh-

bouring towns. Half-a-dozen assemblymen from villages. Guest of honour: Livius Drusus T.P. ('Harmony').

She asked me why I hadn't mentioned that Harmony had been sitting on a slightly elevated seat in the very middle of the platform like King Strychnine holding a formal audience. 'Did he think he was about to be offered a crown, d'you suppose?' I said I didn't interpret his posture in such a light, and anyway how did she know? She had said she wasn't going to be at the meeting. 'I wasn't,' she retorted, 'but there were various poor old women all wrapped up in their blankets, sitting at the edge of the crowd ... selling hard-boiled eggs, leaves full of nuts, black sausages – I saw *you* buy an *atrocious* sausage, I'm sure it gave you gutsache before the morning was out.' It had: and I was very angry with myself I had failed to recognize her in her disguise. God, I was no good for this work ... Who else could have been in the crowd I ought to have known about? The Stain, even? I wouldn't have put it past him. The horrid old cloak Irene had worn was hanging now on a hook in this very room, it would have covered herself, Cuttlefish, *and* Snow-flake, had they all tried to get under it: yet even here, even in our own house, I wouldn't have noticed it, but for the brisk gesture with which her hand as it were *beckoned* me to it.

I *had*, nonetheless, tried to do the job methodically.

1st speech: the mayor.
Regrettable situation: City has allowed highway police to usurp legitimate powers. Hope this is purely isolated incident. Strongest possible protest to be made.
Brief historical survey: Walls of Love never submitted to formidable Hannibal in Great War, foundation of municipal fortunes being establishment of Latin ex-soldier colony here at early stage of City's extension to south Italy. So much to be regretted that man illegally scourged to death was descendant of one such pioneer colonist. Fullest sympathy to friends and relatives.
Press for immediate and utmost compensation.

Interruptions: 'More than compensation – bring the criminal highway police butchers to trial!' 'Forget about your piss-willy protests, let's have some action: *now*!' ... etcetera.

Mayor unable to proceed because of intensity of heckling.

'Why the hell,' said Irene, 'was he talking there anyway? I thought the whole point about this flabby mayor was that he was asked to take chair but *not speak*. Somebody pulling the usual shifty deal to bring him in despite everyone. It didn't matter though – he got his come-uppance.'

Disturbance quelled by CRAC volunteers. Quelling-process itself quelled by arrival of actress *ex machina* –

'Oh make sure you keep that in – flatter the silvery bastard with a flash of the old Latin. "Ex machina". What the devil does it mean?' She knew perfectly well what it meant.

– *ex machina* over the stage-house. Euripides speech exactly on right emotional nerve – public unanimously aroused – tears down every cheek – standing ovation.

'And wasn't her costume *marvellous*? That uncovered right tit like an Amazon *triumphant* in everyone's eye! God but she was *good*: you mean-spirited little turd, Ivory, why couldn't you say so? Second thoughts, better not. He wants an objective summary.'

2nd speech: faction-boss (Latin).
Representative of largest population element, all of them outraged by scourging, most of them farmers in similar position to dead man. Has their forefathers' courageous selfless service to City been finally for ever thus disregarded, to be cast back in their nostrils, etcetera. Let the blood of their glorious race etcetera –

'He doesn't want all this. Of course the whole meeting was carried on in backwoods rhetoric. Just say whether or not you thought he meant what he said.'

Rhetoric judged moderately sincere.

'Will that do?' 'It lacks bite. But so did the rhetoric.'

Speaker announced he was chairman of CRAC organization, begged all other speakers to avoid ethnic divisions, accept CRAC as legitimate voice of protest on main issue.
Attack on City by *Latins* in such terms could be significant?
3rd Speech: faction-boss (Greek).
After years of internal disagreements, Greek inhabitants now united with Latin interlopers –

'Did he *say* "interlopers"? No he didn't: a sweeping

assertion for reasons of your lousy brevity, cut it out. We do *not* want to let him think factions are still at feud.' 'All right then: correction. "United with Latin newcomers"?' 'Better: but you ought to have learned a shorthand.'

> – united with Latin newcomers in stern defence of town's independent constitutional rights. All Greeks committed to constitutional rights. Inventors of democracy. Pericles: Demosthenes: Socrates, etcetera. Let the City beware, it has opened a can of worms.

> 4th Speech: faction-boss (Etruscan).
> Etruscan community the result of refugee problems after City's takeover of Etruscan native centres further north. Wholeheartedly welcomed in Walls of Love. Original northern centres under similar threat today, threat to very existence. Solidarity for all independent towns throughout Italy.

Irene jabbed her finger-nail into the wax of my tablet: 'Underline that last sentence. Very important. And reemphasise the number of times he said "northern".' I made the addition:

> He said 'northern' a number of times: as though expecting manifestations there. If there have been any, this observer has not heard of them – yet.

'Oh crafty bugger Ivory. Keep yourself *well* clear . . .'

> 5th Speech: faction-boss (Samnite).
> Samnite people the only legitimate inhabitants of this area.
> Samnite people destroyed armies from City in war after war.
> Samnite people prepared to sink differences with Greeks, Latins, Etruscans etcetera, in fight against common enemy. The goddess just now in theatrical interlude shown carrying spear of just retribution: let this not be mere poetical figment – we all appreciate poetry, even in Greek, though Samnite bards world-famous – but what we want now is action: real spears, real swords, Samnites always ready – thousands of clansmen in mountains – give the word and they will march!
> Rhetoric not judged to be backed up by adequate political reality.

'Who says? Have you been in those mountains lately?' 'Now you know I have had no opportunity to –' 'Then don't speculate. Cut out that last bit.'

'Correction, Irene: "rhetoric judged highly suggestive of tribal disaffection in mountains, but no figures given of prospective number of armed Samnites available". Tendentious enough for you?'

6th Speech: chief seer of (numerically insignificant) Aboriginal community. These people work as craftsmen-and-women in service of goddess, maintaining temple appointments, etcetera: they manufacture sacred souvenirs for pilgrims.
Speech took form of ritual hymn in Aboriginal language.
Fellow-Aboriginals in audience moaned and groaned in ecstasy.
Intervention judged of no political importance –

'If this is a new bit you've just added in for me, finish it off. "Except in so far as – "?'

– except in so far as it indicates total support for defence of town's ancient privileges against City.

Interruption from floor: 'What about the franchise then?'

Confusion among platform-party. Apparently this is controversial subject which by mutual agreement was not to be raised at this juncture. Interruption proved severe, an obviously pre-planned series of hecklers (mostly Samnites) jumping up and putting question over and over.

Mayor ineffective at dealing with it.

CRAC chairman took over podium: 'My friends, the crucial issue of the franchise is not one which we in CRAC believe can be usefully discussed in this emotional atmosphere. We are here dependent upon our friends in the City who themselves are at the mercy of unscrupulous political intriguers there: and any provocative manifestations here can only increase their already massive difficulties – '

Greek faction-boss hinted that City *sought* provocations in the Walls of Love in order to have pretext for eroding Civil Liberties even further and crushing all potential dissent: highway police excesses etcetera (he guessed) of deliberate design, to this end: we must therefore be very very careful.

'Greeks always say that, Ivory. *You're* always saying it.'

Then: a sort of pantomime during which it became clear that Harmony by some strange chance was reluctantly but generously prepared to say something about the franchise – to prevent anyone else from being embarrassed by having to say it. Whole thing seemed to this observer deliberately built up in order to exonerate Harmony from addressing meeting on this subject, if at any stage he was to be taken to task for it. He could, however, now say he was compelled to do so in order to head off a riot.

Colour given to such an excuse by a group of teenage louts getting onto the stage and pulling down some hangings, for which they were ostentatiously expelled by CRAC volunteer guards.

Harmony: austere, young middle-aged, bald, long-jawed, pinch-mouthed, an expression all the time as though he had just sucked a sharp lemon, his voice cold and scholarly to the point of dreariness, his gestures infrequent and restrained.

He spoke all the time of 'the law' as other men will speak of god – each time he mentioned it his eyes became diamonds.

He explained, without malice, without innuendo, how the 'popular' policies of the 'new crowd' were not really aimed to assist the common people (still less the Italians outside the City) as men like the Mule-driver pretended: the only ones to benefit from them were tax-racketeers and financial cartels making huge profits out of provincial exploitation.

'Jampots, and Hooks – ' Irene was poking me in the small of my back: ' – and someone's sainted father in Pergamus – and you want to tell me that *you're* not involved?'

On the other hand the 'old crowd', despite sterling individuals such as the maltreated Redhead, seemed totally blind to the genuine demands for full political participation now pouring in from all sides, the City multitude and the discriminated-against townspeople of such places as the Walls of Love, to say nothing of the provincials overseas. The last 'old crowd' administration had deliberately passed a bill refusing all hope that the Italian franchise would ever be granted at their hands. Significantly the present 'new crowd' government had made no effort to repeal this iniquitous legislation. Nevertheless, as things stood, it was *the law* and could only be overthrown by constitutional methods.

Interruptions at this point: 'Total waste of time – exercise in futility – crawling to the bastards . . . etcetera.'
Harmony waved these aside with one of his few gestures.

In some northern towns (he said) the struggle for the franchise had taken the form of secret societies pledged to forward the

aspiration by any method, legitimate or other. This could not
be too strongly condemned.

He had (he said) come to the conclusion that the Italian franchise – equal rights for all allied towns with the voters of
the One City – was not only justified but was in fact logically
determined by the course of the City's politics over the past
century . . .

This observer didn't understand this bit too well. Harmony
became very legalistic. I know nothing about the City's laws.
Most of the audience, though, clearly followed him in detail.

Anyway, he ended by demonstrating to his own satisfaction
that his own political campaign for the franchise, coupled with
improved rights for ex-soldiers, manual labourers, the un-
employed, and the children of resident foreigners in the City (I
think?), had put the 'new crowd' in a cleft stick vis-à-vis the
'old crowd', from which they could only extricate themselves
by supporting Harmony's new bill – or bills – I'm honestly not
quite sure –

'Look, Irene, I'm sorry: but it all got too difficult, I mean,
with my not having the shorthand – I – I had expected
you'd give me time to get it all written up once I came
home.'

'So that's all that you've got. About half-way through the
meeting. Marvellous. Oh stop looking so sorry for yourself.
Surely the main thing you need to say is that this man Harmony had worked out an absurdly elaborate scheme for
giving Italians the Roman vote, which was going to take at
least three years to get moving, and which was entirely dependent for success on his own unproved ability to manipu-
late the City factions. The people here had thought he was
coming as a liberator. He spoke for two hours and now they
didn't know what in hell they should think!'

I wrote this down exactly as she had said it. I may have
demurred a little at its cynical dismissal of Harmony's
idealism – I had been quite impressed by him. 'Dry-arsed
pomposity!' she said, 'Or, "law", was it, "law", that you liked
so much to hear about, you sweet little creature? Or did his
exposure of the rackets strike a heart-warming chord? Fine,
so he exposed them: but how many tax-merchants are going
to gaol? Not even those dung-beetles in Ephesus that the

Stain hunted out in dead of night. Jampot and the Hook were renegade notched pennies, that's why *they* were killed. All the rest are back together for another wallow in the warm tureen, splashing the gravy up their fundaments ... Now look here, what happened afterwards? I didn't stay any longer than the heckling after Harmony's devotional address. I saw the Samnites all shouting and pointing up to the troops on the high-town –'

The soldiers, in shirt-sleeves, had indeed been looking down (and trying, fruitlessly, to spit) upon us from the citadel walls; and this had infuriated the crowd, which gave vent to wild cat-calls about the utter uselessness of 'constitutional method'. I told her that at this point a message had been passed onto the stage –

'Oh yes, I know that: that's why I slipped away. I wanted to hear what the message had said before it was censored and only partially read out to you all. I had some words with some men backstage. It was more provocations, wasn't it? News of a chief magistrate in one of the northern towns who'd been scourged because he gave a burnt dinner to a City politico's wife? They read all that out?'

'They did and it caused an uproar. Somebody shouted, "a chief magistrate with a laddered back and you think it's more fucking serious than a stone-dead farmer? They should bloody scourge all chief magistrates and start wi' some of ours begod!"'

'Exactly: they'd missed the point. If the whole message had been read out, they'd have *known* it was more fucking serious. All right, the chief magistrate was only given ten lashes. But when they gave 'em to him, do you know what the army commander of that district had said to him? "A well-whipped cook will be careful to douse his fire ..." He had found out, you see, that the chief magistrate was chairman of the secret CRAC groups in his area. It was a very precise warning: and they *didn't* read it all out. Why not?'

I couldn't answer this, so she answered for me: 'Because no-one's supposed to know that there's a secret CRAC as well as an overt one. And it's this that has been worrying Harmony so much. Overt CRAC, in this town, has in effect assumed all the functions of the town council: but no-one knows what are the functions of the secret part of it, nor yet who are its members. And *that*, of course, is what Silver-hair most desperately wants to know. All right, you and I would like to know it too, but we don't. So what you must do in the final draft of your report is to hint all the time that whatever's going on here is big, really big, hidden, immeasurably dangerous to the City. Tell him all about the bits of the message that weren't read out. Tell him that the resolutions passed at the end of the meeting –' (there had been several of these, dealing with local defence committees; agreeing to await results from Harmony's policy; sending CRAC delegates, overtly, to visit several other towns in parallel predicaments) ' – tell him they seem to bear little relation to what is really being undertaken. Tell him that all these slogans scrawled on the walls these last few weeks – ' (I had seen them and disregarded them as the work of infantile street-gangs: "CRAC-boys conquest hooray!" – imbecilities of that sort) ' – tell him they seem to have precise esoteric meanings. Tell him anything you like: but make him even more afraid than he already is. Because if he *wasn't* afraid – blood of the bull, my darling, d'you suppose he'd have endeavoured to re-recruit *you* . . .?'

She then reminded me that Silver-hair had said that 'means' would be found for me to pass the report to the proper quarters. 'Right,' she said, 'I am the means. Copy it out and leave it with me.'

9   Irene I am Damned

Three days later I wrote out a memorandum headed 'Things I must say to Irene'. But I felt she would give me no chance to say them: so I slipped it, instead, under the door of her room.

Irene I am damned if I'm going to be treated like this any more. Cuttlefish has converted herself into an impossible incarnation of self-assumed divinity: does nothing but squat in her room (it used to be *my* room too) and inhale some toxic concoction she had Snowflake go and get for her – from the Aboriginal seer, for god's sake. It sends her into trances and the rest of the time she's rambling through tirades from the Raven's old repertoire, and clapping her hands to the tunes. Snowflake's no better: in there all day with C., and when she comes out she moans in the corner about her uncle.

Horsefury has disappeared. I had to look after the mules *myself* yesterday. Are you worried about Horsefury? I only ask because he's yours, you paid a high price for him, it's in the ledger.

And I simply do not know what attitude to take towards you, Irene, you. It is evident to me now that you are deeply enmeshed in the politics of this appalling country: and that you were enmeshed in them *before we even came here*. I don't know who you are working for, in what interest, for what advantage or payment; and I certainly don't know why you should expect me to enmesh myself likewise.

Irene: if I am to be of use to you – and god knows, I would wish to be, for I have very long recollections of you, I never *liked* you all that much, but you were always a sort of a friend – why cannot you see that you ought to tell me everything? If I cannot go along with it, I swear I will go home to Asia.

This Italy is none of my business: I don't want to betray anyone. But you have me enmeshed: and it is not fair to fold the net round me time and again *in the dark*. Irene: there is one other thing.

WHEN ARE WE GOING TO RESUME OUR RE-HEARSALS?

The theatre will be open again the end of the week if there is no more trouble. You already had the playbills out before all this began: do you seriously intend to disappoint your public? I would never have thought it of you – such unprofessional behaviour from you would be as impossible as the very idea that you (of all people) would be working *for the City* . . .? Please read this and give me an answer.

10 *Fulfilment, Satiety, Sleep*

Not that day did she give me an answer. Nor the next one. She didn't avoid me exactly, either: but there seemed no possibility of *contact* in any way with her, about the house or down in the town.

On the third day, at nightfall: I had a headache, I could not sleep, my couch injected pains all along my spine from loin to nape of neck. I would have gone for a walk, but the streets were no longer safe. The army's security patrols were everywhere, and people sometimes tried rioting against them, in the seedier districts.

I went out into the yard.

Irene, in the yard, wrapped up in a kind of blood-red curtain. Bare feet. Finger to lips. Hand out of the curtain, grabs hold of my wrist. Strong as a pair of pincers.

'Ivory, why couldn't I find you? I've been seeking you three days since you wrote me that letter. You've been seeking *me*, shall I suppose, a dozen years? I'm a liar: at least fifteen.'

I climb up into the wagon. She had already sprung up there in front of me, helps me in with a painful pull: bad leg jams on the tail-board. Inside, under the canvas, wagon all prepared for us, our little house on four wheels; a carpet spread, cushions, wine-bottle, cups (two), a charcoal brazier (November is chilly in the hill-towns) – but it's not charcoal making all that purple smoke – what is it? Cuttlefish's hairy-man incense? Or something else? Into the back of my nostrils and up through the caves of my brain like a grapnel.

'Now then, after all these years, you can unwind me, so.' The curtain is all in one piece. She hands me the loose end. Soft, easy, pull at it. A spiral: she stands in the middle, turns herself, it falls all around her. Nothing on underneath but her jewels and her hair – her own hair for once (cut short to show the complete shape of her head with a band of pearls tied round it and little sprays of smaller pearls dangling at each ear), in its own proper colours (rusty brown with streaks of silver – I hadn't known about the streaks of silver). No paint on her face and the lines in it pronounced in the exaggerated false light (she has hung a dim lamp from the wagon-tilt) like the scratches a plasterer makes in a yellow-buff wall when he needs a key for the second coat. Her small breasts have never sagged.

I had not remembered quite how hairy her legs were, her armpits, her groin, like the recesses of a cat's body. Now she crouches like a cat, strokes me down with her, finds us a position for coupling such as Cuttlefish and I were never able to discover – my leg hardly hurts me at all: and no cramp.

The fumes from her wicked brazier lead me away into the patterns of the carpet underneath us – patterns of gardens with symmetrical intricate paths and avenues, leading every time through the maze to a central fountain between stone walls among cool dark trees: outside the walls the dead desert mile upon mile where men and camels fall dead and turn into white house-frames of bone for the sand to blow through and the hot wind to live in, whistling in vain for fellow-lodgers. Ha, how the fountain incessantly, repetitively, sprays upward its glistening power.

'Ivory, I have understood that you will have to understand. If I tell you the truth, how much will you believe? Because you say if you do believe it and then you don't want it, you will go away to Asia. Oh . . .? Asia . . .? No you won't. Not any more, oh Asia will be *no place*: no place for you at all. Now: knock on the door again – quiet, or you wake up the house. Come in, here's the threshold – in. Take off your shoes and walk delicately like that man in the Jews' book . . . oh oh but they chopped *him* in pieces . . .'

After this more than once this, after this: 'Ivory, my sweetest lover – do you know, you were by far my youngest sweetest lover? – I am employed by King Strychnine. To create such war in Italy that not one City soldier can be kept inside Asia. And when they are brought back to deal with Italy, he is to give all the Greeks, all the Syrians, all the Persians, their own green fields, white cities, hard mountains (hard as my Ivory, hard and strong), all for their own for as long as they choose to live in them. Do you believe him? He said so, anyway. Believe him or not, I want every Roman finished with. So should you.'

I looked out across the sand-dunes and saw King Strychnine's barbarous horsemen under a laughing cloud of black flags, from end to end of the sun's journey, covering the world with liberty: and the foam from the horses' teeth flew behind them to make the stars and the moon. *I* had a laugh too. Irene had a laugh. We lay back on the deep cushions. King Strychnine was king of the world.

Fulfilment. Satiety. Sleep.

11   *Herostratus*

In the very early morning, the closed wagon, stale and grimy, soot from the brazier smeared on the bright fabrics, thick over-breathed air, harsh taste behind our sour teeth, repentant stomachs: Irene lay on her back, her limbs flung out shamelessly, her mouth wide open and dribbling, small cakes of dirty sweat drying in the folds of her neck, her pearl headband slipped down and hanging from one ear. She snored. The cushions beneath us were stained, and all our clothes mixed into them in a greasy confusion.

She woke up and looked at me. I was aware that what she saw was far worse than what I could see. I pulled up my shirt from the floor to cover myself. She grinned, an accomplice's naughty grin, one school-truant to another (*my* truancies had always been alone . . .). 'You don't need to do that.' Her voice was hoarse. 'I know who you are and I don't care. Let me talk to you about Cuttlefish.'

She explained that Cuttlefish now conceived herself so much a part of her goddess-under-threat that no individual – least of all me – could be in any way relevant to her for a long time to come: if, indeed, ever. What did I think of that?

I thought, I retorted, that the goddess was a *love*-goddess, not an impregnable virgin. Irene said that at this stage there was very little difference. 'When the soldiers have left the high-town, when the City respects the legal status of the Walls of Love, then, perhaps you might find humanity, mortality, once again, between the thighs of your true-love. In the meantime – '

'In the meantime, Irene, you – on behalf of your vicious
Strychnine – are doing your damnedest to make sure there
will be no such "respect". If Cuttlefish herself were to be
cut to pieces at the whipping-post it would all be to the
good as far as *you* are concerned. Or have I not understood?'

I had not understood. Irene thought chiefly (and why
not? it was her own land) of the liberties of Asia. C. had no
feeling for Asia (she had been *owned*, if I troubled to remember it, by purchasing and inheriting strangers there):
her liberty was tied up with her Lady's high-town, and her
Lady was now in danger. But in both cases, the City was
the enemy to be fought. Let them try to kill C., they would
have to kill Irene first, whatever the King of Pont might
think about it. She hoped they would also have to kill *me*.

I said indeed they would.

She told me I was no hero, and I ought not to make
boasts. But she would like very much she and I remained
lovers. I was irrelevant to C: but C. had no reason to wish
me unhappy. Did I not know that C. knew all about last
night? 'We really ought to get washed, this wagon is reeking
like the drain-sump of a third-rate whorehouse.' But she
made no move towards any wash-bowl. Instead she lifted
the folds of shirt away from my body, bent down, and made
it impossible for me – for some considerable space of time –
to raise any further objections to her totally dishonest view
of the world and the behaviour that it gave rise to.

Why on earth had she chosen to talk about Cuttlefish,
anyway?

I said, 'You still have not told me what you intend to do
about our theatre-work?'

She grunted that next day she would of course resume
rehearsals. She supposed the Cuttlefish would take part,
though she anticipated some difficulties. . . . In the meantime, how much had I found out about Harmony's doings?
(Word had it he had already left for the City?).

'Oh, Ivory, by the way: you remember that Herostratus
song? You do know who he was?'

'Wasn't he the man who set fire to the Mother's great

temple at Ephesus in order to get his name in the history books?'

'He was, and he did. Such a very silly bugger. Look, boy, you mustn't think I'm a kind of female version. When I say we want war in Italy, that's what Strychnine wants, fair enough. He doesn't much care who wins, so long as *he* wins, where he is. I want the war to be won *here*, as well as there. And if possible – why not? – without bloodshed. A breaking-apart of a solid stone pillar is a breaking-apart: that's all. That's what we look for.'

I said I didn't see how bloodshed could be avoided, if the City remained intransigent. She wiped herself crudely in her fork with a wet towel and said that neither could she.

I would lie with Irene any time she asked me, even until we were eighty or ninety years old, I think. I could never *live* with her. And I don't suppose I would ever ask *her* to lie with *me*.

12 *More Agitations, and Bribes*

In return for the most flagrant sexual bribes, I had now, it appeared, agreed to hold fast to the purposes of the remote King of Pont. Do not suppose that this contented me, but my relief that Irene was not in collusion with the men of the City was so great that I would have helped anyone any-where – at her instigation – to do anything. Her carnal grapnels brought me into a state of almost permanent pria-pism during the next few weeks – I was back again at the age of thirteen with all the energy, intention, and – would you believe? – the gaiety that had once accompanied the acquirement and exercise of my skills as a comic actor.

I put into order my notes upon Harmony's recent doings with a brisk new feeling for what it was all about.

This town was a Latin town and therefore likely to keep to the very last some genuine hopes of responsible friend-ship with the City. The Greek towns in the Toe and Heel of the country would attempt to avoid all involvement in trouble; the Samnites and other peoples to our west and north were already on the edge of open rebellion: *but if* (Irene calculated) the Walls of Love could be drawn into a real commitment, then the Greeks would have no choice but involve themselves as well. The Walls of Love was therefore the key to a united revolt: she had chosen it (as I suspected), with considerable geographical and ethnographical acumen.

Despite his ostensible control of the overt CRAC, the Latin faction-boss was not accepted in private as senior partner in the committee's deliberations.

If Irene could bribe me, so could I bribe other people. Not of course with her class of commodity, nor yet with money, but I had my resources, and was able to obtain the services of an informant from inside the committee itself. He was a Greek bank-manager – let me call him Strato – his firm maintained branches in many of the peninsular towns, and his CRAC function was liaison with other influential Greeks in all these places. He was scared of violence, but also aware of the financial possibilities of co-ordinated and successful rebellion. But he needed an insurance – if the City prevailed, someone had to let them know that he had really been working for *their* interests all this time, doing his best within CRAC to sabotage subversive efforts etcetera ... I gave him reason to believe that I was a City agent, and could – if need be – provide such insurance. (He took me for a Syrian – alas, my Arabian colouring, my sweaty hands, my nervousness – and therefore automatically assumed I was a deep double-dealer).

Here is a synopsis of Strato's recollection of the CRAC meeting behind closed doors which took place the day after the public meeting in the theatre.

The Samnites (the most bellicose group) dominated the discussion. Forget all that nonsense about clansmen in the hills – their real strength lay in their alliance with the Lucanians down the west coast, and innumerable towns there were in immediate confederation. 'Secret CRAC' – never mind who started it, but it wasn't in the Walls of Love – had built up a series of strong links and armed cells in all these places, and also in more northerly towns to the east of the City. The real purpose of this meeting – how far can we trust the majority population to understand the true ruthlessness of City policy? Or how far will they have been seduced by constitutional and 'legal' expectations held out by Harmony?

The Latins, it appeared, had wanted to be impressed by Harmony. But they were also pessimistic of the City's good faith. The scourging – deliberate provocation or stupid insensitivity – had seriously alarmed them. So they were not now prepared, their spokesmen thought, to dispute the necessity of military readiness, if that was what the Samnites were up to.

The Greeks had no trust in anything to do with the City's constitution: they had always regarded it as a barbarous pseudo-Greek fraud that existed only to provide a cover for naked aggression. But naked aggression tended to be successful, and they begged the Samnites to take care. Challenging it could be more dangerous than submitting to it.

The Etruscans agreed with the Samnites – if their cities in the north were becoming involved, then here we too should not attempt to slide aside.

The Aboriginals had not been a fighting power for about a thousand years: but if their goddess was insulted, they were all ready to immolate themselves in the flames of her burning temple.

Questions put to Samnites:
Was there a date fixed for general outbreak?
Yes, there was, but it mustn't be specified. We would all know when the hour arrived.
What could happen to defer this date?
The grant of the full franchise, obviously. Serious apology for military and highway police excesses might help, if accompanied by substantial compensation.
How could the Walls of Love prepare itself for war with this new garrison in the town?
Outnumber the garrison and take over their weapons.
How?
There were ways, don't ask awkward questions at this juncture, use your sense.

Harmony was then invited to come in and say a few words before he went home. Everyone most polite to him, though only the Latins were cordial. He had been genuinely shocked by the mood of the townspeople. Of course this was only to be expected in view of the outrages etc. Was it too much for him to ask them to trust him? They must understand that their feelings of oppression were exactly the same as those dominating the minds of the submerged City masses, to whom the 'new crowd' has made such specious and ultimately unfulfilled undertakings. A violent assertion of the towns against the City, without regard for the struggle for class-harmony within the City, could only lead to tragedy.

There were many communal leaders from the poorer districts of the City with whom the towns' leaders must urgently be put in touch – reciprocal delegations etc. It was simply not true to say that a City proletarian faction-boss could always be bought off by giving him a commissary's warrant in a regiment headed for loot. Today they were dealing there with men of proven integrity – he begged them once again to trust him: and took his leave, assuring the meeting that the fight for a just settlement of the Italian franchise question was on the edge of final achievement.

The Samnites told him on the doorstep they would give him one month, if there were no further outrages. After that, they could not hold themselves responsible for what might happen.

Once he was off the premises, the Samnites said that they were not at all sure their people could wait even that long.

Strato also offered me a report of a very secret meeting that he was not able to get into. Some small-scale Samnite faction-bosses came together in a shebeen in the town's red-light district (an officially-unacknowledged extension of the Love-goddess's commercial interests, looked after by low-caste Aboriginals). Here they held discussions late into the night with a number of hairy-men, to whom they had to make extensive promises about the eventual handing-over of certain tracts of land in the hills, occupied now by Samnite clans, but originally part of the Aboriginal hunting-grounds. The Samnites had begrudged these concessions. What the hairy-men would do in return for them was not reported to Strato: but it must have been of great value to Samnite plans.[*]

*

[*] the hairy-men. Was it possible that Irene could trace her ancestry in part to this enigmatic stock? When she was naked she certainly looked very much like the Aboriginal women one saw washing clothes in the river below the town, their gowns pulled up and their bare legs dark with wet curls. I must ask her one day. I really know so little about her: but if this guess is true, then her commitment to *Asia* might not in fact be absolute? But it's too late now, anyway.

Strato also heard of another occult meeting, during which a CRAC volunteer-guard leader made enquiries from Strato's informant (one of his own clerks) about the strongroom at the bank, and the identities of the bank's most affluent customers. This worried Strato intensely. The CRAC-man in question was from a very run-down ward of the town where unskilled labourers of all ethnic groups led a promiscuously insanitary life in a rotting pile of slum tenements. There seemed here to be revolution-within-a-revolution in preparation, and god knew what might come of it.

My methods of obtaining information. I will not disguise from you that (a) I knew Strato to be in love – unrequited – with the boy at the theatre who was assistant to the stage-manager, and (b) through exploiting this situation I found out that Strato had been embezzling his employers' funds. These two facts gave me a hold over him, which I used to the utmost.

Do my methods of work seem to you disgraceful? They did to me: but the furred and tawny body of Irene, its serpentine evolutions, the little bunches of golden acorns on a sequinned ribbon that she wore across it, low down, just over the cleft of her tail when she showed herself stripped, back-view, all this in the upshot abolished remorse . . . grapnels.

She said: 'These reports are just right. One point you haven't made, it would do him good to read it: most of the leaders of the CRAC volunteers are also NCOs in the official town militia. Once the City understands their so-called regional security-reserve is totally unreliable, they may begin to take us seriously.'

'Where is Silver-hair anyway?'

'God knows. Horsefury will find him: he's been taking all my messages.'

'Who does Silver-hair work for?'

'The City.'

'I know that. But who in the City? Harmony, for instance, or Harmony's opponents?'

'Impossible to say. I should think he works for all of

them. Whichever of them is nearest the top of the pile. Now Harmony is climbing strongly: these reports might well help him the last few feet – at least I hope so. Of course, dear old Strychnine won't want him there very long. Divide-and-rule, King Strychnine says: no other way in the world to deal with these bastards of Rome. I wonder why nobody tried it?'

13   Druid-woman at the Theatre

About three weeks later. No change in the situation, except that the weather has gone wicked on us. Rain, wind, land-slides in the hills, even snow (most unusual). Rehearsals in the theatre impossible, we have to use the largest room in our house. But only a few more days and the new show will be ready. Theatre manager delighted, he feared that with all the tension we might have upped sticks. He's had book-ing after booking cancelled since the army came to town.

(The army on the whole have behaved themselves, save for a few late-night riots and brutalities, followed by a form of apology from the colonel in command.) Horsefury has returned from his travels and he now is allowed his longed-for drum-solo. Snowflake turns out to be a virtuoso on the castanets, which raises her morale enormously. We are now in effect a company of four. Cuttlefish has emerged from 'behind the goddess's curtain' and works with a steady de-termination, though she hardly ever speaks to us outside immediate rehearsal requirements. Irene wants *me* to return to the boards(!) with one of my old comic drag-act monologues about a servant girl in trouble with a soldier – it has some satirical relevance to the troops in the Walls of Love: which would go down well. But I am doubtful. I'd have to do it more or less from a fixed position, and make the part depend chiefly on the verbal gags, and that's not something I ever had much experience with. Perhaps I'll save it for a later date.

Amazing: we get out of bed, the sun is bright, the wind fallen, the overnight rain drying up in the yard even as we look at it.

'Horsefury, Snowflake! Costume-baskets and follow us down – we're using the theatre today! Thank god!' Irene on her pattens click-clacks along, arm linked into mine, so fast I can hardly keep up. Cuttlefish surges silently forward, wrapped in a dark shawl, her eyes on the far distance.

At the theatre, dismay. The place is full of soldiers. The manager wringing his hands – bloody fool, he had assured us that no-one would be using it all this week. 'So sorry, sir, madame, madame – the officer was so insistent . . .' The officer paid him double-rent, more like; and for what? Practice run-through, if you please, for the regimental Games . . .! Two snarling defaulters, involuntarily enrolled to beat each other to pulp with wooden clubs, are warily circling in the middle of the orchestra like street-corner dogs . . . here, in *our* theatre!

I try to argue. Irene launches herself at a long languid streak of an unprepared young officer, telling him all in the one sentence who his mother was, what his father did to get himself sent to the galleys, why his sister was run out of the knocking-shops of Marseilles.

The officer blusters, calls up another officer, a scar-faced old sweat. This wooden-headed slob says that the theatre is officially commandeered by order of the colonel and flourishes a scrap of paper. Irene tears it out of his hand and throws it away. I snatch it up and look at it. Of course it says no such thing. 'The commanding officer requests facilities for the recreation of his men'. The second officer repeats that that means commandeered. I tell him we are not in a war-zone, whatever he may have been told by the morons who gave him his orders. He says that by the treatment his men have received in this town, he might just as well be in the Basque country. If it rested with him he'd damn well do to us what he did to the Basques.

Things become ugly, menacing: are we going to be arrested? Beaten up? God, I'd not put it past them.

At this point, the Cuttlefish, who has been standing aloof at one corner of the stage, suddenly gives tongue. She throws off her shawl, revealing her black limbs fresh from her morning bath all gleaming with oil, her face taut and transfigured, the ritual marks on her cheekbones livid in the sunlight. She jerks her chin upward, stretching the muscles of her neck, opens her mouth, and commences to ululate. Then broken utterances of strange words, linked by an ecstatic rhythm. She seems to be giving a sort of version of Cassandra's speech from *Agamemnon*: but it is not Greek. A good deal of it sounds like Latin, which she does not normally speak. At all events, the soldiers seem to understand much of it. Not all of it – if I had not known that she was brought from Africa at a very early age, I would suppose she had reverted to her native language.

> Late at night, last night, late at night, last night . . .
> only this morning do they find him late at night . . .
> only now only now only this morning here is the sun
> ho he walks like the street-cleaner shovelling dung in the gutter . . .
> sun can find, red-hot shovel to uncover discover
> hold him up hold him out bring him home . . .
> on the red-hot sunstroke for breakfast . . .
> home home
> bring him home to the tears of vinegar and sulphur
> they make gores in the cheeks of the women
> deep deep in the cheeks and hearts
> of the women of the City . . . and where is the man
> with his smooth heart hard as glue
> glazed like a black pot, no cut in it nor crack when
> he cut open the heart of last night . . .
> last night with his knife he cut open the heart of the saviour
> . . . only this morning do they know and I see them discover
>   him
> oh oh oh where he lies on the shovel of the dung-roasting sun –

On and on and on – more and more rhythmic, less and less coherent.

The effect on the soldiers unexpected, instantaneous: they pull away from stage and orchestra, retreating like nervous children backwards through the tiers, crowding together, muttering. Making charms with their fingers. So am I. I am frankly terrified by the white flecks upon her lips, the rolling of her eyes, the pupils have altogether disappeared.

Irene too is clearly shaken. Whatever this is, it is not something Cuttlefish is doing of her own volition. (I remember the young dancer in the cave of the Seven Sleepers.)

Cuttlefish subsides to the floor of the stage, writhing, twisting, throwing out arms and legs, and – particularly horrible – vomiting, vomiting, a torrent of green bile. The young officer pulls himself together, his uniform must maintain its authority, he strides over to her, hand raised to slap her face. Someone must have told him this – 'woman in a state, slap her in the face'. The other officer runs up behind him, grabs him by the arm – 'no!' I hear the word 'witchcraft'. Soldiers of course are nearly as superstitious as actors: officers no less than men. But not good for the men for officers to show it.

The two of them leave the stage and the older one starts to swear at the lower ranks. Sheepishly these assemble themselves, come timidly down the tiers, fall-in in the orchestra, and file at the double out of the theatre with ill-disciplined over-the-shoulder glances at Cuttlefish, still at her thrashings and gulpings.

Irene and I helpless to do anything. We try to stroke her head, make soothing noises: no result. Horsefury gently takes hold of our hands and puts them away from her. He shakes his head. 'In my country they would call her a druid-woman.'

'Druid-woman be damned,' snaps Irene, 'She's an actress and we're here to rehearse. Will she be fit or won't she?'

'Oh in a short while she will sleep. There, she is lowering herself already. She will sleep, she will of course.' And so she does, spread out on the stage. We carry her into the greenroom and attempt to proceed without her. But no good. 'Goddammit, it's no damned use, we might just as well finish with it!' Irene brings the work to an end after two hours of redundant frustration.

She storms into the greenroom to find the Cuttlefish sitting up and stretching herself blearily. Irene's anger drops away at once, she falls on her knees beside the couch and takes Cuttlefish by the hand . 'Now sweetheart,' she says, 'take it easy, don't move too soon. Do you think you can walk home, or shall I send for a sedan?' Cuttlefish looks at her slowly, recognizes her, and vehemently kisses her, clinging to her hands as though they had just drawn her from drowning.

'I'm sorry,' her voice wavering, 'so sorry, I don't know what went wrong, I – I think – I think I must have been *taken*.'

'Taken? Taken where, my love?'

'I think Africa. Would you believe that. To a river – a great wide river, full of reeds as tall as a house, and there were reed boats there with black men. They stood in the boats on one leg and made noises with their mouths – cluck cluck-cluck. Someone told me – who told me? – someone told me they meant "welcome back home" . . .?'

She stood up shakily, leaning on Snowflake to keep her balance. She might have been bed-ridden for months. All her strength seemed drained: she sat down again, before she fell. 'Wait a moment,' she muttered, 'Before Africa. Where was I?'

'Sweetheart you were here, the theatre – '

'No, no. After that. After that and before Africa. There was a dirty dark place, they caught hold of this man, walking: from behind, they grabbed his neck with a scarf, spun him round and put the knife in. They said, 'Leave him there, they'll find him in the morning when they come with the rubbish cart: and then, me boys, oh scandal and horror.' They were laughing in the dark . . . I don't think I can walk, you know. Yes please, I think, a sedan.'

We had to make up our minds she would not be fit to perform before we opened: so we must rearrange the bill. It was necessary after all for me to get up my Servant-girl act: I had great trouble reaccustoming my memory and my nerves to theatrical requirements. I was angry that Irene seemed to take my unlooked-for ordeal so calmly. I thought I was being singularly heroic, well beyond the call of normal trouper's duty.

Horsefury took occasion to tell me something more about 'druid-women'. 'In my country all the kings would be coming to her to offer her armfuls of golden rings and the chief places at their tables. They would be in fear of her, indeed: but occasion of such *honour* to have her word for all their doings, her rebukes, do you understand, her fore-warnings, even her *curses* they would be seeking – anything but to endure her ignoring them: to be ignored by such a woman – oh the shame of the great man who must suffer it. I'll tell you one thing they would never do – they would never run like rabbits from her in the fashion of these white-scut Romans. No.'

She would ask us at intervals how the work was progressing. A wistful interest, as though she longed to be with us, but I noticed she never listened to the replies. She sat for hours in quiet under the garden porch, staring at the roofs of the high-town. She attended our first performance, but disappeared before it was over, leaving a note of apology at the stage-door, explaining she had felt poorly: she would be in bed when we got home. The message had a post-script, or rather two post-scripts:

'PS: Ivory: I remember now who it was, when I was *taken*, who was telling me what the men said in the reed boats – it was Raven. Would you believe that.

PPS: I have to go home now because I don't want to be in the theatre when the news comes. I know it already.'

14 *Killings*

This was the news that was brought to the theatre only a few minutes after our (more or less) successful first performance. We had just left the stage, the public were just leaving the tiers. A man – no-one knew who he was – came pushing amongst them, jumped up on the stage and shouted it over and over –

'Harmony: they've murdered Harmony!'

When they heard it, the people broke up into angry and excited groups and ran dispersedly all out about the town. If they had not done that, they would have kept together and rioted. Either way, we were all terrified. Anything could come next. We hurried home as fast as we could. Cuttlefish, in bed, had nothing to say, turned her face to the wall.

A few hours later, the news was officially confirmed from the town hall. Harmony, the austere tribune, had indeed been assassinated. In a City back-alley. It was thought that he was on his way home after addressing a big rally of his

supporters, where his policies had been endorsed by en-
thusiastic and even threatening acclamation. His assassins
were not discovered. The body was found an hour after
dawn, exactly the same hour, the same day, that Cuttlefish
had been *taken*.

The City police department floated a theory that the
murderers were Italians unwilling to have Harmony settle
the dispute about the franchise in a constitutional manner.
This theory was not accepted by many in the Walls of
Love.

The garrison was immediately confined to the citadel:
except for increased street-patrols and an extra guard on
the town gates. That evening the first soldier was killed – a
patrol, advancing out of a narrow street into a small square,
walked straight into a volley of arrows. The NCO in command was struck in the neck and immediately bled to death.
Two of his men were wounded. The attackers fled into the
shadows. Within an hour a reinforced body of troops came
back to the square, broke into the houses that overlooked it,
ransacked them, and unrestrainedly maltreated the inhabitants. An old man died of the blows they laid on him, and a
boy and a middle-aged woman were severely hurt. Two
younger women claimed they had been violated; though, in
a statement issued from the citadel, the colonel denied this.
He did not deny the other assaults, but excused them in a
bare-faced manner. He demanded that the 'terrorist
bowmen' be sought out and given up to military justice.
The mayor, prompted by the Civil Rights Action Committee, replied that he thought this would be as difficult for
the town's police as the apprehension of Harmony's killers
obviously was for those in the City.

The colonel imposed a dusk-to-dawn curfew, and said if
it was not observed he would be compelled to seize hostages.
He sent out men to commandeer warehouses and granaries
about the town, and fortify them, so that his troops were
not all located in one central place. The effect of these
measures was to keep armed soldiers continuously on the
streets. This brought renewed attacks on them – by day
they were mobbed by women and stone-throwing children:

at night arrows and throwing-knives came at them without warning. Some more of them were killed, and their comrades made more widespread reprisals. Funeral processions became commonplace, and took on the character of political demonstrations.

The important families got together to form a law-and-order committee. They demanded that the Civil Rights Action Committee, CRAC (of which many of them were also members), should denounce irresponsible hooliganism and put a stop to acts of terror. CRAC split over the contradiction, most of the Latins supporting the law-and-order committee (LOC), while the Samnites called for bigger and more militant marches and demonstrations.

A Samnite march to deliver a letter of remonstrance to the citadel was stopped half-way up the high-town hill and chased down again into the town, with many of its participants injured by the soldiers' bludgeons. A popular young athlete (CRAC volunteer guard and municipal militia-serjeant) was stabbed to death by an army javelin. His funeral was enormous, and dispersed by the soldiers with great violence (and sacrilege to the dead body).

There was fearful recrimination about this, which split CRAC even further. That night the curfew was broken again: no fewer than six soldiers were killed in an attack upon a garrison party bringing rations to one of the outposts in a down-town oil-bottling plant. The colonel then took his hostages – all of them members, or relatives of members of LOC. The CRAC militants were delighted. The colonel realized very soon that no militant was going to behave himself on account of *these* hostages: but he nevertheless refused to release them. He was afraid of losing face. The law-and-order committee went into secret session: and sent for me.

15   Secret Session in the Empty House

The way this was done was odd. I discussed it, of course, at each stage with Irene. Her instructions were cold and 'objective': 'Don't talk to them, let them talk to you. *They* want *you*, not the reverse. Find out what they're up to, and go along with them, if you must. Be oblique, if you can.'

A man he had never seen before accosted Horsefury early in the morning when he was ordering fodder in the market for our mules, and told him that he should 'tell the lame leg from Ephesus that the stooping man with grey hair is no good to him, but other men may be:' and then shoved a paper into his sleeve. This proved to have an address and an hour (mid-day the same day) on it. Half an hour afterwards someone else drifted into our yard and told Snowflake that a few of the magistrates wanted to see me on the subject of the theatre's imminent closure and our residence-permit, which required attention because of the 'emergency'. The address was not, as one might have expected, the town hall, but the one given to Horsefury: and the hour was one hour *after* mid-day.

I went there at noon. An apparently uninhabited house at the bottom of a weed-filled cul-de-sac with an ancient 'to let' notice hanging on the gate. When I knocked I was admitted by a caretaker person. Inside the house it was all dark except for what light came in through missing and broken panels in the tightly-closed shutters. In a small room that might once have been an office sat a fat man I had met before. At Ephesus in the Stain's headquarters.

I attempted not to show surprise. He said, 'Were you noticed on the way here by any patrols?'

'What patrols? The garrison, or the CRAC volunteers?' (The latter had taken to making their own intimidatory rounds of the town in defiance of the City troops).

'Either.'

'I don't think so.'

'Good. Always best to be secure about security. Do you know who I am? No, you don't.' He could see perfectly well that I did. 'I will tell you. I travel for a firm of wine-merchants in Naples. I have known you on and off for some years. We met in the street last night by mere chance. It is only by chance that I am here at all. The emergency has caught me unawares, but I am anxious to do what I can for friends and suppliers in the Walls of Love. You have been asked to meet the magistrates, but they will not exactly be gathered in their official capacity. For instance, I shall be with them. Now: the stooping man with grey hair. You've had a message about him? Good. You will not tell him anything about what happens here.'

'Is he in town then, or where is he?'

'Don't ask questions. Remember how you wet yourself the last time we met. And then you were in your own part of the world. Here, you are in *mine*.'

I pretended to be as frightened as I had been then. But wonderful, I was not – well, not quite. I was *trusting* Irene.

'You see,' he went on, 'the reports you gave that man were used by the military. You will have seen to what advantage. Your opinion, please, of the colonel's recent actions?'

'I – I – do you really want my opinion?'

'You have been living here: I have not.'

'I – sir – I do not think the colonel has handled things as – as adroitly perhaps as he could have done. I – '

'The colonel is an obstinate idiot. He should have released all those hostages as soon as he knew who they were. Your reports no doubt made it clear who they were? We know he received them: were they perhaps doctored? All I say to you is this: no more of them to the stooping man. Instead you will send them to me. A means will be found for it. The solution to the problems here is political, not military: the garrison's reactions, in future, are to be *politically* determined.' A long silence: then –

'Don't assume though I am taking orders from some specifically political source. We regard politicians as *colleagues* in our service of the City, and only accept instruction from them when instructed to do so.' Another silence: then –

'By the way, your charming employer. She has a most capacious cunt. Does she use *it*: or does it use *her*? Quick: I want an answer!'

I was totally taken aback. As usual with these bloody people, I had no idea of how much he could possibly know. I recollected Miriam and the Jampot. I said, 'She's never been one to miss out on the main chance, Irene. If she fucks, then you can take it she fucks to some purpose.'

'Ah yes, but what purpose? Or *whose*? The stooping man's?'

'Most likely not. Most likely some foreign agency.'

He smiled, thick lips, wet, a wet tongue. 'No, no. I had a chat with her in Ephesus, remember? I am accustomed to the intimacies of actresses. I know the main chance they favour. A good strong pair of ballocks and a well-ballasted bank-account. If all goes well I could do her some good. Do you some good too. You might think about it.'

So after all, his interest in her was purely non-professional? He had only put the question so as to be on the safe side – to be secure about security . . .

Back to work: 'Where were we? Ah: political. The colonel believes that by holding Latin hostages he can hold Latin loyalty. Bullshit. The Latins would be only too glad to work with him against the Samnites, if it were properly put to them. No-one has even *tried* to put it: idiots. What else is the LOC all about? That's who you're meeting today, by the way. But the committee cannot serve the interests of the City without appearing to be informers. They'll shy away from it. But if information is given to them – it'll put them on a spot. What'll they do with it? They don't need to be intimidated from above: pressure from below would work far better. And what could be lower than an Asiatic theatre-pimp? I'll tell you what you're to do.'

He gave me a careful coaching. Then he told me to wait a half-hour and went upstairs. After half an hour the caretaker came and brought me upstairs too.

The upper room was just as dark as the rest of the house. The fat man was at a table with five or six others. They all looked grim and disturbed. One of them was the Latin faction-boss. He said, 'This is the man. I am told by our friend here – ' (indicating the fat man) ' – that he has something to tell us that might help.'

The fat man said, 'The theatre, like the wine-trade, has a vested interest in stability. I do think you ought to listen to him.' They all looked at me. I cleared my throat and began.

It had come to my attention, I said, that some of a – a certain faction had been involved in the disgraceful terrorist violence that had been disfiguring the town. I had rather not say how it had come to my attention. I hinted some salacity about the stage-manager's assistant: they licked their lips and nodded. They understood theatrical goings-on. I then changed my tone and blurted out a list of names – mostly Samnite. Those present were all Latin or Greek.

Then I waited.

The faction-boss asked me why I had volunteered this to them. He seemed in command of the situation, though the others were clearly alarmed. I replied that if I took my information to the security forces, innocent men might be placed in jeopardy. I was sure that responsible municipal leaders could handle the affair without blundering. The theatre had already been closed once: I had an obvious personal concern that peace should be brought back on the streets. The faction-boss said that the theatre was being closed again, anyway, as from tomorrow.

They whispered earnestly together. One of them spluttered: 'He has no right, absolutely no right to make these unfounded allegations.' Another one said, 'We can't act on this. If the Samnites find out we have betrayed their – '

'It is not a question of betraying the Samnites,' (the faction-boss, providing the required cover): 'Terrorism itself is a betrayal of *all* the Samnites, the majority of whom are as law-abiding as any Latin. Certain names, that's all – flush them out: the Samnites in general will be deeply beholden to us.'

'We are here talking of a small element,' said the fat man, 'deliberately trying to discredit the constitutional methods of your CRAC. Flush it out, root it out, demonstrate your town worthy of the City's franchise. I recommend, as an interested friend.'

They then sent me home – the faction-boss telling me as I left that our residence-permits could remain valid until it was possible to re-open the theatre. This, I took it, was by way of reward for my municipal high-mindedness.

Well, I had given the names. I forced myself to remember that most of them were the same as those on a list I had seen before all the emergency-business began – a list of Samnite notables who wanted the theatre permanently closed and replaced by a fighting-ring for regular virile Games. That attempt had been diverted by a Greek-dominated 'cultural bloc' on the council: but it had nearly kept us out of this town altogether . . . So: they had wanted Roman Games, let the Romans play games with them.

Later on, as Irene took off my clothes and put her lips to various urgent places, I told her what had developed. She immediately bit me, in uncontrolled excitement.

'Ah!' I yelled out, in uncontrollable pain.

'Ah ha aha!' she cried back at me, 'I was *waiting* for this! Fat-man means the Stain, isn't that right? Twenty-to-one they're putting the Stain in charge of the 'pacification' of these towns. Twenty-to-one he's caught his moment, with Harmony dead, to make the Italian franchise his own public step-ladder! He fixes the Latins in collusion with the army to keep the Walls of Love clinging tight to the City's tit. Precious little milk they'll be able to swallow — but for a while he has them sucking — suck-suckling suck . . . Yah.' I asked her so what. She slapped and bit me again in a sort of frenzy.

'So what? So the Stain will need soldiers. So where are his regiments? Bloody *Asia*, that's where. Twenty-to – no – one-hundred-to-one he has the ships rigged already in Brindisi to go and fetch 'em!'

But with the Latins supporting him, there won't be any war here, so what would the soldiers do?

'Who says there'll be no war? This is the quietest town in Italy today, didn't you know that? What d'you think they're doing in all the *real* Samnite towns since Harmony got his supper-knife?' She rolled me about as it might have been pastry, I had to scream to her to stop.

'The question now remains: if Fat-man is the Stain's man, whose do we think Silver-hair is? Mule-driver's? Why not? If what you were just told is the truth, your reports went up to the citadel reworked to bring about complete confrontation between all local CRAC groupings and the garrison. No doubt something similar everywhere else. So what better chance for the Mule-driver to assemble all *his* old regiments and save the City once again? Do you suppose they might fight each other for the privilege of fighting the subject-peoples? Ho it could come to that yet. Let's see how we can help it . . . So what do we do now? I know what we'll do . . . we'll take *this* and we'll put it *here,* knock knock, you're on the threshold . . .' etcetera, for an hour or two, altogether devoid of politics.

We were startled out of our consequent affectionate lethargy by a great shouting, trumpet-blaring, horse-hoof-thundering uproar at the town-gate only twenty yards from Irene's bedroom window. She was immediately off the bed and at the window, peering breathlessly out, unheeding of how much privacy she displayed to the general world. I pressed under her elbow, struggling to see what was happening outside. A party of cavalry, covered in dust and lather, came through the gate and into the street without even a pause to accept the salutes of the turned-out guard. They went on, up and through the town, like the messengers of hell to carry off a condemned matricide.

'Oh that,' she said, calculating, click-click-click of her brain, 'that's a *very* urgent message. How long before we know what it says?'

We put on our clothes and went out at the back to our roof-garden terrace, from which we could see the high-town. The plumes of the horsemen where already on the steep ascent. Cuttlefish came out to us, a sleep-walking deadness under her eyelids.

'Do you know,' she was murmuring, 'how they dealt with the hostages up there? They have put them in Our Lady's temple: they have them chained by the elbows each one to a pillar. The chains are fixed too low to permit them to stand and too high to let them lie down, or even sit. They are never allowed the chains off, for any reason whatever. Her statue looks at this, every hour of the day and night. It is not yet the worst, though, not yet the worst . . .' We were not clear whether someone had told her this, or whether she had *seen* it, with the vision of her new strange dreams, or whatever.

Within half an hour things began happening: we saw more helmets on the high-town slope, coming down in among the houses, helmets and javelin-points. Bugles were sounded in different outposts all around the town. There was shouting and some screams carried towards us on the breeze. No-one came into our street, and the guard at the gate remained quiet.

Then we saw the helmets again – not all of them – climbing the hill once more – it looked as though they had people with them, people driven, people being beaten, people dragged.

'Ah,' said Irene, 'Your Samnites, poor buggers – they've lifted them in the middle of siesta.' Her face was like the Medea-mask in the theatre-wardrobe: she seemed to turn from me in revulsion. Then she shivered, swung around again, pressed my arm hard. 'No: you couldn't help it. It would have happened in any case. God, but there will be a payment.'

There was now tumult growing from one end of the town to the other. 'Yes, they will riot,' I said, 'They may even burn houses, their own houses as like as not: the Latins will not help them and will very likely riot against them.'

'Divide-and-rule.' Irene contorted her mouth. 'As usual, their turn first. This time: *ours* comes, afterward.'

Later on, Snowflake ran to us, white-faced. Where was Horsefury? There was terrible things in the streets, oh god, madam, where was Horsefury? Irene took her in her arms and said gently that Horsefury knew his business: no better man for slipping safely through a crowd, did she not know that yet? She was right: but it was long after dark – a dark broken by evil red flames and thickened over our heads with a dense cloud of black smoke (the oil-bottling plant had been fired) – when Horsefury darted from doorpost to doorpost and over our yard-wall before the sentry immediately opposite even knew he had passed him.

The boy was in a condition of extreme exaltation: his hair stood all in points, his moustache glittered and bristled as though it was made of lightning-sparks. Face and shirt were smeared with soot, and also with something I thought might be blood.

'War . . .!' He made the word sound like a lion taking note of an intruder into his jungle. 'War. Did not these iron

horsemen bring it today from the north? There is war in
the north: his death by cold knife in the City, as soon as the
men of the north heard his death, they have made the red
war, so they have. And in one certain place, only one yet,
but tomorrow all of them, they say *all* – in the one place the
good men are after taking the spear, and an end to every
Roman who has feet in their green fields. True, true, true –'
(he was almost singing it) ' - every Roman with a spear
in him: and the chief man of all of them with the three-
pointed spear of the fisher six times through the sack of his
gut . . .!'

That was about all we could get from him there and then
in terms of transparent narrative: later the next day we
began to hear the full story.

16   *War*

Not everyone whom the army allowed into the town (and
access was now rigidly controlled) was disposed to tell us
nothing but lies. In effect, the situation proved to be this:
the murder of Harmony had sprung-off outright rebellion
in a number of towns all at once, most of them to the north
of us, many of them Samnite. In one town, every man who
came from, was thought to come from, or held any official
contact with, the City, was killed in a vast outburst of
popular rage. Among the dead, the general in command
there: he was rumoured to have met his end at the hand and
weapon of a man condemned to the net-and-trident fighting
for some crime against the City. It struck home to the imagination: the notion of the arrogant officer trapped by a
mere convict, pierced like a tuna-fish on three spikes –
before long there began to appear on the wall-space of our
town scribbled images of this trident, with or without a
human-headed fish impaled on it.

The City's reaction was obtuse: they had already said that
the best memorial to the murdered Harmony would be a
very firm line taken against any attempt to exploit his
constitutional integrity by unprincipled men-of-violence:
and they held to this despite all. No, there could be no com-

promise: concessions to the Italians could only be given once the latter had – all of them – thoroughly renounced all forms of armed struggle: *terrorism*, in City vocabulary.

However, after the one night's destructive rioting and burning (there had been a long list of casualties, both towns-people and security-forces), the Walls of Love remained in a state of uneasy peace – 'de-stabilized' as the CRAC militants kept insisting, but none-the-less peaceful. The seizure of the Samnite leaders had been effectively intimidating. The more so, when (after the assassination of an incautious army catering-serjeant who had ventured into the market to buy delicacies for the officers' mess) six of the new hostages were disgustingly crucified by the colonel upon the walls of the citadel. But the streets were now swamped with troops – rioters could no longer assemble – and the Latins, in private, congratulated themselves.

The sacerdotal staff had now left the temple-precinct altogether and were living 'in exile' in a tenement made available to them in the Aboriginal quarter. Cuttlefish surprised us by going out, unescorted, to visit them. She repeated this frequently, but took no harm in the perilous streets. We were, none-the-less, very worried about her: but she would not listen to our protestations.

The chief priestess had not left the high-town. She was said to have locked herself into the small garden sanctuary up there: not even the soldiers dared interfere with her in such an ominous place. There were stories told of her ravaged figure appearing now and then on the parapet walls under the moon, howling curses into the air, her tangled locks flying in the wind. She was apparently surviving out-of-doors in the increasingly bitter winter weather: but she was not so far rapt into supernatural commination as to fail to provide for her food-supply. Every day she would lower a basket on the end of a rope towards the houses underneath: people would fill the basket as an act of devotion, and of passive defiance of the City. The military police made a spot-check sometimes to see was she passing messages. All they ever found was little notes saying things like 'The pickled sardines were too salt', or 'Please do not send stale bread except when I ask for it specially to feed the goldfish', and in the end they left her alone.

The garrison was strongly reinforced and a large regimental camp was established straddling the post-road down in the plain. Yes, Irene had it correctly. The general in command of this part of Italy was indeed the Stain – all charges against him had been dropped, and most of his Asian troops had been fetched over to him without delay. Once the new year came in, he waged a determined war upon all the rebellious towns within his immediate reach. The Walls of Love district became his base of operations, the Greek towns further south housed his reserves, he himself was up at the front line, though we heard he was sometimes personally installed in the encampment down below in the plain. If he ever entered the town, he did so discreetly and the population was not told of it. The 'obstinate idiot' still controlled the citadel and town; no doubt the Stain thought he was close enough to him to obviate further stupidities: the Latin hostages, one by one, were released, impaired for ever in their health, but at least alive. A Latin-dominated town council administered the Walls of Love, under firm curb from the military: and the birds of prey consumed the corpses of the Samnites on their high-town gallows-crosses.

Underneath these dreadful disintegrating relics, the theatre re-opened. Irene said we were to put on some light-comedy material and enjoy it, whether we wanted to or not. Things had not quite happened according to her calculated schedule, but the Walls of Love would eventually take its place in her hair-raising perspective of murderous insurrection: in the meantime we must conduct ourselves as unobtrusively as possible. The weather was cold, Cuttlefish was unwilling to perform, the audiences were small and when they laughed at the jokes the effect was unpleasantly hysterical. We did not make much money. Throughout the winter I had not been approached by any more notched-penny men.

After his night of riotous mayhem, Horsefury became sweet and docile, and most attentive to Snowflake. She expanded like a flower in the light of his love. He would make up little songs for her and they would teach each other endearments in their own exotic languages. She still said countless prayers to the love-goddess, not without reason.

She confided to Irene and Cuttlefish that she was pregnant. She begged them not to tell Horsefury, just yet, for would not the baby belong not to him but to Irene? Irene said, nonsense: the baby would be free. Snowflake and Horsefury would be free, too, but this was not a suitable time. She felt responsible for her household under conditions of war: it would be better they should all wait. Snowflake still said she did not want Horsefury told. She was mistrustful of ill luck.

Towards the end of winter we heard talk of a newly-established confederacy of Italian towns hostile to the City: a new *nation* – people said – to be formally known as 'The Nation of Italy' with a capital in the middle of the peninsula, an old town renamed *Italica* – or, as enthusiasts would have liked us to call it, 'the Only One City'. I am no authority upon political systems – no-one had ever, for instance, offered me a vote: but I could not help feeling that this was a *nation* in nothing but name. There was, for example, no unified army, and the war against the City was obviously hindered very much by this.

Nor was the City's army altogether unified either. Generals came and went, battles were lost and won, strategies were confounded and radically re-appraised. Only the Stain seemed to have consistent good fortune. He made slow but undeniable gains every month. Mule-driver, we heard, was active in the north, not perhaps to the best effect: though he did turn a colleague's disaster into one of his own blood-drenched victories with an unexpected surge of his old vigour.

Irene insisted that the Walls of Love could still be the *key*: but we must wait. Only wait for the chance in this one town, seize it, and the Stain was finished. Remember, King Strychnine needed the Stain totally embroiled before he could move in the east: and this was, little by little, coming to pass. She fancied herself as a general. I was not so certain: I thought she had probably fucked-up, as she would put it, but I preferred not to argue with her. We were still as amorous as ever, perhaps at a steadier pace.

17 *What the Devil Was I Playing At?*

One evening we were at dinner, Irene, the Cuttlefish, me. (Horsefury and Snowflake these days ate with us, but tonight they had gone early to bed – Snowflake felt poorly.) Irene said something about the pregnancy. 'She's going to have to tell him one day: I cannot think why she doesn't now – that boy would be so excited I declare he would kill every Roman in the citadel with his bare hands before breakfast.'

I said that that might well be what Snowflake was afraid of.

Cuttlefish said, suddenly: 'She is afraid of the whole world for her child – she would strangle it at birth to spare it the life *she* has had.' Then she relapsed into her usual brooding. She sat cutting a roast turnip into very small slices, eating each one with a snap of her jaws and taking a long pause before reaching for the next.

I put a question to Irene: why did she hate the City so much? I had never heard that she had ever actually experienced any *personal* oppression from that source? In our profession, surely –

'Oh. Oh, Ivory, our profession. When I went away from old Shoulderbone's troupe after a better offer had been made to me by a manager in Rhodes, how old d'you think I was? Seventeen, eighteen? Then a gap of – do your own sodding sum – anyway a good gap till the next time we met. Things happened in those years. One of them was a shit of a Roman. There was in fact no manager in Rhodes. But this shit of a juvenile nobleman in the Roman resident's entourage, who had promised me he loved me and would treat me like a queen. It's an odd thing, this conversation. I mean, Snowflake and her baby. Because he *did* treat me like a queen: I presumed upon that treatment and allowed myself to breed.

'About the time that the creature was born, he heard that his wife had been chosen for him in the City: he had to go home and marry her – all very in-keeping with his status, I foresaw it but could not reasonably object. But I did venture to say to him, "What about me and your daughter?" You know what his solution was? To pension me off with just enough cash to get to Miletus and no further: and to fucking sell the creature into the kennels of – of an agency, supply of orphans, if they lived, to the child-brothels of – of Antioch and points east. Moreover, I let him do it because I did not know till too late what it was that he was doing. It seemed that this – agency was run by a character with some hold over him: a series of vile dealings there I had never even had an inkling of. He had – *frequented* the child-houses, too often, before he met me. *I* was his attempt to reaccustom himself to – to nature, before his marriage, that was what I was. So: I found out too late, and where is Irene's daughter . . .?

'Which reminds me: Fat-man had something to say to you about my cunt and his ballocks. He's been seen again in town, I hear. Perhaps I can do something for his amusement – certainly for *mine* . . .' She licked a plate clean of sauce, with her tongue; and then broke it into two and dropped the pieces on the floor.

She got to her feet: 'Oh Ivory, why didn't I tell you *why* I was going to Rhodes? You would surely have come and rescued me, such a generous boy you were. I didn't want to hurt you by telling you about a nobleman. You worked so hard at your career: it might have stopped your talent there and then.' She left the room, very quickly.

I stayed in my place and began to weep. Cuttlefish, to my surprise, came quietly round the table and put her arms about me warm and close.

'Oh my dear,' she was murmuring, 'don't cry, my dear, how can I comfort you? Lost love, so long ago, lost love and your tall young body, and no-one knows how long ago. How can I comfort you, how can I comfort *her* . . .? You made me free, between you both. Between you both, I have lost you both, I think. I was *taken*, by this goddess, and I have lost all my good people . . .'

I was lying on one elbow on a couch at the end of the dinner-table. Without saying anything else, the Cuttlefish slid up beside me, stretched her long dark arm and snuffed out the lamp in the middle of the table. Moonlight alone was left in the room. She unfastened her gown at the shoulders and pressed her breasts against my wet cheek. I sobbed and turned away. I might have been a little drunk . . . But she lay there and stroked my thinning hairs, and then my face, and then my body.

I did not want to make love to her.

I was filled with Irene. Perhaps I was thinking Irene into Cuttlefish. Perhaps both of them were the same woman. Perhaps the haggard shape of the priestess railing from the rock was the same woman too . . .

Perhaps it would have been better if I had preferred my own sex, like that decent man Roscius, that excellent loyal man, Roscius my friend.

Perhaps I am only a self-indulgent bastard as both Irene and Cuttlefish at different times have called me.

I should *never* have allowed such a half-wit to be in control of the rope-ladder at so crucial a moment of the play. If I was still a straight-legged actor with bounce and strut and comic swagger, there's not a woman in the world I could not have had: and felt nothing for it afterwards but the warm flush of well-being.

I was filled with Irene: I filled Cuttlefish there and then. What the devil did I think I was playing at?

18   Such Joy

Oh god and she got pregnant. She wasn't like Snowflake. She told me. And she told me with such joy.

'It is after all the goddess – she has brought me alive into the centre of the world . . . and here she has made life out of my life . . .!'

19   Secret Session (Once Again) in the Empty House

Irene swore to me she would not be jealous. Swore the Cuttlefish was her dearest friend, even more so than I was, so why jealous? Had she not shared the great Strychnine with nearly a thousand eastern wives? She was, however, jealous: and as arbitrary with it as a wasp.

She stung me, she stung Cuttlefish, with words and abrupt silences. She made sapphic love to Cuttlefish, and at one time I thought she would have embroiled poor little Snowflake by making love to Horsefury. Through all of it she swore she loved us all to distraction. Our theatre work fell to tatters as the spring wore on and the news of the fighting outside the town came in again redoubled. Cuttlefish still visited her friends among the hairy-men, and she would return charged with messages which she whispered to Irene. Whenever this happened, they went into a bedroom and I was firmly excluded.

The public baths were only moderately safe these days – but on the whole the City security-enforcement only made arrests in them as a last resort, they were used by all the collaborating Latins who ought not to be 'alienated'. One day of great heat, the house being plagued with insects, I swallowed my nervousness and went there to freshen myself. In the hot-room I found myself on the next slab to a hunk of great pink pork, of an outline that seemed familiar. He had a towel over his face, but I felt sure it was Fat-man. I tried to move to another section, but he must have been watching me covertly. A man with a hip like mine cannot pass unnoticed in a bath-house.

He laid a hand on my shoulder, friendly. Had I thought any more about what he had said to me about Irene? I promised to take a message. He gave me an address for the reply. I was afraid there would be more: but no, that was it.

I arrived home as sweaty as when I had gone out. Snowflake told me Irene was with Cuttlefish upstairs. I scrambled up, feeling savage, the door was latched, I rattled it open. The two of them lay naked under a mosquito-net: Irene smoothing her hand up and down Cuttlefish's belly. She was murmuring a tune in her ear. Did Irene consider it *her* child, for god's sake? Its shape was already discernible, to the informed eye.

'I am sorry,' I said, stammering. They lay perfectly still and said nothing, a painted sculpture of Two Muses inspiring one another, or something of some such erotic-allegorical variety. 'I am sorry. I met Fat-man.' I was struck to the heart by the beauty of the sight of them. 'Irene, he seems to want you.'

Imagine what she said? 'I will have to shave my legs and put on a wig. Only for my friends do I show myself as I am.' She got up to get dressed. 'Ivory,' she said, 'I had a dream. Who is an old man with a huge hooked nose, dyed black hair and a blood-stained cloak . . .? Oh yes, you *do* know him. It is the Raven, is it not?'

Cuttlefish muttered that of course it was the Raven, she'd often told Irene about him, a dream about the Raven was not of importance.

'But Ivory thinks it is. Ivory is trembling.' Irene left the room and drew me with her. Outside she put her mouth to my ear and spoke between her teeth: 'Ivory, he came and told me that that child in her womb belongs to *him* and he will have it.' There was horror on her face, but she put it away again and looked sly. 'Tonight he wants to see me? Really tonight? Why, tonight is the very night I need to know what he knows and no-one but me can find out.'

At sunset a sedan came to the door, escorted by bulky footmen with bludgeons. A smooth flunkey offered her his master's effusive compliments. She was attired very high-style for the assignation, paint, a dark red wig, eyelashes the length of centipedes, her most gallant draperies of smuggled silk. As she stepped into the conveyance, she suddenly lifted her hem to show me a glimpse of her legs: shaven. She gave me one of her truant's grins. Horsefury went with her, at her instruction, trotting along behind, completely ignoring the footmen.

Cuttlefish was moody, but she asked me to sleep with her. There were some holes in the mosquito-nets that caused us great annoyance. We were still lying awake, bitten and irritable, when we heard the front door open, and rapid footsteps through the house. It was Horsefury. He looked very anxious and distressed. 'I think you should come. It is not a good place. I do not like it at all, that place where she has gone.' It appeared that Irene had been taken, not to the

address Fat-man gave me at the baths, but to the deserted
house where I had met him 'in committee'. The flunkey
had told her it was a more discreet rendezvous than the
other, and had apologized for its seedy appearance. Irene
had whispered to Horsefury to go straight home and let me
know if he felt there might be need.

She went upstairs with the flunkey, and the footmen and
Horsefury were given drinks in the kitchen by the caretaker.
Then they were all told to leave. Horsefury had prowled
about a bit, however: and had been bothered by the fact
that the caretaker seemed to be packing everything up as
though making ready to leave the house that very night.
The kitchen itself was fully equipped but none of the other
downstairs rooms were furnished at all. He did not know
what it was like upstairs, but the hall and passages were
thick with dust. There was a meal for two on a tray – an
elaborate small supper – and the flunkey had taken this
upstairs immediately before the caretaker packed up all the
cooking-pots and utensils. There seemed no-one else at all
in the house. Horsefury had then come straight to find me:
said we should go back and make sure she was safe. I
wondered what we could do if she were not. Cuttlefish said
for god's sake not to waste any time. I wondered whether
Horsefury would be able to protect me as well as his mistress. He said he could do all of it by himself, but not if he
had to talk Latin: therefore I must come with him.

Dodging the patrols, not too easy for me with my damn
stick and my limp, and avoiding dogs that might bark and
houses with lights in them, we hastened through the town.
I had the feeling there were other shadowy people moving
here and there in the dark in the same direction as ourselves.
At one place – ('wait here, so') – Horsefury slipped into an
entry and conferred in a violent undertone with some
hidden person, before hurrying me on again. We took an
unexplained detour through the Aboriginal quarter and
Horsefury made bird-like whistles under several dark
windows.

In the cul-de-sac were two men, stood a little way back
in a gap in the boarded fence. They jumped out and blocked

our passage. Horsefury gave a coughing gasp and immediately killed them: a two-fold darting flick of a short weapon he had held under his coat. I have never seen anything quite so fast, nor so fearsome. But he did not let me pause to admire him for it. The gate was locked, he swarmed it like a squirrel and unlocked it for me from within. There was a light under the side door of the empty house. Horsefury gestured me to stand back, went to the door, and knocked, as it were timidly. A voice asked who was there. Horsefury replied with something deliberately incomprehensible, and knocked again, even more timidly. The door was slowly opened. Horsefury killed the caretaker, holding him up so that his falling body made no noise.

We tip-toed into the house, through the kitchen, into the hall. No doubt at all this place was exceedingly queer. When we fetched the kitchen candle we found that there were no lamps disposed anywhere for us to light. Horsefury, now barefoot, motioned me to take off my shoes. He began to creep upstairs. He left the candle with me, and signed to me to stand back and hold it so that he could see his way. I did so, clutching my private parts, praying to all manner of divinity.

The candle-light made a huge shadow of him on the rotting plaster as he climbed. At the head of the stair he stood, listening. There was a certain noise, not loud, coming from a room out of my range of vision. It did not sound like conversation, nor yet altogether like love-making (though one can never be sure about other people's variations of desire). It did remind me of my sister-in-law and the yellow dwarf . . . Horsefury disappeared round the corner of the landing.

I began to count, one two three, maybe as far as twelve. Then a violent crash as a door was burst open, a spread of light across the landing, a roar from Horsefury, footsteps springing and banging about, furniture falling over, more roars (not all from Horsefury), and a man came hurtling down the stairs towards me. I could see he was not Horsefury, so I came out of my alcove and put my walking-stick between his legs. He fell forward from the last two steps and full length onto the crumbling terrazzo. I hit him hard at the back of the skull with the knobbed head of my stick. He was the smooth fellow, the flunkey: I hit him four times before I was persuaded he was dead.

Horsefury at the stair-top – 'Come, come, you damfool, why do you wait!' – a bedroom door was broken down; inside the room a burning lamp showed walls hung with tapestry, expensive chairs and tables, all upset; the fat man lying across the floor with the carpet, a luxurious carpet, dragged sideways and rolled up with his legs: Irene spread out on the bed, a gag – her own breast-band – stuffed in her mouth, her silk dress pulled up to her armpits, her wig off, her wrists lashed to the bedposts with torn shreds of mosquito-net. She was unconscious.

Horsefury cut the lashings and undid the gag. I looked to see was she wounded – it seemed, oh thank god, not: a few vicious toothmarks, bruises, two deep scratches on her thighs, but no strong bleeding. Horsefury found a bowl of water and a sponge. As I wiped, I spoke to her. 'Come back to me, Irene, it's Ivory here, oh my heart, it's all right, oh my darling, here I am – ' a good deal of all that. I pulled the clothes back over her body.

On a curtained shelf beside the bed lay a short whip, a pair of slender canes, and one or two curious little metal appliances, with spiked screws and hooks and padlocks attached to them. I had never seen anything quite like them before.

After a while Irene sat up, muzzy, confused, but able to drink some of a bottle of wine that was in the room. We took stock of the fat man. Gashes in his groin and stomach, and in his throat: a great quantity of blood. He was dressed only in an open-fronted gown and stank of perfume. Horsefury said: 'I gave him two wounds. Stomach and throat. Two.' He wiped his falchion, looking puzzled. Irene reached over from the bed and groped on the carpet: she picked up a small fruit-knife, very sharp. 'Blood of the bull: missed by two inches, no more than a notch in his groin! Oh get me home, quick. Wait: *can* we get home? Who else is in the house?'

Horsefury said, 'Ah,' with a sort of triumph. Sudden soft

footsteps on the stairs, and three hairy-men into the room, smiling from ear to ear when they saw Irene. Horsefury embraced them, but said nothing: he picked Irene up and carried her downstairs. Fat-man's sedan stood in the hall: more hairy-men around it: we put Irene in it and immediately brought her home. Great speed all the way, surrounded by at least two dozen Aboriginals, changing places at street-corners all through the town. We went so fast I could not keep up. They put me as well into the sedan, crammed me in with Irene. She was cursing in rapid Persian all the way and shivering violently.

The last thing she said, as we laid her in her own bed, was 'What has been done? It has to be done now, *now* it has to be done, I should not have let you fetch me home before I knew, oh what has been done?'

Horsefury told her – pulling out his falchion with an odd kind of soldier's salute – 'Oh they are doing it. Do not take distress: there is nothing to be done that will not now be done before the sun shall jump over the mountain.' We left her, then, to sleep.

20   Questions and Answers

What had happened to Irene?

On arriving upstairs in the empty house, she had found Fat-man waiting to greet her with an admirably-prepared supper. The smooth flunkey at once withdrew, and her host made polite conversation as they ate. She drew him on to talk politics, though he made every effort to talk love. This irritated him and he said things he ought not to have said at that stage. He had clearly expected the evening's proceedings to be at *his* command: and was thrown out when she took the initiative.

She deduced from his sporadic admissions and evasions (a) that he knew that an attempt (of *some sort*) was to be made very soon against the garrison, and (b) that he had probably swopped factions. She thought he now worked for Mule-driver; and wanted to use events in the Walls of Love to discredit the Stain.

Irene in turn made the mistake of letting him see that she had seen this. He then let *her* see that he knew that she was implicated with Pont: he deliberately let slip a quote from a secret letter she had sent some weeks before to a man in Brindisi. Irene became frightened; understanding she had walked into a trap: was she going to be able to walk out of it, and, if so, at what price? All this through the conventions of extra-marital flirtation: and, without shifting the convention – indeed between mouthfuls of preserved ginger and sips of wine – Fat-man named his terms.

He was to be informed of every detail of the plan against the garrison, was to be enabled himself covertly to determine the date for it: and Irene was to accept his sexual demands for an indefinite period. These were now specified: without any euphemistic gallantry. Irene was to submit herself, in private, and in semi-public (when he had a select audience of like-minded friends for her), to almost everything inflicted during the Games upon the most degraded class of female criminal. The alternative was that it should happen in fact at the Games, and she would not survive it. She pretended to agree: and then, as he prepared himself at his ease for the preliminaries, she took up the fruit-knife and slashed at his tumid genitals. (' "Burn the bastards' balls off" – d'you remember we used to say it? I thought cutting might be quicker'). His huge paunch misled her, her aim was diverted, she only notched his groin, 'without even catching his damnēd artery!' At that, the flunkey, from hiding behind the tapestry, came in and caught hold of her. She struggled like a snared leopard, was thrown against the bed-end, hit her temple on the carved ornament; she passed out.

What did Horsefury see through the keyhole before he broke open the door?

He saw the flunkey holding the fruit-knife, poised over Irene's legs; while Fat-man, on his knees beside the bed, was moving his face and one wide hand up and down her torso. His other hand, blood trickling between the fingers, was in the fold of his groin: whether to press against the wound, or for a different purpose, he could not tell. Fat-

man made a noise like an ox grazing a meadow and the
flunkey was whistling through a gap in his teeth. Whatever
they were proposing to do had clearly only just begun.

What was to happen 'before the sun shall jump'?
The attempt against the citadel. It was scheduled for some
days later, and then hurriedly brought forward because of
the killings in the empty house. Irene, Cuttlefish, and
Horsefury were into some of the secrets: would *I* have
been confided in? Not on your life . . .
An extremely deadly poison had been prepared by the
Aboriginals, and passed, by way of the food-basket, to the
priestess in her sanctuary. This, on receipt of a signal from
below, she was to insert into the Archimedes-screw that
controlled her water-supply, and run it down into the cisterns below. The garrison drew its own water, with a screw
of their own, from the same basic reservoirs: the soldiers
were not aware that all the cisterns were inter-connected. It
is a wonder that that frail old woman found the strength to
work the screw: normally it needed the efforts of three
strapping hairy-men. Who helped her? The enamelled-
bronze goddess? The stag-headed wooden cockstander? Or
neither of them: merely the power of unrestrained ven-
detta?

Did it happen?
Oh yes. About noon the next day the priestess stood on
her parapet waving a strip of cloth. That meant she knew
the garrison had been at their water, and were already suffering from it (she could hear, but not see, much of what
passed in the citadel: the groans and cries of the afflicted
men were not muted). Samnite CRAC volunteers ambushed
a relief party from the army's town outposts (the colonel
had hoisted a signal of distress): they killed them all among
the houses out of sight of the citadel and took their uni-
forms.
The guard at the high-town gate, dazed with internal
pain, opened to them unquestioningly: and in a very few
minutes the citadel was captured. The garrison and its
attached whores (they had brought these women in their
baggage-train) were thrown over the precipice, dead or

dying. The priestess gleefully supervised this. Then she led the way into her desecrated temple and released what was left of the hostages. She said it was a pity the soldiers had not died of the draining of their blood, the goddess would have preferred it. As Horsefury, however, had caused Fat-man to die in this way, perhaps the Lady was compensated.

There was fighting in the town all day with the outpost troops, but before night they were subdued. The camp in the plain had very few men in it – the Stain had called all his regiments out on a big offensive – and they did not dare to intervene. The leaders of the pro-City Latins, and some Greeks, were massacred all over the town. They included the LOC-men whom I had met. This was a great relief to me, a guilty relief, guilty. There was no-one else, outside our household, who knew what I had done on that occasion.

Most of the ordinary people were happy to accept the new situation. They offered their loyalty to CRAC, and CRAC gave notice that the Walls of Love was now a fully-integrated part of the 'Nation of Italy'.

What did we do now?
Irene had achieved her purpose. How much was due to her own efforts, and how much would have happened anyway, seemed scarcely worth analysing. She said the next thing would be the siege, by the Stain's main army, of the Walls of Love: and we had better get out before it took place. She said we must go – go – go. She was frighteningly unhinged by her experience with Fat-man: she had never known such terror in her life, she said. Could we not now see she was not in the best of health? She fell into fever and acute depression, she was at times suicidal. She cursed herself for her clumsiness with the fruit-knife, and made a similar attack on me, which nearly succeeded. She said we must go – go – go.

But with her in such a state, how could we go anywhere? And then, one night, she disappeared. Just like that. She was in bed, tended by Snowflake. About midnight she stopped raving and tossing about, and fell into a semblance of sleep. Snowflake, who had watched her for hours, fell asleep too. When she woke up, an hour or so later, she found the bed empty, Irene's clothes gone from the cupboard, no trace of her anywhere in the house. Her strongbox was in my room, and no-one had tried to interfere with it. I'll say this for CRAC, they did everything they could to find her. The whole town was searched block by block. A reward was offered and then increased: no result.

Cuttlefish was *taken* again. She was 'brought to' a green forest, and there she saw Irene dressed in all her Persian clothes, with a crown on her head, dancing and laughing and flourishing a tambourine. The dream was not repeated: and not even the Aboriginal seer could interpret it definitively.

The only practical clue we had was an ear-ring of Irene's found on our roof-terrace. It was just possible for an active person to climb from here onto the town-wall, and from the wall there were various ways of descent to the outside of the town. But the gate-guard should have seen something. Once outside, there were all the horrid possibilities of a countryside in the midst of internecine war. I made up my mind that Irene was dead. If not dead, then what had come to her might not bear thinking of.

Consequences of Irene's disappearance?

Snowflake was so distressed by her responsibility for her mistress's fate that she ate a herb gathered from the high-town hillside. She knew it was poisonous: and told no-one what she had done until too late. She died in Horsefury's arms. He then discovered she had been with child all this time; said nothing to anyone for five whole days: then got blind drunk and set fire to the house from which he had rescued Irene. The fire was put out before it caught any neighbouring buildings: but the CRAC police officer called to the incident told us that Horsefury had been destroyed in its flames.

'We tried to bring him out: he climbed high into the blazing rafters, he was singing in a strange language. Somewhere in the ruins his body must be now, the whole place fell down about him, we haven't the men to spare these days to pull the heap out piece by piece to search for him. What was he – one of these Gauls? Ah, they all run amok in the end.'

The Stain moved his army to surround the Walls of Love. I could not make up my mind whether to stay or go. I did not much care. But then Cuttlefish, who had been spending several days in the temple, came down to me one morning in great haste. She said: 'We go – go – go ...!' When I persuaded her into some coherence, she explained that she had heard from one of her hairy-men that word had got out I had had something to do with the seizure of the Samnite hostages. I could not think how – it was now three weeks since the massacre of the pro-City faction – but if people were talking then somebody would believe them.

(Maybe Fat-man had left information about his informants as a posthumous divide-and-rule delayed-action weapon: and if I did not look sharp it would be into my neck.)

Until this moment I had been a sort of hero – Irene's ordeal had established her as a heroine (ventured her chastity, so they said, for the town's deliverance!): and I was associated with her glory. Not any more.

Where would we go?
We did not even discuss it. There was only one road, anyway, known not to be closed by City troops, the mountain-track to the west: so we took it. We had Irene's strongbox and the two mules. We left the wagon behind. The track was thronged with refugees. CRAC was glad to let them go (useless mouths in a siege).

Cuttlefish said to me: 'Should I kill this child now, before she grows any bigger inside me? If once she is born, I shall not have the heart to be rid of her.' Neither did *I* have the heart to put her to any sort of abortion, and I think this was the answer she hoped for. Though perhaps an abortion might have been wisest. But within the month we had lost three dear and noble friends. I did not have the heart.

Cuttlefish said to me: 'Because that man switched himself to the Mule-driver, he set his trap for Irene. It is therefore the Mule-driver who is to be drained of his blood. Yes.' She said this several times, as we rode.

During the journey – a difficult one, avoiding all manner of wartime dangers – I had an idea that the Raven was riding in the same direction, within hail, on a curious black animal (whether horse, mule, or something less natural, I could not tell). He did not approach us directly, and I felt that his intentions were unusually benign. Cuttlefish seemed not to know of him.

The last time she mentioned Mule-driver was, as I remember, when we came over a hill and saw the sea in front of us, stretching out to the rim of the . . .

What happened then: and why has the Raven changed his shape?

We had not determined where we would go: only to the coast and then let fate determine. It did: it sent a fierce gang of armed men of all colours out of the underbrush onto us as we paused and looked at the glittering blue sea. We were among a small company – peasants moving their stock out of the route of a rumoured army, refugee families, deserters from all the armies. But we were not enough.

We scattered and fled in every direction. I was flung off my bucking mule and fell almost into the middle of the attackers. They tied me up in a bundle with practised dexterity and ran on in their pursuit of the others. I had no idea where Cuttlefish went – she was, incidentally, carrying the cashbox – I was half-stunned and my nose was broken. Soon afterwards some of the gang came back and picked up all those whom they had left on the ground. We were carried through the woods to the sea-shore and heaved into boats. The Cuttlefish was not amongst us.

We were rowed out on the choppy waves and I was sick into the cloth they had wrapped around my face for attempting to bite the man carrying me. There were three pirate galleys backing water a little way off-shore. We were taken aboard the largest of these and dumped under the focsle deck. One of the mates looked us over.

Those men of us who could give no evidence of being worth a respectable ransom were stripped and put to work at the rowing-benches. It was torture to my lame leg. When the bosun saw this he ordered his men to throw me overboard. I screamed so loud – god knows why: with Irene gone and Cuttlefish gone, why on earth should I want to live? – that the captain heard me and came up onto the poop from his cabin to find what was the matter.

As soon as I saw him, I recognized him, and cried out to him of the *Lady Ruth* and the passage I had made in her just over a year before. He said that I had seemed at the time a man of no good luck: but he had done so well since then, that perhaps he had been mistaken. I could live.

This captain (Habbakuk) had abandoned peaceful seafaring because, now the Stain's regiments were withdrawn, the east was so unstable that the trade-routes had become impossible. A circumstance craftily anticipated by a partnership of Joppa shipowners, who had made a joint investment with him in this new-built galley, *Lady Jael*. She sailed under letters-of-marque from King Strychnine, who was not formally at war with anyone, and therefore should have needed no warships. She was a lateen-rigged two-master, carried three banks of twenty-five oars each along each side, mounted two hurling-engines in the prow. She pleased Habbakuk immensely: he dragged me roughly all over the vessel, boastfully inciting my praise for her on every deck.

I was not too sure, though, about my luck. Raven was aboard. He was one of the mates: he was also pulling an oar on the lower bank: he squatted upon the fighting-bridge helping the sailmaker to patch some old canvas. He had cast off his black cloak, and now, it was evident, would be always changing his shape to keep an eye on me everywhere. I assumed this was because I had lost Cuttlefish. How long would it be before her misfortunes caused his revenge to culminate? In the meantime, I must work.

What at?
What does a landsman always have to work at when he finds himself unwillingly aboard ship? Cook's boy, of course: and they would even let me have a pair of sea-trousers to keep my cock out of the soup. Get on with it: report for duty.

BOOK THREE

The 'Lady Jael'

'A check no doubt was kept on the buccaneers of the Adriatic and Tyrrene Seas; but Crete and Cilicia became the recognized home of organized bands of pirates. The Roman government merely looked on.'

Mommsen

1 On Board, and Ashore

I was two years with those pirates. And with the Raven.
Against expectation, the latter did not bother me much. He
was there all the time, of course, on ship-board and ashore:
every day I would notice him as a sailor, a fighting-man, a
captive, a dockyard matey, even a prostitute in a waterfront
bar: but he never *said* anything, and, once he had caught
my eye, he always turned away again quickly as though to
imply, 'Not yet, friend: be comfortable a little while yet.' I
did my best.

Before long I was afraid of him only at night when he
came into my sleep. And the life I had to lead was so strenuous that it was not often anyone could come into my sleep.
Dreams disappear when your pillow is the plank of a wet
deck.

The crew soon found out that I had been an actor, and a
transvestite comic actor at that. They did not care that all
the women I could impersonate had to walk with a hop-
skip-and-jump: to their simple tastes this made me all the
funnier. I was constantly employed in catering for these
tastes: impromptus at all hours in any available cranny of
the ship. They found a name for me: 'Judy Split-arse'. On
one famous occasion, when we were hard-driven by an
enemy five-banker, and the oarsmen were fainting at their
task, the bosun decided that he could not effectively whip
them any longer, but maybe the poor beasts could be
laughed into one last effort to save all our lives. He had me
prance along the gangway between the benches, waving my
bottom and abusing him like an Ephesus market-woman. It
must have worked – at any rate the hostile galley gave up
the chase: and I received the credit. I also had to revive
what little skill I had as a musician and singer – this was
not my strongest line: but I found, if I dressed in a spangled
green gown from the ship's booty, I could competently

enough burlesque the old Herostratus-song, remembering how Chloe would sing the heavy bits, and Irene – oh breaking heart – Irene would twist her slender shoulders, jerk her head like a bird, and come in staccato on the shrill portions.

They particularly laughed at my version of Irene.

The ship, as it happened, was lacking a shantyman (the last one had been killed in a fight with a coastguard cutter off Capri just before I joined the crew). I did not know any sailormen's work-songs: but they soon taught me. My style was never quite right, I think: they tolerated it. When we were under sail, they said, no right hauling at the ropes could ever be accomplished without music.

With all this, my occupation in the cook's department: not an easy one. The captain, half his officers, most of the crew, were Judaeans: and, although they sailed (as Habbakuk put it) 'a point or two to leeward' of the full rigour of the Jewish religion, they none the less demanded all manner of complication when it came to their food. They had their own cook, a sour young pedant from Tyre, who would never let me so much as touch a single one of his utensils or even come near him when he was at work. The stores were allegedly kept separate – Jewish and non-Jewish – but in the conditions below-deck, it was impossible they should never get mixed up. There was moreover only a single cooking-area – a small clay-lined firepit on the main-deck: but this fanatic insisted on dividing it into two. Non-Jews ate the same rations as the Jews, but on no account, ever, were the two sets of food to be prepared in conjunction. This made enormous difficulties: my popularity as an entertainer was all but cancelled-out by the complaints I incurred over the food.

After a few weeks I ventured to apply for a share of the ship's profits. I claimed that my double role (as non-Jew cook's boy and ship's clown – the second part entered into on a voluntary basis to everyone's advantage) meant that I had now transcended the status of captive, and should be considered a regular crew-member. This was put to the vote. Votes for all free hands are a regular part of a pirate-ship's articles. And the vote fell in my favour. Naturally the share was not a large one. In return I had to sign, committing myself for the duration of the cruise, to be renewed each time we put into land for a division of plunder. From all my theatrical-contract expertise, I looked over the documents with care: they were admirably egalitarian. The penalty, on either side, for breach-of-contract was to be made to walk the plank. I was assured that our captain was an honourable man who always abided by his word, and that the *Lady Jael* was therefore an enviable ship on which to serve.

A few words about our habit of life. We attempted to capture all ships we met at sea, unless they belonged to Pont, or could show an (expensive) exemption-ticket from the pirates' grand council. We were especially concerned to pursue City vessels. We took any cargo we could stow in our hold and sell for a worth-while price. We took any captive who could raise a ransom greater than his or her keep. When we needed new oarsmen, we took captives for this purpose. In general, though, Habbakuk did not do business as a slave-stealer. He felt that the trade was already in glut, and to add to it would only enrich the oppressive domination of the City, which he hated. We made raids for booty or ransom-money on undefended coasts.

We frequently returned to our home-port to refit and provision. The pirate community controlled the south-east coast of Asia, Crete, and many other islands. We were an independent self-governing confederacy, ruled over by our grand council, which was elected by a singularly democratic system involving all the associated crews as well as their officers. The alliance with King Strychnine was not binding on all crews: captains made their own arrangements, subject to agreement from their men. But Habbakuk was an enthusiast for it. He held that if the east (for the inscrutable purposes of a punitive divinity) had to be dominated by some powerful 'son of Belial', then Strychnine was the best of the bunch – provided his rule was not to last too long. Strychnine had, it seemed, an exceptional respect for the Judaean god and his unusual requirements. There was

already in Trebizond an empty house, paid for by the king,
where Judaeans could assemble to read the word of their
invisible Lord. This *word* was the only knowledge anyone
had of him. Habbakuk took it utterly on trust. He even
had a book of it in his cabin, which he sometimes read to
the crew. It was a very daunting narrative: I preferred
Homer.

There is much misunderstanding about life in a pirates'
port. People think it is all violence, brawling, drinking, rape.
But the settlement we were based upon proved to be as
well-ordered as any town I have ever lived in, because of
the ruthlessly democratic justice that prevailed. The sentences (either drowning or relegation to the rowing-benches,
or, for lesser offences, removal from the voting-lists) were
not imposed by any single judge: and the motley crews,
perhaps just because they were so motley, discovered as
jurymen an instinctive balance, their own good-natured
equity against all the 'civilized' world. Rules governing
women were particularly precise. Women had no voice in
the democracy. But then they never do. I think a few Irenes
would have done the pirates a lot of good . . .

During my two years I took part in many battles. Or
rather, the ship did. I was permitted, because of my dis-
ability, to keep guard over the more valuable captives in the
bilge. Everyone knew that a lame man on a fighting-bridge
would only incommode the agile ones.

I often saw Raven in the bilge during sea-fights, and his
eyes would glisten horribly.

Our captain was a formidable warrior – in his previous
life as a merchant skipper he had been so much at the beck
and call of so much 'Belialite' authority that he derived
enormous relish from its physical destruction. He was not
unduly cruel. Torture beyond immediate need (for information, usually), and the wanton forcing of women, were
abhorrent to him. His hero was a certain Samson (of his
own tribe, apparently, a legendary ancestor) who had been
a jovial and bawdy giant, much in favour with his Lord
until lechery diminished his morale.

*

How is it that I can speak so coolly of such savage dealings? Because I took part in them, that's how. We attacked, and defended ourselves, on the sickening swaying waves, and I cowered among the body's filth (a chained rowing-crew shits where it works, so the bilge under its foot-boards is in all senses the sink of existence) while death was determined above me. And then I would come up again into the salt air, slimy with the crust of my shame, to find myself there and then amid the only celebration of preserved life possible for such men at such a time – savagery, beasts of prey, yes. Our life had been saved that we might make prey of others: our legitimate delight was to consume that prey.

All that I loved had been preyed upon and taken from me: all that I knew of decent creative art and craft had been made mute as the laws themselves. Except for pirates' laws: and pirates' arts. Judy Split-arse who used to be Ivory, who could interpret Menander's most delicate passages till audiences wept and laughed together. The pirates' tastes were now my tastes: they had to be, dammit – was I not the man who *gave names* to a time-serving committee of delation and betrayal? And had not those names chased me here? *Hypocrite*, if you speak Greek – our common language on board was a sort of bastard sea-coast Greek (with admixture of Aramaic) – is a pompous word for 'actor': very well, I embraced it. At all events I took care that no-one would call me miserable.

And then I took care to attain rapid promotion. From cook's boy to crew's supercargo, from supercargo to captain's clerk. In the latter capacity I berthed in the stern-cabin among the selected luxury of every ship taken between Gibraltar and the Black Sea.

On shore I made a modest comportment. I rented a house in our usual harbour-town with three or four young women in it and a eunuch to look after them while *Lady Jael* was at sea. I behaved to these people most of the time with what I think was a distant courtesy. I could not bear to encourage an intimate friendship, to have anyone ask me questions about who I was before I became what I was. The women were established pirates' women, which meant they had come to accept our society and looked to gain from it as

much as was available. Clothes, jewels, sensual pleasure. I
gave my jolly ladies what they wanted in good measure.
When I needed to lie with them I never courted them with
romantic diffidence: I made them drunk, I made them
laugh, we sang choruses together and fell about in a warm
bath. I was remembering more of my old slapstick than I
ever thought I could have learned.

They must have seen me as an unpredictable companion
– half the time I was as grave and reserved as a magistrate
in the throes of a difficult verdict: the other half, an ithy-
phallic buffoon like a satyr on a vase. They deceived me left
and right – why not? – offered themselves when I was away
to any of the crews in harbour, and I never reproached them
for it. It was none of my business, really.

I did once have an unhappiness with one of these girls, a
roly-poly irrepressible from Illyria. I had her beaten, (by
the eunuch: and also, I am sorry to say, by me), quite hard,
with a rope's end, because she continued to be boisterous
when I was in my quiet mood. After that they all learned to
take their cues correctly. I was sorry I had hurt her. I gave
her a bag of gold as big as her bum, and looked the other
way when I saw her in a dramshop with the bosun's hand
up her skirt.

I never took to love-making with boys or young men,
though there were scores within reach, had I wanted them.
I could not cope with such relationships. I often wondered
why. It is not that male bodies have ever seemed less desirable to me than female, but . . .

Not necessary to remember this *now*, I used to tell myself:
'you are a pirate, you can have anything or anyone you can
adorn or keep fed' . . . but . . .

Not even in the good days before my accident did I enjoy
a boy lover. For even then, even in the heated romance of
the greenrooms, always the same catch in the back of my
rising desire that would bring down the strongest erection
in less time than it took to remind myself of it, that would
leave a kiss more decisively curdled than milk in a thunderstorm. I am not now going to talk of my childhood again
– it was Ivory's, not Judy's: but just this one grapnel

thought. So many ways have schoolboys to humiliate the
son of the most unpopular man in town, some of them are
bound to stick to him through all of his life . . . through all
of his *lives* . . . even extending into the one I was now leading.

With the girls, quite a different matter. I never spoke to
them at all before I left my father's house, you see. And
when I did, it was – it was – it was Irene, as you well know.

My father's house. My father's *methods* served me well in
this new society. Supercargo, captain's clerk – I knew how
to make myself rich with my inventories in my hand and
the piles of plunder on the deck under my literate eye. I did
not *cheat* my shipmates: but I understood the main chance
where they perhaps might not have noticed it, and the merry
buttocks in my house were attired in accordance. I hope I
was more agreeable, though, than either my father or my
brother: and if my eunuch had been at all like that yellow
dwarf, I would have sold him on the spot.

All this I have just written, I look it over and despise
myself. Ponderous exculpations, psychological speculation,
sexual self-titillation: and all to tell you what?

That whatever had happened to the Cuttlefish and our
child was *outside my control:* and that Raven had better
come to terms with it. Let him see how I lived: I was free
of the provisos of his will. The legal phrase 'an Act of
God': pirates are an act of god. Certainly Habbakuk thought
he was. I renounced responsibility.

There was pleasure in the work too – I mean real pleasure
reminiscent of the good days. I was put in charge of the re-
decoration of the ship during the long storm-season. I had
oar-blades tipped with silver, gold braid tassels spliced to
the ropes' ends, satin spread on deck-awnings, new paint-
work like a popinjay's feathers. I even persuaded Habbakuk
that a carved figurehead of Lady Jael herself would not be a
'graven image' within the meaning of his book: and that
despite all the furious objections of the ritualistic man from
Tyre. Chloe would have been proud of me.

I also became brave and ceased to spend sea-fights in the

bilge. I would stand instead at Habbakuk's elbow, recording
every order he gave. He wanted a poem made of his career.
The old Hebrew philosopher who was to write it was too
infirm to come to sea, so Judy Split-arse must supply him
with a veracious history. My name of course would not
appear in the poem. There was to be nothing uncouth about
it – the central character indeed was not Habbakuk himself
but his 'Lord God of Hosts' whose main concern was the
scattering of enemies. Habbakuk's enemies. *Lady Jael's*.
Mine.

And also King Strychnine's. In the middle of the second
year he made his decisive move and took over the whole of
the Province of Asia. He was welcomed with flowers and
flute-girls. He and his men and the Asians themselves killed
every man in the place, every woman with every man in the
place, who came from, was thought to come from, or held
any official contact with, the City. The number of dead was
guessed at no less than eighty thousand. Were my parents
among them? My brother? Who can say? Don't ask me
whether I think they deserved to be.

From Asia the king moved on across the islands, and
threw open the slave-pens of Delos, admitting their desperate contents into his army or the ranks of his camp-
followers. The agents and overseers were killed. Then he
absorbed Greece. Athens rebelled, killed all the men of the
City, and the faction that supported them. Euboea and
Macedon welcomed Strychnine's horde.

When I heard all this – we were doing our own good
work on behalf of the good work between Corsica and the
Balearics – I had Irene in my head night after night wailing
for Herostratus – oh he had carried his fire and she was not
there any more to receive it . . .!

★

And then the day came when I made the discovery that
the Cuttlefish was not dead.

We were hove-to, awaiting consorts, hull-down off the
mouth of the yellow river, Tiber river, the City's river.
Habbakuk projected a raid on the port of Ostia. The City, a

few miles inland, was, we had heard, in the midst of riot and turmoil, factions were clashing, great men about to be toppled. Who should be looking at such a time for a stroke from the sea? But he needed to be certain: he needed an intelligent spy. He needed me. He sent me ashore under cover of night to spend twenty-four hours in Ostia and report on the town's security.

And now, for the first time in all my many boat-trips from ship to shore, the Raven, who was as usual at the steering-oar, actually spoke to me. The name of the shape he had taken on this occasion was (something like) Phut, a hatchet-faced Egyptian mariner who hardly ever spoke to anyone. We were half-way to the beach, he bent his head and said swiftly and quietly into my ear, 'Have a good time, Judy, in Ostia. If you see any o' them blackskin tarts rolling it around in the boozers there, you make a note of 'em for me. There's always good hot jig-a-jig from the top-end of the old Nile.'

Phut, to my knowledge, altogether disliked any congress with black flesh: most Egyptians do, they think it lowers their superior status. The remark therefore came from the Raven: I looked at him, his eyes were bright, they were fixed on me, and remained fixed on me, despite all the exigencies of the steering-oar, until our prow ran up onto the sand. As I scrambled ashore he said again, 'Have a good time. And Judy – remember: you've got a commission.'

Cuttlefish was surely in Ostia.

2   *Cuttlefish in Ostia?*

By daylight I was in the town with a clear notion of my business there. I had got inside without hindrance, which told me something already about the defences: now I moved purposefully through the main streets, down to the harbour, round the quays, back again into the streets. The place was thick with security-enforcement, and not a few squads of soldiers. But it puzzled me: they were clearly preparing for some emergency, though not at all the sort we planned to bring them. The landward gates were closely watched, but

towards the sea there was scarcely a single picket mounted.
But there might be a catch in it. I had done this sort of job
for Habbakuk several times before, being now equally con-
versant with landsmen's and seamen's ways. I must find
someone to talk to and extend my amphibious talents.

But what about Cuttlefish? Never mind about Cuttlefish.
If I was to meet her, she would be met. But the Raven's
word did direct my steps – no, I would have gone there
anyway, the obvious place to visit first – 'rolling it around
in a boozer' – ridiculous even to think of it – I went to a
seamen's tavern, *The Tarpaulin Jacket* in a narrow entry
near the harbour.

The potboy was sweeping the steps, and a horrid smell of
last night's excesses wafted out over the pavement. Inside,
of course, no Cuttlefish, only a slovenly woman with a
bosom like a pair of vegetable marrows, slopping a wet rag
along the top of the bar. I ordered something nasty to drink,
and a slice of bread and olive-oil. The house was perhaps
not so bad after all, they put garlic on the bread and did not
charge extra for it. The woman made it clear it was too
early for her conversation.

Some of her overnight lodgers were coming down the
stairs and making a fuss about paying their bills. One of
them cursed her for waking him too soon. The *Flower of
Leghorn* was not to sail until the sun was over the yardarm
and if that bastard mate wanted his crowd aboard before
then he could sodding well send to Elba for them, because
he wouldn't find 'em here. A bugger turned out of bed and
his bint let lie-in, what sort of fairity was that? The bint,
who was *not* Cuttlefish, stuck a head like a floor-mop round
the top of the stair and screeched that he had paid for his
use of the house, and of her, and must abide by its rule.
The landlady screeched up to her that the boys was wanting
breakfast, so stop that sodding hollering and look after
the kitchen stove. The leisurely man from Leghorn asked
what *was* for sodding breakfast and ordered a long rake of
fried dishes. He sat down over against me, to wait for their
arrival.

He cast a dull eye over my traveller's hat and dusty harp-
case – I purported to be an itinerant ballad-man – and said,

I wasn't the bugger making the music last night, so where had I come from? At a venture I told him Naples. He said that now the Samnite buggers was all but drove into the sodding ground, he dared say Naples would be three ha'pence the less lively. Nothing like a bastard war to keep the cunt at a low price and sailormen as well as sodding soldiers could get the benefit, wasn't that right?

I suggested that the place to be for that class of thing would be Greece and the islands, there was war enough and to spare. He said, 'Be advised, keep out of it, matey. As soon as the Mule-driver gets his regiments out east, fucking Strychnine and all his wogs'll be running like fucking ducks. No room there for no consequential Syrian buggers with mouldy old harps and cripples' crutches, I can tell you: watch it.'

His aggression was modified by the arrival of his breakfast. As he munched I tentatively put forward my next thought: to the effect that some of the Naples men had been surprised that the Stain was not to get the military command after all, seeing how much better than the Mule-driver he had handled the Italian war, seeing how much experience he already had in Asia. Perhaps he was needed to finish off the Italians first?

'Don't you believe it, matey, they've finished off themselves. Ah the City sodding knew how to sort out the like o' that – drive the buggers into the ground and then give 'em what they asked for: sodding franchise, why not? And it was Mule-driver gave it, no-one else. We was glad of it in Leghorn, I can tell you, sodding well ten years too late. I suppose Naples never joined the war at all, ain't that right? Fucking crowd of slick Greekoes, selling cunt and playing harps till the war was lost and the franchise given. All except for them thick Samnites. But we'll soon sort out the likes of them.' It was hard to be sure where his sympathies lay. Perhaps he did not have any, only contradictory prejudices. I tried him again about Mule-driver, as his black teeth clashed into a reeking sausage. What did they think of him in Leghorn?

'How should I know, I've not been in sodding Leghorn for months. I was up in the sodding City with a whole crowd of the boys, doing street-riots for the factions. We was paid off from it last week, once the commands of the army was finally allocated: we'd done what we was asked to do, got the Asian job reversed and given to Mule-driver. God but the Stain's crowd was wild. My belief, they should of kept us on, they sodding should. It's not by no means all over yet.

'But like I say, we was paid-off, and I find along the quay here this crank hooker – the *Flower* – from my old home port, so what's the odds, I sign articles. Loading salt she is, and taking ages at it. All of Ostia's upside down. You tell me you've never seen the Mule-driver, honest? Ah you've missed a glittering sight, you have. Not a man in the sodding City ever did more for the poor worker – you'd expect it, of course, he was born rough himself, wasn't he? You've never seen him? You're downright ignorant. Go and fucking see him today: go and see him and see a *man*!'

For the Mule-driver was coming to Ostia. The very hour that the *Flower* would be preparing to make sail, he would be in the sports-field outside the wall, a passing-out parade for the Marine Guards, his own son was one of the young officers to be given their badge and belt-buckle. Of course the old bugger would be there, proud as Perseus of his sons he was – though that wasn't to say that a commission in the marines wasn't a load of nonsense, covering-up like for the sodding fact that the coasts was so ill-protected they wasn't genuine protected at all – look at the port-security here, for an instance, you could sail a five-bank Punic battle-wagon into the harbour and out again and not so much as a 'who goes there?' – though need I wonder all the rozzers in the town was on edge in the *other* sodding direction: if the Stain's faction-bosses had detailed a crowd here today to go for Mule-driver, by god there'd be some ruction.

'But *I* shall be out of it, that bastard mate put the call out last night. As soon as the sun's over the yardarm. Hi-o for the lays of Leghorn.' He asked me did I know the song, and insisted I sang it. To prove my bona fides, I did.

> Hi-o for the lays of Leghorn-o
> Hi-o for the lays of Leghorn.

Pull taut on your sheet and your halliard
We're sailing away on the storm.

Fierce winds on the wild narrow wa-ter
Make bowsprit and topmast to droop:
Them ironclad tarts of Leghorn-o
Take sailormen all in a troop . . .

And a number of similar rubbish-items, all well-known to
the *Lady Jaels*. He waddled off down to the dock. The bastard mate would be about ready for him. I asked the landlady the way to the sportsfield. I had found out already
most of what I was sent to find. This was a diversion, for
my own curiosity.

A considerable throng of Ostians was also headed that
way. When we got there we found the ceremonies already
begun. Ranks of marines enfolding the open space, and
security-enforcement with bludgeons to bully the noisy
spectators. I had difficulty looking over the heads of the
people. There was a blare of military music, the tramp of
hobnailed boots. I could see the flash and flourish of colours
being carried past, helmet-plumes waving, javelin-spikes in
fence-like array.

I struggled through the press to get a fuller view, using
my stick like a screwdriver to prise myself forward, and at
last found myself up against the two-inch gap between the
elbows of a pair of marines in the crowd-cordon. I had seen
parades too many times before: oh theatrical, but I mis-
trusted them. It was Mule-driver I wanted to see.

'Where's Mule-driver?' I asked an old woman on my
right. She pointed through the gap, across the field. There
was a clump of brazen officers on a platform in front of a
sort of gilded clothes-horse with eagles perched all over it.
The central officer, who was taking the salute, was a short
bow-legged red-faced white-stubbled pop-eyed old bullfrog
with corrugated forearms like a ship's hawsers. At this distance it was hard to be sure, but I had the impression he
was more or less toothless.

'That's him,' said the old woman, 'There he is, my lovely
Mule-driver, there he is, the people's darling. You wait till

he starts to speak; god, *he's* going to tell 'em the tale.' She looked at me acutely: and I saw she was the Raven.

Then the crowd surged, the cordon hit out at us, the Raven had gone.

I began to shake. 'God, he's going to tell 'em the tale' . . .? Tell *me* the tale, surely: his speech, whatever it was, would be – would be what? A City general would never talk about the Cuttlefish . . .? I must be light-headed, sick, maybe – had something been wrong with that bitter wine they had given me in *The Tarpaulin Jacket*?

The parade was over. The troops were now to regale us with a gymnastic display. They came running onto the field in loincloths (as dictated by their prudish Cato-culture), tossing balls one to the other, hurling discs, leaping over wooden trestles. To my surprise I saw Mule-driver undressing himself on his platform. His cloak, his cuirass, his plated apron, and then the clothes he wore underneath, all of them came off and were smartly picked up by an attentive aide-de-camp. Clad only in his brief underwear, he stood in front of all of us, and solemnly flexed his muscles. Applause. His chest was a mahogany barrel, dense with grey hair: but the belly beneath it was also a barrel, and his rump hung down embarrassingly.

He stepped off the dais, and strutted out into the field. A squad of young marines were lined up to throw the heavy sea-fighting darts at a target. Their general came amongst them, took one of the darts, and weighed it in his hand. Then he signed to the first man: throw. About half of them, in turn, made their casts, some accurately, others less so.

The Mule-driver took his own place, poised his weapon, dragged his torso back with a sense of great strain, and hurled.

It fell about three feet short.

A trickle of dubious applause.

He went all thick and dark from the neck upward: demanded another missile. This time: five feet short, and a full yard to one side. The Mule-driver bent over, shoulders heaving – I could hear him gasp from where I stood. This time: not even a trickle. The marines, I thought, seemed ashamed. I felt ashamed myself to be watching him.

(A quick flash to my mind: Irene in Trebizond on her knees beside his sodden drunkard's bed.)

A young officer ran out to him with a cloak and fastened it round him. 'That's his son,' said a voice behind me, 'You know, the old devil oughtn't to have tried it, makes him seem like he's made a fool of himself.' Another voice, farther off, less sympathetic: 'Good old Stain could hit the apple-core five times while this one was still fumbling which end o' the spear was which!' More calls, far from jocular, invoking the 'good old Stain'. Counter-calls, the swirl of a scuffle, bludgeons going up and thumping down, a youth with a bloody head dashing out into the field, pursued, beaten down by the security-enforcement. Another minute, there'd be a full-scale riot.

Then: just as they say in the Jews' book, *then:* the Lord God called 'out of the midst of the cloud' – except it wasn't the Lord God, it was Mule-driver: and in no cloud but on the third step of a reviewing-platform, half-dressed and smoking with sweat.

'ALL RIGHT,' he informed us, 'ALL RIGHT!' and we were stopped in our tracks. 'RIGHT, WE'VE HAD ENOUGH OF IT: SO WE'LL ALL STAND NICE AND QUIET AND WE'LL HEAR WHAT I'VE GOT TO SAY . . . I have been consul of Rome, by your suffrages, six times. I have destroyed the enemies of Rome, in Spain and in Africa, and beyond the Alps and this side of the Alps, and up and down the spine of Italy: AND I'M NOT HAVING NONSENSE. Right. I have reformed the constitution, I have broke the usurped power of the lineage-proud leeches who sucked themselves full of the life-blood of our free yeomen, I have year upon year brought corn into the City to nourish the impoverished multitude, and – *by the same token* – to enrich the prosperous commerce of the port and town of – OSTIA – through which these cargoes are led . . .! I'm not asking for your vote, I've had it and I'm grateful, that grateful you'd never believe – what I'm asking for today is your *confidence*: and your *support*: and your continued careful *vigilance* over all of our liberties, while I take up my burden under the hot skies of the distant orient to strike down yet again the enemies of Rome . . .'

It was coarse beyond all parody: but by god it was effective. Towards the end he got on to religion.

'I am not telling you I lay claim to any presumptuous message from god: you're men of sense and you stand no nonsense. No: but I don't pull punches, I give it you straight from the shoulder – now this here is scientific, it is laid down by divine prophecy, there can be no contradiction of it. I *know* that I am destined not only to save but finally to magnify to unimaginable extremes the strength and glory of our historic Republic – I am assured of this by a proven confidant of the sublime mysteries beyond the clouds.'

His harsh rustic accent had subdued itself to a long low rumble, yet we could hear every word all over the field. He looked majestically sincere, and as simple as a god-fearing cowman. The mystic digression was obviously a regular feature of his addresses. The audience took it most seriously. So seriously that the outnumbered Stain-faction forebore to catcall. One or two people cried out 'He knows . . . he has been told . . . the wise-woman has told him . . .' – things like that. It was an ignorant crowd: the few educated sceptics were a minority and kept quiet.

Mule-driver held up his hand for silence. We could hear the sound of flutes. A pair of white mules, harnessed to a carriage all hung with purple draperies, came trotting onto the field. In this vehicle, behind the driver, sat two painted boys in long silver capes, playing the music. They were on either side of a canopied throne, also draped in purple. Upon the throne, holding a silver trident, and wrapped all in purple, was a hooded female figure.

Her head was bowed, her trident extended forward towards the sky. The hand that emerged, holding it, from the folds of her robe, was a black hand, strong, long-nailed, but delicate, and the poise of its fingers – my heart missed a beat.

He had 'told us the tale', she had appeared on the instant – it *must* be her – surely . . .?

The trident was now pointing towards Mule-driver. He knelt beside the halted car. The silver prongs touched his head, lightly. Then he sprang to his feet: cried out 'DES-

TINY!' in his hugest voice, and snapped his fingers to his son just behind him. He in turn snapped his, and a serjeant came forward with Mule-driver's horse. The old man swung himself, ungainly, into the saddle. Heedless of his state of half-undress, he set the horse in a caracole, and plunged off the field through roaring cheers with a species of circus panache.

The wise-woman in her car followed, more gently, after him. She still had not shown me her face: but her figure was now erect within her purple veils, and to me it was unmistakeable.

She was alive, she was thriving, she was the Mule-driver's trusted seer? Oh yes, she might well be. If she still had in mind the draining of his blood, no better point of vantage to supervise it from.

No: I was not going to have anything to do with her.

No: by act-of-god I was removed from my care of her. I had a duty to the *Lady Jael*. Raven could go bugger himself – or, failing the requisite contortionist skill (he was always very stiff on the stage), he could go bugger a fellow-shade. God knows, in the Further World, they must do something with one another to alleviate the monotony. Did Aristophanes have a joke about it? I made up one for him in my mind: if I ever took a role again in one of his plays, I would insert it as an ad-lib – it would go very well into *The Frogs*. Why, already I was laughing at it myself; it would be bound to please the public. . . .

Giggling obsessively, I got out of that sports-field as though Nemesis in her dark chariot had arisen in front of my eyes. She had, of course, yes indeed. 'But don't think of it now.' To Habbakuk: I had duty.

3   When the Government Falls

Habbakuk's plans were sound, I had concluded: but he would certainly need more than the one ship, and the sooner the better: once all the Mule-driver/Stain political excitement had subsided, the port might be more carefully guarded. Let us hope that our consorts had arrived.

I had seen all I wanted to see, so I found an inn of a better class than *The Tarpaulin Jacket*, ordered a mid-day meal and a bed, and rested through the afternoon. Towards evening I came down for a drink in the bar. As I entered the room, I was immediately conscious of a tension, a suppressed fluster and nervousness among the largely middle-class customers. Heads together, whispers, perturbed exclamations. Odd phrases of anxiety – 'What'll he do, he'll never hold it . . . impossible he can't hold it, my god, not even Hannibal . . . they'll never go through with it, it'd discredit the Stain for ever . . .' I asked the barman what had happened. 'It's the news from the City, we've only just heard it, god help us if they come here.' And then he bustled away.

I caught a man's eye over the shoulder of the man he was talking to. Silver-grey hair, the stoop: and an unwonted expression of feverish agitation. He recognized me at once, put a hand up to me – 'Just a moment,' it said, 'I'll be with you in a moment.' He continued his conversation, very fast, very emphatic. The other man was refusing him something, first apologetically, then positive. Finally he moved away.

Silver-hair, dismayed but dogged, came rapidly over to me – I could save a situation for him?

'You've heard the news?'

'No.'

'You must have heard, it's all over town for two hours, where have you been? Look here, are you still with me? You have to be, my god, it's an emergency. What are you doing here anyway, how long have you been here, you wouldn't – no you wouldn't – you wouldn't possibly have any contacts with the shipping business for god's sake? I am grasping at straws, man, godsake, you've got to help us . . .!'

What had happened was this. On his way back to the City, about the time I was eating my lunch, the Mule-driver had been intercepted by a messenger who told him (a) that the Stain had refused to hand over the allotted regiments that the Mule-driver was to take to Asia, (b) that the officers sent, to the Stain's camp some miles south of the City, to

relieve him of his command, had been set upon by the soldiers and killed, at the Stain's instigation; and (c) that the
regiments were now marching upon the City with colours
spread and javelin-points uncased, and unmistakably
aggressive intent.

Mule-driver had made all speed to the City to organize
resistance but Silver-hair despaired of his success. There
were no regular troops in the place at all, it appeared. Silver-
hair must bespeak a ship to get Mule-driver out of the
country. He expected that Mule-driver – if nobody had
killed him – would arrive in Ostia any time during the next
forty-eight hours, an exhausted fugitive, proscribed and
abandoned: he must have a ship. All these time-servers here
were afraid of the twitch of their own eyelids. The man he
had been talking to – he owned a fleet of twelve grain-
carriers – his entire fortune was due to the Mule-driver's
patronage – he'd rejected him outright. Was there *nobody* I
could think of? For god's sake I was a notched-penny, didn't
I realize the state was in danger – for a general of Rome to
march against Rome was – was – for god's sake it had never
been done since the time of the tyrant kings!

'Yes,' I said, 'Yes . . .' I thought at once of the *Lady Jael*.
No business of mine to tell Habbakuk what to do: but surely
not a pirate on the Middle Sea but would jump at the chance
of an enormous Roman general between his decks and at
his mercy. Worth ten times the ransom the whole of Ostia
could bring in.

'Yes,' I said, 'I know a ship.' On an afterthought – 'How
big is the party? I mean, he's not bringing all the marines?'
I had suddenly this fear – was it a fear, was it a *hope*? – he
might – just possibly, just conceivably – refuse to flee without his wise-woman . . .

'How big? Oh not the marines – not after that fiasco with
the darts this morning, of course they're all as superstitious
as a pack of old wives – the Stain's agitators are already in
the barracks to seduce their loyalty. By nightfall they'll put
an embargo on every ship in the port to stop Mule-driver
getting out of here. If you can find a ship, it'll have to pick
him up some distance down the coast. No, it'll be at all
events a very small party, his son, if he can get away, one or

two others, family, friends, maybe some political associates, I don't know. Godsake I expect no more than you'd put into a fishing-smack. But a fishing-smack's no good. He'll have to go a long way – Spain – Africa – I don't know.'

I enquired about payment. His first reaction was absurd: 'Payment? To you? I was under the impression you were a sworn agent of the Republic.'

'If you like, but which Republic? One of them appears to have thrown the other one out . . .' In my best theatrical-agency style I laid down some terms – a solid fee for the ship and a sound personal commission for myself, the indispensable middle-man. He haggled, but he was desperate: and I pocketed the money. Then *he* had an afterthought – he must have been utterly in shock – to a man of his trade it ought surely to have been his first forethought. 'How do I know I can trust you?'

'You don't. I don't imagine there's *anyone* you can trust. That's what it's like when the government falls. Don't pretend you've not seen it before. Console yourself with this notion: in Ostia there's nothing not a matter of business. Good business demands some measure of confidence. Ask yourself, and let *him* ask himself, is the business good?'

I then worked out an arrangement for him, a rendezvous along the coast, times, places, signals. No, I couldn't tell him the name of the ship, it might be this one, it might be the other: but I'd do for him what I could. So he left.

One more afterthought. Suppose Mule-driver, mad with rage because his seer had given him false prophecy, had already murdered Cuttlefish? From what I had heard of him, it would be just the sort of thing he would do. And how come Cuttlefish had grown so thick with him, when Silver-hair in the entourage would have known who she was? He had seen her in the Walls of Love, had he forgotten? He had not forgotten *me*. Or had something taken place that made it impossible for two and two to be put together? But if two and two were put together, what would *four* signify to Silver-hair?

Wrung out like a damp dishcloth with all these anxieties, I began to think about how much I should propose to Habbakuk. It probably depended on his calculations of the sack of Ostia. He had two opportunities now for immediate advantage. Could he use both? Or would one have to cancel the other?

4 *Passengers Embarking*

'No, there'll be no consorts,' spat Habbakuk as I came up the ship's side. 'They sent a pinnace to let me know they was ambushed off Sardinia by City cruisers. They beat 'em off and got away, but Cap'n Bargates has had to put into safe haven with a hole rammed in his starboard quarter, and Cap'n Iphicles lost nearly all of his upper oar-bank, snapped off short to the outrigger – so they can't come and you've wasted your day, Judy. I'm not going into Ostia with only one ship, let the place be never so open. We'll have to save it for another time. There was a slow-moving sail went up-coast towards Leghorn some hours since: if we get after her now, we might very like overhaul her . . . Ready the oars, mister: and make sail to catch what wind there is – slap it about, now!'

I told him the *Flower* was only carrying salt, we could let her alone. I told him about Mule-driver.

An immediate excited officers' council in the cabin.

'What'll you do, Cap'n?'

'What'll I do? What d'you think that I'll do? Lay him aboard and sell him to Strychnine, of course!'

'Wait a minute, Captain – ' I was nervous, offering comments among the officers, but the matter was too important to leave to their limited political imaginations. 'If you don't mind . . . There's no doubt King Strychnine would pay something for him, but how much? I mean, what is he worth to Pont in these present circumstances? He's old, he's discredited, the man they really want is the Stain and we can't gather *him* for them just yet. No: I've been thinking. Suppose we were to take him on a straightforward basis as a fare-paying passenger and run him to safety, just as he asks for? My guess is, if we can do that, he will make his way home again, and sooner rather than later, to re-assemble all his friends and get the power back into his hands.'

Frowns, shaken heads, pursed lips, they didn't catch on.

The mate said, 'He's old, discredited, you said so your-self: a man like that don't ever get back.'

'I've seen him, I saw him today: old he may be, but as tough as his own truncheon. Gentlemen, he believes as cer-tain as day and night, it is *his destiny* to control the world. And the Stain and all his regiments already bound for Asia – who can they leave in charge of the City while they're gone? The two king-pricks of the entire heap both absent from office – first one home'll be the winner!'

By god I was these days as cute as Irene.

Habbakuk got it. He said, 'I've got it! We'll do as Judy says. We'll take him aboard and I'll make him a bargain. Azrael, Samael: we'll squeeze him like a pomegranate!'

Two nights later, beating on and off the rendezvous, our boat picked the bedraggled general from off a deserted beach. The Stain's cavalry were hard behind him, and the coastguard cutters only missed us because of the deteriorat-ing weather. Habbakuk held *Lady Jael*, heaving and pitch-ing, carefully away from what was now a dangerous lee-shore. Mule-driver's party was even smaller than we had expected. His son had failed to get to him in time – maybe arrested, maybe already dead. His wife and other relatives he had had to leave behind in their country villa. Did Romans strike at their rivals by murdering their womenfolk? If so, then the losses would have to be cut. He had with him a corrupt-looking political son-in-law; a disconsolate staff-colonel; Silver-hair in a state of barely-concealed palsy: and the Cuttlefish.

I had been right of course, it was her. She stood on our streaming outrigger in the gathering gale and appalled the crew. 'Get that damn black witch-wife off of my deck,' howled Habbakuk, 'before she sinks us keel and strake!' No-one dared lay hand on her: she moved into the eyes of the ship and stayed there glaring forward through the moon-shot darkness like a supernumerary figurehead.

Habbakuk took a swift look for pursuing coastguards, saw that they had put back into Ostia in fear of the weight of the squalls: decided that had the Cuttlefish been a seriously

malign influence, *Lady Jael* would not now be riding out
the weather with such tenacity. He did not press his point.
Instead, he beckoned the Mule-driver into the stern-cabin
and ordered me there as well, to interpret. Habbakuk spoke
but little Latin, and Mule-driver, we discovered, made a
virtue of knowing no Greek.

I had had no time to make myself known to Cuttlefish:
from what I glimpsed of her, briefly, in the light of the
storm-lanterns, I had no great wish to do so. Indeed, I was
so filled with horror, I found it hard to keep my mind on
the job. But Habbakuk required an immediate and close
attention: I must force myself to comply. He was the captain: this whole scheme had been my own idea: disgraceful
to neglect my contribution to its furtherance.

'Now: welcome aboard, general: and what are we to do
with you?'

They sat there and bristled, one at the other, the land-
pirate and the sea-thief, balancing their threats and promises.

Mule-driver took swift note of the opulent cabin-furni-
ture: 'Don't think I don't know what kind of a ship I'm
decoyed onto,' he growled, 'I'll plant the gallows-crosses
for you and your precious crew every milestone from Rome
down to Ostia – '

Habbakuk was having none of this. He didn't growl,
rather he whispered like the beginnings of a gale in his own
rigging. 'I can sell you to the Stain, I can sell you to King
Strychnine, I can work you to death on my oar-benches: or
I can get you to where you want to be at the price I lay
down. Question is, can you meet that price?'

The mate came into the cabin, with Mule-driver's son-
in-law, and a duffle-bag packed full of little bags, each one
of them clinking with coin. Habbakuk opened a couple of
them and weighed them all, one by one, in his tarry hands.
'Right,' he said, 'this the lot?' It was obvious from the two
Roman faces that it was not only the lot but far more than
they had wished to offer. (The mate gleefully informed us
he had caught the son-in-law trying to hide the duffle-bag
in a coil of rope on deck). 'No,' grinned Habbakuk, 'I'm
sorry, but it ain't enough. Oh very like you'll tell me it's the
full content of the City's treasury: but it ain't enough. No.'

Mule-driver's jaw snapped left and right, he could have been chewing gristly meat. His jowl and neck were swelling, his hand trembled, he checked it with a slap on the chart-table. 'Name your terms,' he bolted the words out as though the gristle was finally swallowed.

Our captain did so, smooth and easy. 'Safe-conduct and pardon, perpetual, for this ship, with every Roman who accepts your authority – assuming that one o' these days you'll *have* some authority once again. Next: a letter-of-marque with the regular financial incentives for *Lady Jael* to take the seas on behalf of your faction against any other City faction. But not against Pontic ships till my terms with King Strychnine are up for renewal. Third: an understanding that the City of Rome, when once again beneath your governance, accept delegated ambassadors from the Free Seafarers' Confederacy – '

'You mean pirates!'

'I mean pirates. You accept our ambassadors and in good faith endeavour to work out a treaty of mutual advantage.'

'You mean, pay you protection-money.'

Habbakuk smiled, forebearingly. 'There's decent form in these matters. We don't call it that. You understand these things pretty well, I'm sure. Judy, where's them papers? I've all these terms wrote down, all you need to do is to put your name, here and now. Judy: pen-and-ink. But before the pen-and-ink – where in the wide world do you want me to carry you? Name your port.'

A vehement small rush from his stool by Mule-driver, broken off short as he bethought himself: the six-times consul bowed his head. 'Carthage,' he said, 'Is that possible?' Habbakuk looked surprised.

'There's nothing at Carthage but ruins. And your City soldiers made 'em. You sure you want to go there?'

Mule-driver said: 'Gimme the pen. The pen, boy – !' (this to me) ' – don't bugger about!' He signed: and was fearfully seasick.

Habbakuk said, 'You can trust me, I'm a man of honour. I'm a Judaean; of the tribe of Dan, spread abroad all over the waters by the just wrath of the Lord. I never go back on agreements. Carthage. But the wind is foul. I can't promise a quick passage. Judy, a bowl and napkins, send the steward in here to mop up.'

On deck, I picked my way forward along the fighting-bridge, till I came to where I could take a private inspection of Cuttlefish, who now sat cross-legged, murmuring to herself, upon the focsle. I stopped behind the beam of one of the hurling-engines, and decided, no, it was not strange that Silver-hair had failed to recognize her. Her purple mantle was half-fallen off, regardless of the wind and spray. Under it she was covered only by a cluster of filthy rags about her loins and a rusted iron chain wrapped round and round her waist, spikes at the joints of it lacerating her emaciated body. Every bone's-end in her skeleton seemed to be visible, her skin was flaked all over with a horrible series of scabs. The old scars on her cheeks were unnaturally pronounced, they stood out like the ridges of a soldier's cuirass. Her hair had grown till it hung in vile black flags down towards the small of her back. Her nails, uncut, were curved inwards like pot-hooks. Her eyes in the moonlight were oozing whitey-yellow pits, covered with some film-substance, no apparent sight in them, though I did not think she could be actually blind – she had climbed the ship's side smartly enough. She gave the impression she was turning her strong gaze upon the interior of her skull rather than the outside world – how to guess what she saw there? Something else that *I* saw: straight down her dried-up belly jaggedly from the navel, till it was lost behind the rags of her loincloth, was a gleaming new scar, a thumb-breadth wide, lighter than her black skin, a surgical cleft through which some bloody hands (but whose? when? where?) could have dragged out a new-made child. Dead child, or living? Was it possible she would ever tell me? Was it possible she would ever be her own person again, ever again?

At that moment, I hoped not. And moreover, I was per-suaded that since her feet had touched *Lady Jael's* deck – say an hour ago, no more – the Raven had ceased to be on board.

Sick to both heart and stomach, I turned about and pitched myself aft down the short focsle ladder and thence

towards the poop where Habbakuk might have some task for
me.

5   Passengers on Board

Five days of unseasonable tempest – our eastern-water rig
enabled Habbakuk to keep us out to sea for most of this
time, though by no means towards Africa. Mule-driver and
his three forlorn aides vomited their ugly lives out in the
cabin with scarcely a respite. I had now and then to go
amongst them to tell them the news of our heavy voyage. A
certain fatuous trust grew up between me and the old villain
in consequence. Habbakuk was too occupied with the safety
of the ship to take much account of his passengers – they
were to be treated as first-class fare-paying guests, and that
was that – and the ship's officers obligingly (though by no
means happily) snatched their turns of sleep in the focsle.
So the great cabin was all Roman, and my god, did it not
smell like it. Cuttlefish stayed out of sight – maybe the bilge?
– I did not enquire. Once I found her beside Mule-driver's
cot, wiping his feverish brow, a horrid grin contradicting
her apparently compassionate hands. She slipped out without even glancing at me. (The cook from Tyre complained
one day that a cockerel was missing from the ship's hen-
coop: some feathers and claws were later discovered in a
sail-locker, but all hands were so perturbed by a savage new
shift of the storm-gusts that investigation was indefinitely
postponed. I had a dreadful suspicion that Cuttlefish had
been performing a class of divinatory rite that would be
anathema on anyone's ship, let alone a Judaean's. But I
kept my thoughts to myself.)

The Mule-driver sometimes talked to me, in between his
bouts of sickness. He would, I daresay, have talked to
anyone: he was in reality addressing himself, as he used to
in Trebizond, if Irene was to be believed. Sometimes he
sang snatches of songs which sounded as though he had
learned them on his father's farm years before, though maybe
he made them up himself, I don't know. They came in pat
enough, however, to illustrate his political reflections.

'Right,' he would mutter, 'I'm a sick man, nearly seventy years old, and I never had more education than you'd stick on a pikeman's helmet-knob. And yet: six times consul. And in every town in Italy the old soldiers of my regiments at the first call will rise up and haul their spears once again in *my* war – I've only to give the word and that City will crumble like cake. You'll see. So why didn't I give the word? Because I work constitutional. I do *not* carry arms un-provoked against the City that I saved and that gave me my greatness. I wait, like a crafty bugger, for the long-nosed "old crowd" bastards to put themselves in the wrong: I wait and I watch and I bloody well wait. And hey-presto, he does it, the long-nosed bastard Stain does it, and all the world takes note:

> Red fox inside your hen-run
> Blood and feathers in his teeth –'

(How much did he know of what Cuttlefish had been up to in *our* hen-coop, perhaps that very morning? Maybe, even, he had told her to do it . . .?)

> 'What more than that d'you need to know
> That he's the sneaking thief?

Because that's all that he is now, your Greeko-groping Stain. The whole world can take note of it. The day I come back, boy, them gates of their own accord as wide gaping open as one of the Stain's own high-stipend harlots. You'll see.'

But at other times he seemed to doubt his own assurances. 'The Stain has walked out o'Rome: Mule-driver walks back in. But who with? My old soldiers? Ah, but they're old: broken men, weary of it, I daresay. So who else? Who out of all the terrorist rebels have refused the clement terms as was laid down for them by a glorious City? The bandit Samnites, that's who. Recalcitrant, refractory, hard-core men o' violence, and no-one can turn 'em off it. The Stain has a whole damned regiment – more – squadrons and com-panies more – still in them mountains fighting Samnites and Lucanians every day, though the folk in the City haven't heard a word of it – dirties the fair face of peace just a bit too blotchy, don't it? Now, Hercules-god, what's to stop me using them stubborn Samnites to break open Rome for me, hey? Do you tell me they won't have a *motive*? You'll see.'

Once he seemed to say that he had had Harmony murdered. Perhaps I misunderstood him, because his face was flattened on the top of the chart-table at the time and his arms crooked over the back of his skull like a child weeping at a school desk. 'Harmony had to go. Give him his way, he'd have legalistically conceded the lot: to the right to the left to the Italian colonials: oh my brothers but I had my furrow to dig – I couldn't leave *my* field to be seeded grown and reaped by him before I'd even got out my ploughshare! No trouble at all to find the right knife for the dark. The trick only is, to slot it into the right man's hand without giving him a sight of whose hand it was that handed it . . .'

He would sing about this furrow of his and his inborn ability to drive it:

> 'Sheep-dung and goat-leather
> Cold weather hot weather
> Grape-feeding solid soil
> Sunburnt neck and backbreak toil –

I was the first ever of the "new crowd" to make consular rank, who came one-hundred percent fifty-carat gold from the authentic Roman people. All the rest of 'em that tried the same game before me were not born into the "new crowd" at all – they came in out of the "old" out of what they called "social duty", either that or calculation – each single one of 'em had his throat or his brain-pan cleft open as the end of all his efforts.'

He was obsessed with his anticipated arrival in Carthage, he erected enormous hopes upon it: 'Oh there's regiments there that know me. But more than that: Sextilius. He's governor there: *my* appointment, *I* fixed it for him: and moreover I saved his life in the war against the northmen. Same as I do, he comes from the authentic people: he'll never forget a good friend. Aye aye, we reach Carthage, the flag goes up, you'll see . . .'

He drank a great quantity of the ship's wine, abusing it, of course, as 'piss of a bilge-rat, what else'd you look for in a bowel-belching Punic gut-bucket the like o'this?' (though as Habbakuk never plundered any but the very best vintages, this dispraise did not carry much conviction). When he was drunk, and not being seasick, he reminisced about his amorous adventures, which were crude enough in all conscience. His wife, by the way, was an aristocratic lady whom he had deliberately chosen as a means of overcoming the political disadvantages of his sheep-dung and goat-leather past: he sneered sometimes at her venereal capacity, which was apparently not as great as his own – or was it? Some of his comments upon her suggested otherwise: he was clearly a most jealous husband. One of his vaunted exploits was familiar enough to me:

'Not a woman on this ship but that wild blackskin horror. What I'd like at this moment is a white-toothed little cat-mouthed Persian with a tongue you could sharpen a knife on, oh but she knew how to tickle with it where it's sweetest. You could never be quite sure, though, but that devil of Strychnine hadn't poisoned her gums for you.'

⋆

He spent some hours painfully writing away at a lengthy document. He was seasick all over it in the end and crumpled it up and left it lying on the deck-boards. I carefully wiped it as clean as I could and kept it as a souvenir. Here is about one-third of it, deletions, marginal comments, footnotes, all complete.

Revered and most honourable Roman Fathers: most honourable Citizens of Rome: elected thus to your highest office ... by your noble suffrages selected thus to your most powerful office ... made consul, by you, as a result of my indefatigable endurance, for the seventh time: I will tell you what I will do for you.

The illegal usurpation of authority in this City by Lucius Cornelius Sulla (known as the Stain) shall be utterly reversed. Measures shall at once be taken to abolish ... liquidate ... eliminate ... all legal measures are to be put in hand for the *depreciation* of all those found guilty of aiding abetting conspiring-with or inciting the said L. Cornelius to overthrow your constitution . . .

. . . the utmost rigour of the law

. . . draconian legislation

. . . regrettable that all my life I have sought to render Romans free from tyranny

. . . yet here and now I am ~~regrettably compelled~~

. . . I make no apologies.

Treason must be chastised. Special courts, special procedures of trial, special sentences for those ~~found guilty~~ . . . known to be guilty.

For L. Cornelius: ~~banishment~~ . . . ~~death~~ . . . ~~recall from command of your army to stand trial~~ . . . sentenced in absence and a new commander sent out to take over your army from him. If the troops refuse obedience then a new army to be mustered.

> (Right: but who's going to look after Strychnine in the meantime? Leave it till later: maybe the Stain'll beat him first, OR BE BEATEN BY HIM.

You have awarded me my seventh consulate in order that I may put into effect all that legislation I previously attempted, only to see it reversed illegally by L. Cornelius when he drove me into affliction and unmerited exile.

This legislation includes the extension of the corn subsidies to all needy citizens, the extension of full* social rights *and citizenship* to all Italians, ~~explicitly including~~ . . . *with additional privileges† for* the Samnite and Lucanian peoples who have aided me to resume my right; and the reform of the jury system, whereby the listing of citizens to judge constitutional issues shall be once and for all taken out of the hands of the hereditary aristocracy and placed where it belongs, with the authentic Roman people.

Party factions hostile to the legitimate interests of the authentic Roman people shall be prohibited from exercising ~~disruptive influence in the assemblies~~ any influence at all in any of the assemblies.

Senators, Citizens, YOU NEED NO LONGER FEAR DIC-

---

*. . . NB: as qualified by provisos to be subsequently detailed, in full.

† We'll talk about these later. Very like the buggers will ask far too much.

TATORSHIP, PROVIDED YOU ALL UNDERTAKE
TO ~~DO EXACTLY AS YOU ARE TOLD~~ ...
RESPECT THE LAWS AND THE CONSTITUTION.

(Rewards? Someone ought to be rewarded? I've got
the Samnites wrote down. Who else. The pirates?
~~Fuck them~~. Why not the pirates? Leave it open.

REWARDS for loyal friends. Lavish. Spectacular. Day after
day of the sword-fights and circus games. Hand-outs. Free wine
from all the fountains. Dedicate a new temple. Give thanks.

I HAVE COME HOME ...

*

Speaking once, and once only, of the son he had been
forced to leave behind to the mercy of the Stain's men, he
said: 'I seem to have lost him. Hercules-god, you don't think
they could have cut him off? Roman Fortitude, boy: we
don't talk about *that* ...!'

Between him and his aides there was practically no communication. He treated them like dogs in need of the whip,
and they responded like whipped dogs. He was said to have
been, in earlier days, a jovial down-to-earth comradely
leader with an appropriate encouraging quip for one and
all. Not any more. He was, of course, old.

6   *I Was in Charge Now*

On the murky sixth dawn, our close-reefed sails in tatters,
our rowers slumping half-conscious on the benches, we saw
the long grey Italian coastline surging once again inevitably
towards us on the lee bow: there was nothing we could do,
it seemed, to prevent shipwreck.

'Not without,' said Habbakuk, 'not without we can
weather the headland. Get that general up here quick sharp.'

The mate and the steward between them hauled Mule-
driver onto the poop, he fell over his feet on the lurch of
the deck, they took him by the collar and lodged him like a
bolt of canvas between the taffrail and the carved support-
bracket of the stern-ornament. From this gyrating notch he

glowered around at the race of the waves, at the terrifying shore-line almost under our elbows. He peered forward at the headland.

'Look here – ' he forced his words out, as though he had never wanted to speak again, 'look here, I'm not a sailor. I'm not one of your Greekoes, your Punics, your – what are you? – the tribe of Dan. When I fight I bloody march to it. I don't stand nonsense. Feet on the ground and pack on my back, they don't call me the Mule-driver for nothing. I don't give a cut cod for risk, but *my* risk, a soldier's risk, not yours nor your damned gut-bucket's with a leak at every seam and your canvas blown to ribbons. I'll take my risk on shore, use my wits where I know how to use 'em. On keep the bloody gold, man, keep your agreement, just let me off out o' this, anywhere – anything . . .' He interrupted himself with a paroxysm over the rail, then dragged his entrails back to the business in hand. ' – anything rather than lose any more of myself here commanded hand and foot by water-rats and damned salt water. Get me ashore. Do it now.'

Habbakuk was only too glad. He needed a safe haven, he needed urgent replenishment and repairs for ship and crew. He thought he knew where to find them. But until he could get them, Carthage was a lunacy. 'Right,' he said, 'let's weather the cape. If we can, God of Moses. I put you all four – all five, God of Abraham – ashore in the bay. There'll be shelter enough for it. I'm in grief not to do any more for you. I like to stand by my word. If you do meet with friends, re-assemble the old muster, launch yourself back into your cheering City, remember this ship. We owe you three-quarters of a cruise: we'll be happy to fulfil it, provided there's mutual fairity. No gallows-crosses at no milestones, know what I mean? Mister – ' (to the mate) ' – have the boat's crew to station. Weather-oars to back water, lee-oars full ahead – so, keep her so, and we've a chance to clear them reefs!'

God bless her smooth haunches, *Lady Jael* slipped round the point within one narrow fathom of the rocks that could tear her heart out: we dropped anchor in quiet water. As the boat's crew busied themselves and Mule-driver's party came whingeing and moaning out of the cabin, quarrelling over their luggage, Habbakuk stamped with frustration: 'Why dammit, it makes me wild, if we could ha' got these buggers to Carthage, we'd have set ourselves up for life: mister, you and me could ha' been grand-admirals, think of that!'

Cuttlefish, up from the nasty depths, cocked her head like a heron, pointing her harsh bony profile this way and that, smelling the danger of the Italian coast. She had gone out of my life, she came back into my life, now she went out of it once more: none of it might ever have happened. I could forget: I would forget. I wanted to forget and damn quickly.

But: the firebrand of Prometheus . . . of Herostratus . . . rush, flounder and sudden decision: I took the balcony rail at one jump; was-there-wasn't-there the tub full of water beneath it? Resounding clap-trapping splash, a standing ovation; or merely a grotesque shock of pain, and lifelong crippling injury? Close both eyes: do it.

I touched Habbakuk on the elbow. Put it to him, tentatively, that all was not, perhaps, hopeless. Give two or three days, let the weather have time to moderate (it surely was due to moderate), he could conclude his replenishments: and then, if he was lucky, could meet Mule-driver down the coast somewhere – not here – there were City garrisons quite close, and it was no place to be hanging about – fetch him and his people aboard again: and then, Carthage after all, and a full reward! What did he think?

I put it that maybe I should accompany the party to make sure they made the rendezvous, left to themselves they would very likely fail, not understanding about wind and weather, proper anchorages and all that. What did he think?

He was doubtful. He had to work sideways to the wind south-west till he found a group of islands he knew of for his safe haven: he could not tell how long it would take him. And besides, he needed me aboard. I had ship's business to attend to. I rapidly outlined a whole set of possible arrangements that all of a fluster came into my head. They seemed to make sense.

'Wait though, Judy, no. You'll have to cover maybe forty miles of dry land on foot without provisions and lumbered with those damfool soldiers: I can't give you anything more than a bag of ship's biscuit to help you on your way – *you* know the state of the stores. And the country is crawling with troops – we're no more than twenty leagues south of Ostia, you know that?' I knew it. 'And why should you imagine a ferocious old grave-digger the like o' that Mule-driver'll take a blind bit o' notice of anything *you* might want him to do?' I said because if he didn't, he might very well die. Up to me to persuade him, at all events. He laughed: 'Dance for him then, Judy, dance him back upon my deck . . . But not the black one. Not her. She was the one brought down on us this storm. Mind you, she didn't sink us: I was wrong there. But she don't come back on board.'

I gathered a small kitbag, put into it what I thought I would need, made all my evil-averting signs, and attached myself to the great general. As we were rowed to the shore, he swore at me, sneered at me, kicked me on my bad leg: and accepted my presence. I told Silver-hair, confidentially, that I stood to gain advancement among the crew if I carried out my mission effectively. *I* was in charge of *him* now, and he needed to be told. He was too sick to pay much heed – the small boat in the sheltered bay had a worse motion than the ship at sea. But I told him none the less, because my motives required explaining. I mean, they required explaining to *me*.

I was dumbfounded at my own idiocy. I kept my head turned away from the Cuttlefish. From the possessed obsessed wild animal that used once to be the Cuttlefish. Would the Raven let me kill her?, I wondered – hating every inch of her befouled malodorous ruined body. If so, the best solution . . .?

Mule-driver kept his eyes on her, all the way from the ship to the strand, half-closed bleary eyes, the flesh around them all puffy and discoloured with lack of sleep, anxiety, illness, excess of wine: their pupils reduced to hard little black dots, flies lying upon pats of rancid butter. He said:

'Seven consulates: she guarantees it. Three-times-two-plus-
one. Will you look at her, smell the stink off of her, dead to
all decency – who could doubt such a wildwood widdershin
to be owt else but authentic genuine?'

7   Wise-woman Along the Shore

I will not go into much detail about the Mule-driver's Great
Escape. He himself told the story, cumulatively exaggerated,
to any indigent rhetorician who applied to him for a hand-
out during his short-lived seventh consulate – and it has
thence travelled into the history-books. He attributed much
importance to the favourable omens that encompassed him
(so he said, though I don't remember most of them)
throughout his perilous adventure. He failed utterly to
mention me, *Lady Jael*, or the Cuttlefish. Of course, by
then, he was anxious not to have to keep any bargain with
pirates, and could not admit to having been helped by them.
As for Cuttlefish, I think he had become afraid of the very
memory of this woman. He must surely have begun to ask
himself, was the destiny she expounded to him divine or
demonic?

Did I say, by the way, that the name he knew her by was
'Martha'? It had been the name of another wise-woman he
had employed years before, when he defeated the hordes
of the northmen. No sooner had he met Cuttlefish than he
took her for a reincarnation. By all accounts the first Martha
had been a genteel middle-aged Syrian with a taste for sentimental novels and the cleanliness of a vestal virgin: but
that made no difference. She had prophesied good things,
they came true. Cuttlefish likewise, or so he convinced himself. The spirit of heaven's truth was in them both and his
name for it was 'Martha'. QED.

We wandered through the countryside, half-starved and
fearful, for a number of days. We came unexpectedly on a
herdsman on a desolate moor who recognized Mule-driver
and ran away before we could catch him. Our small bag of
food was stolen (by a man, by a fox?) as we slept one night

in a wood. Several miles short of the rendezvous, and time wasting fast, we were sighted in broad daylight by a military patrol as we stumbled strung out along a beach. I had begged the old fool to stay hidden until dark, but he shouted that he was a tactical expert, he had marched regiments thousands of miles: if a foraging party was needed, he was damn well going to lead it – no Greeko would tell him what to do in his own Italy – we were on a strand: we could catch fish!

He was running a high fever and not really responsible for his actions: but his three useless subordinates had totally abandoned all common sense with him, they let him rave wherever he wanted to. Only a few days without feeding their guts, their courage and brains ran out at their back passages. Of course, they were Roman gentlemen, with the habit of command. Their new situation as harried helpless fugitives was outside any possible experience: but they didn't even try. It is a situation a lot of Roman gentlemen will be discovering for themselves these days and in the near future. . . .

As soon as the cavalry sighted us, and guessed who we were, they came down at us at the gallop from over a low hill. They scattered us like field-mice out of reaped corn. All except Cuttlefish. She continued her precise and even stride till she came to a rock at the water's edge: and there she sat down, her back and neck erect, her hair blowing horizontally out in front of her and across her face. Do you know, through all these days, I had seen her neither eat nor drink, and I do not believe she even slept. And she spoke not one word. Mule-driver said she prophesied. So no doubt she was not dumb. But in my hearing, never a word.

I do not know where Mule-driver and the other three fled to. I heard later they were chased into the sea and swam out to some friendly fishing-boats – or rather, to some fishing-boats unfriendly to the City's security forces. But I did not see this. I had hobbled frantically back the way we came and had hidden among some large boulders. The cavalry were so occupied with the pursuit of Mule-driver that they missed me altogether – I was, after all, in the rear, I had such savagery in my mind about all of them.

From my refuge I could see one of the troopers wheel

round and come charging towards Cuttlefish. She stood up, thrust out her trident, and threw her mantle onto the sand in front of the charging hoofs. At this sudden revelation of her skeletal black nakedness with all its attendant grotesqueries, he pulled up short and nearly fell to the ground. Thereupon she screamed with laughter, spreading her feet, bending her knees slightly outward; she tore off her loinrags and urinated copiously all over that rock like a mare in a paddock. The soldier tugged at his rein and made all haste to follow his comrades. I covered my eyes with my hatbrim: I was lost: I was finished. What to do?

After maybe fifteen minutes I forced myself to look up. The bare strand stretched before me, and the bare dunes covered with coarse grass rose up behind it. To my right the Middle Sea sparkled with foam-spurts under a sharp breeze – the weather had indeed moderated. In the centre of the strand, nothing, except the hoof-prints and footprints, and the forked silhouette of Cuttlefish, still straddled upon her rock.

As I watched her lonely shape and remembered all sorts of things I did not choose to remember, she turned to the water and slowly walked towards it, into it, and straight on, till it came up to her knees, her thighs, her hollow buttocks, creeping with each step a hand-span up her taut back – now her hair was floating out all round her and her shoulders were covered by each successive wave. Then her head went under. Two forearms still above the surface, the long fingers pointing upward. Then they too disappeared. I crouched immobile, incapable of intervention.

I looked at the sea where she had been, at the strand where she had been. Did I say nothing but tracks of men and horses? Not quite so. Her purple mantle lay there, and her rags, clotted with sand; and beside them her silver trident.

I looked back to the water. The sun had gone in, a freakish dark cloud in an otherwise empty sky. Without warning it began to rain, fast hard heavy rain, battering into the sea, spotting the flat sand with innumerable little stabs and splashes. For a few moments visibility was cut to no more than fifty yards. Then, as quickly as it had come, the rain passed, swinging swiftly away from the land, an opaque veil between my eyes and the horizon. In the very middle of it, maybe a quarter of a mile from the beach, a black round head shot shining up, a slender neck, shoulders and arms cleaving strongly through the water – Cuttlefish swimming to shore, directly towards me.

Her feet touched bottom, she stood up straight, and came on running, through a rainbow of bright splashes. She flung up one arm and cast her hair out of her eyes as she finally sped clear of the sea. Her paces were long and rhythmic, she looked as though she had run all day and could carry on until nightfall. The sand spurted at her broad heels.

I was on my feet and waiting for her, chill with apprehension.

I had lost my walking-stick, my ankle was twisted, painfully; my hat slipped down sideways from my head. For the first time since Ostia I could see clearly who she was and I could see that her eyes could see me. She stopped just a little way below me, and waited to regain her breath. She smiled. Nervously? She looked down at her feet. Her loincloth having gone, she put a hand over her pubis; and another one over the two withered leaves that had once been her beautiful round breasts.

'Has he gone?' she asked quietly, as in an ordinary chat that had continued for some time.

It took me a minute to make any sound with my gaping mouth.

'Wh – wh – who – ? You – you mean Mule-driver . . .? Yes, I suppose. I – I don't know quite where . . .'

'Will you find me my cloak, please: I am cold, and not good to look at like this.'

She was plucking at the chain round her waist.

'This ought not to be here. It hurts me. I can't get it off.' I made a move to help her, but she waved me away. 'No,' she said, 'no: my cloak, I said. Do what I say.' I fetched the cloak. When I got back with it she had unfastened the chain. She wrapped the cloak round her, more like a civilized costume than she had worn it before, though it had become so torn and filthy during our wanderings she still looked unutterably weird. She then walked to the trident, picked it up, tangled it into the chain, and threw both of them into the sea with a great sweep of her meagre right arm.

'There,' she said, 'that'll do.'

She sat down on the rock and howled with long-pent misery. I put my arm around her, trying to comfort her, but I did not know what to say. Had she, as it were, come back to me after these lost years? Were we to re-gather our life as though nothing had happened to us? What in fact had been our life together? I could hardly remember – when I thought of it, nothing seemed to come into my mind but the teeth of *Irene* biting my shoulders, scarcely germane; the hard little nipples of *Irene* between my lips: what the hell was going on in my imagination?

I called Cuttlefish my dear, as she had called me – but not until after things had become so disordered, surely? I called her by her name, but I am not sure she recognized it. It suddenly jumped to my heart – *did* she in fact know me? I enquired, very cautiously, did she know who I was? She checked her interminable sobbing after a while: her blubbered desolate face came out of her hands.

'No,' she replied, 'I'm not sure. Did we meet ever? I was in Antioch.' I told her I was Ivory, and the town had been Ephesus. 'Oh. Of course. Ephesus. Ivory. I *do* remember. You were his agent, weren't you, you were always trying to fiddle rather more than your ten percent. He said to me often you were too clever by half, but he couldn't do without you because if he went to the managers they would cheat him worse than you did.' Raven, of course . . . I had never heard her offer me these excerpts from his pillow-talk before. She went on: 'He wants very much to play Orestes at the Festival of Legal Justice, and he says you are trying to dissuade him? Why? Don't you think he can deal with a juvenile role any more? His body is as trim as a sprinter's, of course his face is all wrinkles and old leather, but why should that matter when he's in the mask? Is it his voice? Orestes may be a young part, but my god it's mature – oh don't be such a fool – how can a man of twenty ever get to the heart of the role of a *matricide* – he *must* play it!'

'He did play it,' I told her, 'He played it outrageously: the best critic in Sardis said he played it like a washer-woman. He should have taken my advice. It was nothing to do with his age. His temperament, don't you see that? He is a man for mad warriors, brooding despots, aspiring de-moniac tyrants who murder their way to the throne. Orestes, goddammit, is a singularly feeble introvert. When Raven acts a hero stricken with remorse, he has first to have *earned* the remorse, achievement from his crime – power, gold, women, you name it: he has to be high, high, high, before he can fall! I told him not to attempt Orestes, I was right, he should apologize!'

I was getting myself as excited as I had been the first time we had this conversation – was it five years ago? And it was only at this point that I realized that that first time had also been the first time that Cuttlefish and I had . . . she had come on a message to me about Raven's bloody ten percent, we had fallen into dispute over his roles, she had lost her temper at me because I scorned her revered master's judgement (and why not? it was terrible) – I had launched into my own impression of what his washerwoman Orestes had been like for the unfortunate audiences: she had started to laugh, despite herself; we had both laughed, we had clutched at one another in the extent of our hilarity: it was at least a full hour before we had withdrawn from that clutch. Now, here we were, on a dreadful empty beach, among nobody but enemies, marooned.

If this were a light romance, all that had been between us would at once be made known, all difficulties resolved, maybe the Love-goddess herself out of the sea would tower up over us, the gay garland of a *happy ending* outstretched in her white hand . . . It was not a romance.

Cuttlefish simply withdrew into an embittered silence, saying: 'I told Raven he should not trust you. Your judge-ment of his interpretation is very superficial. Hippodamus says his Orestes is the most subtly complex set of insights he has ever seen.' (Hippodamus was the worst critic in Sardis.)

I waited a little; she got up, moodily, and began, without

apparent aim, to wander away along the sand. I trudged
doubtfully beside her – well, beside her and a little behind.
I had to – as it were – put her in the position of looking at
me as I had *really* been. (I was determined not to accept the
possibility that this was the exact position she now held.)

Had we made love in Ephesus that afternoon, or had we
merely quarrelled? I knew that physically we had kissed
and coupled, yes: but in god's historic truth? Maybe we
had done no more than cover over with sexual wrigglings
an essential continued quarrel – a knife-full of honey
smeared across a slice of sour bread – and today the con-
tinuation was resumed? This was absolute nonsense, I was
not going to give way to it. I caught her up.

'My dear – ' I panted (she was going too fast for me
now), 'Cuttlefish, dear Cuttlefish, listen to me: I am Ivory,
I am your lover, we have lived together for several years – '
(why, when I most needed it, could I not recollect exactly
how many?) ' – you were in my service, I made you free, we
were going to – we were going to – ' (but how could I tell
her what we were going to do? I had never even decided in
my own mind, let alone agreed it with her. *Irene's* fault of
course. But *Irene* is not now germane).

She stopped and measured me with a cold glance. 'Oh
yes, you made me free. You had to do it, didn't you: because
otherwise Irene would have given you the sack.' (Irene after
all *is* germane. Oh where *is* that bloody Love-goddess?) I
decided I would pursue this line of talk no longer. If I was
a shady agent with ulterior motives, then that, for the time
being was what I was.

'Cuttlefish, don't walk away till you know where you are
walking to. There is business to be discussed.'

'Ah. Very well. Keep it short though: I've a lot to attend
to.'

'You have? Perhaps to begin with, you could tell me
what?'

'Why?'

'Because I may be in some way connected with it, just
possible our interests are in part identical – '

'I doubt it.'

'I said "just possible": but at least, will you give me the

chance to find out?' Habbakuk was sending his pinnace to a rendezvous three or four miles from this place, just before dawn tomorrow. I could meet them there, tell them Mule-driver had been taken by the cavalry, get back to my piracy, leave this unknown mad African to attend to her own personal concerns: I could see she could harbour no objections; why, she would miss me no more than a lettuce-leaf misses the slug.

However, she thought best to answer my last question.

Speaking slowly, picking her words, uncertainty, maybe fear underneath the uncertainty?

'For some time – I don't know how long – I have belonged outside my body. Which is why I have become so – so repulsive. You will have noticed? Never mind that. During all this time – if indeed it has been *time* – I have been *taken*: to all sorts of people, places, things. Not always told what they are. Sometimes he explains. If you had not tried to cheat him out of the extra percentage, perhaps then he would not be *taking* me to these – things. Never mind that . . . Do you know this Mule-driver man? I have told *him* all he wanted to know. Not my fault if he misunderstands it, my pleasure though, ha-ha. Why don't you laugh? If Raven could act Mule-driver, even you would approve. He is, you said, *earning* – achievement from his crime, will earn more and more yet: I can't stop him, don't want to: he must *grow*. High, high, high . . .? But he don't need me any more. Have I left him? Never mind that. But I was, lately, *taken*, to see one more – thing. There is a town, I don't know where – you are a business-agent, you'll have travelled all these places? – do you know a small seaport town with the police-barracks at the edge of the poor people's houses, dirty houses, near the fishermen's slipways, nets out to dry, goats among nettles, broken pottery, dust? And between this and the stone pier, a small grove, old dead trees, dried shit, nettles again, and an altar . . . To a stone lady with her head flaked away by the salt wind? You don't know it? That's odd. It must be very close: I was *taken* there and I saw Mule-driver. I saw a man he was to meet. In the barracks, in the grove. That's why he don't need me. But I should be there, this one last time. Have you a sharp knife? Don't look so stupid. I said "knife". What's in your bag?'

There was no knife in my bag, but I did have one in the side of my boot (a fighter of Habbakuk's told me what to do with a pirate-knife in a boot, but I never in fact used it as instructed: novices don't win). I offered it to the Cuttlefish wondering would she stab me. I'd not be surprised. But she waved it away: 'I don't want it. For you: cut my hair. Short to the head.' When I had finished this, she did take the knife, and pared her disgusting nails.

'Now,' she said, 'have you money? Good. Go to the town, buy me some clothes. Eastern trousers, if they have them: strong skirts to go over them, a hat and a cape to keep out the rain. Boots. I've a long way to travel. Do you think I am thin enough to be taken for a boy? Then get me some boy's clothes as well. Tell them you are buying for your out-of-doors servants, they'll know what to offer you. And buy a kitbag like the one you carry. I'll meet you in the grove, after dark. Keep it secret. These places are not safe.'

All of this in the tones of a brisk business-woman – say, big Chloe – ordering her underlings about. An underling, I nodded my head, repeated the orders, and went. Tomorrow I would meet the pinnace: but until then, why not do what she wanted? No harm. No doubt, in the town there *would* be a police-barracks – I had never seen a civilized settlement without one. There might even be a grove.

8   The Man in the Town

The man in the town (yes, it did prove to be the town to which Cuttlefish had been *taken*, police-barracks, fishing-nets, slums, the lot) was Horsefury.

He had not been burnt in the burning house. Instead he had had a vision of Irene in the flames, she had had Snowflake at her side with a baby to her breast, and had led Horsefury up and away from his death. At first he had thought she was conveying him to the Land of Young Heroes (a place known to his people, with apple-orchards, and beautiful red-haired queens to rule over it): but no, she was telling him to go and kill Romans, not himself. Mule-driver in particular, if he could find him. So he escaped from the Walls of Love, and fought a single-handed guerrilla war against the City for many months, tended and supplied by mountainy-men.

He proved very effective at this, picking off with his arrows one man, or two men, or more, from passing columns; sliding into camps at night and cutting men's throats, and so forth. Then one day he was captured by a patrol of the Stain's infantry. He passed himself off as a straggler from one of Mule-driver's cavalry squadrons (which were largely made up from Celtic mercenaries, so his tale was plausible). He allowed himself to be re-mustered into a similar outfit under the Stain's command. He sank into himself, obeyed his officers, bided his time. He expected very soon that the Stain's men would be fighting Mule-driver's.

He was eventually posted to this harbour-garrison (coastal security in aid of the civil power). He sat alone in the evening in the police-barracks, singing one of his songs to his sword:

> The three hottest flames to be seen in any fire:
>   Snowflake
>   Her man-child
>   The fierce sword of Horsefury.
>
> Three mortal glories for Horsefury to cut short with his sword:
>   The life of the cruel chief
>   The peace of the cruel chief
>   The cruel chief's hope of an heroic death.
>
> Three rat-wives beneath the corner-post of the highest house
>   in the City:
>   The black rat
>   The hairy-shanks
>   The steel-tooth rat in the long hand of Horsefury.

Two hours before midnight the troopers were called out to find Mule-driver: he had been seen and chased on the beach, had boarded a fishing-boat, and now was supposed to have been put ashore again. A report came in that he was hiding in a marsh not far from the town. Horsefury was not among the men who waded into the rushes and mire and pulled the collapsed old braggart out onto dry land, quaking with ague, dribbling uncharacteristically in sheer terror and despair, dripping black mud from head to foot. A rope around his hands and caught up to a serjeant's saddle-girth, they dragged him like a runaway bullock to the barracks and threw him into the lock-up.

Then they wanted to know what to do with him.

The captain-of-horse said 'kill him', but he was one of the Stain's officers, and simple-minded towards his duties. The police-inspector, a Latin, said 'send him to the City: they want him for trial.' The mayor, also a Latin, but one whose loyalty in the late war had been suspected of wavering between the City and the 'new nation', said 'let him go: the Stain is already in Brindisi embarking for Asia. The friends he has left to take care of the City's politics are not perhaps so friendly as he thinks. They might be glad of a preserved Mule-driver. And besides, who made the laws by which they want to try him? Cooked-up overnight. Legally-speaking, they've nothing on him, and everyone knows it.' The town-councillors, dragged out of bed in the small hours to agree with the mayor, agreed with him at once. The police-inspector agreed with him too, because the tax-collector (who feared dismissal under one of these new 'laws') told him he should.

The captain-of-horse decided privately that if Mule-driver were killed-while-attempting-to-escape, a great deal of trouble would be saved. He asked for one of his men to do this. But the troopers, being Celts, men of the north, said no. Mule-driver had beaten their people, years before, in two great battles. He was a terrible enemy, a cruel chief – if they were to kill him, they must be allowed to select a champion to fight him hand-to-hand in public, for the sake of their warriors' honour.

Now Horsefury was not exactly of the same people as these other horse-soldiers. He had been taken by western-ocean pirates from the coast of his native land – a large green island far out on the world's rim, which no-one in the City had heard of. Within weeks of his capture (he was about fourteen), he was *in* the City, for sale on a sordid platform, amid clamour and confusion, and a swarm of greedy lip-licking faces. These were not men: they were lice and carnivorous reptiles, how could any of them be an occasion for honour? Mule-driver's man had been Fat-man: and Fat-man's man had been the smooth flunkey with the fruit-knife: what had any of these to do with gold-adorned war-chiefs and the glory of single combat? Confidentially, to his captain: let Horsefury and his rat-wife sword be let into the lock-up. . . .

In the dark cell he could see nothing: and then, as his sight adjusted, he became aware of a solid lump of old man heaped in sickness on the sleeping-bench. Two wild red gooseberry eyes and a black gap of an agonized mouth. *Heracles Raving:* Horsefury remembered the battered stage-mask I had inherited . . .

A hair-raising voice came grinding at him out of the black mouth. 'My name is Gaius Marius. I am here for you to kill me. DO YOU DARE . . .?' Horsefury laughed. Of course he dared. But, after all, did he want to? There were Latin orderlies outside the cell, they had heard those words through the ventilation-grill, they had heard how this savage superannuated tortoise was meeting his murderer with unexpected magnificence, so different from the demeaning babble he had uttered when they thrust him in there. Let a poet get hold of his words, they would make him into a great war-chief against all truth and reason, while Horsefury would be seen as a – as a flunkey with a fruit-knife.

So he refused his task.

But, as he had volunteered for it in the first place, he felt it would not be honourable for him to wear his uniform any more: so he deserted there and then. His loyalties were getting altogether too crossed in their purposes, and he was very relieved to be rid of the uniform. He kept the sword, of course. He had as it were *married* the sword in lieu of poor suicide Snowflake. He tossed the uniform into the privy and went over the barrack-wall in nothing but his undershirt.

He would shortly burgle a house and find something else to wear. In the meantime it would be desirable to lie low close to the barracks to see if anyone missed him and came out to search for him. So he hid among the unkempt thorn-bushes and weeds of the dreary little grove between the barracks and the pier.

No-one came out of the barracks: but Cuttlefish came into the grove.

He was springing up to kill her with his sword, when he saw who she was. He was amazed: but not really surprised. Irene, he assumed, had brought them together in order to secure revenge for Snowflake and her baby.

He embraced Cuttlefish and told her what was happening. She told him she knew it already, more or less. And then she told him some other things that she knew, and asked him to be on the alert. I was in the grove too. Not so much in it as near it, hidden among the rubbish-heaps, worried about dogs. I had bought the clothes for Cuttlefish, but stayed clear of her when I saw her with Horsefury. Things were becoming too complicated: I wanted to find out this and that before I showed myself. Habbakuk's pinnace was due in a few hours, at an inlet among the marshes, very close to this town. I had still plenty of time in hand, though I was totally exhausted and did not know how I would keep my strength up for much longer.

In the end Cuttlefish crept out to the rubbish-heaps – *she* knew where I had couched myself, she was worse than any dog – she took the bag of clothes and told me to tell the pinnace to sail straight into the town's harbour. I did not think the pirates would like this: but there were no other big ships against the pier – just one or two scruffy coasters – and if the cavalry tried anything, the pinnace could keep her distance. This whole stretch of shore seemed mercifully free of coastguard craft at present. So I went on my errand.

At about sunrise they brought Mule-driver out of the barracks. The captain's device had failed, and – dubiously enough – he fell in with the mayor's arrangements. Be it noted, he was *not* willing to kill Mule-driver with his own hand – he had served under him once, and had a scruple. It would have been all right though, had a barbarian done it. His ethics were no odder than those of most professional soldiers in the City's service. Very few of them had at this time accustomed themselves to the principles of civil war. It has not taken long for such attitudes to change.

Mule-driver, in borrowed clothes, supported between two provost-corporals (he really was very ill), was greeted in the early-morning street by an anxious little gang of leading townsmen. They were servile. He told them: 'You sent a man to kill me: he couldn't do it, could he? He knew who I was, didn't he? I know who *you* are. I don't have to talk to you. You don't want me to talk to you. You want me to get out and leave you to your peace and quiet. Leave you alone to the free exercise of the electoral franchise I was good enough to make sure you had. You can't use it, not *yet*, in my favour: oh but you'll get your chance. Might even get it before you're ready for it, I shouldn't wonder. The way you conduct yourselves here, I'd be surprised if you ever was ready for anything. There was someone said something about a civic banquet this afternoon. By all means have a banquet, eat it, get drunk at it, I won't be there. I want a ship. I want it now. Is it ready?'

This caused a problem: there was no ship in the port and not likely to be for some days. If Mule-driver had to stay here, he would put himself in peril, he would put the whole town in peril. So when, at that very juncture, *Lady Jael's* second mate, in command of the pinnace, with myself sitting next to him in the stern-sheets, gave a hail to the pier-head and asked the harbour watchman, uproariously and ironically, did he have any important passengers for Africa, no-one cared to enquire too closely into his credentials. *Lady Jael* was hove-to, within easy reach, but out of sight. The wind was fair; Habbakuk had completed his replenishments among the islands; Mule-driver's son-in-law and the other two had been picked up from the edge of the marshes, where the cavalry had failed to find them: nothing could have worked out more conveniently.

A sedan was sent for by the mayor to carry Mule-driver to the pier. He refused it. Sick he might have been, but his eye to his own particular reputation was undimmed. 'No,' he said, 'walk! I've marched regiments thousands of miles.'

There were two ways to reach the harbour from the barracks, the long route through the centre of town, the short
one through the slums and around the grove. They expected
him to take the long way – apart from anything else they
wanted to show him off to the people, and to show their
amenities off to him. Again he refused. As a banished man
he must now demonstrate himself so sure of himself that
popular acclaim was unnecessary.

He shook off the provost-corporals and strode vigorously
– if, to the close observer, a little erratically – down the
street. This street soon became an acrid little lane, he caught
his hand to his face against the smells. Now: he was at the
edge of the rubbish-heaps, to his right the lane bent to avoid
the grove. The direct way to the pier was straight through
the grove: Mule-driver began to take it.

A troubled flurry among the townspeople. Did the general not know, please, there was an omen involved here?
Black bad luck for all ship-taking travellers who set foot in
this grove. Time immemorial, no-one knew why; no-one ever
knew the name of the goddess or nymph whose crumbling
statue dominated the ancient altar there. But it was true:
and everyone always respected it. It was their town, their
grove: please . . .?

At the word 'omen' Mule-driver had halted. At any other
time he would certainly have obeyed it, omens all his life
had ruled every step of his life. But . . . to turn aside now
would be to dissolve the monolithic political impact he had
so accurately constructed. Whereas, to walk straight
through – whatever befell him afterwards, all these people
would see him as doomed: politically that would be no less
of a disaster.

He stood non-plussed: let his eyes roll left and right in
search of anything to help him out.

Cuttlefish came towards him over the rubbish-dump, the
scavenging birds rising noisily at her approach. Her newly
humanized appearance did not affect him: he was well
enough used to the vagaries of seers and wise-women. He
simply looked his strong question at her, and waited for her
solution. He was confident, whichever way she might lead
him would be correct. She too did not speak: she extended

her arm in a most elegant theatrical manner, sweeping him
forward, you might say, into the midst of the grove.

And there, in the midst of the grove, stood Horsefury:
between the statue and the rough-hewn altar-stone, in a
bright white garment short enough to reveal (so strange an
effect of unearthly heroic power) the filled cluster of his
young man's secret parts above long bare thighs; and all
around him the long bare trunks of dead trees, his sword in
his hand, the new-risen sun firing up his yellow hair into a
halo. Mule-driver halted again (again a troubled flurry
through the people): 'Shape of a man: I have seen it already.
Last night? *Why is he here . . .?*'

He seemed in touch for a moment with something more
than usually dangerous, something he did not think he could
deal with – could not fathom. His fever blurred his vision,
his hand wiped across his sweating brow. Horsefury came
towards him, held out the sword, hilt-foremost.

'I am the young man who was not to be the man to put an
end to your life. I had on the red coat of these soldier-men
for my bread and salt. Not any more. But, sir, if you can
employ me, I would wear any coat you would give.'

Mule-driver snorted: 'I'll give you a coat, boy. I'll have
no wild bare-arse northmen at *my* beck-an-call. Hercules-
god, d'you think we're in Ultima Thule? Where's that
horse-captain?' The captain came, with deference. Mule-
driver gave a plunge of his rheumatic elbow towards
Horsefury: 'He's a deserter, self-confessed. Apart from
that, what's his character? I daresay *you* won't want him
back again. He knows *you* inside-out. So you might as well
leave him with me. A strong bugger, well shaped. What's
his character?' The captain said, excellent as far as he knew.
Mule-driver nodded, used his elbow once more to order
Horsefury behind him, and once more began to enter the
grove.

The townspeople cried out, and one or two of them
actually laid hands on him to stop him. Then the Cuttlefish
threw up her arms and uttered the required oracle:

> Here is a thing that appeared:
>   out of your grove into the man's hand.

Send in the thing then first:
 to walk straight through the trees to the far side.

Ill fortune cleave to the thing:
 good luck to the man who shall follow.

How can a thing suffer luck?
 all doom that it bears shall be made void.

Horsefury accepted his role, marched slowly – a 'thing', in no way his own property, but the new chattel of Mule-driver – marched slowly, sacrificially, through the grove and out of it, followed by the 'man', Mule-driver; followed by everyone else.

Someone began to sing a hymn to the nameless lady of the grove. Someone else wondered aloud if Horsefury, manifesting himself so emphatically, might be not so much a 'thing' as some supernatural emanation of the lady's divinity, her son, maybe her sacred bedfellow? Indeed, he did call to mind the stark potency of a child's dream . . . With chanting and hand-clapping, the procession moved on to the port.

Mule-driver thought it best, as they all came down along the pier, to make one final political statement: a deposit account, as it were, to accumulate psychological interest until he should be able to return and draw upon it in triumph. No great tricks of rhetoric; simplicity, an embittered precision: 'All of my years I've stood for nowt else but popular liberty. Aye and it's well-known. *I'll* bring back liberty to the authentic Roman people if I've to cut every throat in that City to do it. You'll see.'

When Mule-driver had been lowered into the pinnace by his new well-shaped bugger (after all this effort, he was on the point of passing-out, he missed his footing three times on the pier), it was observed that Cuttlefish was nowhere to be seen, and that no-one had seen where she had gone to. Mule-driver muttered, 'Leave her, she's accomplished what I brought her for: I never was able to order her, not that one . . .' The second mate, anyway, had been told not to take her aboard, so that was that.

Except not quite. I tossed my kitbag up onto the pier and scrambled out of the boat after it. The second mate called

out: 'Judy – where the hell d'you think you're going?' 'Don't
worry,' I called back to him, 'I've jumped ship, that's all
I've done. Tell the captain my share is divided among the
crew just as though I'd been drowned. That house of mine,
and the girls and so forth – have the grand council sell them,
divide the proceeds the same way. I can't help it. If I stay
with *Lady Jael* I'm a dead man: I had an omen. Good luck,
boys, and fair cruising.' Then I pushed through the people
on the pier-head and made all haste away from that place.
No-one followed me, they were all too bewildered by
everything that had just happened, the last thing any of
them wanted was any prolonged repercussion.

Had I had an omen? In strict truth, I suppose, no. But it
was suitable excuse to offer sailormen: always accepted as a
sound reason for odd behaviour – Habbakuk had a story
from his book about a man called Jonas or some such who
would have drowned an entire crew if he hadn't confessed
to his omens. And yet, in strict truth, I knew that the *Lady
Jael* was no longer a fit place for me: if I could not live
aboard her, then logically, if I stayed aboard, I must die.
QED.

But my real reason? Herostratus, Prometheus, once again,
the tub of water? In my hurried passage round the edge of
the town it crossed my mind that if I could not live any
more with the pirates, then it must be because I could not
live without Cuttlefish. She, as she said, had been *taken*:
now she had *taken* me. Years and years and years ago, as it
seemed, I had made free a beautiful young actress for the
furtherance of her profession (and also for the hindrance of
an ugly, old, dead actor: but the Raven, just now, had
nothing to do with it). *I* now needed to be made free of *her*:
and I could not achieve it by simply allowing ourselves to
be separated yet once again. I could not. So that was my
reason: fidelity? Protestations and eternal vows in one of
Menander's last acts are not necessarily taken at face value
by the audience: but they create an acceptable illusion to
get the company off the stage, the public out of the theatre,
with a sense of *fulfilled artistic form*. Aristotle has some
words about it, somewhere. No serious critic, not even
Hippodamus, could honestly praise the dramatic shape of

the last few years of my life. I *had* been a good craftsman: let me return, and at once, to my workshop.

In the meantime, where was she? Oh god, where had she got to? She told me she had a long way to travel – where, why? What circumstance had developed, through all that obliterated length of time, that she could not now ignore? No, I must not think of that horrible rough incision down the centre of her abdomen: the possibilities it gave rise to were far too – diverse.

So – east-by-south towards the place where Habbakuk's fighters had laid hands on me, cutting off my life, and hers, with the one swift assault? Or west-by-north towards the City, where somehow she had provided herself with white mules, a gorgeous chariot, two little flute-boys in cloth-of-silver?

There was a third road, across country into the hills – if she had taken it, it might eventually bring her to the Walls of Love: yes, that too was a possibility.

I stood at the junction of these three ways, and searched the landscape for a sign.

Not finding one, I began to play oracles, omens; enough of them you might think, already, for one day: but they had their uses. I spoke a silly charm I remembered Proteus telling me once – it was supposed to let you know where to go to pick up the easiest girls –

> Stick, stick, high as the skies:
> Fall between my lady's thighs!

– and then with a special twirl of the wrist I sent my walking-stick (I had found it again on that beach after my absurd conversation with Cuttlefish) spinning above my head. When it landed, the ferrule was pointing east-by-south.

I set off at once in this direction. A quarter-mile further on was a small hill and beyond it the wide marshes, with the sea to the right hand. From the top of the rise I could see the paved post-road curving for a long distance across the pools and reedbeds by means of a causeway. This early in the morning it was empty of travellers. Except not quite – a determined dark figure in a wide-brimmed hat, half-walking, half-running: oh there she was, clear enough.

But how could I catch her? If she expected me to follow, she had forgotten my limp. But then she had no reason to expect anything of the sort, and I had no reason to expect that she should: still less that she might even hope for it. I looked out to sea – there, on the far side of a low foreland, lay Habbakuk's splendid (if hastily and crudely patched-up) galley, her furled sails ready to be spread, her oar-blades gently paddling to keep her steady where she lay. Skimming lightly towards her, the brown lugsail of the pinnace was also in view, just the top of it, over the tall green rushes.

I put one foot in front of the other, caught my painful breath, and – with a filthy word for every step – gave myself up to the pursuit. Judy Split-arse was done with: but Ivory? Did he still exist? And if he did, could he be found? I was chasing him as well as Cuttlefish.

BOOK FOUR

The Mule-driver

'No-one was ever so popular with the masses . . . both on account of his thorough honesty and disinterestedness, and of his boorish uncouthness.

Marius, in the eyes of the populace . . . was the one man capable of averting the ruin of the state, and of substituting in the place of the effete oligarchy a new and vigorous administration.

He died in full possession of what he called power and honour, and in his bed, but Nemesis assumes various shapes, and does not always requite blood with blood. Was there no sort of retaliation in the fact that Rome and Italy now breathed more freely on the news of the death of the famous deliverer of the people, than at the tidings of the battle on the Raudine plain?'

Mommsen

1 *The Desolated Lands*

It is not of importance how I overtook her or by what arguments I persuaded her to let me travel with her, to whatever destination she was bound – she would not tell me, and I did not try to ask more than two or three times. Because she had no money, she tolerated my company – otherwise, she would have begged, stolen, prostituted herself even: so determined, so obsessed she was, to keep moving, towards the south, towards the mountains of Samnium and Lucania, the last bestial alcove of the allegedly concluded war.

The more militarized the landscape through which we had to pass, the more insecure became our presence in it. To begin with I was able to bluff our way past illiterate and corruptible NCOs at the road-blocks (I made myself a passable forgery of an official tablet proclaiming me a 'commissariat commissioner travelling on government business with wife'): but I could not hope to impose upon any seriously-instructed security personnel. I did have a notched penny – Silver-hair's: I had lifted it from him during our peregrinations along the sea-shore – but I forebore to use it until absolutely forced to: I didn't know what complications it might bring down on us.

Although Cuttlefish maintained a resolute silence whenever I questioned her about her purposes, she did tell me from day to day her immediate plans. She would say, 'Does that road branch off to Naples? I don't need Naples. Keep straight on and we reach Nola, is that correct? So let's keep moving.' I had money enough for the time being for wheeled transport: but towards the war-zone this became less easy. Horses and conveyances had been commandeered by the army; grooms and postilions killed, conscripted, or frightened away: and many post-houses were closed to all but official clients.

Nevertheless, she never stopped going, hardly even to eat or sleep. My own strength surprised me: but hers was unnatural and I dreaded what might be the end of it. Her purple-black features were grey-green with the intense strain and her breath hissed as she drove herself forward. A lot of the time I suspected that she still did not totally know who she was, who I was, or at what time of our lives we were living. She more than once broke yet again into that daft dispute about Raven and my ten percent. Another time she told me all about a love-affair she was having (against her will? not clear) with the agent of her honourable master, as though I were some sympathetic young actress she had made friends with in the theatre-portico.

Through one whole day of nightmare cross-purposes, she believed she was Irene, and talked about King Strychnine's anatomy with vehement obscenity. And when, the next morning, I tried, oh so tactfully, to find out whether she was still under this gruesome delusion, she looked at me, wide-eyed, a self-willed child, and said, 'I don't know what you are talking about, of course I am Irene. I am her, and I am myself. I'd have thought you had the sense to know that.'

But she never lost sight of the central concept of a *journey*. I began to understand she did not know where she was headed, except that it was beyond – or in the midst of – the mountains of the south-west. She used to stop at shrines and temples and make enquiries of the priests. She would not allow me to be present at these discussions.

One day I determined to overhear. We were among rain and thunder, late in the evening, coming down to a ford in a barren valley. We saw there half-a-dozen gallows-poles with fragments of dead men nailed to them (a common sight in these foot-hills), and a small round stone building with a conical thatched roof. Inside, a clumsy statue of some local travellers'-god – at least, he had the hat and boots. We made an offering, which was immediately scooped up by a sly-voiced hunchback from a nearby hovel (the only habitable place in all that desolate spot) who came scuttling in to see who we were. He was one of the self-appointed holy-men sometimes to be met with battening on these country shrines and extorting contributions from strangers.

Cuttlefish said she wanted to talk to him, and ordered me out. I crept close to the wall of the shrine, and managed to hear some of their words. The holy-man was saying something about a river. 'Ah, no,' he pattered, 'no river. Not at that place. The wood was there right enough, till the army chopped it down to make a stockade. Are you sure about this river?'

Cuttlefish spoke rapidly, too low for me to catch.

'I see, I see, dear lady, you insist on this river. Wait a minute, there was a place: I've never been to it myself. A lot higher up in the hills. River, wood, temple, settlement of houses like cash-boxes all up the slope, one above the other ... Now, what did they call it ...? My memory's feeble these days. The blessed god does his best for me, but what can he do of any use when so few people come with an offering for him? If I were to promise him a nice young goat, now, he might just be able to get my memory going, he hasn't had fresh meat since, ohoh dear, I don't know when ...'

This was typical. I could hear her counting coins into his greedy dish. The next thing I heard was his asking her who the lame man outside was – her servant maybe? – and would there be any possibility of her making the blessed god fruit-ful with a real fair lady's offering like no-one else could ever give? I don't know whether she would in fact have consented to lie with the obsequious creature if that was the only way to find what she wanted to know: but the lame man was not going to allow the hunchback to take liberties. I went into the shrine, caught him by the throat, put my pirate-knife against his eyeball, and told him to make the god fruitful there and then, without any more help from *my wife*.

He did. The temple that the lady had enquired about could be reached by three days' journeying up such and such a valley: and he swore, he swore screeching, that it had not been destroyed by any armies. I then emptied his offertory-bowl into my pocket, grabbed Cuttlefish by the wrist, and pulled her out into the storm. Perhaps now if I

urged her forward, instead of the other way round, she
might accept my initiative and explain what it was all about.
But not at all – she still kept her cramped silence. Yet I
know she had heard the word 'wife'.

The valleys became thick with moving columns of troops:
most of the time we dodged them by keeping to the upper
slopes, which were constantly veiled in rain and cloud. But
a number of frightening incidents took place. As we
survived them, they are not worth recounting: but one
episode was to have its consequence.

We were held for examination by a desperate-eyed picket
of unshaven and exhausted infantrymen who stopped us in
a ruined village (all but depopulated). They took us to a
hard angry staff-serjeant on intelligence duty. He refused
altogether to accept my 'commissariat' tale. 'Nonsense:
there is no commissariat here. Here the men eat what they
can loot and that's it. If you don't tell me your real business,
I'll work it out of the woman. Don't think I don't know
how. Moreover, my soldiers know.'

Incontrovertibly, an occasion for the notched penny. He
knew what it was: and abused me for not being up to my
job. 'Commissariat rubbish, what kind of a shithead cover-
story is that? How long have you been at this work, limp-
leg? And who's the woman?' I had already picked up some
superficial knowledge of the nature of the campaign in this
district, so I made use of it. I told him I had met Cuttlefish
at one of the base-camps, she had fled there from the Lucanian rebels. She used to be the servant of a leader of theirs,
a much sought-for terrorist captain called God's-hope. She
was now in the process of accompanying me to a place where
some prisoners had been taken, to see if she could identify
him. I put great circumstantial detail into this, but he
sneered.

'You can be sure whoever they've caught, it won't be that
God's-hope killer. Where is this 'place', anyhow? *I* haven't
heard of any suspected leaders in the cages – our men tend
to nail 'em up as soon as they get hands on 'em. As an
intelligence-procedure, totally self-defeating: but it satis-
fies.'

I invented a long account of some advanced unit that had set up its field HQ a few impassable ravines to the east: and he grudgingly let us go. It was obvious that his own understanding of the troop-dispositions across this awful waste was limited in the extreme: I had the impression that the City's army was very far from winning its war, and that everything had bogged down into a series of savage little murders among isolated corners of wilderness with little or no central control. As we left, he said to me – 'Do us all a fucking favour, will you: once you've been up there and out again, if ever you *do* get out, have a full account ready of everyone you see, our people or terrorists: and anyone like me you run up against, tell 'em all of it. The only way to save our lives here is to know everything about everywhere. That notched coin of yours isn't just for the ponces in GHQ to polish their statistics on, you know. God, we could do with the Stain here again.'

After this encounter I made Cuttlefish change into her boy's clothing. She looked moderately like a boy in it – a badly-nourished circus-hand, perhaps, brought over to look after the African animals, an odd sort of person to be wandering the war-zone: but then any civilians, male or female, were anomalous in the war-zone, and I hoped that the disguise would at least prevent immediate notice being drawn to her. The 'holy-man' had been alarming, and the staff-serjeant's idea of interrogation-persuasion was even more so: maybe there'd be no more of that. I misjudged things.

The 'holy-man's' three days was an understatement, it took us nearly a week, and by the end of that time we were starving, our clothes in shreds, our bodies abraded and bruised, our feet in their worn-out boots like lumps of putrid black-pudding.

Cuttlefish saw the temple first, as she went over the summit of a saw-edged ridge ahead of me. She sank down among rocks and thorns, staring into the next deep valley, waiting for me to drag myself up to her.

Well: indeed there *had* been a temple, the stone columns were still erect: and some of the rafters – a black spider-straddle – reared out of the shapeless heap of collapsed mud-brick wall and fallen rooftiles. Behind it on the far slope were the remains of the 'settlement'. Cash-boxes? Maybe once: now they looked like honey-comb that had been trampled by a horse. The wood was still there: thick stunted trees in the valley-bottom, untended undergrowth strangling the abandoned precinct. And there too was the river – in spate: it had rained incessantly since the day at the shrine.

Cuttlefish was muttering: in a low voice to begin with, then rapidly climbing the scale in deranged crescendo: 'Nothing,' she said, 'nothing, nothing at all, nothing, all gone, gone gone gone – NO . . .!' And with a final high-pitched scream, she flung herself forward, fast as a thrown javelin, over boulders, shale, vertical drops, bouncing and tumbling, ripping unhindered through bushes and tangles of weed till she disappeared from my view in the foliage far down below.

I followed, very cautiously. My bad leg knew far too much about hillsides like this. When I got to the bottom I was blocked by the furious river. Yet Cuttlefish somehow had crossed over, I could hear her voice crying out like a wolf through the trees on the far side.

If she could do it, I could – god help us, I *had* to: the strong cold water surged up to my chest, hitting heart and lungs like a hammer, my feet staggered among huge stones and small ones, I went under in the middle and was very nearly swept away: but I got there. I lay on the edge of the bank, half-in, half-out of the torrent, unable to go any farther. I could just see, ahead of me between the soaking leaves, Cuttlefish running round the precinct, stopping short here and there to identify some known landmark, statue-plinth, flight of steps, and then hurrying on to the next one, a spiral course of mounting despair as she took in the full range of the waste and ravaged sanctuary. Then uphill towards the ruined houses, still running and scrambling, still howling.

Three famished mountainy-men, in uncured goatskins and random items of soldiers' equipment, came out from behind a broken wall and silently stood in her way. At the same moment, more of them – seven or eight, I didn't bother to count – were here upon the river-bank not a yard from my outstretched arms.

Even had I been able to move, I could not have evaded them.

In the cellar of a destroyed house they presented us to their commander. He was God's-hope, the infamous Lucanian: and, once his men had discovered the forged 'commissariat' tablet in the midst of my waterlogged sack, he showed no intention of allowing us the comfort of *any* hope.

'I see, you talk Greek, and you work for the Romans. Which makes it even worse than if you were a Roman yourself. I suppose you've lost your way – there's no City commissariat here. My young men have made certain of that. A fair number of you people have lost your way around these mountains lately: that's because they are *our* mountains and we don't deliver their secrets. Now you may or may not have any secrets yourself: but it's my business to find out before you die.'

He was a small dark wedge-faced man, quite young, with a voice like a university lecturer's, reasonable, unemotional, comprehending of others' incomprehension. His shaggy hair and coal-black whiskers, his swashbuckling bandit's accoutrements, seemed irrelevant and accidental, as though he had inadvertently dressed himself in an actor's costume instead of his own and would discover the mistake any minute.

He said, 'Of course you people have given me a great reputation as a torturer. Not true. We do try to hurt you very considerably, but we have neither time nor interest in elaborate techniques. We'll start with the young one, and see how you feel about him – that's the Roman way, isn't it? I suppose he's your servant? So watch what it means to be *yours*, in *our* moutains.'

He took my walking-stick, which I had been clutching all this time without even being aware of it, it had clenched itself between my fingers, so numbed they were by the cold river. His men tore Cuttlefish's clothing off her upper body with a single pull. They saw immediately she was a woman, one of them gave a sharp laugh, that was all the indication of surprise they chose to utter: and at once God's-hope started to hit Cuttlefish all over, front and back, with astonishing great force. She rolled onto the ground, a curious hedgehog shape: she was whining a little, the saliva ran out at the side of her mouth.

He stopped as abruptly as he had begun, and looked at me searchingly: 'I see: you don't care to watch it. You have feeling for her, of course; why else would you have changed her clothes? You are a Greek, not a Roman – or a Syrian, no? I'll carry on.' But he didn't. Cuttlefish's odd passivity disturbed him, or perhaps puzzled him. He said, 'Is she sick?'

'In her mind,' I told him. 'You'll get nothing out of her. It's not – it's not decent to beat a poor madwoman.'

My voice failed as I said it.

'Of course it's not,' he answered me, 'but it works. You're going to talk, aren't you?'

He began again lashing at her: only, once again, to stop short. 'It occurs to me that a Roman agent would not travel this region with a lunatic for any serious military purpose. Would you care to explain her before I hurt her any more? It might be she is really one of our own people, and I am making a mistake.' He sat down on a pile of bricks and waited for me to reply. I stared at him hopelessly. An explanation to this pitiless man?

'Of course she's one of your people,' was all I could blurt out. 'Don't you understand *anything* when you see a woman like this – ?'

'No,' he said, 'How should I? I'm a terrorist, not a doctor. I'm waiting for you to tell me. Begin at the beginning.'

But where was the beginning? The Walls of Love? Ephesus? Pergamus even? I made a number of false starts: until he lost patience, had *me* stripped, as well; and started in on me with the stick, taking a special care to hit my bad hip. Because I was screaming and trying to shield myself, I did not see Cuttlefish get up and I did not hear her begin to speak. By the time God's-hope allowed me a respite, she was already standing with her back pressed into a corner, and talking very fast: hoarse, emphatic, she even seemed half-rational.

She was telling this cruel devil what she had refused to tell me: she was telling him why she had come seeking this temple, she was sure she had been here before, she knew what the place looked like, had lost all trace of its name or its whereabouts, all trace of why she had been here, except that it was *life*, her entire *life*, she could not *live* until she found out.

'If I knew why I had been here, I would know what was the reason for *this*.'

She dragged at her sodden waistband, and pulled down the front of her trousers, displaying to us all the great scar.

'There,' she said, 'there, when did that happen? Where? What was it for? And why do I dream of it in the same dream as this temple, this wood, river, houses: why . . .? And oh god who pulled this place to pieces and where are all the people?'

2   Rabid

Without change of expression, save for a certain speculative sucking-in of his cheeks, he put the stick down and answered her last question. '*We* pulled it to pieces, because the Romans were in it. The people had all gone away before that time – most of them safely enough, I believe. It was a sanctuary of a goddess of childbirth, also a hospital; and an orphanage for children whose parents refused to keep them but would not expose them to the kites on the naked hill. The priestesses were well-spoken-of for their medical art and midwifery – they purveyed spells to remedy infertility, and also to procure abortion. It may well have been possible for them to have cut open the womb of a living woman and extracted a child: but I don't know enough of the matter to say why they should have done such a thing. As you know, I am not a doctor.'

He addressed these words to me, as though expecting me to interpret them for the understanding of a madwoman. But I did not know how to do this, so I kept my silence, as far as chattering teeth and tremors of pain would permit me. But Cuttlefish seemed to have gathered the gist of his account: she sat slowly down, still pressed tight into the corner, and swayed her body from side to side, clutching her arms around her breasts and shoulders. She did not try to pull her clothes back on, the rags of them lay spread around her on the floor. She spoke as though to herself: 'No no there was nothing, it was the fantasy of Raven, he gave me the appearance, swollen, puffed out, so that I *thought*, oh oh god how could I *not* have thought, she had made life out of my life: but puffed out, empty water, mockery gurgles of air: and here, when I could bring forth nothing, did they search for it with their knives . . .?'

But if she was prepared to believe that, I wasn't. I took courage from God's-hope's face – it was not exactly softening, but I could have sworn the bastard was *interested*. I would damn well exploit his interest then – it couldn't make matters any the worse. I said, 'You must know where some of the people went to. The priests – '

'Priestesses, mostly. There were a few men – eunuchs, I think.'

'But where did they go – and who took care of the children?'

'To be frank I neither know nor care. My job, to burn this place and kill all the Romans who had garrisoned it. And I did. You'll find their corpses in the undergrowth even today. *I* left them there. *I* did: and *I* had been born here – my mother having miscarried so many times that they feared her death if she went into labour again without special attendance. It would have been better had they let her alone.'

I was not going to dispute *that*. But I had to keep his interest, I was most apprehensive lest he suddenly shake off this new mood of brooding melancholy (which was not at all in accord with his character of guerrilla-captain) and decide to put in some more work on one or both of us with the stick. I urged him to tell us, was it in any way possible that some children from the hospital could have been got out of the valley alive – it had surely been more than a year ago, surely the Romans at that time had not closed off the entire country as they had now?

His men were getting restless, they did not understand

Greek, they thought perhaps I was cooking up some treacherous deal with their leader outside their rights of consultation. This irritated him: and he turned on them angrily. Having quelled them, he clearly found it necessary to continue our conversation just to make clear who was in charge.

So he informed me, at some length, and almost considerately, that indeed most of the children would have been taken safely away – 'If they weren't, then no doubt they were captured and sold. Well, wherever they are now, servile or free, they are to be envied, are they not? They are out of here, all of them, far away out of these mad mountains. The sanctuary is abolished. The only ones left here are mad, mad as your blackwoman. What else can we be? We take hold of you and flog you with rods for no better reason than that we do not know your faces. When every road that leads towards us, here, in our lunatic's lair, is hedged with burnt villages and rows of rotting gallows-poles, what else does the sane world expect? I'm an educated man, I speak very good Greek – ?'

Indeed he did, I hastened to assure him.

'And yet I have covered your body with stripes. And hers. Yet tell me what else I could do?'

We were all three, for no good reason, squatting on the floor by now – Cuttlefish in the corner, myself a few feet away facing her, God's-hope to the side and in between us, looking fiercely from one face to the other – his last sentence was directed solely at her. He was clothed, and armed: we two were naked, or almost so, with blood all over us: oh, a bizarre grouping, no apparent way to resolve it for whatever fool stage-manager had so casually blocked it out. And around us, the Lucanian fighters, standing back against the steps that led up from the cellar, fingering their weapons, puzzled, nervous, all too likely to spring on us at some undetectable sign from their chief.

Cuttlefish stared into God's-hope's eyes, her own were wide and wild and her mouth was half-open.

She spoke from deep down in her throat. One word at a time, as though gradually dragging up all she ever remembered and, piece by piece, making sense of it. 'You . . .

are . . . not . . . mad. You are . . . killing . . . the City. *That* is not . . . mad.'

He laughed at her, a great spit of laughter that splashed on her scarred cheek.

'No,' she went on, 'no . . .' Her voice was speeding up a little and the words became more connected. 'All the rest became tired: stopped killing: flocks and herds, gave themselves to the City for the City to put them once again to the pasture. All the rest, all of them, all except *you* . . .'

'Indeed, indeed – ' God's-hope was breathing fast, excited: he saw that veiled though her comprehension might be, she understood him, at a certain important depth, 'indeed,' he said, 'yes: the City said "the franchise", they said "your liberties", they said "your citizenship": they went even further – they said "a treaty" – unpicked the Italian nation after all our long fighting, into a little small handful of pieces when before, all those years, they had been able to accomplish nothing with their cruelty and intransigence but confirm us in the stand that we took. But *we* – I mean just *us* – ' (he waved his arm to include his men and the narrow bounds of the cellar) ' – and a few hundreds more – *we* in these mountains took a look at that hope we were offered and saw nothing of what we had fought for. The City with their treaties are seeking a way to rule Italy to their advantage by making a Roman out of every Italian – indeed it is what we had thought that we wanted – *once*. But not any more. Because now we can see them seeking to rule the whole world by making their armies for ever out of all our young men. Whereas, in the meantime, we, of our own resources, we had built ourselves a *nation*! Or the dream of a nation. Hope of one. It was enough . . . So, rather than flocks and herds, we will turn ourselves into wild beasts. Rabid: we are mad and we make mad. It's our only claim to existence. If we stopped it tomorrow, and made peace, where should we be? No-one would ever hear of Lucania again.'

One of his men said something, impatiently. God's-hope rose to his feet with a jerk and a clang of harness. 'Very well,' he snapped in his own dialect, 'that's enough, you can kill them, they're no use to us.' The dialect, though

akin to Latin, was not easy for me to understand, I may
have got it wrong, but I chose not to run any risk of complacency. I too leaped upright, shouting and yelling that we
were not from the City and that we had no wish whatever
that any Lucanian should ever be persuaded to make
peace with anyone anywhere, *please* . . .!

Perhaps I *had* misunderstood him, because none of his
men had moved, and he himself started to laugh again, this
time showering me with his spittle. His mirth was not
in balance, he roared and hooted and barked. And then
Cuttlefish joined in. She laughed until the tears ran,
shaking herself as she sat there as though she wanted all her
teeth to be rattled out.

Through her gulps and sobs she was speaking, indistinc-
tly, but there was sense to it, of a sort. She told him, in a
flurry of disjointed flying phrases, that if he did stop his
fighting he would die and the City would live, unless . . .
unless . . . 'unless you left them a testament, a last will, why
don't you? a bequest . . . leave to them all of it, all rabid
mad in one good gift . . .?' She reached forward and laid
hold of my coat, where it lay on the wet mud floor. Her
fingers prowled along the seam, until she found what I had
hidden there (I did not know she knew where it was): my
notched penny. She pulled at the stitches, they gave, and
the coin fell out. God's-hope, no longer laughing, pounced
on it like a great swift cat. He understood about notched
pennies. So did his men. Now: they would kill.

But they didn't.

God's-hope asked Cuttlefish, very quietly, if *she* understood what she had given him. She told him, no less quietly,
that she did: the notched penny, she said, was the mark of
Mule-driver by way of Silver-hair and Mule-driver needed
God's-hope and God's-hope needed him. But she, the
Cuttlefish, needed neither of them. If she was to tell him how
to use the notched penny to find his way out of the mad
mountains, then he must tell her what she wanted to be told.
There was a sideways cunning in her voice and behind it a
desperate thrust of her sideways mind in all its trouble.

He left us alone then, left us our clothes, and went out to

confer with his fighters. I sat on the floor and hated him: I had never seen any of the pirates beat a woman the way he had served Cuttlefish.

She lay on the floor, curled up under her cape. She moaned a little to herself and then went to sleep, without having said a word to me.

3   A Fair Exchange

I was unable to sleep, I felt so conturbed with pain and rage. Not only did I hate this fanatic God's-hope, I also hated Cuttlefish. I could think of her only with disgust and resentment: I had believed that these emotions might have faded away after her bath in the sea and her apparent return to something like this present world. But such had not proved to be the case.

I did not ask myself what I would have felt had we found the temple undamaged and flourishing, with, for example, a green lawn covered with tumbling children, and one of them, one of them . . . him? her? what name might the priestesses have given it? For example, *God's-hope*? Well, if that had happened, my thoughts would no doubt have been shaped in accordance. As it was, the shape was Lucanian. Last bloody ditch Lucanian and the Cuttlefish was their confederate. Perhaps I did wrong to blame her: she must have lost all standard of comparison. Irene was the one to blame. King Strychnine's Irene. If it had not been for Irene. . . .

I thought about Irene, and – for the first time since *Lady Jael* arrived off Ostia – I felt the battle-flag of my listless sex stirring, you might say, in the breeze. Considering how hard I had been hit between the legs, this was something of a wonder: but not at all an agreeable wonder. To be rising up erect inside my trousers at such a juncture: and for the memory, no less, of how I had allowed myself to be moulded, patted, sucked, licked, scratched, into libertine subservience when every bubble of my brain informed me that the only reasonable thing to do was to get out of the Walls of Love, and get out of it fast – this was worse than humiliating: it was not at all consonant with my identity as

an 'image of god' (Habbakuk's book, I think: I don't recollect any of *our* philosophers putting it quite like that):
moreover it only told me that Irene was – abolished, like
this temple? Like the Lucanians.

So she was.

But my cock stood on end and something had to be done for
it. I would as soon have stuck the clamorous creature into
Mule-driver's toothless gob as into any part of Cuttlefish just
now. I switched my meditations, briefly, to my fat boisterous
Illyrian, remembered how she had squealed that time we laid
into her white hindquarters with my belt and the rope's end,
how red her round whitenesses had glowed, how angrily but
gratefully I had shoved myself in up her naughty little arse-
hole immediately afterwards . . . ah, that was better, no
problems with a *pirate's* memories: I could toss myself off
now without further self-contempt, and I did.

What sort of a foul man was I?

Two of the Lucanians unbolted the door of the cellar,
came in and shook Cuttlefish awake, told her she must go
with them to talk to God's-hope. I asked them if they could
possibly find something for us to eat, and did they not realize how wet and cold we were? We would be dying of pneu-
monia. They told me I was no worse off than they were: if
you took to the hills, then that was what you took to, and
you had to make the best of it. When they went out, they
bolted the door again.

Later on – it was already dark – God's-hope himself came
in. Cuttlefish was with him. He carried a feeble dark-lan-
tern. He said: apart from the lantern, no fires, no lights in
these hide-outs, there were too many Romans in the area,
some of them might even have got up on the mountain-
slope to spy out the land: they did behave efficiently from
time to time.

I said, 'We're in a cellar.' He said, 'It's a principle. Once
you allow it in one instance, men get casual, forget, leave
open doors, show smoke in daytime. Every hour, every day,
we are compelled to compel ourselves . . .'

I asked him what he had been before the war, a schoolmaster? He ignored my sarcasm, and answered as though I

had meant it.

'No, sir: I was a lawyer. A founder-member of CRAC in my town. I specialized in constitutional law and had a great deal to do advising Harmony about his deliberations over the franchise in the City legislature. But the City rejected all constitutional reform, and then murdered Harmony. I came to the conclusion that law was now *abolished*. I looked for another profession, and found it: today, as you see, I am unable to leave it.

'However, it appears that our friend Mule-driver has a use for me and my hungry young men. It was one of his subordinates, by the way, who fixed on this sanctuary as an appropriate place to install soldiers. His skull is on a spike inside the ruins of the temple, where the statue of the goddess used to be: I don't think you will have had time to see it. And Mule-driver himself is in Africa? Well, it will be a little while before he can come back. If we are still here, we will convey him your notched penny and offer our services. You are certain he *will* throw open the full privileges of the City to us: in reward? I mean *full*? We must make of it what we can. Our last will and testament. Why not?'

I did not entirely understand, though I had a glimmering. So I nodded . . .

At about this stage in his discourse I felt cold all over – a quite different class of chill from the one that had gripped me all day. It was due, you see, to his being the Raven.

He had not been, earlier: and as the light from the lantern did not catch his features, it is hard for me to explain how I knew he was now. His voice had not changed, his words were entirely appropriate to God's-hope.

But oh yes, he was Raven all right: and I went cold: and I sweated.

He said: '*My* part of the bargain. I have done what I can for this lady. The fire that destroyed the hospital did not totally consume all the recent archives. Many of these were inscribed on clay tiles in the ancient manner – temple-clerks are conservative. The language is not easy to read: but the lady was able to decipher enough to convince her that two years ago she was here: and she did give birth. We also have made a guess about what happened to the child.

'At the time of the evacuation, it was taken away by one of the temple servants, the archivist Cluilius, separately from the other children. She will tell you about it, in due course – if she wants to. I have given her the essential inscriptions. Tomorrow you will be set on your way by some of my young men. They will insert you far enough through the Roman lines to ensure that you will not need to produce your notched penny. It would be awkward if you had need of it, because I shall be keeping it – I shall require it to make myself known in confidence to this Silver-hair, whenever I see him. I will let you take your baggage: and some of your money. We need money: if only to bribe people with. So I have to expropriate a portion of yours. Oh: about your baggage. We found this, at the bottom of your sack. It's very wet, almost disintegrated.'

It was the vomit-and-wine-stained draft of Mule-driver's projected address to the senate. God's-hope seemed to be smiling. He handed the pulpy mess to me and added, 'I was just able to make the words out. It helped me to derive sense from what your lady was trying to tell me, she is still not altogether exact in her speech. She has been speaking now and then as though she were my pupil, which is odd, under the circumstances. I was thinking of keeping this piece of writing and using it to strengthen me when I come to make my bargain. 'Very like the buggers will ask too much . . .' Revealing, the heel of Achilles, show him I know all about it . . .? But no: I am a lawyer: documents-in-the-case require proof of authorship. This one hasn't . . . But I gather you were both associated with the theatre? I daresay that this could be a speech for a good comic actor, a strong voice of satirical intonation? I would like very much now to hear a piece of a real play, a tragic play. And I make an exception: we will allow light to be kindled. Come.'

He led us out of the cellar, through a labyrinth of ruins under moonlight – the rain had stopped – until he reached the one building with an unbroken roof. It was a large low littered stable – some of the horse-stalls were still there: their shadowy angles flickering in the light of two crude torches stuck into pots at the far end.

A dozen or so of his fighters sat about on the rotted straw, waiting. He brought Cuttlefish down the middle, to stand between the torches. Their flames on his face showed me clearly that he *was* Raven.

I wondered what the hell was to happen. I could not think it possible here and now she could be capable of any sort of *performance*: indeed, her eyes were as blank as bottle-tops, she opened her mouth like a fish, helpless, distressed. I started forward to try and prevent it going any further.

Two Lucanians had their daggers against the pit of my stomach. I stood where I was.

God, but this was a trap. A trap in the form of a surprise test: if she does not do what they expect of her, they will assume she is a fraud, and what sort of fraud but that of a Roman notched penny? God alone knew how slowly they would murder us. Oh once again, here I was, a leaking double-agent in the Stain's tumbled bed-chamber; a pre-varicating tax-evader in my father's 'back room': a mute child cornered at playtime against the wall of the school latrine. . . .

4   *Darius Emperor*

God's-hope leaned against the post, his glittering eyes-of-Raven fixed hard upon the Cuttlefish as she slumped in front of him, her feet inexpressively apart, hands sagging loosely down beside her thighs, head slightly stooped.

'This is not the sharpest setting for tragic poetry,' he said: 'The stage needs to be dressed.' As he spoke, one of his men came in, carrying something under his cloak. 'I gave orders for at least a token of the presence of Melpomene.' The fighter opened his cloak and brought out a leprous skull: not a clean skull, it was smeared with slimy morsels of its old flesh, there were black hairs hanging from it. It stank. The head of the spear that had killed its owner was jammed through one of the eye-sockets and projected out at the back.

God's-hope forced the spear-point into the wainscot of the stable wall, high up behind Cuttlefish.

'Now,' he said, 'act.' 'Now,' he said, 'stage-fright? come

on, child, you're not new to the business: Aeschylus – let him live: recollect him, and you, yourself – *live!*' 'Now,' he said, 'the majestic Aeschylus: ta-tum, ta-tum, ta-tum – ta-*tum*!' He thrust his head forward at her like the blade of a halberd, he clapped his hands together in the age-old metric beat: he was Raven, and his little prize pupil was about to put him to shame before the public: he would not tolerate it. She shuddered, blinked, shook her head: and all of a sudden was taken over by his fierce torch-lit dominance. Metamorphosis of posture, of stature, of expression, all in one moment. The Ghost of Darius, Emperor, filling the stage with huge retribution at the climax of *The Persians*. I did not think this was a speech she had ever learned, certainly I had never heard her repeat it – but she had it now in her mouth and she had it word-perfect. And moreover, it was not any longer a speech about Xerxes the Persian. The swollen neck of Mule-driver thickened through every syllable.

> So many went to war: so few return.
> Art-magic tells the prophecy of god
> Which thus interpreted for earthly wit
> According to these tidings shall fulfil
> Each last calamity. King Xerxes' hope
> Is hollow: let him flee from vengeful Greece
> And leave behind him noblest horse and foot,
> He shall not hear again the brazen clang
> Of their proud harness nor their trumpets' howl:
> He shall not spy their banners where they droop
> Lamenting in Boeotia by the flood
> Of quick Asopus river 'thwart the plain:
> He shall not pace their heart-dishevelled march
> Through dried-up Grecian fields, with doom of death
> A-track the spoor of their failed insolence.
> From north to south they tore the temples down,
> Dragged altars to the ground, upheaved to hurl
> In flying shards of wreck each graven god
> That godlike statuaries had set up
> For human praise and worship. Sacrilege
> By vile and Persian hand is mated now
> With Persian pain and terror in those fields.
> And more is yet to come: the spurting fount

Of hot catastrophe still pours
Unplugged and red beneath Plataean walls,
Where thrusting pikes of Doria shall outrupt
Th'Iranian breast in blood immeasurable.
Heap upon heap of dead: a wordless word
To all posterity that mortal man
In pride must be brought sprawling down:
His splendid flower is wind-blown foolishness,
His jocund harvest, reaped with song cut short,
Shall strangulate the croaking throat of grief.

She finished. There was total silence. I looked round, shrewd manager assessing the mood of my client's public. The grimy haggard Lucanian faces were furrowed with tears. God's-hope, who was not any more Raven but his sole self, sat cross-legged, bowed over with his head in his hands. It was a *moment*.

Not, though, a moment for conventional applause. But it did need something: after Aeschylus, the satyr-play. These men were fighters now, not social theorists, their spirits must be raised up, they must laugh themselves forward to their horrible task. You might well ask, what business it was of mine to be spurring the morale of this malevolent troop? All I can say is – I responded to the immediate theatrical need: instinctive, that's all. I still hated them. None the less, I gave them a macaronic shanty from the hatch-boards of the *Lady Jael*: I was determined to get their hands and feet going – will you believe that I succeeded?

> King Strychnine put a ship to sea
> > *Hey-o the Pontic water*
> The crankest ship you ever did see
> > *A-sailing through the islands-o*
>
> > *The islands-o the islands-o*
> > *He swam his daughter in the Pontic water*
> > *A-sailing through the islands-o.*
>
> Her captain's hair is flaming tar
> His thick neck bone a capstan bar.
>
> He carries his eyeballs in each hand
> To cast his light on sea and land . . .

– and so on, another six or seven physiological stanzas, some
cruder than others. Then the song dropped certain sophisticated political hints – alliances, confederacies, etcetera . . .

> The man who sails with Strychnine's fleet
> Will wear red shoes on both his feet.

> The man who sails with him to Rome
> Will never need another home.

> There was a Roman drove a mule
> He lost his load in Strychnine's pool.

> There was a Roman stained his cheek
> His bum-boy drowned in Strychnine's creek.

– so far, primarily, a sailors' tribute – oh artless enough – to
the potentate who issued them their roving commission. I
added an improvised stanza to suit present company and to
confirm the political hints (I never claimed to be a poet):

> Lucanian goats are harsh and wild
> *Hey-o the Pontic water*
> They lead King Strychnine like a child
> *A-sailing through the islands-o*

> *The islands-o the islands-o*
> *Lucania lifts her hand on land*
> *And sets her feet on the islands-o.*

It was all very sufficiently pointless and idiotic: but the
air and the refrain got into their itching dissatisfied skins
and they roared it out after me, shoving in their own stanzas
(neither better nor worse than mine), and – in the end –
joining hands and stamping round and round the stable till
the torch-flames shuddered and God's-hope tetchily warned
them to make less noise and remember where they were.
But I could see he admired me for the impudence of the
performance – he was not going to beat me again, he was
not going to kill me: and Cuttlefish at last had thrown open
wide to us her spirit, thank god, she had thrown it open . . .

They gave us food (mouldy oatmeal and cold water) and we
slept in the straw – among the bunch of them, warm and close,
arm over thigh – as though it were the bed of a satrap.

★

An hour before dawn Cuttlefish and I were woken up by one of God's-hope's 'young men'. He was not so very young, being an ill-tempered wiry veteran with stubbly grey hair, a battlement of broken teeth in the countenance of a man-eating monkey, all puckered with scars and venomous intent. He said, in as few words as possible, that it was his business to see we got safe out of the war-zone, that their scouts had let them know that the City's troops had been moving in closer upon the valley and its approaches during the last twenty-four hours, and that we would not be able to go out the same way we had come in.

'Twice as long,' he said, 'twice as steep, three times as difficult. Prepare yourselves. But I can always see *them* before they see me, you'll not get detected.' I asked him why, if Lucanian scouting was so expert, Cuttlefish and myself had managed to reach the temple unobserved?

He looked as though he had just eaten a piece of poison-ivy: 'You were seen, Greeko; ten miles back, you were seen. We wanted to watch where you came to, that's all: and make sure there was no more than the pair of you.' He had a bag with some hard rations, and he ordered us to leave most of our own gear behind. 'Don't matter a damn what the chief said last night. It'll clutter you and get you caught, and you're not bringing it. You do nothing these next few days except what I tell you to do. Got it?'

I said, 'Got it.' And we set off. We did not see God's-hope to say good-bye.

He led us a terrible journey. We travelled mostly by night. During daylight we hid in caves and under bushes, and once in-and-out of the water of a small lake. Now and then we made contacts with Lucanian sentinels, perched high up among the rocks to keep watch upon Roman patrols in the valleys. Sometimes one of these men would leave his post and come with us, shepherding us carefully past some new danger that had sprung up since our guide had last passed that way.

We had neither time nor energy to converse, though I did ask Monkey-face once about the military situation: if the City's forces were now occupying so much new country, how long before God's-hope's band was compelled to move elsewhere, and where could it go? He had once been chief-of-scouts in a regular City regiment: he knew what he was talking about. 'These columns can't come into one part of the hills without coming away from another part: they leave the place empty, we move ourselves in. No trouble: we get fewer every day, we need less space. And *they* get fewer too. That Stain of theirs fetched most of the bastards out of it, to Asia: I tell you it was a damnsight worse for us before he went. We'll live, or enough of us will, to help out your Mule-driver back into his City. And then begod, he'll know who his friends are. Or will he? . . . Of course, Greeko, they could astonish us, they could always find a new general, another Stain maybe, and then really come into us. Greeko, if that happens, we'll die. Very like take a regiment with us.'

I was worried about the Cuttlefish. Her strength at last, and suddenly, was beginning to fail. It was no longer a matter of her surging ahead, leaving me to fling myself desperately after her all the time. She had discovered what she had come to discover; had fixed what she had come to fix; had returned to her skill as an actress: she was left with no resources. Monkey-face and I found ourselves pulling her up between us through the worst places, and we had to stop for frequent rests. Her courage was no less, and she even made little bitter jokes about her incapacity; but it was more and more doubtful whether she was going to be able to complete the journey. Monkey-face told her she must. He had his orders: they were to be obeyed. If she could not walk, he would carry her on his back, he would carry her till she damn well died.

There was no question of *my* carrying her: I could barely convey myself. But our earlier ordeal had hardened rather than weakened me, I was able at least to *endure* the state of affairs. Her attitude to me was non-committal, she treated me as a friendly companion but nothing more. Neither affection nor contempt, and indeed it is hard to see how she would have had the time for either. These were not the circumstances for self-indulgent reflection upon our personal relationships.

After one final day of brutalizing effort under the oven-door sun that had replaced the vicious rain, we came down an easy slope through cattle-pasture (almost empty of

beasts), vineyards and olive-groves, not all of them destroyed. We were very nearly at the sea-coast. The post-
road to the City ran approximately north and south.
Monkey-face took us to a disreputable little inn in a lane
about quarter of a mile from the road.

Here he knew the people, who had been useful to God's-
hope in the past and would now take care of us until we were
ready to proceed on our own. We hid in a ditch and waited for
darkness. When the inn was lit up, he crept to the window
and spied out who was there. It seemed safe enough, so he
knocked on the door, whispered a while to the grim woman
who opened it, and then called us over.

I held up Cuttlefish in my arm and struggled across the
threshold with her. The woman and I laid her down on a
bed in the inner room. When I went back into the kitchen
to fetch her a cup of wine, Monkey-face had gone.

About three hours after midnight, my Cuttlefish died.

5   Rational Sense

*What Cuttlefish said to me before she died. These remarks were
uttered in moments of lucidity, they were not always entirely coherent. I have edited them in places to make rational sense of them.
I believe that she wished them to make rational sense, and only her
physical weakness prevented this. There were, however, occasions
when she thought I was the Raven. Perhaps I was, I don't know.
But she was talking rational sense to the Raven, and I have
recorded it equally with the words she spoke to me when she knew
I was Ivory.*

Ivory, dear Ivory, when I belonged to you, I loved you.
When you made me free, I found it necessary to be free of
that love as well. If the war had not begun during those
months in the Walls of Love, I might slowly have become
able to find a new love for you, my dear, that would not
have been dependent upon the kindness you showed me
when I was your property. You know I was only *taken* because of the war – the goddess, the Raven, someone, took
me out of it to Africa where everyone was free – at least free
of the City – so that I could come back and *take* the City. I
will tell you before I go where the City is to be taken to.

That's a joke, dear Ivory: laugh at it. I don't want to go without having seen you laugh again.

I want to speak to the Raven: he was here a few minutes ago, he can't have gone without saying good-bye? Ah, there he is.

('Sir, I did manage to get through the Darius speech without any dries or fluffing: it *worked*. I know you always said these long male orations were outside my range: but if you had been there and heard me you would have had to agree you were mistaken. No sir, I am not challenging your years of experience. You were there when I began the speech: if you had not worked me into it, I could never have got started – if you'd really thought me unsuited to it, you would not have done that. Sir, I will do as you say and leave the kings and ghosts of Aeschylus to you in future. But for that audience, what other possible speech? You were there, but you wouldn't do it yourself, so *I* had to do it. Apologies, but don't beat me for it: I am too old in the business now to be beaten by you any more. Even *you* must admit: I am mistress of my craft. You'd be ashamed if you tried to beat an artist of my class, oh you would.

'Sir, I slept willingly with you, in gratitude for your patience with me ever since you brought me out of Antioch. I deceived you with Ivory because I had found myself defending your interests against his chicanery. And so: I became aware of him, quite a young man, bad leg and all, he made me laugh at your pomposity, made me challenge the demands of the gratitude I felt towards you. For my body to cheat you was to make my spirit free of you. To learn the great roles of the poets was to make myself free of you, too. You were enraged by the one: you encouraged the other. Not logical: and that enflamed my secret parts, oh yes it had to, every time I looked at Ivory. But you knew about your lack of logic, how else could you have written that will?')

Now listen, Ivory, carefully, carefully, you have got to get this right. He gave me the clay tablets – if you can't read them let me tell you what they say. Find them for me, show me them – god it's so dark in here – I'll pick out the letters with my fingers, so, so. This word is *Lanuvium*. Where is

Lanuvium? It's a town, I think, to the north. The temple archivist went there with a baby that was left behind when they all had to flee. He had friends in Lanuvium: and the last thing he did, before he set out, the last man to leave – he entered it all up on the tablet: he wanted the records up-to-date for someone to discover after the war. Conscientious: why should he not have been just as careful in looking after my baby? I know it was my baby because of the number he gives her – no name, just the temple's number, and that sign means a little girl. Now, check it with this other tablet: the number again and the date of birth. It says here 'the Ethiop woman, found by the temple's shepherd on the slope of Mount something: no name: out of her mind: and the baby nine full months inside her upside down: experimental surgery: total success.' And then, after that, this sign, five marks like the petals of a flower. It means that the baby was kept in their orphanage to be brought up as a priestess. If I could remember I am sure I would remember that I had given her to the temple in recompense for the goddess saving both of our lives. But now, there is no temple. I do not know if there is a baby. Try to find her. Lanuvium. Try to find her, and see in Lanuvium in what way through her life the debt to the goddess can be repaid. Try.

Ivory, she is your daughter. Raven says she is his. *This must not, please, be a cause for dispute between you.* If you like, she had two fathers, comedy, and tragedy.

When I go, I will go to Africa. The men in their little boats have told me they will welcome me. They know I have shown that just by existing we can all tear to pieces the glee of the City. That will not make them happy: but it will keep them from thinking they are nothing in all the world but black blank nakedness in foolish boats. Horsefury too: in his apple orchards the same knowledge. His work is yet to be finished.

Horsefury is with Mule-driver. Then, soon, God's-hope will be with Mule-driver. I was with him. Between the three of us, Mule-driver will have broken the glee of the City. If you can help them, help. If you are too frightened, then keep yourself safe: I do not want, oh my dear, to run you into any more danger. You have done your share, you brought Mule-driver onto your ship.

Irene is still dancing. In the green forest: I have been watching her again. When you entered her body, you came into mine as well: my daughter is her daughter. If you like, she has two mothers, freedom, and servitude.

Ivory, hold my hand: kiss me, I can hardly see you. Andromache, farewell to Hector, pathetic, reproachful, I used to speak it so well. But, Hector, farewell to Andromache – the answer to it, or half-answer – I never tried that one. Listen:

> If I crept like a coward
> > from the compulsion of this fight
> How could I again meet mute reproaches
> > of the men of Troy?
> How face the failed worship
> > of fair women in flowing gowns?
> Must warp my heart, oh such weakness;
> > for I have worked always,
> A fighter, to find place
> > in the front of the line or nowhere:
> For my kinfolk, for country,
> > to carve out duty, for my own content . . .
> Deadly fear not so much for my own future now
> > as for you, without me, flung Greekward
> Slave-spoil savagely dragged
> > into Argos to sweat at another woman's loom,
> Carry water from a foreigner's well,
> > without will of your own, toil.
> Oh grant that the ground heaped up
> > over my grave
> Cover me for ever before I can count
> > your cries as they carry you away!

Sick to buggery of all these poets writing nothing but appeals from the women for all their men to stay out of it, keep house, defend them. It never happens the other way round? Ask Irene.

Ivory, d'you know what I see? These last few days, in all

these wolf-keeping mountains? You've lost all your fat. If it wasn't for your leg, you would look like a lovely young actor, if it wasn't for your bald head. You're even thinner than I was when Mule-driver was making his life by my word. Seven consulates, remember, he will have them: watch what happens, but keep out of his way Lanuvium. You will try. Kiss me: I cannot see you. Take hold of my hand, sweetheart, put it under your clothes – my hand, not Irene's. There, that's good luck.

Ivory, when you find her, take her way away out, out of Italy – not to Asia, not to the pirates, somewhere out, out, out – beyond the rim: maybe apple orchards, or the wide wide rivers ... they stand on one leg in their little boats, the brilliant birds are all about them. Cluck-cluck, they are saying, cluck. ...

6 On the Road North

Lanuvium is a Latin town, twenty miles south of Rome and about two hundred and sixty miles north-west of the Lucanian ranges. A well-to-do place, very much in support of the City during the franchise war – a privileged community. I had not been long on the road towards it when I found myself having an unsought conversation with the intelligence-squad staff-serjeant I had run up against earlier. He was now, it seemed, in billets, upon the line of communication, and he was making it his business to ask all manner of questions of all manner of travellers.

'I hope you've got something to tell me, god you're the worse for wear, man, wherever you've been.'

I reminded myself we were ten miles from any fighting: their information was likely to be at least as far away from any truth. Of course, the first thing he wanted to know: had I identified God's-hope? Then, where was the nigger woman? What units had I come up against in which mountains, and how was the terrorist picture? He'd been pulled out of the line for a few days for briefings at HQ, now he was about to return into action: and as usual he badly needed hard facts.

Oh, easy to tell you I spun him another yarn, sent the army on a wild-goose chase all the wrong way – courage, nobility, resourcefulness, solidarity of the unbreakable resistance, all of that, so easy. Advantageous to me, too. Recoup my reputation with posthumous readers. Alas, no advantage in my letting you know how badly I desired to betray God's-hope to these Romans. *That* would have been the easy thing for me to do just at that time.

The constitutional lawyer, his taste for majestic Aeschylus, his unwavering determination to reject all form of compromise lest it somehow convince him that City government might sometimes govern in the interests of some of its dominated subject people: this man, as I travelled, had hung hour after hour, day-long, night-long, in the pit of my imaginings, had hung upon his gallows-cross like a putrefying skull pinned up against the wall of a disordered abandoned stable. With my stick in his hands he had beaten Cuttlefish to death – a delayed death, deferred death, there were other factors, oh yes – I didn't want to argue. It was *his* hand.

I would now tell City intelligence all they wanted to know.

I had seen God's-hope's sentinels, been led over his escape-route, visited his safe-house: surely more than sufficient to secure his immediate capture. I would tell: and he would hang. In the pit of my imaginings, the nails crashed into him, sinew and bone.

Then he (the serjeant) made a mistake. They had brought me the bean-soup he had called for, there was mutton-offal in it: he cracked a nondescript soldier's joke about lions chewing God's-hope's genitals. Now I would not care if they served him to the wild beasts: *except for the fact* that I had dreamed of him on the cross. His skull in my mind had been the Roman skull he'd thought appropriate to Darius Emperor: his death linked thereby, I suppose, to the death of my Cuttlefish. Lions had nothing to do with it. I can't tell you by what quirk of vindictive thought I had settled for nails or nothing: but settled I had, and I was now thrown off-balance.

And, once off-balance, I began to consider. My hatred for God's-hope was personal, directly personal. Revenge.

And wrapped up with personal revenge, a general rage against his fanatical intransigence, an intransigence I associated with Cuttlefish ever since she was first *taken*, in the theatre of the Walls of Love, no – further back, ever since Irene put it to me I was unduly delaying her liberation. When I told her she was a free woman, had she flung herself into my arms? And what about Irene? Put in her thumb and pull out King Strychnine's plum – me, of course, who else? But both of these women, gone from me, dragged from me, through no fault of my own. Relief combined with grief, in both cases: bereavement with liberation: horror with – with nothing. I had hated the pair of them, I loved them both beyond measure.

I had promised, I would find the child. If all was true. But could I *love* the child, now, after such confusion of lost love? This would be shown to me, in due course. First, I must search for her. I could not even have begun to search had God's-hope not made it possible. And I hated him: and here I had my chance to destroy him.

Let me be responsible (out of character, but nevertheless) and look at the public grounds – beyond the personal – for taking this chance. His terrible continued Lucanian war – oh but the effects of it, I had seen them. The land had a right to be granted some peace, at last. Of course, it was not *my* land (which was full of Strychnine and the Stain, don't think about *that*): its suffering strictly no business of mine. But if I could conclude the suffering by giving the information – surely better for the world at large I should do so, here and now.

And yet, the man said 'lions'. 'Lions' was the Roman Games, the disgusting intruder with the face and fangs of Jampot that sat down stage-centre in the very theatre that had been my life ever since I first heard Irene and generous Chloe clamouring in libidinous counterpoint for Herostratus and his torch. 'Lions' would not do.

And now I came to think of it, the gallows-cross would not do either. What about those dripping crosses directly above the orchestra of the theatre in the Walls of Love? Streaks of blood, shit, and liquidated flesh trickling down the high-town crags to where we tried to make the people laugh . . .?

If God's-hope's hand with my stick in it had murdered my Cuttlefish, it was the City after all that had wielded that hand.

No: I would not tell them anything: let them find their own enemies whatever way they could, and if they could not find them, let them live with them still alive. So I prevaricated with this serjeant, said that Cuttlefish was dead and the prisoner she had been brought to see had not been God's-hope at all.

'She's dead . . .?' He was incredulous. 'She can't be dead. Look here, for godsake think about it. All right, she may not have found him, but she knows him, don't she, that's unique: hardly anyone outside the mountains can be absolutely sure what the bastard looks like, we don't even know the name he had, the town he came from, before he went on the run against us. That nigger was unique, Hercules-god, she can't be dead! Why, the man that had her in his pocket, it could be worth – it could be worth, why bloody thousands to him.'

I understood, all in a flash, that ever since our first meeting he had been cursing himself for his stupidity in letting us go: had chewed over and over throughout his frustrated work on the possibilities of once again running across the Cuttlefish: he was consumed with irrational avarice at the very notion of her. And now, without a second thought, I had told him the useless truth.

Then I bore in mind again how Jampot disregarded the true tale that Miriam told him, because on principle in the intelligence service the truth was never true. Would this be the case here? Yes, it was. For he said, 'All right, play it cautious, why not, it's your trade. But don't think I'm not capable of making it worth your while.' 'Worth my while' was enough money to get me to Lanuvium. I named a figure. His eyes glistened and he began to beat me down a few percent. He was talking of government funds, not his pay-packet, so he didn't try very hard. We settled at an adequately split difference.

So then I spun him the wild-goose yarn I ought to have done half-an-hour ago, according to the poets of nobility. Plausible, realistic; he checked it out by maps and papers he called for from the operations room. I invented a captain who had taken delivery of Cuttlefish.

'Marcus Claudius? Don't know him. Hey – any of you in there heard of an M. Claudius, captain, attached staff-duties to the Fourteenth?' Nobody had, which bothered him for a moment (and *me* for more than a moment, I hadn't expected all this checking). Then he thought it out and solved it. 'Ah, yes, of course, on secondment very like from the Twenty-fourth, I'd heard they were shovelling some of 'em around like that, bloody rubbish – god but the Twenty-fourth haven't known arse-from-elbow since God's-hope's gang broke 'em last month at the Ram's Horn Fork. And *that's* all to the good, begod, no shit-head from the Twenty-fourth'll have the least idea what to do with your nigger-bint: I'll fix a deal with him easy as wanking, and after that she's all mine!'

Comradely hopes between us of further co-operation once my present assignment was completed ... and so north, with adequate funds, to Lanuvium.

7   *Gracelady*

He was an old and dreary pedant, or rather he would have been if he had not, in his decrepit age, become unexpectedly besotted with this tiny little copper-skinned black-eyed black-haired maiden he had rescued from the war. He was a self-inflicted eunuch, like so many of the goddess's servants, and had never known the warmth of family affections, at least not since his own childhood so many years before. His vocation at the temple had confined him to office and library, he had had no contact with the children who were cared for there: he had, I believe, astonished himself by the fierce determination developing into love with which he carried her through the war-zone and the starving mountains till he fetched her to this place of safety. He named her Gathered-Up-Alive-By-The-Grace-Of-Our-Lady, pious but unduly circumstantial. To him, in their intimacy, she was Gracelady: to everyone else, just Grace.

A distant relative, now deceased, had owned land near Lanuvium: this had been inherited by Cluilius, and – now he had no temple settlement to live and work in – he was free to settle down here and await his death upon a comfortable income. I found him in an unpretentious cottage on the outskirts of the town: he was sitting in a folding-chair in his garden, pretending to read, watching the sun go down, and watching his little Gracelady playing ball with her nurse among the bushes, the last game of the day before she was whisked protesting off to bed.

I leaned upon the gate, unnoticed, and took in the whole scene.

The child was eventually caught by the nurse, laughing and struggling, brought to the archivist for a trembling old man's embrace, and taken into the house. I waited for a minute or two, assembling my feelings – don't ask me what they were: I felt as though I had been watching Cuttlefish before the Antioch agents had laid hands on her in her African village, and all the clarity of what I was to say to Cluilius had been swept out of my head. Then I plucked up courage and entered the garden.

I was not a very presentable figure, to be sure. My clothes were those of a southern farmer of only moderate means, and travel-worn at that: moreover a farmer with the shifty unreliable 'Syrian' demeanour that so many Latins at once took note of. I held in my hand the two clay tablets.

'Sir,' I began, 'I have reason to believe that these documents are the work of your hand?' He blinked mildly at me, took the tablets, and held them close to his rheumy old eyes.

'Oh, yes,' he replied, 'it would seem so . . . you have been to the temple? Tell me, is it true? The whole place is all utterly in ruins . . .?' I nodded. He looked at them again.

He took in the particular message they conveyed. His soft round white features sagged with apprehension, he half rose in his chair, and then feebly sat down again, his mouth opening and shutting with sudden distress of breathing.

'What do you want? Why do you come here? You have come for the child? You have authority? From the government? You are – not the *police* . . .!'

'No, no, no-no – ' I tried to reassure him, but he did not listen.

'I have done nothing wrong, she is the property of the

goddess – I have done nothing more than bring her out of
danger, I never had part, nor did the temple have part, in
any of the rebellion, we were only concerned to give worship
to the goddess; and the medical work, to all who needed it
. . . *please* . . .!' He fell forward onto the grass and knelt at
my feet. It was dreadful. I had expected he would assume I
was some kind of commercial tout, a confidence-trick man,
a shyster lawyer: but that I should seem a secret-police
operative had never entered my head. Of course, I was
now about as old as my father had been when I left home,
and I ought to have borne in mind the impression that *he*
would have made . . .

I took hold of Cluilius's hands, as gently as I could, raised
him from his knees, sat him quietly in his chair, squatted
beside him, as submissively as I could, and began to explain.
Explain some of it, anyway. How I was a member of a
theatrical troupe scattered by the rebellion, how Cuttlefish
and I had been separated in our flight from the Walls of
Love, how I took two whole years to discover what had
happened to her. (I missed out pirates, witch-wives, Mule-
driver, and all of that: it would only have confused him.) I
did tell him she was dead. He stared at me helplessly.

'And you say that you think you are her father . . .? You
have come here to claim her? To take her away from me?
You have seen her?' I told him, yes, just now, just this
evening: I was sure she was her mother's daughter.

He said, 'Sir, I remember her mother. Not my business
as the archivist to be in and out of the hospital or orphanage
very much, but that lady, I do remember. No-one knew
what to do with her, she knew nothing of where she was
when they brought her in, the gynaecological complications,
I recollect, were extreme. Besides, as she was an Ethiopian,
we were all naturally curious: how could she have come to
the place where she was found? By the shepherds, I believe,
on the upper ranges. Extraordinary. The surgical task, unprecedented, as you know: had it happened in normal peace-
time, the temple would have been able to achieve great
renown from its publication, but, alas . . . She had money
and some jewels, which, when she was in part recovered,
she insisted on paying to our treasurer as a recompense,

and a dowry for little Gracelady: she was to be brought up to serve the temple, while the mother – the mother, I think, kept saying she had work to do elsewhere – the draining of blood . . .? Oh a fearful thing for her to say so often, we supposed she was disturbed in her mind about the operation carried out on her, we felt she should not be allowed to depart in such a condition: but she would have none of it and she took herself off despite all argument. The priestess who cut her open was exceedingly distressed: and often talked about her afterwards. Then the battle came into the valley and all our life and work was finished.

'But now, what will you do? If I do not let you have the child, you will claim her at law? You have proof of your paternity?' He peered at me very sharply: oh indeed he was an archivist, he knew the worth of documents, he was not going to let the case slide by default, so much was very clear.

'No, sir, I have no proof. I can therefore lay no claim.' I thought it best to be direct – can a man who looks like a Syrian ever hope to appear honest to a Latin? – but I would try. 'She believes she is your daughter – '

He smiled, for the first time: 'Not quite, she calls me grandfather; when she is old enough to learn what a eunuch is, I will explain I am really a grand-uncle, I suppose. I have no wish to present myself other than I am.'

'Nevertheless, sir, she believes you are her kinsman and her guardian, and it seems from what I saw that she is happy in your care. I have not had good luck: I am certainly not capable of maintaining her in any security. I cannot see reason why I should endeavour to force her from you. I would, however, wish to be brought to get to know her – for the sake of her mother – and to be in a position to do what good for her I can, as soon as it is in my power.'

I had no idea what all this meant: I could foresee no immediate future for myself, least of all in Lanuvium, which was obviously a tightly-knit small town where a stranger would find it hard to establish himself from nothing at all. But now I had seen Grace, I could not turn blankly away from her – she was, as it were, an anchor for my life, if only I could find out a way to attach myself to the cable . . .

*

I must have looked as helpless as he had a few minutes before. He smiled again – relief, and some cautious complacency, perhaps – this beggarly fellow at his gate was not after all such a threat. Then his countenance straitened a little – the proprieties of the professional temple-official asserting themselves.

'You say that you and her mother were theatricals, is not that so? I do not wish to appear censorious: but I must ask, do you have any intention that at some future time she should be put upon the public stage? I could not agree to that. She is my child, unofficially, you have conceded so much indeed: officially, and I am confident the courts would uphold it, she is the servant of the goddess. Whether she marries or goes abroad, or whatever she does, she must do so with the approval of the priestly establishment. There is a temple in this town: I am very well acquainted with the ladies who administer it, they have already undertaken to become Gracelady's guardians in the event of my death – which will not be long delayed, as of course you have already calculated. The public stage, I regret to say, though an enjoyable institution for those who witness the plays, and even on occasions an opportunity for pious testimony, is not, in my poor opinion, conducive to the moral stature of those who practise its mysteries for financial reward. They are for the most part persons of servile or recently-servile status: and, whatever her ancestry, my Gracelady is now adopted into an altogether superior social caste. I do not wish to offend: I have personal intercourse of a most gracious and intellectual nature with at least one distinguished actor: but that is not at all the same thing as welcoming him as a member of my family, you do understand? I mean, even supposing my excellent friend Roscius himself were to ask me, for example, if he might be betrothed at some future date to Gracelady, I would have to tell even him – '

He went rambling on, but I caught at the name. 'Roscius? You know *Roscius*!'

'Certainly. He was born quite near this town and he still maintains a household here, though for the most part he is on tour or at work in the City. You are aware of his reputation?'

I told him indeed I was, I was most anxious to see him again, was there any possibility – ?

'Certainly: you are in luck, he is in Lanuvium now, he is even mounting a show at the theatre here – well, they call it a theatre, though for those of us who have lived in the south, it is perhaps something of a makeshift affair, though Roscius has in mind, I believe, to subsidize its improvement once the civil disorders have died down. There is, you see, no certainty about government in the City, Lucius Cornelius Sulla put all his own people into offices of power, but since he has departed to the Pontic war, it is feared that once again the 'new crowd' – such a vulgar phrase – will achieve dominance and we shall all be thrown, once again, into turmoil and confusion, oh dear I do hope not . . . Excuse me, I digress. I was asking you your intentions about Gracelady: sir, I must know.'

In the end I agreed with him that I would make no formal claim, that I would not go against the wishes of the priestesses, that I would in return be allowed to get to know the child, but as a friend, not a father, and that he would not prevent me devoting some of my fortune – assuming I ever earned any ever again – to her upbringing, no strings attached. All this to be written down, signed and sealed, in presence of a lawyer, and of one of the ladies from the local temple, and all to be conditional on the absence of any other claimant to the parentage – after all I had no proof even that Cuttlefish was dead, only God's-hope could help me there, I could hardly bring *him* into the discussion. It was little enough to have travelled all those miles for: but I did feel that old Cluilius was more or less persuaded that I was who I said I was.

Perhaps the very thinness of my story had helped to convince him: no confidence-man would have come so shallowly prepared to cheat him out of – well, out of what? He could not think of a motive for my deceiving him: and therefore he was disposed to believe.

I promised I would return the next evening, and bade him a most respectful good-night. I did respect him, too: he was something of a saint, the poor old gelding: and

besides, I had seen the pathetic ruins of the Lucanian
temple he had loved and served so devotedly. I spent the
night at a cheap inn. In the morning I went straight to the
theatre.

8   *The Incomparable Roscius*

Just as he had said, it was something of a makeshift – a
horseshoe-shaped fenced enclosure on a slope running up
to the base of the town walls. The seating was boards raised
on timber scaffolds, and the stage-house a combination of
wooden hut and gaily-coloured pavilion. The scaffolds were
just now being re-erected after storage under cover since
the last presentation. Carpenters swarmed all over the site,
carrying planks and rolls of canvas, hammering nails, stretching ropes, chasing inquisitive children.

A large banner announced: 'The Incomparable Roscius:
with his Unparalleled Comedians: by Special Request of
the Mayor and Corporation of this Peerless Artist's Native
Town . . .' etcetera. The show was to be in three days' time,
and would include – could I believe my eyes – 'for the first
time upon any Italian Stage, the Exotic Eastern Dance-
ritual of the Syrian Sisters!' There were several more
advertized items, of course, but none of the others meant
anything to me.

The whole thing was clearly to be a big municipal occasion, and expense (comparatively-speaking) no object. One
of the carpenters told me it was in honour of the mayor's
birthday. He also told me that none of the actors was here
this morning, because of the technical preparations, though
he was sure Roscius would put in an appearance, it being
well-known that he never left anything to chance. 'But he's
a bright lad and no denying of it: and most of what he
wants isn't as daft as what it seems, not in the long run
anyway, when once you've come to realize he had it all in his
mind from the start and was there, you might say, half-an-
hour before the rest copped on.'

I sat in the sun and waited, watching the busy scene with
almost unbearable nostalgia. Suddenly, from the battle-
ments high up behind the seating-tiers, a well-remembered

stentorian voice: 'Petronius, oh Petronius, if you hang that banner where you're hanging it, it will flap right into the eyes of His Worship the Mayor and all he'll be able to see of *me* upon the upper stage'll be two shapely legs and one cheek of an arse! Pursue the other actors, if you must, with your practical criticism; prudence alone, my dear, dictates that your manager should be exempt!' Everyone broke into laughter, the shame-faced stage-hand made haste to re-position the offending flag: and Roscius, younger and more athletic than ever, leapt down from the wall to the top of the scaffold, and thence with great graceful bounds to the middle of the orchestra. I stood up and moved slightly into his way, unaccountably nervous. Surely he would not have forgotten me? But surely, if reminded of me, in his own town, in pride and fame among his childhood companions and present-day worshippers, he would not care to acknow-ledge me? If only I could have brought to this reunion an equivalent celebrity? Oh god I was so little removed from a beggar: but I did try to adopt not too much of a mendicant attitude; my walking-stick, my dismal clothes notwith-standing.

Of course, I did him an injustice. He recognized me at once, checked in his rapid stride, swivelled on his heel, and thrust both hands into mine with a cry of apparently un-diluted delight. Swept immediately into a flood of his im-pressionistic Greek – 'Ivory, you are well come, oh my friend, how so much in the nick you have arrived, look here now, no time to waste, all is hell-bent in Lanuvium, His Worship the Mayor, incredible birthdays, splendour and debauchery, untold liberalities of our cultural largesse, oh Ephesus and the Stain's gala all over again! Look here now, you must help me, no better man in all Italy, the very man I was remembering ever since all this hulla-balloo began, straightaway let me tell you all that we need you to do . . .!' He took me by the hand, rushed me into the greenroom, whipped a parcel of documents out of his satchel, spread them with a flourish of his hands along a wide trestle table. Cast-lists, costume-invoices, stage-manager's property-schedules, pieces of script, rehearsal-times, musical-arrangements, indecipherable pages of cues.

'Without paper-work, my dear friend, I am perished like the beasts of the sea: my assistant has malaria – calls it malaria – the venereal pox, for heaven's sake, and don't tell me I don't know where he caught it – but hush, we must not say so: dear friend, you are my saviour, please tell me you will have all this damn nonsense in order before dinner-time, of course you will!' I stopped him short before he could go any further.

'Roscius, I must come straight with you. I – I don't have any money – I mean, no money at all. I stayed last night at *The Golden Chariot* and I don't even dare go back because I haven't enough for the bill . . .'

'Money?' he said, 'Money?' – his squint eye revolved, and for an instant I feared the worst – 'Did you not hear what I said to you? Ivory, it is the mayor's *birthday*. Lanuvium is *unbounded* –it had better be, or most-famous-son-of-this-town will know the reasons why! Here – we'll send a boy to pay the grasping hostelry, despatch your baggage to *my* house: guest of Roscius, companion-friend to the Incomparable and Unparalleled: and on my payroll head-of-the-list, as from this immediate instance! Oh oh, but you will reproach me: I have had to do terrible things to our old darlings the Sisters Syrian – Cato-nonsense like as always: they will be dancing in opaque breech-clouts! But here at the theatre only – in the house of Roscius they are themselves alone!'

Later on, in the midst of our work, he said, suddenly, in a sombre tone: 'I am finished with the Stain, you know that? All concluded. He has married again. For love? For money? A great rich bitch of a senator's divorced lady, and ho on the spot and at once, pitched out-of-house all boys girls and inbetweens that made him the human being – oh head-over-heels, the pack of us, my goodness, she saw to that, sharp! And, do you know, all this blood-drinking march-upon-Rome, surrender-the-power-or-die – to tell truth, I did *not* care for it, not at all a happy affair and terrible bad for the comedy-business . . . But maybe one day he comes home and forgives all round. Until then, my own resources; and be damned to his damn patronage.'

And then again, towards the end of the day, as we were packing up and making ready to leave the theatre: 'Oh but god I am so selfish, I ask you nothing about your own people – Irene, my tight little gutter-rat: and your – Cuttlefish, yes? – with the round round head upon that neck of hers like a great tall vase of glorious black treacle – where are they? Alive and joyful?'

I told him, at length. He put his arm around me, and said he would come with me to see Cluilius this very moment, there would certainly be something he could help do for me about Grace . . . 'Dear Ivory, do not distress: we are in comedy, both of us always, and in comedy above everything there must be always the Happy End . . .!'

9   The Happy End?

How different the manner of Cluilius when I came to him arm-in-arm with Roscius! I daresay he had been sceptical – and who could blame him? – of my so suddenly-proclaimed acquaintance with the famous actor. But now, it was all made clear – I was flattered and deferred to, not a mention any more of the moral and social deficiencies of the profession. Instead we talked at large about this playwright and that performer, and regretted most profoundly the debased tastes of the City, as opposed to the more enlightened practice in the south. My accounts of the Asian theatre were listened to with admiration, and I was careful to expatiate upon the generosity of the Stain when he came into Ephesus – I had already deduced Cluilius as something of a partisan of the 'old crowd', in so far as he troubled himself about politics at all. Certainly his years in Lucania had bred in him little sympathy for the aspirations of CRAC: and I kept strictly quiet about God's-hope and his associates.

Roscius then very discreetly led the conversation round to Gracelady and her future. The old man – who had set before us a hospitable side-table of shortcake and sweet wine – was profuse in his apologies that he had not yet sent for her to meet us – she was out for the afternoon with her nurse, visiting some little friends of her own age. I thought it probable he had arranged this on purpose, and that the meeting in an hour or so between myself and the lawyer and priestess was designed to take place without any emotional confusions caused by the presence of its principle subject.

But Roscius being there created quite a new situation for him, and he immediately had a servant running down the lane to fetch Gracelady home, all muddy and sticky as she was.

Well, what can I tell you about what I did and said then? There is not much a strange adult can accomplish with a child of two, except ask her silly riddles and bump her up and down on his knee, let her play with his walking-stick – ride-a-cock-horse-to-King-Tarquin's-house – all that sort of thing. Roscius was a good deal better at it than I was, and he had the sense to buy a handful of sweets which he surreptitiously passed to me, so that I could give them to Grace as if I were the one who had thought of them. Moreover he started her off on a series of singing-rhymes, which she loved – he had after all the advantage of having met her and played with her before – and this was something I could handle very adeptly myself, once I understood what was required. It was not so very different from the shantyman's job on the *Lady Jael*.

The old archivist sat watching it all with his dreamy benign smile, now and then interspersing one of his strange dry little jokes into the conversation, which always dissolved Grace into paroxysms of laughter. He also had a complicated geometrical game with her, involving clothes' pegs and bits of string, and howls of delight each time an amazing new shape was created from an apparently irresoluble tangle.

Then the lawyer was announced, a sharp precise person, very acute towards the interests of his client Cluilius: and, shortly after his arrival, a sedan was brought into the garden, containing the priestess. She was not at all like her opposite number in the Walls of Love, being a stout sensual lady in early middle-age, curled, perfumed, and vaguely benevolent, extremely sentimental towards Grace, and given to elegant gestures of her fleshy white ring-laden fingers.

After some preliminary chit-chat, Grace was sent off to bed – good-night kisses all round, a promise of a bedtime story from me, once our business was over (I had advanced far into her favour, thanks to the good work of Roscius) – and then we all sat round with our wine and looked at one another.

During this slightly embarrassed pause, I glanced towards Roscius, and was startled to see the Raven.

Now I note here and mark it as a significant fact, that this was the very last occasion the Raven has appeared to me up to the time of writing. RIP.

He said, in the Greek of Roscius (we were in 'cultural' Lanuvium, and there was also the specific courtesy towards me): 'You see, my dear Cluilius, the late wife of our good friend Ivory was a very very dear person to me, oh yes she was. And an artist of – oh, such astonishment and perceptions – all Asia was euphoric for her: I have directed her myself there and I know so well her quality! Why, Lucius Sulla, magnanimous patron, had no eyes for any other when she was commanding the stage. And you well understand *his* judgements in these things.' (Indeed they did: very obvious that the name carried great weight in the best circles here.) 'Such tragedy that in the south towns she was fated to display her talents – in very stomach of this terrible war! She was of course from Africa, and her husband from – Sardis?'

'Pergamus,' I corrected him.

'Ah yes, it makes small difference: I put only the position that neither of them at all Italian, not even of the City, cosmopolitan though it may now be. Is it not—I do put it so forcible, my dear friend Cluilius, because I desire you should understand – is it not therefore most appropriate that her darling child should in the end be returned to her own people?'

'To *Africa* . . .?' – the priestess, in a horrified tone.

'Oh no no, dear madame, oh not at all to Africa! I mean only to the company of the artists among whom she was conceived and born, or would have been born had this terrible war not destructed all our comradeships. I am not too

easy about bringing this truth into the consideration – '
(dropping his voice, very wise and discreet) ' – but we have
seen the dear child, her complexion; the *sculpture*, shall I
say, of her sweet features . . . Now; for a Latin citizen of
pride and good lineage, who seeks perhaps a wife for his
fortunate son: should you suppose a girl so – *dark*. . . .' He
let his voice trail away and his hands described the elaborate
parabola I had last seen when he played the Uxorious Usurer
in Ephesus.

Cluilius frowned. 'Do you suggest, sir, that my Gracelady
would be scorned? You have surely a poor idea of the taste
and discrimination of the families with whom I consort.
They would be aware of *my* name: and I cannot think they
would look any further.'

'Of course, of course, yes . . . but we are speaking, are we
not, of some fifteen years ahead . . .?'

Cluilius frowned again, this time with more sadness than
resentment. 'I know what you mean, you mean I shall be
dead, forgotten very probably, and my pretty Gracelady
must fend for herself *as* herself, oh I know what you mean.
Perhaps I would rather not have had to take such a circumstance into consideration. But, on the other hand, our dear
lady, the holy priestess . . .'

The priestess smiled and shrugged: 'Of course we would
do everything to facilitate the child's prospects, but there *is*
a certain truth . . . There would of course be no reason why
she should not be enrolled as a liturgical virgin at the
temple. I understood that the mother did express such a
wish – '

The lawyer, seeing Cluilius looking very dubious at this,
decided to put in a word: 'There is actually no document to
such an effect, is not that so? You were unable, I believe,
sir, to carry away the archives in your haste to rescue the
child from the war-zone, is not that so?'

Now indeed, it had been so: and indeed Cluilius knew
that it was so no longer.

I had brought him the very tablets and had left them, the
previous evening, in his possession – I had had no choice,
he was after all as archivist their official curator. I opened
my mouth to say so – I had nothing to gain from petty

deceptions here – and he saw me open my mouth. He held up a tremulous hand, motioning me to silence. His own mouth opened and shut in short indecision, which he covered by clearing his throat, coughing, wiping his eyes: then he made up his mind.

'No,' he said, 'No. There are no documents that have any bearing upon that. This young man brought me *one* tablet that says simply that I conveyed such and such a new-born child towards this place upon such a date. By comparison with the calendar and – with other evidences – he was able to discover that the child must have been his. But that is all.'

'Then in that case,' pronounced the lawyer, 'it seems clear that if you are prepared to accept this gentleman as the father, it is entirely up to yourselves what arrangements you make for the little girl's upbringing. You have no written pledge to the temple here, I take it?'

'An oral understanding,' said the priestess, 'There has certainly been that. Our respected Cluilius expressed a definite intention that upon his death the child should be placed in the temple's care, with a commensurate dowry. I can hardly believe he would wish to go back upon his word, I have always known him as a most honourable gentleman.'

'Madame,' said Cluilius gravely, 'you need have no fear. But supposing that upon reflection I have come to the conclusion that the girl is not after all entirely suited to the religious life, you would surely not desire me to impose it upon her willy-nilly? But please be assured, absolutely assured, that in no case will the dowry, or an equivalent donation, or an even more extensive donation, be omitted from my will. I am, after all, a man of means.'

'Oh, in *that* case . . .' said the priestess, waving all her twelve rings, and smiling with much relief. And that was all that she said.

In a remarkably short time we had reached complete agreement. Cluilius was to look after Grace until he died or became too infirm. If I were within reach at such a time, I – her acknowledged father – would immediately assume her care and custody. If I were not within reach – here I had to

pretend my theatrical services were in constant demand –
then the priestess would accept temporary guardianship
until she could get in touch with me. Roscius interrupted –
'But surely no difficulty: Ivory and I are to become partners, at all times where I am, dear Ivory will be within my
call!'

He winked at me – 'not to comment!' I was altogether too
flabbergasted to have done so, in any case . . .

If Gracelady wished to embark on a theatrical career at
the age, say, of fourteen, then no obstacle was to be placed
in her way.

The lawyer drew up an appropriate document, which was
signed by all three parties, and witnessed by Roscius and a
neighbour called in especially for the purpose.

We then dispersed, amid great protestations of mutual
esteem. I went into the house and told Grace her promised
story – she was sitting up wide awake waiting for it with an
insistent faith in my reliability (no anti-Syrian prejudice for
her). The story was about a little black girl who lived by a
great wide river where tall men stood on one leg in small
boats and speared the fishes.

I found it hard to express my gratitude to Cluilius. He
found it hard to respond to my expressions. We stammered at
each other, clasped hands, and muttered something about
seeing each other again tomorrow. The old man was greatly
upset. It occurred to me, with a new force, that he could
not have long to live, that it might be a matter of days
rather than months or years.

Then Roscius, not any more the Raven, took me to his house
in the middle of town. Miriam, Rachel and Abigail were his
guests. We found them sitting round a table, sewing beads
upon their new costumes (the regrettable Cato-clouts). We
embraced, and we laughed, we shed tears, and we drank wine;
and we danced, in the new costumes, and the old costumes,
and, by the end of the evening (which was very disgraceful
after such serious emotions) in more or less no costumes at all.

Happy End . . .?

I wish I could say so.

It is true that throughout the winter and the following

spring I lived in Lanuvium, in Roscius's sumptuous house, and worked hard as his partner in all his theatrical ventures. On tour; in Lanuvium itself; and, at least once a month, in the City, where Roscius still hoped to found a regular theatre, and where he was embarking on an ambitious pro- gramme of training young apprentices for a permanent re- pertory company – without which, he held, any talk about theatre-*buildings* would only be so much 'piss-and-bull'.

But all this vigorous activity was constantly over- shadowed by political instability. We worked in hope, but without confidence, which is not a good state of affairs. If there is one thing the theatre requires for the development of its energies, it is some sense of security of status: and no- one that year in the City could enjoy any such luxury.

Rumours all the time, about the government, the war in the east, the Mule-driver on his travels, the Samnite-Luca- nian war, any of them any day sufficient to cause contractors to fail in deliveries of promised material, performances to be cancelled by official decree, visiting artists to cry off. More about these rumours later.

In my private life, I was indeed happy, as happy as a man can be whose bereavement is assuaged by the constant close companionship of the child of his loins: I mean, every time I talked to, or played with, Gracelady, I saw the Cuttlefish, or heard her: I cannot say for certain whether that made for happiness or grief.

Cluilius died at mid-winter, during the raucous seasonal festival: he had dressed up in one of our theatre costumes and masks to impersonate the red-cloaked old man who comes in through the house-roof to give the children their annual presents. Gracelady seemed absolutely to believe in this mystic visitor – the Latins call him Old Saturn – but, as Cluilius had had half the mask cut away so that she would not be frightened (most of his face was thus clearly visible), we could not be sure she did not recognize him. But, if she did, it was as a Cluilius metamorphosed on purpose to offer her a very special kind of relationship, and that meant she had to take care not to let him know that she knew who he was . . .

He had danced around the room with her, had sung her a

mid-winter song, had sat her on his knee and let her feed him with currants and hot cider: and then he had said simply, 'Old Saturn is tired, my dear: I had to travel so far to get here over all the mountains, you won't mind if I go to sleep . . .?' He lay down on his couch, and his life stopped.

His little girl from that moment was my little girl, a circumstance she accepted with surprisingly small distress. It made perfect sense to her that when Old Saturn – or, for that matter, Grandfather – was tired, he would have to go to sleep; and a new person, a Father, would be in charge till he woke up. For a long time she talked to me about him from this point of view – 'When Grand-dad has had his rest, Daddy, we shall go on the picnic,' or, 'when Grand-dad comes out of his sleeping-house he will take me to see the dancing bear?' (the 'sleeping-house' being an austere marble tomb the old man had built for himself beside the post-road not far from his own garden gate) – but eventually she accustomed herself to the idea that there would be no more Cluilius: and she snuggled up close to me with exactly the same soft warmth of affection that her mother had once shown.

Cluilius bequeathed the old nurse to me in his will. I brought the nurse and Gracelady to live with me in Roscius's house: when we were out of town the priestess at the temple would take them both in, and spoil the child dreadfully. She was in many ways a silly cow, the priestess, and greedy moreover: but her kindness to children could not be faulted. I trusted her completely with Gracelady.

Oh yes, all this was happy. But in no wise was it an ending.

10   Rumours and Truth

The political rumours. Some of them were true. All of them were frightening. Here is what I think happened, then, and later in the year, with most of the distortions, propagandist claims, and misunderstandings omitted.

When the Stain had left Italy to go and fight against King Strychnine, he had had to ensure that the City's government was going to remain loyal to him, the more so as Mule-driver had slipped out of his clutches. But the men he had placed in charge of affairs (through manipulation of the elections) had been faced with an impossible duality of political tasks.

(a) They had had to restore as much of the 'old crowd's' traditional legislation – subverted by Mule-driver's season of power – as was practical:

(b) They had had to mop up the last vestiges of the Italian war.

Task (b) could only be accomplished by further (and extreme) concessions – I knew this to be true from my own observations of the Lucanian resistance – while task (a) necessarily involved a 'firm stand' against any more softening of the rigorous attitude of central government towards the subject peoples.

At the same time, the City masses had gained great benefits (at least, they thought they had) from the 'new crowd's' social measures, and any interference with these 'historic proletarian rights', as they were now termed by the faction-bosses, was bound to arouse furious resentment. The result was, within a year, the Stain's nominees nearly all lost their positions at the annual polls for office: and, of the two newly-elected consuls, who were supposed to hold the City safe to his interest, one was an overt enemy, and the other (Gnaeus Octavius) a verbose trimmer who had for the time being staked his reputation on the legal validity of the 'old crowd's' constitutional views – he was always doing this, and indeed was notorious for the number of ambiguous juridical precedents he was able to invoke within five lines of a peroration.

The overt enemy was called 'Ashes', and looked it. I saw him once, at the City's temporary theatre when he officially graced one of Roscius's performances. He did not laugh throughout the entire comedy. His deathly-white face, with deep-set eyes like two holes punched into a paper bag, seemed to float in the midst of the audience, a smudge of some noxious vapour. Upon taking office, he had been compelled, by the terms of a mutual-blackmail deal hashed up between himself and the Stain's faction, to take a powerful and ancient oath that in no way would he oppose the Stain's intentions. This was quite illegal: and of course he did not consider himself bound by it.

So as soon as it became clear that the Strychnine war was going to be a lengthy and toilsome affair, Ashes began proceedings in the City to *depreciate* the Stain's supporters. The vapidity of his colleague Gnaeus Octavius made it all the easier for him to do this. Some of his attempts were through the courts and the legislature. Others involved extensive deployment of secret police and security-enforcement, arrests, confiscation of property; and also some murders. The murders struck terror among everyone ('old crowd' or 'new') because of their inexplicably random nature. The authorities ascribed them to 'bandit elements', sometimes: at other times to 'politically-motivated anti-constitutional terrorist groups'. The respectable townsfolk of Lanuvium were fully persuaded the killings were committed by members of the security-enforcement in order to deter any sort of public utterance or debate upon political matters.

Cluilius's lawyer, for instance, was one of the victims. He was found early one morning, head down in a horse-trough in the town square. His body was covered with bruises, and marks in the manure around the trough showed that he had been dragged there by at least two men. A more sober person never lived: but the police-superintendent said he must have fallen in and drowned while under the influence of drink. No-one chose to comment on this ridiculous verdict, not even Roscius, who was commonly very free in his speech. The funeral was attended only by immediate relatives: and we all felt extremely ashamed.

Then, a few days later, Roscius informed me in a nervous whisper that three houses – one in the City and two in the neighbouring countryside – that belonged to the Stain had unaccountably burnt to the ground. The Stain's wife and children had left Italy – no-one knew their destination, but it was assumed they had gone to join her husband at the Asian front. This meant that before long the Stain would be coming home again *and with his army*, Strychnine or no Strychnine, to avenge himself upon somebody.

*

The two consuls – who for months had done their best to avoid one another, both politically and personally – now fell into open feud. There was an outbreak of uncontrolled rioting – the faction-bosses seemed to have lost all ability to keep it contained within the usual small area of the City among the usual semi-professional class of subsidized activists. Ashes, whose partisans were routed all up and down the seven hills, fled south: to raise an army.

He fled through Lanuvium, and no-one tried to stop him, although almost the entire town was in favour of his pro-Stain rival. The reason for this apathy was the large number of self-proclaimed 'security-enforcement' men, who arrived mysteriously from nowhere to tell the townspeople that if they left their houses between sunrise and mid-day they were liable to end up in horse-troughs or worse. We accordingly stayed indoors and heard the hoofbeats thunder through. Ashes in his flight seemed to be taking with him the complete City gendarmerie, all well-mounted and clattering with so much armour they sounded like a whole kitchen of pots and pans being hurled downstairs.

Gn. Octavius, left behind and allegedly supreme, issued a long-winded declaration of the incontrovertible constitutionality of his government, and appointed a replacement consul. This man, an L. Merula (known as the 'Acolyte' from the scrupulosity of his religious observances), already occupied a priestly office that prevented him ever holding any military command: so what would happen if the Stain failed to arrive with troops and a determination to defend the state's integrity – which he had already decisively breached – by killing his fellow-citizens, no-one could tell.

After all this excitement: the next major rumour. At least, it began as a rumour, then it became an ascertained fact, and then, finally, it was announced from the City by way of the Lanuvium town hall as a *government-established* fact, which no doubt made it true. The Mule-driver had landed in Etruria, north of the City, with a large squadron of African horse, amounting to a half-regiment. He was said to have marched inland away from the City, consolidating his position, and increasing his force. He did this by liberating the inmates of several enormous convict-barracks, which

housed chain-gangs condemned to man the public works
and the great agricultural ranges of absentee noblemen.

Meanwhile in the south Ashes was reported as having
taken over command of most of the troops engaged (supposedly) against the rebels there. He also took over – or was
offered – the command of the rebels themselves: and
combined his two armies into one. The one army was
coming north. I wondered to what extent my notched penny
via God's-hope had contributed to this circumstance.

I also wondered about stories that a fleet of pirates was
cruising up and down the west coast in support of Ashes
and the Mule-driver. They had started to intercept the
City's corn-carriers on their way from Egypt and Sicily,
and people began to talk anxiously of famine. I heard of one
big galley which had been observed and chased in vain by
the Ostia coastguard: it had a figurehead of a 'wild-haired
Fury' brandishing an axe. Or was it a hammer? If a hammer,
it was surely *Lady Jael* . . .? But then again, they were
rumours: we were several miles from the sea: I had not
myself set eyes upon any of these ships.

There was fear of epidemic fever in City. There always
was, each summer, but this year it seemed to be worse.

But I was preparing myself to direct a new comedy (I
had written it all out of my own head, and Roscius had
helped me translate it into Latin – who would have imagined
I would discover such an ability?): and Grace's third birthday would very soon be upon us. We had planned a spectacular celebration: the Syrian girls were making her a complete outfit of the most gorgeous new clothes after the
fashions of Damascus. Altogether we had more than enough
to keep us busy.

The best thing to do with rumours is to remember that
they are more often false than true. The only thing to do
with true rumours is to hope that those in a position to
handle their consequences are well-equipped with both
wisdom and physical resources. I could not be confident of
either.

And I did not like to see Roscius so frightened: I had
always thought of him as totally imperturbable. But he had

long been known as the Stain's man: whereas I was the man who had been frightened *by* the Stain into wetting myself, oh I so well remembered. Maybe the one occasion for fear would, as it were, cancel out the other. Again, I had no great confidence.

11 *Nemesis in the War-meadow*

The military power of the 'new crowd' came all of a sudden upon an unprepared City. Of course it ought to have been prepared, there was no excuse whatever for the dubiously-assertive 'constitutional' authorities: and, in view of my own experiences, even less excuse for me.

I ought never to have gone there at that time, nor would I have, had I even for an hour or two had the courage to think straight: but how could I? I was with Roscius, my child was restored to me, I was beginning my life all over again, I simply could not afford to look at what I saw (or so I told myself). But nonetheless I affronted my own deepest convictions by agreeing to work with Roscius upon a re-munerative but (for me) most ominous project – a lavish programme of spectacle, pantomime and comedy in con-nection with the Civic Games: and you all know that I knew what my opinions were upon Roman Games.

The whole affair was to take place in the War-meadow, the famous parade-ground between the walls of the City and the river, long-honoured as the site from which the Pious Founder, King Romulus (a notorious fratricide), had ascended to heaven – it was also in these modern times the favourite holiday haunt of the City's pickpockets.

Roscius argued that he liked the notion of sword-fighting and the barbarities of the wild-beast shows no better than I did, but if we rejected the commission (it derived from no less a personage than the Stain's unreliable nominee, Gnaeus Octavius) we would be putting ourselves outside all hope of establishing our claim upon the Stain for a permanent theatre-building, and I knew how many years he had been struggling to that almost-attained and highly-desirable end.

I pointed out that the Stain had sent him packing. He replied that that was purely personal, that Gn. Octavius represented the *public* face of his ex-patron, and the public face had never been anything but extremely enlightened. Did I want to ruin his chances for ever by my squeamishness, we were partners, we must pull together! He did not add that I owed him a vast debt of gratitude: my own awareness of the fact closed my mouth upon further protest. I also realized that if he secured the public patronage of the Stain's consul, the renewed private friendship of the great man himself might not be long withheld, and who was I to intrude my begrudgings into so august a consummation?

At the same time I did look sharply enough to my own main chance: at last I had a hope of moderate prosperity; not too moderate, I was deluding myself, to exclude the thoughts of marriage. I had already begun to make approaches to Miriam: despite my ungainly physique, I believed her receptive – at times, it seemed, too receptive – she actually put forward the notion that I should marry Abigail and Rachel as well; they did these things in Syria, she said, Roman law was out-of-date, the eastern family was a wholly progressive institution, in Damascus it would have been out of the question for me to offer to maintain one sister without accommodating the others. I was very fond of all three of them: but there were obstacles, quite apart from the law. I would certainly need far more money than I could at present dispose of: and I did not think the exterior unanimity of the ladies was altogether reflected by total harmony within doors – when they quarrelled the roof-beams shook. I had had enough of that with Cuttlefish and Irene, thank you kindly . . .

Yes, this digression *is* chiefly due to my embarrassment at having to admit that in all these internal debates I deliberately ignored the political implications of work in Rome, just at this juncture, in direct collusion with the pro-Stain faction. We had all of us, from relief, complacency, self-induced negligence, allowed ourselves to accept as true the thoroughly misleading rumours that Mule-driver had shifted his operations to the far north, to the Po valley; that Ashes and the southern army were held up by some of Gn. Octavius's regiments on the far side of Naples: and that both of these rebel forces were thus *safely contained* (Octavius's own phrase, so consoling to his supporters).

The interminable angry queuès outside the bread-shops and the ever-growing numbers of refugees from the countryside crowding into the City should have told us a different tale. Indeed, the presence of the latter made it impossible for us to find decent accommodation during our rehearsal-period.

We were – I suppose – so preoccupied with the work that we scarcely ever wondered why we all had to cram ourselves into a pokey little apartment overlooking and inhaling the cattle-market – not only me and Roscius, but three actors (two of whom alternated, very jealously indeed, as Roscius's lovers), thé Syrians (more or less permanently attached now to our management), two servants who slept on the common landing of the stair, and a pair of Etruscan mask-makers, man and wife, who filled the place with papier-mâché and sticky pools of varnish and allowed glue to get into the cooking-pots. Gracelady was in Lanuvium, and glad I was to be that I had let her remain there, though to begin with I was chiefly concerned to keep her away from the fever (it had begun to spread in the cattle-market ward, and these tenements were very vulnerable).

But for the rest, as Roscius said, on one of his days for putting all his fears aside – 'If we all waited for the politics to lay themselves down before we got out of bed, Seven Sleepers of your Ephesus would by now be Seven Million . . .' Another way of putting my own personal opiate – do the next thing to the thing you have been doing: and I did.

There was an amount of ill-feeling between ourselves and the contractors responsible for the sword-fighting animal-gutting aspect of the Games. They were erecting a fighting-ring close beside out theatre-scaffolds – for several reasons, not least our need to rehearse without being interrupted by menagerie-officials with wheeled cages full of slavering carnivores, it was decided not to use the one structure for both purposes. But each group constantly got in the other's way, and there were disputes about the right to draw freely upon the City's supplies of timber, canvas, and so forth. This led to frequent pilfering of materials by workmen who did not want to have to go to the trouble of sending wagons through the City to the warehouses and builders' yards. This in turn led to free fights and unseemly sabotage, and the intervention of the police.

The police were under-manned, because of the defection of Ashes and his partisans, so it was agreed that some of Roscius's people should keep regular watch in the War-meadow to prevent such incidents, sleeping in our half-finished auditorium, and having a store of clubs and knuckle-dusters to hand. I was appalled by such a necessity, but Roscius airily said it was normal City practice – I didn't have to fight anyone myself, but our workmen needed a person in authority there all the time to tell them whom to beat up. Usually the stage-manager filled this role: but there came one night when he had responsibilities elsewhere, and I found myself under canvas among scantlings and scaffold-poles, with a dozen thuggish labourers sleeping like turtles all around me.

The War-meadow in the early morning is often thick with white mist that rises from the river – a great place to catch the fever – and I awoke about dawn to discover I could not see more than twenty yards in front of my hand. The workman on sentry-go was standing motionless in the fog, leaning against a dripping awning-post, his head cocked suggestively forward.

'What's the matter, do you hear anything?' I whispered in some alarm.

'I don't know,' he growled back at me, 'What do you think? There's certainly something . . .'

We both held our breaths, stood dead still, extended our ears – oh certainly something – but what?

'Nay, they'd never send *that* many o' the buggers to lift an armful of planks,' said the sentry, 'That's hundreds of boots I can hear, horses an' all, what in fuck's going on, d'you reckon?'

'Whoever it is, they're coming down the northern post-road – ' (it ran beside the War-meadow, and then turned off to the left to enter the walls) ' – but they don't seem to be going in through the gate.'

'Gate won't be bloody open, this hour of the morning: we'd have heard 'em give the challenge if anyone wanted in . . .'

Both of us knew at the same moment what was happening – our eyes met and our wet faces exchanged a vapour of cold fear. Before we could put it into words, a small shifting breeze came up, out of the hills behind the City, and the mist began to split. In five minutes the plain was clear of it, except here and there some swirling patches that hid very little. The sun was not fully up, but the grey light was more than sufficient to show us who our intruding neighbours were.

Right across the far end of the meadow, where the post-road and the river closed together its eastern and western boundaries into the point of a triangle, was a mass of armed men. They had assembled so furtively that only ourselves actually upon the meadow could have heard them, and then only because we were taking pains to keep ears open. The guards on the City walls knew nothing of their arrival until this moment of the clearing fog. A trumpet-call from the gate-tower showed us that they had seen, there was shouting and confusion there, and more trumpets from further away.

We made haste to awake our companions – 'On your feet, into the City, quick – it's an attack!' But too slow – as we took to our heels across the damp spongey ground, a group of horse-soldiers came galloping towards us and cut off our retreat. They were swarthy snarling men with large ear-rings and curved swords – Africans of some sort, I guessed: I guessed Mule-driver. But some of the infantry were correctly-uniformed City troops, and I recognized also the equipment, or semi-equipment, of Samnite-Lucanian irregulars (oh I knew all that too well), and that meant Ashes. The two rebel armies, so far apart, according to all report, had somehow managed to meet, join, and invest the secure City. From the north road alone? It seemed not. Across the river, advancing upon the far end of the wooden bridge, was another column; and the increasing wind brought a flurry of trumpets from what sounded like the north-east gate and the road that led inland towards the Sabine Hills.

*

Nobody tried to kill us. The officers we were taken to were anxious to find out about the defences and the garrison and the mood of the City's leaders. We told them all we knew, as quickly as we could, uneasily aware that it was very little indeed, and hoping that they would not think that by torture they could extract more. Fortunately they were not really interested in us; as soon as they found out who we were, and why we had been camping out in the War-meadow, they began to laugh, and promised us that if all went as well with their operations as they expected, we could put on our shows within the week as a welcome to the new government.

But they would not let us back into the City: and we had to hang around their lines, hungry and apprehensive, until the situation clarified. We sat through the hot morning under clouds of mosquitoes, watching company after company file onto the meadow from the post-road. Some of the units pitched tents while others appropriated the theatre and fighting-ring timber-stacks to reinforce their routine stockade. They made my labourers help with this, though I was excused (my bad leg, as usual). They occupied the theatre greenroom-pavilion as a temporary staff HQ: in and out of it all their officers, great bustle and demonstrative competence. I saw God's-hope, on a horse, clean-shaven, looking deadly wicked, with LLL on his shield ('Liberatio Luminosa Lucanica' – the new official designation of his regularized irregular force, it seemed). I saw Ashes, shuffling maps and personnel-rosters on a table intended for our stage-manager to work at.

And then, shortly after mid-day, I saw Mule-driver. At least I assumed it was he, from the shower of salutes from very senior ranks. He was carried across the bridge onto the meadow in a covered sedan surrounded by a shoulder-to-shoulder hedge of orderlies, scores of them, not in uniform, and of a most menacing appearance. The sedan was taken straight into the greenroom: Ashes and other officers thronged in behind it: most of the orderlies came out again and looked aggressive around the theatre's half-built stage. The curtains of the greenroom were closed: the army awaited events.

Some colour-serjeants filled in the time by setting up their banners at the corner of the stage, with stamping and shouting and all the rest of their nauseous ritual. There seemed no serious preparation for either an assault on the City or a siege: I was puzzled by the lack of action on the walls.

At last a small wicket-gate beside the main post-road gate was opened, and some horsemen rode out with a flag of truce. They dismounted, walked into the theatre, and their two officers were admitted to the greenroom. The others stayed outside in easy attitudes. I dared to approach one of them – an NCO of the City garrison – he had helped me a few days ago with an army fatigue party who came to dig a drainage ditch round our site. Fortunately he remembered who I was and did not rebuff me when I asked for information.

'No bother,' he said, 'no trouble at all, barring foul-ups: the faction-bosses have it all sorted out right-all-right, the only one inclined to stick an elbow in is down-and-out with the plague-fever – one problem is, we was expecting another week, and old Mule-driver took us a bit short this morning, right? There – d'ye hear that?' There was a muffled roar on the breeze, from somewhere inside the walls, it sounded like our daily awakening in the cattle-market. 'That'll be Law-preacher Gnaeus took away where he belongs to, right-all-right: after that, me boys – all polished and done-with, bacon and booze for all ranks . . .!' The other men of the flag-of-truce party smacked their hands together and laughed knowingly. And why not, when so very clearly the whole thing had been fixed beforehand? There was money involved here, I guessed, and big money. King Strychnine?

At last came the deputation from the City: a downcast clump of solemn notables, their gowns drawn over their heads. One of them was the Acolyte: Gnaeus Octavius was not there. A whistle blew somewhere and at once the half-built theatre was filled with a thousand or so soldiers, imperilling unreinforced scaffolds as they swarmed all over the benches. I made myself unobtrusive, underneath the scaffolds, where I could see everything on the stage without being seen myself. The Acolyte and the other senators came to the front of the orchestra, their breasts up against the stage, and waited, while the troops on the benches jeered at them.

Then the greenroom curtains opened, and Ashes emerged, to take his seat on one of two stools placed on-stage by an NCO. Some officers came after and stood in a ring behind him. Then another pause. Then a bellow from a colour-serjeant and the banners flashed up and down. Mule-driver lurched painfully out of the greenroom, supported by a young man and hemmed in by his gang of orderlies. The young man was in the battle-gear of a Celtic tribal fighter, that is to say in nothing but plaid trousers and a gold neck-ring: his face and torso were covered with outlandish patterns of blue paint.

I was nonetheless able to recognize Horsefury. His strong teeth were bared in an impacable smile, and he carried a naked sword.

He helped Mule-driver to the second stool: but the old man ignored it, remained standing at one side, upstaging everyone else, his arms grimly folded; he was a desperate and amazing sight. He wore torn and stained sailor's work-clothes, carelessly covered with a patched boat-cloak of black tarpaulin that dragged upon the ground behind him. His white beard was down to his chest and his sparse tangled hair spread over his stooped shoulders. His feet were bare and dirty, his features a dull mottled yellow with red boils breaking out of them, one eye was affected by some sort of cataract, his mouth twitched and chewed without respite.

In the shadow of the greenroom lurked some more decorous associates – Mule-driver's son, and his son-in-law, I saw: and the wraith-like figure of Silver-hair.

The exiles had returned: a dead silence hung over the crowd.

Ashes spoke first, in his horrible rasping whisper. As far as I could tell, he was informing Lucius Merula ('self-styled consul') that Gaius Marius, saviour of the state, required total annulment of the sentence passed against him, illegally;

during his absence: that until this was done, Gaius Marius, saviour of the state, six-times consul, and illegally-degraded hero of the republic, would not enter the City: that if Gaius Marius did not enter the City, the troops of Gaius Marius would: and there would be no-one to control their ferocity – for he, Ashes, would most certainly not presume. There were sufficient of the senate present to form a quorate committee. He, Ashes, had been properly elected consul and would now resume his duties. He wanted an immediate vote, please, upon the status of Gaius Marius. Oh, by the way, where was Gnaeus Octavius? He too was properly elected consul, and should be here.

A roar of laughter from the crowd, immediately silenced as Mule-driver's dreadful eyes, under the broken brim of his rascally hat, swept round the theatre.

One of the deputation stumbled into some words about the late consul Gnaeus having unfortunately lost his life during 'a tumult' that very morning. 'Murdered!' shouted Lucius Merula in a sudden shriek. Mule-driver twitched one hand about half-an-inch towards Horsefury, who stepped down among the senators: and cut off the Acolyte's head.

It bounced like a football onto the stage and fetched up against Mule-driver's unshod toes. He knocked it aside, like a football-game expert, with the slightest of kicks.

There were streaks of blood all over Roscius's new pearl-grey stage-cloth. There was blood on Mule-driver's grotesquely mis-shapen ankle, there was blood upon the white gowns of the distinguished gentlemen who had been standing beside Merula, there was a flash of gleaming blood right across Horsefury's breast.

The crowd reacted with a shocked gasp, a kind of collective catch in the throat: and then, starting with the Lucanian troopers in the topmost tiers, they began to applaud, exactly as they would have done at a play after one of Roscius's celebrated double-takes. Once again, Mule-driver's eyes travelled, once again a deathly silence.

Ashes was speaking again as though there had been no interruption. He said that if Gnaeus Octavius (consul) were dead, then an election was pending: it appeared that a quorate popular assembly might be deemed to be in session: he felt sure that in view of the urgency of the situation the Senate and People of Rome would overlook any small irregularities. Three votes, therefore, to be taken at once.

One: to repeal sentences illegally passed against Gaius Marius.

Two: to elect Gaius Marius to the consulship.

Three: to refer the results of votes *one* and *two* to a full session of the legislature for ratification as soon as circumstances allowed: but in the meanwhile by means of an enabling decree to permit all needful measures to be dealt with during this time of crisis by a special committee to be appointed by the two consuls.

All three motions passed in something like thirty seconds by 'unanimous acclamation'.

A number of staff-officers and civilian dignitaries who had apparently arrived with the insurgent army made speeches, welcoming the return of justice and good order, outlining what they thought might be the benefit to the common citizen. Some of the senators who had come with the Acolyte attempted to make similar speeches, welcoming on behalf of the common citizen the return of justice and good order, expressing delight that there was now a legitimate government in Rome. The troops shortened most of this with volleys of slow handclaps. Horsefury, at a sign from Mule-driver, cut off the head of the last speaker (a persistent and importunate turncoat) just as he reached his peroration.

With that, public business for the day concluded.

Trumpets, bugles, bawling of officers and NCOs, most of the colours parading out of the auditorium: and the army fell-in, with not too much disorder, on the trodden grass of the war-meadow. The City gates were now wide open and people came pouring to greet the government. They made a vast hysterical throng between the regiments and the walls: orderlies with bludgeons ran forward to bash out an avenue for the soldiers to march through.

Mule-driver was still on the stage, waiting immovable. Horsefury sheathed his weapon, picked up the severed heads, tied them together by holes he pierced in their ears, and slung the loop over his shoulder. This was quite a slow process, and left Ashes with nothing particular to do. He clearly did not want to leave the stage until Mule-driver made the first move, and I thought he was rather paler than usual, though admittedly it was hard to tell. The officers standing with him were certainly white and trembling: I saw Silver-hair being discreetly sick into the prompt-corner. Mule-driver's son looked like a man who had taken drugs.

Mule-driver himself was beginning to laugh. 'Why,' he said, 'Seven times consul, exact as was promised, seven times: and I never had to make one word of a speech to obtain it! Are them regiments fell-in yet? Colour-sar'nt, where are you?' A gorgeous glittering eagle was swung up in front of his nose with stamping and shouting. 'Bugler!' A gaudy flourish of soldiers' music. 'Hercules-god but it's hot. They've got fever in the City, they tell me. Do us good, purge our bloods, get rid of damn nonsense. No, we won't have no sedan: I've marched regiments thousands of miles. Walk!'

He humped himself down from the stage, thrust away Horsefury's helping hand, and so out onto the meadow in his foul neglected clothes in the midst of his brazen officers.

He shambled along the line of troops, now and then jerking up his arm in perfunctory salute, while the men cheered him end to end of the formation. The civilians cheered him too, faction-bosses and bludgeon-men out in front orchestrating the clamour. Ashes was close beside him: but I think no-one now noticed Ashes.

When Mule-driver reached the extremity of the line, he paused. The troops were called by their officers into column. He did not look back while the drill was taking place, obviously confident that every company would be in the right order. When the movement was complete, another bugle-call: Mule-driver said, quite quietly, 'March': and he led his soldiers into Rome.

Horsefury and the bodyguard-orderlies walked closer to him than Ashes, and everyone noticed *them*.

12   Horsefury's Narrative (1)

Part of a short account by Horsefury of incidents during the exile of the Mule-driver. (He told it to me in person, under circumstances I will describe in the next chapter).

Because first it had been my purpose to kill this great chief, and then after that, not to kill him at all, I had a strong keenness to observe him at all times of his fortune. We went in that ship to the place called Sicily: the men said they needed water to drink. They had not been able to fill their barrels at the first place, because the river near the town where they took us aboard was black with the bog that was in it: they had a distaste for such water.

In Sicily there was a great fight with soldiers of Rome: they would have seized hold of the Mule-driver, but I, Horsefury, killed so many of them that they had small pleasure to continue. That time I did not only *not* kill the chief: I saved his life against his enemies, and he placed his hand on my head, calling me 'brother'.

After that, we went in the ship to the place called Africa. This, I was saying to myself, was the country of black Cuttle-fish: but the people there were white, so perhaps there was a mistake. In this Africa of the white people is a city and the men said, 'Carthage'. I told them they were not to mock me, for I, Horsefury, knew all about Carthage: Carthage was made of gold and built by giants. 'No,' they said, the soldiers of Rome had set it on fire, and all that was left of it was the place that we saw.

There was no gold and very few people: nothing but fallen stones and old streets covered with sand and little huts like the huts of my own country built here and there among the sand and fallen stones. And a great wind blew: and I heard the voices in the wind of all the men who had lived there: they cried 'Woe'. They cried that they had murdered themselves and their wives and children in fear of the Romans and they had now no place at all to go throughout all the Further World: they must fly in the wind for ever. Some poets should write of these people, they will have been splendid chiefs surely, the extent of their fallen city was so wide.

In one corner of it the soldiers of Rome had set up a stockade. They came out of it to us, asking us who we were and what we did there. There was one man, a strong warrior, his name was Sextilius. Mule-driver had called him at one time 'brother' and now looked to him with certainty for a brother's help. Mule-driver said to him: 'Ho: I am cast out by my enemies, help me with men to return and cut off their heads.' He laughed as he said it, and danced on the sand like a frog, he put his arms round this warrior, trusting in his honour and why wouldn't he? For Mule-driver had saved his life as I had saved Mule-driver's: there is concordance of honour, so, among chiefs about such matters.

Mule-driver at this meeting wore the old cape of a shipman, and a shipman's straw hat: he had no shoes on his feet and his ankles were swollen. Had he desired, he could have found better clothes in the ship: he chose these to make clear to Sextilius his brother the great need he had for his help. I myself would have done the same thing: there is a concordance in these matters. Moreover Mule-driver had not shaved since I went into him in that prison. At first because of the sea-sickness: but he kept his beard on the Carthage shore for the same reasons he wore the old clothes. Oh he knew what the poets would be needing to say about him.

Sextilius wore the red soldier's coat and every inch of him as clean as a white bone: but I saw that his clothes were old, and so were those of his men – old, but all mended with care and their harness well-polished. All their faces were yellow, thin-pinched, teeth chattered, flesh was meagre: they knew the fever in their camp, I do not think the City had given them much succour: Carthage was a place of many ancient deaths and these soldiers had them all upon their backs. I saw this.

But Sextilius was as high as a giant above Mule-driver. He said to him: 'Go away.' He said to him: 'I am the man of the City and the City says go away: you are its enemy and no brother.' He said to him: 'You saved my life? Ho: I have forgotten it. Go away or I will kill you.'

And then he rode back into his stockade and we stood there.

I said to Mule-driver, 'I could kill him?' and he said to me, 'No good.'

We stood there three hours in the very hot sun. Even though the wind blew, the sun pressed hard onto our heads and no sensible man would have endured it. But Mule-driver was not sensible: he was a great chief, mindful of poets: he stood. So of course I must stand with him too. In the fourth hour he fainted, and I led him to a heap of broken stone with a tall pillar above it – it was all that was left of the high sanctuary of the men of Carthage, and the soldiers of Rome had scratched their marks on it – pictures of men's yards thrust against the secret parts of women, and such-like foolishness. Paid soldiers will make such marks always: it is a sign of their low condition.

All this time Mule-driver had spoken not one word except once – the second hour – when he said to me: 'Boy, my son is the same age as you: is he dead, do you think? If not dead, then where is he? Oh better for him to be dead.'

And then, as it grew cool, out of the stockade came a soldier – not Sextilius, but one of his dogs. This dog-man said that Sextilius had told Mule-driver to go: and he had not gone. What therefore did he intend? The dog-man must return to Sextilius with Mule-driver's answer: he must immediately hear what Mule-driver had to say.

Mule-driver said nothing for a long while: and he grinned as I saw him grin that time I was to have killed him in the prison. At last he spoke, his straw hat was so down over his face that nothing of his face could be seen by the dog-man. He said: 'Tell Sextilius that here Gaius Marius sits, among Carthage in ruins, and his clothes are as they are. You have seen this, tell Sextilius: it is to be sure sufficient answer.'

The dog-man went away then.

Mule-driver rose to his feet. He said to me, 'Come. If that ship will still receive me, we shall at once go back on board. Now I know I have no brother, I need have no fear of fratricide. All men are mine to destroy if I wish.' He forgot that in Sicily he had called *me* his brother. I did not forget: but my under-standing of these matters of honour may not be altogether the same as is his – I come from a different country, so.

After that, the ship-captain laid hold of a book he will be keeping: he would decide what to do next by searching with his eyes closed for any letters in the book upon which his finger should chance, by chance, to fall – he said, when his god's face was turned in distaste away from mortal men, he would some-times nevertheless guide a man's fingers to discover his secret intentions. I have seen druids in my own country do much the same thing: they call it 'casting the ogham-sticks' – but you wouldn't have too much knowledge of all that, I daresay.

The ship-captain's finger did at all events prick out a few words – if I remember them, now . . .?

> . . . and it came to pass, when all the kings which were on this side Jordan, in the hills and in the valleys and in *all the coasts of the great sea over against Lebanon* –

(and that was the very particular line of words under his finger-nail)

> – the Hittite and the Amorite the Canaanite the Perizzite the Hivite and the Jebusite heard thereof –

(Oh such names of strange peoples, I think some of them, by the word of the poets, will be the ancestors of *my* people, though I have forgotten too much of my country's good poets)

> – that they gathered themselves together to fight with Joshua and with Israel, with one accord.

By which he understood that there were no great ships to the east of us but the ships of enemies: so he should sail west and look there for friends, which he did, and brought Mule-driver with him. We were not two days along the coast when we met with many ships: they were pirates, and of our own companionship, so the men said.

From the shipmen on board of them we heard that Mule-driver's son was still alive, and with friends, in that part of Africa: so we sailed there and placed the father and son together as they wished to be.

Then the ships sailed away again to pursue their own glory together in the great sea over against Lebanon, just so, the book had said, there being so many enemies there – I think the ships of the man called Stain, against whom they must fight to earn gold from King Strychnine. Mule-driver and his son stayed in Africa all the winter, and I, Horsefury, with them: we obtained soldiers from a king there and made ready to return to Italy.

But all that time Mule-driver cut neither his hair nor his beard, nor did he bathe, nor change his clothes. He said it was a token: there was no fratricide no more, he said: oh let them think of that. He began to smell bad, as some of the druids do. Bear in mind, please, the black Cuttlefish. . . .

Oh, and this other thing, this great thing I must tell you. . . .

*

I'll come to the great thing in a moment. I need to explain first about all the other things that happened before it was made possible for Horsefury to meet with me and tell me anything. It was only a matter of a few hours, really: but god, such appalling hours – I shall never forget them.

13   Nemesis Upon the City

After the terror of the events in the War-meadow I knew exactly what to expect in the City. Had I not seen it at Ephesus? (And also at the Walls of Love; though there, during the massacres, I had not gone out-of-doors.) And indeed, as I followed the tail-end of the crowd, behind the tail-end of the military procession, through the gates and into the warren of little streets and entries that gave access to the cattle-market, much of it was already in gruesome evidence. I saw a Stain-faction political wine-shop being raided by security-enforcement men, led by one of the Samnite officers: I saw a group of apparently innocuous passers-by separated deftly from their companions, put up against a wall, searched, and beaten-up, by a squad of Lucanian irregulars: I saw a young man with frantic eyes and bursting lungs chased into what I knew to be a cul-de-sac by more of the security-enforcement.

The main difference between this and my previous experience of administrative change was that here, as opposed to Ephesus, the people of the streets were themselves playing the main part in the violence of the day's work. Twice in one hundred yards men were lynched – whether they died or not, I did not stop to see: I think they must have done – by screaming fist-and-brickbat-waving quicksets of angry mob. I touched all the corner-posts I could reach, and as I did so I waved my stick yelling 'Up with Ashes, up with Mule-driver, "new crowd" for ever!' – and so arrived home unscathed.

Roscius was in a condition of frenzied distress: he had been in the Great Square during the morning and had witnessed the death of Gnaeus Octavius. The latter had endeavoured to summon the citizens to help the security forces man the walls and repel the insurgents. The security forces themselves had pulled him from the speaker's stand, and –

as Roscius described it – 'ran over him . . . he was there on
the flagstones, on one knee, trying to stand up, and they all
ran, out of their ranks, Ivory, in their hob-nailed boots –
they ran: and he wasn't there any longer . . .'

The ground-floor flat in our building had already been
raided. The tenant, a well-known musician who had often
played at the Acolyte's discriminating dinner-parties, had
been taken away no-one knew where – 'listen, you can hear
his wife now. She's been howling all the day.' Miriam said,
'We tried to go in to help her if we could, but she keeps all
the bolts on her door and is opening to nobody. She has
three little children in there: we think they might have been
killed, no noise from them at all.' Roscius said, 'Why didn't
the dirty bastards come up here? I should have thought as
an actor-manager I was more important than a fiddler. What
the devil's going on, they haven't come to lift *me*?' I said
that perhaps they didn't know where he lived. He was
furious. Shrieking at me, how dare I suggest he was of no
political importance! His role as the producer of the pro-
Stain Civic Games was notorious among the factions – there
were two explanations only: one, that they were saving him
for a huge show-trial on some trumped-up conspiracy
charge: or, two, that his talents were so highly regarded
that they were about to offer him the directorship of a permanent theatre under the new government.

The first idea made him cower and moan, the second
sent him dancing round the apartment snapping his fingers
and exploding with laughter. I had never seen him like this,
nor had any of the others. He kept reverting to the murder
of Octavius.

One of the three actors said the only way to find out was
to go out, one of us, and find out. The mask-maker couldn't
go, because he was down with fever (the epidemic fever?
god, we hoped not), and his wife was looking after him in
bed in the inner room: the Syrian girls mustn't go because
Roscius had seen what he thought was the rape of Octavius's
daughter immediately after her father was 'run over': the
actors refused to go because there was nothing in their contracts about such errands.

One of them left the flat, saying that he had 'new crowd'

friends to look after him so bugger *us* (Roscius and he had been deeply in love for a fortnight). Roscius then threw plates and knives at the other two (one of them had been in love with him all through the past two months), and drove them out and down the stairs, tossing their bedrolls and mask-satchels after them. Rachel emptied a bowl of cold water over his head, and he sat down on the couch and began to giggle.

'Oh god, Ivory, you and me. Either you, either me – which?' I thought his laughter at last was more genuinely comic than manic. This relieved me. He was, after all, the manager, and if he could not keep his head, who could? He jumped to his feet, assumed a tragical pose (incorrigibly hilarious), and announced: 'I must go: I am responsible: I have dragged you all to death with my inexcusable syco-phancy. And when I think how that woman – ' (he meant the Stain's wife) ' – insulted my genius before the faces of six senators . . .' He draped his clothes around him and strode to the door like Regulus at the docks enquiring which was the Carthage boat.

I told him I knew very well what he was at. He was trad-ing on my friendship, believing I would never take him at his word and let him go. But dammit he was wrong, my gratitude stopped somewhere and here today was the place. If he had volunteered, then volunteered he had, let him thrust himself in jeopardy: *I* wasn't ashamed to be fright-ened. Then Miriam got in between us and out at the door. Roscius and I flew after her down the stairs and stopped her by main force. We struggled in the hall, heroism against heroism, fear against fear, while the fiddler's wife wailed behind her locks and bolts. At last, to my utter fury (and panic), I found myself on the street, on my way to the new government to plead for Roscius's life, or whatever would need to be done.

I had known all the time it would have to be me. How could I have avoided it? I had brought the Mule-driver half-way to Africa, I might even be in favour with the regime. But anything, anything, this evening of all evenings, not to have to go and find out. . . .

Upon Miriam as I went, I vented curse after private

curse. I touched door and corner posts. I yelled for the 'new crowd'. I saw mobs, lynchings, arrests, widespread looting, and the beginnings of co-ordinated arson. The seventh consulate of Mule-driver was already more and more overtly the first consulate of God's-hope and of all others who sought the dereliction of the One City. If I had no business here but to observe, like a god from a cloud, I would have rejoiced. Or perhaps not. It was hard to see how *my* freedom was about to be secured by any of all this.

I met the Mule-driver himself; in a wide boulevard fringed with trees and sprinkled with rhetorical statues ('the central thoroughfare of the whole world', a cockahoop tourist-guide had announced it to me on my first day in the City). He was proceeding on his evening stroll, all formalities of his installation as joint-chief-magistrate having now been completed. As he lumbered along, a crowd of some hundreds kept pace with him, baying their delight at his virulent demeanour. He had replaced his shipwrecked-sailor outfit with formal robes of office; but, as these were all slovenly arranged and splashed with his recent dinner, and as he had still neither shaved nor cut his hair, the incongruity of his appearance was scarcely diminished. His consular wardens, carrying their official bundles of rods, preceded him with deadpan faces. They were most careful not to turn their heads lest they should see (and, no doubt, more importantly, be *seen* to see) his extraordinary method of conducting constitutional business.

It was not reassuring.

His feet were wrapped in dirty rolls of bandage: he leant heavily on the arm of Horsefury (still clad and painted as a Hyperborean cattle-thief). Behind him walked Silver-hair, carrying a dossier. Behind Silver-hair were the bodyguards, each man with club or butcher's cleaver. These – I was informed by an excited child at my elbow, who knew everything he should not have known at his age, as street-brats always do – were recruited from the chain-gang convicts he had released in Etruria: they now formed what was officially styled his 'Bureau of Political Research'. Throughout his sluggish parade, the consul was continually accosted by a series of well-dressed quivering gentlemen, all most anxious to salute him and thereby prove their loyalty. Instead of immediately returning the greeting, Mule-driver would turn to Silver-hair, who would consult his dossier. If he gave a nod, Mule-driver with contemptuous dismissal said 'Good evening,' and passed on. If he shook his head, Mule-driver jabbed a pair of knuckles, swollen like oak-apples, into Horsefury's upper arm. Horsefury would either cut the gentleman's head off himself, or signal to the 'Bureau' to beat him down or slash him to ribbons.

The choice of method seemed to lie with Horsefury.

I kept pace with the little procession and saw this happen five times. The corpses were left in the street: but the severed heads went into string-bags carried by the body-guard. The child told me Horsefury was going to chat to the heads when he got home – 'he's one of them Germans, mister, they all do it up there, on account of their religion, see: like, he'll be asking them who's to be killed tomorrow. Oooh . . .'

The stock of suppliant gentlemen began to decrease: but the crowd took care of that, catching them as they tried to slip away, and hauling them aggressively forward for Silver-hair's inspection. Other victims seemed to have been fetched protesting out of their homes to be part of this dire cere-mony. The street was lined here with fine houses of the noble families who ruled the world. The mob surged in and out of garden-gates and forecourts as though they them-selves controlled everything and all of us, from this day forward.

They were wrong. Horsefury was the man with the sword. God's-hope was in their streets, enforcing security. Cuttlefish had declared the inevitability of seven consulates. Habbakuk and his crews had blockaded Ostia, brought near-famine to the City, and thereby caused the mutiny that killed Gnaeus Octavius and opened the gates to Mule-driver's army. Pont, if I guessed correctly, had provided the cash. The world ruled the City today: and the City accordingly was eating its own heart. I ought to have rejoiced, but instead I thought of Roscius, and did whatever came next.

What came next was to catch the eye of Silver-hair; if I dared. Horsefury's demonic glare was uncatchable: and his sword was so swift I did not trust him to recollect any old times but bad ones. Mule-driver was in a blood-veiled trance. It had to be Silver-hair.

I extruded myself from the crowd's hem and made a gesture with my stick. He saw me, and knew me. As he looked up at me over his fearful papers, I realized that he himself was quaking with terror. His cold deliberation was an actor's mask, that was all: the man was stricken to the very bowels by the enormity of what he was doing.

He stepped aside, and whispered: 'I can't talk about it now. I begged the captains to wait in Ostia. All will be settled in due course, but there *must* be a degree of patience. These things take time.' For a moment I was baffled: then I understood he thought I was still connected with Habbakuk. Clearly the new regime was in process of repudiating its promises to the pirates. That was no concern of mine. I told him hurriedly he had made a mistake, I was now an actor once again, and that Roscius (whom some people inaccurately associated with the Stain) possessed a quality of artistry that surely overcame all political prejudice, he was as much a favourite of the popular audience as the Mule-driver was of the same audience when it assembled at the polling booths; and, to clinch it, he had preserved my life in Ephesus from the violence of the Stain (not quite true, but near enough) just as I had saved Mule-driver when he so badly required a ship. Could I please have a letter to give to the faction-bosses to assure my partner's safety? Please. 'Whatever you think of Habbakuk, we did get you all to Africa.' I was sure that the consul would remember . . .

The consul had heard the word 'actor': looked glowering round at me: spat out, 'Actors? Arse-hole merchants, all of 'em. Greeko trade, don't like it, won't have it. Where's my man?' He dug the knuckles into Horsefury, clearly intending my immediate decapitation. I clung shamelessly to my penis under the concealment of my cloak, and exerted every essence of my internal will-power to force Horsefury to see who I was.

I succeeded. His dreadful smile became the confiding dimple of a schoolboy caught with fingers in the jam (I mean a schoolboy whose parents love him). He shook his golden locks (well, I knew they were golden, but now he had stiffened them with white clay till they stood out in a circle of bristling spikes – the custom of his people when head-hunting, I suppose). Mule-driver laughed at his refusal and spat, and continued on up the street. The bodyguards growled and passed me by, muttering threats and jibes against the world at large.

Silver-hair paused for a moment, scribbled something on a tablet, shoved it into my hand in haste and terror, whispered, 'That ought to do, now go away, and please don't come again, please. He doesn't like it.'

The Stain's work in Ephesus had lost me the control of my bladder. Mule-driver this evening gave me jumping diarrhoea. I just had time to get myself down a side-entry between two elegant mansions. I augmented a manure-heap outside a garden-wall: and then straight home without looking at anything I saw. There was blood on my shoes, I discovered, as I climbed our common stairs. I had honestly no idea whose murder I must have trodden in.

The tablet worked. I presented it to the armed potboy-cum-chucker-out at the nearest 'new crowd' tavern, who passed me on to a superannuated professional sword-fighter holding court in the back bar. He assured me that his word was sovereign with the security-enforcement in the cattle-market ward. If we had any trouble, let him know, he'd see us right. He called me 'sir' and cadged drinks all round for 'the boys', which I was only too glad to order. He warned me, however, to watch out for 'them knife-happy Lucanians'. They didn't, it appeared, know a right Roman from a wrong one, and old Ashes was already getting pissed-off with them. But he'd sort 'em out right-all-right, all in his own good time, Ashes knew the score. He also gave me a sort of leather badge with a number burnt into it. It entitled us to a ration-ticket, if shown to the proper ward-agent (the food shortage was now being dealt with, but of course on a basis of political priorities); and, if nailed up on the apartment door, would protect us from well-intentioned but ignorant partisan harassment. He cadged another round of drinks, but I didn't stop to share them.

Late that night, to the absolute horror of everyone in the flat but myself, Horsefury paid us a visit. He simply flung open the door, bursting our inadequate bolt, and stood there in the opening until Roscius and all the others had acceded to my urgent request and gone out onto the landing. Then, in a grave low voice, he told me all that I have already recorded, together with all his other adventures since he left the Walls of Love, plus this:

14 Horsefury's Narrative (2)

Oh, and this other thing, this great thing I must tell you . . .

The ships came back to us in Africa, in the early summer, and we heard of the wars of Strychnine, which had in part gone well for them, though many had been killed, and ships broken. They guessed that the man called Stain could never of his own strength gather the victory: all the less so, if his enemies were to help the Mule-driver return to Rome.

One of the shipmen let me know, after strong drink and a roaring night in a wine-house, that King Strychnine's new wife had much to do with this: that the king himself had been fierce to keep the ships in the east to be part of his own battle, but she over-ruled his judgement altogether and made him send them to Africa the very day that the storms were finished.

So I said to him, 'What new wife?' Oh god here is a strange thing. Bear in mind that the man had drink taken and none of what he said was the words of a man of sense at all, at all . . . *but*: he said this. She was the 'woman brought out of Italy three years ago in the hard weather' – not on his ship she had been carried, but their consort in the same voyage – she was put there by a man who had wanted her conveyed by treachery to the markets at Delos for a great price, though she herself had believed she was to travel at his charges, and free, to the coasts of Bithynia.

But she so wrought upon the shipmen towards their pleasure . . . he said she danced upon the poop in such and such a manner during the – the 'dog-watches', do they call them? and a good name for them, so – and while he told me, he gave out so much indecent laughter, I would not have believed him one word . . .

but: he said this. 'Hairy-legs,' he said, 'for to twitch up the short hairs on every one of their own pelts, ho, the buggers.' And in such a way, do you see, she persuaded them to bring her after all to Bithynia, and much more great reward in it from the time that King Strychnine took her and made her his wife.

She has nothing but good for these pirates through the heart of the king, it would seem.

'Hairy-legs' – is it possible? I mean, you know, and I know – ?

I saw Snowflake in one of my dreams and I asked her, was it possible? She said of course and why wouldn't it be? But when all's said, I can't clear my mind to it. I asked the shipman, from where in Italy? He said, Taranto. He knew no more of it, sure the fellow was rolling against the wall. But I did ask him the name of his consort-ship.

Oh let you remember it now: you will need of course to follow your own questions, for I will not cease mine. The *Chimaera*, a ship of Crete – Captain Dolon, I think the name, but I never had chance to be finding him. It was time for us all to be sailing, do you hear? and our own ship was not at all in the same portion of the fleet as *Chimaera*, I never had the chance, man, do you hear me? To be straight with you, I too had drink taken that night: I would tear out five fingers, man, to have been sober, so I would . . .

Oh indeed, it could be possible: she could still live, and all his filthiness could have been no more than the drink and his dirty manners. I tell you, the day I know it for certain to be true, I myself for the joy of it will kill this Mule-driver and put end to it at once.

For then there will be no more need for all that I must do for him. Until then, I continue: I throw up my long right hand with my steel-tooth rat-wife fixed into it, every time he commands me: and every time, the heads fly – Roman heads, I make my count for him: so many more gone from this City, gone gone to the Further World at behest of their own brother – or do they not rather return along the wind like the dead men of Carthage?

So many more, count them: and then comes the Stain again, and he has his own brothers, and he too has his long right hand, and once again the count to make.

I, HORSEFURY, DO ALL THAT THEY ORDER FOR I
FORESEE WHERE IT BRINGS THEM . . . so I do.

If only, though, I could *know*. 'Hairy-legs' – oh it could be
possible . . .?

*

At the end he heard a noise from the inner room. It was
the unfortunate sick mask-maker, delirious and gabbling,
unable to understand the terrified restraint of his wife.
Horsefury – who had been about to kill him, under the
impression he must be a spy – checked himself in the nick
of time, went softly across to his bedside, gave him a solemn
cavalry salute with his sword, touched the point of the
sword with severe respect against an awe-inspiring Pallas
Athene mask on a shelf above the bed, kissed the wife with
the utmost decorum, and went away upon careful tip-toe.

He had no more words, except, passing Roscius on the
stairs, he laid one hand on his shoulder, and said: 'Tell
your man I don't think I shall have so very much more
time. He must discover her himself. Tell him that.'

For a week we lived in this City of fulfilled revenge and
death. On the eighth riotous night, old Ashes, indeed
pissed-off, had his more responsible troops fall upon the
Bureau of Political Research while they slept in their quarters – most of them in camp on the War-meadow, but the
leaders in the servants' wing of Mule-driver's mansion (a
house commandeered from a *depreciated* rival: his own
having been burnt down when the Stain drove him out the
previous year). Every one of the chain-gang assassins had
his throat cut. Horsefury alone put up a noteworthy fight,
all over the rooftops and gardens and ornamental terraces of
the smart end of town, killing nearly a score of the soldiers.

In the end he evaded them by scaling the fifty-seven foot
high Liberators' Monument (erected to the republican
heroes who expelled the tyrant-kings), where he roared out
poetry in his own language and dodged the arrows that they
shot at him. He was unable to dodge all of them. Sprouting
innumerable shafts and barbs, he sang one final defiant
couplet three or four times over – I think it was the one
about –

Little mules, when they brought me in chains to this free
country,
Did they think I would scrub your unfree pelts for ever?

– and then plunged head first to the marble podium. To his
death? To his apple-orchards, to his Snowflake, upon the
far western bound of the ocean . . .

Mule-driver had him buried with full military honours,
which scandalized many: but as he did not otherwise issue
any statement upon his consular colleague's 'police-action',
it was assumed that the Terror was – for the time – finished,
and that more recognizable concepts of normal law-and-
order were once again to be applied.

Samnite and Lucanian units were withdrawn from the
security-enforcement detail and posted to outlying garrisons. Before they left, they were given assurances that the
civil rights of their communities were finally confirmed. I
could not believe that a man like God's-hope would be
trusting of such assurances. But perhaps he did not need to
be. He had left the legacy of his intransigence in the bosom
of the hated City, and was no doubt quite content to turn
his back and let it breed. He had shown no sign of wishing
to leave military affairs and return to a legal career. About a
year later he was assassinated during an unexplained little
mutiny in a transit camp somewhere near Rimini. I guessed
he had used his stick once too often on a refractory subordinate in pursuance of the City's alien discipline. Or
maybe the notched-pennies thought it was time he too was
depreciated. I never heard the full story.

After Horsefury's death I decided to go to Ostia, and find
out what was what with the pirates. Habbakuk's ship was
no longer there. There was only one crew in harbour, and
they were making ready to sail. Their decks were cleared
for action and their fighters were all armed and lining the
bulwarks. They obviously feared an attempt by the coast-
guard-marines to prevent their departure. I was known to
their second mate: and after some shouting from the quay
and general cross-purposes, he allowed me to board.

He told me that all the effort they had expended on

bringing Mule-driver to Italy, and securing his success, had been, as far as he could see, a complete waste of time. There was no likelihood of Ashes ratifying Mule-driver's treaty with their confederacy, and so long as Mule-driver remained in his present state of health, he could not think that any further pressure could be brought upon Ashes through him. They had considered blockading the Italian coast again: but had decided, for strategical reasons, that it probably would not do.

The crews had been very angry, and had sacked part of Ostia two days before. The marines had not interfered to prevent it, and even yet were all confined to their camp. But a surprise attack by them on this last remaining ship could not be ruled out. She would have sailed with the others but had sprung a leak at the last moment.

He was, on the whole, extremely philosophical about it all. He said that Strychnine had more than enough for them to do in eastern waters, where they were much happier anyway, and it had been great while it lasted. He himself had spent a day and a night in the City and had never been so drunk in his life.

Oh yes, he did know something about Dolon and the *Chimaera*. He'd even sailed on her once, a few years ago, steersman he was in those days. Taranto? Yes, he remembered Taranto. A woman? Hairy legs? Oh he'd never forget *her*. He told me a tale that sent me straight back to see Silver-hair. I was on fire, both brain and body.

15   Nemesis Upon Mule-driver

I was also unafraid; or shall I say I did not give myself time to be thinking of fear. I had come out to the harbour-town in a hired post-chaise: I offered the man untold wealth if he got me back to the City before dark – Roscius's money, but dammit I had saved his life – at least, I claimed to have saved his life, and neither he nor I could ever really know how far among the artists the 'new crowd' purge would have extended if I had not achieved our immunity.

The tablet of immunity I had been given was in my

pocket – it spoke of 'services to the state' rendered by me, Roscius, and all our associates, and was signed with a group of letters – some sort of cypher. I assumed it still held good: so I clutched it in my hand, boldly, and hurried on foot up the boulevard towards Mule-driver's house. Wheeled traffic was prohibited here – for now the Bureau was no more, ordinary police regulations were once again in force. There was a constable on duty outside the mansion. My tablet got me past him with no more than a modest bribe.

The foyer was in a shocking state. It still bore the marks of the violent eviction of its legitimate but pro-Stain occupants. Ornaments were smashed, there were bloodstains on the plaster, and smears of excrement (who is it that always manages to find a handful of shit to dispense on these occasions?): and it looked as though someone had made a cooking-fire in the middle of the mosaic floor.

Despite these uncouth circumstances, the room was full of dependants, petitioners, faction-bosses, contractors, senators, soothsayers, bothered clerks running in and out. The atmosphere was tense. It seemed that everyone had been waiting all day to see the consul, and no-one knew why he had seen nobody. It was almost sunset, and servants were bringing in lamp-standards. I pushed through the nervously nattering throng and caught hold of a clerk. I demanded Silver-hair, showed him my tablet, and said I wanted him *now*. The man brushed me off and told me to wait my turn. I said, 'Where is he, where is he, don't you *know*, you damn fool, the consul's life may be in danger . . .!?'

As I guessed, this upset him even more than he was already upset, and he cast a quick glance over his shoulder, showing me at least where he *thought* Silver-hair might be. He recovered himself, gave me a tablet and a stylo, and told me to write down my business and he'd see what he could do. He then turned away to deal with a man who insisted that he knew of a plot to murder *both* consuls – the attempted queue-jumping was becoming imaginative.

The door the clerk had glanced at was guarded by a Samnite ruffian. I looked carefully towards him, calculating how

possible it would be, the next time the door was opened, to
dodge past him without getting his knife in my kidneys.
Then I saw that he was not a Samnite at all but a Lucanian
and I knew him, he was Monkey-face. I went confidently
up to him, wreathing myself in abundant and prosperous
smiles, and greeted him like an old friend. He was a surly
old bastard, but the cartload of teeth he shoved out of his
mouth at me might have been meant in good-fellowship.

'Nice change to see even a Greeko,' he said, 'These City
sods make me vomit. You can't go in. There's trouble.'

'I must go in. There'll be more trouble if I don't.' I told
him I had to see Silver-hair – was he with the consul or
where was he?

He looked anxious, afraid to be overheard, talked out of
the side of his lips: 'Look, this lot mustn't know it, not even
the clerks. The old bugger's on his death-bed, and they
don't know what in hell to do about it in there. *I* could tell
'em what to do. Cut their own throats here and now, leave
Italy to the Italians, *we'd* run their show for them so they'd
never forget it, never. God's-hope's a damnfool, getting
himself eased out of here just before it all opens up for us.
But dammit, we've no coherence, the City'll take all, right
out of our fingers' ends, same as they always do – flocks
and herds, didn't he say? He was right and now he's one of
'em. Is *this* what your blackamoor wanted?'

'If you'd stayed in your mountains you'd be skull and
bones already,' I told him, 'She got you this far: don't despise it.'

'I don't; she was a *queen*, I don't never forget the way she
made those last five miles. Did you bury her all right? I'd
no choice but to slide out of it, you know that, God's-hope's
orders.' There was maybe a third of a tear-drop in the
corner of his vitriolic eyelid. Under its influence he took
one step to the side, opened the door behind him a surreptitious crack, let me through, and then shut it the instant I
was in.

In the next room a horde of bureaucrats in an agitated
conference, files of papers all over the place, and the door
beyond half-open. I made straight for it, Silver-hair's name

vigorously on my lips, and ignored their attempts to prevent me. The guard at the half-open door was in awe of my preoccupied manner and assumed I knew my business, so he too let me ignore him.

In the third room, Ashes and the son of Mule-driver, and Silver-hair and Mule-driver's son-in-law, and maybe one or two others: the entire government, indeed, bar one. I acted as though I was that one, went straight over to Silver-hair – who gaped at me, incredulous – I said: 'I've just come from Ostia. I spoke with a ship's officer. I must speak with you, alone please!' I made it sound as though all the pirates were about to sail up-river. The lot of them began talking at once. They all thought the pirates were about to sail up-river, serve them right if they did, Habbakuk's treaty had been a real treaty, they had no right to repudiate it.

But that was not my business: my business was to get Silver-hair alone and find out once for all was it or was it not Irene aboard *Chimaera*: whoever it had been, with her hairy legs however exposed, I now knew for certain that the cargo had been shipped by this grey-faced stooping con-triver, and I was permitting no evasions. Contorted with all the discreet omniscience of a respected intelligence-oper-ative, he caught hold of my arm and fetched me at once into a private cabinet opening out of the room at one corner.

I shut the door behind me and put the ferrule of my walking-stick against his adam's-apple, his back pressed hard to the wall. In my other hand was a knife – a fruit-knife, oh yes, I had eaten a picnic on my way down to Ostia that morning. If the police were any good, I should have been searched for weapons at the house-door. Perhaps that had been Monkey-face's job: if he shirked it, I daresay he'd had reasons – he was not altogether absorbed yet into flocks-and-herds. The knife came, with dexterity, from out of my right boot.

'Now,' I breathed at Silver-hair, making a frightening point of not quite opening my lips as I breathed it: 'there's no Research Bureau to back you up and these Lucanians don't know a right Roman from a wrong one. I don't want you dead: but I do want the truth, and I'd as soon die myself as not have it. You came in at her window when she was sick and alone in bed, you fetched her out of the Walls of Love and you fetched her to Taranto. Why?'

His eyes followed the track of my knife as I waved it about in tight circles in front of his face, and he gobbled with the pressure of the stick. I relaxed it a little. He proffered a thin dribble of a smile. He spoke very rapidly, all sorts of excuses – all amounting to the same excuse – overriding demands of the national security, about which he seemed to imagine I would care more than a cockerel's fart. He told me the tale: or *a* tale.

Had I expected him to deny it had been Irene? If so, I misjudged his knowledge of how much I knew. He made no bones about her identity. He explained, at great length, with every implausible elaboration of intrigue, that Fat-man's death, when he heard of it, meant that Irene had become known as an agent of King Strychnine's, and therefore that he (Silver-hair) was also implicated as her associate in very dodgy Pontic contacts – which was true, up to a point, but dangerous for himself, and embarrassing for the Mule-driver. So Irene must be got out of Italy. Did I not understand that he had paid Dolon to take her to safety in Bithynia? How could I believe he meant her any harm? How was it his fault he had been double-crossed, and the pirates had sold her in Delos?

When I told him he lied, he got going on another story. This one might have been true. Irene had willingly accompanied his snatch-men, in secret, to Taranto, where he was waiting for her: but the message he wished her to take to Strychnine (breaking off all covert arrangements that might or might not obtain between Mule-driver and Pont) had angered her. She had had some deal or other fixed-up with Silver-hair (she never told *me* of course), and now – she said – he was reneging on it. Silver-hair was astonished to discover she was determined, as Strychnine's agent, to work for Strychnine's interest rather than Silver-hair's, and was not going to be manipulated by Rome out of the country when she did not choose to go. I think he had so entangled himself in his own complications that he thought all agents he had ever intrigued with were thereafter to be seen as *his* agents. He had forgotten that Strychnine was the enemy first-and-foremost of *all* Romans, 'old crowd' or 'new'. When he realized his error he had had her drugged and run aboard ship, he paid the pirates to sell her, not to the highest bidder in Delos, but to the one whose principals lay furthest away from the City's sphere of influence. He assumed this had been done. 'Of course, you do appreciate,' he snuffled, 'she was suffering from nervous collapse – absolutely out of the question to trust her discretion any more in such delicate transactions . . .' He was sorry, but there it was – would I please let him go now, or the officer behind me would cleave my skull into two pieces.

The crescendo of his torrential narrative had prevented me hearing the slight creak of the door at my back. The officer was Mule-driver's (immensely strong) son. He whipped me out of the cabinet and spilled me into the middle of the main room. Someone else picked up my stick and knife. Mule-driver's son whirled his sword about, measuring the distance to my neck. I shouted out: 'Just one more question!' The sword paused for a moment, I saw Silver-hair motion to the young man to let me speak. Of course, I could not speak, I could only stammer, there had been no question in my mind, only a frantic effort to withhold catastrophe for one small moment. But then, yes of course, indeed there *was* a question, though what good to me the answer would be at this stage I could not imagine. Nonetheless I really did want to know. I had after all been a notched penny myself, and had – to a degree – become genuinely curious about the mental state of the organization that was now about to finish me off. So I asked Silver-hair, trying not to let my voice quaver: 'Why all that chancy nonsense with unreliable pirates? You could have killed her there and then?'

He gave me in reply his world-weary shrug, so sorry for me that for all these years he had been unable to relieve my mind. 'I had to think about future relations with Strychnine, of course. I obtained a receipt from Captain Dolon that she had been properly shipped for Bithynia. It would never do for Pont to suppose we had been deliberately *depreciating* their operatives. They might even have attempted reprisals. Perhaps it was a misjudgement: for we are now going to have to *depreciate* you, which is really not economical. But you are obviously very negative in your approach to us from now on, you must see we can't have that.'

So, here we were. I would never see Gracelady again (nor indeed Irene, though there the hope was anyway but small). All such nonsense. And when I got to the Further World, would I even see Cuttlefish? That cranky curmudgeon of a Raven would have his grip of her there, he would never let me near her.

I knelt on the parquet and waited for the sword. Burn the bastards' balls off, blood-of-the-bull, such nonsense . . .

From behind a door at the far end of the room came a noise like fighting rhinoceroses. The door was flung open, a woman appeared – slender, fine-featured, white-haired – a beautiful woman perhaps – with black rings of utter weariness and despair around her eyes. Mule-driver's son dropped the sword and started across to her – 'No, mother – not now – !' The unearthly roaring and trampling continued beyond. The woman said, 'It's happening again, I can't keep him quiet, it is as though he were already dead and oh god *he will not die* . . .!'

For an instant the doorway was filled with a tumultuous struggle, a vast tormented figure, apparently all bundled in bedclothes, waving what looked like six or seven arms with a lackey hanging on to each one – the statue at Pergamus, the famous one, what was its name? an old man and two young ones enveloped in serpent, it gave me nightmares as a child, god what a nasty thing to have set up in the publc square – then as quickly as it had shown itself, the horrible tableau vanished, the medical staff determined to get Mule-driver back into bed and safe out of the view of the nation.

Mother and son clutched each other, talking fast and distracted: Ashes and Silver-hair and the others swirled about, forgetting me, rearranging the government yet again in irresolute panic.

There was one way out of here and that was through Mule-driver's quarters – bad leg or not, without my stick where was it? – I launched myself at the still open door and plunged through. Plunged through the folds of heavy curtains, into a dark and shuttered chamber; a suffocation odour of everything that could go wrong with, or come pouring out of, the decaying human body; slop-bowls, and basins full of pus-covered lint; a kettle steaming on a small brazier; a dreadful disordered quagmire of a bed: and Mule-driver being forced into it, against his will and screaming.

I was only in the room for five seconds, not counting the ten seconds it took me to break open the shutters upon the window and eject myself across the sill: but the thick words that came out from his throat as I scrambled – there was no other route, the space was so cluttered – right over the end of his bed, over his threshing legs, and under the arm of one of his doctors or nurses or keepers or whoever they were – stayed in my ears and stuck there: I can write them with an absolute precision:

'Lucius Sulla. Lucius Sulla. So many I have killed and yet he will come. I saved the state from all but him: when I looked for him, where was he? I should have met him in the street, he wasn't there.'

As I pitched myself from the window upon a mess of untended brambles, I heard my pursuers bursting into the sickroom, and – from the sounds – prevented from crossing it by Mule-driver once again heaving himself up from his bed.

He was now quoting poetry in his oracular folk-bard manner, you could hear it all over the gardens:

> When empty stands the lion's den
> And all damfools make out he's gone,
> He lies and lurks some otherwhere:
> Beware beware the voided lair –

His fifth line tailed away into unmetrical incoherence, and concluded with a broken cadence of imbecilic giggling, like a drunk falling up against porticos late at night on his way home:

> O Lucius Sulla, how we taught him, we've all taught him,
> taught by masters,
> to learn him how to
> maul and – maul and – tear!

'It's all right,' he said, '*Tear* . . . I did find the rhyme in the end there . . . ha ha. Close it off with the right rhyme. Your genuine goat-leather men always need to make sure that it rhymes . . .'

I suppose, with all the noise from the house, the guards who should have been watching the garden and the back lane had run round to the side door to see if they were wanted, or whatever. At all events, I was able to pull myself up onto a water-barrel next to a potting-shed, and thence to the roof of the shed, and so over the wall without either hurting myself too much or being seen by the police.

Perhaps I was protected . . . for having dodged for some minutes among narrow alleys between and behind the grand houses, I emerged unexpectedly into the main boulevard, and here there *were* police, running about in groups, and yelling; with lanterns, and, I thought, dogs: and yet I escaped them.

'Here, brother, duck down here, you'll be pierced else, like *a squid on a harpoon* . . .!' It was an old woman, a withered negress, who kept a little stall all bright with coloured lights under one of the trees that lined the pavement, she sold sweets, gingerbread, fruits, needles and thread, that sort of thing, she was – I found out later – a well-known street-character, had been established there for years. She fixed me under her stall till the pursuit had diverted itself elsewhere. Then she shooed me away urgently and would accept no payment.

Conceivable, for those few minutes, she had been *taken* by Cuttlefish? Forget it. I got away, nor did they come after me later. They had other things to think of.

Abigail, through some obscure underworld contact – where did those Syrian girls pick up their disreputable friends, they themselves were always, ostensibly, of such inhibiting social rectitude? – found me a foetid cellar to hide out in, under a thieves'-kitchen tenement block, until the news at last came that Gaius Marius Mule-driver was finally irrevocably dead, and his dealings with Pont need no longer fear exposure. His end came after a massive internal hemorrhage. Drained of his blood. Yes.

His seventh consulate had lasted seventeen days.

I left the City and have never returned. Ashes promised the electorate that all would now proceed according to the best principles of republican legality, which meant quantities of highly divisive radical-populist reform. He raised a new regular army to make war against the Stain, if that proved necessary. He settled the remaining problems of the Italian franchise in a way satisfactory even to the Samnite-Lucanian irredentists (or most of them – guerrilla-bands still haunted the wildest areas, and probably always will). It was a solution that – offered some six years previously – would have prevented thousands of deaths.

The Stain fought interminably against Strychnine, eventually with a measure of success. His Greek-loving tendencies were pleasantly demonstrated by his sack of Athens and his massacre of vast numbers of her citizens.

I remained in Lanuvium, where Roscius obtained me a living: permanent manager of the theatre. I married Miriam. I employed my best talents as an artists' agent in the negotiation of one fruitless marriage-agreement after another for her two sisters, who were determined to be choosy, and good luck to them: they deserved well. In the end we found the right men for them – musicians of high quality, one Greek, one Egyptian (Latins were not even considered, however rich and well-thought-of).

Happy End . . .?

I wish I could say so. Oh I worked at my genial and pointless profession: and I waited. For the next wave of the revenge of the world's rim against the City to work its way back to us from over the sea.

Beware beware the voided lair.

16   She Sent Me a Letter

After two years or so the Stain had achieved enough out of his eastern war to enable him to proclaim Strychnine finally beaten. This was by no means true: but it served. Greece and Asia at least were cleared of Pontic rule. He fined Asia millions of gold pieces (reparations for rebellion), and flooded the ruined province with more men of my father's stamp to ensure that it was paid. Strychnine surrendered his fleet. But as most of the crews were of the pirate confederacy, with impregnable havens of their own, very few ships actually turned up to turn themselves in. The Stain did not wait for them, he set sail out of Greece with seven seasoned and exorbitant regiments; and marched north from the Heel of Italy, as ominous as the Raven in the climactic last scene of one of his most acclaimed roles.

In the course of a prolonged series of campaigns, Ashes was assassinated, the son of Mule-driver ritually eviscerated himself, their army fled all over the map: only the Lucanian-Samnite troops held firm – until the Stain broke them to pieces in a final frenzied engagement under the very walls of the City. He then penned-up six thousand prisoners within the boundary-fence of the race-course: and had them all sliced to death throughout one fear-drenched afternoon. While this was taking place, he made a decorous speech to the senate in the precinct of a nearby temple. He told his listeners not to let themselves be distracted by the noise – 'It is only a few criminals receiving due punishment. Please resume your seats, gentlemen, I will not detain you much longer.'

After that he outlined a great rake of reactionary and divisive legislation, and put his refurbished notched-penny and security-enforcement organizations immediately to work. I have written so much about this kind of thing I have really no more words to expend upon the subject.

Except, this time, it was the worst ever.

Some of it by process of law, some of it by public proscription and incitement to lynching-parties, some of it by secret murder-gangs. It hasn't stopped yet.

Thousands upon thousands, they say. Totally arbitrary.

Yesterday Abigail's new husband became one of them, they found him in the river. My stage-manager last week found crucified against the back-stage scaffold-poles when we arrived for rehearsal in the morning. It happens all over Italy. The ports have been closed. There is nowhere to go.

I have just been notified by the town clerk's secretary that 'someone high up' in the City has passed on an informal 'recommendation' that I should be replaced in my job. He did not suggest that such a recommendation could be ignored, although of course he is aware it can have no legal force. Nor did *I* suggest it: and I was suitably grateful for all the kind words the man had for my artistic achievements here.

I am going to have to go into hiding.

I cannot trouble Abigail just now to renew her low-life contacts for me. She is a brave and resilient girl: but I must respect her days of grief. There is an actor in the company who amused us all recently with his accounts of an un-savoury love-affair he had been having with a young, violent, but resourceful ex-sword-fighter. 'Ex' because he had escaped from the barracks where he was in bondage and had taken up with one of the smuggling-gangs in Ostia. Unsavoury indeed, and dangerous without doubt: but I shall explore the possibilities. I know that the actor has no pro-Stain sympathies.

*

I hide. I am in no position to write any more – just these few last lines: and I have found a messenger who will get them back to Miriam. She will put them with the rest of my papers and keep them concealed until – well, until.

Roscius sends a message that he thinks he can save my life, as I saved his. I am afraid he may have to sleep with the Stain again to do it. Could I bear to be friends with him afterwards if he did?

Oh Irene, what do you think of it? Are you glad for what goes on?

The war being over, she sent me a letter, it came to my shuddering hand the very day I was to meet the sword-fighter (he is certainly helpful, though I am nearly as frightened of him as I was of the Hook that time). Irene's word reaches me by a most tortuous route: and I am now quite unable to answer it, being about to go on the move to god knows where, and with no facilities for getting in touch with her unorthodox postal service. Miriam has the letter in safe keeping. I want her to act upon it, but I understand she is unwilling to do so until she can be more certain about what is happening to me. I believe she has come to love me, although I know (indeed she told me, very honestly told me) that she married me for my position and for the sake of Cuttlefish's child. Oh god but I hope my messenger will impress on her my urgency that there is *no time to be lost*!

Irene, it appears, is glad, and she is not glad. She wrote in Aramaic, using a mixture of Hebrew and Persian characters. Miriam will be able to transpose it into Greek.

I hide: and Irene extends herself, beyond the rim of the world.

*

Irene's Letter:

To the lame Greek Ivory supposedly at Lanuvium. If not there, check with Bagoas (last heard of in Naples) and pass to him for final delivery via personal courier-system. Trebizond requires immediate action.

Do you carry your fire, Herostratus, even yet – red head of the torch etcetera . . .? I lie and write this in the King's warm bath, and think about it. Debate it with my body (stretched out under my eyes) *how long and how far* are such combustibles capable of travel. They tell me *she* died. I survive and am fortunate. You cannot be fortunate (oh we hear the news of the Stain's *rearrangements*: so wise a new ruler to *select* his subjects so carefully), but it is possible you survive. I know you survive. Certain portions of me, under the King's warm water, but clear water, I can see them, all nudge me and assure me you do. What about *your* portions?

I have heard you did at last speak with Dolon's sometime steersman. 'Hairy-legs', indeed . . . Crude little fucker, but good-hearted. A liar, though. I did *not* find it necessary to whore myself round that crew to get them to get me where I am. There were arrangements of a *political* (highly sophisticated) nature being made. Pont needed a fleet, the fleet needed Pont. Haggling, nit-picking, meticulous terms.

Those sailors could prong anyone's cunt, any port from Ophir to Morocco, they didn't need Irene's. A relief to your mind, fire-carrier?

Silver-hair should by now have been *rearranged* by the Stain. Or maybe he's worked himself from under and come out a *rearranger*. I was yards in front of him at every step, I don't think he ever knew quite how far.

Sailors always think that all of a King's ladies are Queens. Not true. He has one *Queen*. Changes her now and then, according to her breeding-pattern, but she's never Irene. Irene don't breed – not ever no more again, you know why not. Irene is business. Business is sometimes pleasure. Pleasure is sometimes power. I mustn't tell you any more. Couriers read letters. If I find they read Irene's, though, balls get burnt off. Literally. This King *hurts* people. Never Irene though. He swore it. He has certain kinds of oaths. One kind he always keeps, and Irene knows which kind. Religion-business, eastern; you never bothered to study such things. Much better not to. Irene is *safe* here. If he decides to *rearrange* (*depreciate*? Which word is better? City agents have different vocabulary from Trebizond boys. You're a playwright now, they tell me. You should discriminate among words) – if he decides to *rearrange* Irene, the poison will be *instantaneous*. He swore it. I wouldn't mind that at all.

Eastern he may be, but he doesn't play Fat-man games. Herostratus, that was the most danger of all my life. But brain is balanced now. It took months, and maybe on board *Chimaera* things *did* happen. I remember haggling, nit-picking, not much more. No room in brain those days for anything more; and, after all, I *won*.

For me, meticulous terms; for your black squid, religion-business: for you – Judy Split-arse (Dolon told me about it. Told me last year). Madness always leaves one yard of space for *one* sort of sane action. But because it's all there is, it looks even madder than the madness.

When the King feels Greek, he says 'balance': when he's

Persian, he poisons people. (One thing: he's never Roman –
if he were, he'd say 'balance', and poison at the one same
time, and *that* I could never endure). Which side of him is
the mad side? He conquered Asia and Greece, talking
Greek, with a Persian horde: and the people all said 'Liberator'. I am, strictly, his property: available for command,
for any purpose. And yet I am free. Why? Because until he
dies the sodding City is *not, not, not safe*.

Maybe the Stain says, 'I beat him'. Maybe the next Stain
says the same, maybe a third or fourth after that. It won't
be true. So long as he lives, the City dies a little. And he'll
live longer than Irene, longer than you, so why care what
happens when he dies? There'll always be another one,
somewhere else. 'Balance' is the mad side: it petrifies. Out
of the Stain's *rearrangements*, the City will search for balance. Won't find it, will find immobility: the outside will
in the end break in. Hundreds of years? Why not? We've
seen it in our own life, it'll be seen by our children. And by
theirs. I have no children. You have.

They tell me they call her 'Lady-grace', something of that
sort. I like that. Your daughter – my black squid's daughter
– Miriam's daughter, in a sense. In another sense, *my*
daughter: my sweet Snowflake's daughter, even: any one of
us could have conceived her, if our lusts and your looseness
and some sort of thought from the goddess had coincided
all at the right time. Oh I know you left Snowflake strictly
to her golden savage. But she did say to me once what a
'kind old gentleman' you were. I'm sure you never knew of
her talent for burlesque. It belonged only to my bedroom,
when she was arranging my wigs. It worried her, your
crooked hip. She used to ask me how I thought you and
your dead squid *managed*. 'Sitting?' she said once, 'it must
be very uncomfortable.' Yet, the two of you *did* make
three.

I dream of the third one, often. Dreams that started even
before I was told she had been born.

If you yourself, Herostratus, your torch, its long flame,
etcetera, cannot bring yourself to come, here, here, here,

etcetera, think about the squid-daughter. *I want an answer to this*. Agents can organize. Bagoas, for instance. She ought to be out of it, beyond the rim. Irene is not a Queen. Squid-daughter could be: though not married to any of these poisoning Kings, I wouldn't have that. (I mean a Queen of Freedom, and I could teach her). Send her, if you can bear it.

Now, tomorrow, day after, year after, any time, oh my love, my true lover, my first ever of such long sweetness. Please.

King calls for me, out of the bath, out of this letter, into his words from the Jews' book: he has a man that sings them, thus:

> How beautiful are thy feet with shoes, O prince's daughter
> The joints of thy thighs are like jewels
> The work of the hands of a cunning workman.
> Thy navel is like a round goblet
> Which wanteth not liquor . . .
>
> Now also thy breasts shall be as clusters of the vine
> And the smell of thy nose like apples
> And the roof of thy mouth like the best wine.

I shall go into him, processional, with music of harp and cymbal, three maidens to bear my train, four eunuchs on either side: and then he will be talking to Irene. He makes Pont into Elysium for no-one but Irene. I am fortunate and survive. You are unfortunate, *but* survive.

Oh god, Ivory, send her quick. I am so lonely in this silly palace.

I kiss the red head of your torch; and the joints of thy thighs – yes, you daft limp-leg, *your* thighs, who else's? – are like jewels. How beautiful my legs with hair: how beautiful my Ivory who fucked-up every job I gave him.

EPILOGUE

Letter From a Handmaiden

'The ruler of the kingdom of Pontus was, at this time, Mithradates VI . . . Eastern legend ascribed to him a stature more than human, strength and swiftness surpassing that of all other men . . . He, alone among the princes of the East, was able seriously to contend with the Roman power.'

Mommsen

To
His Inestimable Sublimity: *Mithradates*, King of Pont; Lord of
Bithynia, Cappadocia, Galatia, Paphlagonia, Inner and Outer
Thrace; Protector of Armenia; Suzerain of Asia, Rhodes, Cyprus,
Cilicia; Guardian of Pan-Hellas, Crete and the Thousand Isles;
Guarantor of Syria, Lebanon and Judaea; Regulator of the Cau-
casus; Regulator of the Crimea; Sworn Brother to the Great King
of Kings throughout all Persia as far as the Hindoo Khoosh;
Friend of Egypt; Servant of Mithras; Descendant of Zeus; Bond-
man of Jehovah:

From
His submissive handmaiden, the Lady *Peace-upon-Earth*; con-
ductress of the House of Flowers; Governess of the Royal Cypher-
cabinet; maintainer of the Secret Bosom; disposer of the Gardens
of Paradise:

By the hand of
Bacchides, Chamberlain of All the Confidences:

In
This Palace of *Trebizond*:

Upon
The *third* day of the Manifesting of Dionysus, this *thirty-ninth*
year of the auspicious reign of Mithradates, King of Pont,
etcetera:

Greetings and Duty.

Sublimity, I have received response, alas long delayed, to
the second letter I wrote, with Your Sublimity's gracious
permission, to the man Ivory (the lame Greek), of whom
you and I have often spoken, and whom I last heard of in
Italian Lanuvium. My courier was aware that Ivory was no
longer employed to manage the municipal theatre there,
having been compelled to resign his modest responsibilities
in the face of the displeasure of the Roman Dictator, L.
Cornelius Sulla, about whom Your Sublimity requires no
further information.

My courier discovered that the man Ivory had been the
subject of many appeals to the Dictator (that he should not
be thus dismissed and cast out of favour), from innumerable
friends and associates in the same profession, many of them
persons close to and intimate with the Dictator himself. But
all in vain, for it had become known that Ivory had

materially connected himself with the late Consul of infamous memory, Gaius Marius, about whom Your Sublimity requires no further information.

My courier discovered that Ivory had abandoned his house, his wife and daughter, to flee no man knew whither. Your Sublimity needs not to be told of the frequency of such flights these present days in Italy.

My courier thereupon transferred his responsibilities concerning my letter and its delivery to Your Sublimity's servant Bagoas, accredited commercial and diplomatic agent of the Kingdom of Pont upon the coasts of Italy. Bagoas has his own methods, and his own men, and he did not fail to uncover the truth.

Ivory was dead.

At least, Bagoas was forced so to conclude, when he heard how this man, under an assumed name and occupation in a distant town (Milan of the Gaulish north), had left his unworthy lodging in cover of darkness to purchase some few necessaries, and had never returned. Many men in Milan who went out that night failed similarly to come home. Articles of clothing were found in a municipal midden, and some human remains, none of which were definitely identified as belonging to any particular individual. Such macabre and mysterious circumstances have been a frequent feature of the proceedings of the servants of L. Sulla; and I must acknowledge the evident truth: Ivory is dead.

My Lord King, I weep. Forgiveness, Lord, for my sorrow. All my heart is the King's heart by reason of the King's great goodness to me. Nevertheless, I weep.

Your Sublimity's servant Bagoas, upon receipt of this intelligence, immediately sent men to the widow and daughter of the lame Greek, informed them of the presumed death, and conveyed to them Your Sublimity's most gracious invitation to travel as soon as was convenient into your Sublimity's dominions, here to make their home as Your Sublimity's humble (and grateful) suppliants and the friends of my bosom. The closure of the Italian ports presented no obstacle to the ways and means of Bagoas, who has his own arrangements.

They are now arrived in Trebizond, and bear with them abundant documents with which Your Sublimity no doubt will desire to divert your leisure and instruct your policy. These papers are herewith delivered to Your Sublimity by Your Sublimity's Chamberlain, Excellency Bacchides.

The final document in the collection is, as Your Sublimity will not fail to notice, the first letter that Your Sublimity permitted me to write to Ivory, which he was 'unable to answer'. Your Sublimity in your infinite mercy will forgive – yet again – the indiscretion of your wicked handmaid (me), but will remember (a) that I am a Greek and like to laugh (I know Your Sublimity likes me to laugh), and (b) that my showing you the letter also shows you that I am not keeping the creatures of my incontinent imagination as a disloyal secret within my own breast.

My breast, as Your Sublimity well knows, is always available for Your Sublimity's divine inspection (not tonight, though. It is my time of the month. I'll let you know as soon as the ritual is done with. Religion-business: I know how you feel about it, I always take good care).

As for Ivory's widow and child. The widow has been a dancer, I know her work, she is very very good, in the Levantine manner, though she also has experience of the Greek and Etruscan styles. She will be an ornament to the Gardens of Paradise. She is not yet out of her youth, but soon will be, alas. She will then make an excellent instructress for the young dancers of the Gardens and will be worth a great wage: I expect you to give her one. Oh, she has brought one of her sisters with her, she too a widow, because of L. Sulla. Everything I just said applies to the sister as well. Look after them both.

As for the child: oh she is of surpassing beauty, and were it not for her step-mother being with her I would rear her as my own. Instead I must be content with the role of loving and eccentric aunt. She is about nine years old and *must not be incorporated into the harem*. I have Your Sublimity's word for this, as you very well know: if you break it, beware of *Furies*! You grab at them younger and younger every year, which is all very well if they have no-one to look after their interests: but this one has. I intend she shall be trained, her mother would have wished it, as an independent dramatic actress of the Greek works, and, if she shows talent for it (I think she does), as a poet. I look to Your Sublimity's generosity to assign her the best teachers and philosophers to that end.

For the death of Ivory I weep.

For Your Sublimity's love and forbearance, I dance. You have crowned my life with flowers. Very soon I shall be too old and the blossoms will wither and fall: it will disgust you to see me naked. Perhaps it does already, though I have just looked at myself in the mirror and can't really believe it. To see Your Sublimity naked even when you are aged and grey will always infuse me with insatiate desire: dammit, you are a poetry-book oriental, you *need* all this flattery to keep you going, don't deny it.

And moreover, no-one but you can still be called, always, the Breaker of Romans. Whatever you do: discouragement, never!

By the way, this ambassador come over from Egypt to talk grain-sales: the prices he's quoting to you bear no relation *whatever* to the current rates on the Alex corn-exchange. I've taken pains to find them out for you. The man's a crook, we must not let him get away with it. No reason to assume our Scythian harvests are likely to fail us just yet.

Your devoted lady takes her leave and kisses Your Sublimity's hands: and lovingly, loyally, obediently, kisses also the hands of your most beautiful and gracious Queen, the Mother of your Princely Sons (to whom all respect). She, not I, is the Moon of Your Sublimity's life: and it is right it should be so.

PS: Ivory in his writings does not always tell the truth. I am of a much higher character than the one he assigns to me, but you know that anyway, don't you?

I am not, even yet, sure that he is really dead. I too disappeared, from the Walls of Love: and here I am, all these years afterwards, alive, and in Pont. Next week, all being well, alive and in the *bed* of Pont. Who knows that the old lame leg may not, in the end, find some way of hobbling here? Do not blame me if I hope.

Three kisses, no more no less, in the places you and I know best –

   Irene.

   ★   ★   ★

'The gods of blessing seemed all of them to have ascended to Olympus, and to have left the miserable earth (the . . . nations united in the Roman state) at the mercy of official or volunteer plunderers and tormentors.'

           Mommsen